THE
POSTCOLONIAL
BILDUNGSROMAN

Narratives of Youth, Representational Politics, and Aesthetic Reinventions

THE POSTCOLONIAL BILDUNGSROMAN

EDITED BY
ARNAB DUTTA ROY
AND PAUL UGOR

UNIVERSITY of ALBERTA PRESS

Published by

University of Alberta Press
1-16 Rutherford Library South
11204 89 Avenue NW
Edmonton, Alberta, Canada T6G 2J4
amiskwaciwâskahikan | Treaty 6 |
Métis Territory
ualbertapress.ca | uapress@ualberta.ca

Copyright © 2025 University of Alberta Press

Library and Archives Canada Cataloguing in Publication

Title: The postcolonial Bildungsroman : narratives of youth, representational politics, and aesthetic reinventions / edited by Arnab Dutta Roy and Paul Ugor.
Names: Roy, Arnab Dutta, editor. | Ugor, Paul, editor.
Description: Includes bibliographical references and index.
Identifiers: Canadiana (print) 20250165112 | Canadiana (ebook) 20250165155 | ISBN 9781772127706 (softcover) | ISBN 9781772128413 (EPUB) | ISBN 9781772128420 (PDF)
Subjects: LCSH: Bildungsromans—History and criticism. | LCSH: Postcolonialism in literature.
Classification: LCC PN3448.B54 P67 2025 | DDC 809.3/9354—dc23

First edition, first printing, 2025.
First printed and bound in Canada by Rapido Books, Montreal, Quebec.
Copyediting and proofreading by Kirsten Craven.
Indexing by Paula Butler.

All rights reserved. No part of this publication may be reproduced, stored in a retrieval system, or transmitted in any form or by any means (electronic, mechanical, photocopying, recording, generative artificial intelligence [AI] training, or otherwise) without prior written consent. Contact University of Alberta Press for further details.

University of Alberta Press supports copyright. Copyright fuels creativity, encourages diverse voices, promotes free speech, and creates a vibrant culture. Thank you for buying an authorized edition of this book and for complying with the copyright laws by not reproducing, scanning, or distributing any part of it in any form without permission. You are supporting writers and allowing University of Alberta Press to continue to publish books for every reader.

GPSR: Easy Access System Europe | Mustamäe tee 50, 10621 Tallinn, Estonia | gpsr.requests@easproject.com

University of Alberta Press gratefully acknowledges the support received for its publishing program from the Government of Canada, the Canada Council for the Arts, and the Government of Alberta through the Alberta Media Fund.

Arnab would like to thank his partner-in-crime, Shivangi Jain, for her invaluable support, insight, patience, and encouragement.

Paul would like to thank Behakong Ugor, Unimahsi Ugor, Unimke Ugor, and Andokie Ugor—this one is dedicated to you.

CONTENTS

Acknowledgements xi

Introduction xiii
Arnab Dutta Roy and Paul Ugor

I   Historicizing the Postcolonial Bildungsroman

1 | Reading the Classical Bildungsroman as a Colonial Genre   3
     José-Santiago Fernández-Vázquez

2 | "Couldn't you be broken and still bring change?":
     Nnedi Okorafor's Binti Trilogy   29
     Ericka A. Hoagland

II   Coloniality, Postcoloniality, Cosmopolitanism, and the Bildungsroman

3 | Contextualizing the Postcolonial Bildungsroman   55
     Feroza Jussawalla

4 | "Sono un crocevia":
     Igiaba Scego's *La mia casa è dove sono* as Diaspora Bildungsroman   83
     Simone Maria Puleo

5 | The Cosmopolitan Bildungsroman   107
     Antonette Talaue-Arogo

III Childhood, Nation, and Narration

6 | History as Murmur:
Derek Walcott's *Another Life* as Postcolonial Bildungsroman 131
Andrew David King

7 | Upendranath Ashk's *Falling Walls*:
Bildungsroman of the Lost Youth of Independent India 159
Aruna Krishnamurthy

8 | Recovering Those Who "Trod":
Reclaiming the Bildungsroman in Shūsaku Endō's *Silence* 183
Maria Su Wang and Bethany Williamson

9 | The Truth and Reconciliation Commission, the Bildungsroman, and the "New" South African Subject 207
Deena Dinat

10 | "We Come too Late to the Scene":
Goh Poh Seng, Developmental Time, and the Singapore Story 227
Peter Ribic

IV Modernity and the Postcolonial Bildungsroman

11 | Bad Modernization:
The Carceral States Bildungsroman in Postcolonial Africa 251
Craig Smith

12 | "For Every Child, Every Right":
Reading Postcolonial Bildungsromane of the 1990s across the United Nations Convention on the Rights of the Child 271
Prathim-Maya Dora-Laskey

13 | Organi(ci)zation of the African Intellectual:
Bildung and Representativeness in the Fiction of Chimamanda Ngozi Adichie 299
David Babcock

14 | (Be)Coming of Age in Postmillennial Hong Kong Literature:
Between Humans and Things in Hon Lai-chu's Works 323
Helena Wu

V   Identity Politics and the Postcolonial Bildungsroman

15 | Amos Tutuola and the Novel of Transformation   349
   Gregory Byala

16 | Coming of Age with Ambiguous Identities and a Sense of Shame:
   Zoë Wicomb's *You Can't Get Lost in Cape Town* and David Dabydeen's
   The Intended   371
   Elizabeth Jackson

17 | "No sign of improvement anywhere":
   Phantom Development in Seamus Deane's *Reading in the Dark*   391
   Julieann Veronica Ulin

18 | Replotting the Bildungsroman through a Queer Poetics:
   Ocean Vuong's *On Earth We're Briefly Gorgeous*   415
   Rachel Ann Walsh

19 | Childlessness and the Female Nigerian Bildungsroman   437
   Julia Wurr

   Afterword   465
   Sarah Brouillette

   Contributors   473

   Index   481

ACKNOWLEDGEMENTS

We would like to thank the contributors of this volume who have been such wonderful interlocutors since we started this project in the past three years. We are also deeply indebted to our editor at University of Alberta Press, Michelle Lobkowicz, who has offered support and advice at every stage of the project. We would also like to thank our student research assistants, Mathew Reyes, Ezra Wilson, and Kriti Upreti, who provided crucial help with tasks such as copy-editing the volume at different stages, communicating with the contributors, and organizing the project.

Arnab Dutta Roy would particularly like to thank his university, Florida Gulf Coast University, for providing a generous grant for covering the cost of book indexing, two research assistants, and for providing protected time for research (through two course releases) that enabled the completion of this book. An earlier version of certain discussions on the South Asian Bildungsroman featured in the introduction have appeared elsewhere: "From Modernizing Tradition to Traditionalizing Modernity: U.R. Ananthamurthy's Samskara as Postcolonial Bildungsroman," *Genre: Forms of Discourse and Culture*, vol. 57, no. 2, July 2024, pp. 143–68.

Paul Ugor is grateful to the department of English Language and Literature at the University of Waterloo for the provision of a research assistant, a generous book subvention to support the publication of the volume, and two course releases that gave him time to work on this project.

INTRODUCTION

Arnab Dutta Roy and Paul Ugor

Originally an eighteenth-century German innovation, the Bildungsroman became a popular literary genre across the Anglo-American world during the nineteenth century. Narratively framed as a "coming of age" novel about young adults in search of meaning and happiness, the Bildungsroman was the literary medium of choice for many prominent writers from the Euro-American world—including Mark Twain, Charles Dickens, Jane Austen, and Rudyard Kipling—looking to explore the moral and psychological developments and social adventures of characters traversing unfamiliar worlds, and thereby encountering new challenges and experiences. With many European colonies attaining political independence in the mid-twentieth century, there was a revival of interest in this genre in the Global South. Writers and thinkers from postcolonies across Asia, Europe, Africa, the Americas, and New Zealand turned to the Bildungsroman to explore new stories about childhood growth, belonging, identity, self-determinacy, cultural authenticity, and spiritual awakening. South Asian writers such as Salman Rushdie, Amitav Ghosh, U.R. Ananthamurthy, and Anita Desai, for instance, engaged and reinvented the genre by drawing on literary tropes such as the pilgrimage from classical Hindu, Sufi, and Buddhist mythical traditions. These writers often deployed the genre to explore how youth in India and other South-Asian contexts confronted questions of decolonization, independence, and self-determinacy. Similarly, writers from Africa and the African diaspora such as Ngũgĩ wa Thiong'o, Tsitsi Dangarembga, and Abdulrazak Gurnah found the Bildungsroman to be an effective platform for exploring revolution and radical social change in relation to socio-political developments in Kenya, Zimbabwe, and Tanzania. While Maori writers such as Witi Ihimaera also employed the genre to express conflicts between modernity and tradition facing Maori youth in contemporary New Zealand, Indigenous writers in Canada such as Tomson Highway used the genre to unearth the psycho-social struggles of young people traumatized by the residential school system in Canada, which lasted from the late nineteenth centry to 1996.

This efflorescence of the Bildungsroman in the postcolonies has inspired a thriving body of work in critical theory. The human rights scholar Joseph Slaughter has identified in the Bildungsroman an influential model that "normalizes the story of enfranchisement" by making socially marginal figures representative (*Encyclopedia of the Novel* 94). This critical observation is particularly insightful because it accounts for the popularity of the genre in former European colonies where colonial subjects were denied any form of political-economic rights. So part of the genre's cultural appeal in the postcolony in the wake of decolonization has been the ways in which it has offered new opportunities for the social and cultural agency of the postcolonial subject. It is also for this reason that Mark Stein, in tracing modern Black British fiction's departure from classical literary models, has argued that the postcolonial Bildungsroman should be best understood as a novel of transformation and adaptation rather than as a novel of formation and development. Clearly, the genre has become a formidable literary instrument of individual and collective transformation by social subjects in societies once denied human dignity, cultural identity, citizenship rights, and economic opportunities. As scholar Pramod Nayar poignantly affirms, the protagonists of the postcolonial Bildungsroman, who come from marginalized backgrounds, are "knowing subalterns" who reject oppressive social orders and consciously align themselves with fellow victims who are also "outside the social order" (127). This political valence of the Bildungsroman makes it, according to Nayar, a crucial aesthetic tool for interrogating concerns surrounding Dalit identity, culture, and "coming of age" within modern contexts of South Asian literature, culture, and politics.

The main aim of this book, then, is to examine how an eighteenth-century literary genre, originally meant for expressing local European concerns around childhood development, has now been resurrected by postcolonial writers as one of the most cosmopolitan mediums for addressing and pondering a wide range of global ideas. The book brings together essays from prominent Bildungsroman scholars on diverse topics of literature, narrative, and critical theory that interrogate the different articulations of the postcolonial Bildungsroman and examine the intersection of traditional forms with modern questions of social disruption and identity. In the midst of a rapidly changing, intricately interconnected, and skewed globalized world marked by novel forms of neocolonial exploitations, socio-economic inequities, and new existential threats, and the myriad of limitations they impose on social subjects who inhabit the margins of the global order, *The Postcolonial Bildungsroman* explores the aesthetic and political reinventions that have accompanied the Bildungsroman as a poignant site of renegotiating power relations between marginalized groups/individuals and contemporary forces of unchecked power. The different chapters highlight how the Bildungsroman is reimagined by writers from a wide range of formerly colonized regions across the globe including South, Southeast, and East Asia, the Middle East, the US, Latin America, Canada, regions across Africa and the African diaspora, the Caribbean, Australia, and New Zealand. Contributors consider a wide range of questions as starting points of their exploration of the genre. These include how focusing on the "coming of age" story cycle engages, for instance, recent concerns highlighted by eco-critical, queer, and/or Marxist readings of twentieth- and twenty-first-century texts; in what ways the genre informs contemporary readings of human rights and personhood; and, finally, how examining texts through Bildungsroman generic explications amplifies voices reacting to colonial pasts and their unrelenting grip on the present. The next section surveys definitions of the Bildungsroman, along with its historical trajectory. We then turn to discussions on the colonial and postcolonial variants of the genre, focusing on their departures from the original German model. Following this, we discuss the broader methodology the book adopts in approaching the postcolonial Bildungsroman, before finally transitioning to a discussion on the different chapters in the book.

Definitions and History

"Bildungsroman" is a German word in which *roman* stands for "novel," and *Bildung*, as Sarah Graham notes, connotes a wide range of ideas including "formation, development, growth, or education" (2). Scholars generally agree that the Bildungsroman is a rite-of-passage novel about a protagonist's journey from youthfulness to adulthood. There is, however, little consensus regarding anything else pertaining to the genre, including its literary scope, what the journey of the protagonist entails, and what the journey means for the protagonist. Joseph Slaughter, reflecting on the scope of the novel, observes that the Bildungsroman can be simultaneously located within extremely broad and narrow socio-historical contexts. As a rite-of-passage novel, the term "can be capacious enough to cover any story of social initiation...found in any culture" (*Encyclopedia of the Novel* 93). At the same time, quoting the scholar Jeffrey Sammons, he humorously observes that genre can be defined so narrowly as to cover only "three and a half examples...of late eighteenth-century German novels" (93).

As a literary genre, the Bildungsroman has lived many lives. The genesis of its novelistic form (in Europe) can be traced back to the writings of a small number of German idealists from the late eighteenth century including Christoph Martin Wieland, Johann Wolfgang von Goethe, and Gottfried Keller. However, Goethe is generally believed to be the prime architect of the genre, and his novel *Wilhelm Meisters Lehrjahre* (*The Apprenticeship of Wilhelm Meister*) is considered the urtext of the genre. In this German iteration, the Bildungsroman narrated the story of "the reconciliation of problematic individual... with concrete social reality" (Lukács 132). It aimed at achieving a harmonious, even idealistic, cohabitation between a protagonist's interiority, the unruly domain of personal dreams, ambitions, desires, and hopes, and the external reality of "professions, classes, ranks, etc." (133). Novels such as *Wilhelm Meisters* showed that this reconciliation, while difficult, is not impossible, and must be sought by the protagonist through "hard struggles and dangerous adventures" (133). In many ways, the Bildungsroman was a modern model of fiction most suited to and concerned with exploring the everyday conflicts central to the efforts of individuals seeking to reconcile themselves with the established cultural values and social paradoxes of the societies they've been thrust into by the accident of birth. The Bildungsroman did not, of course, remain exclusively tied to Germany. In the nineteenth century, its popularity rapidly consumed the Western world, including Europe and North America. In the pan-European iteration, the novel lost much of its idealism (i.e., its belief in the amicable reconciliation between the individual and the wider culture) and became more experimental, and acquired an ironic flavour in which the protagonists confronted the contradictions and extremities of modernity.

The nineteenth-century Bildungsroman was reimagined by writers such as Charles Dickins, Jane Austen, George Eliot, James Joyce, and Rudyard Kipling. In their hands, the scope of the genre witnessed a significant expansion, and the plot became more ironic in highlighting "the harsh social realities and stratifications of modern...life" (Slaughter, *Encyclopedia of the Novel* 94). Writers such as Austen and Eliot, for instance, introduced the female Bildungsroman, which employed irony to highlight "some of the exclusionary assumptions behind the bourgeois male norms of the genre; splitting the storyline into a surface plot, which affirms social conventions, and a submerged plot, which encodes rebellion" (94). These interventions allowed the genre to become a fertile aesthetic tool for questioning culture and authority rather than being an avenue for reconciling individuals with the surrounding forces enveloping and shaping their lives. Thus, if the genre began as a narrative instrument of cultural reconciliation and integration, it morphed into a site of critique, protest, and cultural disaggregation. The nineteenth century also witnessed the rise of the colonial Bildungsroman that, as scholar Jed Esty notes, reworked the "narrative time" of the genre from temporal transition to "youthful protagonists who conspicuously do not grow up" (2). These texts, he insists, blocked or deferred the attainment of a mature social role through plots of colonial migration and displacement (2). In other words, the colonial variant, by shifting the focus from the European heartlands to the global expanse of Europe's colonies, "Conrad's Asian straits, Woolf's South American riverway, and Joyce's Irish backwater," unsettled the conceptual and aesthetic boundaries of the "Bildungsroman and its humanist ideals, producing jagged effects on both the politics and poetics of subject formation" (2).

The latest version of the genre is the postcolonial Bildungsroman, which both thematically and formalistically marks a radical departure from classical European forms. Slaughter reflects that this variation of the genre, which emerges from diverse postcolonial situations across the globe, altogether abandons the goals of enlightenment for the protagonist. He adds that postcolonial examples of the genre are pessimistic and often adopt a mocking stance towards "the dominant generic conventions to show how the promises of liberal humanism remain unfulfilled, and are un-fulfillable, under exploitative systems" (Slaughter, *Encyclopedia of the Novel* 95). This moment marks a major aesthetic shift in the trajectory of the Bildungsroman, as Indigenous beneficiaries of colonial modernity use the genre to unearth and interrogate the illogicalities of modernity or European civilization. Irked by the oppressive structures associated with colonialism and disillusioned by the excesses of the new Indigenous ruling elite, postcolonial writers have transformed the Bildungsroman into a veritable aesthetic tool of anti-colonial and postcolonial literary activism.

The scholar José-Santiago Fernández-Vázquez similarly points out that the postcolonial Bildungsroman disrupts the motif of the "hero's compromise," which is a central feature of the traditional model. The classical European model was based on a dialectical process seen through "the protagonist['s]...profound disagreement with his family or society" (87). In the end, there was invariably a resolution to the opposition through the establishment of a compromise between the protagonist and society. Fernández-Vázquez points out that this dialectical structure, within a postcolonial context, does not respond similarly to the needs of "women, racial and sexual minorities, or to the historical experience of the colonized peoples" (87). He, therefore, states that for postcolonial writers of the Bildungsroman such as Ben Okri and Dangarembga, there is often no scope or context for writing a resolution or compromise: "the protagonists...find themselves incapable of choosing between two sets of values, an internal conflict which remains unsolved at the end of the narrative" (87). So that, while the Bildungsroman was always a narrative of acculturation or gradual absorption into a dominant political and socio-cultural system after a process of initial suspicion and questioning, the postcolonial iteration became an aesthetic vehicle of unsettling the status quo and making room for characters who inaugurate and sustain difficult conversations about unequal structures of power in any society or culture. While the initial form of the genre documented the gradual and turbulent process of change for the protagonist, the postcolonial form prefigures characters who seek to effect seismic change to culture by calling attention to its intrinsic inequities, contradictions, and abuses.

The Colonialist Bildungsroman

Both the colonial and postcolonial models of the Bildungsroman engage colonialism, albeit in different ways. The former, Jed Esty points out, navigated ideas of social mobility and progress through the ethos of colonial modernity: "Colonial modernity unsettled the progressive and stabilizing discourse of national culture by breaking up cherished continuities between a people and its language, territory, and polity" (6). The latter, Fernández-Vázquez notes, intentionally engages the colonial ethos "to incorporate the master codes of imperialism into the text, in order to sabotage them more effectively" (88). Scholars, including Esty, Fernández-Vázquez, Feroza Jussawalla, and Erika Hoagland, agree that both the colonial and postcolonial models are intimately interlinked because they deal with a singular Euro-American master narrative, but from different perspectives and with different political ambitions and cultural aspirations. Therefore, to understand the latter, they suggest it is necessary to confront the former. Thus, these scholars do not just provide innovative and often contradictory ways of approaching the colonial Bildungsroman but also offer prescient insights on understanding the interconnectedness of the models and their varied discursive and interventionist potentials.

Esty notes that the colonialist Bildungsroman radically disrupted the tropes of development found in the older eighteenth-century models of the genre. He states that in the colonialist Bildungsroman the youthful protagonists did not grow old and remained perpetually liminal, temporally and socio-spatially. According to him, "such novels tend to present youthful protagonists who die young, remain suspended in time, eschew vocational and sexual closure, refuse social adjustment, or establish themselves as evergreen souls via the tender offices of the 'Künstlerroman'" (3). The theme of "anti-development," Esty suggests, was rooted in colonial modernity. He explains that the older models followed more parochial standards of historical time set in European national culture: "the concept of Bildung evolved within the intellectual context of romantic nationalism…based on an ideal of organic culture [and] reflected in the developing personality [of the protagonist]" (5). Modern imperialism, in contrast, created a rupture in this understanding because it "was a culture-diluting practice that violated 'national-historical time' and set capitalism loose across the globe in ways that would come to disturb…inevitable, and yet measured, human progress" (6). He thus notes that the figure of youth, in the novels of Joyce, Kipling, Conrad, and Woolf, became "the dilated/stunted adolescence of a never-quite-modernized periphery reflecting the global asymmetries of capitalism" (7).

Fernández-Vázquez offers a different approach to the colonialist Bildungsroman. He does not identify with it, a radical break from the older eighteenth-century models. Rather, he states that both the colonialist and the eighteenth-century Bildungsromane promoted the coming-of-age narrative through colonialist ideologies of childhood. He explains that, in the eighteenth-century model, a central focus was on the theme of the development of a single protagonist, "who moves 'from unformed childhood' toward the emergence of a total personality in adulthood" (86). This understanding of development, derived from Western humanism and European enlightenment, also formed the core of the colonialist ethos that drove the colonialist Bildungsroman. Fernández-Vázquez explains that the whole idea of evolving from childhood to adulthood, "from a primitive to a fully developed state of being—constitutes one of the images that has made the colonial enterprise possible" (86). In clearer terms, the figure of the child, a being "not fully evolved or consequential subject," allowed the justification for a colonial intervention "dedicated to...the improvement of colonized peoples" (176).

Along with an emphasis on childhood, the colonialist Bildungsroman highlighted the importance of education in the process of development and growth of a child. Fernández-Vázquez points out that in the Bildungsroman one can identify the construction of legitimate and nonlegitimate forms of knowledge. In most cases, "the values of rationalism, materialism, and pragmatism" were extolled as the cornerstones of legitimate knowledge (90). Whereas "spirituality, fantasy, and myth" were rejected as "worthless superstitions" (90). This practice of categorizing knowledge, as Fernández-Vázquez explains, was central to the imperial project to constructing the Other: "the distinction between a rational West and the fantastic Orient...as a means to deprive Oriental peoples of the right to make their own decisions" (90). In the Bildungsroman, Fernández-Vázquez demonstrates, the dismissal of otherness was evoked through the creation of "an opposition between realistic and fantastic features." In novels such as *Great Expectations* and *Jane Eyre*, the protagonists such as Pip and Jane underwent a systematic regime of education to cast off the influence of superstitions and fantasies; "Pip 'must learn the limitations of the fairy tales he projects for himself'...[Jane] is scolded when she declares that she has seen a ghost" (90). Conversely, these ideological oppositions allowed a distinction between these protagonists, and their "othered counterparts," Magwitch and Bertha; "they are rejected by the dominant discourse, which represents them as 'others' through supernatural imagery: Magwitch...is compared to a ghost...Bertha is described as a 'demon' or as a 'goblin'" (91). The colonialist Bildungsroman became a poignant aesthetic formation that allowed nineteenth-century writers not only to convey but to bolster colonial modernity's disenchantment with spirituality and nature associated with the pre-Enlightenment era, and in the process promote the values of scientific positivism and secular rationalism associated with Euro-American civilization.

Comparison with the Postcolonial Bildungsroman

Despite their different approaches to the colonialist Bildungsroman, both Esty and Fernández-Vázquez, along with others such as Slaughter and Jussawalla, agree that the colonialist and postcolonial Bildungsroman share common grounds. Esty, for instance, states that the theme of "frozen youth" does not end with the colonialist Bildungsroman. It persists in postcolonial forms to "expose modernity's temporal contradictions, particularly in zones of colonial encounter" (36). Citing examples of literary works by a range of postcolonial writers including Salman Rushdie, Mulk Raj Anand, and Gabriel García Márquez, Esty clarifies that contemporary narratives of anti-development, however, unlike the colonialist counterparts, are often not tethered to Eurocentric modernity or historicism. Instead, they are narratives of alternative modernities committed to "autonomizing youth into a trope with no fixed destination…stripped of the moralizing…rhetoric of national progress, civilizing mission" (210). Fernández-Vázquez notes that the trope of childhood that makes the Bildungsroman particularly vulnerable to colonialist co-option is also a feature that makes the genre popular in postcolonial situations. Thus, postcolonial writers, in his view, turn to the Bildungsroman because the "rite of passage" model compliments the postcolonial agenda of charting the origin stories of a newly liberated nation: "the Bildungsroman offers to those writers who wish to situate their stories in the first years following independence, in order to draw parallels between the experience of the new nations and their young characters" (86).

In Slaughter's opinion, both the idealist and postcolonial variants of the Bildungsroman are similar because they are inherently about the colonial encounter. Like Fernández-Vázquez, he observes that the idealist Bildungsroman, typified in the writings of Goethe and subsequent writers from Europe, supports both "imperialism and civilizing mission" through the deployment of problematic ideological tropes of childhood and maturity: "European 'civilizing' colonialism persisted on the technical difference between…the putative civic virtue of the colonizer's father-feeling and the 'childish' incivility of the colonized" (124). In contrast, the postcolonial Bildungsroman, he finds, interacts with the colonialist legacy in more ambiguous ways. In some instances, such as in Marjorie Oludhe Macgoye's novel *Coming to Birth*, the postcolonial novel affirms certain aspects of the colonial structures within a postcolonial setting to envision a post-independent future; "legitimate authority by normalizing the dominant sociopolitical practices and patterns of nation-statist modernity" (124). In other cases, such as the novels of Ngũgĩ wa Thiong'o, it aspires to be a "narrative model for enfranchising the disenfranchised, for un-problematizing the problematic individual, for keeping the broken emancipatory promise of the Enlightenment by repairing the citizen–subject divide" (133–34). In the postcolonial Bildungsroman, the protagonist is not so much a problem to the dominant culture as s/he is an aspirant seeking to be granted the freedoms, rights, and privileges promoted by modernity.

For Jussawalla, all putative differences between the classical and postcolonial Bildungsromane are ultimately facile. Works such as Kipling's *Kim* and Mark Twain's *The Adventures of Huckleberry Finn*, which typically get classified as colonialist, are, in fact, according to Jussawalla, "postcolonial" (30). This is because they not only channel anti-colonial impulses but also share certain characteristics such as "linguistic experimentation and assertion of an indigenous selfhood" that are unique to postcolonial texts (30). Aspects of Twain's novels such as "a growth towards Americanism, selfhood, and the effort to free oneself from British imperialism" make them, in Jussawalla's view, identical in structure to the postcolonial works of Chinua Achebe, R.K. Narayan, and Rushdie that feature "growing up stories… that express the indigenous selfhood as the desired condition to aspire towards" (30). Jussawalla acknowledges that Kipling himself held colonialist views. Nonetheless, she asserts that his novel *Kim*, like Twain's works, also demonstrates "the growth of his character Kim towards Indianness and his desire not to be identified with the British imperialists" (30). Jussawalla concludes that a comparative analysis of the colonialist and the postcolonial Bildungsromane reveals such categorizations to be unstable, and thus highlights the need for a different approach to understanding the intersections of "postcolonial and non-post-colonial, canonical and noncanonical" (31).

Postcolonial Bildungsroman and Anti-Colonialism

Despite sharing generic similarities, the postcolonial Bildungsroman, in many significant ways, signals a radical break from the classical form. This is because it addresses the realities of a world very different from the one(s) inhabited by the heroes of eighteenth- and nineteenth-century novels. Reflecting on the realities of postcolonial writers in the global literary economy, Sarah Brouillette rightly notes that an author's work is "based in a set of significations that mediate between the writer in the world and the world of the work" (44–45). For most postcolonial writers, the world they inhabit is one marked by colonial injuries and prolonged trauma amid a global political economy marked by precarity and uncertainty. In those insufferable conditions, life for the postcolonial subject is one of daily survival based on patchwork and the continued renegotiation of culture. Hoagland notes that when we attend to the Bildungsroman in a postcolonial setting, we automatically recognize that "'culture' is a far more transient and hybrid entity" than it ever was in the past (226). If the classical Bildungsroman highlighted the story of a protagonist confronting urgent matters of his time, including the emergence of a national consciousness in Europe and the cultural transformations from colonial modernity, the postcolonial Bildungsroman narrates what it means to grow up in the world of today. One that is radically altered by colonialism, changed by "the ever-growing reach of globalization" (and the increasing economic disparity that accompanies it), and marked by the violence and instability of "the post-millennium rise in terrorism and wide-scale political disenfranchisement" (226). The result of such changes, as Hoagland notes, is a wholescale dismantling of "the Bildungsroman's core suppositions" occurring "alongside the continued instabilities perpetuated by sharply uneven power dynamics" (226). The new Bildungsroman thus presents an ideologically distinct expression of the Bildungsroman that frequently coheres, "if not wholly in spirit, then in basic design," to the classical model (226).

The Bildungsroman, as one of the most popular literary genres today, has been adapted widely across diverse socio-cultural settings around the world. Understandably, it has been re-envisioned in multiple ways to accommodate/speak to the specific cultural and historical contexts of its production. Nonetheless, almost all Bildungsromane written today share certain features that not only make the genre stand on its own, distinctively from the European model, but that also allow it to uniquely speak to global postcolonial realities. Perhaps the most persistent theme across all variants of the postcolonial Bildungsroman is the engagement with colonialism, its after-effects or continuities. Contemporary scholars of the Bildungsroman generally agree that the genre advances a strong motif of anti-colonialism. Hoagland, for instance, states that the postcolonial Bildungsroman highlights "an act of subversion and inversion, a political act of counter-colonization, a reimagining and reinvention, a process of becoming through the act of unmaking its predecessor and unmasking the Bildungsroman's ideological flaw" (225). Pheng Cheah suggests the anti-colonialism of the Bildungsroman is encoded in its narrative goals of alleviating "the sense of homelessness experienced by those without a sense of community or nation as a consequence of...colonialism" (242). Kaisa Ilmonen, on a similar note, echoes Salman Rushdie's idea of "Empire Writing Back" in stating that writers of the postcolonial Bildungsroman "talk back" to the colonial legacy of the genre by "making use of it for their own purposes" (61). In other words, the genre undergoes, as she identifies, a process of "creolization" that transforms it into a medium capable of "expressing the originality arising from creolized cultural conditions" (62).

Genealogically and discursively, therefore, the postcolonial Bildungsroman is a form of aesthetic adaptation. According to Francesco Casetti, an adaptation is not just the reproduction of an original text or narrative form but "the reappearance of discourse" (82). By "discourse," Casetti elaborates, "what we are dealing with is the reappearance, in another discursive field, of an element... that has previously appeared elsewhere" (82). The "reappeared" discourse then reinserts itself in a new moment, addressing old issues in the light of new presents. Put differently, the "discourse" is made continuously relevant through the acknowledgement that the moment has changed—the adaptation only emerges to address a "new" time and space in the light of current realities. So adaptation, as a cultural phenomenon, functions primarily, Casetti argues, as a "recontextual-ization of the text [genre]" (83). It is worth noting that when discourses "reappear," they do not do so in a static and unchanged mode: they are reinvented anew. But this reinvention still embodies the structural frame and ideological foundations of the old "discourse." Like all forms of adaptation, then, the postcolonial Bildungsroman features in the contemporary world of global letters as the reappearance of an old Euro-American genre in a new time and place in which the discourse of colonialism amenable to the old genre is revisited, recontextualized, reinterrogated, rethought, and challenged in ways that unsettle the intrinsic assumptions that underpinned the original colonialist form and the ideologies it espoused.

Identity Politics

The theme of anti-colonialism in the postcolonial Bildungsroman is most prominently expressed in three ways: 1) through a re-envisioning of its identity politics; 2) through a re-envisioning of the conventional coming-of-age plot; and 3) through a re-envisioning of the protagonist's place in the community. Postcolonial writers of the Bildungsroman radically rethink the identity politics of the original genre. Today, the Bildungsroman is no longer exclusively about stories of white, middle-class, heterosexual, cis-gendered, male heroes from the Western world. Rather, the genre extends itself as a global platform for highlighting voices from the diverse subject positions of race, ethnicity, gender, sexuality, socio-economic status, histories, and cultural backgrounds. Sissy Helff emphasizes this idea by pointing out that the postcolonial "novel of formation...invests heavily in narrating the growth to maturity" of non-white and non-Western protagonists (109). South Asian novelists such as Shobhaa De, Monica Ali, and Hanif Kureishi, she insists, masterfully infuse techniques such as "episodic story-telling, magical realism, and transcultural unreliable narration" into the Bildungsroman model to transform the genre into an effective medium for communicating "the experience of growing up in diasporic home-worlds" (109).

The postcolonial Bildungsroman is not just recruited to highlight racially, ethnically, and culturally diverse experiences. It is also deployed to represent voices of diverse gendered and sexual identities. Scholars including Maroula Joannou and Fiona McCulloch have noted that, while the female Bildungsroman was a popular variation of the classical model in nineteenth-century Europe, novels written under its banner largely echoed a "male-dominant" ethos of "marriage" as a metaphor for fulfillment and happiness. These scholars note that in the twentieth century the female Bildungsroman has been reprogrammed to contest the central ideas on which the classical Bildungsroman was premised; "happiness is the subjective symptom of an objectively completed socialization" (Joannou 200). Joannou observes that twentieth-century women writers including Dorothy Richardson, Doris Lessing, Angela Carter, Jeannette Winterson, and Sarah Waters have "disputed the ameliorative optimism of the form" by eschewing its realism through a variety of "non-realist genres such as the gothic and the grotesque, the utopian and the dystopian, the fantastic, the fable and the fairy tale" (200). McCulloch, on a similar note, observes that the female Bildungsroman has reinvigorated the genre in a postcolonial setting by injecting it with the "political and theoretical impetus from feminism, postmodernism and so on" (176). The postcolonial conditions of the twentieth century have also given rise to the queer Bildungsroman. Meredith Miller notes lesbian, gay, and transgender writers today "strategically deploy existing discourses of sexology and psychoanalysis within the framework of the Bildungsroman…to pit the sexually dissident self against the social world" (243). In a postcolonial context particularly, many writers deploy the queer coming-of-age narratives to encounter what Sandeep Bakshi identifies as the tensions of "queer adolescence, adulthood, and postcolonial modernity" (1).

Rethinking the Coming-of-Age Plot

Postcolonial writers largely rethink the coming-of-age plot. Hoagland expresses this point succinctly. She states that the plots of both classical and the postcolonial Bildungsromane struggle with the inherent conflict between the "ideal of self-determination and the equally imperious demands of socialization" (220). Nonetheless, in the case of the latter, she points out the conflict is intensified "by the shadow of colonialism, the brutality of civil war, widespread disenfranchisement, and fractured family politics" (220). Berthold Schoene-Harwood, reflecting comparatively on the protagonist's journey in both models, states that the postcolonial coming-of-age story is radically altered by events such as globalization, migration, exile, and diaspora. Emphasizing on the difference, he states that in the classical Bildungsroman, while protagonists grow and evolve, "they do not in fact change, but remain essentially identical with whom they were at the outset" (159). This, as he notes, is not true for the growing-up experiences of youth in a postcolonial setting. Insisting that the "narrative inevitability of being eventually granted conclusive social integration is irreparably punctured by the postcolonial experience of cultural dislocation," he suggests that, for the postcolonial youth, "the self is cast adrift and denied the kind of reassuring, conclusive identity warranted by the seamless past/present/future continuum of cultural traditionality" (160). Miller, in thinking of queer Bildungsromane, also agrees that the coming-of-age story of today has lost the narrative optimism and the linear sense of progression found in the original novel; "the queer Bildungsroman…might trace the ways in which novels of the lesbian, gay and transgender…refused those non-literary discourses which systematized the sexual subject" (244). Today, Miller insists, writers refuse the unified protagonist and remove from the narrative "any manner of instrumentalization beyond the reproduction of its own position" (244).

Cross-Cultural Models

Because the postcolonial Bildungsroman disengages unified coming-of-age narratives, there is no singular model or formula that sheds light on its formalistic and thematic constitution. However, there are multiple traditions of Bildungsromane that have developed across the postcolonial world, and that have acquired local flavours and qualities distinctive of their regions/cultures of emergence. The Arabic Bildungsroman, for instance, expresses certain themes, structures, and tensions that predominantly feature in literary works produced in the Arab world. Nedal M. Al-Mousa notes that a wide range of coming-of-age novels from the Arab world, including ones by canonical novelists such as Tawfiq al-Hakim, Dhu al-Nun Ayyub, Suhayl Idris, and al-Tayib Salih, reveal common themes such as cross-cultural conflicts, spiritual crisis, and the quest for love (223). Al-Mousa thus reflects that in the Arabic Bildungsroman the protagonist typically journeys to the West where "he undergoes experiences...including love affairs which are part of his initiation into life" (224). The themes of transnationalism feature predominately in Bildungsromane from other postcolonial locations as well. In Caribbean literature a prominent strain of female Bildungsroman is dedicated to exploring "a shared, collective Caribbean past" and rewriting a "previously repressed history of Caribbean women" (Ilmonen 62). Recalling coming-of-age novels such as Trinidadian-born Shani Mootoo's *Cereus Blooms at Night*, Ilmonen observes that the Bildungsroman in such settings becomes a transnationally located genre that creates within Caribbean cultural contexts "transnational spaces, migrant identities, queer and feminist topics, deconstructed essentialisms, and hybridities" (63).

If there are Bildungsroman traditions dedicated to voicing the postcolonial experiences of cultural dislocation, then there are traditions of the genre that are more committed to exploring coming-of-age narratives within more bounded frameworks of national, regional, and familial history. Chengzhang xiaoshuo, Hua Li asserts, is a good example of this variation within modern Chinese literature. The genre, Li reflects, responds to "the rise of a new identity of youth as a key stage of life...to build a newly modernizing nation-state" (27). Thus, within the framework of national culture, chengzhang xiaoshuo reveals a dynamic interaction between a protagonist's outward experiences and inner life. Referring to the novels of Su Tong and Yu Hua, Li observes that the chengzhang xiaoshuo juxtaposes "the complexity of individual potentiality" upon the broader domains of "practical realities such as marriage, family, and career," which are deemed as necessary conditions for "the young hero's self-realization" (31).

Both Africa and South Asia also have robust postcolonial traditions of the Bildungsroman that situate a protagonist's search for self-development within local contexts of history and culture. There are two common variants of the genre within African literature where this is observable. One variant, Hoagland identifies, can be found in African war narratives, which present "a violent coming of age for those caught in the crossfire" (234). The African war Bildungsroman tells the story of a "stunted Bildung process" as an inevitable consequence of "the civil wars that marked the post-decolonization period throughout Africa" (234). Hoagland observes that this variant of the Bildungsroman, which narrates the life of a protagonist "who has significantly misunderstood the politics and reality of war and warmaking," commonly manifests "in the memoirs and fictionalized accounts of the child soldier experience" (234). Some prominent examples she identifies include Emmanuel Dongala's *Johnny Mad Dog*, Uzodinma Iweala's *Beasts of No Nation*, Ahmadou Kourouma's *Allah Is Not Obliged*, Chris Abani's *Song for Night*, Chimamanda Ngozi Adichie's *Half of a Yellow Sun*, and the memoirs *A Long Way Gone: Memoirs of a Boy Soldier* by Ishmael Beah and *War Child: A Child Soldier's Story* by Emmanuel Jal.

The other postcolonial variant that operates within traditional African settings is the AIDS Bildungsroman. Novels such as Violet Kala's *Waste Not Your Tears* and Carolyne Adalla's *Confessions of an AIDS Victim*, Hoagland notes, chart a particular *Bildung* process that revolves around the revelation of the protagonist's HIV-positive status and how the protagonist responds to this knowledge (235). These novels are often didactic. In addition to offering textual critiques of "patriarchal privilege, gender inequality and misogyny" that make responding to AIDS difficult within traditional African settings, these novels "highlight the ubiquity of the virus itself" (235). The protagonists in these novels, Hoagland clarifies, typically assume an "'Everyman' quality" and journey towards a self-realization that involves a "deeper, and significantly, correct information about a virus steeped in rumor and misinformation" (235).

In South Asia, the Bildungsroman is a popular medium for narrating the history of the nation's transition from a colonized territory under the British to independence. Many postcolonial writers including Narayan, Rushdie, Bapsi Sidhwa, Kamala Markandaya, and Raja Rao make use of the genre to gesture a "turning away from colonizing culture" in the direction of Indigenousness (Jussawalla 36). Several scholars have noted that Indian writers have transformed the genre by infusing it with local traditions of storytelling and narrative forms. Ralph Crane, for instance, notes that Rushdie's *Midnight's Children*, one of the first autobiographical Bildungsromane from India, "sabotages the very form in which it is written" by merging elements of the Bildungsroman with features from oral storytelling (170). Echoing the scholar Michael Harris, Crane observes that Rushdie, in the novel, merges the coming-of-age plot with local techniques of storytelling such as narrative digressions, character summaries, and linguistic innovation that are characteristic of Hindi cinema: "Rushdie takes the language popularized by Hindi cinema with its street-slang, fast pace, melodrama, romance, and action, and fuses it into his narrative to render a surprisingly modern, energetic view of India" (170). According to Crane, this combination of Eastern and Western influences gives *Midnight's Children* "its status as a world novel, with universal application to twentieth-century life" (170).

The scholar Makarand Paranjape suggests that while both Indian and Western Bildungsromane concern the education of youth, they are guided by distinct features and attributes. The Western Bildungsroman is set in a realistic mode and its emphasis is on the development of the ego, i.e., the self-conscious and independent Kantian subject (53). In contrast, he states, there is a predominant variant of the coming-of-age novel in India that sets fantasy and myths as its backdrop and emphasizes an educational process that promotes disassociation from egotistical attachments. The Western Bildungsroman, Paranjape adds, often follows a chronological progression from childhood to adulthood. This trope, he insists, is also disrupted in the Indian version, which often features protagonists who are adults confronting socio-cultural and economic situations that force them to undertake journeys of self-discovery (see Dutta Roy). The most significant aspect of the Indian Bildungsroman, Paranjape states, is that its narrative devices are often inspired by classical and folk models of storytelling. A good example of this can be found in M. Anantanarayanan's 1960 novel *The Silver Pilgrimage*. The novel follows the story of a prince from medieval Sri Lanka who embarks on a journey to find his true potential as the future king and guardian of his kingdom. While retaining some structural similarities, it departs from the European model in two fundamental ways: One, it traces the protagonist's return to religious orthodoxy, thus inverting the European journey-trajectory that typically begins with orthodoxy and moves towards secularization. Two, it rejects the rags-to-riches storyline of the Western model and adopts the folk narrative device of pilgrimage and exile drawn from precolonial fables composed originally in Sanskrit, such as the *Panchatantra* and the *Hitopadesha*.

Postcolonial Bildungsroman and Human Rights
The postcolonial Bildungsroman is recruited by writers to address larger sociological concerns of social justice, human rights, and climate change. Slaughter is perhaps among the most notable scholars to draw a common genealogy of the development of contemporary human rights laws and the emergence of the Bildungsroman. He notes that contemporary human rights laws function to regulate the relations between individual and state, where the latter is simultaneously imagined as a "predator that must be contained" and a democratic institution that "administers legal personality to human beings" (*Human Rights, Inc.* 89). Thus, he observes both human rights law and the Bildungsroman, a novel concerned with resolving human-state conflicts, share this basic plot structure that manages the pressures of both human rebellion and state legitimation (90–91).

This comparative approach not only enables Slaughter to highlight how the Bildungsroman today engages the intersections of the genre and human rights in a broader postcolonial setting, but it also allows him to revisit the classical models from the perspectives of such concerns. He observes that the idealist eighteenth-century model, represented in *Wilhelm Meister's Apprenticeship*, promotes German-idealist solutions to the perceived conflict between individual and society; "the integration of a particular 'I' into the general subjectivity of a community, and thus, finally, into the universal subjectivity of humanity" (*Encyclopedia of the Novel* 93). Nonetheless, he finds that the classical genre's egalitarian goals to "normalize the social formations and relations of a rights-based nation-state" are starkly contrasted against its historical affirmation of European imperialism and its "civilizing mission" (94). Evoking Maria Lima's study of the postcolonial Bildungsroman, Slaughter observes that contemporary authors of the Bildungsroman such as Dangarembga not only reject the solutions of the classical model but also demonstrate that "colonialism made Bildung improbable, and the desired pedagogical effect of the Bildungsroman was to produce compliant colonial subjects" (96).

Postcolonial Bildungsroman and the Environment

In his book, *Postcolonial Environments*, Upamanyu Pablo Mukherjee states that "postcolonial" as a condition does not just affect humans. Rather, it signals histories, situations, practices, and experiences that highlight "intensified and sustained exploitation" of humans, nonhumans, and ecological spaces "of the former colonies" in the Global South (5). He therefore suggests that literature cannot truly confront the effects of colonialism by focusing exclusively on human experiences. He insists that literature must encounter the intertwining of "postcolonial" and "environment" to understand the current state of the world and its materials strata, which is composed of "soil, water, plants, crops, animals (both domestic and wild)" (5). The postcolonial Bildungsroman has been recruited by many authors to precisely address this intertwining. The environment, as Rob Nixon suggests, plays a crucial role in shaping a protagonist's process of coming of age in a postcolonial setting. Nixon points out that the connection between nature and the process of growing up is clearly observable in Dangarembga's *Nervous Conditions*, a Bildungsroman set in colonial Rhodesia. In it the protagonist Tambu's transition from a rural background to a "middle-class possibility" is expressed through her inhibiting two environmental spaces, one signalling a garden belonging to "the books, the wealthy, and to those at liberty to treat the earth as an aesthetic canvas," and the other, rooted in "her childhood soil, fraught with survival's urgent chores" (27–28).

The intertwining of "postcolonial" and "environment" is also reflected in Helena Feder's articulation of the Bildungsroman as the story about the process of human separateness from nature, human supremacy over nature, and "the struggle for and anxiety about this supremacy" (21). This theme, Feder insists, is expressed in contemporary works including Jamaica Kincaid's *A Small Place*, where readers, addressed as "you," assume the subject positions of tourists who travel to Antigua only to learn they have been cast into the Other's experience of the dominated world; "Positioned rhetorically as a naïve tourist, 'you,'…travel to Antigua…carry your home with you, that you are another colonist, that everything here (as at home) is on your terms, that as you stop to admire beauty, which to you has no history and which you cannot understand, you are an 'ugly' thing" (22). Feder explains that Kinkaid's Bildungsroman thus links that genre's tropes of travel and self-development to "the current ecological and socio-economic realities of tourism and the maldevelopment of the postcolonial world" in telling a story about "those that have been invaded and relocated, those that are too poor to travel and too poor to live properly in the place they live" (19).

If the old European empires have reinvented themselves into invisible and uncontainable transnational corporations as Michael Hardt and Antonio Negri have so eloquently argued in *Empire*, the ruthless exploitations and other forms of oppression associated with colonialism have now found new outlets in the extractivist activities of late capitalist institutions and other entities driven primarily by primitive accumulation. Part of what now constitutes the perniciousness of neoliberal globalization that resembles the ruthlessness intrinsic to colonialism is the slow and invisible nature of its violence in postcolonial settings all over the world where Indigenous lands are appropriated from local inhabitants, exploited of their natural resources, and poisoned by toxic wastes that threaten the lives of both the young and the old (Nixon). The postcolonial Bildungsroman thus emerges in the current context of slow environmental violence as a formidable genre that traces and unravels the devastations and immiserations wrought by new imperial entities in the developing world that endanger and unsettle postcolonial youth.

Bildungsroman and Narrative Forms

According to Franco Moretti, the Bildungsroman has a brief lifespan. The genre lasts no more than the span of eighty years that separates *Wilhelm Meisters Lehrjahre* from George Eliot's *Daniel Deronda*, after which the genre becomes unstable and unsustainable (1906). This position is however contradicted by many who find that the Bildungsroman exceeds far beyond the recognizable boundaries of the "genre proper" in offering narrative sequences and situations that compliment modern culture (1097). This introduction has already highlighted how postcolonial writers transform the Bildungsroman by re-envisioning the classical theme of growing up in a variety of different ways. Scholars such as John Frow, Melissa Hardie, and Vanessa Smith, however, remind us that, along with theme, the formal contours of the Bildungsroman have also been subject to "transformation...historical revision and formal experimentation" within "post-colonial and post-settler" contexts (1096). The African Bildungsroman offers a good example of this. Hoagland observes that many Bildungsromane written in Africa break away from the fictional mound of the classical genre. In fact, she states that Camara Laye's *L'Enfant Noir* (*The African Child*), which is arguably the urtext of the African Bildungsroman, is not fictional at all. Rather, it is an autobiographical narrative that draws from a well-established tradition of nonfictional Indigenous writing that maps realistic representations of childhood "onto representations of the constraints of African history" (230). Hoagland observes that because the African Bildungsroman is so deeply indebted to the local traditions of autobiographical writing, it inevitably breaks the classical rule that "Bildungsromane are fictional texts," and presumably "threatens an aesthetic cornerstone of the genre" (229).

Friedrich Kittler notes that "media ecologies" play a major role in the development and sustenance of the Bildungsroman. More precisely, he notes that the Bildungsroman is mediated through a) available technological environments of communication, and b) new discursive modes of engaging ideas of coming of age. The original European roots of the genre, he observes, were "in the rise of the nuclear family" and in the new pedagogic technologies "with which mothers home-schooled their children" (1908). Today, he insists, the Bildungsroman is subject to a radically different technological environment and is mediated through a wide range of new socio-cultural contexts of engaging coming-of-age narratives. In other words, the Bildungsroman, he remarks, "becomes television shows, graphic novels, and films, and they feature new communities of characters...in the glory of their individuality or particularity" (1908). Perhaps, the mediation of the Bildungsroman form happens most prominently today through comic books and graphic narratives. Ian Gordan insists that graphic narratives are ideal mediums for expressing the coming-of-age motif because they not only possess the "capacity to harness a powerful repertoire of images around adolescence, growth, and the assumption of responsibility," but also appeal "both to youthful readers and adults with an investment in how cultural representations of youth and growing up are organized" (268). Citing examples such as Art Spiegelman's *Maus*, Gene Luen Yang's *American Born Chinese*, and Alison Bechdel's *Fun Home*, Gordan notes that the "graphic novel as Bildungsroman" is not simply a story told (271). Rather, it is a story revealed "through a medium that allows self-reflexive representation in a liminal space, often as tightly focused as a moment captured in a single panel" (271). In clearer terms, he explains that the process of maturation is not just told or shown, but "through the pages of the comic takes effect" (271). He remarks that other mediums, including prose novels, can do this, "but it is the immediacy of comic art that sets graphic novels apart" (271).

Summary of Contributions and Thematic Threads
The vast and perceptive theoretical and analytical yields that have emerged from the chapters in this book not only point to the profundity and malleability of the Bildungsroman as a narrative genre but also the ways in which this unique mode of imaginative expression have served both as a powerful critique of politics and culture in various historical and global contexts. In each chapter, we see how the Bildungsroman simultaneously responds to and shapes particular social histories and the philosophical and cultural assumptions underlying them.

Organized thematically, part one of the book historicizes the genre, both in the colonial and postcolonial contexts. Drawing on what he sees as the ideological proximities inherent in the classical Bildungsroman, Fernández-Vázquez sketches out the cultural and ideological foundations of the genre, arguing that a "certain ideological affinity can indeed be established between the classical forms of the Bildungsroman and colonial discourses." Ericka A. Hoagland also undrapes the complex genealogy of the Bildungsroman but does so to pinpoint the genre's lack of aesthetic purity. While the content of the genre itself is always about identity trans/formation, the form itself embodies the thematic concerns of growth and social changes it enfolds. Given the rapidity of social change, high risks, and uncertainty of futurity associated with a postmodern global order where the certainties of the past are no longer guaranteed, Hoagland shows how the inherent hybrid nature of the Bildungsroman makes it a suitable mode of cultural expression to deal with the vexing "identity-centred" issues associated with a volatile postmodern, posthuman age, "which by necessity means re-imagining not just the self, but the body containing the self."

Part two addresses the postcolonial Bildungsroman more specifically, especially how the classical genre has been reinvented and reimagined in postcolonial contexts to address unique historical conditions. Feroza Jussawalla's chapter identifies a characteristic feature of this adapted mode of narrativization in the postcolony, noting how, in the wake of liberationist movements and the emergence of new nation-states in the 1960s, the Bildungsroman became the preferred genre of writers in India and Africa to convey the excitements about freedom through the voices of young protagonists. The main difference here is how the genre was marked by a search for the soul of the new nation rather than that of an individual in search of meaning and identity in the classical tradition of the Bildungsroman. Simone Maria Puleo shifts the locus of debate from the postcolony to the imperial centre, Rome, unveiling how, in a globalized world in which postcolonial subjects who have been forced by economic, environmental, or security imperatives to move transnationally, the "diaspora Bildungsroman" becomes the perfect medium to capture the struggles of subjects produced out of a "border culture in which the processes of maturation are always interrelated with the burdens of migration and cultural hybridity." In this perplexing context of growth, Puleo argues "coming of age involves mediating the sociopolitical dynamics of assimilation and integration, allegiance and belonging, residence and citizenship." It is the same context of migrancy that informs Filipino American Randy Ribay's novel *Patron Saints of Nothing*, which Antonette Talaue-Arogo argues captures "how the self-productivity of the Bildungsroman has been deployed to resistant ends by less privileged groups, particularly formerly colonized peoples in aid of identity and nation formation." What unites the chapters in this section of the book is that whether in the margins of the postcolony, settler colony, or at the heart of the empire in Europe, the Bildungsroman serves as a very pithy response to what Simon Gikandi has termed "the colonial factor." The postcolonial Bildungsroman was produced out of, and in turn continues to respond powerfully to, the lingering immiserations and contradictions of neo/colonialism.

Part three privileges very important insights into how the postcolonial Bildungsroman deepens the links between childhood, nation, and narration. In the feverish excitement that marked new postcolonial nations, egregious blind spots inherent in the Indigenous culture and liberal democracies emerging in the postcolonies were overlooked. The concerns and anxieties of those on the margins of the new nation, such as minorities, the lower classes, women, the disabled, and other marginalized groups, were ignored. Andrew David King's contribution opens this section and it combines a deep reflection on both form and genre. Honing in on Derek Walcott's autobiography, *Another Life*, he argues that the text "suggests its own reading as a postcolonial Bildungsroman and can indeed be read as one." Part of the wider critique King provides is an exhortation to avoid imposing external generic conventions on text and to read locally situated aesthetic responses to a set of issues, even if on the outside they seem to be some fixed narrative or genre. He ultimately argues, "It is works like *Another Life*…that necessitate and interrogate Frye's 'almost'—and that prompt us to 'recover a sense of the variety of literary forms'" (Fowler v). Aruna Krishnamurthy's brilliant analysis of Upendranath Ashk's *Falling Walls* demonstrates how the text served as terse "class critique, highlighting the inefficacy of stultifying traditions, repressive family hierarchies, regimented reformist movements, and lack of material resources as its mainstay" in India. The Bildungsroman became the poignant genre to highlight and challenge the hypocrisies of an Indigenous culture and its elite searching for freedom and social justice while harbouring and nurturing repressive practices directed at the most vulnerable among them. Maria Su Wang and Bethany

Williamson propose the concept of "spiritual Bildungsroman" to capture the journeys of *other* silent subjectivities whose struggles are beyond the predictable "nation-centric individualism" of the Bildungsroman. Through their analysis of Shūsaku Endō's *Silence*, they unpack how the text skillfully "shows the difficulty of *spiritual* formation (rather than the traditional physical and social coming-of-age) when emissaries from multiple would-be empires clash with each other."

The next chapter in this part is thematized around the discourse of human rights in the context of national healing and reconciliation in South Africa. After forty years of an inhuman political system and racial capitalism founded on racial segregation and the exploitation of non-white subjects under apartheid South Africa, by 1994 the nation sought to reinvent itself through a process of national truth and reconciliation. Deena Dinat's contribution demonstrates how the Bildungsroman became the ideal genre to both forge the ethos of national truth seeking, healing, and reconciliation associated with South Africa's TRC process, as well as the lingering injustices of a biopolitical, post-apartheid society. As he so eloquently shows, if Nadia Davids's *An Imperfect Blessing* "provides a paradigmatic example of how the Commission's norms dominate the possibilities for imagining the young post-apartheid subject," he also calls attention to how K. Sello Duiker's *Thirteen Cents* represents the Bildungroman's aesthetic potential to expose the necropolitical power that underpins contemporary South Africa. If the nation is a cultural product fashioned out of a process of conscious employment strategies as Homi Bhabha argues, the chapters in part three of the book undrape how the aestheticization of nationhood works through the narrative trope of the coming-of-age. Finally, Peter Ribic's chapter demonstrates the imaginative contestations between a single story of national formation and development agenda by the Singaporean state in the 1960s and Goh Poh Seng's first novel, *If We Dream Too Long*, which served as a kind of "reprieve from the homogenizing and synchronizing effects of Singapore's authoritarian model of state-directed economic growth: an unregulated time within which to achieve what Goh describes as a temporary 'spaciousness' (*Dream* 24) amid the calculated tumult of Singapore in the 1960s."

In part four, the contributors expound on the various ways in which the postcolonial Bildungsroman takes on a myriad of issues associated with global modernity such as biopower, temporality, uncertainty, risks, subjectivity, and meaning. Focusing on Helon Habila's *Waiting for an Angel* and Alain Mabanckou's *Black Moses*, Craig Smith unwraps the unique poetics of the "carceral Bildungsroman," which "make carceral enclosure—rather than a 'traditional plot of libidinal closure' (Esty 22)—the central site/rite of maturation." In *Waiting for an Angel*, as well as *Black Moses*, we witness a ruthless modern Nigerian postcolony in which the coming-of-age experience is under the shadow of a brute treasonous state, rather than a compassionate care-taker state. And if the postcolonial Bildungsroman initially sought to imaginatively create and promote nationalist aspirations through a young protagonist that challenges Euro-American colonial values, the context of post-independence disillusionment in Africa from about the 1970s onwards saw the emergence of different character protypes in the African Bildungsroman. Prathim-Maya Dora-Laskey's chapter attempts to answer a very bold question: What happens when a universalist, ethical, and legalistic framework of childhood is applied to South Asian Bildungsromane? Signed into law in September 1990, the UN Convention on the Rights of the Child was seen as a major legal victory for children. It offered a powerful legal instrument to protect and insulate children from the prejudices and chronic indifference of a violent adult world. Using two canonical South Asian Bildungsromane, Dora-Laskey demonstrates how literary narratives can function "as a key reflection of the discourse on human rights."

In his contribution, David Babcock illustrates how Adichie ingeniously recontextualizes the Bildungsroman by "rethinking the ways that aspiring intellectuals figure their relationship to the community, abandoning a concept of the intellectual as authoritative voice of the people in favour of one where the intellectual acts as a conduit for a dense network of interpersonal traces." Helena Wu, too, elaborates on the recontextualization of the Bildungsroman amid the uncertainties and fragmentations of the coming-of-age experience in Hong Kong. The rapidity of global social change has meant that modern-day societies are now beset by uncertainty, unpredictability, and increasing degrees of risk, and young people are at the centre of the ongoing discussions regarding the anxieties assorted with a globalized world. Wu's chapter raises and addresses a very poignant question: "How do we position the postcolonial Bildungsroman in the context of Hong Kong when the goal of coming of age and the society's value system have become increasingly divergent?" Her contribution provides very fascinating insights into the ways in which the aesthetics of magical realism have been central to how Hon Lai-chu, a post-millennial writer, narrativizes the fluidities, destabilizations, and uncertainties that characterize young people's lives in modern-day Hong Kong.

The final part of the book shows the perspicacity of the Bildungsroman as it takes on various social debates and identity questions in diverse postcolonial contexts. Gregory Byala's chapter concentrates on Amos Tutuola's *My Life in the Bush of Ghosts*, noting that the text is not so much a narrative of formation as it is about "transformation," wherein the process of "maturation has produced a liminal subject, pulled in two directions." It is this same experience or feeling of fragmentation, rather than coherent formation and integration into a dominant culture and society, that Elizabeth Jackson unveils in her brilliant analysis of two novels set in Cape Town, South Africa, and London, UK. What her chapter establishes is how the Bildungsroman documents and bears witness to the existential struggles of young postcolonial subjects (of mixed heritage) navigating the challenges posed by their sense of ambiguity towards their cultural identities. These young heroes grapple with the arbitrariness of racism, especially the devastating impacts of racial stereotypes on young people seeking to find a social anchor for their lives in a mean-spirited and bigoted society. Julieann Veronica Ulin's chapter deepens the theme of incompleteness and fragmentation in the coming-of-age experience. Through an ingenious combination of detailed close reading and painstaking theoretical work, Ulin sheds important insights on the complex ways in which Seamus Deane's *Reading in the Dark* interrogates the gripping power of history on the present. The chapter is exemplary in terms of exploring how tensions of past and present, colonial and postcolonial, history and memory, tradition and modernity, real and imagined underscore postcolonial motifs of development/rite of passage.

Rachel Ann Walsh's chapter draws out the paradoxes of a genre concerned with linear development as she examines Ocean Vuong's *On Earth We're Briefly Gorgeous*. Set in the United States, Vuong's novel questions America's national myth of freedom and prosperity for a young protagonist with alternative ethnic and sexual identities. She argues that Vuong's novel deploys both queer poetics and animals as a leitmotif to document "moments of exposure, care, and trauma shared between multiracial and queer subjects whose precarity is determined by their historically uncertain relationship to the category of the human" in America. Julia Wurr concludes the book with her scintillating analysis of texts by three Nigerian feminist writers—Sefi Atta, Flora Nwapa, and Buchi Emecheta. Wurr notes how all the "texts critically explore the great procreative pressure which their female protagonists have to endure from their adolescence onwards." Although not opposed to motherhood as such, what these writers emphasize through the coming-of-age narrative is "how the pressure to have children informs their protagonists' development from childhood to adulthood." Taken together, many of the chapters in the book exemplify how the postcolonial Bildungsroman, as Byala notes, often responds to "the material, economic, and social conditions of its production."

Both in terms of geopolitical and thematic coverage, this book is expansive, tracing not just the originations but also the varied reinventions of the Bildungroman across different postcolonial settings. But the outcome of such a capacious survey of the aesthetic shifts and political and cultural interventions of a very popular genre across three centuries is that we are beginning to witness its ultimate reckoning. In her afterword, Sarah Brouillette rightly notes, "The Bildungsroman has been a key novel genre—if not the urgenre of the novel, as the very *story of stories*, with its generative narrativity of beginning, middle, and conclusive end." But the historical realities that enveloped and shaped the Bildungsroman, especially in the post-imperial, late-capitalist, and postcolonial contexts, have changed remarkably. The certainty of futurity that once served as the captivating premise for the genre no longer exists. Brouillette's coda is a prescient reflection on the body of chapters gathered in this book, as well as a powerful commentary on the near uselesslessness of a genre about futurity when our current historical realities no longer guarantee any futures. It is a brilliant take that challenges us to rethink the exigency of the Bildungsroman in the context of global uncertainties, enormous social risks, unconscionable indifference to human suffering, and unmitigated violence causing planetary ruination.

Works Cited

Al-Mousa, Nedal M. "The Arabic bildungsroman: A generic appraisal." *International Journal of Middle East Studies*, vol. 25, no. 2, 1993, pp. 223–40.

Bakshi, Sandeep. "The Crisis of Postcolonial Modernity: Queer Adolescence in Shyam Selvadurai's *Funny Boy* and P. Parivaraj's *Shiva and Arun*." *Commonwealth Essays and Studies*, vol. 42, no. 1, 2019, pp. 1–14.

Bhabha, Homi. *Nation and Narration*. Routledge, 1994.

Brouillette, Sarah. *Postcolonial Writers in the Global Literary Marketplace*. Palgrave Macmillan, 2007.

Casetti, Francesco. *Theories of Cinema, 1945–1995*. University of Texas Press, 1999.

Cheah, Pheng. *Spectral Nationality: Passages of Freedom from Kant to Postcolonial Literatures of Liberation*. Columbia University Press, 2003.

Crane, Ralph J. "The Chutnification of History." *Inventing India: A History of India in English-Language Fiction*, Palgrave Macmillan, 1992, pp. 170–89.

Dutta Roy, Arnab. "From Modernizing Tradition to Traditionalizing Modernity: U.R. Ananthamurthy's Samskara as Postcolonial Bildungsroman." *Genre: Forms of Discourse and Culture*, vol. 57, no. 2, 2024, pp. 143–68.

Esty, Jed. *Unseasonable Youth: Modernism, Colonialism, and the Fiction of Development*. Oxford University Press, 2012.

Feder, Helena. *Ecocriticism and the Idea of Culture: Biology and the Bildungsroman*. Taylor & Francis, 2016.

Fernández-Vázquez, José-Santiago. "Recharting the Geography of Genre: Ben Okri's *The Famished Road* as a Postcolonial Bildungsroman." *The Journal of Commonwealth Literature*, vol. 37, no. 2, 2002, pp. 85–106.

Fowler, Alastair. *Kinds of Literature: An Introduction to the Theory of Genres and Modes*. Oxford University Press, 1985.

Frow, John, et al. "The Bildungsroman: Form and Transformations." *Textual Practice*, vol. 34, no. 12, 2020, pp. 1905–10.

Gikandi, Simon. "African Literature and the Colonial Factor." *The Cambridge History of African and Caribbean Literature*. Vol. 1, edited by F. Abiola Irele and Simon Gikandi, Cambridge University Press, 2000, pp. 379–97.

Gordan, Ian. "Bildungsromane and Graphic Narratives." Graham, pp. 267–82.

Graham, Sarah, editor. *A History of the Bildungsroman*. Cambridge University Press, 2019.

Graham, Sarah. Introduction. Graham, pp. 1–9.

Helff, Sissy. "Growing Up in Transcultural Diasporic Worlds." *Unreliable Truths: Transcultural Homeworlds in Indian Women's Fiction of the Diaspora*. Cross/Cultures, Vol. 155, Brill, 2013, pp. 107–46.

Hoagland, Erika. "The Postcolonial Bildungsroman." Graham, pp. 217–38.

Ilmonen, Kaisa. "Talking Back to the Bildungsroman: Caribbean Literature and the Dis/location of the Genre." *Journal of West Indian Literature*, vol. 25, no. 1, 2017, pp. 60–76.

Joannou, Maroula. "The Female Bildungsroman in the Twentieth Century." Graham, pp. 200–16.

Jussawalla, Feroza. "Kim, Huck and Naipaul: Using the Postcolonial Bildungsroman to (Re)define Postcoloniality." *Links & Letters*, vol. 4, 1997, pp. 25–38.

Kittler, Friedrich A. *Gramophone, Film, Typewriter*. Stanford University Press, 1999.

Li, Hua. "Bildungsroman/Chengzhang Xiaoshuo as a Literary Genre." *Contemporary Chinese Fiction by Su Tong and Yu Hua: Coming of Age in Troubled Times*. Sinica Leidensia, Vol. 102, Brill, 2011, pp. 13–32.

Lukács, Georg. *The Theory of the Novel*. Merlin Press, 1971.

McCulloch, Fiona. "Bildungsromane for Children and Young Adults." Graham, pp. 174–99.

Miller, Meredith. "Lesbian, Gay and Trans Bildungsromane." Graham, pp. 239–66.

Moretti, Franco. *The Way of the World: The Bildungsroman in European Culture*. Translated by Albert Sbragia. New Edition, Verso, 2000.

Mukherjee, Upamanyu P. *Postcolonial Environments: Nature, Culture and the Contemporary Indian Novel in English*. Palgrave Macmillan, 2010.

Nayar, P.K. *Writing Wrongs: The Cultural Construction of Human Rights in India*. Taylor & Francis, 2014.

Negri, Antonio, and Michael Hardt. *Empire*. Harvard University Press, 2001.

Nixon, Rob. *Slow Violence and the Environmentalism of the Poor*. Harvard University Press, 2011.

Paranjape, Makarand. *Another Canon: Indian Texts and Traditions in English*. Anthem Press, 2009.

Schoene-Harwood, Berthold. "Beyond (T)race: Bildung and Proprioception in Meera Syal's *Anita and Me*." *The Journal of Commonwealth Literature*, vol. 34, no. 1, 1999, pp. 159–68.

Slaughter, Joseph R. *The Encyclopedia of the Novel*. Wiley, 2014.

Slaughter, Joseph R. *Human Rights, Inc.: The World Novel, Narrative Form, and International Law*. Fordham University Press, 2007.

Stein, Mark. *Black British Literature: Novels of Transformation*. Ohio State University Press, 2004.

von Goethe, Johann Wolfgang. *Wilhelm Meisters Lehrjahre*. Tredition GmbH, 2012.

I

HISTORICIZING THE
POSTCOLONIAL BILDUNGSROMAN

1

READING THE CLASSICAL BILDUNGSROMAN AS A COLONIAL GENRE

José-Santiago Fernández-Vázquez

The Classical Bildungsroman as an Expression of Western Modernity
Coming-of-age novels, also described as "novels of formation," "development," or "initiation," have always been among the most popular literary genres in the postcolonial world, from pre- and post-independence classics, such as R.K. Narayan's *Swami and Friends*, George Lamming's *In the Castle of My Skin*, or Ngũgĩ wa Thiong'o's *Weep Not, Child*, to name but a few, to more recent literary productions, such as Uzodinma Iweala's *Beasts of No Nation*, Chimamanda Ngozi Adichie's *Purple Hibiscus*, Kopano Matlawa's *Coconut*, or Romesh Gunesekera's *Suncatcher*, among others. In fact, a great deal of the novels written by the winner of the 2021 Nobel Prize for Literature, Abdulrazak Gurnah, fall within this category, including *Memory of Departure*, *Paradise*, and *Gravel Heart*. The extraordinary success of these types of narratives, which find their main source in the German tradition of the Bildungsroman and its Anglo-American reworkings in the nineteenth century, has been explained in different ways. Critics generally link the development of the postcolonial Bildungsroman to the creation of "national allegories" (Jameson 69), or they refer to

the need these writers have to connect with an international reading public, a goal which would even work as a way of normalizing a narrow universalism (Slaughter 1419). In their readings of specific texts or regional literature, some scholars have also suggested that the postcolonial Bildungsroman constitutes an "identity political tool" (Ilmonen 61), an instrument that is deliberately used to engage in an oppositional dialogue with former colonial masters. The popularity of this literary form in the postcolonial world could then be interpreted as an attempt to appropriate a "master genre."

While I do not think that all postcolonial Bildungsromane must be read necessarily within this "writing back" framework, I would like to argue that a certain ideological affinity can indeed be established between the classical forms of the Bildungsroman and colonial discourses. This "ideological affinity" is an expression of what Edward Said has called a "structure of attitude and reference" (*Culture and Imperialism* 52), that is, the adjacency of different cultural manifestations that, although formally independent, converge with one another, like different branches of the same tree (Said, *Beginnings* 351–52). As Paul Bové has put it, "various 'sciences' might be institutionally and even conceptually discontinuous…and yet given their 'adjacencies' make up a coherent system of thought" (55). Taking Said's methodological approach into account, this chapter examines the cultural and ideological roots of the classical Bildungsroman as a Western-based genre that promotes a colonial ideology. Using Johann Wolfgang von Goethe's urtext *Wilhelm Meister's Apprenticeship* and Charles Dickens's *Great Expectations* as examples, I suggest there is an adjacency between the major narrative conventions of the male classical Bildungsroman and the ideological and epistemological background that characterizes Western modernity and gave rise to colonialism.

A word of caution is necessary, however, before we jump to analyze the colonial undertones of the classical Bildungsroman. As it has been said, the origins of this genre are generally identified with German (pre)Romanticism, having Goethe's *Wilhelm Meister* as the genre's major representative and Victorian British literature as one of its most popular expressions. Yet coming-of-age narratives go beyond the Western tradition, with Goethe's novel being more of a "turning point" in the history of an earlier literary system than the birth of an unprecedented literary form (Golban 4). To give a few examples, in the early twelfth century the Andalusian Muslim philosopher Ibn Tufail already published an allegorical text, *Hayi ibn Yaqdhan*, in which he describes the growing-up process of a young boy living on a desert island and his evolution from ignorance to greater knowledge and maturity. This philosophical text, which was translated into Latin and English in the late seventeenth century, probably influenced Daniel Defoe's *Robinson Crusoe*, which in turn may be considered an example of the Bildungsroman story. If we look at a totally different tradition, we may also find some of the attributes of the Bildungsroman in pre-modern Chinese biography, including the tension between a young protagonist's individuality and the requirements of socialization (Li 33). Even if we were to constrain ourselves to the Western tradition, it would be impossible to ignore the influence that the epic and the picaresque genres have exerted on the evolution of the Bildungsroman. At the same time, however, classical Bildungsromane that flourished in Europe during the late eighteenth and nineteenth centuries have some specific characteristics, which are partly a consequence of the development of Western modernity. This association with modernity opens the path to trace a connection between the genre of the Bildungsroman, in its classical male Western form, and the promotion of the colonial ethos.

The Colonial Affinities of the Classical Bildungsroman

The relationship between colonialist discourse and the Bildungsroman can be seen already in the major narrative development that characterizes the latter. The passage of the hero of the Bildungsroman, the *Bildungsheld*, from ignorance to knowledge—"from unformed childhood towards the emergence of a 'total personality' in adulthood," as Peterson tells us (21)—runs parallel to the development that colonized populations were to undergo as a result of the civilizing project of the Europeans. In this sense, as Jo-Ann Wallace has seen, the idea of "childhood," as a primitive state of consciousness in which the tutelage of others is needed, is one of the images that made the occupation of foreign territories possible, used by some to justify colonial plunder.

As Wallace puts it,

> an idea of "the child" is a *necessary precondition* of imperialism—that is, that the West had to invent for itself "the child" before it could think a specifically colonialist imperialism...This construction of "the child" coincides with the apogee of English colonial imperialism; indeed, it was an idea of "the child"—of the not yet fully evolved or consequential subject—which made thinkable a colonial apparatus dedicated to, in [Thomas] Macaulay's words, "the improvement of colonized peoples." (176)

The use of the notion of "immaturity" to underpin imperialist philosophy took various forms throughout European colonial rule. Sometimes colonizers resorted to the supposed lack of intellectual development of the "Natives" (analogous to infantile or juvenile immaturity) to argue they lacked the feelings of the white man and could therefore be deprived of the rights inherent in the Western (adult) subject. This is, for example, the reasoning used by L.W. Lyde to justify the enslavement of the African population.[1] "It was just because Negroes never attained an 'age' when personal dignity or self-respect became conscious beyond the degree in which they are conscious in the average child, that slavery was a matter of *relatively* little moment to them" (qtd. in Spurr 162). At other times, more subtle but no less damaging arguments were used, such as the extension of the mother-child bond to the realm of the relations between cultures or nations, by means of a clearly incongruous comparison, which forms part of what Spivak has called the epistemic violence of imperialism (139). The identification of the metropolis with a beneficent mother watching over the development of her offspring appears in various colonial writings, but it is perhaps George Lamming, in *In the Castle of My Skin*, who has best expressed the way in which this parallelism was put at the service of the colonial enterprise: "Three hundred years, more than the memory could hold, Big England had met and held Little England and Little England like a sensitive child had accepted" (32).

A supremacy similar to that which the colonizers seek to impose on the colonized nations is exercised by the mentor who tutors the protagonist's development in the classical Bildungsroman. Like the colonizers, the mentor justifies his actions by the benefit derived from them for the protagonist, even if his actions also entail, as in the case of colonial tutelage, an undermining of the individual's freedom. This coincidence is not fortuitous. In both cases—the construction of the colonial subject and the supervision of the protagonist of the Bildungsroman—we are faced with the same pedagogical project in which the influence of Enlightenment thought can be traced. It is significant, in this respect, that when Kant was forced to define what was to be understood by "Enlightenment," in response to the question posed by a Berlin newspaper, he resorted precisely to the idea of "guardianship" or childhood. In his answer, Kant blamed those who, in his opinion, were incapable of accessing the historical maturity he identified with rationalism:

> Enlightenment is man's release from his self-incurred tutelage. Tutelage is man's inability to make use of his understanding without direction from another…Laziness and cowardice are the reasons why so great a portion of mankind…remains under lifelong tutelage, and why it is so easy for others to set themselves up as their guardians. It is so easy not to be of age. (85)

We must warn, with Michel Foucault (35), that the Kantian definition carries an implicit defence of the imperialist mentality. This defence becomes evident from the moment in which Kant excludes some individuals from the benefits of the Enlightenment and claims they should remain under the tutelage of other human beings, as long as they continue to maintain their infantilism.

Kant's thesis, according to which there are a number of individuals who must be governed by others by virtue of their immaturity, found a place in Goethe's ideology, who would also resort to the idea of childhood to justify the absolutist use of power. According to Goethe, and I'm quoting the original words in German, to be completely exact, "*Wir brauchen in unserer Sprache ein Wort, das, wie Kindheit sich zu Kind verhält, so das Verhältnis Volkheit zum Volke ausdrückt. Der Erzieher muss die Kindheit hören, nicht das Kind; der Gesetzgeber und*

Regent die Volkheit, nicht das Volk" (We need in our language a word that expresses, in the same way that childhood relates to the child, the relationship between the people and the concept of the people. The educator has to listen to the child, not to the child; the legislator and ruler, that which concerns the people, not the people) (qtd. in Smith 12). The enlightened absolutism that Goethe defends in this passage was transplanted to the Bildungsroman, where the mentor acts for the benefit of the protagonist but without listening to his opinion, and where the Kantian hierarchy is reproduced between those subjects who are ready to enjoy freedom and those who lack the determination to be free. This is the case in *Wilhem Meister's Apprenticeship*, where a secret society, the Tower Society, tutors the young protagonist and leads him along the path previously marked out, regardless of his desires and inclinations. According to the educational principles of this society, not all men devote their attention to prosper in their perfection, as they should. It is therefore the responsibility of the teachers and members of the society to instruct them in their "proper duties" (Goethe book VIII, ch. V).

From a historical point of view, the concept of "*Bildung*" that gives the Bildungsroman its name refers both to the idea of an organic development and to a set of principles and values that should guide the formation of the individual in society. Among these principles are the belief in progress (an idea that manifests itself in the teleological structure of the Bildungsroman, based on successive stages), and the humanist ideal that developed in Germany during the eighteenth century (*Humanitätsideal*). The philosophy of the *Humanitätsideal* assumes there is a universal subjectivity, a single human nature, that would manifest itself differently in different peoples and cultures. From this arises the need to treat all human beings with respect, since the harm caused to one of them is also an affront to the spirit shared by all. However, as several critics have argued, beyond the egalitarianism it claims to defend, humanism masks a form of reductionist thinking, whereby the attributes of a "centred subject" (masculine and European) are imposed on the rest of the individuals. As Leela Gandhi observes: "The humanist valorisation of man is almost always accompanied by a barely discernible corollary which suggests that some human beings are more human than others" (29). The humanitarian ideal proper to the concept of *Bildung* responds to this excluding philosophy. Johann Herder, promoter of the German pre-Romanticism Goethe later developed, considered that any individual possessed the necessary potential to carry out the organic development he advocated, whose literary manifestation is the Bildungsroman itself. In practice, however, the apprenticeship program envisaged by the German thinkers was limited to the upper classes and excluded women and other minority social groups (Kontje 6–7; Cocalis 404). Schiller, for example, argued that, although the "universal man" remains latent in all individuals, only a few have fully developed their humanity (qtd. in Redfield 51). It would be the responsibility of this chosen group to devise a method of instruction that would ensure the actualization of the universal powers that exist in all human beings. This civilizing project is transferred to the classical Bildungsroman, where, as we have just said, a chosen few are expected to act as models for the other individuals, forcing them to develop their potentialities. This is the main purpose of the Tower Society, as one of its members explains to young Wilhem:

> I felt no interest in men, but to know them as they were. With the same taste I gradually infected all the best of our associates; and this circumstance had almost given a false direction to our plan of culture. For we now began to look at nothing but the errors and the narrowness of others, and to think ourselves a set of highly-gifted personages. Here the Abbé came to our assistance: he taught us, that we never should inspect the conduct of men, unless we at the same time took an interest in improving it. (Goethe book VIII, ch. V)

The intent that the members of the Tower Society express to use a "plan of culture" for the benefit of humankind illustrates the semantic change the notion of culture underwent during the last decades of the eighteenth century. Raymond Williams has shown how the social, political, and economic transformation that Europe experienced during this period gave a new meaning to some common words, such as "industry," "democracy," "class," "art," and above all "culture." The word "culture," which had been used mostly to refer to the "tending of natural growth," started to be understood as a "general state or habit of the mind," a whole way of living, closely associated to an imperative of human perfection (xvi–xviii). This work of perfection, which strictly speaking went beyond a utilitarian tendency, implied that human beings had to be educated for their own benefit so they achieved the highest ideals of cultivation and learning. At the same time, the principles of education and culture worked as the best possible remedy for social disorder and anarchy, as Matthew Arnold would eventually argue (Williams 113–14). As the power of religion diminished in modern European societies, it was necessary to look for alternatives to protect Western "civilization" and to promote social control. The classical Bildungsroman articulates this need for social control through its educational principles, which require the protagonist to submit to the larger social values the mentor represents. In this sense, the mentors who plan the development of the Bildungsroman protagonist in Goethe's and later Bildungsromane appear as the narrative manifestation of the social technicians who, from the eighteenth century onwards, began to devise new methods of disciplining the individual. As Marc Redfield (50–51) has argued, this process ran parallel to the development of a colonialist system. From this point of view, the Bildungsroman can be interpreted, in accordance with poststructuralist assumptions, as a literary form aimed at justifying the "interpellation processes" through which power constructs subjectivity.

The relationship between the education of the individual and the tutelage or subjugation of entire peoples can also be perceived in the fact that the Tower Society does not limit itself only to the education of the protagonist but also intends to transfer its educational project to other lands. The theme of educational development is thus linked to the topic of geographical expansion, whose colonial resonances are even clearer. In *Wilhelm Meister's Apprenticeship*, for example, there are several passages that connect geographical expansion and economic profit. In one of them, the members of the Tower Society decide to support each other in protecting their interests in different countries through a cooperation agreement that bears some resemblance to the division of the world agreed to at the Berlin Conference and in other colonial treaties: "As matters go, it is anything but prudent to have property in only one place, to commit your money to a single spot; and it is difficult again to guide it well in many. We have therefore thought of something else. From our old tower there is a society to issue, which must spread itself through every quarter of the world" (Goethe book VIII, ch. VII). Similarly, in an earlier scene, the narrator links Wilhelm's acceptance of the values of bourgeois society to his discovery of the possibilities offered by commercial activity to establish control over other territories:

> He now, for the first time, felt how pleasant and how useful it might be to become participator in so many trades and requisitions, and to take a hand in diffusing activity and life into the deepest nooks of the mountains and forests of Europe. The busy trading town in which he was; the unrest of Laertes, who dragged him about to examine everything, afforded him the most impressive image of a mighty centre, from which everything was flowing out, to which everything was coming back; and it was the first time that his spirit, in contemplating this species of activity, had really felt delight. (Goethe book IX, ch. XIX)

Wilhelm's words indirectly hint at the link between the mercantile capitalism promoted by bourgeois society and the colonization of other territories, a link that is made explicit in *Great Expectations*, where one of the protagonist's friends plans to enrich himself through trade with the West Indies (Dickens, ch. 22). Ultimately, the "impressive image of a mighty center, from which everything was flowing out, to which everything was coming back," which so fascinates Wilhelm, evokes an "imperialist geometry" based on the distinction between centre and periphery (compare Ashcroft et al. 88). At the same time, geographical mobility dominates one of the major narrative principles in Goethe's novel and in the classical Bildungsroman in general: the motif of travel as an essential part of the protagonist's apprenticeship (*Bildungsreise*).

The hero of the classical Bildungsroman often moves from the countryside to the city (as in *Great Expectations*) or decides to set out on a journey along the roads of his homeland (the case of *Wilhelm Meister's Apprenticeship*). By linking the protagonist's initiation to the exploration of a new geography, the Bildungsroman contributes to the success of the colonial enterprise, paving the way for the spread of its stories of conquest and adventure in distant territories. In the British Bildungsroman, for example, the city is often presented as a land of opportunity where the hero is offered the chance to succeed and to achieve individual enlightenment and refinement, even at the cost of some risk (Pip would never have become a gentleman had he remained in the countryside). In this way, the benefits geographical mobility can bring to the individual are emphasized, establishing an indirect analogy with the reward that, according to the official discourse, awaited all those who took part in the colonizing feat. In fact, in some Bildungsromane, once the protagonist's apprenticeship has been completed, the hero decides to undertake a second journey, which takes him to more distant territories (as in *Great Expectations*, where Pip travels to the East, or in Goethe's novel, the second part of which is devoted entirely to narrating Wilhelm's travels). This second displacement highlights the importance of geographical mobility for the construction of the protagonist's subjectivity, as is also suggested by the fact that Wilhelm's father considers that an essential part of his son's education consists in keeping a travel diary (Goethe, book IV, ch. XVII). In some cases, the emphasis given to the travel motif in the Bildungsroman even makes it possible to establish a link between this literary form and travel narratives, a genre associated with the dissemination of colonialist ideology (Said, *Culture and Imperialism* 310). This is the case, for example, in *Contarini Fleming*, a Bildungsroman written by Benjamin Disraeli in imitation of *Wilhelm Meister*, where the protagonist's apprenticeship is linked to his adventures in different countries of the world, and which reproduces the stereotypes of Orientalist discourse.

During the course of the journeys he undertakes, the protagonist of the classical Bildungsroman experiences a personal transformation: he gains maturity and self-confidence, and eventually he comes to accept the privileged place he is called to occupy within society. The process of transformation that the hero undergoes benefits society, but this evolution is ultimately governed by the defence of individualistic values. A certain egocentrism may even emerge, as it can be appreciated in Contarini's self-description: "When I search into my own breast, and trace the development of my own intellect, and the formation of my own character, all is light and order. The luminous succeeds to the obscure, the certain to the doubtful, the intelligent to the illogical" (Disraeli 2). The importance of individualism in the Bildungsroman goes so far that Lee Erwin does not hesitate to call this genre "the most individualistic of all the individualistic Western forms" (90). Along these lines, Hartmut Steinecke has proposed replacing the term Bildungsroman with *Individualroman* (94). The defence of individualism in the classical Bildungsroman is manifested in the central position occupied by the hero in relation to other characters (it is significant, for example, that the protagonist is almost always the only child, or that his siblings are in the background). Individualist philosophy can also be perceived in the importance given to the moment of choice in the structure of the novel, through which the hero must decide whether to renounce his youthful rebelliousness and accept the dominant social values in a decision that marks his entry into maturity. The defence of individualism is consistent with the bourgeois principles that gave rise to the genre, but it is also, by extension, consistent with the maintenance of the imperialist order. Frantz Fanon observes that "the native intellectual had learnt from his masters that the individual ought to express himself fully. The colonialist bourgeoisie had hammered into the native's mind the idea of a society of individuals where each person shuts himself up in his own subjectivity" (47). The fundamental purpose of inculcating the values of individualism in the colonized subjects was to prevent the formation of a collective consciousness that would facilitate rebellion against the European invaders. But, beyond this specific objective, the individualism of the Bildungsroman is also a fetish of Western culture and, above all, one of the characteristics that frequently differentiates Western philosophy from the Indigenous cultures of the former colonies.[2]

The interest of the Bildungsroman in the social construction of the subject, geographical mobility, and the defence of individualism, which we have examined in the previous paragraphs, connects this genre to imperialist discourse. However, it is paradoxical to note that the Bildungsromane that were written in Europe in the eighteenth century, when the foundations of imperialist philosophy were laid, as well as in the nineteenth century, when Western empires were at their height, seem to pay little attention to colonialism. This impression fades when a closer reading of these novels is made, but only in part. The colonial world, which must necessarily have played a fundamental role in the societies in which the classical Bildungsroman flourished, is almost always incorporated into the text in an indirect or symbolic way. This is the case in *Wilhelm Meister's Apprenticeship* with images of geographical expansion. In *Great Expectations*, the continent of Australia, where Magwitch is serving his sentence, is given a secondary role. But there are also other, less well-known references, which prove the influence of imperialism on young Pip's formation: in chapter twenty, for example, Pip alludes to the superiority of the British people over other civilizations, observing how "we Britons had at that time particularly settled that it was treasonable to doubt our having and our being the best of everything." This statement also reflects the younger self's naïveté, and it deviates from the skepticism that the mature narrator shows (a skepticism also noticeable in the ironic "great expectations" of the title). Shortly afterwards, a secondary character tries to convince Pip about the goodness of trade with Ceylon and the West Indies (ch. 22), an activity the protagonist rejects but replaces with the idea of serving as a soldier in India (ch. 40) and, later, with his journey to "the East" (ch. 59). Sometimes even the descriptions of everyday objects show the influence of colonialism, so that the clothes of those attending Pip's sister's funeral are black "like an African baby" (ch. 35).

All these references prove colonial reality was an omnipresent factor in the everyday life of British society, even if the most brutal aspects about the colonial mission were deliberately ignored. This ignorance is not confined to the Bildungsroman alone, but affects the entire nineteenth-century English novel, as Said has shown in *Culture and Imperialism*. In this work, the Palestinian writer defends the need for "contrapuntal readings" capable of exposing the complicity of the realist novel with colonial discourse (66). As an example, Said offers us an interpretation of Jane Austen's novel *Mansfied Park*, where the economic well-being enjoyed by the Bertram family is guaranteed by a plantation on the Caribbean island of Antigua, run, in all probability, by means of slaves. The link Austen establishes between domestic prosperity in England and the possession of overseas territories thus illustrates, according to Said, the subjugation of the colonies to the metropolis:

> More clearly than anywhere else in her fiction, Austen synchronizes domestic with international authority, making it plain that the values associated with such higher things as ordination, law, and propriety must be grounded firmly in actual rule over and possession of territory. She sees clearly that to hold and rule Mansfield Park is to hold and rule an imperial state in close, not to say inevitable association with it. What assures the domestic tranquility and attractive harmony of one is the productivity and regulated discipline of the other. (*Culture and Imperialism* 87)

A fundamental aspect in this analysis is that, despite the important role it plays in the plot of *Mansfield Park*, the Antigua plantation is mentioned very superficially in the novel, as if the author wanted to deny its existence. This desire to dispense with the details of daily life in the colonies has, in itself, a double ideological significance. First, by omitting any reference to colonial societies, the metropolitan writers follow the slogan mentioned by Pip, which was to emphasize Britain's superiority:

> An apparent indifference about Empire in a work of art indicated not so much a remoteness from imperial involvements as acceptance: the assumption that with Britain at the helm all was right with the world... Where the rest of the world was ignored in a novel, it was because the rest, the non-West, was assumed to be marginal and secondary to the metropolis. (Boehmer 24)

Secondly, this omission has the purpose of reducing to silence all those who might threaten the "normality" of European civilization. As Pierre Macherey has pointed out, the statements that give coherence to the dominant discourse can be articulated only thanks to the existence of certain silences: "For in order to say anything, there are other things *which must not be said*" (95). In the Bildungsroman, this oppressive silence aims to inculcate in the reader the belief in a centred and unitary subject, created from the repression of other forms of subjectivity, which are confined to the margins of the novel.

In *The Colonial Rise of the Novel*, Firdous Azim has attempted to establish a correlation between the emergence of the novel and the colonial project.[3] As a starting point, Azim defines this genre as a narrative characterized by the defence of a unitary subject in accordance with the philosophical principles of the Enlightenment. Then, following Lacanian theses, Azim states that the construction of a homogeneous personality goes hand in hand with the annihilation of "otherness," which makes the novel one of the manifestations of imperialist discourse:

> The translation of imperialism into the novelistic genre is not limited to its thematic concerns, but refers to the formation of the subjective positions of the coloniser and the colonised within the colonial terrain. The narration in the novel is also dependent on the centrality of the narrating subject. The notion of the centrality of this subject and the homogeneity of its narration has also come into being within the colonising enterprise…The central subject who weaves the narrative is also based on the forceful negation of other elements, deliberately ignoring other subject-positions. Thus, the novel is an imperialist project, based on the forceful eradication and obliteration of the Other. (31, 37)

For Azim, the image of unity conveyed to the reader is a chimera. Otherness is always present in the Western narrative, threatening the position of hegemonic discourses. This threat can take various forms: femininity, sexual deviance, criminality, savagery, irrationality.

In line with Azim's thesis, we should note that in the classical Bildungsroman the protagonists reject all those who embody otherness, even when they have played a decisive role in the protagonist's formation. This is the case in Charlotte Brontë's *Jane Eyre*, where Jane describes Bertha as a savage (ch. 25) or a hyena (ch. 26), despite the fact that Jane literally depends on Bertha (or her unfortunate death) in order to marry and carry out her social ascent. As Gayatri Spivak has observed in one of her best-known essays:

> In this fictive England, she [Bertha] must play out her role, act out the transformation of her "self" into that fictive Other, set fire to the house and kill herself, so that Jane Eyre can become the feminist individualist heroine of British fiction. I must read this as an allegory of the general epistemic violence of imperialism, the construction of a self-immolating colonial subject for the glorification of the social mission of the colonizer. (139)

The (self-)immolation to which Spivak alludes is also present in *Great Expectations* and in *Wilhelm Meister's Apprenticeship*. In Dickens's novel, Pip becomes a gentleman thanks to Magwitch's help: "I lived rough that you should live smooth; I worked hard that you should be above work" (ch. 39). However, this does not prevent Pip from showing disgust towards his benefactor—whom he compares to a snake (ch. 39)—nor does it prevent Dickens from deciding to end the convict's life in order to prevent him from interfering in the later stages of the protagonist's training. Something similar happens in *Wilhelm Meister's Apprenticeship*, where several characters are sacrificed for the sake of Wilhelm's well-being and his assimilation of the dominant values. One of the clearest examples is that of Mignon, an abandoned child whom Wilhelm adopts. The girl's sexual attraction to the protagonist makes her an obstacle to the triumph of patriarchal ideology. By the end of the novel, Wilhelm has succeeded in forming a traditional family. Mignon does not fit into this project, due to the ambiguity of her status as adopted daughter and lover. Therefore, she must die. And she dies, like Bertha, in a contrived way, a victim of a strange illness.

The deaths of Mignon, Bertha, and Magwitch show that, in the classical Bildungsroman, happy endings are often achieved at the cost of the suppression of certain forms of subjectivity. In Lacanian terms, we could say that the Bildungsroman is trying to disregard the role that otherness plays in the construction of the hero's subjectivity. Perhaps this could explain Pip's ironic reply to Magwitch when he inquires about the place he should occupy in the house: "'Where will you put me?...I must be put somewheres, dear boy.' 'To sleep?' said I" (ch. 39). According to some critics, this process of repression of otherness would be seen, above all, in the construction of the protagonist's sexual identity. Moretti (28n28) and Tobin (252), for example, have drawn attention to the intense bonds of friendship that are established between the hero of the Bildungsroman and other young people. We would find ourselves, according to them, before a homoerotic attraction, which would be diffused by a later displacement of desire. This displacement can induce the hero, for example, to marry the sister of his best friend, as happens in *Wilhelm Meister's Apprenticeship* (where Werner marries Wilhelm's sister and where Wilhelm marries Lotario's sister). In Goethe's novel, moreover, references abound that show Wilhelm is interested in women in male clothes, such as Mignon herself (Tobin 253). Similarly, Wilhelm embraces his beloved Mariana for the first time when she is wearing a military uniform (book I, ch. I). And before he marries Natalia, he is attracted to Therese, who is described as "a lady such as you will rarely see...a genuine Amazon; while others are but pretty counterfeits, that wander up and down the world in that ambiguous dress" (book VII, ch. IV). To all this we should also add the accusations that the protagonist himself displays androgynous traits (Minden 3).

Another example of the repression of otherness is to be found in the treatment given to the world of fantasy and the supernatural. Due to its bourgeois origin,[4] as well as the influence of the Enlightenment, the Bildungsroman revolves around a positivist philosophy. Consequently, the hero's education is based, among other precepts, on the rejection of "myth," understanding as such everything that departs from a rational explanation (the only exception to this principle would be the assimilation of religious ideas). In *Wilhelm Meister's Apprenticeship*, for example, the members of the Tower Society urge the protagonist to discard his faith in chance. In *Great Expectations*, Pip hides from

Estella that he has seen in the garden the figure of a hanged man (ch. 8), and in *Jane Eyre*, considered by many to be the prototype of the female Bildungsroman, the heroine is reprimanded because she claims to have seen a ghost: "I saw Mr. Lloyd smile and frown at the same time: 'Ghost! What, you are a baby after all! You are afraid of ghosts?'" (ch. 3). Once again, therefore, we can see how the classical Bildungsroman helps to endorse the principles of the Enlightenment, including its disenchantment with nature and spirituality and the promotion of the secular rationalism that characterizes Western modernity.

In addition to making a defence of positivism as the guiding principle of the hero's education, the Bildungsroman corroborates the validity of rationalist philosophy through the way in which fantastic events are described. Generally, the author evokes the fantasy world indirectly, but without the mythical elements ever materializing. In *Jane Eyre*, for example, one can find aspects of the iconography of fairy tales or gothic tales: storms, messages from the beyond, premonitory dreams, etc. (Moretti 187). However, there is no episode that clearly confirms the presence of a supernatural entity, since the appearance of the ghost is attributed, as we have just seen, to the overflowing imagination of the protagonist and, later, to the existence of the first wife of the owner of the house. The same happens in *Wilhelm Meister's Apprenticeship*, where fantastic imagery is used ironically to describe a perfectly plausible event: the initiation ritual into a secret society.[5] Similarly, in *Great Expectations* the description of a terrifying landscape at the beginning of the novel culminates not with the appearance of a supernatural being, as one might expect, but with that of a convict. The lack of development of fantastic symbolism in these stories responds to contradictory dialectics. On the one hand, the attempt to conceal the presence of supernatural elements, associating them with a logical explanation, shows the intention to uphold a rationalist subjectivity at all costs. On the other hand, the fact that mythical elements infiltrate a realistic narrative is proof of the inability of the dominant discourse to impose its will and suggests that otherness can never be completely eliminated.

The survival of fantastic elements in the classical Bildungsroman also indicates that, despite the rejection of irrationalism by Enlightenment thought, European subjectivity continues to be attracted to myth. The desire to deny this evidence causes irrationality to be projected onto other realms outside the Western subject, which would explain the indirect association established between fantastic discourse and the colonial experience. In Dickens's novel, for example, Magwitch's first appearance takes place in a graveyard and, later, when he returns from his exile in Australia, the character is compared to a ghost (ch. 47). In *Jane Eyre*, Rochester's wife of Caribbean origin is described as a "demon" or a "goblin" who haunts the heroine with her "ghastly visits" (ch. 27) and behaves like a vampire: "She sucked the blood: she said she'd drain my heart" (ch. 20).

The use of myth to describe the characters linked to the colonies implicitly reproduces the orientalist schemes Said has brought to light, according to which a distinction must be established between the rational West and an oriental world attached to fantasy, incapable of reaching the highest heights of scientific thought. This argument, based on the traditional distinction between "Myth" and "Logos," has been used, for example, to attribute the origin of philosophy to the Greeks, to the detriment of "oriental" civilizations (Bonnín Aguiló 25). Or to defend the subordination of primitive forms of thought, distinguishing between the rationality of "civilized man" and the superstition of the "savages." However, in contrast to the pejorative vision of myth that predominates in contemporary Western societies, there is a very different conception, which considers fantastic or supernatural experiences as instruments for attaining knowledge and reaffirming collective identity. In this second understanding, myth is identified with the cultural heritage of the community and is often linked to oral traditions. Indeed, in several of the former European colonies in Africa, the Caribbean, or other territories, myth is considered a valuable element.

A final factor brings the Bildungsroman close to imperialist discourse: the analogy between the structure of this type of novel and the linear and teleological pattern of development advocated by historicism—understanding this term in its historiographical sense, that is, as one of the main paradigms to interpret and order the events of the past. It has already been pointed out that the Bildungsroman has a purpose-oriented structure, in which each of the stages of the hero's apprenticeship forms the basis for a subsequent stage. Thus, in the classical Bildungsroman we can distinguish four main stages, which correspond to a large extent to the pattern that the anthropologist Joseph Campbell has identified in traditional rites of passage (30): separation from the dominant social values; initiation, which is usually linked to a geographical displacement; decision to reintegrate into society and accept the hegemonic values; and return. Two aspects of particular interest derive from this teleological structure. First, by describing the hero's apprenticeship through successive stages that complement each other to form a homogeneous whole (the protagonist's process of socialization and integration into the bosom of bourgeois society), the Bildungsroman incorporates the Hegelian notion of *Aufhebung*, as Barney has pointed out: "[the protagonist's *Bildung*] follows the philosophical logic of *Aufhebung*, which defines the ability to absorb and transcend constitutive parts in forming a fully coherent, integral whole" (360). The term *Aufhebung* refers to a process of evolution in which each stage destroys the autonomy of the previous stage but preserves what was valid in it, in the same way that a plant destroys the seed from which it comes in order to develop life. Hegel and other historicist philosophers applied this organic pattern to historical development, arguing history is oriented according to a universal teleology. The rationality that historicism claims for history appears in the Bildungsroman—this would be the second aspect to highlight—thanks to the existence of an educational purpose, which gives meaning to everything that happens. By describing the hero's evolution in a direct line "from error to truth, from confusion to clarity, from uncertainty to certainty" (Tennyson 137), the Bildungsroman contributes to the spread of the historicist thesis that sees progress as the driving force of history.

The thesis that there is universal historical progress, defended by historicism, is clearly inadequate from a postcolonial perspective. The European invaders tried to justify the subjugation of the Indigenous populations under the pretext that Western rule was necessary to contribute to the progress of the colonies. However, as Aimé Césaire and Homi Bhabha suggest, the barbarism into which colonialism degenerated in many cases makes Western civilization morally and spiritually indefensible (Césaire 8) and calls into question the idea that history conforms to a unitary scheme of progress and rationality (Bhabha 41–42). Rather, as Nietzsche argues, history should be conceived as a discontinuous process marked by a "will to power" that leads to the domination of other human beings (78). In his study on the Western concept of history in *White Mythologies*, Robert Young has shown that historicist theses can be sustained only if the least-favoured countries are kept out of the historical process. Hence Hegel's famous statement denying the existence of an African history: "At this point we leave Africa, not to mention it again. For it is no historical part of the world; it has no movement or development to exhibit" (99). A similar argument would be raised by Marx when he claimed, "Indian society has no history," and that what we call its history is merely the history of the foreign powers that have occupied the country and founded their empires "on the passive basis of that unresisting and unchanging society" (217). The exclusion of Africa and India from historical development, by virtue of their alleged "passivity," confirms that historicism conceals a repressive ideology that is detrimental to colonized countries. As Said has repeatedly observed: "So far as Orientalism in particular and European knowledge of other societies in general have been concerned, historicism meant that one human history uniting humanity either culminated in or was observed from the vantage point of Europe, of the West" (Said, *Beginnings* 22). Similarly, Seamus Deane has referred to the way in which historicism links the concepts of historical progress and racial evolution:

> In the nineteenth century, the period in which European imperialism attained its fullest expansion, geographically and ideologically, a Hegelian philosophy of history was invoked to demonstrate that the task of completing human history had been passed on to the European nations…History as a concept was enfolded with race; racial evolution and historical destiny were envisaged as ineluctable forces that marched together in the name of Progress toward the triumph of civilization. (355)

The notion of historical progress that historicism implicitly defends can be maintained, therefore, only if we assume the primacy of the West, which means we should also disregard the history of other nations. The epistemic violence of historicism makes the teleological structure of the Bildungsroman problematic and makes us realize, once again, that the apparently well-ordered progression of the *Bildungsheld* is based on the repression of alternative forms of subjectivity.

Conclusion

As we have seen, several of the characteristic features of the classical Bildungsroman are susceptible to being related to a colonialist ideology. First, the linear and teleological plot that characterizes the traditional Bildungsroman can be connected to the historical theories that favoured the development of European colonialism. By describing the hero's apprenticeship in successive stages that seem to contradict each other, but which in the end form a homogeneous whole, the Bildungsroman incorporates into the text the dialectical vision Hegel and other historicist philosophers used to describe historical development. In turn, the existence of an educational purpose, capable of giving meaning to everything that happens, responds to the teleological model advocated by this philosophical school, claiming the existence of a universal historical rationality. The idea that there is a unitary progress to which all nations must submit, defended by historicism, was used as a pretext to justify the intervention of colonial powers in extra-European territories. A connection can also be drawn between the pedagogical evolution experienced by the protagonist of the Bildungsroman, supervised by a mentor, and the civilizing project based on the Enlightenment that the European colonizers tried to implement in the colonies. The existence of a link between the colonialist ethos and the classical Bildungsroman is also supported by the theme of geographical mobility and by the repression of certain forms of subjectivity that contradict the bourgeois, rationalist, and individualistic values of the genre. Taking into account the adjacencies that can be traced between the classical Bildungsroman and several of the ideas and concepts that framed colonial discourse, this literary genre becomes an ideological battlefield, a symbolic arena where postcolonial writers can contest the epistemological violence of imperialism. The alternative views of the coming-of-age process that populate some postcolonial Bildungsromane thus challenge the alleged universality of Western genres and make us wonder to what extent the concept of universalism is actually an ideological cover-up.

Notes

1. The quote first appeared in 1910, in *United Empire*, a publication of the Royal Colonial Institute.
2. See in this regard, for example, Achebe (205-07), Obiechina (15), Richetti (xii), and Kirpal (149).
3. From a wider perspective, Gauri Viswanathan has shown how the introduction of English literary studies in British India worked to uphold colonial ideology. Western literature thus appears as "a vital, active instrument of Western hegemony in concert with commercial expansionism and military action" (166-67).
4. Vassilis Lambropoulos observes, "If there was a product of civilization that the bourgeoisie detested, it was myth. If there was a category of thought they renounced, it was myth. If there was one kind of story they found alien to logic, it was myth…[Myth] was the single belief the enlightened class did not tolerate" (162).
5. Compare: "[In *Wilhelm Meister's Apprenticeship*] the miraculous becomes a mystification without a hidden meaning, a strongly emphasized narrative element without real importance, a playful ornament without decorative grace" (Lukács 142).

Works Cited

Achebe, Chinua. "The Nature of the Individual and His Fulfillment." *The Colonial and the Neo-Colonial Encounters in Commonwealth Literature*, edited by H.H. Anniah Gowda, Mysore University Press, 1983, pp. 205-15.

Ashcroft, Bill, et al. *The Empire Writes Back: Theory and Practice in Post-Colonial Literatures*. Routledge, 1989.

Azim, Firdous. *The Colonial Rise of the Novel*. Routledge, 1993.

Barney, Richard A. "Subjectivity, the Novel and the *Bildung* Blocks of Critical Theory." *Genre: Forms of Discourse and Culture*, vol. 26, no. 4, 1993, pp. 359-75.

Bhabha, Homi. *The Location of Culture*. Routledge, 1994.

Boehmer, Elleke. *Colonial and Postcolonial Literature: Migrant Metaphors*. Oxford University Press, 1995.

Bonnín Aguiló, Francisco. *La historia de la filosofía y sus orígenes*. Servicio de Publicaciones de la Universidad de Alcalá, 1992.

Bové, Paul. "Discourse." *Critical Terms for Literary Study*, edited by Frank Lentricchia and Thomas McLaughlin, 2nd ed., The University of Chicago Press, 1995, pp. 50–65.

Brontë, Charlotte. *Jane Eyre*. Penguin, 1966 (1847).

Campbell, Joseph. *The Hero with a Thousand Faces*. Princeton University Press, 1968.

Césaire, Aimé. *Discours sur le colonialisme suivi de Discours sur la Négritude*. Présence Africaine, 1955.

Cocalis, Susan L. "The Transformation of *Bildung* from an Image to an Ideal." *Monastshefte für deutschen Unterricht, deutsche Sprache und Literatur*, vol. 70, no. 4, 1978, pp. 399–413.

Deane, Seamus. "Imperialism/Nationalism." *Critical Terms for Literary Study*, edited by Frank Lentricchia and Thomas McLaughlin, 2nd ed., The University of Chicago Press, 1995, pp. 354–69.

Dickens, Charles. *Great Expectations*. Penguin, 1965 (1861).

Disraeli, Benjamin. *Contarini Fleming: A Psychological Romance*. Longmans, Green & Co., 1845 (1832).

Erwin, Lee. "The re-vision of history in the West Indian Bildungsroman." *World Literature Written in English*, vol. 33, no. 2, 1993, pp. 90–102.

Fanon, Frantz. *The Wretched of the Earth*. Grove Press, 1963.

Foucault, Michel. "What is Enlightenment?" *The Foucault Reader*, edited by Paul Rabinow, Pantheon Books, 1991, pp. 32–50.

Gandhi, Leela. *Postcolonial Theory: A Critical Introduction*. Columbia University Press, 1998.

Golban, Petru. *A History of the Bildungsroman: From Ancient History to Romanticism*. Cambridge Scholars Publishing, 2018.

Hegel, Georg Wilhelm Friedrich. *The Philosophy of History*. Dover Publications, 1956 (1899).

Ilmonen, Kaisa. "Talking Back to the Bildungsroman." *Journal of West Indian Literature*, vol. 25, no. 1, 2017, pp. 60–76.

Jameson, Fredric. *The Political Unconscious: Narrative as a Socially Symbolic Act*. Cornell University Press, 1981.

Kant, Immanuel. "What is Enlightenment?" *Foundations of the Metaphysics of Morals and "What is Enlightenment?"*, The Liberal Arts Press, 1959, pp. 85–92.

Kirpal, Viney. "What is the Modern Third World Novel?" *Journal of Commonwealth Literature*, vol. 23, no. 1, 1988, pp. 144–56.

Kontje, Todd. *The German Bildungsroman: History of a National Genre*. Camden House, 1993.

Lambropoulos, Vassilis. *The Rise of Eurocentrism: Anatomy of Interpretation.* Princeton University Press, 1993.

Lamming, George. *In the Castle of My Skin.* Collier Books, 1970 (1953).

Li, Hua. "The Changing Patterns of the *Bildungsroman* in Modern Chinese Literature." *Contemporary Chinese Fiction by Su Tong and Yu Hua: Coming of Age in Troubled Times.* Brill, 2011, pp. 33–74.

Lukács, Georg. *The Theory of the Novel: A Historico-Philosophical Essay on the Forms of Great Epic Literature.* Merlin Press, 1978.

Macherey, Pierre. *A Theory of Literary Production.* Routledge and Kegan Paul, 1978.

Marx, Karl. "The Future Results of British Rule in India." *Marx & Engels Collected Works.* Vol. 12, Lawrence & Wishart, 2010 (1853), pp. 217–22.

Minden, Michael. *The German Bildungsroman: Incest and Inheritance.* Cambridge University Press, 1997.

Moretti, Franco. *The Way of the World: The Bildungsroman in European Culture.* Translated by Albert Sbragia, Verso, 1987.

Nietzsche, Friedrich. *On the Genealogy of Morals.* Vintage Books, 1989 (1887).

Obiechina, Emmanuel. *Culture, Tradition and Society in the West African Novel.* Cambridge University Press, 1975.

Peterson, Carla L. *The Determined Reader: Gender and Culture in the Novel from Napoleon to Victoria.* Rutgers University Press, 1986.

Redfield, Marc. *Phantom Formations: Aesthetic Ideology and the Bildungsroman.* Cornell University Press, 1996.

Richetti, John, editor. *The Columbia History of the British Novel.* Columbia University Press, 1994.

Said, Edward. *Beginnings: Intention and Method.* Columbia University Press, 1985.

Said, Edward. *Culture and Imperialism.* Vintage Books, 1994.

Slaughter, Joseph R. "Enabling Fictions and Novel Subjects: The 'Bildungsroman' and International Human Rights Law." *PMLA*, vol. 121, no. 5, 2006, pp. 1405–23.

Smith, Marielle Christine. *The Fathers of the German Bildungsroman.* 1995. Harvard University, PhD dissertation.

Spivak, Gayatri Chakravorty. "Three Women's Texts and a Critique of Imperialism." *A Practical Reader in Contemporary Literary Theory*, edited by Peter Brooker and Peter Widdowson, Prentice Hall and Harvester Wheatsheaf, 1996, pp. 133–43.

Spurr, David. *The Rhetoric of Empire: Colonial Discourse in Journalism, Travel Writing and Imperial Administration.* Duke University Press, 1993.

Steinecke, Hartmut. "The Novel and the Individual: The Significance of Goethe's *Wilhelm Meister* in the Debate about the *Bildungsroman*." *Reflection and Action: Essays on the Bildungsroman*, edited by James Hardin, University of South Carolina Press, 1991, pp. 69–96.

Tennyson, G.B. "The *Bildungsroman* in Nineteenth-Century English Literature." *Medieval Epic to the "Epic Theater" of Brecht*, edited by Rosario P. Armato and John M. Spalek, University of Southern California Press, 1968, pp. 135–46.

Tobin, Robert. "Healthy Families: Medicine, Patriarchy, and Heterosexuality in Eighteenth-Century German Novels." *Impure Reason: Dialectic of Enlightenment in Germany*, edited by Daniel W. Wilson and Robert C. Holub, Wayne University Press, 1993, pp. 48–64.

Viswanathan, Gauri. *Masks of Conquest: Literary Study and British Rule in India*. Columbia University Press, 1989.

von Goethe, Johann Wolfgang. *Wilhelm Meister's Apprenticeship*. P.F. Collier & Son, 1917 (1795).

Wallace, Jo-Ann. "De-Scribing *The Water-Babies*: 'The Child' in Post-Colonial Theory." *De-Scribing Empire: Post-Colonialism and Textuality*, edited by Chris Tiffin and Alan Lawson, Routledge, 1994, pp. 171–84.

Williams, Raymond. *Culture and Society: Coleridge to Orwell*. The Hogarth Press, 1987 (1958).

Young, Robert C. *White Mythologies: Writing History and the West*. Routledge, 1990.

2

"COULDN'T YOU BE BROKEN AND STILL BRING CHANGE?"

Nnedi Okorafor's Binti Trilogy

Ericka A. Hoagland

"If adolescence is the time when one considers what it means to be human," Elaine Ostry observes, "then there has never been a period of history when it has been more difficult to figure this out than now" (222). This is especially true if we accept that we are on the cusp of— if not already in—a "posthuman" age, one in which "what it means to be human has never been more flexible, manipulated, or in question" (Ostry 222). Texts like Nnedi Okorafor's Binti trilogy, a complex mix of YA, science fiction (SF), and Bildungsroman, inflected by Okorafor's "Africanfuturist" philosophy, and featuring a heroine whose molecular self is manipulated multiple times by either alien DNA or advanced biotechnology, are especially important for how they illuminate a multitude of identity-centred concerns, ones shared by both YA literature and postcolonial texts featuring adolescent protagonists, as well as posthuman narratives. These include navigating a physical body in flux while at the same time negotiating social spaces that are variously indifferent, confusing, and hostile; coming to terms with familial and cultural truths that often throw into question the very bonds of affiliation that have defined the self; and reconciling past experiences with the hard-won knowledge of the present, all in the face of a potentially uncertain future. In the discussion that follows, I consider the Binti series within a framework informed by Okorafor's Africanfuturism, posthumanist concerns, trauma theory, and in active dialogue with the science fiction and Bildungsroman traditions. It is through the integration of the former—Africanfuturism and posthumanism in particular—that Okorafor reconstitutes the postcolonial Bildungsroman as science fiction, and the science fiction Bildungsroman as postcolonial, as well as posthuman, in the Binti series.

In the opening scenes of the series, the trilogy's heroine and namesake, Binti, a sixteen-year-old Himba girl, makes her way in the pre-dawn hours from her family's home to the launch port that will propel her into space. She is bound for Oomza University, an intergalactic institution of higher education specializing in advanced mathematics, science, and weapons technology. There is a simple reason she has left her home so early and without her family: they do not know that their daughter and sister, a "master harmonizer" highly gifted in mathematics, has resolved to leave her home and planet, regardless of her family's and community's disapproval, to do and be "more." It is that single word, "more," that encompasses much of what Binti's journey effectively is: desiring more than marriage and being the family master harmonizer, and building and selling complex and beautiful astrolabs, Binti has set herself in direct opposition not just to her family's expectations, but to the traditions of her people, who, she tells the reader, "don't travel. We stay put" (Okorafor, *Binti* 13). But that desire, Binti reveals, was "an urge so strong that it was mathematical." And "those numbers," Binti tells us, "added up to the sum of my destiny" (*Binti* 29). It is in wanting "more" for herself that Binti inevitably becomes more, far more than she expected, just as she finds herself a part of something far more significant than seeking a university degree, even a degree as prestigious as one from Oomza Uni.

For Noah Berlatsky, "*Binti* is, most directly, a coming-of-age story, about how a girl from a rural backwater comes to the urban center of the universe. But it also challenges science fiction to see that journey as an answer to its apocalyptic invasion obsessions. Every cultural exchange doesn't have to be a genocide—and, in fact, people from other cultures are not hard to find. There are different people everywhere." Indeed, it does not take a particularly discerning reader to notice that Binti regularly refers to the various aliens she encounters as "people": even as she describes their physical otherness—the Meduse's jellyfish-like bodies, or the spider-like body of Oomza University's president—she insists upon that word, on recognizing every alien's personhood. Berlatsky also describes the series as a twist on the reverse colonialism story, noting Binti "is exactly the sort of person who doesn't show up at all" in those stories, which in science fiction frequently depicts an "oddly monocultural" Earth. A monocultural Earth, like that depicted in the *Star Trek* franchise, for example, is held up as a glorious egalitarian achievement, rather than the culture-voiding maneuver it actually is. The "final frontier" of space is, with few exceptions, not that diverse at all, as alien race after alien race is humanoid, with only a few modifications made to the face and head (and sometimes the hands and skin). *Binti*'s universe, by contrast, is wildly, satisfyingly diverse; so diverse, in fact, that Binti's humanoid form is hardly the rule. The diversity of descriptors for the trilogy—an "interstellar coming-of-age story," a story of reverse colonialism, a "story of synthesis"—appear to line up with the universe Okorafor has created.

Yet the Binti trilogy ultimately—and I think, rightly—resists easy categorization, or as Sandra Lindow notes of Okorafor's fiction more generally, "it is not easy to pigeonhole" (46). Attempts to label the trilogy on the one hand appear to be exercises in futility, and on the other, delimiting a trilogy that appears to be deliberately genre-resistant. The challenges posed by the text to categorize it echo, as we will see, the ongoing efforts to define and redefine the Bildungsroman, efforts that become all the more complex when the genre is fused with other forms. Nevertheless, Lindow's description of Okorafor's works as "*thought-experiments* regarding young women who challenge the hierarchical power structures and cultural traditions that hinder their moral development" is a good place to start, if not to label the Binti trilogy outright, then to place it within its most important context (46, emphasis added). This raises the question: Why am I arguing that the series should be read as a postcolonial science fiction Bildungsroman? Why try to "pigeonhole" it? Or, to put it another way, what can be gained from reading the series through this lens? And is there a danger in doing so that may actually limit the text rather than showcase its complexity?

Let me initially respond by arguing that something that "resists easy categorization" most importantly reminds us of the fallibility of categories, to, if you will, "proceed with caution." Challenging texts like the Binti series allows us to test the boundaries of categories or genres, a practice that can assure a category's continued use, or if a category is found wanting, to expose its limits, and if need be, to cast it aside for something better. In thinking through the appropriateness of the label "Bildungsroman" for the Binti series, we are both testing the genre's boundaries and infusing it with rich ideas about what constitutes *Bildung* in a posthuman age. It is useful to recall Jed Esty's observation as we proceed that "genres are almost always empty sets that shape literary history by their negation, deviation, variation, and mutation" (18).

If the nineteenth-century saw the consolidation of the Bildungsroman's conservative ideological subtexts, then the twentieth and twenty-first centuries have been exercises in critiquing the genre's limitations, in some cases dismantling the form only to rebuild it to, in Gregory Castle's words, give the Bildungsroman "a new sense of purpose," and make the genre more responsive to, and reflective of, a variety of subjectivities. Maria Helena Lima effectively concurs, noting that, as "the world assumes different configurations," narrative forms require "new topographies." Or, as Michael Ormsbee notes, "no genre is so entrenched that it cannot be overthrown" (1959). Ormsbee's words are influenced by Yury Tynyanov's observation that when "a new phenomenon *supplants* the old one, [and] occupies its place," it is at the same time both the "substitute" of the older phenomenon "without being a 'development' of the old" (qtd. in Ormsbee 1959). Ormsbee refers to the ongoing disputes to properly define the genre as the "battle for the Bildungsroman" (1962), attempts on the one hand to open up the definition to accommodate those other subjectivities and their stories, but which have the potential to dissolve the borders separating the genre from other forms. On the other hand, "too narrow a definition" threatens "to disappear" the genre entirely. This leads Ormsbee to note that "most critics seek a middle ground for their working definitions, one that allows them to include at least *some* narratives without the apparently embarrassing necessity of including them all" (1956).

Where Ormsbee's concern resides largely in explaining the concept of "protagonicity," the process by which a character is recognized as occupying the dominant position among the characters in a text, in order to "answer the question of how to recognise a Bildungsroman" (1956), his working through of the "inclusive" and "exclusive" definitions of the Bildungsroman provides for us a useful space for thinking through how the Binti series figures in the larger conversation, or "battle" attending the Bildungsroman. More "expansive definition[s]" of the Bildungsroman, like Michael Beddows's (who defines the genre simply as a text charting "'the development of a single hero or heroine'") render the genre, in Sarah Graham's words, "'meaningless because [they] are too wide'" (qtd. in Ormsbee 1956). However, it is worth noting that broader definitions of the genre nevertheless serve a crucial purpose in opening the door to texts that otherwise would be ignored, dismissed, or rejected, though they also threaten whatever stability the genre claims to have. Indeed, ongoing additions of texts to the field, ones that challenge, displace, and disrupt the genre's presuppositions and even its form, like postcolonial and SF Bildungsromane, exacerbate rather than ameliorate the concerns of critics like Graham. That would seem to leave us at a bit of an impasse even before attending to the problems of an overly narrow definition of the genre.

These problems reveal themselves to be self-evident: If the genre is defined in relation to a specific cultural moment and space—that is, located within late and post-Enlightenment Europe—then what of texts outside of that moment, or that space, that otherwise reflect all of the generally agreed-upon markers of the Bildungsroman, most significantly an emphasis on the *Bildung* of the protagonist? Scholarship has generally accepted that the Bildungsroman genre persisted beyond the nineteenth century, and literary as well as scholarly interventions into the genre's Eurocentric, androcentric, and bourgeois roots have effectively rendered much of the exclusive definitional claims on the genre passé. Ormsbee's earlier observation regarding a middle ground thus seems all the more reasonable, and like Castle, he advocates for a "renewed commitment to multiplicity," making an intriguing case for redefining the anti-Bildungsroman as a "mode of textual interpretation which responds to the restrictive 'law' of the Bildungsroman" by offering up instead "multiple protagonists, multiple perspectives, and multiple stories" (1963). This allows Ormsbee to acknowledge the continuing necessity for inclusivity in conversations regarding the Bildungsroman, while also allowing him to make his case for "protagonicity" with regard to identifying the "common denominator" between the broad and narrow definitions of the genre. But, in aligning "multiplicity" with the anti-Bildungsroman tradition, one could argue Ormsbee is essentially engaging in his own act of exclusivity, and indirectly reinforcing the very Eurocentric, androcentric, and bourgeois roots of the genre that critics have worked so diligently to expose. In turn, such a maneuver has the potential to undo the genre's own *"Bildung"* over the last century by associating only the anti-Bildungsroman with the most significant, the most crucial development in the genre: that "commitment to multiplicity" that has arguably saved the genre from impotence.

In turn, the blending of the Bildungsroman with other genres, like YA and science fiction, points to an established "genre adjacent" history of the form that explores the possibilities of synthesis. For example, in the science fiction Bildungsroman, symbolism and metaphor are often used to render science fiction tropes as emblems of the *Bildung* process. In "The Young Adult Science Fiction Novel as Bildungsroman," Michael Levy argues that "with its emphasis on change, the discovery of new knowledge, and the conquest of new worlds," science fiction is a "logical medium for the Bildungsroman" (117). He argues the two together "create a powerful vehicle for the symbolic portrayal of many younger readers' most cherished hopes for the future" (117). While I am not entirely on board with Levy's statement that the Bildungsroman is fundamentally an "optimistic genre" (107), his larger point about the fusion between the Bildungsroman and science fiction is sound.

Ender's Game by Orson Scott Card is perhaps the best-known SF Bildungsroman and offers us a solid point of departure for outlining the central characteristics and tropes of this literary hybrid. Pulling from familiar SF tropes, including setting the story of Andrew "Ender" Wiggin in both a technological-advanced future Earth and in the far reaches of space, and applying the common SF plot device of an alien threat to humanity, the novel follows Ender as he is trained along with other exceptional children first at "Battle School" and later at "Command School," both being military facilities preparing the children to eventually take on the alien threat, known as the "buggers." In its revelations about Ender's earlier childhood, his struggles at school on Earth, his conflict with his older brother Peter, and close relationship with his older sister Valentine, *Ender's Game* reads very much like a YA novel, though it is most frequently described as military SF. Yet Peter Hall convincingly demonstrates that *Ender's Game* (as well as two other pieces of military SF, Robert Heinlein's *Starship Troopers* and Joe Haldeman's *The Forever War*) exhibit all the characteristics of *Bildungsweg*, or the path to self-formation, and of Jerome Buckley's "generalized plot synopsis of the Bildungsroman," which Hall describes:

> The adolescent sets out in the world, meets with setbacks usually caused by his own temperament, encounters several guides and mentors, makes false starts in selecting companions and a vocation, until finally he gains enough insight to achieve a personal transformation that allows him to adapt to the demands of his times and environment by finding a vocation in which he may work effectively. (153)

Leaving aside for the moment that Buckley's plot synopsis describes the plot of the Binti series pretty accurately, let's take a closer look at how *Ender's Game* helps us to map out a rough definition of the SF Bildungsroman. Just as with traditional, that is to say, more "earthbound" Bildungsromane, the emphasis on Ender's maturation process, which culminates in his adjustment to the cruel truth of his direct involvement in genocide and his attempts to rectify that action, reflects Hall's words that, like any Bildungsroman, Ender has essentially marshalled "the inner resources of [his] youth...to challenge an unresponsive or hostile environment" (158). In this case, it is the widespread xenophobia towards the buggers, even after their almost complete annihilation, and the desire to make Ender a puppet of his brother Peter's political machinations, that push Ender further into space, towards both possible redemption and a peaceful future where humans and buggers can coexist. Hall argues that, "dislocations in time and space" aside, the SF Bildungsroman should be approached like "any other Bildungsroman" (158). These words are revealing for what they tell us about what a SF Bildungsroman is, and even what it is not.

In insisting upon the SF Bildungsroman's "sameness" in relation to the traditional Bildungsroman, Hall is asserting for texts like *Ender's Game* a place at the table along with other canonical Bildungsromane, including the ones Buckley himself uses to define the genre and establish its socio-cultural and ideological functions. But in doing this, Hall is also implicating the texts he discusses, and the SF Bildungsroman more generally, within the problematic ideological spaces occupied by the Bildungsroman. All of this is to say that those "dislocations in time and space" that Hall downplays when discussing the SF Bildungsroman in favour of its larger connections to the traditional Bildungsroman are absolutely crucial to delineating what distinguishes the SF Bildungsroman from its traditional forebear.

Let's briefly turn our attention to Ashley Maher's interesting work on Naomi Mitchison's 1962 novel, *Memoirs of a Spacewoman*. Not only is Maher's phrase "intergalactic education" an intriguing way to describe Binti's own education in Okorafor's series, but in arguing that Mitchison's use of "future fiction's imaginative resources" to "envision a future social and political organisation in which the Bildungsroman would once again function," in casting the genre out into the "wilds" of space, Mitchison and other writers who blend SF with the Bildungsroman are able to "think beyond the Bildungsroman's traditional containers of nation and empire" (2147). Indeed, this is crucial to Okorafor's trilogy and the "work" it is doing in relation to a remapping of the Bildungsroman, as Okorafor, like Mitchison, "offers a revised model of both subject formation and collective development" (2148). By bringing Binti into contact with different lifeforms and the moral codes that govern them, Okorafor presents endless possibilities for Binti's development, a fact further underscored by Binti's physical evolution.

Maher argues that Mitchison "reclaims the narrative of progress central to the classical Bildungsroman" by upending what Jed Esty describes as "'mainstream developmental discourses of self, nation, and empire'" that have increasingly dominated discussions of the genre, by rendering, at most, narratives of economic development and empire building to subtexts in her novel (2151). This is also the case with the Binti trilogy. While the first novel, *Binti*, does relocate the traditional colonial contact zone out into space with the story of the Meduse chief whose stinger was stolen from him and put on display at Oomza University, the series as a whole is more devoted to Binti's "narrative of progress," one which is crucially shaped by Okorafor's Africanfuturist philosophy and the transhumanist elements she integrates into the larger story. In using speculative fiction to, in the words of Jennifer Wager-Lawlor "intentionally destabilize" the "ideal and ideological teleologies of a classical Bildungsroman text" (Wager-Lawlor 24), the "feminist future fiction" Maher discusses, like *Memoirs of a Spacewoman*, introduces both "new social worlds" and new bodies of knowledge to the genre (2156). This is essential work that directly speaks back to Ormsbee's "commitment to multiplicity," while also gesturing to the very specific "body of knowledge" that organizes Okorafor's "future fiction."

The introduction of other ideologies into the Bildungsroman is an intentional act. It carries with it the "threat" of destabilizing and the promise of rebuilding. This is precisely what Okorafor's definition of "Africanfuturism" does: constructed by Okorafor as a response to the limitations of Afrofuturism, which, as she states, "did not describe what I was doing," Africanfuturism is a deliberate act of destabilizing attempts to define her work as Afrofuturist, while offering a new construction, a new space that more appropriately defines what ideas underpin her stories. Describing Africanfuturism as a "sub-category of science fiction," Okorafor says it "is concerned with visions of the future, is interested in technology, leaves the earth, skews optimistic, is centered on and predominantly written by people of African descent (black people) and it is rooted first and foremost in Africa. It's less concerned with 'what could have been' and more concerned with 'what is and can/will be.' It acknowledges, grapples with and carries 'what has been'" ("Africanfuturism Defined"). In connecting Africanfuturism to science fiction, and also to the Bildungsroman and its work, we can more clearly see how Okorafor's Binti series destabilizes the genre and rebuilds it, just like its protagonist, into something "more."

This "more" is a key motif in the trilogy, beginning—and ending (or more appropriately, continuing)—with Binti herself. As Okorafor observes of her heroine: "She's constantly asking the question, 'Who am I?' This question grows louder and louder with each novella" (Liptak). What began as a desire for more than just the traditional path that had already been determined for her in the first volume becomes more than she bargained for when the alien Meduse take over the ship transporting her to Oomza University. And when the Meduse manipulate her genes in order to communicate with her, they set her on another path, this one of physical "more-ness" that in turn moves Binti and her story into the space of the posthuman. In blurring the lines not only between the human and the technological but the human and the animal, and the human and the alien, Okorafor challenges her reader to both reassess what it means to be human, and humanity's capacity to transcend its physical, epistemological, and cultural limitations: to be "more" like Binti herself. Taken still further, the *posthuman* science fiction Bildungsroman deconstructs what Victoria Flanagan calls "normative understandings of subjectivity" (20), instead positing subjectivity as "networked and collective," as well as "hybridised and fluid" (8, 25).

A bit more on that last point: the posthuman offers a space for thinking about *Bildung*—what it means, what it can be—beyond the human. Rather than "depict an individual who develops...by overcoming hostile environments," as can be seen in traditional Bildungsromane, as well as colonial and postcolonial Bildungsromane, the protagonist of the posthuman science fiction Bildungsroman is "radically transformed by her surroundings" (Maher 2145). As such, *Bildung* is written just as intensely upon the body as within it, and physical transformations have the potential to both fragment and suture. Furthermore, the posthuman lays bare the limits of "bodily masternarratives [that] authorize a very narrow range of responses: that it is maturing or evolving or deteriorating or remaining the same, becoming dependent or independent; that it is threatened by, succumbing to or recovering from illness; that it is gaining or losing, for good or ill, various features or functions (weight, hair, muscles, mobility, etc.); that it is growing, reproducing, dying" (Halberstam and Livingston 18). Just as the postcolonial Bildungsroman frequently engages in recuperative acts of culture and the self, fashioning and refashioning identity against a backdrop of colonial trauma and neocolonial imperatives, the posthuman SF Bildungsroman "attend[s] to the specificity of the human—its ways of being in the world, its ways of knowing, observing, and describing—by…acknowledging that it is fundamentally a prosthetic creature that has coevolved with various forms of technicity and materiality" (Wolfe xxv). What is evident is that, whether we are talking about a postcolonial Bildungsroman or a posthuman Bildungsroman, the fundamental concerns about what makes us human and about how otherness is created and maintained apply. The Binti series explores both, setting part of the trilogy on an earth "fundamentally altered by climate change" and places like Binti's homeland still bearing the marks of "imperialist domination [and] yet persisting and evolving beyond that history" (Crowley 256). Furthermore, the series of transformations Binti undergoes, ones that mark her more "other," as well as posthuman, are also the changes that equip her to survive a maturation process that is deeply marked by trauma and violence. She survives precisely because she mediates, or "harmonizes," the variety of cultures that would define her, and in so doing emerges a Bildungsroman protagonist like no other.

"African science fiction's blood runs deep, and it's old, and it's ready to come forth," Okorafor notes in a 2017 TED Talk. What began as "the need to see an African girl leave the planet on her own terms," the Binti trilogy became, like its protagonist, "more." In its pages, readers can detect Okorafor's observation, "For Africans, homegrown science fiction can be a will to power." It reflects, too, the fact that "not all science fiction has the same ancestral bloodline" ("Sci-Fi

Stories That Imagine a Future Africa"). At once a powerful evocation of the deep African ancestral bloodlines coursing through her writing, Okorafor's work is also a deliberate attempt to draw attention to the "epistemic violence" inflicted by Western cultures, including the "exclusion of African stories and African bodies from its collective visions" of the future (Burnett 122). "Rather than waiting futilely for the crumbs of African futures [that are] doled out occasionally and reluctantly by Western science fiction," Burnett notes, writers like Okorafor "can imagine their own futures" (133), one which foregrounds African creativity and culture towards life-affirming and transformative ends. That Okorafor's trilogy revolves around these concerns should come as no surprise. Just like the tessellating triangles weaving a pattern into Binti's hair that speaks of her family's "bloodline, culture, and history" (*Binti* 23), Okorafor braids into the Binti saga Himba culture, African colonial history, and deep ecology to create a science fiction Bildungsroman that is Africanfuturist, postcolonial, and posthuman.

Inasmuch as Okorafor's trilogy reflects Linda Ng's words that the Bildungsroman is a "future-facing genre" (2167), as well as Dustin Crowley's point that Okorafor is using the science fiction genre "to project and prepossess a future in which African peoples like the Himba are not shut out of technological agency and its posthuman possibilities" (244), much of what defines Binti's *Bildung* is trauma. In fact, I would argue that the *Bildung* process is itself fundamentally a traumatic one, a "violen[t] maturation" that "requires the individual to undertake a kind of self-organising makeover, a metamorphic dissolution in order to be reborn" (Ng 2168, 2172). Such a "makeover" for Binti would appear to be inevitable in the first volume, an action necessary if Binti is to acclimatize to the world Oomza University represents and offers her admittance into, and that is precisely the sort of change Binti's mother most fears, telling her daughter that Oomza "wants you for its own gain. You go to that school and you become its slave" (*Binti* 14). While her mother's words rest heavily on her, they are not enough to dissuade Binti from defying her family's wishes and Himba tradition and leaving home to attend Oomza University. Okorafor is quick to cast Binti's *Bildung* "amongst the stars," and more significantly within the history of imperialist violence, by embroiling her in the first volume in a conflict between the alien Meduse and the very university she is so eager to attend. Five days before arriving at Oomza University, the ship carrying Binti and a few hundred students and professors is attacked by a group of Meduse, a jellyfish-like race who "initially appear to be [the] colonizers, [but] instead become the colonized," as Okorafor positions the Meduse as "Natives" who have been victimized by Oomza University, which has been displaying the stinger of the Meduse chief for many years (Burnett). The Meduse who attack "Third Fish" are on what amounts to a suicide mission to retrieve the stolen stinger, and in so doing, restore the honour of their chief and their people. In a quick but graphic scene, Okorafor depicts the Meduse slaughtering everyone on the ship, leaving only the pilot and Binti alive. The rest of the first volume details Binti's captivity on Third Fish, the sentient, shrimp-like space transport, and later, her successful negotiations between the Meduse and Oomza University.

These two initial sites of trauma, the possible future trauma invoked by Binti's mother, and the more immediate and tangible trauma witnessed by Binti, firmly situate trauma as a significant agent in Binti's maturation process. She must learn to navigate things both seen and not seen, including the various emotional and physical traumas she endures. But it is specifically the slaughter in the dining hall that inaugurates trauma as both a theme and an agent of *Bildung* in the series, and it is the memory of that moment that follows Binti as she makes the voyage back to Earth on Third Fish in the opening of *Binti: Home*. A few dozen pages into the second volume, Binti finds herself just outside the same cabin in which she was held captive by the Meduse a year ago, and she must fight back a mounting panic attack as the memory of the murder of one particular friend, Heru, a brilliant and kind Khoush boy, plays over and over in her mind.

According to Amanda Wicks, "following a traumatic event, any memory associated with that experience registers primarily as implicit memory or memory that 'we do not know we know,' so that it cannot be recalled at will" (Nalbantian qtd. in Wicks 14). While Binti is expecting "nasty flashback[s]" (*Binti: Home* 40), she "needed to go home" (*Binti: Home* 31), thus weighing her desire to be back with her family against the certain distress she will experience by returning to the site of her initial traumas. Like most victims of trauma, Binti has little control over when that memory will assert itself: it is just as likely to wash over her at random, unguarded moments as it is when she is actively facing that terrible time like she does on Third Fish. Moreover, her trauma is all the more heightened by both her survivor's guilt and a feeling of complicity: "I'd become a family with the murderous Meduse," she observes (*Binti: Home* 43). Not only that, but for Binti, "traumatic memory becomes conflated with reality so that it seems to occur in the present" (Wicks 332). In other words, her trauma not only actively and regularly asserts itself, forcing her back to that horrible moment, but it affects Binti's ability to participate in the present, to *be* present. Her trauma threatens to define her; in the words of Susan Brison, "Trauma undoes the self by breaking the ongoing narrative, severing the connections among remembered past, lived present, and anticipated future" (41).

What emerges over the course of the trilogy, then, is Binti trying to make sense of an "ongoing narrative" that is itself constantly in flux, accelerated *and* confounded by a series of revelations, and sharpened by violence and betrayal. The sting that allows her to communicate on behalf of the Meduse also changes her carefully curated locks into the *okuoko* of the Meduse, and apparently wipes away the "code" representing her "family's bloodline, culture, and history" she had braided into the tessellating triangles of her hair (*Binti* 23). What's more is that Binti does not realize the extent of that physical change until she arrives at Oomza University. After successfully negotiating the return of the Meduse chief's stinger that had been stolen years ago by representatives of the university,[1] Binti is asked by a Khoush professor if she will ever return home, since her people "don't like outsiders" (*Binti* 80). It is in that moment that Binti finally "sees" what has happened to her hair, which is now more like tentacles, translucent and glowing "a strong deep blue like the sky back on earth on a clear day" (*Binti* 81). Forced to face her now "strange body," Binti collapses into treeing out of desperation and grief. Later, in a private moment, Binti reapplies *otjize* to her new "hair," and this moment is significant not only because she must actively confront and touch her "strange body," but in putting *otjize* on her *okuoko*, she is also incorporating this new "truth" about her body into her Himba self. That the *otjize* she applies to her hair is made not from the clay near her home but clay from the planet on which Oomza University resides shows Binti once more engaging in the kind of identity negotiations that characterize the *Bildung* process. Binti is not only assured that she can recreate the *otjize* away from home, but the *otjize* itself acts as a kind of suture, helping to heal Binti's psychic wounds by grounding her in its familiar and comforting touch and smell. Even the distinct differences between earth-made *otjize* and Oomza-made *otjize* that Binti notices do not undermine its symbolic power, or for that matter, its healing properties, as Binti uses it to heal one of the tentacles of a Meduse, Okwu, with whom she has become friends and who has joined her at Oomza University at the close of the first volume.

The second volume of the trilogy essentially expands on the interlacing of trauma, *Bildung*, and the posthuman by taking Binti back to Earth to reunite with her family and to complete a Himba ritual. Once more, the effective intersections between trauma and the posthuman—and the science fiction Bildungsroman as a vehicle for exploring those intersections—are apparent. As trauma theory "focuses on how psychological trauma affects human consciousness and is inscribed in the body, leading to diverse interpretations and redefinitions of being," and discourses on the posthuman "foreground[s] questions regarding what constitutes the human, exploring the boundaries of subjectivity and the body," we can in turn also see how Binti's *Bildung* is one best described as both traumatic and posthuman (Ferrandez San Miguel 30). The "strange, new world" Binti must learn to navigate is her own body, and it is through those attempts to incorporate those new parts of herself/her self that Binti can begin to heal and be whole again.

For if anything else, the trilogy begins not with a fractured sense of self: Binti may be seeking something beyond what her insular Himba culture can offer when the trilogy begins, but she is not unsure of who she is until she leaves home. Likewise, her return home leads to more, rather than less, destabilizing: the joyous family reunion at the beginning of *Binti: Home* degenerates into an argument between Binti and her older sister, Vera, who accuses Binti of selfishness, of bringing dissonance. Her sister's accusation echoes Binti's own fear, articulated just after she disembarks from Third Fish and into her family's arms: "For a moment I was two people," she thinks, "a Himba girl who knew her history very well and a Himba girl who'd left Earth and become part-Meduse in space. The dissonance left me breathless" (*Binti: Home* 52). Instead of finding reassurance back home, Binti is left more uncertain and resents her family for not understanding what she has been through, even as she struggles to explain it to them, which in turn exposes the limits of language to describe trauma.

Binti is hopeful that going on pilgrimage, a significant rite of passage for Himba girls, and one which her departure from Earth postponed, may offer her the comfort and answers she is seeking. But the night before she begins that pilgrimage, the Night Masquerade, a powerful masked figure representing "the approach of a big change," appears to Binti (*Binti: The Night Masquerade* 56). That "big change" comes the next morning in the form of her father's people, the Enyi Zinariya, or "Desert People," who take her across the desert to their home. The journey to her father's people is not unlike its own pilgrimage, bringing Binti deeper into the desert, farther away from her family, but closer to a heritage that, until her paternal grandmother comes to retrieve her, was hidden from her. She discovers that the Enyi Zinariya are possessed of very old and very advanced alien knowledge and technology. This discovery forces her to acknowledge her own prejudices, as she assumed her father's people were inferior, mistaking their odd hand movements as some form of mental illness. She learns that those movements are actually how the tribe manipulates a virtual reality technology unlocked by the biological nanoids, known as "zinariya," that are written in their DNA. As one of the daughters of the desert people, that alien DNA is in Binti as well; she must undergo an initiation ritual that will allow her to access that technology already inside of her. But just as she is struggling to manage the strong impulses of her Meduse DNA, Binti finds that properly using the biotechnology within her is just as difficult.

She is hardly given any time to adjust, let alone embrace, this new part of herself, however. Back at her family's home, where Binti's Meduse friend Okwu, who has accompanied her on her journey back to Earth, awaits her return, the Khoush, largely figured as the trilogy's primary antagonist and the long-standing enemy of the Meduse, attack Binti's village. When Binti's father refuses to turn over Okwu to the Khoush (Okwu is actually hiding in the nearby lake), the Khoush begin bombing "The Root," Binti's home that has been carved into the roots of an Undying Tree. Binti learns of the attack just as her initiation ritual with the Enyi Zinariya is finishing,[2] thus connecting (while also truncating) a moment of growth with another trauma, another loss.

Consumed with grief over the loss of her family and abandoned by the Himba Elders in the third volume, *Binti: The Night Masquerade*, Binti once more takes on the role of master harmonizer when she returns to her village and attempts to broker a peace between the Khoush and the Meduse. She draws upon the "deep culture" of the Himba during the negotiations, but her efforts, while impressive, are only temporary. The moment the Khoush forces return to their ships, they begin to fire indiscriminately on the village, and Binti's body is torn apart. She does not live to learn that her family survived the attack on The Root after all, and they are left to mourn their extraordinary daughter and sister. Her family is convinced to let Okwu and the daughter of Third Fish, "New Fish," take Binti's body to space, and it is in the breathing chambers of New Fish that Binti undergoes her third transformation, which also resurrects her. Binti learns that New Fish's mother guessed that Binti might be healed by New Fish's microbes, as young Miri-12s still contain many of these life-building cells. Though restored to life, Binti's new "parts" only further confuse her sense of self: "am I really even me?" she asks (*Binti: The Night Masquerade* 192). She even acknowledges just how radical and strange all the changes to her body are: "I don't want all this…this weirdness! It's too heavy! I just want to be" (193). Now permanently tethered to New Fish, just as she is to the Meduse and the Enyi Zinariya, Binti's *Bildung* is hardly complete: just as she must continue to manage the trauma that led to her physical transformations, she must also learn how to exist in a world that has no name for her. So she names herself: "My name is Binti Ekeopara Zuzu Dambu Kaipka Meduse Enyi Zinariya New Fish of Namib" (*Binti: The Night Masquerade* 170).

Throughout the trilogy, Binti's passage into adulthood is regularly, almost perversely, interrupted by traumatic violence and bodily incursions that threaten her subjectivity and disrupt the goals of harmony and synthesis that define the traditional Bildungsroman. Read as metaphors for the changes expected of, and in some cases forced upon, the postcolonial and posthuman subject, the admittedly extreme experiences to which Binti is subjected challenge her abilities as a "master harmonizer" just as they challenge the reader to reflect more deeply on how the self is forged in conflict. Perhaps this is why, as the trilogy comes to a close, Okorafor gives Binti a well-earned happy ending. Back at Oomza University, and joined by Okwu, Mwinyi, and some close school friends, Binti takes one more journey, this time to the falls near the school, something she had long wanted to do. "When we got there, it really was like witnessing a beautiful dream," Binti tells us (*Binti: The Night Masquerade* 203). The nightmares and the flashbacks may not be gone, but for the moment they are replaced by something more hopeful, something that speaks both to who she is and what she yet might be.

Conclusion

Rather than confine "Africa to its colonial past or its neocolonial, fractured present," Andrew Liptak argues that "the *Binti* novels instead insist on Africa's crucial role in humanity's future." By placing Binti at the centre of humanity's future among the stars, Okorafor elevates the Bildungsroman's function: no longer bound by reckoning solely with narrow social systems on Earth, the Binti series contemplates what the *Bildung* process must take into account in an increasingly posthuman age, which by necessity means reimagining not just the self but the body containing the self. Where YA texts "use biotechnology as a metaphor for adolescence," according to Elaine Ostry, Binti's "flexible body that challenges borders" functions more as a metaphor not only for the possibilities suggested by the posthuman body, but by a more flexible understanding of the *Bildung* process itself (223). No longer limited by either a fully human body or by the confines of Earth, Binti's development is more than just ongoing; it is evolving, constantly transforming. Like Naomi Mitchison in *Memoirs of a Spacewoman*, Okorafor seems "interested less in staging the failure of the classical Bildungsroman than in staging the failure of the social and political forces that threaten[ed] and limit[ed] its model of self-formation" (Maher 2147). With Ostry's idea of the flexible body in mind, the *Bildung* process is productively destabilized and rebuilt to accommodate a more expansive idea of humanity that breaks free of "the conventional definition of humanity" that Ostry argues still limits YA science fiction (235).

But whether Binti's destiny to transcend the human—and possibly the mortal—through a fusion with alien DNA and alien technology is the path for humanity in general remains unclear. Like many Bildungsroman and YA protagonists, Binti is presented from the outset as special, already "more" than those around her even before she undergoes her first transformation. This would appear to suggest that Binti's destiny may not be a collective one, and in casting her as a Messiah-like figure in the third volume, Okorafor further sets Binti apart from those around her: human, alien, or sentient species. Okorafor thus collapses organic boundaries for her heroine while erecting others that insure her "more-ness." But as she intimates in the third volume, Binti's merger with New Fish is not one-way: "Your body is partially me," New Fish tells her, and "I am partially you." When Binti fully absorbs this truth, she is able to occupy New Fish's body and "swim" in space, though she is also now tethered to the Miri-12s, meaning she cannot be more than five miles away from New Fish.

Bettina Burger argues, per Emma Dabiri, that when Binti joins the Meduse hive mind, this represents a movement away from "western epistemological traditions that imagine the self as an essential unified being" (Kurtz qtd. in Burger 372). She reminds us that Binti "does not give consent" when the Meduse stinger is plunged into her spine (372), any more than she has given consent to have zinayira technology in her DNA, or New Fish's microbes running through her body. That

Binti's triple transformations are essentially the choices of others for her cannot be overlooked. In that sense, the series does not reconcile an abiding problem in the Bildungsroman, the expectation that the protagonist must conform to the social order to survive. Given no choice but to accept those transformations, Binti must find a way to bring these new parts of her identity into productive, positive synthesis. Binti embodies precisely what Karen Barad argues in *Meeting the Universe Halfway*: she has reached "a point where individuality is itself undone by the specific entanglements of becoming that transcend the distinctions between bios and technics, organic and inorganic, artificial and natural, mind and body" (qtd. in Burger 373).

To return to Peter Hall, this would appear to be the very "dislocations in space and time," and I would add, of the body, that the traditional Bildungsroman form cannot support. At least not without the intervention of science fiction, which is better equipped to address the challenges posed to the Bildungsroman in our posthuman, Anthropocene age. Yet the Bildungsroman remains central to explorations of the self, and why a merging of the two makes so much sense. Just as "*Binti's* mathematics points towards a dismantling of traditional Western concepts of science," and Okorafor's insistence on Africanfuturism "opens up a new category that may be helpful in discussing newer texts of African science fiction," which also are not "dependent on previously established, Western science fiction tropes" (Burger 366), her reconfiguring of the Bildungsroman through a synthesis of the transhuman, the Africanfuturist, and science fiction opens up the genre in ways that, to borrow a phrase from Ashely Maher, expand its "novelistic scale" in ways wholly appropriate and necessary for the post-millennium, posthuman age.

Likewise, Binti herself is the logical next step in the development of Okorafor's female protagonists. Like the liminal spaces of the desert and space in which the trilogy is set, Binti occupies and represents a threshold, a "space between" Okorafor's younger, still physically maturing heroines in *Akata Witch*, *Zahrah the Windseeker*, and *Who Fears Death*, and the adult Binti has not yet become. Like Sandra Lindow's description of Okorafor's fiction as "interstitial," the bodies of Okorafor's heroines are likewise interstitial, sliding, and in some cases erupting, into new forms, and Binti is no exception. In turn, by using the Bildungsroman to rewrite the form, Okorafor is engaging in necessary work for the Bildungsroman, ably moving it into a space where "what it means to be human has never been more flexible, manipulated, or in question." That the Bildungsroman found a home in the world of science fiction long before *Binti* attests to the necessity of this "merger" on the one hand, and on the other, Okorafor's inventive updating of this merger in the Binti series opens the door for more additions to this increasingly significant literary hybrid.

Notes

1. Aside from associating the theft of the Meduse chief's stinger with the story of Saartje Baartman (1789–1815), a Khoekhoe woman with steatopygia who was displayed at various attractions and exhibitions, the Meduse stinger is, like Saartje Baartman's genitalia (which continued to be displayed after her death), a private and sacred part of the body. This makes both the removal of the stinger and its display more than just theft but a violation. This violation is made all the worse by the fact that, as Vajra Chandrasekera points out, the officials at Oomza have "no idea how the stinger ended up in their museum." This stunning lack of responsibility is quite simply a manifestation of the university's "latent violence [and] imperial arrogance" (Chandrasekera). Though it makes promises to remove those Oomza individuals responsible, the university offers no official apology. What is additionally interesting is that the Meduse fail to appreciate the violation they enact upon Binti's body when she is stung. Seen as a practical means to an end, the Meduse cannot see the irony of their own actions any more than Oomza University can see what it had done with the chief's stinger as anything other than an action done in the interests of science.
2. When her father senses Binti has unlocked her latent zinariya technology, he "sends" a message to her that clearly signals his unhappiness: "Oh, no, no, no, what have you done?" (*Binti: Home* 159). Her father's disappointment is almost more than she can bear. "After all I'd already done to him, to everyone, to myself," she despairs (*Binti: Home* 159).

Works Cited

Barad, Karen. *Meeting the Universe Halfway: Quantum Physics and the Entanglement of Matter and Meaning*. Duke University Press, 2007.

Berlatsky, Noah. "Nnedi Okorafor's *Binti* Steers the Reverse-Colonialism Story in a New Direction." *Medium*, 23 Mar. 2017, https://medium.com/@Random_Nerds/nnedi-okorafors-binti-steers-the-reverse-colonialism-story-in-a-new-direction-dd188a89c954.

Brison, Susan J. "Trauma Narratives and the Remaking of the Self." *Acts of Memory: Cultural Recall in the Present*, edited by Mieke Bal et al., University Press of New England, 1999, pp. 39–54.

Burger, Bettina. "Math and Magic: Nnedi Okorafor's *Binti* Trilogy and Its Challenge to the Dominance of Western Science in Science Fiction." *Critical Studies in Media Communication*, vol. 37, no. 4, 2020, pp. 364–77.

Burnett, Joshua Yu. "'Isn't Realist Fiction Enough?' On African Speculative Fiction." *Mosaic: An Interdisciplinary Critical Journal*, vol. 52, no. 3, 2019, pp. 119–35.

Castle, Gregory. "Coming of Age in the Age of Empire: Joyce's Modernist Bildungsroman." *James Joyce Quarterly*, vol. 40, no. 4, 2003, pp. 665–90.

Chandrasekera, Vajra. "Binti by Nnedi Okorafor." *Strange Horizons*, 29 Feb. 2016, http://strangehorizons.com/non-fiction/reviews/binti-by-nnedi-okorafor/.

Crowley, Dustin. "*Binti*'s R/Evolutionary Cosmopolitan Ecologies." *Cambridge Journal of Postcolonial Literary Inquiry*, vol. 6, no. 2, 2019, pp. 237–56.

Dabiri, Emma. *Don't Touch My Hair*. Allen Lane, 2019.

Esty, Jed. *Unseasonable Youth: Modernism, Colonialism, and the Fiction of Development*. Oxford University Press, 2012.

Ferrandez San Miguel, Maria. "Appropriate Bodies: Biopower and the Posthuman in Octavia Butler's 'Bloodchild' and James Tiptree, Jr.'s 'The Girl Who Was Plugged In.'" *Atlantis: Journal of the Spanish Association of Anglo-American Studies*, vol. 40, no. 2, 2018, pp. 27–44.

Flanagan, Victoria. *Technology and Identity in Young Adult Fiction*. Palgrave, 2014.

Halberstam, Judith, and Ira Livingston. *Posthuman Bodies*. Indiana University Press, 1995.

Hall, Peter C. "'The Space Between' in Space: Some Versions of the *Bildungsroman* in Science Fiction." *Extrapolation: A Journal of Science Fiction and Fantasy*, vol. 29, no. 2, 1988, pp. 153–59.

Levy, Michael M. "The Young Adult Science Fiction Novel as Bildungsroman." *Young Adult Science Fiction*, edited by C.W. Sullivan, Greenwood/Praeger, 1999, pp. 98–118.

Lima, Maria Helena. "Decolonizing Genre: Jamaica Kincaid and the Bildungsroman." *Genre: Forms of Discourse and Culture*, vol. 26, no. 4, 1993, pp. 431–59.

Lindow, Sandra. "Nnedi Okorafor: Exploring the Empire of Girls' Moral Empowerment." *Journal of the Fantastic in the Arts*, vol. 28, no. 1, 2017, pp. 46–69.

Liptak, Andrew. "Sci-Fi Author Nnedi Okorafor on Creating an Instellar Coming-of-Age Story." *The Verge*, 25 May 2017, https://www.theverge.com/2017/5/25/

15610998/nnedi-okorafor-binti-home-night-masquerade-cover-interview-read.

Maher, Ashley. "*Memoirs of a Spacewoman*: Naomi Mitchison's Intergalactic Education." *Textual Practice*, vol. 34, no. 12, 2020, pp. 2145–65.

Ng, Linda. "Fixing to Die: Kazuo Ishiguro's Reinvention of the *Bildungsroman*." *Textual Practice*, vol. 34, no. 12, 2020, pp. 2167–83.

Okorafor, Nnedi. "Africanfuturism Defined." *Nnedi's Wahala Zone Blog*, 19 Oct. 2019, http://nnedi.blogspot.com/2019/10/africanfuturism-defined.html.

Okorafor, Nnedi. *Binti*. Tor, 2015.

Okorafor, Nnedi. *Binti: Home*. Tor, 2018.

Okorafor, Nnedi. *Binti: The Night Masquerade*. Tor, 2018.

Okorafor, Nnedi. "Sci-Fi Stories That Imagine a Future Africa." *TED*, 22 Nov. 2017, https://www.youtube.com/ watch?v=MtoPiXLvYlU.

Ormsbee, Michael. "Battle for the Bildungsroman: 'Protagonicity' and National Allegory." *Textual Practice*, vol. 34, no. 12, 2020, pp. 1955–68.

Ostry, Elaine. "'Is He Still Human? Are You?' Young Adult Science Fiction in the Posthuman Age." *The Lion and the Unicorn: A Critical Journal of Children's Literature*, vol. 28, no. 2, 2004, pp. 222–46.

Wager-Lawlor, Jennifer A. *Postmodern Utopias and Feminist Fictions*. Cambridge University Press, 2013.

Wicks, Amanda. "'All this happened, more or less': The Science Fiction of Trauma in *Slaughterhouse-Five*." *Critique: Studies in Contemporary Fiction*, vol. 55, no. 3, 2014, pp. 329–40.

Wolfe, Cary. *What Is Posthumanism?* University of Minnesota Press, 2010.

II

COLONIALITY, POSTCOLONIALITY, COSMOPOLITANISM, AND THE BILDUNGSROMAN

3

CONTEXTUALIZING THE POSTCOLONIAL BILDUNGSROMAN

Feroza Jussawalla

The Bildungsroman is the genre that most defines what we today call "postcolonial literature." The simple growing-up story of a young protagonist coming into a knowledge of themselves, mostly as an individual, or, using the Joseph Campbellian paradigm, a hero's growth into an understanding of their world, was the genre that seemed to appeal the most to writers such as Indian writers R.K. Narayan, Mulk Raj Anand, and Raja Rao, or the African writers Ngũgĩ wa Thiong'o and Chinua Achebe, who had begun to write in English immediately upon the independence of their countries from colonialism. Though English was a second language for the majority of them, whether Indian, Nigerian, or Kenyan, it comprised their colonial education. Gauri Viswanathan's *Masks of Conquest: Literary Study and British Rule in India* shows how British education influenced these up-and-coming writers in their style and genre choices. This led them not only to write in English but mimic the Victorian novels, often Bildungsromane like *David Copperfield*, for instance. That is why, in the context of African cultural production, for example, Simon Gikandi has rightly argued that postcolonial African literature began as a response to what he calls "the colonial factor." Not only were pioneer African writers such as Chinua Achebe, Wole Soyinka, Ngũgĩ wa Thiong'o, and others in their cohort products of colonial institutions, they began their writing careers by responding to colonialist representations about Africa, and colonial institutions and their ideas and policies in the continent. In the case of India, it must be remembered that it was T.B. Macaulay who introduced English to the colonies. In his 1835 minute on English education in India he had written:

> We have to educate a people who cannot at present be educated by means of their mother-tongue. We must teach them some foreign language. The claims of our own language it is hardly necessary to recapitulate. It stands pre-eminent even among the languages of the west...In India English is the language spoken by the ruling class. It is spoken by the higher class of natives at the seat of government. It is likely to become the language of commerce throughout the seas of the East. ("English Education Act 1835")

In the past forty-plus years of teaching what we now call postcolonial literature, and thirty years of producing Salman Rushdie scholarship, I have argued that, even if a novel like *Midnight's Children* (or *The Satanic Verses*, for that matter) seems to be postmodernist in style, at the base of the work is the coming to a realist awareness of belonging to a "nation" and being part of the broader efforts to promote the chosen ideals of that nation (nationalism).

I would like to reiterate that the central theme of *most* postcolonial novels is a coming to an awareness of belonging to a nation, nationality, and Indigenous and local identity, even if that awareness entails an interrogation of the concept of nation derived from colonial ideas/foundations of "the nation." In the case of the Indian subcontinent, it must be remembered that Gandhi, Nehru, and Jinnah were all products of British education, and Gandhi brought the idea of liberation from his English language "reader," edited by a Mr. Bell. Gandhi noted that "Mr. Bell rang the bell of alarm in my ear, and I awoke" (Gandhi 73). In the case of Africa, when I questioned Achebe about whether the Westminster model of government did not prepare them to govern their own countries, he responded by saying,

> It was not the intention of the British to practice their system in the colonies. They practiced a colonial system, a totalitarian system, whether in Africa or India or wherever. So, to expect the colonial subject to have imbibed the Westminster model during the colonial period is farcical. Because there was no Westminster model practiced in the colonies; there was no training…So you have to wrestle with independence—that's really the issue. You don't deal with it by running back to servitude. (Jussawalla and Dasenbrock 66)

So, despite their sense of nation being derived obliquely from colonial models, they do have a sense of a "nation" as an "imagined community" (see Anderson) that embodies their cultures to which they belong. This is what I mean by the writers' sense of nation, nationality, and belonging: their loyalty/attachment to their soil, their cultures, their communities.

Thus, the Bildungsroman as written by writers, grappling with their sense of newly constructed nations, and coming into an identity of their own, becomes the defining trope of postcolonial literature per se. All the novels I am going to write about follow a certain pattern. A young protagonist finds themselves in a cross-cultural situation as a result of colonialism, and the journey is one of finding out where he belongs, what his/her identity is, and, often, the outcome of that endeavour is a nationalistic awareness of belonging in one's country/culture.

The novel form, though sometimes considered foreign to most postcolonial cultures, is the favoured form of both literary and political expression for postcolonial writers. It merged well with the oral storytelling tradition.[1] Thus, we find that more often than not, from the beginning of postcolonial writing, writers turned to the novel form. From the earliest of these novels, R.K. Narayan's *Swami and Friends*, in 1917, to Salman Rushdie's controversial novels *Midnight's Children* and *The Satanic Verses*, the theme is that of a young boy or girl (as in Bapsi Sidhwa's *Cracking India*) growing up under a foreign power; going to school in a British system; learning and adapting to a foreign language, with some introspection of the writer's use of the language; and then, more often than not, coming into an awareness of him/herself as belonging in one's own culture, country, and nation. *Nation* and *nationality* then become major themes not just of the literature but of the theory. How do we define a nation? How is one's nationality shaped? What discriminations does a child/individual face in growing up under the dominance of a different culture as the dominant power? And so it is that the postcolonial Bildungsroman becomes the allegorical representation of not just the experience of the heros but the growing nations themselves.

I have written extensively on the evolution of the Bildungsroman in colonial and postcolonial discourse, both as a genre of realism and national awareness ("Kim, Huck, and Naipaul"; "Reading Barbara Kingsolver's *Poisonwood Bible*"). The genre began in the eighteenth and nineteenth centuries as a novel that depicted a young man's journey into foreign lands and different civilizations to both be educated (*Bildung*) and discover himself. Later, it began to be associated with what Joseph Campbell identified as the hero's journey in search of "the golden fleece," which more often than not was "the self"—self knowing within the hero's psyche. The traditional genre, taking its roots from early folktales, evolved into the nineteenth-century novel of self-discovery. With its German background, it also became a novel of nationalism at a time when nationalism was percolating in Germany in the late nineteenth and early twentieth century. From its early inception, it was the genre of realism, of the portrayal of people, places, and perils that the hero traversed through and that led to the spiritual, emotional, or political growth of the hero or heroine. Women writers like Charlotte Brontë and George Eliot laid the basis for novels that came to be called female Bildungsromane. This incorporation of the female heroine became more sophisticated with, say, Henry James and E.M. Forster's travels of women heroines.

It can safely be said there is a very particular pattern: the protagonist finds themselves in a cross-cultural situation, pulled in two directions by forces that seek to determine whether they want to belong in and among the Westerners, or whether they belong in their Indigenous community. Several factors impact them: there is English language education and the interaction with the colonial educational system, learning English, changing and adapting English to "make it their own" (as in the case of a Joyce or Rushdie); religious education, and its rejection, whether it is the Christianizing effort of the colonial schools or the mission schools; a consequent confusion in the minds of the protagonist; and a necessary journey away from that situation that eventually leads to an awareness of belonging. The journey motif is particularly important in finally deciding where one belongs and where one's allegiances lie. This is true not just of the most simplistic novels, like R.K. Narayan's *Swami and Friends*, but all the way up to Rushdie's experimentations with style and form, and Zadie Smith's more complicated layered narratives as in *White Teeth*.

As said before, in their use of the Bildungsroman, these writers are and were very much influenced by the German form that came down to them through the British use of the form, from their colonial education. In fact, R.K. Narayan, in his 1974 autobiography *My Days*, describes how his uncle admonished the young writer to follow the example of Dickens, particularly *Great Expectations*, which, in itself, is a Bildungsroman. This is also true of Rushdie, who, despite always acknowledging that his father asked him to work from the *Arabian Nights*, says his father also urged him to connect with the British literary tradition. However, Rushdie also claims a more intellectually sophisticated literary heritage. Here is how he traces his literary ancestry:

> Let me suggest that Indian writers in England have access to a second tradition quite apart from their own racial history. It is the culture and political history of the phenomenon of migration, displacement, life in a minority group. We can quite legitimately claim as our ancestors the Huguenots, the Irish, the Jews; the past to which we belong is an English past, the history of immigrant Britain. Swift, Conrad, Marx are as much our literary forebears as Tagore or Ram Mohan Roy. America, a nation of immigrants, has created great literature out of the phenomenon of cultural transplantation, out of examining the ways in which people cope with a new world; it may be that by discovering what we have in common with those who preceded us into this country we can begin to do the same. (Rushdie, *Imaginary Homelands* 20)

Turning from that, Rushdie claims what perhaps can be considered a postmodern heritage:

> My own—selected half-consciously, half-not—include Gogol, Cervantes, Kafka, Melville, Machado de Assis; a polyglot family tree against which I measure myself, and to which I would be honored to belong. (*Imaginary Homelands* 20–21)

Despite this claim of Rushdie's, it is not a leap to say that Indian writers use the trope of the Bildungsroman for nationalistic and realistic purposes just like their German literary ancestors.

Goethe's *Wilhelm Meister*, a historical and social novel, used the Bildungsroman for nationalistic and class analysis. Here the *Bildung* is less a journey of personal growth than, after his "years of apprenticeship," a journey into national identity and sense of the exceptionalism of that identity. Hannah Arendt sees *Wilhelm Meister* as an attempt by educated noblemen and actors to cultivate "personality" in a middle-class hero, "because the bourgeois in his own social sphere is without personality" (169). But at the same time it is also an inculcation of German values, such as pride in their "culture."

In *Signs Taken for Wonders*, Franco Moretti writes,

> At the end of *Wilhelm Meister's Years of Apprenticeship* everything—episodes, characters, values find an unambiguous arrangement within an organic totality. Wilhelm Meister's Bildung—and through him the reader's—consists precisely in recognizing this state of affairs; in feeling integrated and finally finding one's peace there. (231)

Moretti also posited that, in the postmodern world of mass culture, the *Bildung* would be redundant. However, looking at the new novels emerging both in the postcolonies and in the diaspora, even in languages such as Arabic, we see the fascination with and compulsion of the genre. Many contemporary writers, too many to list, whether Indian, or from the African nations, or diaspora writers, or even new, younger writers who express their disaffection with Westernization, do so through the eyes of a young hero. Perhaps they use their own growing-up experiences and desires to come into their identities in their writing. The genre persists and seems ever more relevant.

At the ending of most postcolonial Bildungsromane, the hero, just like Wilhelm Meister, gains a feeling of being at home in one's culture and nation after a journey of cross-cultural interactions and challenges, especially after anti-colonial encounters. Even if that "feeling of being at home" is not so much an acceptance of the conditions of existence, they suggest an acute awareness of the various forces enveloping and defining one's life. The "homeliness" I suggest here is a very conscious formulation of a set of repertoires that allow subjects to successfully navigate those uncertain and perhaps unacceptable spaces and material conditions of the nation. Therefore, the Bildungsroman seems to have become the defining genre of postcolonial literature. It best expresses nationalist sentiment because almost all the characters express dissatisfaction and disaffection with cross-cultural situations and find home in their cultural and national contexts. This sets the pattern for postcolonial Bildungsromane that document an archetypal character's anti-colonial sentiments in the cross-cultural colonized world and then a coming to peace with oneself in one's nationalist identity. Pramod Nayar, in his influential book *Writing Wrongs*, notes, "The Bildungsroman works in much the same way, where it posits an inalienable, immanent self that needs to grow, but also shows how the self is formed through and within a social context" (98). However, he also makes the case for what he calls the "dissensual Bildungsroman," or narratives of "untouchability," "othering by caste" (98).

The dissensual Bildungsroman portrays a self that has not been allowed to grow due to the social contexts it finds itself mired in. The Dalit narratives are "anti-development" texts, tracing the blockages that arrest the growth of the self, akin to what feminist readings of women's texts show as a "growing down" (as opposed to the male protagonist's "growing up") due to hostile contexts (Lazzaro-Weis). The self-cultivation central to the classical Bildungsroman is not possible here. Thus, the dissensual Bildungsroman is a narrative of the dissonance between self-determination and integration. More importantly, it gestures at the social contexts of the self. If in the classical

Bildungsroman trials and circumstances are seen as opportunities to shape an individual's own identity, in postcolonial India—with its caste, class, poverty, and other forms of structural inequalities—they become spaces where identities are predetermined with no agency for the individual to intervene in the process.

Like Nayar, Jed Esty also moves from the traditional Bildungsromane of the modernist period to the anti-development narrative, because he believes the traditional narratives, at this point in history, provide little insight into our current times. However, at the risk of repeating myself, I would say the persistence of the form in the hands of many current and contemporary writers—the continuous emergence of new Bildungsromane—shows the usefulness of the form for those who want to describe the path of their awareness. While there are too many to list, some examples come to mind such as Ali Eteraz's *Native Believer*, Mohja Kahf's *The Girl in the Tangerine Scarf*, or Hanif Kureishi's *The Buddha of Suburbia* or *My Son the Fanatic*. The list could go on.

One would have to classify the anti-Bildungsromane that Nayar and Esty reference as a separate and different genre than the traditional Bildungsroman that allows for the protagonist's growth into self-awareness and national awareness. They do this in the particular form and structure I have emphasized here, repeatedly.

All the novels discussed here are rooted in realism regardless of linguistic, stylistic, and formalistic experimentation. This stylistic experimentation itself is a nationalistic gesture, trying to "make English one's own." To prove this, I turn to Raja Rao's preface to his stylistically experimental novel, *Kanthapura*. Rao attempted to break standard English and write in a varied English that was meant to capture the language as spoken or written by Indians. Interestingly, Rushdie also does this. Rao's manifesto is as follows:

> One has to convey in a language that is not one's own the spirit that is one's own. One has to convey the various shades and omissions of a certain thought movement that looks maltreated in an alien language. I use the word "alien," yet English is not really an alien language to us. It is the language of our intellectual make-up—like Sanskrit or Persian was before—but not of our emotional make-up. We are all instinctively

bilingual, many of us writing in our own language and in English. We cannot write like the English. We should not. We cannot write only as Indians. We have grown to look at the large world as part of us. Our method of expression therefore has to be a dialect which will some day prove to be as distinctive and colorful as the Irish or the American...The tempo of Indian life must be infused into our English expression, even as the tempo of American or Irish life has gone into making theirs. (vii)

Rao used this as a justification for his postcolonial move to break English, which was then also seen as early manifestations of modernism and postmodernism, especially when he was often compared to someone like Joyce, which is a comparison that also follows Rushdie. In fact, both authors are simply representing the "real" Indian English dialect as it exists and expressing "realism."

Similarly, while Rushdie's stylistic and formalistic experimentation can be seen as postmodern in structure and style, it greatly reflects the reality of both the Indian English of the context and the actual history he is attempting to rewrite. Rushdie is often considered postmodern because he is deconstructing the metanarrative of Indian or subcontinental history. Lyotard says, "I define *postmodern* as an incredulity toward metanarratives" (xxiv).

However, if we define the postcolonial Bildungsroman by using the characteristics I lay out, such as challenging the colonizer's language, religion, education, political systems, culminating in a return to one's roots, we can see that Rushdie, like any of the Bildungsroman authors mentioned here, is also very much a realist, and his narratives are also rooted in realism.

A simple study of the development of Indian English in the various locales of India shows just how realistic Rushdie's effort is at capturing the Indian English dialect. It is because of this that Rushdie became extremely popular with his Indian readership, whether in India or abroad, as they could hear the rhythms of the Indian English they grew up with. Furthermore, his depictions of subcontinental politics, politicians, and military officers show his realistic knowledge of subcontinental matters. If Rushdie's depictions had not been as realistic as they were, his work would not have evoked the violent reactions, as well as the frequent "bannings" they experienced. It is important that a reader be familiar with the context to recognize this. I was perhaps the first person to write about Rushdie's stylistic experimentation and capturing of Indian English in my then dissertation published as a book in 1985, *Family Quarrels: Towards a Criticism of Indian Writing in English*.[2] To argue that Rushdie is wholly and solely postmodern does him a disservice. In fact, I have argued that Rushdie became a victim of postmodern interpretations, ie., shifting signs and signifiers that can be read differently in different contexts. Thus, we find that what Rushdie thought was a postmodern construction/production the Ayatollah Khomeini saw as an insult to the real life of the Prophet. We then find him, like Prufrock, saying "This is not what I meant at all." He has had to repeatedly invoke this disclaimer from the initial reaction to *Midnight's Children*, and from there on, *The Satanic Verses*, to the most recent stabbing.[3]

Reading Rushdie as postmodern makes him a victim of the "postmodern condition," of shifting signs and shifting meanings, where meaning is wrested from his authorship and put in the hands of a warring faction of readers. His becomes an actual case of "the death of the author." In "Structure, Sign and Play in the Discourse of the Human Sciences," Derrida argues that one of the premises [of postmodernism] is the "shifting signifier," whereby meaning is not fixed (85). Postmodernism argues for the concept of play. This sense of play contrasts with the sense of realism and historical accuracy of Rushdie's works. In postmodernism, according to Derrida, "there is no transcendental or privileged signified," as there would be in or under realism (85). Derrida argues that the domain or play of signification has no limit "if one erases the radical difference between signifier and signified, it is the word signifier itself which must be abandoned" (85). Under such a system, neither the critic nor the reader can make dogmatic judgments or proclamations about whether a work should be considered postmodern or realistic. As Stanley Fish argues, the reader writes the text he reads; judgments of whether an idea is reductive or not under the postmodern premise are themselves shifting. Derrida argues that there are thus two interpretations of interpretation, of structure, of sign, of play: "the one seeks to decipher dreams of deciphering a truth or an origin which escapes play...the other, which is no longer turned toward the origin, affirms play" (93).

Take for example Rushdie's description of Mrs. Gandhi's hair as "black" and "white," reflecting the black market and the white market of India's economy under her regime. "Her hair, parted in the centre, was snow-white on one side and black as night on the other... Recurrence of the centre-parting in history; and also, economy as analogue of a Prime Ministerial hairstyle" (*Midnight's Children* 386). While it can be seen as a postmodern pun, among other things, like the description of Mrs. Gandhi's behaviour at the death of her son in a plane crash, it caused the novel to be banned by her. Similarly, when one finds one's last name (Jussawalla, among others) mentioned in the narrative (227), it is hard to "excuse-mes" (227) the narrative as postmodern.

So, despite stylistic experimentations, the form postcolonial writers most preferred for their creative expressions of nationalism and telling the stories of their nations, as realistically as they could, was not just that of the novel but particularly the "growing-up" novel or the Bildungsroman. This form became a trope or metaphor for the development of the nation itself. Frederic Jameson calls these "national allegories":

> Third World texts, even those which are seemingly private and invested with a properly libidinal dynamic—necessarily project a political dimension in the form of national allegory: *the story of the private individual destiny is always an allegory of the embattled situation of the public third-world cultures.* (69, emphasis added)

This is perhaps the most important characteristic of postcolonial literature. As writers watched their nations developing and coming into a sense of identity, they wrote about characters who reflected this concern. Swami, in *Swami and Friends*, reflects the growing Indian state, a state struggling with a language crisis and an identity crisis—a state that takes a long reflective look before it identifies itself. Swami is a young boy growing up under British rule. All things British attract him and his friend Rajam: cricket, British novels, doing well in the English language. But Swami has a streak of nationalism in him. He questions the English master about why "*A*" should be for apple, why the mango should not be an equally important fruit, why Jesus is more important than Krishna, and eventually decides to run away from a cricket match. He goes on a long walk into a forest, along a river, only to come out recognizing he does not want to be like the British but like his Indian grandma. He awakens into a sense of "Indianness." Narayan means this to reflect India's awakening into Indianness.

Swami and Friends was first published in 1935, just as the anticolonial movements were beginning in India. In this novel, the young protagonist, Swami, incessantly asserts the superiority of his Indianness as he questions colonialist practices. He goes to a school where the English teacher starts with "A is for Apple," causing Swami to ask what an apple is and whether it is like a mango. The questioning continues with the religion teacher, when Swami asks why, if Christ was superior to Indian gods, was he crucified. In this cross-cultural encounter, while the "English educated" teacher is attempting to inculcate admiration for Western items and icons, the innocent questioning of a young child shows the deep roots and pride in one's own Indian culture.

This spills over into the playing fields over a cricket match and a Westernized friend, causing Swami to run away on a reflective journey into the forest and return only to realize that where he is most comfortable and at peace with himself is with his Indian "Granny." Thus, the pattern for the nationalistic, anti-colonial, postcolonial Bildungsroman is laid. In other subsequent novels we see this pattern repeated, culminating in the superiority of national identity: There is the rejection of the first colonizing method, the teaching or learning of English. Secondly, the rejection of the colonizers' religion, followed by the assertion of the superiority of Indigenous ways. Then there is a reflective journey, usually along a river, and, finally, a coming into a national awareness. We see this pattern in almost all of the early anti-colonial and even later postcolonial novels, such as Ngũgĩ wa Thiong'o's *Weep Not, Child*. This is not to say that all postcolonial novelists follow Narayan, or even, say, James Joyce's *Portrait of the*

Artist as a Young Man, a Bildungsroman of simultaneously nationalist and modernist tendencies, but that they continuingly express the burgeoning of nationalist desires, a sort of nationalist longing for a home to preserve identity. Here the choice of the postcolonial subject is an assertion of cultural sovereignty symbolized by the acceptance and embrace of local culture, rather than colonial culture.

On the other hand, Ericka A. Hoagland, in her dissertation, *Postcolonializing the Bildungsroman: A Study of the Evolution of the Genre*, upon a detailed critical reading of various texts and an examination of the critical history of the genre, posits that "First-Nations authors use the genre to explore how colonialism impaired and destroyed indigenous identity and culture; the genre then is used to reclaim and assert lost histories and identities as the means by which healing on an individual and communal level may be achieved" (iv). This is exactly what we see Narayan doing in the example of asserting, at the very simplistic level, such as the naming of a fruit to reclaim an identity whitewashed by the colonizers. So, while it might seem as though these small particulars are parochial, they are, in fact, from a child's point of view, important. Hoagland further writes that the new life of the genre is that of a resistance narrative, and we can see this resistance at the simplest level through the eyes of the very young children. Slaughter expands "the implicit Bildungsroman narrative of personality development…unfolds the plot for transforming personal rebellion into social legitimation" (92).

Like Narayan's *Swami and Friends*, Thiong'o's *Weep Not, Child* similarly parallels the growth of the hero, Njoroge, with that of the Kenyan state. Just like Swami, Njoroge, as he is growing up, going to school, church, and interacting with Christianity, defines himself by negation, as "not British," not English-speaking, resisting the dominant authority looking forward to a new dawn of Kenya under Jomo Kenyatta. There is an interesting exchange between Mr. Howlands, the colonizer plantation owner and Njoroge's father, Ngotho, the farmhand:

> They went from place to place, a white man and a black man. Now and then they would stop here and there, examine a luxuriant green tea plant, or pull out a weed. Both men admired this *shamba*. For Ngotho felt

responsible for whatever happened to this land. He owed it to the dead, the living and the unborn of his line, to keep guard over this *shamba*. Mr. Howlands always felt a certain amount of victory whenever he walked through it all...

"You like all this?" Mr. Howlands asked absent mindedly...

"It is the best land in the country," Ngotho said emphatically...

"I don't know who will manage it after me..."

"*Kwa nini Bwana*. Are you going back to—?"

"No," Mr. Howlands said unnecessarily loudly...

"My home is here!"

Ngotho was puzzled. Would these people never go? (wa Thiong'o 32)

What wa Thiong'o is communicating here is the poignant situation where the colonizer is oblivious to the ownership of the land, who it belongs to, and the African sense of the ownership of their land, very much like what we see in the United States with Native American lands. Njoroge, in his encounters at school, is constantly trying to convince his classmates of the importance of belonging to and feeling attached to the native lands. There is a continuous refrain of waiting for Jomo Kenyatta, who they see as the "Black Moses," to come and put them in possession of their own lands. In *Swami and Friends*, there is the refrain of "waiting for the Mahatma," and of immense disappointment when he does come. In an attempt to make Kenyan children more aware of their need to belong to their land and Indigenous communities, wa Thiong'o developed children's books, *Njamba Nene and the Flying Bus*, *Njamba Nene and the Cruel Chief*, and others. Njamba Nene is an extension of Njoroge. He is poor, goes to school in tatters, and the more Westernized kids make fun of him. But when their school bus gets stuck and there is no rescue for several days, Njamba Nene helps the other children in the bus survive by knowing which plants are edible and how to survive off of the land. The children are quite taken with him. The lesson being that Indigenous Knowledge is better than Western sophistication.

Mr. Howlands in *Weep Not, Child* is, like Karen Blixen in *Out of Africa*, a settler-colonial. Ngũgĩ wa Thiong'o, in his interview with me, said of Blixen,

> She said, "I love African people." But she loved them in the same way that people love their animals, their house, and goods, and so on. And the sentiment that's expressed in her work as part of the relationship between, let's say, the settler and the Kenyan people, was one of charity, aid, benevolence, which are in fact some of the sentiments which now tend to govern the neo-colonial relationship between the third world and Western countries. (Jussawalla and Dasenbrock 40)

No other postcolonial Bildungsroman makes as compelling a case for indigeneity and coming into Indigenous Knowledge as does *Weep Not, Child*.

Salman Rushdie's novel *Midnight's Children*, a seminal novel in this canon, both broke new ground in linguistic and stylistic experimentation and captured the history of India and its move into the postcolonial world through the eyes of two children born at midnight but switched at birth. Midnight was the hour of India's independence. They grow up in a manner similar to Swami, with all things British and coming to identify themselves as Indian, despite their wanderings through the country during the independence movement and the division of India, and the subsequent corruption of neocolonial India under Mrs. Gandhi (no relation to Mahatma Gandhi) and her sons, particularly Sanjay (see 323) and his failed Maruti car project and enforced vasectomies. It was groundbreaking in many senses of the word, not just in the breakthrough style of the Irish James Joyce or the magic realism of a Kafka or Gunter Grass, but because of its reassessment of the neocolonial nation in a very realistic fashion, despite a postmodern form. It questioned whether independence was really good for these nations rapidly moving into neocolonial corruption. It is this specific criticism of India's politics at the time that makes Rushdie's novel very realistic though rooted in a "post," postmodernist ethic. Finally, though, both of the characters, Saleem and Shiva, come into an awareness of themselves as indigenously rooted in India. In his essay, "The Cultural Politics of Rushdie Criticism: All or Nothing," I have been criticized by Timothy Brennan for my argument of indigeneity and Indianness in Rushdie's work, for having excessively nativistic readings of it. However, as I trace the growing-up awareness of both these characters in *Midnight's Children*, who make up the double Bildungsroman in this narrative, we can see that their final awareness at the end of their "hero's journey" is in their rootedness in India, as Indian, despite the "cracking" of India, the breakdown of India into a Muslim Pakistan and Hindu India (which at that time was more secular than now).

After all their peregrinations, movements, and migrations, through the just-being-formed Pakistan, the just-being-born India, after the ending of the Bangladesh Liberation War and the victory of Field Marshal Sam Maneckshaw, both characters, the original Saleem being called Shiva, and Saleem Sinai our protagonist, come to their awareness as being rooted in India: "Without passport or permit, I returned, cloaked in invisibility, to the land of my birth; believe, don't believe, but even a sceptic will have to provide another explanation for my presence here. Did not Caliph Haroun al-Rashid (in an earlier set of fabulous tales) also wander unseen, invisible, anonymous, cloaked, through the streets of Baghdad?" (Rushdie, *Midnight's Children* 368–69). Similarly, the original Saleem, going through life as Shiva, also makes a "truly synchronous" arrival in India: "Shiva alighted from an army motorcycle; and even through the modest khaki of his army pants" emerges "India's most decorated war hero" (393). Shiva becomes the allegorical god Shiva, symbolizing India. Both men "handcuffed to history" grow into "the incarnation of the new myth of August 15th, the children of ticktock…Midnight's Children" (369). Under all the postmodern facade is the realistic awareness journey of two men who grow into their Indianness, a national sense of belonging. They come into a sense of Indianness and indigeneity. And I believe this is also true of Rushdie himself, even today, after his many peregrinations.

In *Midnight's Children*, Rushdie, it must be remembered, was recording real events, (re)writing actual history under the cover of postmodernism in order not to be censored or called out. But this backfired because Rushdie's depictions are extremely realistic. The narrator, or as Rushdie famously calls him the "unreliable narrator," is Saleem Sinai, supposedly the scion of the Sinai family but is not so because he was switched at birth by his Goan Ayah Mary Perriera, who sought a life of privilege for an underprivileged child. Thus, the real Saleem becomes in the novel the character Shiva, who embodies the mixed lower class and caste of Indians. Mary Perriera had enacted her own private revolutionary act in switching the babies. In this narrative who is there to speak for the poor, the even more oppressed than the colonized? Rushdie had appointed himself the spokesperson. This in turn has gotten him into trouble with almost every book he's written because of the realism of his own "private revolutionary acts," referring to what he calls the private revolutionary act of Mary Perriera in switching the two babies (Rushdie, *Midnight's Children* 116).

Rushdie's creation of two characters born at the same moment and representing two different cultures (Muslim and Hindu), one the national, and the other either the hybrid or the Westernized, but both growing into their sense of indigeneity, has led to a series of novels in which twins growing up reflect the "national allegory," where one represents the Indigenous, nativized perspective arguing for nationalism, while the other, the Westernized perspective, but where both come into an awareness of themselves as rooted in their particular culture and their culture of origin. Sometimes these can be seen as evil twins, where one represents the good points and the other the evil perspective. Take, for example, Arundhati Roy's *The God of Small Things* and Zadie Smith's *White Teeth*. But this trope of the Bildungsroman journey as a journey towards one's indigeneity persists in postcolonial literature per se.

Ernest Renan has said, "A nation is a soul, a spiritual principle" (qtd. in Bhabha, *The Location of Culture* 19). Benedict Andersen has described it as "an imagined community"; that there really is no such thing as a political state or a nation, but it is instead how the residents imagine themselves bound together in a community. We can see this in literature from recently colonized cultures, as also with the current concerns with Chicano literature, Native American literature, and other such literature of marginalized minorities. Nationalism and the need to define the nation and its culture and its forms of narration have been the cornerstone of postcolonialism, now giving way under postmodern approaches of literature and culture to a greater sense of cosmopolitanism, hybridity, and the dismissing of nationalism and identity as "essentialism" or stereotyping and as the pinning of individuals and cultures for an essence that is not quite possible anymore. Jameson discusses this very aptly in his essay, "Third-World Literature in the Era of Multinational Capitalism":

> Judging from recent conversations among third world intellectuals, there is now an obsessive return to the national situation itself, the name of the country that returns again and again like a gong, the collective attention to "us" and what we have to do and how we have to do it, to what we can't do and what we do better than this or that nationality, our unique characteristics, in short, to the level of the "people." This is not the way American intellectuals have been discussing, "America," and indeed one might feel that the whole matter is nothing but that old thing called "nationalism," long since liquidated here and rightly so. Yet, a certain "nationalism" is fundamental in the third world (and also in the most vital areas of the second world), thus making it legitimate to ask whether it is all that bad in the end. (65)

Homi Bhabha, one of a triumvirate of so-called postcolonial critics and theorists, articulates this thus: 1) "nationalist discourses" produce the "idea of the nation"; 2) this draws attention to language and rhetoric; but 3) "the locality of a national culture is neither unified nor unitary in relation to itself, nor must it be seen simply as 'other' in relation to what is outside or beyond it" (*Nation and Narration* 4). Home, identity, nation, and race are all tied together in postcolonialism. Whose home is the land? Where does one belong? Is it the right of the colonizer to remain in the land?

Postcolonial responses to the Empire have contributed much to race studies. Though ideas of racial and cultural equality existed in the United States before Gandhi, his resistance to apartheid in South Africa (see Little; Dekar), from where he originally started his movement of resistance to the Empire and racial inequality, did give much strength to the main figures in the American civil rights movement, as also to Nelson Mandela. It is well known that Gandhi influenced Martin Luther King Jr., especially in his use of nonviolence. Gandhi, on the other hand, was much influenced by the Civil War and the American ideas of the resistance to slavery. It is from this resistance to power, "speaking truth to power," that the nation grows.

An interesting parallel comes from colonial American literature, where the form of the Bildungsroman was associated with the archetypal innocent, "American Adam," coming into an awareness of himself as "American." R.W.B. Lewis posits that, in creating the break from Europe, the move away from England by the Mayflower "pilgrims," we see the beginning of a new myth of America, the innocent clean land, unsullied by the past of English history, making a fresh new beginning, freed of the class structures of the "Old World." In all these gestures, we can see what we now term "postcolonial" in the Americans' break from their past of having been under king and crown. In fact, these are the first intimations of "postcoloniality."

> The American myth saw life and history as just beginning. It described the world as starting up again under a fresh initiative, in a divinely granted second chance for the human race, after the first chance had been so disastrously fumbled in the darkening Old World. It introduced a new kind of hero, the heroic embodiment of a new set of ideal human attributes. (Lewis 5)

The hero of American Bildungsromane defined America's "separation from Europe," i.e., the break from the British strictures that those founding this newly formed country demonstrated as "our national birth" (Lewis 5).

This "American Adam" (harkening back to the biblical Adam of the Christian origin story—the archetype of the new beginning) is very aptly reborn as the hero/heroine of the postcolonial Bildungsroman that expresses both the exceptionalism and the essentialism of the new conceptions of the post-independence nations. The postcolonial heroes are also making a fresh new beginning freed from their colonial pasts. Postcolonial Bildungsromane from nations in the process of gaining independence, i.e., breaking away from colonialism, perhaps taking inspiration from such works as James Joyce's *Portrait of the Artist as a Young Man*, espoused the genre as a means to emphasize their return to origins through the *Bildung*, or journey of a young protagonist. Some readers may not like a comparison that stretches across continents and nations such as comparing Joyce and Irish nationalism with Indian writers, but since colonialism as it was practised across countries and continents was so similar, the forms of resistance, such as those articulating resistance through a young hero's growing-up journey, as the protagonist Stephen Dedalus does in *Portrait*, were very similar. These comparisons are very apt. Whether in Ireland, India, or on the African continent, oppression took the form of erasing language, religion, and cultural ways of being. Stephen resisting his principal's use of standard English and resorting to Irish words such as "tundish" is very similar to what Swami or Njoroge were doing.

These authors meant to distinguish themselves from Western hegemonic discourses. R.K. Narayan's *Swami and Friends* and other works such as Bapsi Sidhwa's *Cracking India* chronicle the development of postcolonialism on the Indian subcontinent. Indian political theorist Partha Chatterjee has long argued against third world nationalisms. In his *Nationalist Thought and the Colonial World*, he attempts to show the connection between nationalism and illiberal regimes. Most telling is his newest, *The Truths and Lies of Nationalism*, which considers a manuscript of mysterious origin, a conversation with a Charvak, perhaps, but not necessarily a representative of the traditional Indian Charvaka materialist philosophy, which also denies India's Vedic origins and connections. He argues that no civilization can claim an ancient historic nationalist identity. Chatterjee writes, "The Indian *rashtra* as a nation-state has only been in existence since the middle of the twentieth century" (*Truths and Lies* 3). This is, of course, the period of colonial resistance, the urge towards postcoloniality and the recreating of a nationalist sense or awareness. Gayatri Spivak calls connections to nationalism a "nostalgia for lost origins" (87). But there would be no postcolonialism without the rise of the nationalist sentiment and the resistance against colonialisms.

The drawing of borders and the consequent effects on peoples form an essential part of the young heroine's Bildungsroman in Bapsi Sidhwa's *Cracking India*. Literarily, borders manifest national literature, even if they are written in English, and often deal with the problems of identity, national pride, and awakening. Out of the sentiment and desire to preserve home, and nation, come borders, both hard and permeable.

The earliest of Bildungsromane concerned with borders is Bapsi Sidhwa's *Cracking India*. Written about the exact moment of Partition, or when the Indian border was being created during the independence movement, it records the horrific violence around the expulsion of Hindus and Muslims from both sides of the border. During the negotiations around India's independence from the British, the Muslims, led primarily by Muhammad Ali Jinnah, foreseeing they would be a minority in Hindu India, wanted a safe territory for themselves, a "*Pak*," or holy, "*istan*" or land.

Cracking India, a female Bildungsroman, is told to us by Lenny, a young Parsi Zoroastrian adolescent. She is the embodiment of hybridity as all the Parsis in India were and are. The Parsis enjoyed a unique position of not belonging to any of the subcontinental religions, neither being Hindu or Muslim. When they arrived in India, fleeing persecution by the Arab Muslims, they promised the Indian Raja they would mix with the Indian people like milk mixes with sugar. Sidhwa does, in fact, tell this oft-repeated folklore in her book (47). The Parsis prided themselves on their ability to assimilate and be hybridized, and that they belonged nowhere and everywhere in their hybridity. Hybridity is a fitting and natural concept for Homi Bhabha, as a Parsi, to espouse in his book, *The Location of Culture*. The Parsi condition "overcomes the grounds of opposition and opens up a space of translation: a place of hybridity...*neither the one nor the other*...and properly alienates our political expectations" (25, emphasis added). It is also interesting to note that Muhammad Ali Jinnah was married to a Parsi woman, Rutti, known in Pakistan as the Madre-e-Millat, or the Mother of the Nation. Due to their hybridity, the Parsis were to some extent protected and could protect the persecuted on either side. It is fitting that this story of Partition is told in their home where Hindus, Muslims, and Sikhs all live and work together. Hiding under the dining table, Lenny, the protagonist, hears that their home was "like Switzerland." But she is not exempt from the violence of what Larry Collins and Dominique Lapierre, in their book *Freedom at Midnight*, called the "Greatest Migration in History," the result of Partition (373–400). They tell the stories of individuals like one Madan Lal who could not get beyond the vision of his mutilated father and wanted revenge (382). Lenny, the little polio-stricken Parsi protagonist, is forced to deal with the dead and mutilated body of her friend the masseur, her *ayah* or nursemaid's friend and companion, who had alleviated the pain in her legs many times. Returning from school one day, there is a swollen and bulging gunny sack in her way: "the sack slowly topples over and Masseur spills out" (Sidhwa 185). His fault, like that of her hunted *ayah*, or nursemaid, Shanta, that of belonging to one religion or another. What India's Partition demonstrated and continues to demonstrate today, and has through India's conflict-ridden seventy-five years of independence, is the brutality of conflicts based on religion, caste, loyalties, and affiliations. Unlike the other Bildungsromane we have looked at thus far, Lenny's awareness results not in nationalism but in her own cultural identity of not belonging to any of the major religious or political factions.

If we approach the issue of nationalism through Deleuze and Guattari's notion of "nomadism," we may believe that colonialism will always be with us as each subsequent wave of colonizers carve out their territories, and while continuing the palimpsest of colonialisms imbue each new layer of colonialism with their sense of superiority. Settler colonialism will continue with new and different settlers, as it has historically done. It is in recognizing global processes of colonialism, hybridity, assimilation, and integration that we can combat these continual uprisings.

Borders that mark out and lay claims to territories tend to enhance tendencies, resulting both in violence, such as that which has plagued the northwest borders of the subcontinent, and others resulting in *precarious* conditions for migrants. Judith Butler writes in *Frames of War*, "Precariousness and precarity are intersecting concepts. Lives are by definition precarious: they can be expunged at will or by accident; their persistence is in no sense guaranteed" (25). We see this in the precarity of borders as violence erupts from challenges to them. Perhaps what would help is what Deleuze and Guattari call "deterritorialization."

With current nationalist trends, there is not only a growing interest in how literature reflects and has reflected these trends but also a renewed interest in reframing the genre of the Bildungsroman, which has been the central genre of choice among postcolonial writers as it is the trope that mirrors growing nations. The most important work in this new critical trend of studying the Bildungsroman is Joseph Slaughter's *Human Rights, Inc.: The World Novel, Narrative Form, and International Law*. Slaughter sees the Bildungsroman as the genre that makes the transition into "modern historical time" (109). What Slaughter says of the Bildungsroman as an imaginative force "to reconcile the forces of rebellion and legitimation" (135) fits in well with seeing how the Bildungsroman works in these early and beginning postcolonial novels, where a rebellion is portrayed through the simple innocent eyes of children. Several younger scholars, including José-Santiago Fernández-Vázquez and Maria Helena Lima, have found new ways to subvert the genre to look at new ways that authors use the genre. I myself have presented papers several times on the "reverse Bildungsroman" in such works as Chitra Banerjee Divakaruni's *The Mistress of Spices*, where an older character comes into a new awareness and metamorphosizes into a younger self. Similarly, Shaul Bassi's "The (Un)making of Saladin Chamcha: Rushdie's Subversion of the *Bildungsroman*" similarly looks at the reverse Bildungsroman.

The awareness of nationality and identity are the pivotal moments that led not only to postcoloniality but to postcolonial literature per se, with particular emphasis on the novels, especially Bildungsromane, that chronicle the journey of a hero or heroine towards a national identity and awareness while paralleling the rise of the nation. They raise among their readers a sense of identity and belonging.

For understanding the nativistic and realistic aspects of the Bildungsroman and the fact that, even with formalistic experimentations, postcolonial Bildungsromane reflect the actual realistic contexts of their countries, we need to go to the critical perspectives promulgated by critics such as Stanley Fish, where it is important to look at the context of situation to establish a proper interpretive community that understands and explains the context. It is not possible to proceed on the Derridian notion of *il n'y a pas de hors-texte*, because a knowledge of the context leads to greater understanding of the text itself. Western hegemonic readings, even committed by critics from the cultural background but married to Western theoretical perspectives divorcing the text from context, sometimes cause misinterpretations.

One of the earliest critics of Indian writing in English, the late Syd Harrex, had written,

> [A]n appreciation of Indian cultural and social backgrounds is necessary to an understanding of Indian fiction, and...a non-Indian critic's knowledge of these backgrounds is not only restricted but also impaired by occidental fallibilities. (1–2)

It behooves us to revisit his injunction when looking at the genre of the postcolonial Bildungsroman. So I'm arguing that, given the historical contexts that shaped the emergence and growth of the postcolonial Bildungsroman in India, the genre has to be seen as one that not only defines nationalistic leanings but as one that is the predominant genre of what we today call "postcolonial literature." It is a genre that reflects the postcolonial authors' realistic representations of their contexts and histories, and serves as a tool for arousing ideas of nationalistic belonging and indigeneity. In defining it thus, I am conforming to Bakhtin's concept of the Bildungsroman as *"an image of a man growing in national-historical time"* (qtd. in Esty 3, emphasis added). For Bakhtin, the Bildungsroman provides an image of a man in the process of becoming. And, for me, becoming a nationalistic hero. This justifies Bakhtin's recognition of the Bildungsroman's pride of place in the history of realism (qtd. in Esty 5).

Notes

1. In refuting my essay claiming that the form of *The Satanic Verses* is more an indigenous form, Timothy Brennan, in his essay, "The Cultural Politics of Rushdie Criticism: All or Nothing," claims the novel form is foreign to India.
2. Canadian Uma Parameswaran was perhaps the first critic to conduct an interview with Rushdie in which she asked him what category he would see

himself belonging to. Rushdie indirectly addresses her questions in his essay, "'Commonwealth' Literature Does Not Exist."

3. See Jussawalla, "Post-Joycean/Sub-Joycean," "Resurrecting the Prophet," and "Rushdie's Dastan-e-Dilruba." I have consistently claimed that when Rushdie is rooted in a contextual reading, we can see that the facade of postmodernism crumbles.

Works Cited

Anderson, Benedict. *Imagined Communities: Reflections on the Origin and Spread of Nationalism.* Verso Publishing, 2016.

Arendt, Hannah. *The Origins of Totalitarianism.* Houghton Mifflin Harcourt Publishing Company, 1968.

Banerjee Divakaruni, Chitra. *The Mistress of Spices.* Anchor Books, 1998.

Bassi, Shaul. "The (Un)making of Saladin Chamcha: Rushdie's Subversion of the *Bildungsroman.*" *Salman Rushdie: New Critical Insights*, edited by Rajeshwar Mittapalli and Joel Kuortti, Atlantic, 2003, pp. 72–86.

Bhabha, Homi. *The Location of Culture.* Routledge, 1994.

Bhabha, Homi. *Nation and Narration.* Routledge, 1990.

Brennan, Timothy. "The Cultural Politics of Rushdie Criticism: All or Nothing." *Critical Essays on Salman Rushdie*, edited by Keith Booker, G.K. Hall, 1999, pp. 107–28.

Butler, Judith. *Frames of War: When Is Life Grievable?* Verso, 2009.

Campbell, Joseph. *The Hero with a Thousand Faces.* New World Library, 2008 (1949).

Chatterjee, Partha. *Nationalist Thought and the Colonial World: A Derivative Discourse.* University of Minnesota Press, 1993.

Chatterjee, Partha. *The Truths and Lies of Nationalism: As Narrated by Charvak.* SUNY Press, 2022.

Collins, Larry, and Dominique Lapierre. *Freedom at Midnight.* Simon & Schuster, 1975.

Dekar, Paul. "Gandhi's Influence on the Civil Rights Movement in the United States." Fellowship of Reconciliation, written for the Gandhi Peace Festival, 2020, https://forusa.org/gandhis-influence-on-the-civil-rights-movement-in-the-united-states-2/.

Deleuze, Gilles, and Félix Guattari. *A Thousand Plateaus: Capitalism and Schizophrenia.* Translated by Brian Massumi, University of Minnesota Press, 1987.

Derrida, Jacques. "Structure, Sign and Play in the Discourse of the Human Sciences." *Critical Theory since 1965*, edited by Hazard Adams and Leroy Searle, Florida State University Press, 1986, pp. 83–96.

"English Education Act 1835." Wikipedia, https://en.wikipedia.org/wiki/English_Education_Act_1835.

Esty, Jed. *Unseasonable Youth: Modernism, Colonialism, and the Fiction of Development*. Oxford University Press, 2012.

Fernández-Vázquez, José-Santiago. *Reescrituras postcoloniales del Bildungsroman*. Verbum Editorial, 2003.

Fish, Stanley. *Is There a Text in This Class?* Harvard University Press, 1980.

Gandhi, Mohandas K. *An Autobiography, or The Story of My Experiments with Truth*. Translated by Mahadev Desai, Navajivan Mudranalaya, 1940. https://www.mkgandhi.org/autobio/chap15.htm.

Gikandi, Simon. "African Literature and the Colonial Factor." *The Cambridge History of African and Caribbean Literature*. Vol. 1, edited by F. Abiola Irele and Simon Gikandi, Cambridge University Press, 2000, pp. 379–97.

Harrex, Syd C. *The Fire and the Offering: The English-Language Novel of India, 1935–1970*. Kolkata, Writers Workshop, 1977, pp. 1–2.

Hoagland, Ericka A. *Postcolonializing the Bildungsroman: A Study of the Evolution of the Genre*. Purdue University, PhD dissertation, ProQuest Dissertations Publishing, 2006.

Jameson, Fredric. "Third-World Literature in the Era of Multinational Capitalism." *Social Text*, no. 15, 1986, pp. 65–88.

Jussawalla, Feroza. *Family Quarrels: Towards a Criticism of Indian Writing in English*. Peter Lang, 1985.

Jussawalla, Feroza. "Post-Joycean/Sub-Joycean: The Reverses of Mr. Rushdie's Tricks in *The Satanic Verses*." *The New Indian Novel in English: A Study of the 1980s*, edited by Viney Kirpal, Allied, 1990, pp. 227–37.

Jussawalla, Feroza. "Resurrecting the Prophet: The Case of Salman, the Otherwise." *Public Culture*, vol. 2, no. 1, Fall 1989, pp. 106–17.

Jussawalla, Feroza. "The Reverse Bildungsroman as Globalization Device: The Case of *The Mistress of Spices*." *Focus India: Postcolonial Narratives of the Nation*, edited by T. Vijay Kumar et al., Pencraft, 2007, pp. 220–30.

Jussawalla, Feroza. "Rushdie's Dastan-e-Dilruba: *The Satanic Verses* as Rushdie's Love-Letter to Islam." *Diacritics*, vol. 26, no. 1, Spring 1996, pp. 50–73.

Jussawalla, Feroza, and Reed Way Dasenbrock, editors. *Interviews with Writers of the Postcolonial World*. University Press of Mississippi, 1992.

Lazzaro-Weis, Carol. "The Female *Bildungsroman*: Calling It into Question." *NWSA Journal*, vol. 2, no. 1, Winter 1990, 16–34.

Lewis, R.W.B. *The American Adam: Innocence, Tragedy, and Tradition in the Nineteenth Century*. University of Chicago Press, 1955.

Lima, Maria Helena. "Decolonizing Genre: Jamaica Kincaid and the Bildungsroman." *Genre: Forms of Discourse and Culture*, vol. 26, no. 4, 1993, pp. 431–59.

Little, Becky. "How Martin Luther King Jr. Took Inspiration from Gandhi on Nonviolence." Biography.com, 19 Jan. 2021, https://www.biography.com/activists/martin-luther-king-jr-gandhi-nonviolence-inspiration.

Lyotard, Jean-François. *The Postmodern Condition: A Report of Knowledge* (*La Condition postmoderne: Rapport sur le savoir*). Translated by Geoff Bennington and Brian Massumi, University of Minnesota Press, 1984.

Moretti, Franco. *Signs Taken for Wonders: Essays in the Sociology of Literary Forms*. Verso Books and NLB, 1983.

Narayan, R.K. *My Days*. Harper Collins, 2013.

Narayan, R.K. *Swami and Friends*. University of Chicago Press, 1980 (1935).

Nayar, Pramod K. *Writing Wrongs: The Cultural Construction of Human Rights in India*. Routledge, 2012.

Rao, Raja. *Kanthapura*. New Directions, 1963.

Rushdie, Salman. "'Commonwealth' Literature Does Not Exist." *Imaginary Homelands: Essays and Criticism 1981–1991*, Granta Books, 1991, pp. 61–70.

Rushdie, Salman. *Imaginary Homelands: Essays and Criticism 1981–1991*. Granta Books, 1991.

Rushdie, Salman. *Midnight's Children*. Alfred Knopf, 1981.

Rushdie, Salman. *The Satanic Verses*. Viking, 1988.

Sidhwa, Bapsi. *Cracking India: A Novel*. Milkweed Editions, 1991.

Slaughter, Joseph R. *Human Rights, Inc.: The World Novel, Narrative Form, and International Law*. Fordham University Press, 2007.

Spivak, Gayatri C. "Can the Subaltern Speak?" *Colonial Discourse and Post-Colonial Theory*, edited by Patrick Williams and Laura Chrisman, Columbia University Press, 1994, pp. 66–111.

Thiong'o, Ngũgĩ wa. *Njamba Nene and the Cruel Chief* (*Njamba Nene na Chibu King'ang'i*). Translated by Wangui wa Goro, Heinemann Kenya, 1988.

Thiong'o, Ngũgĩ wa. *Njamba Nene and the Flying Bus* (*Njamba Nene na Mbaathi i Mathagu*). Translated by Wangui wa Goro, Heinemann Kenya, 1986.

Thiong'o, Ngũgĩ wa. *Weep Not, Child*. Heinemann Educational Books, 1964.

Viswanathan, Gauri. *Masks of Conquest: Literary Study and British Rule in India*. Columbia University Press, 2015.

von Goethe, Johann Wolfgang. *Wilhelm Meister's Apprenticeship*. P.F. Collier & Son, 1917 (1795).

4

"SONO UN CROCEVIA"

Igiaba Scego's *La mia casa è dove sono* as Diaspora Bildungsroman

Simone Maria Puleo

In a review of Igiaba Scego's *La mia casa è dove sono* for *Internazionale*, Michael Braun—a correspondent from the German magazine *Die Tageszeitung*—writes: "In her own way, what Igiaba Scego proposes is a Bildungsroman, a novel of formation" (qtd. in Scego 235). Braun makes an insightful proposition, but what does he mean by "in her own way"? Perhaps, Braun is thinking through a Germanist lens, and Scego's book simply reminds him of that classic genre so central in German literary tradition. But is there something about Scego's Bildungsroman that is distinctive from other Bildungsromane, at least in the German iteration? If we are to follow Braun's idea, the next question would be: What type of Bildungsroman[1] did Scego write?

In recent decades, genre scholarship on the Bildungsroman has taken a postcolonial turn, spurred by the work of Jed Esty, Sarah Graham, Ericka A. Hoagland, Maria Helena Lima, Joseph Slaughter, and José-Santiago Fernández-Vázquez, among others. In the words of Graham, "the Bildungsroman, originally concerned with young, white, privileged, heterosexual men, came to give expression to the marginalized and silenced, in writing about the formative experiences of women, LGBTQ people, and postcolonial populations" (1).

The Bildungsroman's potential for sociopolitical commentary, which was first levied by European men to reflect on their own self-worth in a society speeding headlong towards an age of revolution, has been harnessed by authors whose own coming-of-age stories had for too long been deemed irrelevant and unworthy of telling.

Postcolonial Bildungsromane are not nearly as idealistic as their eighteenth- and nineteenth-century predecessors. According to Hoagland, "closure, at least in the way we would understand it in the European Bildungsroman, is neither forthcoming nor assured" (220). In the postcolonial Bildungsroman, crossing the finish line (i.e., maturity, inclusion, reconciliation) is never entirely certain as characters continue to wrestle with how their lives have been affected by colonialism and its abiding legacies. That is not to say that the postcolonial Bildungsroman is merely a reactionary or pessimistic inversion of the traditional model. The genre appropriates the concept of *Bildung* to reflect on the complex reality of coming of age in a postcolonial context. As such, one of the key distinctions between the traditional and postcolonial models is that the latter are not rife with the philosophical triumphalism implicit in the maturation of the traditional Bildungsroman protagonist. In contrast, the postcolonial Bildungsroman treats thematic issues such as "hybridity, ambivalence, and trauma" (Hoagland 224) as ongoing processes. The "essential *becoming*," as Bakhtin (20) once described, is deferred and exists in a state of negotiation or compromise.

Igiaba Scego's *La mia casa è dove sono* intersects with the discourse of the postcolonial Bildungsroman at various axes—the details of which are explored in the forthcoming sections. Born and raised in Rome, Scego is the daughter of Somali political refugees—her parents, Kadija Hussein and Alì Omar Scego, fled Mogadishu in the aftermath of Siad Barre's coup d'état in 1969. In her autobiographical work, *La mia casa è dove sono*, she recounts episodes from her childhood in Rome, "the land of the ex-colonizers" as she puts it (19) and meditates on paradoxical situations she confronted living the contact zone of her hybrid Somali Italian identity. Through a blend of personal anecdotes and historical exposition, *La mia casa è dove sono* accounts for how the history of Italian colonialism in Somalia, Barre's regime, and the Somali civil wars all shaped not only the adult but also the writer Scego would become.[2] Furthermore, Scego exposes the racism and prejudice she often faced as a Black Muslim woman in a predominantly white, majority-Catholic Italian society. Writing in Italian, she addresses a readership that was (and still is) ignorant of—and/or apathetic to—the nation's colonial past and the government's dehumanizing treatment of migrants, refugees, and the broader diasporic community. *La mia casa è dove sono* acts, not as a testament to the assimilation of Somali immigrants into Italian society, but as a testimony to coming of age in a contentious middle space between cultures, "un crocevia," or a crossroads, as Scego declares.

As such, this chapter introduces the term "diaspora Bildungsroman" to describe how Scego adapts the genre to the contours of diaspora experience. Many postcolonial Bildungsromane such as Nuruddin Farah's *Maps* or Tsitsi Dangarembga's *Nervous Conditions* are set in the formerly colonialized states and examine the struggles of characters as they reckon with the legacies of colonialism and the new realities of decolonization. However, Scego's project is distinct since she is a second-generation Somali immigrant in Italy, a colonizer state. Scego writes from a liminal position as both insider and outsider, native and non-native, Italian and Somali—from the "intervening space 'beyond,'" to echo Homi Bhabha (7). As we see repeatedly in *La mia casa è dove sono*, the diaspora Bildungsroman expresses the confounding experience of a person being seen and treated as foreign in the very place where they were born and raised. The work's title *La mia casa è dove sono*, or "my home is where I am,"[3] doubly evokes the comfort and discomfort of diaspora, of dislodging one's conception of home from a particular place and binding it instead to the migratory self. Though Italy and Somalia are not neighbouring states, Scego nevertheless narrates her story from what Gloria Anzaldúa famously described as a "psychological borderland" (iv), a space that emerges from the author's Somali Italian identity. In contrast to many postcolonial Bildungromane, the diaspora Bildungsroman is thus a product of border culture in which the processes of maturation are always interrelated with the burdens of migration and cultural hybridity. In the diaspora Bildungsroman, coming of age involves mediating the

Simone Maria Puleo 85

socio-political dynamics of assimilation and integration, allegiance and belonging, residence and citizenship.

The forthcoming sections elaborate these ideas as they run through the pages of Scego's *La mia casa è dove sono*. The first section, "Recovering Italy's Colonial Past," examines the historical circumstances through which Scego's family first arrived in Italy, as well as the author's perception of the Italian public's understanding—better yet, misunderstanding—of Italian colonial history. The following section, "Interrogating the Present," discusses the racism and discrimination to which Scego was subjected, while also managing anxieties provoked by ongoing conflicts in Somalia. Both sections highlight the didactic function of the Bildungsroman as the author offers the Italian reading public a glimpse into the intricate reality of coming of age as a Black, Muslim, second-generation Somali immigrant woman in Italy.

Recovering Italy's Colonial Past

For generations, the history of Italian colonialism remained at the margins of Italian public memory, academic discourse, and literary and artistic production. In the Italian education system, the chapter on colonialism was conveniently excluded from the history books.[4] Only in the 1990s did certain writers and public intellectuals begin to open a meaningful discussion about Italy's colonial pursuits in Eritrea, Ethiopia, Libya, Somalia, and elsewhere. To name one glaring example of the systemic obfuscation of Italy's colonial past, *Lion in the Desert*, Moustapha Akkad's 1981 biopic about the Libyan resistance leader Umar al-Mukhtar and the Second Italo-Senussi War, was promptly banned by the Italian government—today, the film remains largely obscure. At the time of the film's release, the Undersecretary of Foreign Affairs Raffaele Costa, who was centrally responsible for blocking its distribution, commented that the film "damaged the honor of the Italian Army" (qtd. in Del Boca, "The Obligations of Italy Toward Libya" 197). The film's censorship exemplifies a systemic effort to suppress discussion of this shameful period in Italy's national history. The censorship of *Lion in the Desert* is but one example of how the Italian government worked to blot out the memory of its colonial past, or as Sandra Ponzanesi puts it, how in Italy, "the postcolonial moment [had] been, so to say, suspended or delayed" (qtd. in Sansalvadore 63).

In *La mia casa è dove sono*, Scego frequently highlights the erasure of colonial history from Italian public consciousness, embedding moments of critique and socio-cultural analysis into familial anecdotes and memories of her upbringing. The book opens with a memory of Scego visiting her brother Abdulcadir in the UK—they were joined by their cousin O, who at the time had settled in Finland. Their meeting was like the opening of a *barzelletta*: that is to say, "an Englishman, an Italian, and a Finn walk into a bar..." (16).[5] Her brother (like other Somali folks in the UK) did not quite understand why Scego would choose to remain in Italy, the "land of the ex-colonizers," where Somali refugees were not provided with government assistance, housing, or subsidies of any kind (19). At times, even the sexual dynamics of colonialism had been brought into discussion as she recalls being asked, "Do you want to be a madam like those poor women during colonialism? The lovers of the Italians who at the end of the mission would be abandoned, left with problems and the babies?" (19). The thorny question gives readers a historical insight into the abuse of Somali women under Italian colonial rule, many of whom were treated as concubines by colonial officers, but it also speaks to how the legacy of that abuse continues to haunt Scego (like other women with roots in formerly colonized spaces) in the present. The question of "Why Italy?" frames the story's central conflict, that is, Scego's quest to find her place in the present world, to untangle some of its gravest contradictions, to come to terms with the painful inheritance of the colonial past.

Scego's journey to Italy did not begin with Scego herself but with her father, Alì Omar. Born in the coastal city of Brava, Alì Omar Scego came of age in the postwar British Military Administration (1941–1950), when the Big Four powers (UK, France, USA, USSR) seized control of Italian Somaliland. The British eased many restrictions that had been installed by the Fascists, and during this period, Alì Omar, like many of his generation, took an interest in *siyaasi* or politics, to use Scego's words (43). He was a member of the Somali Youth League (SYL), the nationalist political party that would play a key role in Somalia's transition towards independence. In 1950, the British proposed the Bevin Plan, which aimed to unite all the "Somalilands" (Italian Somaliland, British Somaliland, Ogaden, North Frontier District, and Djibouti) into a single self-governing state. However, the Bevin Plan for a Greater Somalia was rejected, and Somalia was placed under UN trusteeship, to be administered by the new Republic of Italy for ten years (a period known in Italy as *Amministrazione fiduciaria*). The UN Resolution 289 that established the trusteeship included the condition that the Italians support the Somalis in their transition towards democratic self-governance. Scego comments, "No one can teach you democracy, least of all your ex colonial boss" (46). Nevertheless, in accordance with the resolution, the Italian government sent members of Somalia's burgeoning political class to study "democracy" in Italy—Scego's father and Abdirashid Ali Sharmarke were among the first delegation of Somalis to arrive in Rome. Those trips to Rome in the 1950s were special to Scego's father: "You ate, you read, you flirted with the receptionist, and you studied democracy" (52). During one of his last trips to Rome, Scego's father saw Nat King Cole perform at the Teatro Sistina. From the stage and through the brilliant stage lights, Mr. Unforgettable miraculously recognized Alì Omar and two of his colleagues. Scego jokes: "three black dots in a sea of white" (56). Nat King Cole shook their hands and graciously invited them to sit in the front row—a magical moment of Black solidarity.

In 1960, Somalia gained its independence and the Somali Republic was formed. Alì Omar took public office, serving positions including ambassador and foreign minister. But his life would drastically change in 1969 with the assassination of Somali President Abdirashid Ali Sharmarke and Siad Barre's subsequent coup d'état. Scego explains that "his choices were to support Siad Barre's military dictatorship or be eliminated. My father chose exile and a new homeland, Italy" (51). More than just Italy, Alì Omar Scego resettled in Rome, where the magic he had experienced years prior helped him to believe he could start over (93). Alì Omar Scego's incredible life story is emblematic of Somalia's complex process of decolonization; his life runs parallel with the life of the nation. In *La mia casa è dove sono*, his story functions as a Bildungsroman within a Bildungsroman, connecting individual with state, past with present, father with daughter. It offers a valuable lesson to readers about the transitional political processes Somalia underwent in the movement towards independence, but also speaks to political processes that compel one family to leave their homeland in search of another.

Answering the question "Why Italy?" is more complicated for Scego than it is for the rest of her family because she was born and raised in Rome, and therefore harbours nostalgia and even a touch of pride for her birthplace. She acknowledges that a declaration of unreflective patriotism such as "I love Italy!" would not survive critical scrutiny but admits that "Italy [is] my country. Full of defects, certainly, but my country" (19). Though Scego communicates her feelings of national attachment and her robust sense of Italianità, she blunts the patriotism of her pronouncement by showing an awareness of the country's many problems and faults. And she similarly approaches her love for Somalia, "which [has] plenty of its own defects" (19). In any case, the pull of multiple allegiances is a hallmark of cultural hybridity and often an emotional topic for refugees, immigrants, and members of diasporic communities since it can spur feelings of guilt, betrayal, or even treason. The discourse of nationalism has entrenched a strict belief that people have one true homeplace, and therefore cultural hybridity can cause friction as it rubs against a person's deeply engrained sense of national identity.

Despite her love of country, Scego concedes a major point to Italy's critics: "Italy had forgotten its colonial past. It had forgotten that it had put Somalis, Eritreans, Libyans, and Ethiopians through hell. It simply washed away that story with a sponge" (20). Discussion of colonial history's erasure—a key proposition of Italian postcolonial studies—is effortlessly woven into Scego's personal memories. It is important to highlight that, at the time of *La mia casa è dove sono*'s publication in 2010, awareness of colonial history was very limited in Italian public consciousness, relegated largely to cultural scholars and historians. Scego's writing thus becomes a means to expose postcolonial discourse to common Italian readers who might not read academic journals or monographs, but who might grab Scego's nonfiction off the shelf at a local bookstore, since, in recent years, so-called migrant literature has become a popular genre in Italy.

La mia casa è dove sono also discusses Italy's sordid relationship with its colonial history in comparison to other colonizer nations. Scego sets the record straight, responding to myths about Italian colonialism that had been instrumental in distinguishing Italy from other colonizer nations, and thereby justifying the silence:

> This doesn't mean that the Italians were worse than other colonizers. They were the same as the others. The Italians had raped, killed, derided, polluted, plundered, and humiliated the peoples with whom they made contact. They were like the English, the French, the Belgians, the Germans, the Americans, the Spanish, and the Portuguese. But in many of these other countries, after the end of the Second World War, there had been a discussion, there had been arguments, glances were bitter and forceful; imperialism and its criminals were scrutinized; studies were published; the debate influenced literary production, essay-writing, film, music. Yet, in Italy, silence. As if nothing had happened. (20)

Unlike other nations during the postwar moment, where the abuses of colonialism were revealed and, in some measure, publicly decried, the Italian government "actively impeded the emergence of truth," to use of the words of Angelo Del Boca ("The Myths, Suppressions, Denials, and Defaults of Italian Colonialism" 18). That is not to say that other European governments gladly admitted their wrongdoings, but by the intellectual vigour and courage of previously colonialized subjects like Frantz Fanon and Albert Memmi, for example, a serious discussion about the atrocities of colonialism was had and a credible historical record was created. For various reasons, the same did not take place in Italy.[6] Instead, the Italian Ministry of Foreign Affairs financed the publication of *L'Italia in Africa*, a fifty-volume work of historical revisionism that mitigated the violence committed, and in its treatment of certain colonial officers, verged on hagiography (Del Boca 18). Efforts such as *L'Italia in Africa* were responsible not only for the acquittal of war criminals such as Benito Mussolini and Rodolfo Graziani, neither of whom were officially indicted, but they also gave rise to egregious misconceptions about Italian colonialism, namely the *Italiani brava gente* myth (good-hearted Italians): the idea that Italian colonialism had not been as bad as other colonialisms, that it had not lasted as long, that it had even resulted in prosperity and social progress, and that friendly relations had existed between colonizer and colonized. That was never the case. The Italians were no better or worse than other colonizers. They were, in fact, the same, as Scego points out.

La mia casa è dove sono is not a book of postcolonial theory, after all, so these observations represent a conflict in Scego's coming-of-age story. The history of Italian colonialism is a cause of personal consternation for Scego. In addition to her cultural identification with the city of Rome, or her delight at seeing Roma compete at Stadio Olimpico (127), she had become an Italian citizen in the 1980s and had since enjoyed the privileges afforded by the state's recognition. Despite feelings of happiness and relief, Scego is aware of how lucky she and her brother had been, especially by comparison to others of her generation (111), whose access had been severely restricted by the Italian government's adoption of *jus sanguinis* legislation.[7] Enjoying some measure of integration as an Italian citizen, Scego questions the degree to which she is implicated in the state's past colonial terror or its ongoing violence towards migrants and refugees. She wonders where she fits in a nation that had been responsible for so much pain during colonialism, and a nation that continues to trample the human rights of African asylum seekers landing on her shores.

Similar insecurities are brought into relief when Scego remembers her grandfather, Omar, who was "*quasi bianco*" (almost white) and who had worked as an interpreter for one of Italy's most ruthless colonizers, Rodolfo Graziani (80). She describes seeing her grandfather in an old family photo, noting she could very well have "mistaken him for an Iranian or one of those Portuguese colonizers from the fifteenth century who landed in Brava with Vasco da Gama" (80). His light skin troubled Scego: "it threw the sense of African pride into crisis" (81). She wonders if there is a Portuguese ancestor in her genealogical tree, and whether her discomfort at that possibility is a sign that she, like Malcolm X, had "learned to hate every drop of that rapist's blood in [her]" (qtd. in Scego 81). Yet, thinking fondly of her grandfather, she settles on a less essentialist understanding of race and identity: "No one is pure in this world. We are never just black or just white" (81)—a clever double entendre, which, on the one hand, refers to skin colour, and on the other, is suggestive of treating racial identity with nuance rather than black and white binaries. To Scego, we are all the fruit of an encounter (*incontro*) or a match (*scontro*); we are a crossroads, points of passage, bridges (*crocevia, punti di passaggio, ponti*) (81). Such moments of clarity reveal a universalist strain in Scego's thought that resists colourism and counteracts notions of racial purity that can exist on both sides of the colour line.

Perhaps more unsettling for Scego is her grandfather's association with Graziani, *il macellaio del Fezzan* (the butcher of Fezzan). Graziani was a heinous military officer and colonial governor responsible for innumerable war crimes and human rights abuses during his missions in Ethiopia and Libya. Graziani used chemical weapons to suppress the Senussi revolt in Cyrenaica, resulting in the arrest and execution of resistance leader Omar al-Mukhtar. According to Dominik J. Schaller, up to one hundred thousand Bedouin Cyrenaicans were forcibly displaced from their settlements in Djebel al-Akhdar (358). Women, children, and the elderly were interned in Italian concentration camps; Libyan civilians lost their lives in mass executions. Years later, Graziani adopted similar methods in Ethiopia. After a failed assassination attempt on Graziani in February 1937, he ordered a reign of terror on the Ethiopians, known now as Yekatit 12. Entire neighbourhoods of Addis Ababa were destroyed, and according to a recent study, approximately nineteen thousand Ethiopians lost their lives in the ensuing massacre, with thousands more imprisoned or interned (Campbell 323). Scego comments that many *cantastorie* or griot were targeted by fascist mobs because Graziani believed the *cantastorie* to be subverting his authority (85). In the following months, paranoiac Graziani ordered an attack on the Debre Libanos monastery: nine hundred Ethiopian Orthodox monks and priests, together with 125 deacons and around one thousand visiting clergy, laymen, and pilgrims, all perished (Campbell xlii). Scego covers Graziani's crimes in conjunction with remembrances of her grandfather to serve a didactic function. In other words, she provides a history of Graziani for Italian readers who may have never learned about his abuses in school and elsewhere in the public sphere.

She also reflects on her grandfather's association with Graziani as a proxy of her confrontation with hybrid identity and the politics of being Somali Italian in the present day. Like his granddaughter, Omar Scego had a gift for language, and while many young boys of his generation were conscripted by the Italians as *àscari* (askari), he had been fortunate to work as an interpreter and translator, eventually for Graziani himself. Scego remembers her father remarking that many of the words her grandfather had to translate were "molto dure" (very hard) (87). Scego is arguably implying the moral dimension of the words, not the linguistic difficulty of the translation process. The big question is trod out more explicitly: "Was my grandfather then a fascist? Better yet, was he complicit in fascism? Was he guilty of the crimes he had to translate?" (86). These questions echo her own personal struggle with the guilt of being an Italian citizen—culturally and on paper—when the state had done so much harm to her people and other African peoples. She recognizes, however, that her grandfather had done what was necessary: "my grandfather had understood that translating was the key to survival in that subjugated country" (86). Scego speaks to the pragmatism of survival, especially under the gruelling conditions of colonial rule. Like her grandfather had done in Italian Somaliland, Scego, too, had to survive as a second-generation Somali in present-day Italy, which for her meant speaking the language, getting an education, and becoming a citizen, e.g., integrating into the society. Though she did so of her own volition, the guilt of integration is not lost on Scego.

Scego's journey of self-discovery bears similarity to other postcolonial Bildungsromane in which "the inherent conflict between the 'ideal of *self-determination* and the equally imperious demands of *socialization*'…is often intensified by the shadow of colonialism" (Hoagland 220). The story of *La mia casa è dove sono* is the story of Scego seeking to reconcile her Italianità and her Somali heritage, despite the haunting spectre of colonialism, which represents an obstacle she may never completely overcome. In this regard, Scego reminds us of Askar, the young character in Nuruddin Farah's novel, *Maps*, whom Hoagland describes as "fated never to stop searching, never to stop wondering who they are and where they belong" (218). But Scego is different from Askar because she is more optimistic about her searching, a kind of being-in-motion: "In the end I am only my story. I am me and my feet" (34). She banks on these powerful emblems—her story and her feet—symbolic of movement, distance, and pace.

Another equally important function, as I've outlined throughout the section, is Scego's determination to impart the history of Italian colonialism to her readers. Martini, Slaughter, and others have described the Bildungsroman as "a didactic genre that performs what it thematizes, encouraging the reader's cultivation through its depiction of the protagonist's development" (Slaughter 96). *La mia casa è dove sono* enacts Bildungsroman didacticism by recovering the marginalized history of Italian colonialism. In sharing her own coming-of-age story and family history, Scego simultaneously educates readers about Italian colonialism: a redacted history that had been largely suppressed in Italian schools, institutions of learning, and the public sphere. Building upon the work of authors such as Mohamed Bouchane, Pap Khouma, and Gabriella Ghermandi, the writings of Scego and others of her generation, such as Cristina Ali Farah and Gabriella Kuruvilla, are signs the delay is finally over. Postcolonialism has settled in Italy.

Interrogating the Present

For Scego, Italian colonialism exists as a powerful memory that reverberates into the present—an inherited experience that conditions her sense of heritage, her sense of family, and her general world view. Unlike her parents and grandparents, Scego did not live through the colonial era, nor did she, like her older brother, reside in postcolonial Somalia for an extended period. In contrast with postcolonial Bildungsromane such as Chimamanda Ngozi Adichie's *Purple Hibiscus*, which is set in decolonized Nigeria, Scego's writing approaches Somalia through the lens of the African diaspora experience in Italy. *La mia casa è dove sono* offers readers insight into the life of a young Black woman of Somali heritage coming of age in Italy's predominately monocultural society.[8]

As a Black child in Italy in the '70s and '80s, Scego often dealt with racism. She remembers being told by a classmate: "You have black skin which carries germs and disease. My mom told me not to play with you, otherwise I'll get really sick and die" (152). The memory reveals how Scego was often subject to racist attacks from an early age and how racism was taught to white Italian children. She is careful to explain that the children were parroting racist stereotypes they had been told by their parents. She suggests that, in this regard, not much has changed in Italy since she was a child. Certain Italian families continue to complain about "bambini di origine straniera" (children of foreign origin) being in the same classroom as their children (i.e., white Italian children). Scego notes that when these parents are called out as racist, they deny the accusation and argue they are only concerned because so-called foreign children "limit the school's productivity" (152). She recalls being referred to frequently as "sporca negra" (dirty n*****) or "Kunta Kinte" (152), a reference to the American television miniseries *Roots*. Many Italians, however, had failed to understand the program's critical commentary. Instead of saying "we admire Kunta Kinte, he is a hero," they would say "you are just like Kunta Kinte, a dirty n*****, and we will whip you, you were born to be a slave" (153). As with the history of Italian colonialism, Scego exposes racism in Italy in the '70s and '80s, a predominately monocultural society with an ethnically homogenous population, where discussions of racial prejudice were similarly marginalized.[9]

Scego continued to deal with racist remarks and microaggressions during her high school years in the early '90s. Her gym teacher would ask, "How did you get so tan, Igiaba? What do you use in the morning before coming to school?" (147). To make matters worse, the gym teacher repeated the vile joke for three years. Readers are shown the prominence of casual racism, which can take place in the school gymnasium, as well as the highest office of government. For instance, on November 6, 2008, in an interview on national television, Prime Minister Silvio Berlusconi made a similar racist joke about newly elected US President Barack Obama, remarking "è giovane, è bello, ed è anche abbronzato" (he is young, handsome, and also tan). Berlusconi's comment stirred up a few liberal-leaning pundits in Italy and the United States, but the reaction was mild. Many dismissed its gravity and treated it as "just a harmless joke."

Scego, however, would not let her gym teacher go unchecked. In the last week of classes, she brought a tin of shoe polish to school and said, "Prof, I finally brought you that product. I use this every morning. I rub it on real good for a few hours. It works like a charm" (148). The teacher's face showed his "vergogna" (shame) (148). Scego's unwillingness to accept the abuse, and her choice to fire back at the ignorant schoolteacher, are signs of her growth and self-determination, of her *Bildung*. But those moments of assertion were sporadic and often fleeting. Encounters with racism occurred frequently in Scego's life, and she admits, "I didn't always have the mind to respond. I didn't want problems. I just wanted some peace" (148). In contrast with the triumphalism of the European Bildungsroman, *La mia casa è dove sono* offers small victories. Scego's vulnerable admission that she was sometimes too tired to fight, nonetheless, sends a powerful message to readers that all people regardless of race deserve to be treated with respect and dignity.

As an immigrant child with a basic need to feel accepted by her peers, Scego was subject to the social pressures of assimilation. She had not yet become "an African proud of her black skin" (151), and she reasoned that, while she could not rid herself of the black skin that had caused her so much pain—racists had caused her pain, not her skin, she later understood—she could work on her command of the Italian language (151). Around the age of four or five, she thus decided to cease speaking Somali. Refusing to speak her mother tongue was her "bizarre way of saying 'love me'" (152). Reflecting years later, Scego realizes her "choice" did not result in the desired effect. Yet her language assimilation had other unintended consequences: Scego was a bookish teenager and more well-read than most of her peers. She knew everything about Italian poets like Leopardi and D'Annunzio, and she cared very little for rock singers like Freddie Mercury and Vasco Rossi (139). Scego implies that the pressure of language assimilation in part contributed to her skill set as an author—the author who comes to write the story being read.

It was not until Scego visited Somalia years later that she recovered her love for Somali. After a few months immersed in her ancestral homeland, where "the word has a place of honor" (151), she found herself speaking Somali "very well" (157). Writing from the present, Scego seems happy to report having "two mother tongues that love her in equal measure" (157). With a subtle reference to Pablo Neruda's poem "Oda a las gracias," she declares, "Grazie alla parola ora sono quello che sono" (Thanks to the word I now am what I am) (157). In these moments, *La mia casa è dove sono* acts as a diaspora Künstlerroman, documenting how the impact of language assimilation on the one hand, and homeland travel on the other, shaped Scego as a writer.

Racism and the pressures of assimilation not only affected Scego's relationship with language but also her self-image. In her adolescence, Scego internalized white European ideals of feminine beauty. Measuring herself against a set of culturally biased beauty norms, adolescent Scego often felt insecure and unattractive. She writes, "At sixteen, my difference weighed on me. My skin, my hair, my decidedly African derriere were obstacles" (140). Her feelings of self-doubt fuelled a desire to erase or neutralize those bodily markers of Blackness. She never dreamt of being white, but she dreamt of being "transparent" (140). The notion of "transparency" corresponds directly with the pressure of assimilation and a yearning to vanish into the host culture. The psychological harm that white feminine beauty standards caused Scego bears similarity to the experience of Black women in the United States. Like Scego, college-age African American women "struggle with physical features that are considered to be more African than European" (Sekayi 469). Though Scego herself may be suspicious of such a far-reaching comparison, this connection is particularly germane within the generic context of the internationalist Bildungsroman, especially the women's and postcolonial subgenres.[10] In this regard, *La mia casa è dove sono* reveals how a Black woman's journey towards self-affirmation in Italy, as in the United States, can be impeded by white feminine beauty ideals promoted in both countries by media apparatus that, in the pursuit of profit, replicate normative ideology and frame whiteness in the cultural centre.

In addition to expressing the ways in which certain European ideological structures had affected Scego personally, *La mia casa è dove sono* details her acquaintance with the African diaspora in Italy and her growing consciousness of its treatment by government institutions, aid organizations, and the Italian public. Scego remembers a time in her high school years when the family was struggling financially—her father had been granted amnesty and was back in Somalia building a business that could support the family if they were to eventually repatriate. Scego and her mother often relied upon aid organizations such as Caritas. At an aid centre near Santa Maria in Trastevere, they found themselves among other members of the diaspora, Somalis, Filipinos, Eritreans, Cape Verdeans, Roma, as well as some Italians (121). Scego was ashamed to be asking for charity, but her mother pulled her aside and wisely explained that many of the women there had been professionals or government functionaries or diplomats, and that they did not feel humiliated to ask for help. There is nothing wrong with asking for help, her mother assured her (121). Scego comments: "there weren't sad faces; there were people who were having a tough time, but who had every intention of getting past it" (121). These moments highlight Scego's maturity: the development of moral fortitude and optimism in the face of immensely difficult living conditions. They were provided with pasta and canned goods, and Scego even found a sweater with a yellow stripe that her schoolmates considered uber chic. This episode offers a positive look at the work of aid organizations such as Caritas but also shows what integration often involves on a daily basis for diasporic communities in Italy.

However, not all her interactions with aid organizations had been positive. Fellow Somalis had recommended another church, Giustiniana, where Scego's mother might also find leads on housekeeping work. Yet Scego instantly felt a different vibe than she had felt at Trastevere. She recounts:

> They didn't give you a package. If you wanted to eat, you had to wash your hands and sit at the table. But first you had sit through mass. Even

the Muslims, and if you didn't, the priest wouldn't give you any leads for work. I thought what the priest was doing was so stupid. (122)

The Giustiniana and its head priest were enacting a neocolonial Christianizing mission by requiring aid seekers to participate in Catholic religious observance. They leveraged aid to ensnarl the less fortunate members of the African diaspora as a means of bolstering the falling numbers of their own congregation. And they saw converting Muslims to Catholicism as another benefit of their scheme. Scego remembers wanting to tell the priest that "spirituality must come from inside. It cannot be imposed by force. If by Christian charity, you want to help us, do so, but you must do so without asking for a mass in return" (123). Readers see Scego becoming wise to the exploitative practices of certain aid organizations and developing a critical consciousness of the predation to which the African diaspora was often subject in Italy.

Her father did return to Rome, but the family's plans to repatriate were thwarted by the ousting of Siad Barre, the fall of the Democratic Republic of Somalia, and the outbreak of civil war. In the late 1960s, the ascension of Barre's regime had sent the family into exile, and in the early 1990s, his removal paradoxically prohibited their return. Hoagland indicates that "a variant of the African postcolonial Bildungsroman can be found among texts that belong to another significant genre of the African novel: the war narrative, which frequently presents a violent coming of age for those caught in the crossfire" (234). In contrast, as a diaspora Bildungsroman, *La mia casa è dove sono* narrates the traumatic effect of civil war on members of the Somali diaspora in Italy like Scego. Though not literally "caught in the crossfire," members of the diaspora felt the cost of war vis-à-vis family, friends, and community ties. Scego remembers attending what she calls a "funeral," a vigil for thirteen Somalis who perished off the coast of Lampedusa in October 2003. Their remains were transported to Rome per the request of Mayor Walter Veltroni, after a campaign by the Somali community. "We had never asked for anything from Italy that had colonized us," Scego writes, "but that day we demanded our right" (100). The thirteen who lost their lives were fleeing the ravages of civil war—violence, famine, disorder—crossing the Mediterranean in search of asylum. The Somali community felt it their responsibility to secure their compatriots a proper burial and the reading of a surah in the Quran (100). They came together that day at the Piazza del Campidoglio to honour the dead, but for Scego questions remained. Those who had been lost had "my same nose, my same mouth, my same elbows...why did they die and why are we alive?" (100). The guilt of having survived, of having built a life abroad, in Italy of all places, plagues Scego as she looks upon the remains of those who had not been as fortunate.

The extreme hardship of the civil wars also depersonalized relations between Somalia and the diaspora. Scego explains that "in a country with no infrastructure, public life, opportunity, only money can open the doors of survival; money is better than I care about you, euros were excellent for saying I love you" (133). Relationships that were once based in kinship ties and shared culture are reduced to financial exchanges due to the desperate circumstances of civil war. Members of the diaspora like Scego get second jobs at call centres or drive taxis to send the earnings to those affected by war in their home country. According to Scego, sending money is how the diaspora manages the guilt of not "sharing in the disaster of war" (133). She was safe from war in Italy, but she was nonetheless disturbed by the thought that she could have been "those relatives, those uncles and aunts, those cousins, nieces and nephews" (133). Why was she more deserving of safety than those relations?

Scego's coming-of-age story arguably culminates with the absence of her mother, which is the episode that marks her passage into adulthood. After her father had prepared the business, her mother returned to Somalia to ready the home into which the family would resettle. No one could have predicted that a civil war would begin and separate her mother from the family for a period of two years. Scego recounts that in those early times of her mother's absence, communication was very limited. In the entire two-year period of her absence, she only spoke with her mother once. Scego and her father would be periodically notified by a family friend that someone had seen Kadija—that "she was alive, at least a month ago" (143). They prayed for her safe return but were powerless. All they could do was wait. Scego had to continue with her daily life in Rome, studying and socializing, but the mammoth stress of the situation caused great emotional harm. During this period, Scego struggled with bulimia: eating and then regurgitating "ciambelloni confezionati" (big donuts) (144). When her mother Kadija returned to Rome, alive and well, Scego was overwhelmed with joy. She wrote a poem to recite for her mother at the airport but was unable to utter the words; she wanted so desperately to show her love but could not. Scego did not want to "contaminate" her mother because, in her mother's absence, the young lady felt she had become a "persona strana" (strange person) (149). A year and a half after her mother's return, Scego recovered from her bulimia, but the absence had left an indelible mark. The maturation of the diaspora Bildungsroman hero is not teleological in nature but an ongoing venture through war and peace, sorrow and joy, loss and recovery.

Conclusion

The value of an Italian diaspora Bildungsroman such as Igiaba Scego's *La mia casa è dove sono* cannot be understated. Italy as a nation desperately needs voices that can speak to the legacies of colonialism and the injustices the African diaspora continues to face. While much of the text traces Scego's memories of the past, the implications undoubtedly "seek meaning in the future" (5) to echo Franco Moretti. The Loescher edition (which is cited throughout) is a teaching edition, designed for high school students. It contains discussion questions, interviews, reviews, and other pieces of context. I cannot think of a better book for Italian high school students of all backgrounds—for students to be exposed to this diaspora Bildungsroman at such a crucial moment in their own coming-of-age story. Adolescent members of the African diaspora in Italy deserve to have someone who speaks to and from that reality represented in curriculum—especially Italian Black girls. And it is also important for white Italian students to gain a deeper and more nuanced understanding of colonial history and the struggles that their friends and neighbours of the African diaspora have and continue to face. Igiaba Scego often jokes that she sees herself as a writer, despite critics and interviewers who label her as an activist. As I see it, her writing intrinsically enacts a kind of cultural activism that advocates for a more inclusive, more empathetic, and more just Italy.

Notes

1. In *The Glossary of Literary Terms*, M.H. Abrams defines the Bildungsroman as a novel about "the development of the protagonist's mind and character, in the passage from childhood through varied experiences—and often through a spiritual crisis—into maturity, which usually involves recognition of one's identity and role in the world" (93). Abrams articulates the Bildungsroman's primary narrative endeavour: to novelize the coming-of-age story—a basic mode of storytelling that exists across most world cultures. His narratological definition speaks to the core conflict the Bildungsroman hinges upon—that is, a spiritual or existential crisis the protagonist must confront as they begin to ask questions about their place in the state or society or the world writ large.
2. *La mia casa è dove sono* participates in the Künstlerroman subgenre, in which the writer describes the "acquisition of the skills, habits, experiences, and attitudes necessary to write that story after the fact" (Slaughter 93).
3. All of the English translations in the chapter, including passages from Scego's novel, are my own.
4. According to Leone and Mastrovito, "the presence of Fascism and Italian colonialism in Italian school history textbooks is quite recent. In 1960, a ministerial decree stated that the secondary school teaching program must cover historical events up to 1957, and in 1996 a new ministerial decree again strongly recommended the teaching of twentieth-century history. These institutional exhortations reflect a general reluctance in Italian history teaching to face such controversial memories" (20). Leone and Mastrovito's findings suggest that Italian history books continue to obfuscate colonial endeavours and atrocities. Many of the history books analyzed were "still oriented towards interpretative abstraction" and made allowances for Italian colonialism by linking it to the "imperialist politics of other states" (23). For instance, in one of the textbooks under review, Aurelio Lepre's *La storia: Dalla fine dell'Ottocento a oggi*, Fascist Italy's support of Ethiopian colonization is rationalized as a reaction to British imperial maneuvers that aimed to keep Italy from "its place in the Sun" (24).
5. A *barzelletta* is a funny, ironical story in Italian popular culture, often with local and regional nuance. I translate Scego's joke and include "walk into a bar" to approximate the English equivalent of a joke cycle or bit.

6. Over the last two decades, the question of why Italian colonial history was suppressed more than other colonizer states has received a great deal of attention from scholars such as Danielle Comberiati, Caterina Romeo, Cristina Lombardi-Diop, Angelo Del Boca, Sandra Ponzanesi, and Giovanna Sansalvadore, to name a few. Scholars agree that the suppression of Italian colonial history is most strongly linked to the "mainstream postwar rebuilding" (Sansalvadore 64) of Italian identity. After the dismantling of Fascist Italy, many Italians took the mantle of the anti-Fascist resistance, centring the *partigiani* as the spiritual founders of the new republic. Italians disassociated themselves from the Fascist state and its actions, including its colonial missions. Put simply, the postwar revisionism created into a reality in which the mainstream understanding was that Italians weren't colonizers, Fascists were. Not only was this crude historical revisionism but it also obscured the historical fact that Italian colonial expansion began long before Fascism, as early as 1870 when the Rubattino Steamship Company first docked in Eritrea. Other contributors include the virtual inaccessibility of archives as has been suggested by Palumbo and Del Boca, and the contradictory perception of Italy as a formerly colonized state, a powerful myth harkening back to the Risorgimento. Finally, it is important to mention what Lombardi-Diop and Romeo have referred to as "uneven decolonization" (6). Unlike France and Britain, Italy did not experience large-scale immigration from its colonies, neither during the colonial era nor after the postwar dissolution. The absence of postcolonial authors who could speak to Italian colonialism and its legacies contributed greatly to that history's marginalization.

7. The *jus sanguinis* principle that informs current Italian immigration policy has been heavily criticized by immigrants' rights activists for the last two decades. The gravity of the situation is deftly explained by Clarissa Clò: "Italy has a very restrictive citizenship legislation based on *jus sanguinis* (i.e., blood, lineage, and race) so that, even when they are born and raised in Italy, children of immigrants are considered by law immigrants themselves. The extent of the prejudice of this legislation based on descent and ethnic belonging is evident in the restrictions that immigrants from the so-called Third World have to suffer as opposed to others born of Italian or European origins" (275–76). For more on the struggle of second-generation Italian immigrants, see Chiara Marchetti's "'Trees Without Roots': The Reform of Citizenship Challenged by the Children of Immigrants in Italy."

8. In the 1970s and 1980s, Italy was not yet the destination site for immigration that it has become in recent decades. Lombardi-Diop and Romeo suggest that only in the 1980s did Italy become a destination site for global migration, operating as a passageway for southern and eastern migrations during the Cold War (9).

9. For more on the marginalization of discussion pertaining to racial prejudice in Italy, see "Postracial/Postcolonial Italy" in which Cristina Lombardi-Diop argues that "widespread racism permeates the political discourse, the societal behavior, and popular culture, yet race is often unnamed and ultimately silenced" (175).

10. Scego encourages scholars and cultural critics not to conflate the experience of Blackness in Italy with the experience of Blackness elsewhere, particularly in the United States. In a recent interview, Scego has argued that "we need to create a language, a mode, a modality, to speak about being Black in Italy, neri italiani. One that neither retraces the African American forms, nor the debate of the anglophone world, because the risk is that of retracing things that do not really fit with our situation. Numerous scholars and activists parrot the United States discourse about race, whether slogans—I am not talking about 'Black Lives Matter,' that slogan is universally true—or other concepts, which, in a carbon-copy fashion, are applied, here, in Italy" (Riccò). As a white Italian American man, I am keenly aware of the importance of avoiding "carbon-copy" comparisons and have done my best to interpret Scego's writing with respect for the distinct experience of Blackness in Italy.

Works Cited

Abrams, M.H. *The Glossary of Literary Terms*. 7th ed., Heinle and Heinle, 1999.

Anzaldúa, Gloria. *Borderlands/La Frontera: The New Mestiza*. Aunt Lute Books, 1987.

Bakhtin, M.M. *Speech Genres and Other Late Essays*. Translated by Vern W. McGee, University of Texas Press, 1986.

Ben-Ghiat, Ruth, and Mia Fuller, editors. *Italian Colonialism*. Palgrave Macmillan, 2005.

Bhabha, Homi K. *The Location of Culture*. Routledge, 1994.

Campbell, Ian. *The Addis Ababa Massacre: Italy's National Shame*. Oxford University Press, 2017.

Clò, Clarissa. "Hip Pop Italian Style: The Postcolonial Imagination of Second-Generation Authors in Italy." Lombardi-Diop and Romeo, pp. 275–93.

Comberiati, Daniele. "'Missioni': Doubled Identity and Plurilingualism in the Works of Three Female Migrant Writers in Italy." *Migration and Literature in Contemporary Europe*, edited by Mirjam Gebauer and Pia Schwarz Lausten, Peter Lang, 2010, pp. 205–18.

Del Boca, Angelo. "The Myths, Suppressions, Denials, and Defaults of Italian Colonialism." Palumbo, pp. 17–37.

Del Boca, Angelo. "The Obligations of Italy Toward Libya." Ben-Ghiat and Fuller, pp. 195–203.

Graham, Sarah, editor. *A History of the Bildungsroman*. Cambridge University Press, 2019.

Hoagland, Erika A. "Postcolonial Bildungsroman." Graham, pp. 217–39.

Leone, Giovanna, and Tiziana Mastrovito. "Learnings about Our Shameful Past: A Socio-Psychological Analysis of Present-Day Historical Narratives of the Italian Colonial Wars." *International Journal of Conflict and Violence*, vol. 4, no. 1, 2010, pp. 11–27.

Lombardi-Diop, Cristina. "Postracial/Postcolonial Italy." Lombardi-Diop and Romeo, pp. 175–91.

Lombardi-Diop, Cristina, and Caterina Romeo, editors. *Postcolonial Italy: Challenging National Homogeneity*. Palgrave Macmillan, 2012.

Marchetti, Chiara. "'Trees without Roots': The Reform of Citizenship Challenged by the Children of Immigrants in Italy." *Bulletin of Italian Politics*, vol. 2, no. 1, 2010, pp. 45–67.

Moretti, Franco. *The Way of the World: The Bildungsroman in European Culture*. Translated by Albert Sbragia, Verso, 1987.

Palumbo, Patrizia, editor. *A Place in the Sun: Africa in Italian Colonial Culture from Post-Unification to the Present*. University of California Press, 2003.

Ponzanesi, Sandra. "The Past Holds No Terror? Colonial Memories and Afro-Italian Narratives." *Wasafiri*, vol. 15, no. 31, 2000, pp. 16–19.

Riccò, Giulia. "Igiaba Scego on Writing Between History and Literature." Publicbooks.org, 8 Dec. 2020, https://www.publicbooks.org/igiaba-scego-on-writing-between-history-and-literature/.

Sansalvadore, Giovanna. "Coming to Terms with Our Colonial Past: Regina di Fiori e di Perle by Gabriella Ghermandi." *Studi d'italianistica nell'Africa australe*, vol. 26, no. 1, 2013, pp. 63–68.

Scego, Igiaba. *La mia casa è dove sono*. Loescher, 2010.

Schaller, Dominik J. "Genocide and Mass Violence in the 'Heart of Darkness': Africa in the Colonial Period." *The Oxford Handbook of Genocide Studies*, edited by David Bloxham and A. Dirk Moses, Oxford University Press, 2010, pp. 345–65.

Sekayi, Dia. "Aesthetic Resistance to Commercial Influences: The Impact of the Eurocentric Beauty Standard on Black College Women." *The Journal of Negro Education*, vol. 2, no. 4, 2003, pp. 467–77.

Slaughter, Joseph. "Bildungsroman." *Encyclopedia of the Novel*, edited by Peter Melvin Logan, Wiley-Blackwell, 2011, pp. 93–97.

5
THE COSMOPOLITAN BILDUNGSROMAN

Antonette Talaue-Arogo

Colonialism, sublimated as a civilizing mission, rests on the putative impossibility of the full maturation of the colonized, their inability to come of age unlike their colonial masters. Such infantilizing rhetoric translated into policy is evident in Philippine colonial history and its legacies, particularly migration in the post-independence period. Through a close reading of Filipino American Randy Ribay's 2019 novel, *Patron Saints of Nothing*, this chapter argues that the Bildungsroman, a genre that has travelled beyond its German origin to form part of world literature, can be appropriated towards anti-Orientalist ends. Exemplified by the aforementioned book, the Philippine Bildungsroman rewrites the genre through a nuanced representation of the hero's journey. In so doing, it revitalizes the unfinishability of *Bildung* as a moment of positive reconstruction of identity formation and social relations that can be adequately studied under the rubric of inclusionary cosmopolitanism.

Genre of/in Formation

The Bildungsroman is a genre of formation that is in formation. Marc Redfield states, "This genre does not properly exist, and in a sense can be proved not to exist: one can take canonical definitions of Bildung (itself no simple term), go to the novels most frequently called Bildungsromane, and with greater or lesser difficulty show that they exceed, or fall short of, or call into question the process of Bildung which they purportedly serve" (Preface). That the Bildungsroman especially gained currency in the twentieth century is explained by the institutionalization of literary studies in this period. Practical Criticism and New Criticism were the inheritors of Kantian aesthetics that enabled an understanding of literature as disinterested and of the writer as an autonomous subject who transcends material and everyday concerns, capable of seeing and representing what is truly universal. In this Romantic and formalist conception of the writer as genius and literature as timeless can be gleaned the ideology of liberal humanism, an ideal and valuation of being human attained by the enlightened or, after Kant, the mature. This proper subject of history is always already Western, male, bourgeois, and heterosexual, a privilege that is a product of even as it produces the literary canon, or touchstones for Matthew Arnold (824). For Redfield, thus, aesthetics is ideological (Preface).

The theoretical turn in the 1960s designating intersecting paradigms can be seen to critique this aesthetics as ideology (see A. Anderson 1). Owing to its poststructuralist provenance, postcolonial theory enables a critique from within of the ambivalent relationship of desire and disavowal between the colonizer and the colonized and the hegemony of Western modernity condensed in the Cartesian dictum, "I think therefore I am."[1] This is the normative definition of the human being as rational and in possession of proper knowledge, what comprises the humanities today rooted in the classical studies of Renaissance Italy. Leela Gandhi explains the progression of humanism from the sixteenth to the eighteenth centuries against which the turn to theory was mobilized as an expansion in the conceptualization of man from the basis of what he knows to how he knows what he knows. Gandhi uses the word "man" deliberately to foreground that the "humanist valorisation of man is almost always accompanied by a barely discernible corollary which suggests that some human beings are more human than others—either on account of their access to superior learning, or on account of their cognitive faculties" (*Postcolonial Theory* 29). This is a mechanism of power, a way of justifying hierarchization between group identities based on sex, gender, and sexuality; class; race, ethnicity, or nationality; and other categories. Humanity or human-ness is a process of development, a universal maturation for Kant in his response to the question, "What is Enlightenment?" published in 1784. Within the framework of the human being as the rational adult, it comes as no surprise that Orientalist discourses deploy an infantilizing rhetoric, representing colonized peoples as infants, silent subalterns incapable of self-representation and self-knowledge. They are ever developing, not ever coming into full humanity. This opposition between being and becoming, with the West claiming for itself the former subject position by prescribing what makes a human being human, explains Edward W. Said's theorization of Orientalism as discourses across disciplines that codify a fundamental distinction between the Occident and the Orient, positing the latter as the former's negative Other (2–3).

Paradigmatic of Orientalism is Rudyard Kipling's infamous poem, "The White Man's Burden," published in 1899 but completed a year before at the time of the emergence of the United States as a new imperial power. In 1898, the US went to war against Spain precipitated by the explosion of the battleship USS *Maine* in Havana Harbor, sent to Cuba for the safeguarding of American interests in the wake of resistance against Spanish colonial rule. The Spanish–American War eventuated in the Treaty of Paris in December that made Cuba a US protectorate. It also handed the Philippines, Spain's colony for over three hundred years, to the US for the sum of $20 million. The Philippines was then an emerging nation-state, though not recognized as such by both Spain and the US, molded by the reform movement and the revolution leading to the declaration of independence from Spain on June 12, 1898, by the revolutionaries and the formation of the constitutional republic on January 23, 1899. Emilio Aguinaldo, the country's first president, soon declared war against the US. The Philippine–American War "has been described as the United States' first Vietnam War because of its brutality and severity" (Abinales and Amoroso 117). The Americans, through President Theodore Roosevelt, declared victory over the revolutionary government in 1902. The "benevolent assimilation" policy of President William McKinley that sublimated colonization as a matter of instruction in governance and related social aspects, such as education, until the Filipinos demonstrate their capacity for self-rule was pursued. It was for naught that the Philippines staged the "first anticolonial revolution in Asia" (Abinales and Amoroso 113) and established "the first republic" (116) in the region. The colonial masters were the arbiters of the preparedness of the colonized and the latter were judged as not yet ready.

The US colonial administration of the Philippines exemplifies the tropes of belatedness and derivativeness that are the hallmarks of Orientalism as the exercise of power through the production of knowledge about the objects, and subjects in a conversely relational manner, of authority. US paternalism was discursively exercised through the attribution of immaturity to the colonized. This was evident in the designation of the Filipinos as America's "little brown brothers" (Orden) by William Howard Taft who was the first American governor-general of the Philippines before he succeeded President Roosevelt. Kipling memorializes this colonial stereotype in the specific context of US colonialism of the Philippines in these deprecatory lines:

> Your new-caught, sullen peoples,
> Half-devil and half-child. (The Kipling Society)

The colonized are represented as permanently in a state of transition to adulthood, of coming of age but with the *telos* of Enlightenment perpetually in a state of deferral. Any approximation of the colonizer's way of life is but a poor imitation, what Homi K. Bhabha sharply phrases as "almost the same but not white" (89). Or in Redfield's elucidation of aesthetic education: "the subject of aesthetics comes into existence by identifying with an exemplar, and the exemplar is exemplary because of its original spontaneity: what must be imitated is the inimitable" (21).

Backdropped by the US colonialism of the Philippines, one can more fully understand the Bildungsroman as a literary genre in aesthetic ideology (Redfield 4). Man's self-cultivation produces culture, or

Kultur, as the teleological fulfillment of the highest human ideals and capacities (see Cheah, *Spectral Nationality* 7). In colonial pedagogy putatively aimed at the production of proper subjectivity, "the exemplary and developmental temporality of aesthetic history permits the 'native' or, mutatis mutandis, the working-class or feminine subject to be represented as incomplete rather than different—with the unstated proviso that these 'children' will also never grow up: within the harmonious aesthetic universe they are naturally childish" (Redfield 25–26). At the same time, within this historiographic frame, the incompleteness and indeterminacy of the Bildungsroman can be seen as a liberatory space. Its cognate terms of form and model explain why, for Hans-Georg Gadamer, "Bildung (as also the contemporary use of 'formation') describes more the result of this process of becoming than the process itself" (qtd. in Redfield 47). And yet *Bildung*, Gadamer continues, "remains in a constant state of further continued Bildung" (47). The way out of this bind is the very notion of exemplarity that the West as the civilized subject of Enlightenment, having emerged from childhood to reach subjecthood, as the subject who has become Subject, arrogated to itself in contradistinction to the rest. That this exemplarity is constructed rather than reflective of reality, used to prop up unequal social structures, has been compellingly demonstrated by postcolonial scholarship following Said's *Orientalism*, encompassing works in literary history and genre studies.

Franco Moretti, for instance, begins his discussion on distant reading with the observation that the modern novel of the eighteenth to the twentieth century is "a compromise between a western formal influence (usually French or English) and local materials" (58), an example for which he identifies *Noli Me Tangere* by Philippine national hero, José Rizal. Read as a Bildungsroman (see Cheah, *Spectral Nationality* 239–40), the novel was published in 1887 and originally written in the colonial language, Spanish. For Moretti, this compromise is an approach that insists on a mutually transformative relationship between national and world literature. On a similar vector, David Damrosch argues that a literary text becomes a part of world literature by its movement beyond its source culture and its reception by a target culture with its own national traditions. World literature is a hybrid site where negotiations over group identity, relation to otherness, and futurity are undertaken. Rather than accepting the taken-for-granted core to periphery direction, Damrosch makes a case for bidirectionality reinforced by more collaborative pedagogical and research methods. Pheng Cheah sees in Damrosch's framework the narrative arc of the Bildungsroman in which "a literary work is therefore seen as being like a traveler, even a protagonist of a bildungsroman. It enters into a horizon wider than its immediate home. It evolves and grows as it makes its way across the world just as the protagonist gains enlightenment in a developmental process of maturation" (*What Is a World?* 29).

The "autoproduction" (Redfield 55) of the Bildungsroman is applicable to literary texts as well as to interpretive communities. As the literary representation of *Bildung*, the individual development of the protagonist extends to the reader through the latter's own experience of novelistic education, the condition of possibility for the generalizing premise of the Bildungsroman. In understanding the genre as transnational, or more aptly cosmopolitan as will be further discussed, one can better appreciate how the self-productivity of the Bildungsroman has been deployed to resistant ends by less privileged groups, particularly formerly colonized peoples in aid of identity and nation formation. A paradigmatic example for the cosmopolitanization of the genre is the Philippine Bildungsroman that is shaped by the country's history of colonialism and its afterlives, specifically having to do with mobility. Represented by Randy Ribay's *Patron Saints of Nothing*, whose protagonist is an immigrant subject, this novel shows how the genre itself undergoes development, representing historical changes in individual and group identities towards greater inclusivity.

Philippine Bildungsroman

On June 12, 1956, the Philippine government ratified Republic Act No. 1425, also known as the Rizal Bill, which mandated the inclusion of *Noli Me Tangere* and its sequel, *El Filibusterismo*, in the curricula of all public and private schools, colleges, and universities.[2] For Caroline S. Hau, this law lays bare the reciprocal relationship between literature and the nation as acts of imagination produced by social relations and everyday behaviour of individuals who were born into or have moved to a given territory with its own set of historical memory, cultural traditions, and political structures. Furthermore, their co-constitutionality is informed by the state's prescription of didactic criticism, making literary education the tool for the formation of patriotic citizens following the example of Rizal's life and works, and applying these lessons to the challenges of their own period. "Literature," according to Hau, "is utilized strategically in the formation of an educated, 'model' citizen-subject who aids in the transformation of his or her society" (*Necessary Fictions* 16). The state determines what must be read and how this text ought to be read, premised on the notion that literature is at once referential and performative, representing but also bringing into being "the 'Filipino' political subject of truth and action" (*Necessary Fictions* 16). The *Bildung* of Crisostomo Ibarra-cum-Simoun, Rizal's hero, is the *Bildung* of the reader, whose achievement of national character through the Bildungsroman contributes to decolonization and the formation of an independent state. Cheah puts forth a comparable argument:

> One can say that activist postcolonial nationalist novels are conceived as a means for generating a reading public that can be a renewing basis of the nation-people, the medium and substrate in which it can regenerate itself by reflecting upon and knowing itself. Hence, in postcoloniality, the political vocation of culture finds its exemplary performance in and as activist nationalist literature, especially in and as the novelistic genre of the bildungsroman. (*Spectral Nationality* 240)

That nationalism originates in fiction attests to the necessity of such pedagogical imperative, neutralizing the apparent deployment of literature as an ideological state apparatus in the service of critique of the more pernicious colonial ideology.[3] As depicted by many post-independence novels in the Philippines and other formerly colonized countries in the Global South, however, nationalism can be hostaged by native elite interests in alignment with empire in its neocolonial and neoliberal forms. In *Elites and Ilustrados in Philippine Culture*,

Hau patiently historicizes the emergence of this group identity from the colonial to the post-independence periods in the Philippines, facilitated by economic, political, cultural, and intellectual capital. She clarifies that they are a heterogenous group whose constituency changes over time. Identified as the wealthy, the highly educated, and the governing class, segments of the elite approach "leadership not so much as service (hence subservience) to the state as command over (and therefore subordinating of) the state" (3). It is simultaneously a desirable and disavowed subject position, not unlike that of the colonizers. The *ilustrados*, or the enlightened in translation, of the nineteenth century, among them Rizal, were credited with fighting for reform and eventually participating in the revolution. On the other hand, many capitulated and collaborated with the new colonial masters. Such politicking that is driven by personal interests continued after the Third Philippine Republic was inaugurated in 1946, succeeding what was established during the Japanese occupation and after independence from the US. Post-independence politics, especially during the dictatorship of Ferdinand Marcos from the 1970s, would be characterized by crony capitalism. This is a system of collusion between political leaders and the business class that the Philippines and its historical specificity contributed to the understanding of the machinations of political economy (6).

The flexibility of the elite as a group identity defined by the dynamic relations of various kinds of capital, including talent and skill, and global transformations, such as diaspora, allows for an expansive categorization, such that "Overseas Filipino Workers, Overseas Filipino Intellectuals, and Filipino-foreigners in the late twentieth and early twenty-first centuries" (Hau, *Elites and Ilustrados* 11) can now be recognized as elites, able to affect national and international developments. Indeed, they have become the new *ilustrados*, viscerally confronted with the "world of multiple nations—a vision that was clear to the Filipino nationalists in the late nineteenth century but eclipsed under the weight of the US empire" (Aguilar 1). To borrow the phrase of Filomeno V. Aguilar Jr., there has been a "migration revolution" since the Marcos administration, transforming migrants' and nonmigrants' understanding of nationhood and generating experiences that unsettle individual and collective identity. Rolando B. Tolentino provides a succinct overview:

> Since then, the Philippines has become the largest supplier of immigrant professionals to the United States, particularly nurses, doctors, and medical technologists (Catalan 1996). In the 1970s, Marcos intensified the labor export, creating what are called OFW (Overseas Filipino Workers) and OCW (Overseas Contract Workers)—new labor identities for Filipinos doing flexible and 3-D (dirty, dangerous, and difficult) jobs overseas. The OCW phenomenon is so huge that the Philippines is now the third largest exporter of labor and the second biggest receiver of remittances in the world. One out of ten Filipinos is an OCW, at least one-half of Filipinos have a family member who is an OCW, and therefore, at least half of the population is supported by OCW remittances. Confronted with perennial political and economic crises, post-Marcos national administrations have increased the reliance on OCWs as reliable foreign currency suppliers. (78)

These spatial movements reconfigure state and, its synecdochic image, family relations centred on class status and intersected by gender, as well as race and ethnicity (see Tadiar, esp. ch. 1). Upward social mobility is visually demonstrated especially in provinces where remittances are used to build new houses, among other practices (Aguilar 6). Children of migrants, specifically of those who have coupled with other nationalities or the "'Fil-foreign' (as they are referred to in Philippine print media)...are the new mestizos of Philippine society, the fresh new embodiments of modernity from the outside, even as they simultaneously add a new inflection to the question of authenticity of Filipino identity" (6–7).

The politics of nation and identity formation, as well as migration and immigration, form the thematics of *Patron Saints of Nothing*, contextualized in Philippine President Rodrigo Roa Duterte's war on drugs. The novel belongs to the genealogy of Philippine Bildungsroman,[4] with the narrative device of a return as the prompt for the hero's journey towards self-realization at its heart. Traced back to Rizal's novels, the Philippine Bildungsroman not only establishes the central role of writing in imagining the nation and decolonization (Hau, *Necessary Fictions* chs. 1 and 2; Cheah, *Spectral Nationality* ch. 5). Through the trope of the returning hero, it critically engages with the ineluctable elements of mobility, privilege, and foreignness in identity and nation formation. This is taken up by *Patron Saints of Nothing*, in which the hero's subject position as an immigrant and its attendant cultural dislocation is haunted by the charge of and internal struggle with betrayal and insincerity. At the level of authorial intention, the novel itself can be read as an act of return fraught with the same questions. Ribay reflects on the impetus for his work: "What's my role as a Filipino American who's at once connected, but also an outsider to what's happening in the Philippines" ("'Patron Saints of Nothing'")? In grappling with these issues, the novel enables a reframing of the Bildungsroman within a cosmopolitan framework through restoring the experiencing subject to agency, a subject whose homecoming develops an openness to a reconciling and collaborative work on the struggles the Philippines has long endured. The novel is a rejoinder to the colonial discourse of the impossibility of *Bildung* for the colonized, departing from the idiom of failure of an accomplished ideal. Through a revisioning of the hero's journey, it demonstrates that *Bildung*, instead, is a continuing process of learning and unlearning informed by life experiences towards more inclusive attachments and modes of belonging.

Cosmopolitan Subject of Bildung

Patron Saints of Nothing is about the enduring consequences of colonialism, primarily mobility and its effects on subjectivity and social relations, the perception of immigrants of their home country, as well as their relationship with those who remain at home. The novel follows Jay Reguero, a seventeen-year-old "Filipino *American*" (Ribay 26), who goes back to Manila from Michigan under the guise of a vacation before starting college. In reality, he seeks to uncover the true reason behind the death of his intelligent and socially conscious cousin, Jun, with whom he exchanged letters for a time while they were growing up. He soon learns that Jun was killed because of his involvement in drugs. For this reason, Jun's father, Maning, who is a high-ranking member of the police force and an ardent supporter of the president's war, refuses to hold a funeral for his own child. With the help of Jun's sister, Grace, and a romantic interest who is a journalism student, Mia, Jay's investigation leads to an unexpected and undesired revelation of Jun's less than heroic life and Maning's less than villainous character (288–89). This is an unconcealment that proceeds as Jay travels from the city to the province, a movement that brings him ever closer to home as place of origin and that becomes the site of a fragile reconciliation for his deeply divided family. Jun, it is revealed, was indeed using and selling drugs, leaving his girlfriend, Reyna, to shield her from the consequences of such actions. Maning did not order his son's death and did look out for Jun, attempting to remove his name from the police watch list. After this revelation, the family, with Grace's initiative, holds an intimate memorial that Maning, in the end, joins. At this moment, Jay is able to articulate the truth uncovered by his quest: "Truly, none of us is one thing" (300).

This is a moment of epiphany for the protagonist brought about by the painful disillusionment not only about his beloved cousin and country of birth but also his own role and relation to this reality. He is not the saviour come to right the injustices in the Philippines (291). Grace is the one who will take over managing the website Jun was running called GISING NA PH! (Wake Up Philippines!) that documents the alleged abuses of the drug war and humanizes those embroiled in drug use. This is one of the lessons of Jun's death—that good continues to exist in people who suffer from addiction, that they are deserving of help rather than retribution, and that this assistance is the duty of the elected to which they must be held accountable. How effective an intervention this online platform is remains to be seen but, as it has turned out for Jun's family, it is an indispensable tool of personal and, optimistically, national understanding. What is also undeniable is the necessarily collective nature of this truth seeking, one that in due course allowed for even combating individuals—the accused father and the angry nephew, the resentful domestic and the timorous immigrant—to share the same sorrow and mourn together. The novel explores the various facets of what can be called an immigrant disposition. Jay's father feels guilty for leaving, perceived as desertion by Maning and his wife, Ami. Jay, himself, feels lacking in Filipino-ness. He doesn't speak Tagalog and Bikol, he hasn't read the novels of Rizal, and he doesn't know enough about the country's history. In one of the vehement confrontations between Maning and Jay, the former berates the latter:

> You do not live here. You do not speak any of our languages. You do not know our history. Your mother is a white American. Yet, you presume to speak to me as if you knew anything about me, as if you knew anything about my son, as if you knew anything about this country. (160)

The novel's resolution lends validity to Maning's speech that, when heard with the discovery of the truth behind Jun's passing, sounds as if it comes from a place less of anger than pain. However, as Jay has intuited, truth is not just about the inadequacy of the act of representation by the Other of that which is Other to them (155–56). It is that representation—one that is closer to an ethical viewpoint and that makes space for the ambivalence and complexity of identity and social relations—ought to be inclusive and recognize the universality of, as Jay puts it, "some sense of right and wrong about how human beings should be treated that applies no matter where you live, no matter what language you speak" (174). Fittingly, the novel ends with a plan by Mia and Jay to co-write, along with Grace, Jun's story (307). In a moving conclusion, Jay, upon arriving back in the United States, informs his father that he intends to defer college and return once again in order to learn more about the Philippines.

The novel thus opens and closes in the same way, with the hero's journey as the central element of Jay's coming of age, a quest for the truth of his cousin's death at the beginning and a continuing quest for the truth of the state of affairs of his country of nativity, a country he claims as his own with more conviction at the ending. Jay, as with the structure of a quest narrative, is not at all heroic at the onset.[5] In fact, the reader first meets him as a ten-year-old boy on his first visit to the Philippines crying over a dead puppy, somewhat reprimanded by Maning for this supposed weakness of character and comforted by, out of all family members, Jun. It is not so much his emotional response to his first encounter with death that makes the character unheroic at this stage. Jay's reaction is typical of his age and of someone with love for animals—tied to the ethics of otherness and concretized in Jun's socio-political awakening in the novel (258–60)—although Maning's rebuke certainly influenced his exertion of control over his emotions as a teenager (86, 240) and gives an insight into Jay's antagonism towards, and yet fear of, his uncle. What makes the prologue significant, therefore, is the family dynamics immediately mapped by the author and that will explain the act of abandonment by and concomitant feelings of "guilt, shame, and sadness" (19) of the protagonist. Over the years, the cousins write to each other, Jun more persistently, until Jay simply stopped answering. Even his desire to learn more about what happened to Jun is egotistically instantiated by a need for absolution: "that, whatever happened, a few more letters from me wouldn't have made a difference" (21). Moreover, he is ignorant of the political situation in the Philippines that determined his cousin's fate, too unconcerned and too uninterested to read beyond sensational headlines (24). His American friend, Seth, is more knowledgeable about President Duterte. And yet Jay's self-recrimination that moves him to action—from reading up on the drug war to travelling to the Philippines upon receiving a message on Instagram from someone who claims to be Jun's friend sharing information about the victims of the administration's policy—shows the potential for moral development and social consciousness. His distancing from Jun through his nonresponse to the letters, he begins to recognize, is analogous to the silence of Filipinos abroad, a silence of the relief of security from the dangers at home. His father is "just glad" (26) his children grew up and live in America. Jay confronts his possible complicity and gives an accounting of the self: "It strikes me now that I've never truly confronted that question before, that I never had to. But I'm left to wonder, did my parents' silence—and mine—allow Jun's death in some way? Was there anything we could have done from the US" (27)? That he journeys home with the intent to investigate Jun's death suggests that practical action is truly possible if distance, no matter how critical through the double perspective that unhomeliness engenders, is taken in conjunction with the act of return.[6] Put another way, a Fil-foreign retains Filipino-ness and remains a good Filipino by the act of return. It is this movement that signals his heroism, the act that defines a hero in the Philippine literary and historical collective unconscious.

Isagani R. Cruz (qtd. in Aparece) propounds a morphology of Philippine epics and identifies the following recurring actions at the beginning and ending of such works, explaining the collective understanding of heroism: "the hero departs from home" and "the hero goes back home" (146). The country's pantheon of national heroes from Rizal to Benigno Aquino Jr., former senator and opposition leader whose assassination in 1983 culminated in the People Power Revolution in 1986 and the fall of the Marcos dictatorship, is in conformance with this literary representation of a hero who leaves home but, importantly, returns home, even at the risk of personal safety. Reinforcing this archetypal understanding of a hero, President Corazon Aquino, the widow of the slain Aquino, "conferred upon returning migrant workers the status of 'new heroes' (*bagong bayani*) of the Filipino nation-qua-economy" (Aguilar 138). They are heroes because they are the bearers of liberation, political and economic. Particular to different kinds of migrant identities, it must be clarified, are expectations of the fulfillment of this duty to return. For OFWs and OCWs, return is not strictly physical given the context of global capitalism in which remittances and transfer of other goods are valuable, if not more desirable (Hau, *Elites and Ilustrados* 270). For Overseas Filipino Intellectuals and Fil-foreigners or Fil-foreign, the obligation as generally perceived is to actually return (270). This is especially the case for those who are professionally and personally invested in knowledge production about the Philippines and its translation into societal intervention. The following exchange between Jay and his mother shortly after he learns of the circumstances of Jun's death is an acute depiction of the question of representation and, related to this, the critique of Orientalism levelled against foreign scholarship on the Philippines, including works by Overseas Filipino Intellectuals.[7]

"How many people have died?" I ask instead of answering.

She shakes her head. "Some think over ten, maybe twenty, thousand.

But the government says only a few thousand."

Only.

"And Filipinos are still okay with this guy?"

She takes a deep breath. "Jay, it's easy for us to pass judgment. But we don't live there anymore, so we can't grasp the extent to which drugs have affected the country. According to what I've read, most Filipinos believe it's for the greater good. Harsh but necessary. To them, Duterte is someone finally willing to do what it takes to set things right."

"So I'm not allowed to have an opinion? To say it's wrong or inhumane?"

She puts her hands on her hip and flashes me a look that signals I should check my tone. Then, in a low voice, says, "That's not what I'm saying, Jay."

"What are you saying?"

"That you need to make sure that opinion is an informed one." (Ribay 25–26)

Jay's homecoming, then, is significant as a fulfillment of this precondition for what is considered proper representation, which is interiority as opposed to exteriority. It is also the actualization of the promise of liberation, which in the novel is Jay's pursuit of justice on a personal level by allowing the family to uncover the truth about and, in so doing, grieve Jun's death. However, instead of bringing to light what the reader can see is a preconceived truth of what is right and wrong, of who is perpetrator and victim, what unfolds in Jay's truth-seeking sojourn is an anti-heroic journey that reveals ambivalence, prejudice, and complicity. Characters are shown to be fallible, even Jun of keen intelligence and deep empathy, who from a young age showed compassion for the less privileged members of his society and acted on it. Jay, all throughout his stay in the Philippines and as he becomes immersed in retracing the events of Jun's life, carries the discomfiture of an identity crisis signalled by his inadequacy in the native language (208). All the same, there are moments of belongingness as while he's singing karaoke with neighbours or standing by the water's edge and feeling the steady waves of the sea (226–27). Seeing the slums of Metro Manila is at once estranging and familiar to Jay, exceeding photographic and linguistic representations and yet also refusing the stereotype of extreme degeneracy by simply being a space of everyday life and survival (197). Perhaps, most tellingly, he knows fully well that he would not have cared about the drug war had it not affected him personally (194). Danilo, another uncle of Jay's who is a priest, despite great regret over what is happening to the country and the family, retreats to the platitude of the separation of church and state. Chato, Jay's aunt who worked as a lawyer, is resigned to the reality of a corrupt judicial system in the Philippines. But characters are also shown to be redeemable, even the masculinist and chauvinist Maning accused of having a hand in his own son's death. The hero's journey is underlined by a doubleness, the notion that the quest is both meaningful and futile, that people are both right and wrong. In the novel, *Bildung* is not the Enlightenment stadial movement from ignorance to knowledge or, more precisely, knowledge as clearly delineated precepts about reality and, as such, is presented as an accomplished ideal. For Jay, learning is an experiential process of unlearning about the self, others, and reality (288). *Bildung*, indeed, is continued *Bildung*, the yet-to-come actualization of humanity as an ideal that is continuously reshaped by intersecting experiences of misjudgment and epiphany, and the affective dispositions of vulnerability and fortitude.

As sketched out in the first section of this chapter, the incompleteness and indeterminacy of *Bildung* is characteristic of the Bildungsroman that is deployed in the critique from within of humanism as urstructure of colonialism and in imagining the nation in former colonies. In *Patron Saints of Nothing*, the Bildungsroman performs this critique from within to a second degree. *Bildung* is not based on the supposed exemplarity of the colonial master or the diasporic figure or the rooted national but rather on an all too human-ness, the recognition of which allows for speaking with and listening to one another that, in turn, facilitates the suturing of relationships and engenders community (Epilogue). It is this inclusionary ethos that is the basis of the novel's cosmopolitan viewpoint. Kwame Anthony Appiah explains that "cosmopolitanism shouldn't be seen as some exalted attainment: it begins with the simple idea that in the human community, as in national communities, we need to develop habits of coexistence: conversation in its older meaning, of living together, association" (xix). There has been a recuperation of cultural cosmopolitanism in contemporary critical theory since it first emerged in the classical period through to the Enlightenment.[8] It is a paradigm of a "strategic bargain with universalism" (Malcomson 234), necessitated by historical conditions of deterritorialization as with the conquests of Alexander the Great that spurred intercultural exchange during the Hellenistic Age, and the technological inventions and the Industrial Revolution beginning in the eighteenth century that allowed for greater mobility. The acceleration of globalization since the late twentieth century has made possible the large-scale exchange of money, goods, ideas, and people (see Appadurai, ch. 2). In these instances, cosmopolitanism functions as a corrective to the dangers of ethnocentrism, promoting "reflective distance from one's cultural affiliations, a broad understanding of other cultures and customs, and a belief in universal humanity" (A. Anderson 72). The new cosmopolitanisms respond to the limitations of cosmopolitanist frameworks that eliminate rather than integrate difference in pursuit of an abstract universalism that is always already particular to the so-called proper subjects of history.

Correspondingly, cosmopolitans, and in line with the preceding discussion, are privileged individuals and groups possessing economic, political, cultural, and intellectual capital, and because of which they can travel, produce, and communicate with others outside of the nation-state. However, just as there are new elites and *ilustrados* in Philippine culture, cosmopolitanism "has a new cast of characters" (Robbins 1). They are less privileged individuals and groups whose spatial movements may not necessarily be by choice but due to specific conditions of marginalization, such as colonialism, and whose experiences are formative of what a world community means and looks like. In inclusionary cosmopolitanism, universal humanism is deliberately redefined in view of particular cultures. The nation is not set in opposition to but is seen as a part of a widening scale of affiliation towards the transnational. For Martha Nussbaum, classical cosmopolitanism proposes that the individual is "surrounded by a series of concentric circles" ("Patriotism and Cosmopolitanism") from the family to the national and to the whole of humanity. To concretize this movement and ensure inclusiveness are the challenges taken up by the new cosmopolitanisms, oriented towards the practical rather than the philosophical or the theoretical, and are thus "more modest and more worldly" (Robbins 3). In Ribay's novel, this is dramatized by Jay's decision to go on a gap year and once again visit the Philippines, study the country's history, and learn to speak its local languages, that is to carry on and persist in his own life education.

As a migrant identity, Jay possesses a hybrid subjectivity, neither purely Filipino nor purely American but a product of the colonial encounter and its legacies, including alienation. He is a stranger to Seth, in whose mind is ingrained the idea of the Philippines as a country of poor people, as he is a stranger to Maning, who projects onto him the national grievance over US colonialism and his personal animosity towards Jay's father for colluding with the Americans by moving to the empire. Indeed, he is a stranger to himself, having to give up comforting notions of good and evil and the catharsis of moral satisfaction. But, in this Bildungsroman, it is arguably more adequate to look at Jay as a cosmopolitan subject of *Bildung* whose maturation is evinced by his intentional bracketing of the comfort of his subject position as a Fil-foreign distanced from the troubles at home, and of the contentment with the fragile resolution of his journey as a gesture of reparation. He continues in his *Bildung* through a voluntary affiliation with the Other, this country he does not understand and its people he loves and resents but seeks to live with and learn from. Here resistance is less structural as in postcolonial hybridity than intentional and voluntary. If hybridity is a result of the colonial encounter that transforms both cultures of the colonizers and the colonized, then the subversion of colonial power is immanent to the structure of colonialism (Bhabha 112), in which case "the dissolution of colonial division is seen as in some ways inevitable: a matter of temporal unfolding" (Gandhi, *Affective Communities* 5). For Gandhi, not only has history belied this *telos* of freedom given neocolonialism but it also does not recognize the processes of self-problematization that enable modes of being apart from identitarian thinking and that motivate cross-cultural collaborations. While hybridity and the postcolonial tropes of mimicry and ambivalence produce agency, this is "a kind of agency without a subject" (Young 188). The new cosmopolitanisms depart from the negative critique characteristic of the theoretical turn and instead advance positive freedom as oppositional politics, exploring the range of thought styles—cultivation rather than subversion, optimism rather than suspicion—and affective relations between group identities—forgiveness rather than resentment, anger at injustice that transitions to "compassionate hope" (Nussbaum, *Anger and Forgiveness* 31). It is this reconciliation, no matter how precarious, among the members of Jay's family—Maning and Jay, Jay and his father—that serves as condition of possibility for the continued *Bildung* of the individual, the national, and, yes, the cosmopolitan.

Notes

1. My discussion of postcolonialism draws from Gandhi's *Postcolonial Theory: A Critical Introduction*.
2. For an authoritative critical discussion of the relationship between literature and nationalism in the Philippine context, see the works of Hau, especially *Necessary Fictions: Philippine Literature and the Nation, 1946–1980*.
3. See also Benedict Anderson, *The Spectre of Comparisons: Nationalism, Southeast Asia, and the World*. Hau was a former student of Anderson at Cornell University.
4. Hau provides sharp analyses of representative contemporary novels that arguably form the literary tradition of the Philippine Bildungsroman in her body of critical works that examine the relationship between literature and nation. In her most recent book, *Elites and Ilustrados*, the texts she critiques include Miguel Syjuco's *Ilustrado* and Ramon Guillermo's *Ang Makina ni Mang Turing*. See Chapter 4 and Epilogue.
5. According to Thomas Foster (ch. 1), the hero in a quest narrative need not be very heroic to begin with, since the whole reason for the journey is to gain self-knowledge and attain maturity.
6. On the question of critical distance in nation formation, see Said's "Intellectual Exile: Expatriates and Marginals (1993)."
7. On the politics of representation, see Hau (*Elites and Ilustrados* ch. 7).
8. For a succinct and substantive overview of cosmopolitanism, see A. Anderson (ch. 3).

Works Cited

Abinales, Patricio N., and Donna J. Amoroso. *State and Society in the Philippines*. 2nd ed., Ateneo de Manila University Press, 2017.

Aguilar Jr., Filomeno V. *Migration Revolution: Philippine Nationhood and Class Relations in a Globalized Age*. Ateneo de Manila University Press, 2014.

Anderson, Amanda. *The Way We Argue Now: A Study in the Cultures of Theory*. Princeton University Press, 2006.

Anderson, Benedict. *The Spectre of Comparisons: Nationalism, Southeast Asia, and the World*. Verso, 1998.

Aparece, Ulysses B. "Retrieving a Folk Hero through Oral Narratives: The Case of Francisco Dagohoy in the 'Sukdan' Rituals." *Philippine Quarterly of Culture and Society*, vol. 41, no. 3/4, 2013, pp. 143–62. *JSTOR*, http://www.jstor.org/stable/43854726.

Appadurai, Arjun. *Modernity at Large: Cultural Dimensions of Globalization*. University of Minnesota Press, 1996.

Appiah, Kwame Anthony. *Cosmopolitanism: Ethics in a World of Strangers*. W.W. Norton, 2006.

Arnold, Matthew. "The Function of Criticism at the Present Time." *The Norton Anthology of Theory and Criticism*, edited by Vincent B. Leitch et al., W.W. Norton, 2001, pp. 806–25.

Bhabha, Homi K. *The Location of Culture*. Routledge, 1994.

Cheah, Pheng. *Spectral Nationality: Passages of Freedom from Kant to Postcolonial Literatures of Liberation*. Kindle ed., Columbia University Press, 2003.

Cheah, Pheng. *What Is a World? On Postcolonial Literature as World Literature*. Kindle ed., Duke University Press, 2016.

Cheah, Pheng, and Bruce Robbins, editors. *Cosmopolitics: Thinking and Feeling beyond the Nation*. University of Minnesota Press, 1998.

Damrosch, David. "World Literature, National Contexts." *Modern Philology*, vol. 100, no. 4, 2003, pp. 512–31. *The University of Chicago Press Journals*, https://doi.org/10.1086/379981.

Foster, Thomas C. *How to Read Literature Like a Professor: A Lively and Entertaining Guide to Reading Between the Lines*. 2nd ed., Kindle ed., Harper Perennial, 2014.

Gandhi, Leela. *Affective Communities: Anticolonial Thought, Fin-de-siècle Radicalism, and the Politics of Friendship*. Duke University Press, 2006.

Gandhi, Leela. *Postcolonial Theory: A Critical Introduction*. Kindle ed., Routledge, 2020.

Hau, Caroline S. *Elites and Ilustrados in Philippine Culture*. Ateneo de Manila University Press, 2017.

Hau, Caroline S. *Necessary Fictions: Philippine Literature and the Nation, 1946–1980*. Ateneo de Manila University Press, 2000.

The Kipling Society. "The White Man's Burden." https://www.kiplingsociety.co.uk/readers-guide/rg_burden1.htm.

Malcomson, Scott L. "The Varieties of Cosmopolitan Experience." Cheah and Robbins, pp. 233–45.

Moretti, Franco. "Conjectures on World Literature." *New Left Review*, vol. 1, Jan./Feb. 2000, pp. 54–68.

Nussbaum, Martha C. *Anger and Forgiveness: Resentment, Generosity, Justice.* Kindle ed., Oxford University Press, 2016.

Nussbaum, Martha C. "Patriotism and Cosmopolitanism." *Boston Review*, 1 Oct. 1994, https://bostonreview.net/articles/martha-nussbaum-patriotism-and-cosmopolitanism/.

Orden, Vina. "The Little Brown Brother's Burden." *The Margins*, https://aaww.org/the-little-brown-brothers-burden/.

Redfield, Marc. *Phantom Formations: Aesthetic Ideology and the Bildungsroman.* Kindle ed., Cornell University Press, 1996.

Ribay, Randy. *Patron Saints of Nothing*. Kindle ed., Penguin Young Readers Group, 2019.

Ribay, Randy. "'Patron Saints of Nothing' Is a Book for 'The Hyphenated.'" Interview by Noel King and Ashley Westerman, *NPR*, 17 June 2019, https://www.npr.org/2019/06/17/727649223/patron-saints-of-nothing-is-a-book-for-the-hyphenated.

Robbins, Bruce. "Introduction Part I: Actually Existing Cosmopolitanism." Cheah and Robbins, pp. 1–19.

Said, Edward W. "Intellectual Exile: Expatriates and Marginals (1993)." *The Edward Said Reader*, edited by Moustafa Bayoumi and Andrew Rubin, Vintage Books, 2000, pp. 368–81.

Said, Edward W. *Orientalism*. Vintage Books, 1979.

Tadiar, Neferti X.M. *Things Fall Away: Philippine Historical Experience and the Makings of Globalization.* Kindle ed., Duke University Press, 2009.

Tolentino, Rolando B. "Macho Dancing, the Feminization of Labor, and Neoliberalism in the Philippines." *TDR (1988–)*, vol. 53, no. 2, 2009, pp. 77–89. *JSTOR*, http://www.jstor.org/stable/25599475.

Young, Robert J.C. *White Mythologies: Writing History and the West.* 2nd ed., Routledge, 2004.

III

CHILDHOOD, NATION, AND NARRATION

6

HISTORY AS MURMUR

Derek Walcott's *Another Life* as Postcolonial Bildungsroman

Andrew David King

The Question of Genre

How should a literary typologist approach a text like Derek Walcott's 1973 work *Another Life*? Should one simply accept D.J. McClatchy's description of the text, on the back cover of Edward Baugh and Colbert Nepaulsingh's critical edition, as a "long autobiographical" poem? "Long" may seem insufficiently descriptive (is *The Waste Land* long? *Beowulf*?), even as it offers firmer ground than the shifting sands of the "autobiographical," which Northrop Frye claims merges into the novel by series of imperceptible degrees (303–07). In a work whose narrator is so closely identified with its author that the narrator alternates between using characters' fictional names and the historical names of the people they represent, how are we to understand the line between fact and fabulation, let alone how generic expectations inflect, modulate, and construct the text? From one angle, this may seem neither an especially new nor pressing question, one that could be raised equally about much poetry of the last century. But there are two reasons, I will argue, why a concern with genre is particularly salient—and fruitful—with respect to *Another Life*. The first is that the text raises, by formal and thematic means, the question of its own

131

ontology, of which genre is one aspect; it recounts Walcott's upbringing and young adulthood in Castries, Saint Lucia (although I will speak not of Walcott but of "*Another Life*'s narrator" when discussing the voice in the text), not from a settled, external perspective, but from a shifting, internal one. The second is that, in pressuring generic expectations, *Another Life* formally illustrates and complicates some of Walcott's views about postcoloniality and postcolonial subjectivity.

The underlying proposal motivating and unifying these arguments is that *Another Life* suggests its own reading as a postcolonial Bildungsroman and can indeed be read as one. To read *Another Life* in this way is to make at least two leaps: one away from the European genealogy of the Bildungsroman genre, and another from the latter's traditional home in the domain of fiction. Such a reading holds out the prospect of an enriched understanding, and enlarged canon, of postcolonial Bildungsromane, a category given a synoptic overview by scholars like Ericka A. Hoagland, just as it offers a new test case for theories of genre, especially those implicitly or explicitly theorized by Caribbean writers. Frye, in his *Anatomy of Criticism*, hazards that the term "fiction" could be applied to any work of literature "in a radically continuous form"—which, he qualifies, "almost always means a work of art in prose" (303). It is works like *Another Life*, I hope to show, that necessitate and interrogate Frye's "almost"—and that prompt us to "recover a sense of the variety of literary forms" (Fowler v).

The Bildungsroman and Its Postcolonial Stakes

My suggestion is that reading *Another Life* as a Bildungsroman or, alternatively, as a Künstlerroman or Erziehungsroman—I understand the latter two as subtypes of the Bildungsroman—yields insights into Walcott's negotiations of personal and cultural history. More ambitiously, this reading suggests ways that signal works of postcolonial Caribbean Bildungsromane, like George Lamming's *In the Castle of My Skin* and novels by Roger Mais and V.S. Naipaul, may be refracted through the lenses of Walcott's formal and thematic concerns. *Another Life*'s debt to these European forms—both in a genre-specific sense and in the broader sense of what Wittgenstein called a Lebenswelt, or "lifeworld"—is considerable, and has gone largely without remark (11).

Another Life's interrogation of generic distinctions amounts to a means by which Walcott scrutinizes not only the nature of his childhood, adolescence, and young adulthood, but the inseparable, clashing arcs of Caribbean and European history, myth, and time. In reflecting on his own formation as a writer and artist—categories of creative professionalization that *Another Life* both runs together and teases apart, as it does genres—Walcott's formal and thematic appropriation of elements of the Bildungsroman and Künstlerroman becomes a statement about the conditions and limits of agency, with ramifications for Caribbean understandings of colonialism's pasts and postcolonialism's futures.

Kent Puckett describes the Bildungsroman as often being taken to have a dialectical plot, beginning with a protagonist in a "state of naive innocence" who undergoes "a middle education by error" before finally arriving at "some sadder and wiser state of final maturity" (72). Drawing on Franco Moretti's analysis of the genre as representing the achievement of a synthesis between the individual and society, Puckett writes that "the *Bildungsroman* presents this synthesis as a *narrative* of development: to grow up in the *Bildungsroman* is to learn really and truly to want what society wants, to find oneself and one's desires ultimately 'at home' in one's world" (72–73). According to another account of the Bildungsroman, it "follows the development of the hero or heroine from childhood or adolescence into adulthood, through a troubled quest for identity"; this account also suggests that the Künstlerroman is a subgenre of the Bildungsroman (Baldick 35). The theme of a "troubled" quest for identity, with its agonistic overtones, hints at displacement and escape, and perhaps ultimately a rehoming, recalling the narrator's numerous escapes with Gregorias—the name Walcott gives, in *Another Life*, to his friend Dunstan St. Omer—to the coast and forest to paint, or to Harry Simmons's studio to be mentored in the arts. Both moves, recurrent throughout the text and especially in Book II, can be understood as means by which the narrator attempts to stand outside of the social world into which he has been thrown by accident of birth—the zeitgeist or *episteme*, in Foucault's terms in *The Order of Things*, that "defines the conditions of possibility of all knowledge, whether expressed in a theory or silently invested in a practice" (183). The narrator's never-entirely-successful attempts at escape—and the additional externalization that happens when these attempts are viewed omnisciently—reveal the inseparability of his subjectivity's emergence from the emergence of history, a dovetailing Bakhtin held to be key to understanding the Bildungsroman as a "novel of emergence" (23). Hoagland, following Jed Etsy, reads the phenomenon of the postcolonial Bildungsroman as demarcating a third phase of the Bildungsroman after its pre-colonial and colonial phases; in the colonial phase, the genre's relationship with the standard trajectories available to protagonists of Bildungsromane grows uneasy, an uneasiness intensified in the postcolonial Bildungsroman by the traumatic legacy of colonial disenfranchisement (217–38).

Puckett describes the modern novel, of which the Bildungsroman is one permutation, as drawing "dialectically on all the narrative forms that came before" (71). The epistemic situation of *Another Life*'s narrator is likewise generated by an implicit conviction that a modern work of literature, if not a novel, should draw copiously on the array of generic resources that preceded it. The text draws on the resources of theatre and tragedy—as with the memorable procession of the *dramatis personae* of Castries in Book I—as well as those of geography, art and military history, botany, and theology. In this sense, too, *Another Life*, seen through the lens of the Bildungsroman, is distinctively modern. Like Hegel, who was unimpressed with Goethe's 1795 foundational Bildungsroman *Wilhelm Meister's Apprenticeship* for the reason that it provided bourgeois readers a dull mirror with which to view themselves, *Another Life* seeks not merely to reproduce the narrator's environment but to gain knowledge by transcending it, even if doing so completely remains impossible (72). One can hear, in Georg Lukács's description of *Wilhelm Meister's Apprenticeship*, something that the narrator of *Another Life*, whose intellectual development is unintelligible apart from his social, material, and environmental conditions, hopes to achieve: "the education of man for a practical understanding of reality" (59).

A quasi-mythological reconstruction of Walcott's life through middle age, *Another Life* tells of its narrator's upbringing, friendships, tutelage, first love (with Andreuille Alcée, the poem's Anna), later marriage, and departures from, and returns to, Saint Lucia. Book I sketches Castries and the narrator's childhood before the turn, in Book II, to his apprenticeship to painter and humanist Harry Simmons alongside his friend Dunstan St. Omer—to whom he gives the racially "explosive" name Gregorias, "a black Greek's!" (line 3619). Book III focuses on the narrator's relationship with Anna, which is crushed by the juggernaut of the narrator's task of self-definition: the relationship and his love, as well as Anna herself, are transformed into texts, and art sunders love. Like the preceding books, Book IV collects a multitude of distinct times, jumping between them. Its centrepieces are Simmons's suicide and Gregorias's suicide attempt, recollected when the narrator visits the island in middle age. The third agent in a trinity that includes life and death, the narrator concludes the arc of self-development with a celebration of Gregorias—also now aged—as emblematic of the sun-like force of willpower and art, in line with Bakhtin's conception of the Bildungsroman as dealing, at its core, with problems of creative power (24). Hyperconscious of both the necessity and fallibility of memory, the poem is fundamentally concerned with time—and with time's by turns virtuous and vicious relations to narrative, history, myth, and conceptions of the self. Although governed by a narrative logic, the poem thwarts that logic throughout, staging disruptions to linear time that complicate any simplistic reading of the poem's account of its narrator's move from childhood to adulthood. Frye proposed that a key subgenre within autobiography consisted of what he called "the confession form," wherein, from Augustine onward, a narrator constructs a cohesive pattern from dispersed elements (307). The narrator of *Another Life* stands on the cusp of this distinction, dispersing with one hand the sand that the other had gathered.

Along the poem's halting, fractured temporal trajectory, the traditional Bildungsroman and Künstlerroman themes of artistic apprenticeship, friendship, and the cultivation of self-knowledge blend with a number of philosophical concerns. The result is a meditation on the concept of development that both recounts the "plot" of a life—fictional or historical, or fictional *and* historical—and relates that plot to other issues both contained in time (insofar as they appear in the life in question) and outside of time (insofar as they refer to perennial questions, or questions that, at the requisite level of generality, can appear across many lives, or manifest only abstractly). Genre, too, surfaces as a named variable in this meditation, as when the narrator discloses, at the beginning of chapter seven, that provincialism "loves the pseudo-epic" (line 952). The patterning of *Another Life* raises the question of what counts as continuity and what as break—a question made significant in part by the poem's investment in the space of the postcolonial Caribbean as one that must necessarily move into the future. Furthermore, it raises the question of the significance of painting and poetry for humankind in general, as a species of representing and representation-using creatures; of what a given individual's debt to history, or histories, is, and how history and myth (two categories not to be confused in Walcott's cosmology) are to be differentiated; of the relationship between documentations of fact and the inventions of the imagination; and of how to create—in particular, how to write—something with stable meaning within a natural world that relentlessly, and yet inscrutably and chaotically, means and means anew (Walcott, "The Muse of History" 37). *Another Life*'s adoption and interrogation of the Bildungsroman genre amounts to another instance of what Jahan Ramazani describes as Walcott's tireless confounding of "limits set by colonizer and critic" (414).

But the most significant way in which *Another Life* contributes to the conceptual history of the postcolonial Bildungsroman, if we choose to so read it, has to do with its conceptions of history, trauma, and recovery. Walcott's essay "The Muse of History" begins with James Joyce's pronouncement in *Ulysses* that "history is the nightmare from which I am trying to awake," and, as Baugh and Nepaulsingh have meticulously documented, Joycean influence—especially of that foundational Künstlerroman in English, his *A Portrait of the Artist as a Young Man*—suffuses *Another Life*. (The word "ulyseed" even appears as a verb [line 734].) The Joycean epigraph to "The Muse of History" suggests, perhaps, the obvious way out of any nightmare: waking up. But this is not Walcott's strategy, nor is it a strategy available to his narrator. Excoriating the hypothetical poet who conflates history and language and thus "limits his memory to the suffering of the victim," he instead claims that "maturity is the assimilation of the features of every ancestor" ("The Muse of History" 36–38). Consistent with this understanding of West Indian history and literature, *Another Life* attends to the violent aftermath of colonialism without constructing it as the sole force against which the narrator defines himself and his development. To the contrary, in *Another Life*, history is not conceptualized as a unity to be opposed, just as there is no clear division between present and past. In Book II, "Homage to Gregorias," Walcott describes seeing history "through the sea-washed eyes / of our choleric, ginger-haired headmaster" and experiencing nostalgia for "[h]ymns of battles not our own" (lines 1643–44, 1650). Questions of ownership and obligation with respect to history remain unsettled; at times, the narrator of *Another Life* feels he possesses sufficient agency to revert history by means of a kind of anachronistic and atheistic anti-natalism. "I am pounding the faces of gods back into the red clay," he says, not long after recollecting the nostalgic history lessons to which he was subjected as a young student—pounding them "back into what they should never have sprung from," namely the "god-breeding, god-devouring earth!" (lines 1685–87). This sense of history as malleable contrasts with narratives of colonial trauma that see the violence of history as determined and determining, the grounds for an oppositional identity, or both.[1] At this moment in *Another Life*, the narrator flirts with the rejection of Walcott's principle of personal and aesthetic maturity, a pluralism that assimilates the features of every ancestor—though, as I will explore, he will ultimately affirm it both formally and thematically, fashioning *Another Life* into not only the narrative of its protagonist's development but an allegory of the self-actualization of the postcolonial Caribbean as such.

Division, Repetition, and Progress in *Another Life*
The narrator's numerous intellectual and emotional engagements with these questions is structured, I argue, by two logics: the binary logic of division (and its frequent partner, opposition) and the cyclical logic of repetition, each of which complicates and enriches the text's relation to the Bildungsroman genre. The "Divided Child" of Book I's title becomes a divided adult by the end of Book IV, but the persistence

of division does not imply the absence of development; the narrator's achievement is, in part, a new relationship to division. Nor by "division" do I simply mean the logic by which a protagonist, faced with an obstacle, overcomes it: there is no synthesis, in the sense of total resolution, in *Another Life*, and Walcott elsewhere makes clear his negative assessment of what he perceives as an agonism in postcolonial literature that constructs itself solely as a mode of opposition to the bitter enemy of its colonial past ("The Muse of History" 38–39). The divisions in question exist within the narrator as well as without. The loosely autobiographical project of *Another Life* extends rhizomatically into what James Olney calls autophylography, the recounting of a people, before condensing again into singularity, as vines do to form a trunk (Olney; Alabi 3–6). The divisions are also metaphysical: the other life of the title surfaces repeatedly in the text as a motif that invokes both the general possibility that things might be otherwise and the specific history of Christianity—and its moralized afterlife—in Saint Lucia. M. Travis Lane enumerates some of the text's many oppositions, which "all tend to emphasize a harmony based on duality" rather than unity: "the sun and the moon, the earth and the sea, the West Indian reality and the European myth of the tropics, the local and the heroic, the past and the present" (76).

For much of *Another Life*, the effects of these divisions are destructive. Early in Book I, as part of an elaborate description of the environment and history of Castries, the narrator mentions a retired Captain X, "who kept an open grave behind his house, / would shoot on sight. Shot himself, sah!" (lines 907–08). Three divisions are demarcated here: between colonizer and colonized, policed by violence; another internal to individual selves, which here culminates in suicide (and foreshadows the suicide of Harry Simmons and Gregorias's suicide attempt); and a third, internal to the text, marked by the irruption of a voice that is neither the narrator's nor any particular other's ("Shot himself, sah!"). As the narrator moves into middle age, a twofold division marks his understanding of, and relationship with, his Caribbean community. He feels set apart from them—"a people with no moral centre"—both incidentally and by an ethical choice (line 2833). He accuses some among them of pernicious self-undermining, those "who peel, from their own leprous flesh, their names," "whose god is history. *Pax*," he notes with bitter sarcasm (lines 2953, 2965). These are those who, in the narrator's view, fail at the Adamic task the poet is called to take up. With the technobureaucrat's calipers and measurements, these "dividers" take "their measure / of toms, of traitors, of traditional and Afrosaxons" (lines 2970, 2975–76). This eugenic manner of taking stock of the race amounts to a division in itself, a cleaving apart of what should be whole; and while this seems intrinsically objectionable to the narrator, he reserves his fiercest ire for its effects on Gregorias. A prophet unrecognized in his hometown, Gregorias stands as a model of the alienation from "home" as both geographical place and concept that runs through Walcott's corpus:

> but out of its mist, one man,
> whom they will not recognize, emerges
> and staggers towards his lineaments. (lines 2990–92)

Such a social split can be liberatory, as when—in a passage discussed below—it seems a precondition for the narrator's falling in love with art: his "having no care / for truth" is what permits the emergence of the aesthetic commitment that marks the beginning of his life as an artist (lines 1048–49). But the porousness of the boundary between the past and the future that follows truth's demotion also exhausts the narrator, leaving him "[t]ranced" in history lessons, "groggy with dates," with the "fiction / of rusted soldiers fallen on a schoolboy's page"—an image that, like so many others in *Another Life*, analogizes and fuses the textual to the real (lines 1626–27, 1641–42). This exhaustion can lead to a craving for nihilism: "I cursed what the elm remembers," the narrator writes, hoping that the sea will erase the Lockean names written by a "thin, / tortured child"—perhaps himself in an earlier life—"on his slate of wet sand" (lines 1579, 1583–85). Frustration with the palimpsestic text of history, which in *Another Life* absorbs and textualizes natural and social worlds, culminates in a desire for an unobtainable *tabula rasa*. The narrator cannot escape his Adamic task, nor the fact that he cannot, unlike Adam, begin at the beginning. Bernard Stiegler, reading a scene from Rousseau's *Discourse on the Origin of Inequality* in which Rousseau imagines the stable life of the "man of nature," notes there is neither education nor need of it: "everything repeats itself identically" (115). The narrator thus poses a distinctively postcolonial problem for the protagonists of postcolonial Bildungsromane: how to construct the self against the backdrop of an antagonistic or indifferent history that nonetheless fails to provide a stable "before," and how to do so while one's social milieu remains in the throes of oppositional senses of history and utopian visions of returns to nature that mask moral and intellectual paralysis.

Division in *Another Life* destroys and negates but also leads to regeneration, both directly and indirectly; the narrator's productive confrontations with it mark his negotiations with Caribbean discourse as "inextricably tied to a form of creative schizophrenia" (Dash xxvi). At first, division rives the narrator's quest to become an artist, his passion split between writing and painting. "Where did I fail?" he asks in Book II, noting he had the requisite discipline for visual art practice (line 1344). The failure is diagnosed as a consequence of the young artist's ambition; he sought "in every surface...the paradoxical flash of an instant" that captured, crystal-like, the ambiguities of possible meanings, and hoped that "both disciplines"—writing and art—"might / by painful accretion cohere / and finally ignite" (lines 1348–49, 1352–54). Here the narrator draws on the celestial, heliocentric metaphors of sunlight, flame, and illumination with which *Another Life* will climax, modelling what has been described as the "accretion and recovery" of Caribbean creolization (Meehan and Miller 364). He eventually admits he "lived in a different gift, / its element metaphor," but finds in this realization a means to comprehend the divergences between him and Gregorias, who he admires intensely (lines 1355–56). While painting with Gregorias one day, the narrator notices the asylum across the harbour, which leads him to remark that while Gregorias "had his madness, / mine was our history" (lines 1548–49).

Seen against the messiness of that history, Gregorias's private madness seems what Dickinson called divinest sense, such as when he matter-of-factly declares he does not care whether he is understood, and that he loves life while the thanatotic narrator loves death (line 1509). The linkage between Gregorias's "madness" and divinity returns elsewhere: "Yes, God and me, we understand each other," he says (lines 1517–19). But the narrator's sense of distinctness from Gregorias shades into an appreciation of their commonalities as *Another Life* progresses. Both are frustrated artists; neither can deny the facts of history, even as the narrator envies Gregorias's freedom from it, earned by a mixture of gumption and foolhardiness. Their friendship is both a figure for the question of how the postcolonial artist can be reconciled to their society and a means by which the narrator advances his development. In a passage that foreshadows the sun as symbol of astonishment and accomplishment with which *Another Life* ends, the narrator tells of how

> The sun came through our skins,
> and we beheld, at last,
> the exact, sudden definition
> of our shadow. (lines 1790–93)

Separate skins, but a shared shadow: Gregorias and the narrator partake of what Hannah Arendt called "the political kind of insight *par excellence*," in which friendship reveals "how and in what specific articulateness the common world appears to the other, who as a person is forever unequal or different" (83–84). After the death of Gregorias's First World War-veteran father in Book II, their fatherlessness, as well as their artistry and drunkenness, unites them in such a common world (line 1150). In its concern with relationality—the narrator's dyadic relationship with Gregorias, and the pair's triadic relationship with Simmons—*Another Life*, as Maria Cristina Fumagalli has noted, is less like Wordsworth's *The Prelude*, a text with which it is often compared, and more like Dante's *Vita Nuova*. The Greek myths, too, function as obvious points of comparison, with Anna playing Eurydice to the narrator's Orpheus; she appears in the doorway of the abandoned boathouse in the book's first chapter before the narrator climbs the hill to Simmons's studio, set up in an old morgue, to wrestle with his choice between the verbal and visual arts. At the poem's close, division and wholeness, the poles of relationality, are reconciled within the narrator's world view (lines 24–79). Though "I saw with twin heads, / and everything I say is contradicted," the narrator becomes "fluent as water," quoting a translated line from an autobiographical poem by Villon: "'I have swallowed all my hates'" (lines 3278–79, 3280, 3306).

Another Life's concern with cyclicality supplements its obsession with division and opposition, providing, along with its narrative backbone, the bridge across some of division's chasms. This momentum is acquired at a cost, as cyclicality threatens to undermine the notion of development central to the Bildungsroman. Ruminating on his relationship with Anna, the focus of Book III, the narrator recalls a walk they took by the lagoon one afternoon, self-consciously assessing its transience from the perspective of the present: "Where they now stood, others before had stood, / the same lens held them, the repeated wood" (lines 2196–97). Nature's indifference to human approval manifests in "the mangroves plunged to the wrist, repeating / the mangroves plunging to the wrist" (lines 3238–39). Cyclicality corrodes into stasis and sameness, but nonetheless resists the linear development on which the protagonist of the Bildungsroman depends. When the narrator, in Book IV, returns to Saint Lucia, he is hardly shocked to find "the groyned mangroves meeting / the groyned mangroves repeating / their unbroken water-line," telling visually how the island "had not moved from anchor" (lines 3543–47). This sense of repetition as sameness recalls the narrator's earlier years with Gregorias, where days were "welded by the sun's torch into days," or "woven into days" (lines 1166, 1171). But this repetition, which here works against development, also becomes its condition at the poem's close, where the seeming endlessness of time and history reinforce the narrator's celebratory, speechless astonishment at the power of art, his chosen vocation.

It is useful to get a sense of the poem's ending—to which I'll return—in order to appreciate the ways in which its beginning, in cyclical fashion, contains its seeds. Book I offers a catalogue not just of Castries and its coastal surroundings but of its inhabitants, flora and fauna, and the residents and material contents of Walcott's childhood home. While not static, the world possesses an opacity and fixity in the eyes of the young narrator, who perceives in the family home the accretion of lives and epochs incapable of comprehension by his epistemic and aesthetic faculties. Startlingly, these sedimentary deposits return the narrator's gaze: "in turn," he says, "these objects assess us" (line 300). Somehow both autonomous and a projection of human desire, the childhood home becomes an organism ("Skin wrinkles like paint, / the forearm of a balustrade freckles"), one frustrated by the repetition of time ("the flowers keep falling, / and the flowers keep opening, / the allamandas' fallen bugles, but nobody charges") (lines 309–10, 306–08). The second chapter of the first book ends with the narrator accepting the apparent unchangeability of this environment, one in which each object "screams again / to be put down / in its ring of dust," a material universe in which the place of his mother—the addressee—is likewise fixed (lines 329–31):

> I can no more move you from your true alignment,
> mother, than we can move objects in paintings.
>
> Your house sang softly of balance,
> of the rightness of placed things. (lines 333–36)

The human purposiveness praised here contrasts with the apparent—although, as I will argue later on, not actual—stochasticity of the nonhuman universe in *Another Life*. The admiration accorded to Walcott's mother suggests a continuity between her domestic mastery and the mastery of the artist, whose objects, once painted, are immovable, determined by an Adamic creativity. As the narrator notes, the balance at work in the house is a softer one than that perceived after Simmons's suicide—but it is balance nonetheless, and so stands linked thematically to the cosmic balancing of death and life, suffering and *eros*, at the conclusion of *Another Life*. This linkage weds mastery via human purposiveness, whether domestic or artistic, to the mastery exhibited by the flux of forces that govern the universe; the straining, earned mastery of the artist is mimetic of the effortless mastery of nature. In both cases, the perception of this balance produces a generative astonishment—even as, in case of the balance perceived in Book I, it is revealed without much dramatic flourish, the product of a largely plotless, ekphrastic rendering of the scene of childhood.

If the objects of the narrator's childhood home constellate part of the material galaxy against which he constructs his sense of self, then the nested social worlds of Castries, Saint Lucia, and the Caribbean, as well as the natural world, form its remainder. These latter worlds pose an additional challenge of legibility: their significations are much more fluid and transient than the familiar backdrop of childhood, more resistant to memory's lens. *Another Life* is abundant with textual and literary metaphors—metaphors of books, of writing, of languages and sign systems—for natural processes; like the narrator, Saint Lucia itself is in the process of being written, in the double sense of being constituted as well as documented. In the very first lines of Book I, the sea's waves are described as "pages" of "a book left open by an absent master / in the middle of another life," evoking the *in medias res* with which Dante's *Inferno* begins—a text in the background of Book III's elaboration of the narrator's love for Anna—but following it with an invocation of cyclicality:

> I begin here again,
> begin until this ocean's
> a shut book, and, like a bulb
> the white moon's filaments wane. (lines 4–7)

This *in medias res* is any arbitrary point on a circle, a beginning that is always a beginning-again. And each beginning-again is the work of memory, a revision that involves retrieving the past by the aid both of nature and human striving—conflated here in the "filaments" of the moon, part of another repertoire of metaphor in the text whose vehicles consist of technologies of illumination and visual reproduction, including film and printmaking.

The tension between the future and the past in the narrator's youthful aspirations, as well as in the fact that Book I frames *Another Life* as the rekindling of a previously unsuccessful act of recollection, is echoed by several further divisions: between city and country,

Catholicism and animism, and heaven and hell. The "tubers" of an ancient faith exert their hold on the town's "rooted" middle class, "beginning where Africa began: in the body's memory" (lines 558–60). Here memory, in the form of the recollection of colonial displacement, acts as both constituting and dissolving force, blurring the distinction between the natural and the human. The narrator himself is split between thinking that hell is colonial poverty—"two hundred shacks on wooden stilts"—and rejecting the Church "for some ancestral, tribal country," whose "clear tongue over the clean stones" he can hear (lines 873, 985–86). Against this multitude of divisions, Book I concludes with an account of the narrator's awakening to his vocation as an artist, a realization prompted by an experience of ecstatic astonishment. Fourteen years old, having "lost my self [sic] somewhere above a valley," the narrator recounts "dissol[ving] into a trance," being "seized by a pity more profound / than my young body could bear" (lines 996, 1002–04):

> I wept for nothing and for everything,
> I wept for the earth of the hill under my knees,
> for the grass, the pebbles, for the cooking smoke
> above the labourers' houses like a cry,
> for unheard avalanches of white cloud (lines 1010–14)

Even in this moment of transcendent unity, during which the dramatic spur of *Another Life's* Künstlerroman arc emerges, the narrator's identification is dual, oscillating between "nothing" and "everything." This duality seems to underwrite, rather than obscure, an incipient class consciousness, one that finds an objective correlative in the "unheard avalanches" of the clouds. This ecstatic sympathy is followed by the question of whether "blare noon" or twilight is the "true light"—a question, put in terms of the text's recurrent metaphors of illumination, of the world's trustworthiness, but also of the narrator's capacity for self-knowledge, of his power to discern the true from the false (lines 1023–24). Animated by this skeptical question, the narrator declares he "fell in love with art, / and life began," amid Book I's scattered references to Samuel Palmer, Claude, Turner, and Fra Angelico (lines

1055–56, 1025, 1041, 1042, 1062). The narrator's revelation, about a third of the way through the work, amounts to the first moment of what might be called specifically *narrative* drama in the text's account of the narrator's life—which, by his own account, begins with this moment. Despite being the first such moment, it occasions the self-actualization that marks the culmination, rather than the beginning, of a traditional Bildungsroman. *Another Life* thus complicates the received Bildungsroman structure from the outset, placing the achievement of the narrator's identity before his development.

Gregorias, imperfect twin to *Another Life*'s narrator, serves as the main engine of the narrator's development after the latter's quasi-mystical inauguration into life as an artist. The two set themselves lofty artistic goals, swearing "that we would never leave the island / until we had put down, in paint, in words," every "self-pitying inlet / muttering in brackish dialect" (lines 1185–90). Against a history "thickening with amnesia," in an archipelago "like a broken root," the narrator and Gregorias take up their artistic labour, catalyzed by their understanding that "no one had yet written of this landscape / that it was possible" (lines 1223, 1239, 1215–16). Both young men find a mentor in Harry Simmons, but Gregorias becomes the narrator's most immediate and forceful model of mastery; every landscape they encounter appears "already signed with [Gregorias's] name" (line 1384). Although the narrator is mesmerized by Gregorias's powers, the incessant deployment of textual metaphors in *Another Life* implies the power of the narrator's own capabilities—suggesting that writing is "the site of history's enactment" and that history itself consists of the ongoing labour of writing (Scott 793). The idea of the landscape and culture as possessing as-yet-decoded dialects propels Gregorias and the narrator; the speaker simultaneously crafts and discovers the model of the Gregorias who will return, Christ-like, at *Another Life*'s close as the archetype of unruled and unruly—that is, truly free—aesthetic energy.

One, though not the only, challenge to the narrator's artistic development under the tutelage of Simmons and Gregorias arises from the effects of that tutelage on the narrator's romantic life. The same aesthetic capabilities that the narrator yearns to glean from Gregorias destroy his relationship with Anna, who he had fallen in love with as a teenager. Anna, analogized to Dante's Beatrice, was the centre of "the disc of the world," the hub around which spokes and cycles circled (lines 2031, 2941). The narrator, wondering whether "a pen's eye could catch that virginal litheness," grows so distracted by this question that he loses sight of the real Anna: "The hand she held already had betrayed / them by its longing for describing her" (lines 2216–17). Sensing this, Anna, dissatisfied with the island and the relationship, is first transformed in the narrator's imagination into a heron, and then made to speak. "I became a metaphor," he imagines her saying, "but believe me I was unsubtle as salt" (lines 2362–63). As their relationship grows more troubled, the narrator perceives things becoming nonidentical with themselves—a shift away from the sense, in Book I, that things were in their right places. Seen at the beginning of *Another Life* in the door of the boathouse from Harry Simmons's studio, where she was also an artistic subject for the narrator, then learning to paint, the narrator sees her again "rise / from the bright boathouse door," unable to cease objectifying and aestheticizing her (lines 1077–78). Worse, she becomes "all Annas, enduring all good-byes": an empty, repeated signifier from which the real, beloved Anna vanishes (line 2259). The narrator finds himself adrift in dissociated sense impressions, the detritus of history: "A gleam. Her burning grip. The brass shell-cases…forty-one years after the Great War" (lines 2373–75). As love swells with death, the narrator's powers of metaphor wither, and he imagines Gregorias, Anna, and Harry dissolving in his imagination, only to be named—this time with their names as Walcott knew them—afterwards:

> three loves, art, love and death,
> fade from a mirror clouding with this breath,
> not one is real, they cannot live or die,
> they all exist, they never have existed:
>
> Harry, Dunstan, Andreuille. (lines 2720–24)

Concerned with how the artist and writer may perform the Adamic task of "giving things their names" against a backdrop of the duelling forces of existent history and myth, the poem here performs part of that task, even if it swoons in the delirium of imagining that what it names never existed (line 3627). In citing these figures' historical names, the text raises again the question of the distinction between the fictional and the historical. In this, and in its collision of love and death, *Another Life* is at once utopian and anti-utopian: utopian in its refusal to abandon the Adamic task entirely, but anti-utopian in its rejection of European notions of personal and historical progress, and in its nuancing of the renewal with which it concludes with acknowledgments of violence, poverty, suffering, and death. Haunted by the Nietzschean notion of eternal recurrence, a model of history as endless repetition, *Another Life*'s narrator is led by this lateral progression to the doctrine of *amor fati*, the love of fate (*Ecce Homo* 258; *The Gay Science* 157, 194). In Book IV, "The Estranging Sea," after the devastating suicide of Harry Simmons and his learning of Gregorias's suicide attempt, the narrator finds in the brutal flux of nature something that amounts to judiciousness, if not justice:

> Yet, when I continue to see
> the young deaths of others,
> ....
> there is something which balances,
> I see him [Simmons] bent under the weight of the morning,
> against its shafts,
> devout, angelical,
> the easel rifling his shoulder,
> the master of Gregorias and myself,
> I see him standing over the bleached roofs
> of the salt-streaked villages,
> each steeple pricked
> by its own wooden star. (lines 3242–59)

Where a semicolon or period might have appeared, Walcott places a comma. The self-consciously tentative "there is something which balances" leads directly into what might have been a new sentence: the vision of Simmons, who appears as the genius and soul of Castries. Memory's repetition, its invocation of Simmons, folds the timeline on which Simmons has died back onto itself, relying on circularity to turn him into a god. But if he is a god, he is a local one, presiding over a divided realm, as *Another Life*'s narrator inhabits a world constitutively sequestered into segments: "each steeple pricked / by its own wooden star." The potent pairing of a self-isolating individuality with repetition resurfaces across Walcott's corpus. In a late work, *The Prodigal*, Walcott imagines the sublime terror of the annihilating white of the Alps repeating infinitely, a dissolving, fractal pattern intrinsic to nature's metaphysics: "How many more / peaks…Infinite and repetitive as the ridges / patterned like okapi or jaguar" (10). Simmons is not the centre that would otherwise hold together all the world's mere anarchy, but his existence is still one clear counterpoint to the deaths of the young—presumably including Walcott's own father, who died in his early thirties—that mark the world as cruel and unjust.

Anti-Narrative, Anti-Bildungsroman

Rather than descend into quietism, what the narrator achieves at the end of *Another Life* is the enactment of Walcott's declaration in *White Egrets* that "[t]he perpetual ideal is astonishment"—no easy or sanguine state, but one that shares semantic, and sonic, affinity with anguish (8). Neither glee nor horror, the astonishment that marks the culmination of the narrator's development constitutes an erotic response to a perception of the world as sublime—one all the more potentially optimistic for being articulated against a scarred, death-ridden backdrop. A narrative of development riven twofold, by division and by repetition, *Another Life* stands as a kind of anti-Bildungsroman, in the sense that it borrows from the genre's fundamental tropes, structures, and assumptions while creatively defacing them.

If the traditional Bildungsroman culminates in "individual achievement and social integration," *Another Life* calls into question what these criteria mean (Abel et al. 5). But this is not solely because its narrator is "a prodigy of the wrong age and colour," destined for exclusion from the European canon he frequently draws from, although that is no doubt part of the story (line 22). The terminus of the narrator's development—in terms of criteria derived from the European Bildungsroman—is indeterminate and bittersweet, less an arrival at a fixed point than the adoption of a fluctuating perspective on the past. An episode in Book II reveals this, amid the narrator's exuberant account of his *de jure* apprenticeship to Harry Simmons and *de facto* apprenticeship to Gregorias. The narrator asks (note the use of the present-tense "know" to describe the past), "how we could know then, / damned poet and damned painter," that they would resemble the "fisherman and joiner," the other downtrodden inhabitants of Castries, all those whose "fiction of their own lives claimed each one" (lines 1868–72, 919)? The narrator's sense in Book IV—after Harry's suicide, Gregorias's ostracization and suicide attempt, and his own middle-age discontent—that life has not gone as well as he had hoped it would is buttressed by the enthusiasm of astonishment, even as the work of making art and facing history has grown no easier: "with the fierce rush of a furnace door / suddenly opened, history was here" (lines 1899–1900). If the Adamic task that constitutes the true calling of the artist must constantly be redone—the speaker having already done it with an Eve-like Anna in Book III, when "everything stood still for us to name"—this repetition, the narrator decides, can be a source of momentum rather than, or in addition to, despair (line 2061). If the twentieth century, as C.L.R. James argues, cast subjects into a constantly expanding web of relations, the narrator draws power from these ties even while suffering at their behest (247). Having moved from the age of eighteen to forty-one over the course of *Another Life*, the narrator links the figure of Gregorias to the sun, and the power of both to his own powers of repetition in the face of repeating time, the frenzy of history:

> So, I shall repeat myself,
> prayer, same prayer, towards fire, same fire,
> as the sun repeats itself and the thundering waters
>
> for what else is there
> but books, books and the sea,
> verandahs and the pages of the sea (lines 3494–98)

Earlier the sun "explodes into irises," and the narrator rises, Whitmanian, "singing with sunstroke!" (line 1319) The sun serves as model for both Gregorias and the narrator, who, once lit, burn together as the single "light of the world" (line 1867). Gregorias himself, in the final lines of *Another Life*, becomes the narrator's model, with the narrator remaining an apprentice to Gregorias and to his memory. Playing Adam, in the poem's last line the narrator jubilantly dubs Gregorias "Apilo!"—mirroring, in a final gesture by which the apprentice of the Bildungsroman becomes the master, the latter's powers of invention, and rejecting the notion that the inhabitants of the postcolonial world should remain spectators of modernity rather than its creators (line 3637; Chatterjee 5).

I have been suggesting that the animating strands of *Another Life* are both narrative and, in a sense, what might be termed anti-narrative, even as these narrative-corroding elements (division understood as fracture or frustration, cyclicality, and repetition) that frustrate the stable progression so typical of Bildungsromane are put, ultimately, to narrative purposes. "Where else to row, but backward?" the narrator asks (line 1778). Understood as a Bildungsroman, the poem moves by several means: by structural divisions and the attempts to overcome them, by cyclicality and recurrence, and by a stumbling forward despite these. To paraphrase Spivak, one must think ideology before one can think history; *Another Life* stages the nonlinearity of the passage from the former to the latter (54). Its splintered energy still permits the narrator to arrive at some degree of self-understanding and accomplishment—as, at the end of a traditional Bildungsroman, one would expect. But if the traditional Bildungsroman comprises the arc-like history of a fictional life, the crossing of a definite threshold, the postcolonial Bildungsroman must be something else. And this "something else" that it must be is what *Another Life* illuminates, a passing beyond the petty disputes that Rhonda Cobham-Sander argues characterize the Caribbean experience from Walcott's perspective and into the realization that all the perceived betrayals of his fellow Caribbean artists were, in fact, "quarrels with the self," "neither knowing which is liana or trunk, which is the parasite, which is the host" (169). This sense of ontological disorientation may be a pervasive feature of the postcolonial Caribbean experience as represented in the region's poetry and theory. According to Sylvia Wynter, one of Édouard Glissant's most revealing distinctions separates the Antillean and "New World black" experience of colonization from that of the Indochinese or Africans (643). For the latter, "the end of the colonial experience was the *end of an interruption*," but the former experienced it as a cutting loose into history, an uprooting (Wynter 643). In *Another Life*, too, there is no Archimedean point from which the narrator can leverage himself into the future; the haziness of the line between future and past, history and myth, agency and its illusion, precludes that possibility. It is a line that, like a line of verse written in sand, must be rewritten constantly against unpredictable tides—written, erased, written again.

One formal consequence of this uprooting, I want to suggest, is precisely the possibility of the generic cross-pollination that spurs *Another Life*'s engagement with the genre of the Bildungsroman. Ato Quayson, in *Tragedy and Postcolonial Literature*, argues that the commensurability of two objects of literary analysis is not always antecedent to their comparison; the fact of the comparison itself may inaugurate novel kinds of commensurability (303–04). While Quayson's remark pertains to the methodological debates in literary analysis, it seems to me helpful in understanding how the flux of form, genre, and tradition both operates in Walcott's text and is understood by its narrator to operate. Walcott's speaker seems to tacitly believe that colonialism's sundering of boundaries levels hierarchies while nonetheless seeking to establish an overarching one, so that the previously incommensurable becomes, in the chaos of the colonial project, commensurable. In *Another Life*, Walcott's narrator practises his own form of chaotic reconstitution—of self, people, and world. Greek antiquity and European Renaissance cultures are brought in, as in much other work by Walcott, with little preamble, justification, or apology; the speaker's encounters with these traditions is treated as self-explanatory in the context of European hegemony. This elision at first might appear to be the result of an assumption of continuity between the cultures of colonizer and colonized, but it can also be understood as the aesthetic expression of a claim: that the heritage of

Europe and Asia Minor are as much the narrator's materials to use as he sees fit, as are the baubles of his mother's sitting room and the public lives of his neighbours in Castries. The search for a "painful accretion" of artistic modes—painting, poetry—elsewhere in the text finds a structural analogue in the narrator's negotiations of theme and genre (line 1353).

In illustrating the tensions between the determinative vectors of history and the constrained agency of the individual, *Another Life* explores how the apparent fixity of nature and natural laws—the domain of the purposive, but nonhuman and nonhistorical, world—that help to generate these anxieties about agency may paradoxically hold out a solution for Walcott's narrator. That solution, a kind of mimetic activity, is foreshadowed by Hegel, a figure often associated with the theorization of the Bildungsroman in Europe, in a revealing footnote to his preface to the *Philosophy of Right* (Pfau). There, Hegel explains that the difference between laws of nature and the "laws of right" is that the latter, unlike the former, are human inventions (13). The constructed character of the laws of right introduces the possibility that the categories of what exists and what ought to be might diverge. Not only is such a conflict, Hegel insists, "found only in the sphere [*Boden*] of the spirit," but what he terms the "arbitrariness of life"—and perhaps also its mutability, which holds out the possibility that agents may act to change their lives and history—inclines us to turn to nature and take it as our model (13). In the title essay of his collection *What the Twilight Says*, Walcott, writing three years before the 1973 publication of *Another Life*, notes that the "resignation to fate" impelled by being born in "a colonial backwater" led him to think that "the only credible life was nature" (13). Hans-Georg Gadamer similarly asserts that, like nature, "*Bildung*"—a term that, in his usage, crucially contains the term for "image" or "form," *Bild*, and thus foregrounds the relation of art to self-fashioning—has "no goals outside itself" (Gadamer 10–11; Weinsheimer and Marshall xi). In the penultimate chapter of "The Estranging Sea," not far from the narrator's ecstatic renaming of Gregorias, the narrator's aspirations surrender to the *logos* of the natural world. Tree leaves replace the pages of epics and mathematical treatises, the achievements of humanism and science; the speaker, observing his son, sees "a child without history," whose only knowledge is "the knowledge of water runnelling rocks," who "hears nothing, hears everything"—a rhetorical callback to the fourteen-year-old narrator's first aesthetic revelation, which likewise invoked both void and totality—"that the historian cannot hear, the howls / of all the races that crossed the water" in migration or conquest (lines 3382–83, 3387–89).

If the British colonial history to which the narrator was subjected in school was a history "of ennui, defence, disease"—a record of empire as self-infecting pathology—here disability, if not illness, provides the metaphor by which the speaker makes sense of his son's epistemic status outside of history, and the abilities that status affords him (line 1662). The other element of the image comprises the coastal, riparian, and littoral: water meeting rock. Foucault, in the final paragraph of *The Order of Things*, considers the collapse of the *episteme* that authorized the "invention" of humanity; this leads him to envision the human as a figure drawn in sand—precarious, transient, prone to disappearance (422). Following the dissolution of the concept of the "author," he says elsewhere, history "would then develop in the anonymity of a murmur. *We would no longer hear* the questions that have been rehashed for so long" about who speaks, or who an author—who any human being—really is ("What Is an Author?" 222, emphasis added). The narrator's son, who "puts the shell's howl to his ear," understands that, in Rey Chow's reading of Foucault, history appears not as a network of solid connections but through "mutations, ruptures, and breaks" (line 3386; Chow 124). In its final dialectical flourish, *Another Life* transcends dialectic, just as the narrator's son transcends the division between deafness and audition. Its narrator, exhausted, makes the turn to nature Hegel observed, but nature—finally, if ironically—is found to contain the real history of humanity; superficial and partial histories, like the torn-out leaves of a book, fly away.

I want to close with a quotation from Glissant that complements the narrator's astonishment in the face of sublimity at the end of *Another Life*—as if it were its theoretical supplement:

> Experience of the abyss lies inside and outside the abyss. The torment of those who never escaped it: straight from the belly of the slave ship into the violet [sic] belly of the ocean depths they went. But their ordeal did not die; it quickened into this continuous/discontinuous thing: the panic of the new land, the haunting of the former land, finally the alliance with the imposed land, suffered and redeemed. The unconscious memory of the abyss served as the alluvium for these metamorphoses…Thus, the absolute unknown, projected by the abyss and bearing into eternity the womb abyss and the infinite abyss, in the end became knowledge…This is why we stay with poetry. (7–9)

Glissant's abyss is the ocean of the Middle Passage and, less concretely, historical totality itself: an abyss that stares back. It bears some resemblance to the Yoruban metaphysical phenomenon Wole Soyinka terms "the abyss of transition," which, fittingly for Walcott's narrator at the text's close, houses "the ultimate expression of cosmic will" (26). J. Michael Dash claims that Glissant and Walcott share their conception of history as sea-like, "with its constantly changing surface and capacity for infinite renewal" (xxix). The depth of the two thinkers' mutual imbrication is suggested, too, by their standing in chiastic relation via epigraph: Glissant borrows Walcott's phrase "sea is History" as the epigraph for *Poetics of Relation*, and Walcott borrows a paragraph from Glissant's novel *La Lézarde* as the epigraph for *Another Life*. While Glissant writes here of an absolute unknown that "became" knowledge, elsewhere he speaks of "a knowledge becoming," derived from thought's construction of "the imaginary of the past" (n.p., under heading "Imaginary"). Knowledge as becoming, the past continually constructed by the present: these and other temporal knots characterize the time of *Another Life*'s narrator who, despite them, arrives at middle age with his own share of fragile but real knowledge, participating in what Gadamer, explicating Hegel, described as the basic character of *Bildung* as historical spirit: "to reconcile itself with itself, to recognize oneself in another being" (13). With its incessant textual metaphors, *Another Life* proposes, by its own example, that the Bildungsroman is inadequate to postcolonial reality without these knots, and without undertaking the labour of untying and retying them. We might, too, concur with Glissant that poetry bears a special relationship to the abyssal knowledge these operations produce. If it is a Bildungsroman at all, *Another Life* is the Bildungsroman of one who crosses the abyss and yet knows that, to stay afloat, he must keep crossing it—the sun "drumming, drumming" above him (line 1200).

Notes

1. Blossom Fondo interprets Paula Marshall's *Triangular Road* as a Künstlerroman in which the transatlantic slave trade and Marshall's narrative of her own development are set in parallel, with the former structuring the unfolding of the latter. Awareness of the terrors of colonial history suffuses *Another Life*, but these memories' failure to determine either the text's direction or the nature of the narrator's response differentiates it from the kind of developmental novel Fondo takes *Triangular Road* to be, where collective trauma serves as both catalyst and threat to the flourishing of the individual protagonist and their cultivation of identity.

Works Cited

Abel, Elizabeth, et al. Introduction. *The Voyage In: Fictions of Female Development*, edited by Elizabeth Abel et al., University Press of New England, 1983, pp. 3–19.

Alabi, Adetayo. *Telling Our Stories: Continuities and Divergences in Black Autobiographies*. Palgrave Macmillan, 2005.

Arendt, Hannah. "Philosophy and Politics." *Social Research*, vol. 57, no. 1, Spring 1990, pp. 73–103.

Bakhtin, M.M. "The *Bildungsroman* and Its Significance in the History of Realism (Toward a Historical Typology of the Novel)." *Speech Genres and Other Late Essays*. Translated by Vern W. McGee, University of Texas Press, 1986, pp. 10–59.

Baldick, Chris, editor. "Bildungsroman." *Oxford Dictionary of Literary Terms*, Oxford University Press, 2008, p. 35.

Chatterjee, Partha. *The Nation and Its Fragments: Colonial and Postcolonial Histories*. Princeton University Press, 1993.

Chow, Rey. *A Face Drawn in Sand: Humanistic Inquiry and Foucault in the Present*. Columbia University Press, 2021.

Cobham-Sander, Rhonda. *I and I: Epitaphs for the Self in the Work of V.S. Naipaul, Kamau Brathwaite and Derek Walcott*. The University of the West Indies Press, 2016.

Dash, J. Michael. Introduction. *Caribbean Discourse: Selected Essays*, by Édouard Glissant, Caraf Books/University Press of Virginia, 1989, pp. xi–xlv.

Fondo, Blossom. "'I Have Known Rivers': Traumatic Memory and the Postcolonial Künstlerroman: A Reading of Paule Marshall's *Triangular Road*." *Zagadnienia Rodzajów Literackich*, vol. 56, no. 1, 2013, pp. 27–38.

Foucault, Michel. *The Order of Things: An Archeology of the Human Sciences*. Routledge, 2005.

Foucault, Michel. "What Is an Author?" *Aesthetics, Method, and Epistemology*. Vol. 2, by Michel Foucault, edited by James D. Faubion, translated by Robert Hurley et al., The New Press, 1998, pp. 205–22.

Fowler, Alastair. *Kinds of Literature: An Introduction to the Theory of Genres and Modes*. Oxford University Press, 1982.

Frye, Northrop. *Anatomy of Criticism: Four Essays*. Princeton University Press, 1971.

Fumagalli, Maria Cristina. "*Lo Stilo Della Sua Loda* or The Style of Her Praise: Dante's *Vita Nuova* and Walcott's *Another Life*." *Journal of West Indian Literature*, vol. 9, no. 1, Apr. 2000, pp. 42–69.

Gadamer, Hans-Georg. *Truth and Method*. 2nd rev. ed., translated by Joel Weinsheimer and Donald G. Marshall, Bloomsbury Academic, 2013.

Glissant, Édouard. *Poetics of Relation*. Translated by Betsy Wing, University of Michigan Press, 1997.

Hegel, G.W.F. *Elements of the Philosophy of Right*. Edited by Allen W. Wood, translated by H.B. Nisbet, Cambridge University Press, 1991.

Hoagland, Ericka A. "The Postcolonial Bildungsroman." *A History of the Bildungsroman*, edited by Sarah Graham, Cambridge University Press, 2019, pp. 217–38.

James, C.L.R. "Popular Art and the Cultural Tradition." *The C.L.R. James Reader*, edited by Anna Grimshaw, Blackwell, 1992, pp. 247–60.

Lane, M. Travis. "A Different 'Growth of a Poet's Mind': Derek Walcott's *Another Life*." *Ariel*, no. 9, 1978, pp. 65–78.

Lukács, Georg. *Goethe and His Age*. Translated by Robert Anchor, Merlin Press, 1968.

Meehan, Kevin, and Paul B. Miller. "Literature and Popular Culture." *Understanding the Contemporary Caribbean*. 2nd ed., edited by Richard S. Hillman and Thomas J. D'Agostino, Lynne Rienner Publishers, 2009, pp. 339–66.

Nietzsche, Friedrich. *The Gay Science, With a Prelude in German Rhymes and an Appendix of Songs*. Edited by Bernard Williams, translated by Josefine Nauckhoff and Adrian Del Caro, Cambridge University Press, 2001.

Nietzsche, Friedrich. *The Genealogy of Morals and Ecce Homo*. Edited by Walter Kaufmann, translated by Walter Kaufmann and R.J. Hollingdale, Vintage Books, 1989.

Olney, James. "The Value of Autobiography for Comparative Studies: African vs. Western Autobiography." *Comparative Civilizations Review*, Spring 1979, pp. 52–64.

Pfau, Thomas. "*Bildungsroman.*" *The Encyclopedia of Romantic Literature*. Vol. I, Wiley-Blackwell, 2012, pp. 124–32.

Puckett, Kent. *Narrative Theory: A Critical Introduction*. Cambridge University Press, 2016.

Quayson, Ato. *Tragedy and Postcolonial Literature*. Cambridge University Press, 2021.

Ramazani, Jahan. "The Wound of History: Walcott's *Omeros* and the Postcolonial Poetics of Affliction." *PMLA*, vol. 112, no. 3, May 1997, pp. 405–17.

Scott, Joan W. "The Evidence of Experience." *Critical Inquiry*, vol. 17, no. 4, Summer 1991, pp. 773–97.

Soyinka, Wole. *Myth, Literature and the African World*. Cambridge University Press, 1976.

Spivak, Gayatri Chakravorty. *The Post-Colonial Critic: Interviews, Strategies, Dialogues*. Edited by Sarah Harasym, Routledge, 1990.

Stiegler, Bernard. *Technics and Time, 1: The Fault of Epimetheus*. Translated by Richard Beardsworth and George Collins, Stanford University Press, 1998.

Walcott, Derek. *Another Life*. Edited by Edward Baugh and Colbert Nepaulsingh, Lynne Rienner Publishers, 2009.

Walcott, Derek. "The Muse of History." *What the Twilight Says*, Farrar, Straus and Giroux, 1998, pp. 36–64.

Walcott, Derek. *The Prodigal: A Poem*. Farrar, Straus and Giroux, 2004.

Walcott, Derek. "What the Twilight Says." *What the Twilight Says*, by Derek Walcott, Farrar, Straus and Giroux, 1998, pp. 3–35.

Walcott, Derek. *White Egrets*. Farrar, Straus and Giroux, 2010.

Weinsheimer, Joel, and Donald G. Marshall. Translator's Preface. *Truth and Method*. 2nd rev. ed., by Hans-Georg Gadamer, Bloomsbury Academic, 2013, pp. x–xix.

Wittgenstein, Ludwig. *Philosophical Investigations*. Rev. 4th ed., edited by P.M.S. Hacker and Joachim Schulte, translated by G.E.M. Anscombe et al., Wiley-Blackwell, 2009.

Wynter, Sylvia. "Beyond the Word of Man: Glissant and the New Discourse of the Antilles." *World Literature Today*, vol. 63, no. 4, Édouard Glissant Issue, Autumn 1989, pp. 637–48.

7

UPENDRANATH ASHK'S *FALLING WALLS*

Bildungsroman of the Lost Youth of Independent India

Aruna Krishnamurthy

This chapter attempts to bring two disparate literary traditions—the Bildungsroman genre that developed out of Western Enlightenment culture in the eighteenth century, and the nascent Hindi novel of the mid-twentieth century around the time of India's transition from colonial rule to independence—into a mutually critical dialogue to expand the scope of both traditions. As a genre, the Bildungsroman has a well-defined origin point in Goethe's *Wilhelm Meister*, as well as a recognizable (if somewhat contested) trajectory as it evolved from celebrating the individual in eighteenth-century German Romanticism to the more restrictive confines of nineteenth-century realism in the British novel and into the modernist anti-Bildungsroman forms practised by Joyce and Woolf, among others. While a detailed appraisal of the genre and its scholarly treatments are outside the scope of this chapter, it is worth identifying the Continental Bildungsroman as a "novel of formation" or "becoming" (Bakhtin) that "balance[es] social and moral demands with the decisions taken and choices made by free will" (Golban 21), and dramatizes the individual's ability to resist and prevail against the pressures of society and its institutions. This primordial antagonism between the self and society allows the form to expand into a universalist framework; according to Sarah Graham: "The narrative offers privileged access to the psychological development of a central character whose sense of self is in flux, paralleling personal concerns with prevailing values. The Bildungsroman's ability to explore the relationship between self and society accounts for its lasting global appeal" (1).

Alongside this synchronic struggle between self and society, Bildungsroman studies also trace the "rise of feminist, post-colonial and minority studies during the 1980s and 90s [that] led to an expansion of the traditional Bildungsroman definition…from traditional metropolitan novels of formation and social affirmation to increasingly global and fragmentary narratives of transformation and rebellion" (Boes, "Modernist Studies and the Bildungsroman" 231). The afterlife of the genre in the postcolonial imaginary as a challenge to colonial aesthetics and a consequent redefinition of the form through the experience of the colonized or postcolonial subject is one of the most exciting developments and forms the main frame of this chapter that looks at Upendranath Ashk's Hindi novel *Falling Walls*, published in 1947 in India. The novel is set in the years preceding independence, which came in 1947, and traces the story of Chetan, a twenty-one-year-old youth from a lower-class neighbourhood of Jalandhar, Punjab, who, according to Peter Gaeffke is "dominated by his memories and…subdued by the oppressive multiplicity of his world" (57). This first installment of an incomplete five-part series also called *Girti Diwaren* or "falling walls" is built around Chetan's childhood, marriage, sexual desires, struggle for individuation in a repressive and violent household, and his attempts to establish his authority as a writer in his lower-class milieu. Ashk uses the Bildungsroman's plot of self-cultivation to examine the plight of urban, lower-class Indian youth with artistic sensibilities and to examine the fate and identity of the youth that will inherit a free nation. The key features of the Bildungsroman—a young protagonist, aesthetics of interiority, and the epistemology of historicism—connect with the genre of the Hindi novel where Ashk marks the point of intersection between these two disparate traditions. By relocating the drama of growth, maturation, education, and apprenticeship in low-brow localities and habituses of India that are typically neglected by anglophone writers, *Falling Walls* offers a fresh opportunity to study questions of class, gender, mobility, and successful maturation that form the warp and woof of the Bildungsroman, particularly from the perspective of the social margins of colonial India in the years preceding political independence from the British Raj.

Bildungsroman and the Hindi Novel

Bildungsroman scholarship shows a set of overlapping concerns and terminologies, from which I distill a few that are relevant for *Falling Walls*. Franco Moretti's study of the form within the emerging culture of capitalist modernity and its particular focus on the "interiority" and "mobility" of youth is germane for this analysis. Moretti's thesis that the Bildungsroman rises out of a crisis where Europe "plunges into modernity without a culture of modernity" (5) resonates with *Falling Walls*'s historical situation of India on the cusp of independence and self-rule but without well-developed social, political, and cultural institutions that could accompany that transition to egalitarian nationhood and modernity. Like the case of the Irish colonial state in Gregory Castle's analysis of the modernist Bildungsroman, in India, too, "modernization had been at best an uneven process, in large part because colonial rule tended to retard development in some sectors of society and to encourage it in others," and there were "[f]ew bourgeois liberal political institutions and no secular, humanist educational tradition" (*Reading the Modernist Bildungsroman* 57). The literature of modernity that emerged in late-nineteenth-century India was shaped by the double trajectories of anti-colonial nationalism and an internationalist progressive movement, marking the end of tradition and convention (both literary and cultural) in favour of history consciousness (famously articulated by Premchand's manifesto for the Progressive Writers Association in 1935).

This epistemic shift from customary to historical consciousness that created imbricated trajectories of the novel genre and literary realism also shaped the Bildungsroman's "strategies of emplotment" (Boes, *Formative Fictions* 6). Within this nationalist/progressivist/

reformist tradition of the Hindi novel, the genre of the Bildungsroman offered writers such as Agyeya and Ashk an important reframing of (though not a break from) the prevailing "social problems" approach that defined the Premchand generation, as well as progressive writers' movement. Peter Gaeffke points out that both Agyeya and Ashk add psychological complexity and erotic elements to the theme of economic necessity in realist fiction, where the "hero is open to a complex set of influences and the forces which shape him as an individual character and are also experienced in a highly individualistic way" (51). Ashk's adoption of the new aesthetics of interiority, also key to the development of the New Story movement in Hindi literature, marks his own maturation as a writer away from the literary apprenticeship of his influential predecessor, Premchand. Reflecting on his motivations for writing *Falling Walls*, Ashk deploys a modernist terminology of desacralization and innovation to crystallize his new authorial identity:

> I wanted to write a much greater novel than *Godan*...I wanted to write a novel that gave equal time to the inner and outer complications of the hero's life, one that wouldn't fit into the old style of pattern, but I didn't have a new pattern. And so, I began my search for a new pattern. (xxi)

This rethinking of the scope of literature and author through the inner life of a restless and sensitive artist hero is effected through key elements of the Bildungsroman genre, inventoried by Jerome Buckley as "childhood, the conflict of generations, provinciality, the larger society, self-education, alienation, ordeal by love, the search for a vocation and a working philosophy" (qtd. in Boes, *Formative Fictions* 18). But unlike the modernist Künstlerromane of Joyce and Woolf that "keep the social concern to a lesser degree, to show the impossibility of harmony between internal and external factors" (Golban 6–7), Ashk creates a productive tension between the emergence of the Lockean self and the aim of social reform. Gaeffke emphasizes that these novels, while focused on the struggles of the individualized hero, were equally interested in the "whole fabric of society" to ask, "what were the possible options for an Indian individual, and India as a whole under present conditions" (51). This interconnectedness between the fate of the hero and the class and nation he represents is also echoed by Ashk:

> This section of *Falling Walls* is about that time in the hero's development when he doesn't understand what he should do in life...This section of the novel shows the ephemeral dreams that rise up in just a moment after coming into contact with the zeal, tumult, optimism, pessimism and imagination of the life stage of youth, and how they collapse in the next moment when they get a kick from reality, as well as the inner and outer struggles of a lower-middle-class youth. (xxvi)

Moretti's storying of modernity through the figure of dynamic but evanescent youth also shapes the drama of freedom and conformity key to the genre. While the maturation plot (especially in the nineteenth-century English novel) ends the promise of youthful dynamism with a pragmatic reconciliation with prevailing social values, according to Gregory Castle, in the twentieth-century modernist Bildungsroman "the bildungsheld's refusal to sanction the ideal—the result of discovering it to be a sham—becomes the starting point for imagining new modes of self-formation and social belonging that do not depend on achievement and that reward aspiration as a goal in itself" ("The Modernist Bildungsroman" 146). Castle's framework of negative dialectics suggests that the promise/premise of the ideals of "aesthetic education and individual freedom" (*Reading the Modernist Bildungsroman* 1) of the classical Bildungsroman offers the artist hero a way to resist the nineteenth-century bourgeois appropriation of the form, which converts the modernist Bildungsroman's failure to achieve maturation into a "critical triumph" (3). The modernist turn in the Bildungsroman tradition is very relevant for *Falling Walls*, which equally uses the aesthetic sensibility of its protagonist as a way to critique conformity to an emerging national ideal of masculinity. But rather than the anti-bourgeois sensibility of the Western modernist Bildungsroman that took issue with "overly rationalized and bureaucratized societies" (Castle, *Reading the Modernist Bildungsroman* 1), *Falling Walls* is built around class critique, highlighting the inefficacy of stultifying traditions, repressive family hierarchies, regimented reformist movements, and lack of material resources as its mainstay.

Further, where Castle sets up a critical continuity between the ur-Bildungsroman and the modernist variant, Ashk's Bildungsroman necessarily lacks that direct connection to a literary antecedent except in an itinerant way. As a borrowed form written in the Hindi vernacular, it lacks the specific referentiality that a modernist colonized subject might inject into the genre as a critique of empire (more on this later). Nevertheless, two key features of the modernist Bildungsroman play well into the analysis of *Falling Walls*: a protagonist (also representing the emergent youth of the nascent nation) whose aesthetic aspirations and sensibilities are frustrated by existing social and cultural apprenticeships, and his inconclusive *Bildung* that emphasizes a radical critique and rejection of social norms. To the latter point, each installment of the *Falling Walls* cycle ends in an indeterminacy about the fate and fortunes of Chetan, where Ashk exchanges maturation or *telos* for a spiritual homelessness and narrative inconclusiveness in order to refine and redraw the contours of progressivist realism.

Epistemology of Contingency

The modernist Bildungsroman's critical stance is equally important for challenging ideologies of imperialism, where the colonized subject's failure of self-cultivation within the apparatus of the empire exposes the occlusion of them from the universalist rhetoric of the traditional Bildungsroman. Castle shows how James Joyce's Künstlerroman, for instance, dramatizes the outsider status of the Catholic Irish colonial subject whose experience of nonidentity within a disciplinarian colonial culture leads him to choose "exile over social integration" (*Reading the Modernist Bildungsroman* 129). In Erika Hoagland's words, the genre of postcolonial Bildungsroman is defined by "active and regularly subversive engagement with its literary forebear" (218), that (in José-Santiago Fernández-Vázquez's words) "incorporate[s] the master codes of imperialism into the text, in order to sabotage them more effectively" (qtd. in Hoagland 218). While Ashk does address the secondary status of the colonized subject at crucial moments in the novel, the subversive potential of *Falling Walls* lies in its vernacular break from both Eurocentric *and* anglophone postcolonial traditions. In Ashk's novel, it is not so much the dehiscence of the "Native" within repressive colonial culture but the struggles of individuation within the impoverished and ignored bylanes of lower-class neighbourhoods in provincial cities such as Jalandhar, Lahore, and Shimla that create the sense of exile for the aspiring artist.

There are some similarities between Ashk's adaptation and the Künstlerroman tradition, most notably the theme of alienation and failed mentorships, a lot of it deriving from his own struggles as a writer. First, as a Punjabi writer from Jalandhar in Hindi-centric Allahabad (now Prayagraj), Ashk, like fellow modernists, was very much an outsider. Daisy Rockwell highlights "the inter-regional prejudices between Ashk, the outsider and the Punjabi, and the residents of his adopted city, Allahabad" (*Upendranath Ashk* 5) as part of the angst that pervades his identity as a writer, especially at a time when Hindi was being championed as a unifying national language by Mahatma Gandhi and the nationalist movement. Ashk's departure from the accepted standards of literary writing, along with his polyglot style that included a mix of high- and low-brow languages, stretching from standardized Hindi to everyday Khadi Boli, Urdu, and Punjabi, further puts him at odds with the literary establishment that was strengthening Modern Standard Hindi as the language of the emergent nation. In Rockwell's retelling of Ashk's literary legacy, rather than the colonizer's language, it is the hegemonic sway of standardized Hindi and its institutions that led to Ashk's "persecution complex" (32), his lashing out at critics, and his unpopularity with reviewers. Secondly, Ashk's class location, the fact that he grew up in a poor, albeit upper-caste, household under an authoritarian and violent father who placed high expectations on his sons, a pious and long-suffering mother, and was educated in local Arya Samaj schools primarily in Hindi, Urdu, and Sanskrit is key to understanding his identity as a writer. The figure of the punishing and cruel father, so central to *Falling Walls*, is clearly modelled on his own father about whom Ashk says:

> The only thing my reckless and negligent father ever taught us was that we could do whatever we wanted…but we had to be better than anyone else. But what work? What occupation? He never told us that. (qtd. in Rockwell 20)

His lower-class origins also determined his trajectory as a writer, where the struggle for basic necessities of life left him with little time to follow through with his aspirations:

> What I hadn't thought of in my youthful optimism and zeal was that in this commercial age, it's impossible for any lower-middle-class writer to find enough free time for the creation of such a long novel. For that you need the leisure of Tagore, Galsworthy, Tolstoy, or the modern Russian writers. Such leisure is not in the fate of the Indian writer busy in the endless struggle to gather together the minimal necessities of life. (xxiv)

Added to these setbacks, the literary milieu of the 1940s placed enormous hurdles on aspiring writers from humble origins such as Ashk, where, according to Rockwell,

> there were no laws regarding payment of royalties and the publishers could exercise complete control over their writers. They often set up situations where they would commission a work from an author for a flat fee, and then refuse to give the author any of the royalties. Sometimes, a writer desperate for cash might sell all his rights to the publisher. Some writers had been virtually ruined by the system. (26)

The combination of class exclusion and an oppressive childhood influenced Ashk's radical break from the popular *chhayawad* or romanticist style, with its lofty idealized characters, towards forging a style where realism, modernism, and progressivism were in mutually critical dialogue with each other. What emerges from this attempt is a Bildungsroman of failed apprenticeships: unable to exercise control over their choices in a regimented household and unequal society, young men and women in *Falling Walls* shape their self-cultivation around an epistemology of contingency and impromptu adaptations to ever-changing and challenging circumstances that result in makeshift and unmediated routes of social mobility with no clear destination. That epistemology of contingency (also recognizable as the concept of *jugaad* in contemporary North India) may be glimpsed at even in the happenstance nature of Ashk's encounter with the Bildungsroman and modernist genres that influenced his style. Rather than a sustained apprenticeship in European literary traditions that typically informs the anglophone postcolonial traditions of the Bildungsroman, Ashk comes across the genre almost by accident:

> Someone suggested I read Romain Rolland's *Jean Christophe*...I rushed immediately to the shop, but fell silent when I heard the price of *Jean Christophe*...I just went to the shop four or five times and read a hundred and fifty or two hundred pages of the novel at the shop...I also needed a pattern that would enable me to weave together the inner and outer complexities of the hero. I had recently read a novel by Virginia Woolf or some other writer from her group. All the activity in the book was limited to the hero getting out of bed, going to the window, and taking a walk, yet the writer had very cleverly woven the story of his entire life into those actions. This pattern was helpful to me, and so the two of these together served as models for my own novel. (xxii)

This borrowing of styles based on a serendipitous encounter in a neighbourhood bookstore does not quite fall into the parody or mimicry paradigm of the native writer that is key to the postcolonial Bildungsroman, but signifies more a desacralization, creative repurposing, hacking, transculturation, and novelization of the genre within the lower-class habituses of India. Equally, the novel's epistemology of contingency and strategy of improvisation are key to Chetan's *Bildung* and challenge the arrow-marked trajectories of the idealist protagonists of the reformist and progressive literary traditions.

Childhood and Conflict of Generations

Falling Walls is the first of an unfinished cycle of five novels whose grand scale, as well as the "mediocrity and lack of imagination" (Gaeffke 57) of the protagonist, has been compared to Proust's monumental *À la recherche du temps perdu*.[1] For Rockwell, the encyclopedic novel is at once "a cultural history, a literary picaresque, a Partition novel (in its reconstruction of an undivided Punjabi past), a Bildungsroman and a work of satire" (Preface x). *Falling Walls* covers Chetan's trajectory from innocence to maturity dramatized around three centres of experience that are distributed over three locations: the first part, set in Jalandhar, covers the dysfunctional relationship between a restless Chetan and his bullying father, Shadiram, and Chetan's arranged marriage to a woman he is not attracted to; the second, set in Lahore, is built around the struggles of becoming a writer while battling economic necessity as a householder and navigating the world of desire and sexuality as a young man; and the penultimate chapters, set in Shimla, show the end of Chetan's creative journey in failure and his epiphany about the deterministic class realities of his lower-class milieu around the motif of "falling walls." While the plot moves forward in a linear fashion, Chetan's intense memories of an abusive and violent childhood at the hands of his father punctuate the story as impressionist spots of time and bring the novel into the framework of failed mentors and apprenticeships to account for Chetan's crisis of *Bildung*. The combination of outward circumstances linked with his lower-class existence, as well as internal *méconnaissance* that stems from his childhood trauma, leads to a self-estrangement that resonates both as a critique of class barriers, as well as the spiritual breakdown of the sensitive and creative mind.

In the first part of the novel, Chetan's unwilling marriage to Chanda, who is depicted as an "unremarkable, slightly plump, dark-skinned girl" (Ashk 9) and his attraction towards her cousin Neela form the main narrative of the epistemology of contingency. Chetan's inability to take control of his future is transposed into desire towards women who offer the possibility of sexual sublimation, including improvising a romantic but manipulative and predatory fantasy with thirteen-year-old Neela, who pays the price for his recklessness. At the very outset of the novel, we find that Chetan is living a split life, an inner dreamworld of desires, aspirations, and plans, and an outer existence that struggles against the demands of the oppressive social order in the form of an authoritarian father. As a young man with a talent for education and the arts, Chetan displays the boundless vitality and potential that is emblematic of a *Bildungsheld* of modernity, a threshold figure between two generations, one defined by customary authority and the other by individualism:

> Chetan's ambitions grew and grew like the hunger of a man in chains, and he wasn't prepared to have them thus curtailed...He'd been deprived of the experience of college life and therefore he had an intense desire to go to Lahore to experience life, if only for a short while. But he had no way of going, so he'd suppressed this desire. (10)

The socially pragmatic function of education as a vehicle of mobility under colonial rule, also sanctioned by parental approval, clashes with education's promise of unfettered self-exploration for the young emerging out of a freedom struggle. The curbs come in the form of his tearful mother's pleas: "You've studied plenty. You have a job now. Stay with that for a while, get married, settle down and live the way the rest of the world lives" (17). Chetan's inability to take on figures of authority to voice his aspirations, seen in the opening episode of the novel, becomes a pattern of communication breakdown and self-estrangement that recurs at crucial moments in the plot with other mentor figures. In this instance, his crisis of individuation is underscored by a childish act of resistance incongruous with an educated man of marriageable age: "He stomped his feet in rage and stalked off to his room to lie down" (15).

Masculinity, Alienation, and Imagination

As an "old school matric-pass man who worked night and day in the Multan Division of far-off stations, dealing with tickets, passengers and trains" (Ashk 50), Pandit Shadiram's life is defined by lack of social and economic mobility under colonial rule, for which he creates an outlet through debauchery, dissipation, and violence. Though Ashk doesn't delve too deeply into Shadiram's own *Bildung*, his unmitigated cruelty and regimen of discipline towards his family seem to be an amalgam of two different types of toxic masculinities, one stemming from his subservient role as a functionary in the empire (though he claims to have slapped a British officer in anger one time), and the other deriving from the muscular culture of the Hindu nationalist Arya Samaj and Hindu Mahasabha movements that held sway over North India in the early twentieth century. A number of details allow us to see the father's childhood of parental neglect as collateral damage of the colonizer's chokehold on the life of colonized subjects. Under colonial rule, Shadiram's father, who works as a record keeper, had to sacrifice his family obligations to serve his masters:

> When the sub-collector, the superintendent and the revenue officer were on tour, he had to assist his masters and travel all over the district with them…he'd leave his child Shadiram in the care of the clerk and spend the entire day running around. (61–62)

Shadiram's maniacal obsession with his children's educational accomplishments is symptomatic of struggle for mobility under British rule, seen in his narrow idea of the value of education: "If Chetan were to say to him, 'I'm going to Lahore…to take the finance exam and become an ATS [Assistant Traffic Superintendent], his father would understand, because the supervising officer of his TI [Traffic Inspector] was an ATS. But the idea that Chetan planned to become a great writer might be beyond his comprehension" (50). Shadiram enforced the socially pragmatic idea of education through discipline and violence that refused to recognize the individuality of the child, perhaps recreating the colonizer's expectation of obedience from the colonized in his own household. The novel is fairly littered with episodes where Chetan and his older brother, referred to as Bhai Saheb, are beaten mercilessly when they fail to correctly answer Shadiram's impromptu quizzes on math and English, or otherwise obey his instructions. In this narrative of failed apprenticeship, the children develop an action plan of contingency to avoid the clutches of their father:

> [Chetan] always thought of scores of ways to avoid his father's beatings: he made sure to avoid him and to absent himself from the house whenever he was at home. Chetan's younger brother, though young, took full

advantage of Chetan's far-sightedness...He would fall ill so that Chetan would have to take him to the doctor...he'd disappear so Chetan would have to go out looking for him...They also made absolutely sure that if Pandit ji came into the house, not only would there be no books in their hands, no books would be visible in any corner of the house. (21)

Shadiram's disciplinarian attitude and domestic violence ends their childhood prematurely, where Bhai Sahib develops a stubborn insouciance to the trauma of his father's violent rages, a "detachment that's usually caused by daily abuse and beatings as a child" (20). Bhai Saheb's failure to thrive in that household results in his numerous attempts to run away from home; labelled the "old codger," or "the ox," his vitality dulls down to torpid stagnation: "Bhai Sahib devoured the heaps of knowledge contained within those books like a white ant; and like a white ant, his mind remained a total blank, despite having consumed a great trove of literature" (27).

Chetan's childhood trauma of violence haunts him at crucial moments in his life, leading to a spiritual and physical breakdown. While in Shimla, two crucial incidents of violence from his childhood resurface as epiphanies in his own plot of dehiscence between the *innenwelt* and *umwelt* that leaves him unable to speak up and challenge his ill treatment. He recalls an incident from early childhood when he is slapped by his malnourished mother for refusing to drink cow's milk, leaving him with the knowledge that "there was no turning back [from that incident]...[I]n some obscure corner of his impressionable young mind, something was brewing—it wasn't just physical pain that bothered him" (287). In another important episode, when Shadiram tries to show off young Chetan's prowess in English to his colleague, and a nervous Chetan fails to deliver, Shadiram "beat[s] him like a madman" (291), resulting in Chetan's breakdown and alienation from the world around him:

> He wandered about in a fog...He couldn't stop his eyes from filling with tears again and again...The throbbing pain of his cheeks had subsided, but he felt unbearable agony in his wounded heart. (292)

But unlike Bhai Saheb's response, Chetan's anomie releases his "power of imagination" (300) in the form of a family romance to cope with his traumatic childhood:

> [W]hen he felt downcast with sorrow...he imagined that Ram and Sita were there with him. Ram would lovingly stroke his head and Sita would affectionately lay him in her lap, and he'd forget everything—all his father's beatings, taunts and curses...Sometimes he'd go and meet Krishna and his gang of cowherds...and celebrate the raas dance with the beautiful, gentle milkmaids. At night, he'd become the hero of the stories that Ma or Gangadei [his grandmother] had told him during the day. (299)

Much like in the case of the Romantic artist, Chetan's inner resource of imagination comes to heal his fragmented self in nature and art, and also frames the revolutionary vertigo of the modern *Bildungsheld*:

> In his imagination the ocean of life swelled with infinite possibility. He always found himself standing at the shore, staring enthusiastically at the restless waves. He would get a ship and go to the farther shore and frolic amongst these towering waves. That farther shore where there was success, wealth and happiness. (300)

On the flip side, this restorative and restless imagination leads Chetan into modernity's tragedy (or "critical triumph," according to Castle) of what the narrator calls "overblown sentimentality" that prevents him from maturing into a sturdy and socially pragmatic *Bildungsheld*, as he "didn't have the thick skin that usually develops in those growing up in the lower middle classes—that tough hide that suffers mortal insults and lies without feeling a thing, that brown-noses, gives and receives bribes, and cheats and swindles" (336).

As a man driven by sensibility, Chetan represents a new masculine ideal that, with all its faults and missteps, captures the zeitgeist of independent India. As discussed above, Shadiram's violence may stem from the destructive influence of colonial rule, but his disciplinarian attitude towards his sons may be equally influenced by the Arya Samaj, "an activist Hindu revivalist and reformist movement founded in 1875" (Gupta 441) that had a powerful presence in Punjab and North India in the twentieth century. Charu Gupta has analyzed the emergence of the militant phase of the Arya Samaj and Hindu Mahasabha movements in the 1920s as a three-part response to colonial rule: challenging British colonial masculinity by galvanizing a native version; selectively reshaping the identity and imagery of Hindu religion; and crafting a national image of a "new full bodied masculine Hindu male" (442) who would resist both the "rational British colonialist and the lustful muslim." The cult of violence and the culture of gymnasiums or *akhadas* that flourished in the early twentieth century were very much a part of Ashk's childhood as well, where his father, "a huge strong man, and a regular visitor to the akhada, the wrestling arena" tried to raise his sons as *pahalvans* (bodybuilders) to assert their supremacy as upper-caste brahmins (Rockwell 19). This pugilistic attitude combines seamlessly with Samaji ideals in Shadiram, who opines, "'All the problems our country and caste are experiencing are because we've abandoned the old ideals and philosophies'…'All around you see cowardly, weak, pale young boys and girls who can't laugh properly, can't play, can't enjoy life.' Then he'd guffaw and begin sermonizing loudly about the importance of wrestling and playing kabaddi and fencing for the development of the nation" (116).

In contrast, Chetan's identity is constructed within emotional and aesthetic registers and challenges both colonial masculinity of the British, as well as the Hindu reformist male of the Arya Samaj. In addition to rejecting his father and all that he represents, Chetan questions the efficacy of reform movements that dismiss tradition and rituals as excessive but also deprive young people psychic and libidinal release in the beauty and laughter of old customs. His marriage ceremony, conducted according to austere and devotional Arya Samaj rites, leaves him with a sense of dissatisfaction and unfulfilled desires. On the one hand, the threadbare rituals of the Arya Samaj wedding allow the lower-class family to escape the considerable financial burden of an expensive wedding, but on the other, it meant a ban on "joking and joyful laughter at weddings" (144). In the place of the "usual saucy, taunting wedding songs, there was a gramophone belonging to the one and only reformer of the Basti, Master Nandalal, which cried out in its inelegant voice: Oh Lord, please give us all purity...Master Nandalal the reformer disliked women climbing up on roofs at weddings, and whistling and singing dirty songs. He believed these sorts of practices were ripe for reform" (140).

Ordeals of Love

The repressive morality principle of the upper-caste, male-dominated reform movement that sought to purge sexuality, particularly linked with women's identity, and replace beauty and laughter with devotion is seen by Chetan as a disservice to the poor of the nation:

> For the hungry and poor of India, the few hours of weddings and holidays were the only time when people could enjoy themselves a bit...The groom's procession would be welcomed with sweet songs...Chetan wished he could hear those sweet songs, but the gramophone droned on as before on the verandah: Oh Lord, please give us all purity now...Chetan imagined a beautiful wedding goddess stripped of her ornaments by the tyrannical reformer. (140–41)

Denied control over his own life and marriage, Chetan sublimates his disappointments through subterfuge by ensnaring his hapless sister-in-law, Neela, for extramarital flirtation. In his drab marriage scene, Neela stands out in her beauty and gaiety, and though Chetan later becomes well disposed towards his wife, Chanda, for him, "Neela was fire" (148). After his marriage, Chetan manipulates his wife at every opportunity to get physically close to Neela, grooming the thirteen-year-old for his voyeuristic pleasure. When Neela is sent to attend to him, as her customary sister-in-law role demanded, he makes bold advances on her by holding "Neela's hand to his throat and then to his cheeks...[and]...draw[ing] her hand—that was softer than the wings of a dove and whiter than milk—to his lips, when Neela pulled it back" (156). Though there is some evidence of Chanda's stoic silence in the face of her helplessness, we never find out how Neela or Chanda view Chetan's overtures. While Chetan's sexual frisson for Neela is sometimes humanized as a contingent compensation for the tragedy of circumstance, where the prosaic and plump Chanda, and not the beautiful and poetic Neela, is chosen as his wife, Ashk does reserve severe censure for his reckless and selfish behaviour. At the end of the novel, young Neela's life and happiness are frittered away by her family in a hasty marriage to an older, unattractive man of questionable repute as the result of Chetan's precipitous actions and his cowardly victim shaming. Even as Chetan's captation for Neela is framed within the "falling walls" motif as yet another disappointment in the heady plot of modernity, Ashk makes it clear that Neela is a victim of Chetan's failed *Bildung* in a hopelessly conventional society.

The novel extends the plot of desire and sexuality beyond Chetan's desperate overtures towards upper-caste and delicate Neela into a crucial formative experience of maturation in Lahore's community of lower-caste drifters. If, as Gupta points out, Hindu reformist movements "revealed an obsession with Hindu female chastity and purity," where "women were to be protected from the 'other' by invoking Hindu masculinity," (444) the novel shows a range of female characters who defy this orthodoxy with a display of robust sexual desires. In Lahore's "cheerless, filthy, poor neighbourhood" (Ashk 92) of Changar *mohalla*, lusty, lower-caste women with few prospects for self-advancement, such as the horse cart driver's sister Prakasho and dark-complexioned, full-cheeked Kesar, with her "fearless, bold glances" (110), engage in their own contingency plans for self-gratification. While the depictions of these women's frank sexuality border on the grotesque, their gumption and strong drive for self-affirmation form a healthy contrast to the long-suffering upper-caste women of Chetan's family, and exert a subterranean pull on him. Caught between the contrary demands of his celibate and carnal selves, Chetan's insecure masculinity drives him to local quacks such as Munshi Girija Shankar—an ayurvedic doctor *and* literary figure— who capitalized on the identity crisis of displaced young men by offering dubious advice and remedies. Within his own epistemology of contingency, Girija Shankar profits from the failed mentorship of a society given to austerity and celibacy, where, as Bhai Sahib says,

"It's the fault of those of us who should fully explain such things [as sexuality] to young men and women when they come of age, but it's considered a sin even to hint at them" (115).

Portrait of the Artist

Lahore's low-brow heterotopia and its shape-shifting world of writers, publishers, doctors, and pharmacists is where Chetan begins his journey as a novelist. Rockwell highlights Ashk's own literary apprenticeship within similar heterogenous and folksy subcultures in pre-Partition Punjab, where "storytelling was often a street-side affair: Punjabi poets knocked out verses in poetry slams and on street corners, mirasis travelled from town to town telling their tales, Urdu mushairas or poetry gatherings were numerous, and even Ayurvedic sex doctors published literary reviews from their clinics" (Rockwell, Preface xii). Chetan's initiation into the world of letters begins at a young age, when the Arya Samaj's repertoire of devotional songs and stories stirs his aesthetic sensibilities, leading him to create his own songs, and gaining (perhaps misplaced) confidence in his abilities to sway audiences with his art. As he grows older, he develops interest in Punjabi poetry recited at fairs, where the poets were "usually hookah-pipe makers, dyers, motor drivers, snack vendors and men of that class" (Ashk 364). The carnivalesque atmosphere "of the travelling theatres, magicians and madaris" (363) is underscored by the Rabelaisian flavour of these literary gatherings where poets displayed the "splendour of their art..[but] [w]hen the field began to narrow… moved on to curses" that "would become progressively more and more pointed, bitter, plain-spoken and obscene, until one of the poets, or one of their acolytes, would throw a shoe at the abuser. Then the poet-groups would abandon their displays of creative genius and start showing off their physical prowess instead, and a hullabaloo would break out" (366). In this scrappy communitarian setting, Chetan wins a prize for a poetic composition in his teenage years and begins his tutelage in the arts. The low-brow world of his encounters limits his apprenticeship in high art and literature, and the lack of material resources and a room of one's own in which to write place considerable obstacles in his journey as an author.

Often in the Bildungsroman tradition, the turn towards aestheticism comes when, as Castle says, "the protagonist, by resisting the dialectical closure of achieved Bildung, forges new values in the only spaces open to her, inner life and the aesthetic milieu it generates. The portrait of the artist motif captures this transformation of inner culture—the garden of Bildung—into the consolations (or desolations) of aesthetic life" ("The Modernist Bildungsroman" 146). In *Falling Walls*, recourse to art and literature follows a similar trajectory, where Chetan's interest in music and literary arts grows out of a desire for self-affirmation and mobility denied to him in a punishing and impoverished household and within the Arya Samaj cultural apparatus. But unlike the modern artist, it is not the purposeful "transformation of inner culture" but "his habit to take as much advantage as possible of any situation" that motivates him "to spend his free time on creative work" (Ashk 218). Chetan "didn't really know anything about novels and how they were written," as "he had absolutely no money for buying books, and no time to go to libraries and take advantage of the wealth that filled their shelves" (219). In this situation he apprentices himself to a "great writer" he has read about, "who would perfect his nascent stories by filling in the plots and strengthening the outlines when he went out for walks" (219). Chetan's novel-writing episode is a defining moment where his boundless optimism and energy meet insurmountable class obstacles that literally and metaphorically sink his novel. Ashk utilizes this self-reflexive episode to project his own identity shift from a writer "in thrall" of the "powerful and scrupulous tyrant" of literary convention to the "uncircumscribed spirit" (Woolf 160) of the modernist artist. Even before Chetan tragically loses his novel during a thunderstorm, his plan to adopt the sensational style of populist fiction already hints at the ersatz quality of his novel. The protagonist was to be from an upper-class aristocratic family who would rescue his loving father from financial ruin by reluctantly marrying into a wealthy household. The young man would then desert his new wife after securing her jewels and leave home for the life of a wanderer where another woman would fall in love with him. Eventually, he will be restored to his wife and family, but his long-suffering lover would die waiting for him to return. Though Chetan invests considerable energy and effort in writing his novel, even orchestrating a move to a larger residence for privacy, the project is a failure from the start as its subject matter is inauthentic and disconnected from the gritty realities of his life. Under the spell of a "great author's" advice, an exhausted Chetan is so lost in planning the novel during his walk home after a tiring day that he fails to notice that a heavy downpour had engulfed the entire filthy Changar *mohalla* with murky water. Chetan's insistence on "following the course described by the great author," and his continued "absorption in the construction of the plot" even as the roads are filling up with water, lead to that fateful moment when "his foot [gets] caught in the gutter" and the "precious diary" slips and falls into the water and is lost forever. The episode, rendered within Ashk's combination of reformist and modernist frameworks, shows Chetan as a victim of his class situation but equally imprisoned within his mind-forged manacles. For Ashk, a writer is born only through a clear apprehension and appreciation of one's lived reality, which then empowers him to challenge convention. Reflecting on his own passage into authorship, he says:

> I had been living in such an imaginary world before, that I hadn't noticed all the refuse, poverty, hunger, illness and sorrow around me… Many of the poets I enjoyed reading, and whose works moved me… now began to seem completely insipid from the perspective of subject matter…They skimmed the surface of the ocean of life simply and beautifully, like stones skipping across still waters. I didn't want my writing to skim along any more. (xx)

Self-Education and Search for Vocation

While in the next few installments of the series Chetan arrives into his authentic modernist identity as an interpreter of the world for his generation of readers by loading every rift of his experience with ore,[2] *Falling Walls* showcases Chetan's maturation within what Moretti calls modernity's "bewitching and risky process full of 'great expectations' and 'lost illusions'" (5). The final act of the unfolding drama of *Bildung* occurs under the exploitative patronage of the street-smart and smooth-talking Kaviraj, a self-styled author, publisher, sexologist, and champion of young writers, about whom Chetan discovers too late that "the art of doing someone a favour...and getting something in return...was child's play for him" (Ashk 333). After the debacle of the novel, impoverished but still enthusiastic Chetan seeks out Kaviraj as his only recourse for fulfilling his literary ambitions of getting published. Kaviraj's patronage of Chetan was based entirely on a canny understanding of the former's social and psychological vulnerabilities and using that knowledge to advantage himself. Filled with hopes, Chetan relocates from Changar *mohalla* to Ruldu Bhatta in Shimla, but soon finds out that Kaviraj had relegated him to the status of a servant to get Chetan to complete a book project for him. This betrayal crushes Chetan's spirit, leading him to a full realization of the deterministic forces of class exclusion and exploitation he had hitherto escaped using the optimism and energy of his imagination. In Shimla, Chetan "found that the world around him contained two classes—one was the oppressors, the exploiters, and the other was the oppressed, the exploited" (301). Added to this growing awareness, while working for Kaviraj's book, Chetan arrives at a new understanding of the failed parenting of his lower-class community where the unregulated sexual drives of the older generation, such as Shadiram, "[hollowed] out the nation's future generations like weevils" (327). Frustrated by the shortcomings of his community, Chetan "wishe[s] he could somehow get the authority to raze the entire mohalla to the ground," but as a sign of maturation, connects his inner quest for self-fulfillment with the larger fate of the nation in the realization that "the ancient worn-out walls of the entire country would have to be pulled down, and a new country, a new society, a new generation would have to arise" (331).

As a multidimensional motif, falling walls connects Chetan's personal story of optimism and disenchantment and his quest for authority with the larger struggle for freedom of the nation. Rather than privileging a narrowly aesthetic inner life for its *Bildungsheld*, the novel captures the totality of Chetan's experiences that unfold in a multiplicity of milieus and multilayered personas, at once hopeful, sentimental, manipulative, humorous, questioning, subservient, penitent, satirical, and grotesque. The walls he must break down represent the putative "morbid symptoms" of an "interregnum society" on the cusp of transformation; Chetan's Bildungsroman parallels the coming-of-age narrative of the nation itself as it sheds the yoke of colonial rule and its pre-colonial past and struggles for a new identity. The multilayered image of falling walls at the end of the novel prepares the reader for the next chapter in the *Bildungsheld*'s quest for the gestalt of freedom in a nation about to "[plunge] into modernity without a culture of modernity":

> As he lay there staring into the dark void with sleepless eyes, Chetan felt that these walls stood not just between himself and his wife, not just between Neela and Trilok, but that countless similar walls stood between all women and men, classes and castes in this subjugated nation…there was no end to such walls. In that silence cloaked in darkness, Chetan heard the mute sobs of countless souls trapped in the walls with no way out. Where were the foundations for these walls? When would they fall? No matter how hard he thought about it, Chetan could come up with no solution. (486)

Notes

1. Rockwell tells a similar story of chance encounter between Ashk and Proust's work where a fellow writer, Rajinder Bedi, informs Ashk about Proust's "extremely long novel all about his feelings and experiences." Apparently, that impresses Ashk, who resolves to "write a novel just as long" (121).
2. Peter Gaeffke says that "each new development of the series is influenced by the shifts and changes in the literary aesthetics of the 50's, 60's and 70's." He usefully summarizes the progression of the series as follows: "I. Concern with the social and individual barriers which separate the hero from those close to him (Girti Divare); II. Expansion of this concern to include the whole community (Sahar Mein Ghumta Aina); III. Deep interest in the basic experiences of the individual, e.g., death, insanity, and basic values (Ek Nanhi Kindil); [and] IV. Art and love in their very individual and highly differentiated aspects (Badho na nav is thav)" (61).

Works Cited

Ashk, Upendranath. *Falling Walls*. Translated by Daisy Rockwell, Penguin, 2015 (1947).

Bakhtin, M.M. *Speech Genres and Other Late Essays*. Translated by Vern W. McGee, University of Texas Press, 1986.

Boes, Tobias. *Formative Fictions: Nationalism, Cosmopolitanism, and the Bildungsroman*. Cornell University Press, 2012.

Boes, Tobias. "Modernist Studies and the Bildungsroman: A Historical Survey of Critical Trends." *Literature Compass*, vol. 3, no. 2, 2006, pp. 230–43.

Castle, Gregory. "The Modernist Bildungsroman." Graham, 143–73.

Castle, Gregory. *Reading the Modernist Bildungsroman*. University Press of Florida, 2006.

Gaeffke, Peter. *Hindi Literature in the Twentieth Century*. Harrassowitz, 1978.

Golban, Petru. *A History of the Bildungsroman: From Ancient Beginnings to Romanticism*. Cambridge Scholars Publishing, 2018.

Graham, Sarah, editor. *A History of the Bildungsroman*. Cambridge University Press, 2019.

Gupta, Charu. "Anxious Hindu Masculinities in Colonial North India: Shuddhi and Sanghatan Movements." *Cross Currents*, vol. 61, no. 4, Dec. 2011, pp. 441–54.

Hoagland, Erika. "The Postcolonial Bildungsroman." Graham, 217–38.

Moretti, Franco. *The Way of the World: The Bildungsroman in European Culture*. Translated by Albert Sbragia, Verso, 1987.

Rockwell, Daisy. Preface. Ashk, x–xvii.

Rockwell, Daisy. *Upendranath Ashk: A Critical Biography*. Katha, 2004.

Woolf, Virginia. "Modern Fiction." *The Essays of Virginia Woolf*. Vol. 4: 1925–1928, edited by Andrew McNeille, The Hogarth Press, 1984, 157–65.

8

RECOVERING THOSE WHO "TROD"
Reclaiming the Bildungsroman in Shūsaku Endō's *Silence*

Maria Su Wang and Bethany Williamson

The very capaciousness of "Bildungsroman" alludes to an instability at the heart of the genre itself, as well as the criticism that seeks to understand it. A typical Bildungsroman follows an individual's absorption, or accommodation, into a broader social sphere; accordingly, critics read the genre as tracking the process by which a youthful or "immature" individual learns to acculturate into a changing social order.[1] Tellingly, however, critics often define the Bildungsroman in terms of individual character *development* while also contesting its nature and end. For instance, in their introduction to a recent special issue of *Textual Practice*, John Frow, Melissa Hardie, and Vanessa Smith explicitly raise this problem of development as indicative of the genre, asking, "Given the contours of the Bildungsroman in its early form and its reliance on a model of progressive maturation, insight, and social adjustment, how might *ways of being in the world sidelined by this model* institute, instead, counter or contrary Bildungsromane?" (1905, emphasis added). What Frow, Hardie, and Smith acknowledge is that, despite the many attempts to expand or delimit the genre, the category of Bildungsroman still remains heuristically valuable as a "structure"

(1906) by which to examine the internal growth—or lack thereof—of a character who struggles to adapt the self to the space of others.

The problem of adapting the self becomes even more fraught and complicated in colonial, postcolonial, and transcultural contexts, as this book explores. Indeed, as Simon Hay notes, the "postcolonial Bildungsroman" interrogates an already troubled generic category, layering the contradictions of the postcolonial subject on top of what Moretti has identified as the contradictions of "modern socialization" (318). Many twentieth-century iterations of the Bildungsroman feature marginalized individuals from formerly colonized spaces who resist the overwhelming residual force of the colonizing nation; in the process, these individuals reclaim their voices in more or less successful ways. Jed Esty highlights the failures and challenges of such attempts, tracing how globalization works as a destabilizing force for the nation-state and its citizen protagonists (4). By contrast, Erika Hoagland sees the postcolonial Bildungsroman as offering space for "subversion and inversion": the narrative form, as she describes it, can function as "a political act of counter-colonisation, a reimagining and reinvention, a process of becoming through the act of unmaking its predecessor and unmasking the Bildungsroman's ideological flaws" (225).

Yet even as Hoagland and others have highlighted the transformative "unmaking" and "unmasking" of the original form, they continue to reinforce a key building block of the genre—namely, the allegorical link between *individual* and *national* development.[2] We aim to rethink this focus on nation and individual (and the relationship between them) by considering a piece of fiction that engages in a similar work of generic and ideological dismantling while existing outside the explicit temporal-political frame of the postcolonial. We argue that the discourses of "postcolonial" and "Bildungsroman," through their dual emphasis on resistance and reclamation, open up new ways of understanding texts that index the ideologies of empire. To fully understand the value of these discourses-as-genre, we must account for how individual stories of formation are deeply intertwined across national boundaries, cultural values, and religious commitments. Toward this end, we consider a novel that showcases transimperial[3] encounters between Western European and East Asian characters and fruitfully conceptualizes a literary temporality before the advent of the European Bildungsroman.

Imperial Imagination and Cultural Adaptation in Shūsaku Endō's *Silence*
Shūsaku Endō's 1966 historical novel, *Silence*, which explores religious persecution in Edo-era Japan, exemplifies this work of the Bildungsroman by compelling the reader to read through and beyond the typical trajectory of an individual protagonist so as to recognize how individual narratives of growth conflict with and depend on each other. Written in a postcolonial moment by a Japanese Catholic writer who looks at the workings of empire from a spatio-temporal distance, *Silence* features a European protagonist in never-colonized Japan. It shows the difficulty of *spiritual* formation (rather than the traditional physical and social coming of age) when emissaries from multiple would-be empires clash with each other. This clash—and possible development for *multiple* characters simultaneously—disrupts the classic Bildungsroman emphasis on individual formation and opens up new ways of seeing subjectivity emerge in community, beyond the bounds of nation-centric individualism.

In a crucial moment of the novel, Endō's most unlikeable character voices a provocative critique, foreshadowing the protagonist's spectacular failure of Christian loyalty. Kichijiro, this unlikeable Japanese apostate, has repeatedly trampled on the *fumie*, a wooden image of Christ (or Mary) used by the authorities to test Christian loyalty, in order to save himself from persecution. He defends his duplicitous behaviour and continued apostasy with these words: "One who has trod on the sacred image has his say too" (Endō 122). Kichijiro's plea is not only for himself—a clamouring for his individual voice to be heard—but also for the value of recovering the many voices of those who have likewise "trod on the sacred image," ostensibly betraying Christ and renouncing their Christian identity. In fact, Kichijiro's insistence that this perspective needs to be acknowledged reflects one of *Silence*'s dominant themes: the necessity of resisting the Catholic Church's glorification of martyrs and offering instead a counter-history that recovers the psyches of spiritually weak Christians who "failed." Nowhere is this theme more apparent than in the trajectory of the novel's protagonist, Sebastian Rodrigues, a Portuguese priest who enters Japan with idealistic hopes of missionary fruit only to succumb to trampling on the *fumie* himself. As readers come to learn, Rodrigues's social order—and, thus, his behaviour within it—is shaped by Kichijiro's parallel act of trampling. In this regard, the profound achievement of *Silence* is to challenge the reader's assumption that the Western priest's perspective is indeed the only orienting point for the novel, even as Endō crafts his narration with Rodrigues as its primary focalizer.

If we focus only on Rodrigues's plotline, as many of Endō's readers do, it would seem as if the novel traces his spiritual *Bildung* from a place of perceived cultural and spiritual strength to that of apparent weakness, resulting in the dissolution of his Western identity and eventual absorption into the social order of seventeenth-century Japan. Yet by including, even marginally, these other voices—voices of those who *also* trample on the *fumie*—the narration compels us to rethink the Bildungsroman's individualist emphasis and recognize the complexities of assigning individual development when the political, economic, and cultural affiliations and motivations of others are at work. *Silence* ultimately forces readers to confront the question of *scale*—whose perspective, which layer, at which register—when categorizing Bildungsromane. By focusing on this novel, our chapter intervenes not only in the question of "counter or contrary Bildungsroman" (Frow et al. 1905), but also considers how a transimperial text like *Silence* might broaden the purview of the postcolonial Bildungsroman by foregrounding voices beyond that of the protagonist. *Silence* does so, specifically, by including the failed and fractured—yet somehow redemptive—narratives of *other* voices marginalized in stories of empire.

In what follows, we briefly survey how scholars of *Silence* have discussed the novel's East/West encounters in relation to its theological themes. We then complicate the critical focus on Rodrigues's character by considering how the novel invites us to triangulate his perspective with those of two other discursively marginalized characters who have also trampled on the *fumie*: the Japanese apostate

Kichijiro, who tramples explicitly, and the Dutch clerk Jonassen, who does so by implication. By including analyses of the latter two characters, our chapter shows how the novel's inclusion of and attention to these two other cultural voices complicates the Bildungsroman pattern of individual absorption within a social order.

Postcolonial Approaches to Endō's *Silence*

Critics of *Silence* have often focused on Endō's treatment of Rodrigues's cross-cultural accommodation and adaptation as his own Portuguese Catholicism bumps against the hostile skepticism of his Japanese captors. Christopher B. Wachal summarizes this critical conversation in his contention that "we must read Rodrigues's apostasy in light of Endō's global concerns" (94). Building on the work of Van C. Gessel and others, John Netland likewise argues that Endō moves beyond the "simple binarisms" that often inform an Orientalist "oppositional paradigm of East versus West" (179). As Netland puts it, Rodrigues embodies a Christ-like "emptying of cultural particularity" (181), thereby showcasing Endō's nuanced appreciation for "the complexity of cultural hybridity" in light of "an eternal, multicultural kingdom of God" (193).[4] Netland's argument underscores the critical focus on Endō's Rodrigues—and specifically the religious implications of Rodrigues's act of trampling on the *fumie*—as the centre of meaning in the novel.

Both Wachal and Netland emphasize Rodrigues's transformation-through-trampling in order to suggest that Endō's readers, like his protagonist, also have the chance to reject national "structures of power" that shape identity (Wachal 104). Matthew Potts, however, reads Rodrigues's example more skeptically, arguing that "imperialism remains an essential interpretive category" insofar as "empire, race, and religion" work together to shape Rodrigues's understanding of himself and Japan (Potts 192n27). Unlike Netland and Wachal, who see in Endō's work a radical capacity to imagine reconciliation of cultural difference, Potts suggests that "the narrative instability of Christian identity [in *Silence*] leaves it uniquely available not only to relentless redescription as ethnicity but also to ruthless reinscription as empire" (185). Departing from critics who focus on Rodrigues's inner turmoil of belief, Potts argues that "what he is being forced to abandon" in the moment of apostasy is not "his moral integrity or his religious faith" but rather "his whiteness" (199) and its accompanying "privilege" (200). In this regard, Potts offers a helpful corrective to critics who focus exclusively on Rodrigues's apostasy as an act of religious subjectivity and what Netland calls a cultural "emptying" (181).

However, in characterizing Rodrigues's failure as development, Potts follows other critics in neglecting Endō's attention to other *narrative* perspectives on cultural-religious weakness. For instance, Potts's focus on Rodrigues's identity as one of "whiteness" does not fully account for the anxiety white Europeans experienced due to their recognizably supplicant position vis-à-vis Far East Asian economies. Neither does it acknowledge the diversity of European experience, as whiteness is embodied not only by Rodrigues but also by Dutch merchants who appear at the end of Endō's novel. As we will show, decentring Rodrigues's perspective reveals how Rodrigues's story is shaped and destabilized by the stories of others—including that of Kichijiro (who shares Rodrigues's Christian identity but not his European heritage) but also that of a Dutchman (who shares Rodrigues's white identity but not his religious conviction). All three characters struggle to understand their complicity in broader networks of economic and cultural power. And in this sense the clashes and connections between their individual stories illustrate the limits of the Bildungsroman model to account for the intersection of *multiple* emerging national identities.

Indeed, rather than a straightforward critique of "whiteness," Endō's novel weaves together the threads of Rodrigues's Bildungsroman with the implied perspectives of other flawed individuals, both Japanese *and* European, thereby revealing how Rodrigues cannot complete the cycle of his Bildungsroman until he exchanges his false sense of superiority for an actual awareness of his cultural, spiritual, and political weakness. While Rodrigues's own account of Japan is marked by a distinctly Eurocentric *attitude*, the novel as a whole provides ample evidence that seventeenth-century Europe's *practice* of empire was not monolithic. Indeed, the East/West power dynamic Rodrigues embodies is neither neatly Orientalist nor strictly "postcolonial." Not only did Rodrigues's native Portugal never colonize Japan but also, despite rhetorical posturing by ambitious Western nations, the seventeenth-century global power balance was by no means in favour of the West.[5] And even as he views the Japanese peasants to whom he ministers through a hierarchical framework that privileges clear categories of "strong" over "weak" and "saint" over "sinner," Rodrigues exhibits signs of weakness that are inextricably connected to his Western identity (Endō 82). Rodrigues's character does not clearly transform from strength to weakness through an act of self-aware relinquishing, as Netland and others suggest. Rather, he is faced, again and again, with the stark *limits* of his spiritual and cultural imagination as he struggles to embody a spiritual sanctification wholly divested of national-cultural power.

Rodrigues's Perspective: Political Precarity and Spiritual Strength
What is of interest to us in Endō's novel is how the imaginative limits of each character clash with and inform each other, thereby complicating the individual- and nation-centric notions of development associated with the classic Bildungsroman. Before Rodrigues even reaches Japan, the novel's initial setting has troubled his—and readers'—understanding of how his Portuguese and priestly identities intertwine. Such a setting not only shows readers Rodrigues's own competing motivations but also the myriad perspectives at work in this space—perspectives that challenge binary distinctions between white and not-white, Christian and not-Christian, European and Japanese. By showcasing the differences *and* similarities between Rodrigues's perspective and those of others who betray the God they claim to love, Endō invites readers to recognize the dangerous limits of Rodrigues's Westernized spiritual imagination.

The novel's setting underscores both the origins of and threats to that imagination. Endō situates his protagonist in the historical wake of Japan's 1614 "expulsion of all [Christian] missionaries" (2). Since "the Church at Rome" is fully aware "of the straitened circumstances in which the Japanese mission was situated" (1), Rodrigues enters Japan knowing that he is unwelcome and preparing for "the possibility of a glorious martyrdom" (6). Indeed, with the prospect of such "glory" set before him, Rodrigues interprets his precarious position—as an outlawed European missionary in closed Japan—as one of spiritual importance. "Born into the world to render service" to others (18), he and his colleague, Garrpe, perceive themselves to be "the last stepping-stones of the Gospel" (34). Once Garrpe is martyred, Rodrigues sees himself as a "single candle burning in the [dark of the] catacombs" (64).

Even as Rodrigues frames his political weakness in terms of spiritual significance, he, like many of Endō's modern critics, glosses over another form of weakness—namely, the economic anxieties that inflect and undermine his missionary work. According to "the way of thinking that prevailed" in "the Europe of that time," the apostasy of a notable priest is "not simply the failure of one individual but a humiliating defeat for the faith itself and for the whole of Europe" (Endō 6). In this regard, Rodrigues seems to enact the very allegorical link between individual and national destinies that characterizes the classic Bildungsroman: he is the white, European protagonist finding his way and bolstering his identity in a hostile world. Rodrigues bears the weight of the Church's expectations, whose stakes, he comes to find, are felt in Protestant and Catholic Europe alike. His spiritual quest to hear Christ speak—a quest that, fuelled by a personal conviction of divine presence, justifies his missional endeavours in Japan—is a motivation muddied by the fact that he functions as an emissary of one European nation among several that were vying for trade privileges "at the periphery of the world" (6).

Endō offers ample evidence that Rodrigues's experience, and the limited imaginative framework by which he makes sense of it, is shaped by these broader intra-European trade rivalries. What strikes Rodrigues, as he and his fellow travellers preview a map of their upcoming voyage to Japan, is the thrill of exploration—he sees, in his imagination, the "spectacle of an Orient which was literally the end of the earth and of a Japan which was its uttermost limit" (6). Upon arriving in Goa, he and his companions learn that "Japan had cut all trade relations and intercourse with their country" (9). From Macao, Rodrigues writes a letter explaining the status of Portugal's "commercial relationship" with Japan and noting that the risk to Portuguese "trading ships" is heightened by attacks from English and Dutch rivals (11–12). Thus, even before he arrives on his mission field of Japan—the new social order of his Bildungsroman—his religious identity as a priest begins to take a subordinate role to Europe's political-commercial priorities, as Rodrigues moves through a transimperial network.

Though he relates the facts of his travels with objective detachment—insisting that his motivation is purely "the conversion of Japan and the glory of God" (Endō 13)—Rodrigues unwittingly underscores links between the respective work of Europe's merchants and missionaries, insofar as the latter are dependent upon the former's success. In his letter from Macao, Rodrigues exhibits keen awareness of this dependence, as he notes how shifts in the silk trade have complicated global relations. "Ironically enough," he writes, "as a result of the Japanese government's forbidding ships of its own country to go to foreign lands, the monopoly of the silk trade in the whole Far East has now fallen into the hands of the Portuguese merchants in Macao" (14). As he goes on to explain "the total income of this import" (14), he juxtaposes an emphasis on Macao's value to European coffers with more personal observations of its physical misery and the poverty of its Chinese residents who never see the profits of the silk trade. Looking around at the "deserted," "dirty streets" (15) of "this crumbling town in the Far East" (18), he questions but ultimately reaffirms his own priestly purpose in leaving the comforts of home.

Rodrigues's imaginative limits and as-yet-naive perspective are underscored in his later interrogation with Inoue, the notoriously brutal "Lord of Chikugo" (Endō 129). With disarming calm, Inoue presents his perspective on Rodrigues's work through a trenchant metaphor of Christian proselytization as the unwelcome yet "persistent love of an ugly woman" (131). As Inoue describes how "Spain, Portugal, Holland, England and such-like women keep whispering jealous tales of slander into the ear of the man called Japan," Rodrigues "[begins] to realize what Inoue [is] getting at" (130). He reflects on the Church's complicity with colonial ambition, considering "how often he had heard at Goa and Macao how the Protestant countries like England and Holland, and the Catholic countries like Spain and Portugal had come to Japan and, jealous of one another's progress, had spoken calumnies about one another to the Japanese" (130). As he considers how "the missionaries, too, out of rivalry had at one time strictly forbidden their Japanese converts to consort with the English and the Dutch," he begins to acknowledge how the truth of Christianity and the Church's representation of that truth have been entangled with nationalist histories and power structures (130).

Through Rodrigues's perspective, *Silence* depicts the formation of imperial thinking in spaces outside the formal reach of Europe's expanding empires. At the same time, by triangulating two discursively marginalized perspectives with that of Rodrigues, the novel invites the reader to decentre the European protagonist, with his limited imagination and inability to appreciate others' full interiority. Our chapter turns to these perspectives next. The first is that of Kichijiro, one of the Japanese Christians to whom Rodrigues feels called to minister; the second is that of Jonassen, a Dutch clerk who boasts of his access to Japanese trade after the Portuguese are expelled. Both of these voices represent those who, with different motivations and results, have also "trod on the sacred image." Both of these perspectives also shape Rodrigues's own, revealing how this individual's growth and development—that is, his Bildungsroman trajectory—is inextricably shaped and defined by the complex stories of others who occupy his social order. By including these voices, however peripherally, Endō invites us to read against the individualist grain of the story as we expect it to be told.

Kichijiro's Perspective: "The Weak Shoot"

Kichijiro, the Japanese apostate who betrays Rodrigues, emerges as a key figure by the end of the novel. In fact, some critics even argue he serves as a "relational protagonist" alongside Rodrigues, and that this multiplicity is one of Endō's most substantive contributions to modern Japanese literature (Doak 12).[6] Endō's choice to include Kichijiro's vantage, as the "one who has trod on the sacred image," reflects the importance of accounting for *more* perspectives, beyond that of the protagonist, on spiritual failure. Kichijiro's plea is not simply one for inclusion but also for sympathetic expansion. Yet this sympathy is precisely what Rodrigues is unable to offer: he cannot imagine and thus cannot see the full interiority of Kichijiro, and, by extension, Japanese Christians as a whole. Rodrigues thinks his repugnance for Kichijiro is simply because of the latter's spiritual weakness. However, if we have been reading attentively alongside and *through* Rodrigues's perceptions since the beginning of the novel, especially during his epistolary descriptions, we realize it is not only Kichijiro's weakness as a Christian that repels Rodrigues. In fact, Rodrigues is driven by an overall aversion to and inability to appreciate the full humanity of the Japanese Christians. Because the novel remains centred on Rodrigues's vision, we as readers must read *through* his biases and limited imagination in order to access the voices of Kichijiro and his fellow Japanese Christians.

One way the novel signals Rodrigues's aversion to the Japanese Christian peasants is through the images he uses to describe his first and lasting impressions of them. Throughout the early chapters of *Silence*, Rodrigues consistently refers to the peasants he encounters as animals or beast-like. In chapter three, when reflecting on the lives of the Japanese Christian peasants, he remarks, "I tell you the truth— for a long, long time these farmers have worked like horses and cattle; and like horses and cattle they have died" (Endō 31). In the same chapter, when baptizing an infant for the first time, Rodrigues refers to the baby as "it": "this was already a peasant face that would…grow up like its parents and grandparents to eke out a miserable existence face to face with the black sea in this cramped and desolate land; it, too, would live like a beast, and like a beast it would die" (38). When peasants from another village come to visit him and his companion Garrpe, he describes them as "two men dressed in rags as though they were beggars crouched there like dogs" (39). While these observations are framed as initial impressions, they stubbornly and disturbingly persist in shaping Rodrigues's vision, not only in the epistolary chapters, which contain Rodrigues's first-person narration, but also in later chapters that switch to third-person narration. Even after Rodrigues is captured by the Japanese authorities in chapter five, he continues to refer to the Japanese peasants as animals, stating that "children and adults alike, dressed in rags, had kept staring at him with glimmering eyes like animals" (84). He later analogizes them to "a bunch of ignorant beasts [who are] quite unaware of the fate that awaited them" (86).

These observations not only reveal the limits of Rodrigues's sympathetic imagination but also explain for readers how he eventually perceives the apostasy of the Japanese Christians. At this point, in chapter five, the novel has switched to third-person narration but is still focalized through Rodrigues. His earlier observation—that the Japanese peasants seem "like a bunch of ignorant beasts" as they await their fate in captivity—demonstrates how he can only think of their behaviour in terms of instinct. While he can observe and judge them, he can neither fully interact with them as fellow humans nor presume their interiority as people with fears, longings, or shame like himself. In chapter five, after he receives the gift of a small cucumber from Monica, a Japanese peasant who is imprisoned like himself, we can sense Rodrigues's repulsion in his response: "When he bit into it, his mouth was filled with its green stench" (Endō 86). Rather than noting the woman's kindness, he only marks the "stench" of her gift. Later, while reflecting on Monica's Christian name, he observes, "Her answer was somewhat bashful, as though her Christian name was the only ornament she possessed in the whole world. What missionary had given the name of Augustine's mother to this woman whose body was reeking with the stench of fish?" (86–87). Although Rodrigues does not acknowledge his judgment directly, his reflections show how he finds the Christian name of "Monica" incongruous with the Japanese woman's body. Rather than focusing on her generosity or her humanity, he flinches from her smell and class. Rather than recognize their shared Christian faith, he focuses on their cultural difference. These responses make sense when we consider how the novel has revealed Rodrigues's preconceptions of both Japanese and Christian identities at the beginning of the novel. Endō's readers must work to see *beyond* Rodrigues's limited perspective in order to notice the glimmers of humanity the *novel* suggests for the Japanese characters—glimmers that Rodrigues remains unable to recognize.

Nowhere is Rodrigues's partial, incomplete perspective more apparent than in the novel's rendering of his encounters and interactions with Kichijiro. From their first meeting, Rodrigues describes the Japanese man as "reeling from excess of alcohol" with a "crafty look on his face" (Endō 15). Rodrigues continues to cast Kichijiro as a drunkard and coward, noting "those Japanese eyes, drunken and dirty yellow, [which] flashed craftily" (16) and judging him as a "cunning fellow" whose cunning "comes from weakness of character" (18). Yet even as Rodrigues quickly dismisses Kichijiro's "cowardice" and "servile grin" (19), the novel suggests other ways to understand this character. We find out "he was a fisherman from the district of Hizen near Nagasaki" and "had been adrift on the sea and had been picked up by a Portuguese ship" (15). We also discover how he had witnessed Christian persecution in his village: "the spectacle of twenty-four Christians being subject to the water punishment by the local daimyo" (15). Even as the novel provides these hints of trauma and "an open wound" (16), Rodrigues remains committed to his negative impression, dismissing Kichijiro's cowardly behaviour as "far from anything you could call Christian patience" (19). It is because of Kichijiro's expressed fear in the face of potential violence and devastation that Rodrigues begins to doubt both his Japanese and Christian identity: "Was it possible," he asks, "that he was of our faith—this wretch who all through the journey not only failed to help but was even a positive nuisance. No. It was impossible. Faith could not turn a man into such a coward" (23–24). Underlying these remarks is a presumption of Christian faith and identity that leaves no space for human weakness or failing. For Rodrigues, having faith means only being noble, heroic, and courageous in any circumstance.[7]

For Rodrigues, the presumption of heroism and self-sacrificing nobility as the hallmark of Christian witness is directly opposed to the state of beastliness he observes in the Japanese Christians he meets. Rodrigues consistently contrasts the noble work he and Garrpe share with the actions of Kichijiro, whom he characterizes repeatedly as behaving "like a whipped dog" (Endō 82). In chapter four, after he and Garrpe decide to flee separately, Rodrigues reflects, "It was not to hide in the mountains like fieldmice, to receive a lump of food from destitute peasants and to be confined in a charcoal hut without being able even to meet the Christians [that they had come]. What had happened to our glorious dream?" (64). Similarly, while starving and on the run from the Japanese authorities, he eagerly devours his food before having a moment of self-reflective shame: "I'm just like a dog, he reflected as he licked his fingers…And here he was, forgetting even to pray, and pouncing upon his food for dogs" (98–99). Again, in Rodrigues's mind, piety must always supersede any of the baser instincts. Yet in the last conversation Rodrigues has with Kichijiro before he is apprehended by the Japanese authorities, it becomes clear to readers how Rodrigues's thinking actually parallels that of Kichijiro. The passage begins with Kichijiro's words and then continues with Rodrigues's reflections:

> "Mokichi was strong—like a strong shoot. But a weak shoot like me will never grow no matter what you do." He seemed to feel that I had dealt him a severe rebuke, because with a look like a whipped dog he glanced backwards. Yet I had not said these words with the intention of rebuking him; I was only giving expression to a sad reflection that was rising in my mind. Kichijiro was right in saying that all men are not saints and heroes. How many of our Christians, if only they had been born in another age from this persecution would never have been confronted with the problem of apostasy or martyrdom but would have lived blessed lives of faith until the very hour of death…
>
> Men are born in two categories: the strong and the weak, the saints and the commonplace, the heroes and those who respect them. In time of persecution the strong are burnt in the flames and drowned in the sea; but the weak, like Kichijiro, lead a vagabond life in the mountains. As for you (I now spoke to myself) which category do you belong to? Were it not for the consciousness of your priesthood and your pride, perhaps you like Kichijiro would trample on the *fumie*. (81–82)

In this moment, not only does Rodrigues agree with Kichijiro's distinction between being a "strong" versus a "weak shoot" (82), but he also acknowledges explicitly how he, like Kichijiro, might trample on the *fumie* were it not for his "priesthood and [his] pride." In other words, Rodrigues agrees with the fixed categorization of people, regardless of context and circumstances—one is either "strong" or "weak," heroic or subservient, a "saint" or "commonplace." This kind of essentialist world view leaves no space for fluidity, growth, or transformation, and in many ways it parallels his designation of the Japanese Christians as animals, or fixed, bestial creatures simply overcome by instinct. Rodrigues cannot help but see Kichijiro's motivations for apostasy as rooted in the weakness of simple fear, "like a whipped dog," rather than imagine other possible motives—such as shame, embarrassment, and even a tension between cultural rootedness and personal belief—that might compel him to make this choice, again and again. For Rodrigues, cowardice and fear are tied to a state of almost subhuman beastliness, while the implied opposite is a fearless nobility and courage that marks ideal Christian humanity. Thus, later in chapter five, when he notices Kichijiro following him even after he has been captured, Rodrigues remains mystified. As the narrator puts it, "It was Kichijiro...Seeing that the priest had noticed him, he got all excited and tried to hide in the shelter of a tree. The priest was perplexed. Why did this fellow who betrayed him come following after him in this way?" (105). Rodrigues is still unable to imagine a more complex spiritual interiority for Kichijiro—a state, for instance, in which Kichijiro may apostatize out of fear and cowardice and still retain faith.

Even as Rodrigues's gaze remains limited, Endō's novel continues to give readers glimpses of Kijichiro's potentially more complex spiritual interiority. For instance, in chapter six, Kichijiro himself reveals the complicated motivations behind his stepping on the *fumie*:

> "Won't you listen to me, father! I've kept deceiving you. Since you rebuked me I began to hate you and all Christians. Yes, it is true that I trod on the holy image. Mokichi and Ichizo were strong. I can't be strong like them."
>
> The guards, unable to bear it any longer, came out with sticks; and Kichijiro fled away, screaming as he ran.
>
> "But I have my cause to plead! *One who has trod on the sacred image has his say too.* Do you think I trampled on it willingly? My feet ached with the pain. God asks me to imitate the strong, even though he made me weak. Isn't this unreasonable?" (121-22, emphasis added)

With these words, Kichijiro admits his motivations for betraying Rodrigues to the Japanese authorities: he was driven by hatred and revenge towards them, and even self-hatred and resentment towards God. He notes his unwillingness to trample, as well as the emotional anguish of such an action, where his "feet ached with the pain." In his own words he reveals complex, even confused, motives. Yet Rodrigues can only hear and perceive his voice "like the whining of a dog" (121). While Rodrigues treats him like an animal who behaves out of instinct (and thus appropriately belonging to the category of the "weak"), Kichijiro himself insists on his own full interiority and humanity. He comes back to plead his case before the priest and to us as readers.

Jonassen's Perspective: Self-Interest and Abjection

Neither Rodrigues nor Kichijiro is the last of Endō's characters to "have their say." The ending of the novel comes full circle, resituating Rodrigues's apparent spiritual epiphany in impersonal economic terms, as the Appendix details "expenses of [the apostate's] funeral" (Endō 212). It is also here—amid the final chapters' deliberate ambiguity, where readers are left without the clarity of Rodrigues's own perspective—that Endō offers one more perspective on whether the act of trampling the *fumie* is one of strength or weakness, Christian love or unrighteous self-interest, failure or completion of a spiritual Bildungsroman. This perspective comes in the voice of another unlikely character—Jonassen, a Dutch clerk—whose story intersects with those of Rodrigues and Kichijiro.

In the preceding chapter ten, entitled "Extracts from the Diary of Jonassen, a clerk at the Dutch firm, Dejima, Nagasaki," the Dutchman inserts into his narrative of port activities various observations about the situation for Christians in Nagasaki and Rodrigues's role in upholding the Japanese government's persecution of Christians. His detailed descriptions are jarring in their juxtaposition of quotidian trade and acts of violence. In his entry for July 9, for instance, Jonassen offers a second-hand account of Christian "parents [who] had been executed the other day by being hung up by the feet"; in the next sentence, one of several that detail imported commodities and their values, he writes that "toward evening a Chinese junk made port.

Her cargo was sugar, porcelain, and a small quantity of silk textile" (Endō 191). In August, he returns to this same Japanese family's story, describing how a "Chinese junk made port" with a "cargo" of "gossamer, figured satin, crepe-de-chine and other fabrics, the estimated value of which was eighty *kan*"; three days later, he describes how "the two sons of the executed parents I mentioned elsewhere... were beheaded" (193). Jonassen's disturbing juxtaposition of detail shows how the lives of Japanese Christians and the witness of the European missionaries are inextricably linked to the profit margins of the Dutch, who were granted trade privileges denied to the Portuguese by Japanese authorities.

Jonassen's imagination is sharply limited by his obsession with such profit, much like Rodrigues's perspective is limited by his own cultural identity. For Jonassen, even the humanity of a fellow European like Rodrigues is subservient to economic concerns. Jonassen is particularly concerned by reports of illegible Christianity among his countrymen, after Rodrigues's former mentor, Father Ferreira (now notorious for his own apostasy) "testified in Edo to the Supreme Authorities that there are many Roman Catholics among the Dutch and in Holland" (Endō 192). When Jonassen hears, secondhand, that "the apostate was writing various things about the Dutch and the Portuguese," he documents his honest reaction: "I almost wish death on that rascal who ignores God; our Firm will only get into trouble because of him. However God will protect us" (196). Subsequently, he becomes defensive, claiming that "there had never been a single Christian...who spoke Dutch, while I could name at once dozens of Christians who spoke Portuguese" (196). Tellingly, in his disavowal of any such sincere Protestant practice as Inoue associates with Holland, Jonassen hints at his complicity in these acts of violence. While he does not confess to physically trampling on the *fumie*, his betrayal of the Christian faith is just as egregious and self-interested as that of Rodrigues. Through his concluding confessions, Jonassen joins the ranks of those who "have their say" in defending such betrayal—and whose limited perspectives inflect and complicate Rodrigues's own.

Jonassen's persistent use of the passive voice—to describe, for instance, how "it is said that" the "apostate Portuguese" priests "were present at the inquisition" of an accused Japanese Christian (Endō 190)—underscores his effort to maintain objectivity in the face of horrors in which he finds himself complicit. His lapse in self-control—seen when he "wish[es] death" on Rodrigues (196)—reveals a personal anxiety that he, too, covers over with perfunctory, self-interested piety ("God will protect us"). Meanwhile, when he encounters Christian contraband written in *Dutch*, he "decide[s] to keep silent" despite knowing what such objects mean (194). His passivity notably emerges in his diary entry for January 4, where he states that "the *fumie* exercise is performed by the people" (197). He goes on to describe his observations of this "exercise" in some ethnographic detail but with clear distance from any personal stake. What he leaves out altogether is any explanation of how ostensibly Protestant Dutchmen managed to convince the Japanese authorities they do not practise their Christian beliefs and, thus, cannot be considered a threat. In other words, Jonassen leaves out of his account the fact that the Dutch successfully supplanted the Portuguese in Japan because they were willing to perform—in an active and ongoing way—their disavowal of Christian practice. By strategically leaving out this information, Jonassen elides anxious recognition of his complicity with others' persecution, as well as the possibility that he himself participates in the same act of trampling he observes others perform.

Such a possibility aligns with Engelbert Kaempfer's first-hand description, in his *History of Japan*, of Dutch East India Company practices in Edo-era Japan.[8] Kaempfer emphasizes a troubling connection between Christian principles and the pursuit of national profit, explaining how Christianity was commercialized so thoroughly that Japan's "new converted Christians" uneasily perceived "that their Spiritual Fathers aim'd not only at the salvation of their souls, but had an eye also to their money and lands" (158). Kaempfer shows how Portugal's Dutch successors, keenly aware of Japanese antipathy towards Christianity, showed themselves willing to sacrifice every Christian ideal for the sake of national profit. He observes that "so great was the covetousness of the Dutch, and so great the alluring power of the Japanese gold, that rather than to quit the prospect of a trade, indeed most advantageous, they willingly...chose to suffer many hardships in a foreign and heathen country" (174). These hardships not only pertained to their effective imprisonment at Deshima but also to their disavowal of Christian proselytization and practice, including abstaining from Sunday services, public "pray[er] and singing," and other "outward marks of Christianity" (174). Moreover, faced with continued Japanese skepticism about their loyalties, the Dutch merchants showed "submissive readiness" to help the Japanese authorities eradicate Christianity (173). Their performance of disavowal extended even to the point of being willing to trample on the *fumie* themselves.⁹

Kaempfer's first-hand context for Jonassen's fictional diary underscores how Endō's protagonist, Rodrigues, is part of a broader intra-European web of political-economic-religious interests from which he cannot, despite best intentions, extricate himself. Indeed, with his above-mentioned analogy of "jealous" women, Endō's Inoue shows himself to be well aware of how economic *interest* shapes Rodrigues's understanding of East/West distinctions (Endō 130). As a Japanese magistrate, Inoue recognizes—as Rodrigues cannot and Jonassen will not—that the very "categories" of "strong" and "weak" Rodrigues uses to define his sense of self are contingent upon and undermined by his position within this fluctuating and tenuous transimperial web (82). Within this web, the act of trampling on the *fumie* becomes a way of signifying one's position in relation to other people, rather than simply proving a relationship with Christ. And once again, Rodrigues's persistent obsession with his own *individual* Bildungsroman keeps him from grasping and grappling with how his story clashes and connects with others' journeys.

After the diary extracts of chapter ten, Jonassen's voice blurs into the narrator's, and Endō focalizes the final pre-Appendix pages through Rodrigues. We leave Rodrigues in his posthumously documented refusal to accept his own participation in self-interested distortions of the divine. In these final pages, Rodrigues wrestles with Inoue's accusation that Christianity demands an unwavering "strength of heart," whereas "the mercy of the Buddha" acknowledges man's "hopeless weakness" (Endō 200). Readers leave Rodrigues once again meditating on "the face of him whom I have always longed to love" (203) and claiming that, even in the face of his apostasy and God's silence, "my life until this day would have spoken of him" (204). As Rodrigues ponders his position of weakness—not only denied free movement within Japan but also "expelled from the mission" and "regarded as a renegade" by those back home (186)—he experiences the "searing pain" (188) and stark "solitude" of seeing his own situation reflected in his fellow Portuguese apostate, Ferreira (189). He recognizes, while also persistently disavowing, that he and Ferreira have fallen into the same trap as Japanese believers who may have "twisted God to their own way of thinking in a way" (160). While Ferreira claims that "we can never imagine" such thinking, it is clear that both priests—like Jonassen himself—have indeed imagined and extended that distortion (160).

Conclusion

On the face of it, Endō presents a version of the classic Bildungsroman as his Western protagonist dissolves his core religious identity in a new cultural space (indeed, at the novel's conclusion, Rodrigues has literally taken a Japanese name and wife). At the same time, however, Endō asks readers to think more expansively about the story of formation Rodrigues represents. His novel, we conclude, productively interrogates the interaction *between* individuals in a messy, evolving transimperial world. While critics of *Silence* have focused on Rodrigues's development or lack thereof, thus reinforcing the Bildungsroman's focus on an individual protagonist, the novel itself resists such limited thinking. By triangulating the perspectives of Rodrigues, Kichijiro, and Jonassen—three individuals, representing three distinct cultural-national identities, whose betrayals of Christ differently reflect the complexities of this network—Endō emphasizes how cultural and racial myopia keep these individuals from being absorbed neatly into their social order. Rodrigues's struggles are refracted by those of the other characters, and his persistently limited ability to see, imagine, or accommodate the struggles of *others* keeps him from finding resolution in his own Bildungsroman.

While *Silence*'s early modern, East/West negotiations situate the novel outside the strict bounds of colonial and postcolonial experience, the novel accomplishes similar work to that of other postcolonial Bildungsromane. If readers follow Rodrigues's story alone, they may see only a failed Bildungsroman, but once we become attuned to the other voices in the story (even "unlikeable" voices such as Kichijiro's), we see how *Silence* reclaims and "reimagin[es]" the genre (Hoagland 225). The benefits of such a reading, we suggest, may extend beyond Endō's characters, providing a template, of sorts, for the possibility of readerly reimagination.[10] By stubbornly anchoring the reader's perspective in Rodrigues's flawed gaze, the novel compels us to experience his limits and question what he notices. In the end, we are invited to expand our capacity to empathize with *all* those who have "trod on the sacred image." The deliberate ambiguity of Endō's ending leaves the reader in a state of awareness that Rodrigues himself never obtains. To validate the novel's power, readers must not just *sympathize* with Rodrigues as a character, but also *recognize* and *reject* the limits of his perspective (as we might more naturally do for Kichijiro's perspective, or Jonassen's). Whereas Rodrigues is faced with the limits of his spiritual and cultural imagination but never becomes fully aware of them, the reader—forced to read alongside and through his perspective—has the chance to see differently.

Notes

1. Classic studies of the Bildungsroman include Franco Moretti's comparative work, *The Way of the World*, which positions the genre as quintessential of European modernity by casting the youthful protagonist as the "symbolic form" for the volatility and openness of early capitalist society (3). More recent studies maintain ambivalence about its generic boundaries. Michael Ormsbee, for example, begins his article by explicitly raising this problem: "Every critic writing about the Bildungsroman must begin with—or successfully avoid—a question of definition" (1955); see also Aleksandar Stević.
2. For instance, Esty notably pinpoints "the crucial symbolic function of nationhood" in shaping the Bildungsroman (4), while Joseph Slaughter defines the genre as concerned primarily with a nation-centric task of "incorporating the problematic individual into the rights and responsibilities of citizenship, and thereby

2. legitimating the democratic institutions of the emergent rights-based nation state" (94).
3. Pointing to how "the history of empires has, by and large, remained nationalized," Daniel Hedinger and Nadin Heé define a "transimperial approach" as one that considers the "entangled processes" of "imperial competition, cooperation, and connectivity" across global history (429–30).
4. See also Gessel, who underscores this critical consensus on Rodrigues's transformation: "the novel can certainly be read as a journey in which the aggressive, fervently faithful Western priest Rodrigues is transformed by his painful experiences in Japan into a much weaker, more passive, yet significantly more compassionate human being, virtually indistinguishable from Kichijiro by the end of the book" (33).
5. Netland includes a helpful discussion of the pitfalls and possibilities of applying postcolonial theory (including Edward Said's seminal argument in *Orientalism* about Western hegemony after the late eighteenth century) to Endō's work (179). On Asian dominance of the early modern global economy, see work by economic historians Andre Gunder Frank and Kenneth Pomeranz. In his work on seventeenth- and eighteenth-century British literary narratives about the Far East, Robert Markley highlights the significance of these and similar studies for literary analysis, noting that "'traditional' postcolonialism has no way to account for a Sinocentric world, and therefore tends either to ignore Japan and China or read European-Asian encounters in the seventeenth and early eighteenth centuries through the lens of the nineteenth-century European domination of India" (8–9).
6. According to Doak, "Endō's works are characterized by external, multiple relational protagonists" (12). Doak goes on to argue that "while the mainstream of modern Japanese fiction has been within the *watakushi-shosetsu* (I-novel) genre, Endō largely avoided that genre" (12); instead, "Endō regularly locates his characters in a sociality that evokes a coming together with others as liberation, a sociality that underscores the importance of ecclesia or Church in every individual's life" (12).
7. By the end of the novel, Rodrigues notably shifts in this respect, as he comes to recognize how human weakness can still constitute faith; it is this shift in awareness that has led some critics to read *Silence* as a Bildungsroman.
8. Kaempfer, a German physician who worked for the Dutch embassy at Deshima in 1690–1692, documented Portugal's rise and fall in favour with Japanese authorities, as well as lengths its Dutch successors went to maintain their own tenuous trading privilege.
9. Markley argues that the Dutch "abjection" Kaempfer describes includes a "willingness after 1638 to perform the ritual of *yefumi*—literally trampling on the crucifix—in order to maintain their trading privileges in Japan" (241–42).

Dutch "submission," Markley contends, was "neither a single act nor a carefully staged performance during their annual tribute mission to Edo but an ongoing test of their willingness, at any and every moment, to sacrifice religion, national and personal honor, and weaponry to placate Japanese authorities" (254).

10. In his work on Black British literature, Stein similarly asks whether the Bildungsroman might be considered in terms of an "authorial or narrative intent not only to depict a process of education but also to educate the reader" (24).

Works Cited

Dennis, Mark W., and Darren J.N. Middleton, editors. *Approaching Silence: New Perspectives on Shūsaku Endō's Classic Novel*. Bloomsbury, 2015.

Doak, Kevin M. "Before *Silence*: Stumbling Along with Rodrigues and Kichijiro." Dennis and Middleton, pp. 3–23.

Endō, Shūsaku. *Silence*. Translated by William Johnston. Picador Modern Classics, 2017.

Esty, Jed. *Unseasonable Youth: Modernism, Colonialism, and the Fiction of Development*. Oxford University Press, 2012.

Frank, Andre Gunder. *ReOrient: Global Economy in the Asian Age*. University of California Press, 1998.

Frow, John, et al. "The Bildungsroman: Form and Transformations." *Textual Practice*, vol. 34, no. 12, 2020, pp. 1905–10. *Taylor & Francis Online*, https://doi.org/10.1080/0950236X.2020.1834692.

Gessel, Van C. "*Silence* on Opposite Shores: Critical Reactions to the Novel in Japan and the West." Dennis and Middleton, pp. 25–41.

Hay, Simon. "*Nervous Conditions*, Lukács, and the Postcolonial Bildungsroman." *Genre: Forms of Discourse and Culture*, vol. 46, no. 3, 2013, pp. 317–44.

Hedinger, Daniel, and Nadin Heé. "Transimperial History—Connectivity, Cooperation, and Competition." *Journal of Modern European History*, vol. 16, no. 4, 2018, pp. 429–52. *JSTOR*, https://www.jstor.org/stable/26740769.

Hoagland, Ericka A. "The Postcolonial Bildungsroman." *A History of the Bildungsroman*, edited by Sarah Graham, Cambridge University Press, 2019, pp. 217–38.

Kaempfer, Engelbert. *The History of Japan, Together with a Description of the Kingdom of Siam*. Vol. II (1690–92). Translated by J.G. Scheuchzer, James MacLehose and Sons, 1906.

Markley, Robert. *The Far East and the English Imagination, 1600–1730*. Cambridge University Press, 2006.

Moretti, Franco. *The Way of the World: The Bildungsroman in European Culture*. Translated by Albert Sbragia, Verso, 1987.

Netland, John T. "From Resistance to *Kenosis*: Reconciling Cultural Difference in the Fiction of Endō Shūsaku." *Christianity and Literature*, vol. 48, no. 2, 1999, pp. 177–94. *JSTOR*, https://www.jstor.org/stable/44312667.

Ormsbee, Michael. "Battle for the *Bildungsroman*: 'Protagonicity' and National Allegory." *Textual Practice*, vol. 34, no. 12, 2020, pp. 1955–68. *Taylor & Francis Online*, https://www.tandfonline.com/doi/full/10.1080/0950236X.2020.1834704.

Pomeranz, Kenneth. *The Great Divergence: China, Europe, and the Making of the Modern World Economy*. Princeton University Press, 2000.

Potts, Matthew. "Christ, Identity, and Empire in *Silence*." *The Journal of Religion*, vol. 101, no. 2, 2021, pp. 183–204. *The University of Chicago Press Journals*, https://www.journals.uchicago.edu/doi/abs/10.1086/712992.

Slaughter, Joseph R. *Human Rights, Inc.: The World Novel, Narrative Form, and International Law*. Fordham University Press, 2007.

Stein, Mark. *Black British Literature: Novels of Transformation*. Ohio State University Press, 2004.

Stević, Aleksandar. "The Genre of Disobedience: Is the Bildungsroman beyond Discipline?" *Seminar—A Journal of Germanic Studies*, vol. 56, no. 2, 2020, pp. 158–73. *University of Toronto Press*, https://utppublishing.com/doi/abs/10.3138/seminar.56.2.5.

Wachal, Christopher B. "Forbidden Ships to Chartered Tours: Endō, Apostasy, and Globalization." Dennis and Middleton, pp. 93–106.

9

THE TRUTH AND RECONCILIATION COMMISSION, THE BILDUNGSROMAN, AND THE "NEW" SOUTH AFRICAN SUBJECT

Deena Dinat

The South African Truth and Reconciliation Commission (TRC) remains an internationally celebrated mechanism of transitional justice, one designed to put to rest the violent injustice of apartheid's past and inaugurate a multiracial, democratic present. Operating between 1996 and 2003, it sought to "provide for the investigation and the establishment of as complete a picture as possible of the nature, causes and extent of gross violations of human rights" during the apartheid era (Republic of South Africa 1). Public disclosure was the means through which the injustices of the apartheid era would be healed; rituals of confession and forgiveness between victims, perpetrators, and commissioners would help establish a "new" South Africa. The dissemination of testimony through mass media was crucial to the subject- and nation-building ambitions of the commission, echoing Homi Bhabha's description of the nation as a "form of social and textual affiliation," rather than a fixed political entity (292).

Participating in this textual construction allowed the public to share in the act of witnessing, in the process of reconciliation, and in the creation of a new national subject.

The TRC was, however, limited in its ability to address apartheid-era abuses. As Mahmood Mamdani asks, how was it possible that the commission deemed apartheid a crime against humanity and yet only recommended reparations for approximately twenty thousand victims? (35). In its attempt to address the horrors of apartheid—a system of white-minority rule that targeted entire races—the TRC individualized both victims and perpetrators, leaving it only able to address a fraction of those impacted by apartheid. The largely public nature of testimonies, from both victims and perpetrators, offered a means of resolving this contradiction: the experiences of individuals were to become stand-ins for those who would never learn the truth of their losses, nor qualify for the reparations offered by the state. Meanwhile, those who benefitted from centuries of racialized exploitation saw apartheid agents forgiven or punished on their behalf. The TRC relied on an experience of identification and substitution to resolve the limitations of scale Mamdani notes; the spectating subject found in the testimony of a stand-in a version of the self who wept, disclosed, and confessed, cleansing both participant and audience of the past. Adam Sitze, meanwhile, recasts the legal and political intervention made by the TRC, which offered amnesty in exchange for the full disclosure of politically motivated human rights violations: rather than *breaking* with the colonial indemnity jurisprudence of apartheid, in which the state took to "legalizing illegality before, rather than after, the event," the TRC's Amnesty Committee attempted to create "*an indemnity to end all indemnities*" at the threshold of the new South Africa. Instead of marking a rupture in the colonial systems of the past, the TRC relied on the reinstation of "one of the worst juridical conventions of the apartheid state" (9–10). Dina Al-Kassim also asks us to consider "what conceptions of the human are naturalized" by the state through the TRC's use of testimony as a method of national healing (168). These latter critiques identify the commission as a *generative* project rather than a purely retrospective one, a project that produces new forms of state power and new kinds of subjects.

Nowhere is the generative ambition of the TRC more evident than in its treatment of children's testimonies. Commissioners belatedly created special hearings for children to speak before the TRC to recognize the "direct impact of the policies of the former state on young people and the active role they played in opposing apartheid" (TRC 250). It was essential that young subjects participated in the "healing ethos" of the commission "to ensure that [they would be] given the opportunity to participate fully in South Africa's new democratic institutions" (251). Through testimony, the TRC came to offer the subject access to a new process of formation; it offered, in essence, a national *Bildung* plot. The post-apartheid Bildungsroman and the commission both demand a legible, confessing subject who provides an account of the self before a public that ensures its values have been internalized and reproduced. Both set out a path for development, a narrative arc[1] moving from a past of unfreedom towards a future of nonracialism, liberal democracy, and human rights.[2] Ideologically bound, the TRC and the Bildungsroman both allow us to glimpse the construction of the idealized post-apartheid subject, and its constitutive Other.

This chapter turns to radically different texts to explore the relationship between these subject-making mechanisms. Nadia Davids's *An Imperfect Blessing* provides a paradigmatic example of how the commission's norms dominate the possibilities for imagining the young post-apartheid subject. In Davids's coming-of-age narrative, the *Bildung* plot requires the internalization of the TRC's nation-building project: historical conflict can and indeed *must* be resolved through the values embodied by the TRC. K. Sello Duiker's *Thirteen Cents*, meanwhile, mimics the expectations of the genre as a means of revealing the necropolitical nature of state power. While the Bildungsroman traditionally affirms the state's generative, life-bestowing powers, *Thirteen Cents* subverts the *Bildung* plot: violence and death operate as the means of entry into a society of adults. Whereas the normative Bildungsroman works to *obscure* the state's necropolitical foundations, *Thirteen Cents*'s focus on violence as a means of development condemns its young protagonist to the margins of the nation. Neither novel fits within what might be termed "TRC literature," a subsection of post-apartheid literature that directly engages with the events of the commission.[3] Shane Graham's discussion of TRC texts, for example, looks at works that "simultaneously produce and draw attention to the fragmentation of subjectivity experienced by the [apartheid-era] trauma survivor" (12). This bracketing of TRC literature, with its focus on testimony and trauma, affirms the TRC as a *retrospective* project, and as such obfuscates the commission's ongoing influence on contemporary South African literature. Instead, this chapter focuses on texts that come after the establishment of the commission but do not represent it directly. These are texts that demonstrate how the norms established through the TRC have been taken up in ways that exceed representations of the commission itself.

"Coming of Age *with* the Country": *Bildung* as Reconciliation in Nadia Davids's *An Imperfect Blessing*

An Imperfect Blessing tells the story of a Coloured[4] Cape Town family negotiating the rapidly changing landscape of South Africa in 1993 and 1994, a particularly violent period in the transition from white-minority rule to nonracial, multiparty democracy.[5] It is a Bildungsroman tied to real, historical time.[6] The primary narrative concerns the development of teenager Alia Dawood who is grasping for an adult identity amid the racial, religious, and class complications of an emergent nation. Without the teleology of the struggle against apartheid, "it didn't feel like she and the country were in this together" (Davids 19). Yet to be incorporated into the grand sweep of national history, she "had been born too late," the narrator explains; "too late to be a part of the graffiti and the chanting and the defiance. Too late to know what it felt like to lend flesh to a crowd, to spit at the police, to gather in secret corners at school. Too late for all that" (19). The fight against apartheid offers her no *Bildung* plot, adrift at the supposed end of history. Instead, her process of development will centre around the internalization of a new national order, one that works to confine opposition to the state, and contestation over the nature of that state, to South Africa's past. While the characters of the novel are uncertain about the nation to come, the novel knowingly plots Alia's development within the teleology of the post-apartheid dispensation; as such, her development affirms the nation envisioned by the TRC. The task of the Bildungsroman and the commission are, in that sense, one in the same: they allow the subject's entry into a nation as it is remade in the image of that becoming subject.

An early moment in Alia's development demonstrates how the structures of the new South Africa are made intrinsic to the *Bildung* plot of the novel. Her entry into a broader public takes place at HAL's, a nightclub named after Stanley Kubrick's cyclops in *2001: A Space Odyssey*. The gesture to Homer via Kubrick and Arthur C. Clark parodically elevates the young subject to the status of hero; here she will face challenges that must be surmounted if she is to be recognized by the adult world. HAL's had long functioned as a rite of passage for Coloured teenagers, and by 1993 it "held inter-generational memories. Alia's uncles and aunts had all come here and told her how they had bowed at the altar of disco. A decade later her older cousins had pumped their fists," to the radical hip-hop of the 1980s (39). HAL's most significant trial concerns Alia's ability to negotiate the suddenly desegregated spaces of the new South Africa. It is no longer possible to emerge as a national subject through the racial logic of apartheid. Instead, Alia must learn to share a *national* identity with Black South Africans. Watching her fellow Coloured Capetonians dance, Alia feels as though she was in "one of those rooms filled with mirrors where an image is replicated in a dizzying ad infinitum" (46). Her claustrophobia alerts us to the unsustainability of spaces like HAL's, but also the unsustainability of a parochial Coloured identity. The repetition of the familiar image is broken when the narrator notices the presence of Black teenagers: "confined to a corner, as if the dance floor was an abstracted grid of the city and they were still obeying a now abolished law…they danced with their backs to the rest of the club, their movements a seamless blend of American music video sequences and 1950s kwela" (46). They provoke panic in Alia, who "realised with gathering dread that not even her beetle-crushers could make up for the Gothy whiteness of her get-up" (46). As Mohamed Adhikari writes, Coloured identity once found "remarkable" stability during white-minority rule, "spurred [by] hopes of future acceptance into the dominant [white] society" (467). As the end of apartheid neared, this proximity to whiteness would no longer grant the Coloured subject legitimacy, Alia learns. In this historical moment the young Coloured subject remains caught between multiple racial and historical orders: whiteness is suddenly cast as inauthentic while Blackness remains foreign.

These complex questions of identity, race, and belonging are ones the TRC and the electoral process will resolve, the novel assures us; the liberal institutions of the emergent nation will provide a means of confining Alia's racial anxiety to the past. Alia's friends parrot contemporary political debates: one is embarrassed by his parents' continued support for apartheid's National Party, another has parents who have been anti-apartheid African National Congress supporters for decades, while "this one had a mother in the UDF [the anti-apartheid United Democratic Front], this one had a sell-out uncle in the TriCameral Parliament, this one had a cousin who had been in solitary [confinement]" (56). Cape Town's Coloured community, the novel demonstrates, represents the full spectrum of South Africa's political positions. As tensions around the future of the country rise, they are dispersed by a teenager mocking a song on the loudspeaker: "'Jou ma en pa is [Your mother and father are] Ninja Turtles! *OW!* Mandela skop vir Buthelezi [Mandela kicks Buthelezi]! *OW!*'" (58). This pastiche of schoolyard nonsequiturs, pop-culture references, and political commentary makes it clear that Alia's entry into political discourse still has limited consequences. These differences *matter*, but only in so far as they attest to the diversity of the electoral choices that await. Participation in the new political system, not old racial identities, will provide entry into the new South Africa.

As the site of Alia's earliest adult experiences, HAL's serves a function not dissimilar to that of the Bildungsroman itself: it offers a way of bringing together the contradictions and complications of identity in a fast-changing nation while reaffirming the idea that the new South African state will provide the means of resolving what remains of a violent past. As Alia is driven home from HAL's, "she watched the hills of her neighbourhood rise up as if for the first time: something she could not yet name had shifted, changed, been made anew" (59). What she cannot name is the development of her own normative national subjectivity, one coextensive with the South Africa being constructed around her.

Rewriting the New Nation

The novel provides a second *Bildung* plot through the character of Waleed, Alia's uncle. His development has been stalled by apartheid and its slow dismantling. Much of Waleed's story takes place in 1986 through a series of flashbacks that track a political awakening that leaves him adrift in the new South Africa. An itinerant writer and academic, his struggle to come to terms with the changing world is captured in "the realm of agonised imaginings," and his six-year-long doctoral thesis on "*how political trauma limits creative output*" is now an "uneasy obsession" (Davids 67). It is an autobiographical obsession: Waleed "felt his life and his work had been royally fucked by apartheid; he was convinced that the conclusion of the research was dependent on the end of the system" (67). Familial conflicts stem from the same source; it is clear that apartheid has interrupted his development. Only through the establishment of a new nation and a new subjectivity can these tensions be resolved.

The anti-apartheid movement in Cape Town offered no path for Waleed's normative growth; forays into political action are complicated by his class position and his distaste for the violence of the struggle against apartheid. When he offers to hide Firoze, a teenaged activist on the run, Waleed is wracked with guilt that can only be eased through speculation and, ultimately, fiction: Waleed "pictures jungles and Firoze's slender build…he hears the insistent rhythm of a training song…[h]e layers the imagery with stories of ambush…[h]e agonises…[h]e allows the questions to take the place of action" (198–99). Waleed fictionalizes Firoze's future as a means of narrativizing his uncertainty. This series of narrative leaps—his attempt to imagine a future for Firoze, to write Firoze's Bildungsroman—will become Waleed's strategy for confronting the political questions he cannot address through activism, and this fictive turn will also come to serve his own *Bildung* plot. The political crisis of the late-apartheid era, the novel makes clear, cannot provide the grounds for the emergence of a new South African subject. Instead, the crucial questions the anti-apartheid activists raised—around the nature of power and subjection, the torsions of racial capitalism, the necessity of armed struggle—will be the raw material used to inspire Waleed's autobiographical writing, part of a practice of self-representation that will allow his eventual emergence into the new South Africa. This is the same subject-making procedure central to the TRC: the subject must provide an autobiographical account of the self as a means of recognizing, and thus dispensing with, the past. The nation-state itself provides this *Bildung* plot through the commission, which allows a normative subject to be reclaimed from the violence of history.

The novel ends with both Alia and Waleed writing themselves into the new South Africa; self-representation has become the apotheosis of subject-making. Alia writes a letter to a love interest detailing the nation's first democratic election on April 27, 1994. The date represents a new maturity for both Alia and the nation:

> I think everyone in Walmer Estate registered [to vote] at my old school, Zonnebloem. I hadn't been back since I left and there was something incredibly weird about walking through those gates again…It was as if there were two things going on at the same time, what I was seeing right then and there and then also what I was remembering. (402–03)

She is too young to vote, but returning to a site from her youth to witness the emergence of the new South Africa allows Alia to claim her place as a subject of history, one fully aware of her own experience of the world as it is being formed around, and indeed, through young subjects like her. Election day also works to resolve lingering familial and political squabbles; we are told "Mama got into a fight with her neighbour Auntie May because Auntie May announced really loudly that she would be voting for the Nats, which we now know (sickeningly) is how most of the Western Cape went" (403). As Zoë Wicomb writes, the fact that Coloureds in the Western Cape largely voted for the National Party in 1994 is tied to what she describes as the *shame* of miscegenation, which questions whether Coloureds had bought into "non-racialism, acceptance of African leadership, and a sense of common nationhood" after the end of apartheid (99). Davids's Bildungsroman confines these questions to the past, a matter for grandmothers to bicker over: they will not threaten the development of the "new" Coloured subject. Alia's letter ends by reinscribing the necessity and inevitability of the TRC; she explains that "'seeing' is one of the things that's going to happen, that's *got* to happen...no one will ever be able to say again that they 'didn't know'"[7] (Davids 404). She is now firmly embedded within the language of the TRC: through storytelling and witnessing, she can claim a place in the new nation.

Waleed's *Bildung* plot ends with a public reading of his work. A multiracial audience gathers at a local bar to celebrate his writing centred on the rubble and detritus of District Six, which is now free to be transformed into a narrative act of self-representation. This is the writing, we are told, that has freed him from anxieties of bygone forms of activism. He has finally stopped raging "against readers assuming the biography of his work, saying that it is a ghettoising tool for women, for people of colour. Always, he's refused his own life in his work. But now he sees that there is no shame in acknowledgement. *No, none at all*" (408). Autobiography may have once been dismissed as a bourgeois interest amid the struggle against apartheid, but it is now essential to Waleed's development. As Frederic Jameson observes, the common turn in the "Third World" Bildungsroman toward autobiography marks the emergence of the "'centred subject' who comes into being" over the course of the novel and in so doing invites the reader to reread and resituate "the formation of an intellectual" within a new sociality (183). Transforming from activist to intellectual, Waleed is finally able to cast off the "shame" of the past and enter the new South Africa.

Post-Apartheid Life and Death in K. Sello Duiker's *Thirteen Cents*

Contemporary South Africa, and the variegated forms of capital accumulation that sustain it, requires the creation of a peripheral nonsubject. Whereas the Bildungsroman traditionally works to incorporate the subject into the formal realm of the nation, *Thirteen Cents* critiques both the subject-making functions of the genre and the attempt to create a new South African citizen. Duiker's text confronts the processes of subject-making that have come to define the post-apartheid state, revealing the violence that undergirds the national project.

Readings of the novella often attempt to rescue Azure, the protagonist, from the horrific abuse he suffers throughout the text. Shaun Viljoen's introduction to a 2012 edition, for example, describes the novel as "a bildungsroman of the boy's sexuality in formation," (xii) a Bildungsroman "as much about survival and a sense of self on the urban edges as it is about marginalized sexuality" (xiv). That sexuality only emerges through rape and abuse in the novel is ignored by Viljoen; his reading folds the violence of the text into a *Bildung* arc that makes a national subject. This is a normative reading that reaffirms the Bildungsroman's function as a generative expression of the modern political order, one in which the state operates as a life-giving and -managing power. What of the genre's relationship to the postcolonial nation-state and its claim on violence and, ultimately, death? Pheng Cheah ties the genre to the nation's morbid functions: as the nation allows for the generation of life, it must also distribute death. By the end of the twentieth century, Cheah writes, postcolonial nationalism "ha[d] become the exemplary figure for *death*," not life (226, emphasis added). Similarly, Achille Mbembe challenges normative accounts of state power in which "the ultimate expression of sovereignty is the production of general norms by a body (the demos) made up of free and equal men and women. These men and women are posited as full subjects capable of self-understanding, self-consciousness, and self-representation" (13). Mbembe describes the romance—perhaps the *roman*—of sovereignty as residing in the belief that "the subject is the master and the controlling author of his or her own meaning…a twofold process of *self-institution* and *self-limitation*" (13). However, the postcolony expresses sovereignty through "less abstract and more tactile" categories of life and death (14). This *necropolitical* conception of sovereignty underlies my reading of *Thirteen Cents*, a text that recognizes the production and governance of South African subjects remains entrenched in a violent, death-distributing infrastructure.

In conversation with Fred de Vries in 2004, Duiker highlights the role of *force* in contemporary South Africa:

> Violence is a culture that communicates a certain message. In Thirteen cents [sic] I wanted to explore how violence is not only a way of dominating people, but I also wanted to show that violence is used by people to communicate with each other and to convey a message. The way in which this happens is deplorable. But we are part of a violent culture, and we never knew a period of rest, nor did we receive help to enter into a process of healing after apartheid. (de Vries 23)

In Duiker's description, violence is not merely a trial to be passed before acceptance into the nation. Instead, it forms the substrate through which information is transmitted, through which relations are formed, maintained, and changed. For Azure, the *Bildung* plot cannot be resolved through an ascension into the national sphere; the novella calls our attention to the way in which post-apartheid South Africa remains structured by a politics of death.

"Julle fokken mannetjies moet skool toe gaan": An Education in Precarity

The novella begins with an assertion of subjecthood: "My name is Azure. *Ah-zoo-ray*. That's how you say it" (Duiker 1). "Azure" references his blue eyes that, paired with his dark skin, trouble the racial categorizations still in force after the end of apartheid. With little more than a name—and an insistence that it be articulated—Azure is cast as a figure of precarity, a term Judith Butler establishes to differentiate exposure to violence from a general sense of precariousness, which all living beings experience. Precarity "designates that politically induced condition in which certain populations suffer from failing social and economic networks of support and become differentially exposed to injury, violence, and death" (25). The precarious

> appeal to the state for protection, but the state is precisely that from which they require protection. To be protected from violence by the nation-state is to be exposed to the violence wielded by the nation-state, so to rely on the nation-state for protection *from* violence is precisely to exchange one potential violence for another. (26)

"I live alone," Azure tells the reader, alerting us to his precarious life at the edges of the *polis* (Duiker 1). While he is chastised by adults on the street—"'*julle fokken mannetjies moet skool toe gaan*'" (you fucking little men must go to school)—formal education has only reinforced his exposure to violence and offers him no entry into the nation-state (2). His parents were murdered while, Azure explains, he "was away at school," enmeshing his formative loss within the realm of education (2). The abuse he is subjected to comes to replace traditional schooling; as his chief tormentor Gerald, who later claims to have killed Azure's parents, explains, these experiences ensure that Azure will learn "to live with fear" (68). Living with fear is what will allow him to participate in the necropolitical structure of the city and the ongoing horror of post-apartheid subjugation. If *An Imperfect Blessing* demonstrated the ways in which political violence will soon be subsumed by the nation-building rhetoric of the TRC, *Thirteen Cents* demonstrates that violence remains fundamental to producing the abject subject.

Azure's maturation follows the violent education he has been subjected to. He accepts that a child like him can be abused by adults "because you're a *lytie* [kid] and they are big. You see it's like that. That's how it works here. You must always act like a grown-up. You must speak like them" (3). Enduring and reproducing violence are the conditions of his *Bildung* plot. Azure continually reminds himself and the reader of the rules of survival while relying on a small cast of adults to support him; but, in keeping with the nihilistic tenor of the novel, they are inevitably revealed to be a part of the abusive adult world. Joyce, for example, "understands banks and how they work," and so is trusted to hold Azure's meagre earnings (11). The bank is another adult institution Azure cannot negotiate, as

> Grown-ups ask many questions there. You must remember where you were born and exactly how old you are. You must have an address and it must be one that doesn't keep changing. Like you must stay in the same spot for say maybe five years and when you move you must tell the bank. They must know everything about your movements…If you ask me they are a bit like gangsters, they want to know everything so that you cannot

run away from them. And you must have an ID and a job that pays you regularly. (11–12)

The adult world demands a fixed, stable subject: to belong to the institutions of the nation is to enter the economy, to be traceable, to be known by those who would inflict harm. In Azure's experience there is little to distinguish the legitimate power of banks from the illegitimate power of gangsters. Being recognized does not hold the same promise for Azure as it did for Alia: to be recognized in *Thirteen Cents* is to be exploited. Trapped at the outer limits of the nation, on the cusp of adulthood, between racial categories, Azure is as far away from the normative conception of the subject as he can be without being entirely adrift. It is a position that echoes Foucault's "ship of fools," which Kalyan Sanyal adopts to describe the conditions of postcolonial capitalism (44). Azure is within a long history of colonial expulsion that remains after the end of apartheid, "condemned to a no man's land" amid the "outcastes and rejects of the contemporary third world economies" (46). The threat of violence that underlies the postcolony is exposed by Azure's precarity, by his wandering through the streets of Cape Town. As such, Duiker's text adopts the trappings of the Bildungsroman as a means of deconstructing the generative assumptions of both the genre and the nation.

"I'll Give Him Fire": Death, Excess, and Sacrifice

Cape Town offers no reprieve from the violence Azure experiences. "Grown-ups are fucked up," he declares before being corrected by a confidant, "no, Cape Town is fucked up" (37). Attempting to find the target of his critique, Azure tries again: "it's Cape Town, not the people," only to be corrected by Vincent once more, "and the people. Don't forget about the people. They're also fucked up" (37). In this diagnosis, the city and its inhabitants, its subjects and its infrastructure, are inextricable. In a final attempt to ingratiate himself into the world of adults, Azure turns himself over to Gerald to be raped and tortured before he flees for the refuge of Table Mountain. His experience of Gerald's abuse induces a radical break in what might have been his *Bildung* plot. Drawing a crucifix in excrement on the walls of his cell, he claims he is "getting stronger" (55), and attempts to rationalize his torture, telling himself "this is how they teach me to be strong" (47). It is a strength that will soon be turned against the city and its adults: "I take in their light and destroy them with fire" (47). Later, as his psychosis deepens, his process of education begins to disintegrate. The day of his thirteenth birthday arrives, and while this was supposed to signal his entry into manhood, he knows his education is far from over: "One. Three. I must understand that number. I must understand what it means to be a grown-up if I'm going to survive" (66). To survive he must escape the city.

This escape disrupts Azure's circulation between the men who solicit him for sex, the gangsters who surveil and torture him, and the adults who promise him access to the formal world but exploit him instead. He seeks the only remaining place of safety in "the sleeping mountain above" (100). What he experiences on Table Mountain suggests a final uncoupling of his subjectivity from the world of the normative nation-state; he attempts to become a subject outside of the subject-making processes of society, a coin removed from circulation. In the latter part of the novella, he enters into what Georges Bataille calls "*non-productive expenditure*," the luxury of the nonessential, the excessive, the abundant (168). This escape represents what Jean Baudrillard would go on to refer to as the anti-economy of death, wherein death takes on "the paroxysm of exchanges, superabundance and excess," rather than annihilation or pure negativity (154). We witness, Baudrillard continues, "death as a principle of excess and an anti-economy," one in which "only sumptuous and useless expenditure has meaning; the economy has no meaning, it is only a residue that has been made into the law of life, whereas wealth lies in the luxurious exchange of death" (155–56). "In a system where life is ruled by value and utility," Baudrillard continues, "death becomes a useless luxury, and the only alternative" (156). On the mountain, Azure engages in this exchange of abundance and death: "I'll give them all destruction, I say and start gathering wood. I take the dead ones, the ones that look grey and white from too much drying in the sun. They will burn easily, I say, and leave the brown ones. It is hard work carrying them up and down and through the tunnel but I enjoy it. I work silently.

For the first time I work like I know what I'm doing" (Duiker 107). These branches, which "look like something...arms, legs, bodies, birds, elephants, monsters with many arms and legs and other things," are sacrificed in the fire (108). These are sacrifices "begging for destruction," and transformed by Azure's labour (109). Whereas Mbembe's reading of Hegel suggests that the "human being truly *becomes a subject*" by transforming nature through labour and it "is through this confrontation with death that he or she is cast into the incessant movement of history," *Thirteen Cents* provides a different relationship between labour, death, and the becoming subject (14). Azure's labour is a labour of sacrifice that does not enter him into the normative movements of history nor the nation. This ritual suddenly recasts him as a profligate figure.

Soon Azure sees "total destruction...I just keep climbing, higher and higher. I get excited when I think of this ball of fire growing bigger and destroying everything in its path" (Duiker 105). This marks the final transformation of his development; as he walks past others on the path, he has "nothing to say to them. I'm done with grown-ups. They are full of shit. They want fire. I'll given them fire" (106). He begins to shed the impulse to ingratiate himself into adult society, into the formal economy of value and exchange. Instead, he enacts his own form of ritual violence to radically remake the conditions of his subjection. In fevered dreams he envisions Saartjie Baartman, who shares his experience of exclusion and violence. Initially offering maternal comfort—she has "the lightest smile," and her "long breasts are like fruit, like fat pears"—it soon becomes apparent that Azure and Baartman are bound in an inescapable cycle of gendered colonial violence (119). While she appears to aid Azure at first, identifying Gerald as the "T-rex" tearing apart the city, she eventually reveals that she and Gerald are lovers, and that Azure is "'going to be big just like him'" (122). It is a warning: Azure will eventually reproduce his education of destruction and violence if he completes his *Bildung* arc. As he sets fire to the city beneath him, Azure adopts the right of the sovereign—the adult, the state, the gangster, the police—the right to impose violence, the right to transgress the prohibition on death. He transcends neither his subjection nor his exposure to death. Instead, this brief reversal affirms Duiker's diagnosis of the function of violence in post-apartheid South Africa: violence is the medium through which subject and sovereign are bound.

Whereas Bhabha suggests the nation fills "the void left in the uprooting of communities and kin" by turning "that loss into the language of metaphor" (291), the novel ends with a refrain that recognizes the inability of metaphor to account for death: "My mother is dead. My father is dead" (Duiker 161). This revelation does not end his torment—it is an acknowledgement of its source: "I have seen the slave-driver of darkness and he is a mad bastard. I know his secrets. I know what he does when we sleep. My mother is dead. My father is dead" (164). His education has revealed the ways in which post-apartheid South Africa, beneath the TRC's facade, remains structured through the violence of racial capitalism. Viljoen argues this final acknowledgement means Azure can "begin again on the clean slate emerging beneath his feet" (xvii). It is a reading that aligns with the efforts of the contemporary nation to draw a line under the horrors of the past and obscure the exploitation that makes the nation possible: the notion of a "clean slate" can only reproduce the violence Azure flees, for what could possibly lie beyond that erasure? His *becoming* is only possible through the excesses of death, placing him at odds with the nation's claim over life. At the uncertain end of the novel, the end of his purported *Bildung* plot, Azure remains a revelatory figure—one who exposes the limits of the normative subject and the sovereignty of the nation-state—and as such he *must* remain outside of the national project, and outside of the trajectory of the Bildungsroman.

Conclusion

No genre hews closer to the norms of the state than the Bildungsroman. It is unsurprising then that the TRC would come to adopt its key assumptions, and that the normative Bildungsroman in post-apartheid South Africa often participates in the subject-making project of the commission. As *An Imperfect Blessing* demonstrates, the TRC and the Bildungsroman work in concert to produce the young subject of the nation's future, and both seem to offer a means of resolving the injustices of the past. In this sense, the present becomes the inevitable result of the subject's development, a process through which both nation and narration are naturalized. This process of becoming along with and through national history is upended in *Thirteen Cents*. The novella gestures towards an unspoken national violence, asking what becomes of a subject cast to the margins of a society that no longer simply kills that which it rejects. As such, Duiker demonstrates the ways in which the genre can be made into a tool of radical critique, a means of revealing what underpins attempts to remake the state and the subject. While the TRC fades from the national consciousness, its logics remain embedded in notions of the normative subject. The Bildungsroman thus remains a crucial site in which subjection is contested, a discursive space in which the demands of the TRC and the post-apartheid state—demands for a transparent, confessing, and conciliatory citizen—are challenged, undone, and remade.

Notes

1. This progressive arc is narrativized by the Promotion of National Unity and Reconciliation Act, which describes the commission as part of a "historic bridge between the past of a deeply divided society characterized by strife, conflict, untold suffering and injustice, and a future founded on the recognition of human rights, democracy and peaceful co-existence for all South Africans, irrespective of colour, race, class, belief or sex" (Republic of South Africa 2).
2. The "narrative homology" shared by the Bildungsroman and the modern human rights regime, as Joseph Slaughter has described, is one also shared by the TRC (93). As Samuel Moyn has noted, while most twentieth-century struggles for independence eschewed the language of individual human rights in favour of national sovereignty, South Africa was the exception; freedom was imagined through discourses of human rights rather than self-determination (173). In keeping with this discursive history, the TRC addressed the violence of the apartheid state and the struggle against it as generally equivalent violations of human rights.
3. Examples of TRC literature include nonfiction accounts of the commission— Antjie Krog's *Country of My Skull* and Pumla Gobodo-Madikizela's *A Human Being Died That Night*—as well as works of fiction that directly reference the commission, such as Achmat Dangor's *Bitter Fruit*, and Zoë Wicomb's *Playing in the Light*. Hybrid works incorporated both the fictional and nonfictional,

such as *Ubu and the Truth Commission*, a play written by Jane Taylor and directed by William Kentridge.

4. "Coloured" is used to refer to a multiracial population that draws on varied backgrounds, including but not limited to Indigenous Khoisan, Southeast Asian, African, and white settler communities. A fixed racial category during apartheid, "Coloured" continues to be widely used in South Africa and, while contested, it is not considered derogatory.

5. Franco Moretti historicizes the Bildungsroman within the transition of European societies from aristocratic forms of rule to bourgeois capitalism; the genre represented a way to "heal the rupture" of this historical shift and to "imagine a continuity between the old and the new regime" (viii). The language of "healing" and "transition" was essential to the TRC's mandate, another homology between the commission and the genre.

6. As Mikhail Bakhtin writes, the Bildungsroman produces the subject "*along with the* world and he reflects the historical emergence of the world itself. He is no longer within an epoch, but on the border between two epochs, at the transition point from one to the other" (23). The process of the subject's development is no longer a private affair; the subject emerges in and constitutes the *public*" (23, emphasis added).

7. This assertion repeats TRC Deputy Chairperson Alex Boraine's claim that, because of the commission, "it is no longer possible for so many people to claim that 'they did not know'" (289).

Works Cited

Adhikari, Mohamed. "Hope, Fear, Shame, Frustration: Continuity and Change in the Expression of Coloured Identity in White Supremacist South Africa, 1910–1994." *Journal of Southern African Studies*, vol. 32, no. 3, 2006, pp. 467–87.

Al-Kassim, Dina. "Archiving Resistance: Women's Testimony at the Threshold of the State." *Cultural Dynamics*, vol. 20, no. 2, 2008, pp. 167–92.

Bakhtin, M.M. "The *Bildungsroman* and Its Significance in the History of Realism (Toward a Historical Typology of the Novel)." *Speech Genres and Other Late Essays*. Translated by Vern W. McGee, University of Texas Press, 1986, pp. 10–59.

Bataille, Georges. "The Notion of Expenditure." *Visions of Excess: Selected Writings, 1927–1939*, edited by Alan Stoekl, translated by Alan Stoekl et al., University of Minnesota Press, 1985, pp. 116–29.

Baudrillard, Jean. *Symbolic Exchange and Death*. Translated by Iain Hamilton Grant, Sage, 2000.

Bhabha, Homi K. "DissemiNation: Time, Narrative, and the Margins of the Modern Nation." *Nation and Narration*, edited by Homi K. Bhabha, Routledge, 1990, pp. 291–322.

Boraine, Alex. *A Country Unmasked: Inside South Africa's Truth and Reconciliation Commission*. Oxford University Press, 2000.

Butler, Judith. *Precarious Life: The Powers of Mourning and Violence*. Verso, 2004.

Cheah, Pheng. "Spectral Nationality: The Living on [Sur-Vie] of the Postcolonial Nation in Neocolonial Globalization." *Boundary 2*, vol. 26, no. 3, 1999, pp. 225–52.

Davids, Nadia. *An Imperfect Blessing*. Umuzi, 2014.

de Vries, Fred. "I Try to Be My Own Publicity Manager…" *De Volkskrant*, translated by Eva Rondas, Apr. 2004, pp. 22–24.

Duiker, K. Sello. *Thirteen Cents*. David Philip, 2011.

Graham, Shane. "The Truth Commission and Post-Apartheid Literature in South Africa." *Research in African Literatures*, vol. 34, no. 1, 2003, pp. 11–30.

Jameson, Frederic. "On Literary and Cultural Import-Substitution in the Third World: The Case of the Testimonio." *The Real Thing: Testimonial Discourse and Latin America*, edited by Georg M. Gugelberger, Duke University Press, 1996, pp. 172–91.

Mamdani, Mahmood. "Amnesty of Impunity? A Preliminary Critique of the Report of the Truth and Reconciliation Commission of South Africa (TRC)." *Diacritics*, vol. 32, no. 3/4, Autumn-Winter 2002, pp. 32–59.

Mbembe, Achille. "Necropolitics." *Public Culture*, translated by Libby Meintjes, vol. 15, no. 1, 2003, pp. 11–40.

Moretti, Franco. *The Way of the World: The Bildungsroman in European Culture*. Translated by Albert Sbragia. New Edition, Verso, 2000.

Moyn, Samuel. *The Last Utopia: Human Rights in History*. Harvard University Press, 2010.

Republic of South Africa. The Promotion of National Unity and Reconciliation Act 34 of 1995. www.gov.za, 1995, pp. 1–39. *Republic of South Africa Government Gazette*, chrome-extension://efaidnbmnnnibpcajpcglclefindmkaj/https://www.gov.za/sites/default/files/gcis_document/201409/act34of1995.pdf.

Sanyal, Kalyan. *Rethinking Capitalist Development: Primitive Accumulation, Governmentality and Post-Colonial Capitalism*. Routledge, 2007.

Sitze, Adam. *The Impossible Machine: A Genealogy of South Africa's Truth and Reconciliation Commission*. The University of Michigan Press, 2013.

Slaughter, Joseph R. *Human Rights, Inc.: The World Novel, Narrative Form, and International Law*. Fordham University Press, 2007.

Truth and Reconciliation Commission (TRC). *Truth and Reconciliation Commission of South Africa Report Vol. 4*, 1998. www.justice.gov.za, chrome-extension://efaidnbmnnnibpcajpcglclefindmkaj/https://www.justice.gov.za/trc/report/finalreport/Volume%204.pdf.

Viljoen, Shaun. Introduction. *Thirteen Cents*, by K. Sello Duiker, Ohio University Press, 2013, pp. iv–xxxiii.

Wicomb, Zoë. "Shame and Identity: The Case of the Coloured in South Africa." *Writing South Africa*, edited by Derek Attridge and Rosemary Jolly, Cambridge University Press, 1998, pp. 91–107.

10

"WE COME TOO LATE TO THE SCENE"

Goh Poh Seng, Developmental Time, and the Singapore Story

Peter Ribic

Early in Goh Poh Seng's first novel, *If We Dream Too Long*, an underexamined Bildungsroman set in the months after Singapore's political separation from Malaysia in August 1965, the eighteen-year-old protagonist, Kwang Meng, comes to a curious realization. "There are no real dramatic causes left for our generation," he tells his friends just after their high school graduation, "and what is worse, the ones in power are still young" (9). Kwang Meng's immediate referent is the leadership of the People's Action Party (PAP) and, specifically, Prime Minister Lee Kuan Yew, who came to power after Singapore was granted internal self-governance by the British Empire in 1959 and went on to hold more or less uncontested political authority for the rest of his career. But this sense of generational untimeliness seems to run deeper than the coronation of the newly independent city state's postcolonial political elite. "We come too late to the scene, our generation," his friend Hock Lai adds, "after the action is over" (9). Independence, which corresponds for Goh's young heroes with a symbolic introduction to professional life, signals not a beginning but an ending, the falling action of a "drama" that has already taken place.

Goh's description of generational lateness is remarkable, first, because it cuts against the critical common sense that the postcolonial Bildungsroman is distinguished by a sense of unsettled futurity. For recent critics, the classics of the genre—from George Lamming's *In the Castle of My Skin* to Tsitsi Dangarembga's *Nervous Conditions*—appear so often to resist narrative closure because the formation of postcolonial subjects allegorizes the unfinished and ongoing projects of national formation and development launched across the world in the era of decolonization. As Pheng Cheah writes, "the imperativity of national *Bildung* was invariably personified in the [postcolonial Bildungsroman's] protagonist whose formation...parallels and symbolizes that of the emergent nation" (239). Whether individual texts affirm the possibility of a national coherence to come, as in Lamming's novel, or demystify narratives of development as an "illusion" (Slaughter 245) under the conditions of (neo-)colonial domination, as in Dangarembga's, the genre is animated by its orientation towards a speculative correspondence of individual maturity and national self-determination that has not yet arrived and rarely occurs within the diegetic framework of the postcolonial Bildungsroman itself.

Equally significant here is that after more than fifty years of one-party rule and steady economic growth, Kwang Meng and Hock Lai, it seems, were right about Singapore's undramatic future. As one of the so-called Four Tigers and, more recently, as one of what the World Bank calls "high-performing Asian economies," the city state stands out as a paradigm of successful modernization for the formerly colonized world, verified by the reigning metrics and metonyms of postwar developmentalism. Singapore now boasts, for example, one of the world's highest per capita gross domestic products, as well as globally renowned systems of education, health care, and public housing. While often derided as an irredeemably "boring" place (Gibson) by Euro-American observers, Singapore is increasingly seen as a model for capitalist growth in an age of secular stagnation, both in Southeast Asia and in the erstwhile metropole, where the recent slogan "Singapore-on-Thames" crystalizes the political economic ambitions of post-Brexit neoliberals.

How, then, should one interpret Goh's prophetic disillusionment with Singapore's postcolonial project? How was the story of Singaporean postcoloniality narrated to create the effect of resolved "action" by the time the novel was written in the late 1960s? Focusing on the tangled temporalities of postcolonial development, this chapter reads Goh's novel alongside a competing *Bildung* plot known as the "Singapore Story": a "national myth" (Loh et al.) that began to take shape in the 1960s as an authorized narrative of national formation disseminated by the state, the PAP, and by Lee Kuan Yew, whose memoirs *The Singapore Story: Memoirs of Lee Kuan Yew* and *From Third World to First: The Singapore Story, 1965–2000* comprise the Story's retrospective canon. Narrating national formation as a project to reproduce the institutions, infrastructure, and economic dynamism of the "First World," the Singapore Story projects towards a technocratic future, foreclosing the radical possibilities of the postcolonial event by narrating a sustained "cultural revolution" (Trocki 138) as merely a pragmatic response to the challenges of postcolonial modernization. Goh's novel registers the "depoliticization effects" (Chua 26) of this national Story, but it also attempts to reclaim a measure of what I will call here "developmental time." Ultimately, for Goh, the literary itself offers a reprieve from the homogenizing and synchronizing effects of Singapore's authoritarian model of state-directed economic growth: an unregulated time within which to achieve what Goh describes as a temporary "spaciousness" (*Dream* 24) amid the calculated tumult of Singapore in the 1960s. Goh does not attribute a revolutionary potential to his own work, or to an emergent Singaporean national literature in general. And yet, in a city state where Lee is reported to have said, "poetry is a luxury we cannot afford,"[1] the novel nevertheless amounts to a political event by opening an important, if modest, parenthesis within both the authorized national Story and the global narrative of postwar development.

The Singapore Story

Looking to Lee's accounts of the "political struggles" of the 1960s, one can trace how economic development hardened as the authorized framework for Singaporean *Bildung*. Rather than, for example, securing autonomy and freedom for a postcolonial nation-people, economic growth became the order of the day, a national purpose in whose name nearly all state-directed social reorganization would be undertaken. At the same time, development offered the Singaporean state a narrative framework within which to divest its radical interventions of political content. Just as President Harry Truman inaugurated the development era in 1949 as a neutral "program for making the benefits of...[Euro-American] scientific advances and industrial progress available" to the "underdeveloped areas" (qtd. in Esteva 1), for Lee, Singaporean development was branded, not as process of politicized national striving but as a managerial challenge for local specialists in consultation with global experts. Officially, there would be no need for political struggle, only technocratic tinkering overseen by the state and the PAP, including, in practice, the ruthless suppression of vibrant and viable political alternatives, from Maoism and Malay nationalism to the Bandung-inflected Third Worldist socialism initially championed by the PAP itself (see Trocki and Barr).

It seems Lee understood that Singapore lacked a coherent national identity when it found itself notionally independent, first with the withdrawal of the British Empire and again with the separation from Malaysia, and incorporated this "lack versus other postcolonial nations" (Holden, "Postcolonial Desire" 345) as a founding problematic of the Singapore Story. Referring to the separation from Malaysia, Lee writes (repurposing a line from *Twelfth Night*): "Some countries are born independent. Some achieve independence. Singapore had independence thrust upon it...[W]ith separation, [Singapore] became a heart without a body" (*The Singapore Story* 22–23). The metaphor of an incomplete body recurs throughout Lee's memoirs, sometimes blending with a description of the city state's truncated geography: "We inherited the island," Lee writes in *From Third World to First*, "without its hinterland, a heart without a body" (3). Lee offers here a strange inversion of a dominant metaphor within midcentury anti-colonial discourse. For writers like Frantz Fanon and Amílcar Cabral, as Cheah describes, anti-colonialism is often figured as an "organismic" struggle: "life itself pitted against the imperialist forces and their agents, which are viruses infecting the popular organism" (213). While Lee channels a vitalist current in his image of a "heart without a body," the dynamics of national *Bildung* are, in relation to radical anti-colonial writing of the 1960s and 1970s, crucially reversed. For Lee, midcentury Singapore was not a coherent national organism burdened by an imperial excess, which could then be "eradicated" (Cheah 223) in the process of anti-colonial revolt, but an organ in search of a body. Insofar as Singapore was marked out by a traumatic separation from an integral form, its struggle for postcoloniality would require seeking out prostheses to supplement its constitutive lack.

This figural process would take the concrete form not of delinking from but relinking to the neocolonial powers of the "First World." As Lee writes, "we...found our new hinterland in America, Europe, and Japan" (*From Third World to First* 63). This meant, first, cultivating foreign direct investment by way of the newly established Economic Development Board, whose singular brief was to attract multinational corporations (MNCs) and, in doing so, to facilitate the industrialization of a newly isolated city state and supplement the island's historical *entrepôt* function. To secure these investments, then, the radical dimension of Third Worldist anti-colonialism needed to be variously ignored or repressed. Lee writes:

> The accepted wisdom of development economists at the time was that MNCs were exploiters of cheap land, labor, and raw materials. This "dependency school" of economists argued that MNCs continued the colonial pattern of exploitation that left the developing countries selling raw materials to and buying consumer goods from the advanced countries...Third World leaders believed this theory of neocolonialist exploitation, but [Goh] Keng Swee and I were not impressed. We had a real-life problem to solve and could not afford to be conscripted by any theory or dogma. Anyway, Singapore had no natural resources for MNCs to exploit. All it had were hard-working people, good basic

infrastructure, and a government that was determined to be honest and competent. Our duty was to create a livelihood for two million Singaporeans. (*From Third World to First* 57–58)

Here the political valence of dependency theory—that national self-determination depends not merely upon economic growth but dismantling "the colonial pattern of exploitation" as such—appears as merely a "theoretical" or "dogmatic" layer of postcoloniality, set in opposition to what Lee calls Singapore's "real-life problem." And, as a result, the political concerns of a nation are, for Lee, superseded, at least in the short term, by those of a national population. The task of cultivating freedom and autonomy in relation to a (neo-)colonial system—a task that does not "impress" Lee and his Minister of Finance Goh Keng Swee—is, in other words, replaced by a blinkered commitment to quantitative improvements, supplemented by foreign multinationals, for the "livelihood for two million Singaporeans." By rejecting dependency theory in favour of calculable progress, Third Worldist idealism in favour of dispassionate and depoliticized capitalist realism, the PAP could rise above the political fray and focus on the "simple guiding principle [of] survival" (58).

The other side of this economic project was the deliberate re-engineering of "Third World" subjectivities. "I believed," as Lee writes, alluding to China's Great Leap Forward, "that we could reeducate and reorient our people…If the communists in China could eradicate all flies and sparrows, surely we could get our people to change their Third World habits" (*From Third World to First* 58). In addition to promoting the use of English and Mandarin rather than Chinese dialects in the home (*From Third World to First* 154–55), prohibiting public spitting (173), and regulating popular media in an effort to curb dissent, the state's most ambitious intervention in everyday life was its public housing scheme, undertaken by the Housing Development Board (HDB), which aimed to break up the island's semi-autonomous racial enclaves—Malay *kampongs* at the edges of the city and the "slums" of Chinatown—and resettle their occupants in state-subsidized housing. Expanding the state's power to acquire land, Lee's vision was to clear these spaces "of filth and dilapidation" (*The Singapore Story* 185) and replace them with high-rise apartment complexes on the model of British council estates. "The PAP government was not only carrying out a humanitarian task," as Loh Kah Seng writes, "but...integrating ['squatters'] into the state and the formal economy" (264). And in the state's official discourse, this was not politics but pragmatism: a semantic shift discernable in the buildings themselves. "To the extent that pragmatism has a look," as Rem Koolhaas describes one HDB estate, "it is utilitarian, Anglo-Saxon: the slabs are purely quantitative emblems—modernity stripped of ideology" (1021).

In the aesthetics of "modernity stripped of ideology," one can locate a fundamental contradiction of Singaporean postcoloniality. On the one hand, as Carl A. Trocki puts it, the first decades of PAP power took the form of a "cultural revolution" (138)—in Fredric Jameson's terms, the deliberate "restructuration of collective subjectivities along the logic of a new mode of production" (*Valences* 267). Unlike the Chinese "eleven years," however, "Lee's revolution was not a proletarian but a bourgeois revolution. Rather than mobilizing the masses, Lee and the PAP worked to immobilize them" (Trocki 138), not only through the application of repressive state power but also by securing consensual participation in the regime's new model of authoritarian capitalism. On the other hand, in the contemporaneous *narration* of this cultural revolution, as Beng-Huat Chua writes, "the PAP government may be said simply to have done what was necessary, that is, to adopt the developmentalist programme and attitude in its day-to-day management of the nation...[F]rom the very outset of state formation, the developmentalist strategies have always been identified as the 'natural', the 'necessary', and the 'realistic' solution to the problems of nation-building" (28). As a national *Bildung* plot, the Singapore Story divests this transition of revolutionary content. Beginning with the metaphor of an incomplete national body in need of supplementation, the Story follows what it positions as the only available course of development, a course that is, in turn, naturalized as "necessary" and "realistic." In spite of its subject, the Singapore Story is, in this way, deliberately *"boring,"* as the American novelist William Gibson described his visit to Singapore in the early 1990s, particularly when drawn out in Lee's interminable memoirs, which together amount to nearly fifteen hundred pages of sanitized anecdotes and dreary tabulations of policy successes. But boredom, as a literary and political strategy, has its uses. As Hock Lai puts it in *If We Dream to Long*, it forecloses a sense of "action," creating the effect of a completed national drama in a period marked, in fact, by revolutionary change. And it is into this revolutionary and yet somehow tedious world—what Goh calls "mundane modern Singapore" (*Dream* 66)—that *Dream* releases its protagonist, who immediately notes he "has not been feeling too well since he contracted," among other maladies, a case of "boredom" (1).

If We Dream Too Long and Developmental Time

Born into a middle-class Straits Chinese family in Kuala Lumpur in 1936, and educated in Ireland in the 1950s, Goh Poh Seng lived in Singapore from 1960 to 1986, when he immigrated to Canada, returning to the city state only once before his death in 2010. Goh's quarter century "stuck" in Singapore, as he described the period in an interview at the end of his life ("Goh Poh Seng"), was remarkably productive in a number of fields. While working as a medical doctor and managing his own practice, he published two novels, *If We Dream Too Long* (completed in 1968 and self-published in 1972) and the Vietnam War novel *The Immolation* (published in 1977), as well as three collections of poetry and three plays. He also founded a literary magazine, *Tumasek*, in 1964, and a small literary press in 1972, owned a nightclub, promoted musical acts, and, from 1967 to 1973, served as the chairman of the government's National Theatre Trust.

Frequently cited as the first Singaporean novel in English, *Dream* has gained greater critical recognition in the past few decades as an important, if idiosyncratic, entry in the global archive of postcolonial Bildungsromane. Briefly, the novel follows Kwang Meng, a listless high school graduate, with neither the money nor test scores to attend university, in the six months after Singapore's separation from Malaysia on August 9, 1965. Although Goh does not signpost the correspondence, there is in this way an unmistakable link between Kwang Meng's introduction to professional life and Singapore "going it alone" as an independent nation (Lee, *From Third World to First* 3). And yet, if the

Singapore Story strips away high drama from the project of postcolonial nation building, Goh takes something like the opposite course. Over the novel's twenty-four chapters, very little happens, but the narration, grounded in Kwang Meng's perspective, invests its mundane literary world with an often comically augmented significance. In no fewer than five scenes in the short novel, for instance, Kwang Meng goes to the beach where his swimming strokes are documented with overwrought meticulousness. Elsewhere, and with a similar attention to the quotidian, we find Kwang Meng eating with his parents and siblings in their HDB flat, drinking in local bars with his friends Hock Lai and Nadarajah, working for a shipping company as a "clerk, junior probationary grade" (*Dream* 24), and strolling aimlessly along the Esplanade. In the novel's final pages, Kwang Meng's father, himself a senior clerk for a shipping company, suffers a stroke. After his father's forced retirement, the responsibility to support the family falls to Kwang Meng, whose youthful enervation comes to an abrupt end, replaced by a "strange and new fear that caused his palms to exude cold sweat...He was suddenly frightened of losing his job" (150).

If Goh's novel is largely emptied of action, this lack is redeemed for his critics by the reputed dynamism, skillfully documented, of its literary world. As Koh Tai Ann describes, "the novel...is distinctive for its setting—the new urbanscape of public housing blocks, multistory offices downtown alongside still existing imperial buildings, exclusive clubs and Chinatown slums—and its alertness to a historical shift, the old giving way to the new" ("Goh Poh Seng" xiii). Mirroring the depoliticized nature of Singaporean modernization, however, *Dream*'s representations of "the old giving way to the new" are remarkably muted. While Goh is certainly invested in documenting the transformations of the urban landscape, from the clearance of the Chinatown slums to the land reclamation projects that redrew the boundaries of Singapore Island itself, what is missing from the novel is precisely the sense of "historical shift" that would mark these transformations out as a radical break with the past.

Early in the text, for example, Kwang Meng reflects on the durability of the British colonial infrastructure:

> He walked in the direction of Collyer Quay for the bus stop, the sea to his left. To his right, across the street, the Singapore Cricket Club stood patronizingly at the corner of the Padang. A relic of the colonial past, but still the same syce-driven cars were parked outside in the members-only parking enclosure, and the same English masters were seen going in for their Whiskey Stengahs and their Brandy Drys. He caught a glimpse of the white uniformed Chinese "boys." It's funny how the English can unselfconsciously call these old Hainanese men, "boys." Walking on, Kwang Meng felt that it was not such a relic after all, in spite of Independence. The English are durable, he thought. (4)

For Lee and the PAP, preserving monuments from the colonial period was part of a deliberate strategy to show Singapore's potential foreign investors that "my colleagues and I had no desire to rewrite the past" (*From Third World to First* 50). For Kwang Meng, however, the persistence of not only English colonial architecture but the English "masters" themselves, waited upon here by Hainanese valets (perennially infantilized as "boys") and Indian or Malay chauffeurs, attests to the persistence of colonial patterns of racial hierarchy. Though formally incorporated within the modern state's sphere of harmonious "multiracialism," these men continue to serve more or less the same "function," though now with the added significance that, like the buildings around them, they too are symbols that postcolonial Singapore has "no desire to rewrite the past." In this way, the event of postcoloniality is hollowed out, reduced to a merely formal marker signifying, perhaps, newness (of the government, the developmental institutions of the state, and so forth), but without an authentic historical rupture: independence without the politics of independence, the postcolonial without postcoloniality. "No wonder," as Kwang Meng thinks, "the English still feel very much at home here" (Goh, *Dream* 4).

At the same time, whatever authenticity the city's peripheral enclaves possessed during the colonial period has, for Kwang Meng, been swept away by the tide of modernization. Though he was born "in an old section of Singapore's teeming Chinatown," by the time the novel begins in 1965, his family has lived for two years in an HDB flat on the seventh floor of a twelve-story block "beside the other identical blocks arranged in a pattern of standing dominos" (33–34). In one of the novel's most discussed sequences, his memories of this earlier period in Chinatown bubble to the surface in a brief, "involuntary reverie" (Koh, "Intertextual Selves" 180). While this sensuous scene stands out from the novel's otherwise affectless narration, it also notably resists sentimentality. Kwang Meng remembers, for instance, the "noisy and joyful camaraderie" brought about by living with his extended family, "thirteen souls distributed into the four small rooms" (Goh, *Dream* 34), reduced now, in the HDB flat, to the more legible nuclear unit. But his memories linger, too, with the injustices of the arrangement and, in particular, with Ah Suan, his grandmother's maid, "who had been bought as a child...and who was treated like a slave rather than a servant" (34). He remembers the smells from the provisions shop below, the "dried salted fish, strings of reddish-brown Chinese sausages hanging from wire hooks...boxes of salted ducks' eggs preserved in black ash" (34–35), but he remembers them "mingling with the smells of the often rubbish-choked monsoon gutters" (35).

Juxtaposing this "pungent cornucopia" with the seriality of the HDB flat, Jini Kim Watson reads this scene of recollection as expressive of a "vague yearning for differentiation tied to [Kwang Meng's] nostalgia for an intensely colorful and scented Singapore" (116). Although there is a nostalgic element here, Goh also consistently undercuts this feeling, not only by returning, with each image from childhood, to what Koh calls its "squalid reality" ("Intertextual Selves" 180), but also with a sense that, refracted through his (and Singapore's) new antiseptic modernity, these memories no longer quite belong to him. "That past life in Chinatown," Kwang Meng thinks, "seemed remote now. It was like a scene in a drama in which his present self was not an actor, but a spectator, and a somewhat disinterested spectator at that...They were almost characters of another story, and not his own" (Goh, *Dream* 34). The very act of remembering scenes from his childhood underscores for Kwang Meng not continuity but a historical caesura. As "a spectator, and a somewhat disinterested spectator at that," his past—unlike the colonial past that seems to live on amid the animated "relics" of British rule—is marked out by rupture, here, too, associated with architecture in a split between the abundantly "differentiated" Chinatown shophouses and the "identical blocks" of HDB flats.

Linking this ambivalent reverie to Kwang Meng's earlier reflections on colonial architecture, one can begin to see how a politically charged and formally complex literary temporality congeals within Singapore's postcolonial "urbanscape." Politically, in the "durable" Englishness of downtown Singapore, colonial history is, for Goh's protagonist, all too present. The event that would mark its obsolescence and signal a new course of national history, "Independence," is emptied of significance when considered against the background of colonial architecture. On the other hand, Kwang Meng's experience of his personal history is fractured by a selective, but nevertheless radical, upheaval in the same urban geography. The replacement of sensuous Singapore's Chinatown with "purely quantitative emblems" creates precisely the historical break that "Independence" cannot, leaving Kwang Meng's memories curiously "remote" after only a few years. For Kwang Meng, then, development appears as *both* an extension of colonial patterns of exploitation and the radical remaking of the city state's cultural geography: continuity at the levels of the political and economic combined with turbulence at the level of domestic life.

Crucially, these two perspectives on the past coalesce in what Kwang Meng experiences as a kind of interminable present. Finding himself, when the novel begins, embedded in the routine of a job without "prospects," the days proceed as an "idle succession" (97): "Monday, Tuesday, Wednesday, Thursday, Friday, Saturday and Sunday and Monday and...round and round and round and round" (67). Following the career path of his father, who had worked for twenty-five years in the same shipping firm, Kwang Meng's waking hours are claustrophobically regimented. "His days," as Goh writes, "have no spaciousness" (21). Mirroring the PAP's effort to render its revolutionary remaking of the city state as "natural," "necessary," and "realistic" (Chua 28), Goh narrates the temporal experience of modernization as tedious repetition. Cut off from his personal history and, simultaneously, subject to a colonial presence continuous across the empty marker of "Independence," his story becomes an eventless chronicle: "If only some soul-searing event would happen...would lighten his life, so that he could find his own true voice...What if nothing happens all life long?" (Goh, *Dream* 97).

Extending this final question, the novel's central narrative problem becomes: How does one narrate a *Bildung* plot, and, specifically, the symbolic event of maturity, within an eventless present or what Goh calls Singapore's "mundane modern[ity]" (66)? If, as Jed Esty writes, "the European Bildungsroman's historical vocation was to manage the effects of modernization by representing it within a safe narrative scheme" (4), namely the gradual compromise between the freedom of youth and the normative gravity of maturation, then in the postwar climate of modernizing Singapore the former would seem to be strangely foreclosed in advance. Condemned to rehearse the career of his father (for Franco Moretti, the "classical Bildungsroman" arises at precisely the moment in European history when the cyclical time of generational repetition loses its sway), Kwang Meng cannot even harbour the illusion of a youth marked by "boundless dynamism" (Moretti 6). As a result, Goh is forced to rethink the *Bildung* plot altogether, not in terms of reconciling one's desires with the imperatives of a rigid social order, but of surrendering oneself to a place, understood in advance, within a "changeless" hierarchy. In *If We Dream Too Long*, in other words, *Bildung* becomes a narrative, not of compromise but of "resignation" to the fact that one has "come too late to the scene" (Goh, *Dream* 7).

The clearest articulation of this new narrative system comes later in the novel when Kwang Meng attends a small dinner party with his neighbour, the schoolteacher Boon Teik. Over beer in the living room of Boon Teik's HDB flat, the neighbour offers a bit of hard-won perspective on Kwang Meng's dreary prospects:

> It may seem meaningless, but it really is not. Depends on how you look at it. I believe that it must be viewed from the wide context of society. Man is a social animal, you must first accept that. He lives in society, and it follows that for society to function, there must be different planes of work. But whatever the category, whatever the plane of work, they all fit

> in like the individual pieces of an intricate machinery, the pieces of an intricate clock. In this way, every little piece, every single unit is important…You must understand that modern society is complex; the more modern the form of society, the more complicated and sophisticated it becomes; and in such a society, there must be numerous, necessary forms and categories of human functions, from the most lowly to the most lofty. Indeed, the range of differentiation determines the level of development of that society. (Goh, *Dream* 114)

Notice here Boon Teik's familiar image of an integrated national form composed of interlocking "pieces" and hierarchically distributed "planes of work" seems to operate within two temporal dimensions at once. On the one hand, in the final sentence he appeals to what one might call comparative developmental time: a spectrum of nations arranged by their "level of development." This is the temporality that structures Lee Kuan Yew's narrative of Singaporean growth from "Third World to First." On the other hand, the process of development is experienced cyclically as the social mechanism reproduces itself again and again, growing in complexity and sophistication, perhaps, but maintaining more or less the same form across every iteration. Breaking with what Cheah identifies as the "organismic" metaphor that animated other struggles for postcolonial sovereignty, the "individual piece" here forms part "of an intricate *machinery*, the pieces of an intricate *clock*" circling itself endlessly. This is the modality in which Singaporean modernization is lived by Kwang Meng: a mechanical sequence of days unfolding in "idle succession." And here *Dream* comes closest to theorizing its own reorientation of the *Bildung* plot, which now involves capitulating to the "changelessness" of everyday life while finding "meaning" in the more abstract register of developmental temporality. Maturation, in other words, means a resignation to meaninglessness in the service of the Singapore Story itself.

    With his father's stroke, and the knowledge that he, as the eldest child, will now be responsible for supporting his family, any resistance is, seemingly overnight, replaced by a "fear…that he might lose his job" (150), a "fear" demanding acquiescence to the eventlessness of the Singapore Story as it was lived day to day. "He realized that it must be just this kind of feeling, this kind of terrible fear, that made people the small frightened people they become: the spineless clerks who eke out a dreary job year after year after year" (150). Similarly, in response to his mother's appeal to the family's tragic "fate," Goh's protagonist only nods, thinking, "Things just happen, that's all. So what is there to understand? Things just happen" (148). For Kwang Meng, in other words, there is no redemptive meaning to accompany his inevitable integration into the national mechanism. "Things just happen," "year after year after year," within a temporality policed, not by the "understanding" that his "dreary job" has meaning when viewed from what Boon Teik calls "the wide context of society," but by the "fear" of being left behind.

In his final line, Kwang Meng formalizes his surrender to the temporal order of Singaporean modernization. Approached along the Esplanade by "an old English lady, a tourist," asking for directions to the Raffles Hotel, another architectural symbol of the colonial past, Kwang Meng "couldn't comprehend. Suddenly he replied, 'Yes, Madam. I go with all convenient speed,' and walked away" (155). Quoting a peripheral character, Portia's servant Balthazar, from *The Merchant of Venice*, Kwang Meng offers, first, a performance of ironic servility tuned to the metropole's language and national literature. But it is also an inappropriate performance: a *non sequitur* that reframes the docility of this formerly colonized subject as an incomprehensible affront. "The old English lady tourist," the novel concludes, "looked at the vanishing figure and shook her head, puzzled" (155). At the same time, the line would seem to indicate that Kwang Meng has, finally, become a peripheral character in his own *Bildung* plot. Having played the role of Balthazar in a high school production of Shakespeare's play, Kwang Meng's single line reappears to mark his position within a national character structure centred not on clerks "junior, probationary grade," but the PAP's stalwart managers with Lee Kuan Yew leading the way. If the peripheralization of the protagonist, from Wilhelm Meister to Elizabeth Bennet, traditionally signals the successful integration of the individual as a "simple part of a whole" (Moretti 16), here the suddenness of the line, in words that are not his own, spoken at the wrong time to the wrong audience, suggests Kwang Meng's failure to consent to this development. Accordingly, for Watson, *Dream* amounts to a "failed Bildungsroman plot, where education and experience fall short of bringing the individual in line with his proper place in society" (118). The result may be formally indistinguishable from the conclusion of the "classical Bildungsroman"—indeed, after his father's stroke, Kwang Meng assumes his "proper place in society" to support his family—but it is a result achieved without alternatives. What is more, the conclusion of Goh's "failed Bildungsroman plot" is presented in explicitly temporal terms. Kwang Meng concedes to "go with all convenient *speed*" to perform his social function, in this case, according to the mechanical rhythms of a lived Singaporean time, which is here underscored by the regularized meter of Shakespearean blank verse. More than simply staging a compelled resignation to peripherality, this final line also symbolically synchronizes its protagonist as one piece "of an intricate clock" measuring out an "idle succession."

If Goh's novel fails as a Bildungsroman, then, it may nevertheless successfully allegorize the logic of Singaporean modernization in the 1960s. While Kwang Meng registers that Singapore is being remade, the "richness and dynamism" of the transition from "Third World to First" are lost on him, subsumed by the brutal cadence of economic necessity. Just as the nation's development was stripped of its political valence, reframed as merely a "natural" course of action undertaken by an impersonal, technocratic apparatus, so too is Kwang Meng's narrative deprived of a sense of willed authorship. As a text in which almost nothing happens, in which a hero grows, having no alternative, to accept the nothing new, *If We Dream Too Long* diligently transplants the apparently eventless narrative of the Singapore Story to the level of the citizen.

Conclusion

One should, however, read these lines once more. Recalling Kwang Meng's diagnosis that "there are no real dramatic causes left for our generation" (Goh, *Dream* 9), the novel's final resignation is, by contrast, saliently dramatic: a self-consciously histrionic announcement emphasized by its wry mimicry, contextual inappropriateness, and its speaker's abrupt exit. Positioned at the end of the text, it is a peripheral character's single line, "I go with all convenient speed," amplified by context into a howl—and, in this way, a narrative event in a novel where events of any kind are in short supply. As an impromptu, postcolonial performance of Shakespeare along the Esplanade, it is also, importantly, a *literary* event that finally cuts through the atmosphere of narrative stasis. It is a conclusion that interrupts, if only for a moment, the novel's cyclical temporality at the very same moment its protagonist resigns to it.

The text is dotted with similar literary interruptions, which, though brief and quickly refolded into the eventless present, quietly prepare the reader for this overdetermined conclusion. Early in the text, Kwang Meng's literary education is limited, it seems, to Shakespeare, the comics page of the *Straits Times*, and a few Anglo-American adventure tales taught to him in school: Sir Walter Scott, Robert Lewis Stevenson, and Edgar Rice Burroughs. From these texts, as Holden notes, Kwang Meng draws an image of "colonial masculinity" ("Colonialism's Goblins" 167), against whose "pioneering" "simplicity" he contrasts his own dreary, "complicated" life as a clerk. While driving through Malaysia on one trip to the beach, for example, a landscape of rubber plantations suddenly transforms into a colonial image of tropical frontier: "Kwang Meng could almost imagine the wild boars, the tigers, the tapirs, the elephants, the honey bears and the *pelandoks* or mousedeer, and Tarzan, lord of the green beast-filled jungle, although he knew Tarzan was supposed to be in Africa, darkest Africa, and not in Malaysia" (Goh, *Dream* 90). This image, however, soon becomes a vehicle to reflect on the "eventlessness" of Kwang Meng's professional life. In the rubber plantations he perceives "the smell and sight of pioneering. Pioneering, and me a complicated clerk in a bloody city, Kwang Meng thought. Pioneers are simpler people" (91).

While Holden is right to emphasize the colonial valence of Kwang Meng's early reading habits, the function of literature remains remarkably undifferentiated for Goh's protagonist, even after Boon Teik introduces him to a broader range of "good books" (117) by Narayan, Dostoyevsky, and Sartre. In particular, for Kwang Meng, the effect of literature, from *Tarzan of the Apes* to *The Man-Eater of Malgudi*, is to "steal time." Literature offers, in other words, a temporary deferral, a parenthesis, an unregulated time outside of the regimented hours of the "mundane modern." In what one can only interpret as a self-reflexive joke, Goh underscores this function by setting nearly all of Kwang Meng's engagements with literature in or around a bathroom. Early in the novel, rushing out the door to catch the bus to his office, Kwang Meng realizes he will have to "visit the toilet at the office, on office time…Ha, ha, he pounded his chest in the manner of Tarzan, lord of the green beast-filled jungle, as if he had just challenged the whole world" (23). A few pages later, the moment having arrived at last, "Kwang Meng left his desk, unsentencing himself, reprieving himself, and walked magnificently, majestically, to the office toilet. On office time!" (27). Later in the novel, his tastes having improved, he now uses Narayan to secret away a few minutes before returning to his desk.

> Nowadays he stayed longer than before at the office toilet, stealing office time, reading the books that Book Teik had lent him, so that he didn't have to come out immediately after he was done. The first few mornings he could be heard laughing loudly from within the toilet, and some of his office mates, not colleagues, must have thought him cuckoo. But he was only reading Narayan; and Narayan was indeed very, very funny. (120–21).

It is in a bathroom too—not at the office, but in a local bar—that Kwang Meng makes his first and only attempt at literary writing. An avid reader of lavatory graffiti, he adds, impulsively, his own lyric:

> The days drag by,
> The nights are worse;
> There's nothing to do
> If you don't have fifty dollars. (82)

If "office time" presents itself to Kwang Meng as the paradigmatic modality of modernizing Singapore's interminable present, the lived national temporality in which days simply "drag by," literary texts, undifferentiated by quality, allow Goh's protagonist to recover a small measure of time for himself. Reading and writing, in and of themselves, constitute in this way acts of temporal theft. While there is something furtive and immodest about Kwang Meng's literary habits, hence the bathroom setting, they also seem to provide a source of not simply amusement but of a more meaningful, if still fleeting, "reprieve" from the paradoxical changelessness of daily life. For Kwang Meng, in other words, literature offers an "unsentencing" from the prosaic, which he performs in his lavatory poem by adding line breaks to a description of his eventless time: "The days drag by, / The nights are worse; / There's nothing to do / If you don't have fifty dollars."

By representing the literary as an act of "stealing time" in a founding text of Singaporean literature, Goh asks his readers to recalibrate their understanding of the function of a national literature in general and the postcolonial Bildungsroman in particular within the context of the authoritarian developmental state. As Gwee Li Sui describes, the first generation of Singaporean literature—which includes the work of Goh, Kok Seng Tan, Lloyd Fernando, Edwin Thumboo, Catherine Lim, Robert Yeo, Arthur Yap, and others—has been retrospectively folded into the Singapore Story as part of the cultural dimension of the national *Bildung* plot. "After 1965, the year of Singapore's independence," Gwee writes, "the youthful imagination is...said to have given itself to constructing and enriching the life of a nation" (56). Goh, too, drifts towards this narrative in a 2007 interview with the *Straits Times*. Reflecting on the beginning of his career as a writer, he says, "I realized that all the books I enjoyed were about somewhere else, not my hometown. I thought that we need our own literature in order to know about ourselves. Since there was not much literature about Singapore at the time, I had the temerity to try to write some" (Yap 2007).

One should not, of course, dismiss this conceptualization of an emergent national literature premised upon what Jameson calls "cultural import substitution." Limiting the discussion to these terms, however, would strip Goh's novel of its capacity not only to reflect back a postcolonial nation in the process of formation, but to interrupt, briefly, this same process and to intercede on behalf of those for whom, like Kwang Meng, the experience of the Singapore Story was one of tedious eventlessness. In the context of Singapore's depoliticized "cultural revolution" in the 1960s where, in Lee's terms, "poetry is a luxury we cannot afford," the novel refuses to accommodate the velocity of Singaporean developmentalism. It is not a revolutionary text. But it insists, as a literary object, upon going at a speed that is more convenient.

Note

1. Although widely repeated, it is difficult to attribute this "very quotable quote" to Lee with any certainty. As Philip Holden writes: "Search for that 'famous declaration' in newspapers, in government records, in the national archives, even in the nineteen-volume *Papers of Lee Kuan Yew*, and you find nothing. Try another approach: trace a thread back into the labyrinth of scholarly references. Were those words said in a speech, or let drop as a casual remark? Where? When—in 1968 or 1969?...Even those who heard the words pronounced now cannot agree on when they were uttered, and cannot recall their precise context" ("The Myth" 170).

Works Cited

Barr, Michael D., and Carl A. Trocki, editors. *Paths Not Taken: Political Pluralism in Post-War Singapore*, National University of Singapore Press, 2008.

Cheah, Pheng. *Spectral Nationality: Passages of Freedom from Kant to Postcolonial Literatures of Liberation*. Columbia University Press, 2003.

Chua, Beng-Haut. "Not Depoliticized but Ideologically Successful: The Public Housing Programme in Singapore." *International Journal of Urban and Regional Research*, vol. 15, no. 1, 1991, pp. 24–41.

Esteva, Gustavo. "Development." *The Development Dictionary: A Guide to Knowledge as Power*, edited by Wolfgang Sachs, Zed Books, 2010, pp. 1–23.

Esty, Jed. *Unseasonable Youth: Modernism, Colonialism, and the Fiction of Development*. Oxford University Press, 2012.

Gibson, William. "Disneyland with the Death Penalty." *Wired*, 1 Apr. 1993, https://www.wired.com/1993/04/gibson-2/.

"Goh Poh Seng." *Youtube*, 27 Jan. 2010, https://www.youtube.com/watch?v=5DtS8YoxQXE.

Goh Poh Seng. *If We Dream Too Long*. National University of Singapore Press, 2010 (1972).

Goh Poh Seng. *The Immolation*. Epigram Books, 2011 (1977).

Gwee Li Sui. "Demythologizing Singaporean Literature." *Living with Myths in Singapore*, edited by Loh Kah Seng et al., Ethos Books, 2017, pp. 53–60.

Holden, Philip. "Colonialism's Goblins: Language, Gender, and the Southeast Asian Novel in English at a Time of Nationalism." *Journal of Postcolonial Writing*, vol. 44, no. 2, 2008, pp. 159–70.

Holden, Philip. "The Myth That Dare Not Speak Its Name." *Quarterly Literary Review Singapore*, vol. 14, no. 1, 2015, pp. 159–70.

Holden, Philip. "Postcolonial Desire: Placing Singapore." *Postcolonial Studies*, vol. 11, no. 3, 2008, pp. 345–61.

Jameson, Fredric. "On Literary and Cultural Import-Substitution in the Third World." *The Real Thing: Testimonial Discourse and Latin America*, edited by Georg M. Gugelberger, Duke University Press, 1996, pp. 172–91.

Jameson, Fredric. *Valences of the Dialectic*. Verso, 2009.

Koh Tai Ann. "Goh Poh Seng's *If We Dream Too Long*: An Appreciation." *If We Dream Too Long*, National University of Singapore Press, 2010, pp. vii–xxxvi.

Koh Tai Ann. "Intertextual Selves: Fiction-makers in Two 'Singapore' Novels." *Tropic Crucible: Self and Theory in Language and Literature*, edited by Ranjit Chatterjee and Colin Nicholson, National University of Singapore Press, 1984, pp. 163–92.

Koolhaas, Rem. "Singapore Songlines: Thirty Years of Tabula Rasa." *S,M,L,XL*, edited by Rem Koolhaas and Bruce Mao. Monacelli, 1995, pp. 1008–89.

Lee Kuan Yew. *From Third World to First: The Singapore Story: 1965–2000*. Harper Collins, 2000.

Lee Kuan Yew. *The Singapore Story: Memoirs of Lee Kuan Yew*. Times Editions, 1998.

Loh Kah Seng. *Squatters into Citizens: The 1961 Bukit Ho Swee Fire and the Making of Modern Singapore*. University of Hawai'i Press, 2013.

Loh Kah Seng, et al. "Singapore as a Mythic Nation." Introduction. *Living with Myths in Singapore*, edited by Loh Kah Seng et al., Ethos Books, 2017, pp. 1–14.

Moretti, Franco. *The Way of the World: The Bildungsroman in European Culture*. Translated by Albert Sbragia, Verso, 1987.

Slaughter, Joseph. *Human Rights, Inc: The World Novel, Narrative Form, and International Law*. Fordham University Press, 2007.

Trocki, Carl A. *Singapore: Wealth, Power and the Culture of Control*. Routledge, 2006.

Watson, Jini Kim. *The New Asian City: Three-Dimensional Fictions of Space and Urban Form*. University of Minnesota Press, 2011.

The World Bank. *The East Asian Miracle: Economic Growth and Public Policy*. Oxford University Press, 1993.

Yap, Stephanie. "A Pioneer Returns Home." *Straits Times*. 18 Nov. 2007.

IV

MODERNITY AND THE
POSTCOLONIAL BILDUNGSROMAN

11

BAD MODERNIZATION
The Carceral States Bildungsroman in Postcolonial Africa

Craig Smith

As a form that typically conveys a "hyper-European narrative of the autonomous individual" (Austen 227), the Bildungsroman may not initially present itself as a genre with much to offer postcolonial authors. Indeed, the very act of labelling a text as a postcolonial Bildungsroman may be "inherently contradictory" (Hay 318), for the genre's roots can be located "in a burgeoning nationalism based on an ideal of organic culture whose temporality and harmony could be reflected in the developing personality at the core of the bildungsroman" (Esty 5). As such, the *volk*-ish associations evoked by an organic *nation*-state underwrite the development of the Bildungsroman, but these same associations seem ludicrously and perhaps dangerously out of place in many postcolonial states—legacies of imperialist cartographic invention—that cannot claim descent from a singular, unified nation.

Yet, despite its beginnings in post-Enlightenment European fictions, the Bildungsroman has nevertheless long been an important postcolonial genre. Whatever ubiquity it can claim, the cultural and epistemological politics of the postcolonial Bildungsroman have never been straightforward, as it has functioned both as a model for the colonial emulation of imported values and as a form whose textual subversions serve de-colonial causes. It may be that "writing in a form so identified with the European literary tradition cannot avoid...some cultural compromise with the dominant 'other'" (Austen 226), but any discussion of how the Bildungsroman entered the artistic repertoires of (post)colonial authors as an educational and acculturative component of a broader colonialist agenda is greatly complicated by its historical role as a powerful vehicle for nationalist sentiments. According to Jussawalla, the Bildungsroman remains "a favored form for the postcolonial writer," one that demonstrates "the hero or heroine's developing affirmation of his or her native culture and history" (98), wherein the protagonist's "personal growth and development almost always reflects his or her growing sense of national and ethnic belonging" (98). Similarly, for Stitt, "Postcolonial coming of age narratives...allow authors to couple the development of a child with the rise of independence struggles or postcolonial independence" (181).

As Jussawalla and Stitt demonstrate, then, the Bildungsroman is inextricably linked to the wider development of postcolonial literature. Crucially, however, their words are perhaps especially germane to African literature. In both Western and African Bildungsromane, the central process of youth identity formation or dissolution takes place "in the context of a 'modernizing' world" (Austen 215). Accordingly, the ambivalent appeal of the Bildungsroman as a genre for African writers to draw on, especially during periods of social and political transformation, becomes clear: if, in a European context, "youth was the master trope of modernity itself" (Esty 4), the coming-of-age narrative paradigm, whose "cardinal defining feature...is predicated on change" (Okuyade 363), seems especially well suited to African nations undergoing monumental change and emerging from periods of externally imposed colonial childhood into the promise-filled youth of post-independence nationhood. The "aspect of becoming" that is "of crucial importance for the bildungsroman as a narrative form" (Okuyade 381) invites, perhaps more than other genres, openness to contextualized readings of national allegories.[1] At the same time, this framing highlights how the Bildungsroman's politics in an African context are hopelessly contradictory: given that colonialism in Africa often took the form of paternalistic guardianship of colonies not deemed "ready" for self-governance, this very youth-modernity association makes the "soul-nation allegory" (Esty 44) in African Bildungsromane closely resemble a recognizably Eurocentric point of view. Insofar as the Bildungsroman "constitutes a crucial narrative structure to represent the advancement and development of postcolonial African nations as they are depicted textually, where the maturation of the child body tropes the emergence of the fully-fledged nation state" (Phillips 105) that nevertheless remains part of a "never-quite-modernized periphery" (Esty 7), one might be tempted to conclude that the genre's "idea of successful adulthood is imperialist, colonial and patriarchal" (Hay 322).

Consequently, few postcolonial Bildungsromane "have ever fully invested in the genre's…idealist vision" (Slaughter 26), so that "the African variant of the coming-of-age narrative differs from traditional Western variants" (Okuyade 360). Where, in Barnard's judgment, the Western Bildungsroman "in its affirmative form…proposes a narrative resolution to the tensions between the anarchic predispositions of the individual and the conformist demands of the state" (545), the vexed combination of individualist and integrative qualities that characterize the Bildungsroman finds its idiosyncratic expression in novels in which African youths find or, more frequently, fail to find individual fulfilment and belonging in national, ethnic, linguistic, and religious communities long devalued in colonial discourses. For Okuyade, the general pattern that emerges in African Bidungsromane suggests a bleak resolution to the tensions Barnard identifies:

> African coming-of-age narratives do not emphasize reintegration and harmonious reconciliation of the protagonist with his/her society as the prototypical Western bildungsroman does. Instead, it expresses a variety of forces that inhibit or prevent the protagonist from achieving self-realization in postcolonial African spaces. (360)

Okuyade's gloss on the African Bildungsroman's prevailing pattern demonstrates how easily the genre can contribute to a familiar mood of disillusionment in Africa's post-independence years. As Young puts it, "If one relies on the expectation of 1960 as a measure, African state performance overall is clearly disappointing, particularly when compared to most of Asia and, to a lesser extent, Latin America" (31). Accordingly, if the literature of disillusionment—as articulated most famously in works by authors such as Ayi Kwei Armah and Ngũgĩ wa Thiong'o—catalogues these state and societal disappointments, then the African Bildungsroman both comprises a subgenre of this body of writing and, as I will argue, continues to give particular form to current Afropessimism on a continent in which the "mood pendulum" (Young 23) has historically swung from high hopes to crushing despair.

The Bildungsroman's longevity within postcolonial African literature is a sign of its foundational role. Yet its current function in African postcolonies needs to be (re-)assessed. The question that concerns me here is thus not "What contribution to postcolonial African literature has the Bildungsroman made?" but, rather, "What does the genre's persistence tell us about its continuing ability to meet the changing needs of contemporary postcoloniality in Africa?" This question seems particularly essential because the Bildungsroman in Africa has lately undergone a significant resurgence. Now largely in the hands of Africa's third generation of postcolonial authors, who have taken on the task of "highlighting contemporary realities rather than deconstructing colonialism or its legacy" (Cockley 149), the genre's ubiquity raises crucial questions regarding the provenance of the renewed interest in coming-of-age narratives, its gendered contours in contemporary iterations,[2] and the socio-political implications of its popularity in marketplaces both local and global.

Joseph Slaughter contends that the Bildungsroman shares with human rights law "a conceptual vocabulary, deep narrative grammar, and humanist social vision" (4). Jed Esty similarly notes the genre's "humanist ideals" (2) in its yoking of its "biographical form...to its progressive concept of national destiny" (24). A "sort of novelistic wing of human rights...that demonstrates its norms" (Slaughter 25), the Bildungsroman is thus a fictional form uniquely attuned to late-twentieth- and early-twenty-first-century life, for "ours is at once the Age of Human Rights and the Age of Human Rights Abuses" (Slaughter 2). This general contemporary condition manifests itself in particular and local ways across the African continent. For instance, with an eye on Nigeria, Egya proclaims that the "prolonged military despotism of the 1980s and 1990s" in the country constituted a genuine "age of oppression" (110) ripe with abuses of human rights and with human rights activism.

It is precisely this Nigerian situation that provides the backdrop for Helon Habila's first novel, *Waiting for an Angel*, a narratively disordered Künstlerroman of sorts that begins at its chronological end with the aspiring-novelist-turned-journalist protagonist, Lomba, attempting to resist a "loss of self" (Habila 14) after being arrested for covering a demonstration and imprisoned, without formal charges, as an "anti-government rat" (20). The end point of Lomba's personal and artistic development, his incarceration serves not only as the narrative beginning to Habila's novel but also as my own point of departure for considering what I see as a recurrent trend in a range of twenty-first-century coming-of-age narratives focusing on young and often idealistic male protagonists. In a European context, Esty identifies a recurrent "arrested-development discourse" in modernist iterations of the Bildungsroman, but what are we to make of postcolonial African Bildungsromane, written in English and in French, in which the central event in the protagonist's development *is* a literal arrest by a repressive state? Novels such as Habila's *Waiting for an Angel* and Alain Mabanckou's *Black Moses* make carceral enclosure—rather than a "traditional plot of libidinal closure" (Esty 22)—the central site/rite of maturation. In this way, they suggest a possible third variant of the genre in contemporary African writing, alongside the war and AIDS Bildungsromane variants identified by Hoagland (234–35).

These works make imprisonment a new metaphor for modernization in postcolonial Africa, albeit a form of modernization hopelessly stalled within a "violent colonial political economy that spatializes containment and punishment" (Pfingst and Kamari 707). In a context wherein the "largest audience for postcolonial Bildungsromane from the Global South still resides largely in the literary industrial centers of the North...whose readers seem to have an insatiable appetite for the stories of Third Worlders coming of age" (Slaughter 37–38), the carceral Bildungsromane I consider here are riven by new competing impulses: in them, the critiques of different forms of African modernity draw force from the Bildungsroman's imbrication with Enlightenment ideals of autonomous self-formation, but this proximity to Enlightenment ideals brings the novels perilously close to replicating the Enlightenment's exclusion of Africa from participation in global modernity.

The State Is the Prison: Diffuse Carceral Politics in '90s Nigeria

Though Habila's *Waiting for an Angel* begins with Lomba's "second year in prison" (13), his individual circumstances reflect a "diffusion of the carceral" throughout Nigerian society, resulting in an atmosphere characterized by "brute force, random killings, assassination of opponents, repression of student protests, arbitrary arrests, rape, home invasions, and public torture" (Erritouni 149). Resembling other parts of the continent, the Nigeria of Habila's novel is the inheritor of colonial "institutional...practices that enact punishment on historically punishable bodies" (Pfingst and Kimari 699). It is unsurprising, then, that in the afterword to *Waiting for an Angel* Habila explains that 1990s Nigeria was "a terrible time to be alive, especially if you were young, talented and ambitious—and patriotic" (223). Lomba—the would-be novelist-turned-journalist who becomes, in the state's eyes, one of the "Saboteurs" (Habila 20) responsible for "organizing violence...against the military legal government" (25)—perfectly fits Habila's description as Lomba's story ends with him as one of the prisoners of whom "no record" remains after Nigeria's prisons "swelled with political detainees" (42). Crucially, it is a process both highly particular to Lomba and common to many deemed "pro-democracy activists" (42) by a repressive state, and it engenders in Lomba the formation of a new, politicized identity. To the extent that "the notion of writing as activism drives [*Waiting for an Angel*'s] narrative" (Dunton 74), the regime of General Sani Abacha—"the most horrific military regime to control the government since independence" (Cockley 165) and "Nigeria's nadir in the postcolonial epoch" (Heaton and Falola 10)—plays a constitutive role in Lomba's accepting writing's activist role.

Temperamentally possessed of "a deep sense of fatalism" (Erritouni 146), Lomba is not initially the character whom readers meet in the book's first chapter, a "survivor" whose time in prison teaches him "not to hope too much, not to despair too much" (Habila 43) and whose death is "hard to imagine" (43) for an unidentified narrator wanting to put Lomba's story together after his disappearance. In subsequent chapters, *Waiting for an Angel* "dispense[s] with linear narrative" (Cockley 166) and uses shifting narrative perspectives to account for Lomba's journey from a state of freedom to ever-more-remote Nigerian prisons. While a student, Lomba "abhors politics or political actions" (Egya 119), and his instinctual disinterest in writerly activism becomes apparent when he hears a student boycott leader reference a famed Nigerian dissident: "Remember what Soyinka wrote, 'The man dies in him who stands silent in the face of tyranny'" (Habila 55). Wole Soyinka's words in his prison diary, *The Man Died*, foreshadow what readers already know to be Lomba's future condition, but Lomba remains ironically unmoved by what is meant to be a call to action. Feeling "like an imposter, out of place," Lomba remains "the only one in the crowd who was not jumping up and down and gesticulating and urging Sankara on" (55).

It is, instead, the state's intrusion into a matter of private suffering and grief that acts as a catalyst for Lomba's transformation. After Lomba's friend Bola loses both parents and one of his sisters in a deeply symbolic car accident involving a "military truck carrying the furniture of an officer on transfer from Lagos to Ibadan" (61), Lomba is forced to acknowledge the imbrication of private life—the ostensible focus of his writerly ambitions—with Nigeria's public sphere, which "provides the ultimate setting of Bildungsromane" (Slaughter 33). After a grief-stricken Bola wanders from his home and, in a "fanatical frenzy," takes to the streets to repeat "word for word, Sankara's speech" to a crowd of Lagosian onlookers (Habila 74), Lomba watches helplessly as "Two men, identically dressed in long black coats and dark glasses...plucked [Bola] down from his perch" (75) and take him away in "a black Peugeot 504 with tinted windows" (75). The opacity of the security forces' glasses and car windows ironically make something transparent to Lomba: the cruel indifference of a modern Nigerian state more threatened by Bola's public cry that "the military has failed us" (74) than moved by his obvious inner distress.

Bola's brief and brutal imprisonment prefigures the treatment Lomba receives later, but, more importantly, it also leaves the erstwhile apolitical author—who earlier in life dreams only of writing "novels and poems" and dedicating his "first book" to his girlfriend Alice (98)—"walking down [a] deserted road with nowhere to go" (83) as the artist he planned to be.

The isolated enclave that university life initially appears to represent to Lomba proves illusory, and, as he explains to James Fiki, editor of a local newspaper called *The Dial*, "When school began to look like prison, I had to get out" (112). Journalism represents an escape to the protagonist who, at twenty-five years of age, discovers that "for the past two years I had been locked in this room, in this tenement house, trying to write a novel" (110) and similarly locked in a "hallucination" that "I could cure all of the world's ills through my stories" (167). Lomba's sense of confinement in his ordinary life mobilizes what Fludernik calls "metaphors of imprisonment" (230), wherein Lomba's free life makes sense to him only when understood as a figurative extension of the carceral realities facing the Nigerian people. Economically precarious and creatively moribund, Lomba's turn to journalism is at first a nonideological continuation of his search for an adult "male destiny" (Esty 24) outside of prisons both figurative and literal. As he explains to James, he is "not very political" (Habila 112), in a country where, according to James, even "the very air we breathe is political" (112). Lomba returns home with instructions to write about "the general disillusionment, the lethargy," anything Lomba wants provided that he "stick[s] to the general facts" (113), only to discover his neighbour Nkem, his face "bloody," with "one eye... swollen" (113), being dragged "forcibly to their van" by five police officers (113). As with Bola, then, experience teaches Lomba about the omnipresence of Nigeria's carceral politics.

Bola's and Nkem's encounters with the lived "state of exception in the [Nigerian] postcolony" (Erritouni 149) leaves both of them "blinking" (Habila 83, 113), a physical manifestation of the abuse they suffer and a symbolic reminder of what it was for Nigerians of this era who were forced to stare closely into the inner workings of a state in which "every day came with new limitations, new prisons"

(Habila 224). Though Lomba becomes a journalist and eventually has to go into hiding after the offices of *The Dial* are set on fire, he remains steadfast in his desire not to oppose the state directly, telling a young partygoer, "I don't want to get arrested" (218), despite her advice that he "really must try and get arrested" (218) if he wants to make it as an author. It is only there, she implies, that he will become witness to the effects of what, in a different context, J.M. Coetzee describes as the "dark chamber" where the state "asserts that its own survival takes precedence over the law and ultimately over justice" (362). Essentially, Lomba's commitment to writing falls short of his wanting to see the inside of that chamber. It is not until Lomba visits a museum exhibit devoted to the African slave trade that he realizes "why it is important to agitate against injustice, no matter the consequence" (Habila 168). This epiphany finally commits Lomba to covering the demonstration that leads to his arrest, completing his transformation from reluctant artist-with-a-journalistic-side-job to committed journalist-activist.

Journalism, in Lomba's eyes, does what serious literature cannot. According to James, Lomba "won't find a publisher in this country because it'd be economically unwise for any publisher to waste his scarce paper to publish a novel which nobody would buy, because the people are too poor, too illiterate, and too busy trying to stay out of the way of the police and the army to read" (194). James's words illustrate how significantly Abacha's regime "decimated the publishing industry" (Egbunike 225) in Nigeria. Egya explains, "Under the yoke of tyranny, the educational system collapsed and the reading culture became zero" (111). This complementary decimation of a local publishing industry and of a culture of educated readers is arguably the surest sign of the postcolonial modernity of Nigeria's authoritarian regime, which expresses its "will to power" (Erritouni 146) through its cultivation of a "hostile period during which creativity collapsed in Nigerian literature" (Egya 122). Consequently, Lomba "cannot complete his novel and become the hero he wants to be" (Egya 121). Yet Lomba's very failure to produce a novel in many ways generates *Habila's* novel.

Indeed, it is not so much the possibility of a story like Lomba's being written—by someone other than Lomba—that provides hope for this creative triumph, but a change in the circumstances of publication and dissemination that takes place beyond the frame of Lomba's story. With Nigeria "thrown out of the Commonwealth of Nations" (Habila 195), Lomba finds his potential venues of publication limited, which prevents his participation in an international book market (over)determined by the awarding of prestigious literary prizes such as the "Commonwealth Literary Prize" (195). In contrast, Habila faced no such creatively crippling hindrances writing *Waiting for an Angel*. The narrative trajectory that sees Lomba's novelistic aspirations go unfulfilled as part of a coming-of-age narrative that does "not emphasize [the] reintegration and harmonious reconciliation of the protagonist with his/her society" (Okuyade 360) is precisely what makes *Habila's* novel internationally marketable as a singular iteration of an "increasingly global fictional genre" (Esty 25). As Austen explains, "almost all African bildungsromane are written in European languages and are read at least as much by Europeans and Americans as by Africans" (225). This no doubt allows the genre, which "incorporates" into its tale or personal growth "intimate aspects of local experience" (Austen 227), to fit seamlessly into an exotic and exoticized postcolonial literary and critical "industry" in which authors produce and sell texts that "can be thought of as having a touristic conscience" (Brouillette 5). In this way, *Waiting for an Angel* appeals directly to what Slaughter describes as the "metropolitan literary industry's appetite for Third World Bildungsromane that turns multicultural, postcolonial reading into a kind of humanitarian intervention" (35).

If the act of reading an African Bildungsroman itself *becomes* the activist intervention by the Western reader, this exemplifies how the contemporary, post-independence, coming-of-age narrative shares with its predecessors what might be considered a kind of compromised politics of postcoloniality, to the extent that "there is something awkward or even impossible about a novel being both postcolonial and bildungsroman at once" (Hay 318). *Waiting for an Angel* may offer exonerating comfort to those Western readers who learn about the abuses of the Nigerian state through its pages. According to Erritouni, "jettison[ing] Marxism as an explanatory framework" (144), Habila shows readers "that despotism in Nigeria is an expression of the will to power of the postcolonial rulers" that "has no genealogy or economic rationale" (146), while, for Cockley, Habila "highlight[s] contemporary realities rather than deconstructing colonialism or its legacy" (149). In other words, the novel risks reaffirming the pernicious stereotype that, as Dipo Faloyin irreverently puts it, "in deep dark Africa…deep dark things take place" (83).

In bringing to light the abuses and excesses of late-twentieth-century, post-independence Nigeria *for* a predominately Western readership, Habila shows how the country has failed to cultivate "a democratic humanitarian sensibility" (Slaughter 42) that in a typical affirmative Western Bildungsroman would allow the protagonist to "freely reconcile inner desires with outer demands" (Esty 11). Habila comes to resemble other postcolonial authors, "writing from or about the developing world, and situating their narratives within an often violent political history, [who] are expected to act as interpreters of locations they are connected to through personal biography" (Brouillette 70). That is to say, he bears witness, through a text generically coded as a Bildungsroman, to a parodic African exceptionalism that implicitly reinforces the association of the "moral force" (Slaughter 54) of human rights laws with the normative Western Bildungsroman. As Hay puts it, "For a novel of formation to make sense, its protagonist needs to have both the desire and the opportunity to become something new" (319). While, in *Waiting for an Angel*, Lomba's life story reveals his incessant desire to become something new, it is his emplotment/entrapment within the Nigerian postcolony that prevents his disjointed coming-of-age narrative from taking on a less exotic shape.

Alain Mabanckou and the Exoticist Carceral Bildungsroman

If *Waiting for an Angel*, Habila's first published novel, was the product of an author of whom cosmopolitan literary readers could have few expectations, the same cannot be said of *Black Moses*, a Bildungsroman set in Congo-Brazzaville, the birthplace of Alain Mabanckou, "one of Africa's foremost francophone writers" (Deckard 97). As "perhaps the most visible Black contemporary writer in French publishing at the moment" (Stern 206) who "has recently come to international attention outside the French-speaking world" (203), Mabanckou's contribution to the African Bildungsroman genre invites contextualization in light of his broader life and oeuvre. And it is precisely in that context that *Black Moses* can be seen as rather anomalous.

Mabanckou's identity as an increasingly "transnational" (Stern 202) author, "a citizen of no one place" (Arnett and Wright 240) who "claims the world as his home" (Toivanen 328), is somewhat belied by *Black Moses*, a novel resolutely located in the geographic, historical, and even linguistic particularities of its African time and place. *Black Moses* signals its localized character in an opening paragraph that simultaneously announces its status as Bildungsroman:

> It all began when I was a teenager, and came to wonder about the name I'd been given by Papa Moupelo, the priest at the orphanage in Loango: *Tokumisa Nzambe po Mose yamoyindo abotami namboka ya Bakako*. A long name, which in Lingala means "Thanks be to God, the black Moses is born on the earth of our ancestors", and is still inscribed on my birth certificate today. (Mabanckou 3)

For a nonlocal readership, the foreignness of character and place names, the linguistic particularity of Lingala, and the autochthonic associations of the protagonist's name all highlight *Black Moses*'s specific local focus on Congo-Brazzaville in the latter years of the twentieth century during a period "of uninterrupted army rule" (Young 18). For an author whose texts often "explicitly aspire to universality" (Arnett and Wright 239), the very *particularity* of focus in *Black Moses* is not necessarily unique for Mabanckou, but it is perhaps characteristically idiosyncratic in how it allows him to pursue "an appropriate mix of universalism and national culture," which is for Vivian Steemers "the best guarantee for literary success in a global market" (206). Like Habila's *Waiting for an Angel*, Mabanckou's *Black Moses* is an African Bildungsroman whose assumption of an international readership plays a constitutive role in how it tells and sells its coming-of-age narrative.

Though the novel's title hints at a story of liberation and national (re-)integration, the narrative in *Black Moses*, much like *Waiting for an Angel*, is teleologically governed by a logic of carceral enclosure that prevents its protagonist from finding a place in a nation in which "to be marked nonnormative or nonconforming...is to be vulnerable to punishment, violence, and surveillance" (Kelley 591). Unlike Lomba's story in *Waiting for an Angel*, delivered both in the protagonist's own voice and in an array of first- and third-person accounts, *Black Moses* is narrated solely by Moses. Despite Moses's claim to be "introverted by nature," he ends the novel being "allowed to write, to fill page after endless page, the whole day long" (197). If, in *Waiting for an Angel*, the poetry Lomba writes in prison "is a symbol of freedom, of the ability to cross boundaries" (Eze 102), the writing Moses produces is perhaps more properly seen as a manifestation of a cycle of perpetual enclosure. *Black Moses*'s narrator is ironically named as his story is not one of movement from captivity to freedom but, rather, from one form of confinement to another. Moses makes his ultimate condition known early in the narrative when he reports that he "write[s] these lines, imprisoned in this place that was once so familiar, but is now so very different" (Mabanckou 8), in a narrative "today" (197) that sees Moses writing from "the orphanage where I spent the first thirteen years of my life" (197).

Commenting on the Bildungsroman's frequent use of a "journey motif," Okuyade emphasizes that the intimate "connection between travel and individuation" (362) is a predictable element in coming-of-age narratives. Naturally, Moses's narrative is characterized by almost incessant movement that sees him taking on and casting off a series of identities along the way. Moses begins life in an orphanage in Loango but escapes, ending up in Pointe-Noire sleeping "in the Grande Marché with...other teenagers" (102) whose gang he joins. Moses later "with[draws] to the Côte Sauvage after a widely publicised operation" (113) to drive the youth gangs out of the Grande Marché is organized by "Francois Makélé, the foremost citizen of the town...seeking election for a fourth term" (113), which leads to Moses carrying out odd jobs for a brothel madame named Maman Fiat 500, who procures for him a "job as a dockhand" and "a little place...down by the River Tchinouka" (145) to live in and watch over for her. This point represents Moses's nearest approach to the form of middle-class integration so often found in affirmative Bildungsromane.

This seemingly "normal life" (149) Moses lives is again taken from him by Francois Makélé, now mayor, who, targeting Maman Fiat 500 and her "Zairian whores," once again "choose[s] a group to gang up on, and wage a noisy campaign...with the forces of law and order and the TV cameras" (149). This campaign results in bulldozers being brought in "to destroy the majority of brothels in Pointe-Noire, while soldiers went round coshing the poor women" (150). Notably, it is the grotesque *spectacle* of the forced dispersal that demonstrates the workings of carceral politics in Pointe-Noire. Indeed, Makélé's media-savvy strategy replicates what Kelley describes as the "dominant representations of black female criminality produced by the carceral state and the media" (594) in order to justify the repressive use of force. Though Kelley focuses on carceral politics in an American context, what happens to Maman Fiat and her girls similarly demonstrates how "the racial [and ethno-national] construction of gender and sexual normativity is always a process requiring constraint and containment, ultimately producing regimes of carcerality" (597).

Whether he experiences it or simply bears witness to its effects, it is Congo-Brazzaville's regime of carcerality that determines Moses's dissolution of character as the end point of his maturation. The violent dispersal of Moses's "little family" has seriously deleterious effects on his mental state. He explains, "After that, nothing. I remembered nothing, not even who I was" (Mabanckou 151). Moses's journey reaches its seemingly inevitable terminal point in a "new penitentiary centre for criminals deemed to be 'not responsible for their actions'" (197) after he kills Francois Makélé, "that maggot of a mayor" (197) whom Moses sees as the architect of his mental and familial disintegration, and who is likely responsible for "a mass grave where most of the victims of his campaign" against "'Zairian whores'" (197) end up.

Coming full circle, Moses's story exemplifies the Bildungsroman's "generic debts" to the picaresque novel, which "narrates the story of a perpetual social outcast" who is forever excluded "from the rights franchise" (Slaughter 42). Often coming close to constructing an alternative family structure his orphan origins deny him, but which would enable him to meet "the bildungsroman ideal of smooth progress toward a final, integrated state" (Esty 27), Moses is repeatedly stymied by exclusionary African modernization projects that interrupt "the movement of the subject from pure subjection to self-regulation [that] describes the plot trajectory of the dominant transition narrative of modernization" (Slaughter 9). This pattern begins during Moses's time in Loango as an orphan, when Papa Moupelo, the priest from Zaire responsible for giving Moses "the most kilometrically extended name in...possibly the entire country" (Mabanckou 7), helps Moses and the others "forget who or where we were" (5). Papa Moupelo represents a benign father figure to guide Moses through the Bildungsroman's "closural plot of adulthood" (Esty 13). However, he is ultimately cast as one of the "local lackeys" of a devious capitalist "Imperialism" (Mabanckou 20) and exiled from the orphanage as an archaic danger to the modern "scientific socialism" driving the "Congolese Revolution" (20) that soon has the orphanage authorities uniformly speaking "their own special language...picked up in Moscow...in which every sentence contained the word 'dialectic', or, as an adverb, 'dialectically'" (26–27).

This transformation of a once-diverse institution into one of the nation's many homogenizing "laboratories of the Revolution" (Mabanckou 63) initiates a familiar pattern in the novel: the removal of the Zairian priest from the orphanage, which leads the children to speculate about his death, prefigures Francois Makélé's brutal removal of the sex workers from Zaire in Pointe-Noire. In both cases, the removal of Zairian elements is an exercise of institutional power that regulates and homogenizes the respective polities in the name of modernizing ideology. Similar to Habila's *Waiting for an Angel*, the repressive excesses of the modern African state engender the protagonist's transformation from marginalized insignificance to an individuated oppositional subjectivity that the state must contain and confine. After Makélé's razing of the brothels, Moses spends some time in a maddened state and fittingly "going round and round in circles" (158) before donning "a green outfit...long, pointed shoes" and "a hood... topped with a peacock feather" (189) in hope of becoming "the Robin

Hood of Pointe-Noire" (190). That he does so at age forty, the same age at which the biblical Moses, "appalled by the day-to-day wretchedness of his people...killed an Egyptian foreman who was attacking an Israelite" (189), signifies Mabanckou's protagonist's inability to fulfill the Bildungsroman's "closural plot of adulthood" (Esty 13), for his resistance constitutes nothing more than a form of childish play acting, a holdover from Moses's youthful dreams "of being Robin Hood, adopting his name, possessing...that character's generous heart" (Mabanckou 110). Though the adult Moses takes comfort in believing he has paralleled his biblical namesake by "liberat[ing] the people of Pointe-Noire from Francois Makélé" (197), the conclusion reached at his trial that he "acted under the influence of insanity" (197) undercuts his optimism: his assassination of a hated rival changes nothing structurally, but only brings to fruition the carceral destiny encoded in Moses's coming of age.

In his "tilting at windmills" (161), opposing social and political forces that he can neither join nor overcome, Moses reveals his true literary progenitor to be neither the figure of economic redistribution he dresses up as nor the ethnic/national liberator he is named after. Rather, Moses follows the path of Don Quixote, a picaresque knightly cosplayer who also famously sets himself against a (European) form of bad modernity and is mocked and placed under a kind of psychiatric house arrest because of it. For the cosmopolitan reader, the undeniable particular *strangeness* of the Congolese public sphere that is both backdrop and antagonist to Moses's coming of age ultimately dissipates when located not in the postcolonial milieu from which it emerges but in the Western literary paradigm it Africanizes.

An Uneasy Peace? African Bildungsromane in an Exoticist Postcolonial Literary Market

Waiting for an Angel and *Black Moses* offer their readers a glimpse of outcast life in two African postcolonies. In both novels, readers encounter narratives detailing individual defeat by a repressive state and may find in these novels a "male destiny" (Esty 24) peculiar to African Bildungsromane: the carceral site as the narrative fulfilment of personal development. The typical plot that defines the

Bildungsroman gives way to ambiguously and ambivalently open-ended chronologies that are the by-products of postcolonial states characterized by corruption, cronyism, and cruelty. Consequently, the well-intentioned Western reader may struggle to reconcile the social and political portraits contained within these novels with African literature's long-standing project of deconstructing othering caricatures of Africa as a place of backwardness and unfinished projects of modernization.

Yet it would be a mistake simply to view either carceral Bildungsroman as a text that laments an African nation's belated and misbegotten participation in global modernity. *Waiting for an Angel* places centre stage a politically repressive but economically neoliberal Nigerian nation that reminds us that "neoliberalism is no longer a particular political project but rather the dominant logic of practically the entire earth" (Walker 650). Similarly, in *Black Moses*, Moses is privy to the adoption story of Sabine Niangui, a former orphanage resident who, as an adult, returns to work in her former home. Sabine tells Moses that her adoptive mother "was crazy about my putty-coloured skin, my big eyes and Afro hair…and nicknamed me 'Angela Davis,' after a black American activist you may have heard of. I liked her calling me this, especially when I learned that this woman had fought for the freedom of black people in America" (Mabanckou 66–67). The story Moses hears tacitly reframes his own unsuccessful fight for freedom not as a case of African exceptionalism but, rather, as part of a global "emancipatory politics" (Walker 647) rendered necessary by the racial legacies of carceral colonialism.

The compromised postcoloniality that has always been a feature of the postcolonial Bildungsroman thus arguably rears its head in examples of the genre produced by third-generation African authors. From one perspective, these novels that exhibit a "shift from the postcolonial concern of blame to the inner, transcultural one within the African socio-political set up" (Eze 109) may let their Western readers off the hook when it comes to the colonial legacies that inform African states with problematic human rights records. But from another prospective, the African strangeness that Western readers may look for is undercut by intimations of uncanny resemblance in the carceral Bildungsromane I discuss here. Ultimately, for Slaughter, the

Bildungsroman "serves as the primary enabling fiction for an international reading public that is emerging (I'd like to think) in advance of the administrative structures and social formations that such a sphere ordinarily serves" (33). In novels that in many ways offer such depressing views of postcolonial African life, it may be in this suggestion, more than any other, that tentative hope may be located.

Notes

1. This differs from Fredric Jameson's "sweeping hypothesis," which contends, "All third-world texts are...*national allegories*" in which "*the story of the private individual destiny is always an allegory of the embattled situation of the public third-world culture and society*" (69). Rather than suggesting that postcolonial Bildungsromane lend themselves to being read as national allegories because, per Jameson, that is what "third-world" literature inevitably does, my point is that postcolonial Bildungsromane can be read in terms of national allegory because that is what the Bildungsroman typically does.
2. As this chapter considers the formative role of carceral spaces in the lives of young male characters confronting a new "male destiny" (Esty 24), I do not address the spatial sites of female *Bildung*, beyond noting, "The home in some female bildungsromane is constructed as a colonized space where views of the colonizer/father permeate everyday conversation and relationships" (Okuyade 365).

Works Cited

Arnett, James, and Angela Wright. "Paul's Letter to the Congolese: Allegory, Optimism, and Universality in Alain Mabanckou's *Blue White Red*." *Genre: Forms of Discourse and Culture*, vol. 50, no. 2, 2017, pp. 239–65.

Austen, Ralph A. "Struggling with the African Bildungsroman." *Research in African Literature*, vol. 46, no. 3, 2015, pp. 214–31.

Barnard, Rita. "Tsotsis: On Law, the Outlaw, and the Postcolonial State." *Contemporary Literature*, vol. 49, no. 4, 2008, pp. 541–72.

Brouillette, Sarah. *Postcolonial Writers in the Global Literary Marketplace*. Palgrave Macmillan, 2007.

Cockley, David. "Helon Habila's Neoliberal Nigeria: Free Markets and Subordinate Cultures in *Waiting for an Angel*." *Emerging African Voices: A Study of Contemporary African Literature*, edited by Walter P. Collins, III, Cambria Press, 2010, pp. 147–76.

Coetzee, J.M. "Into the Dark Chamber: The Writer and the South African State." *Doubling the Point: Essays and Interviews*, edited by David Attwell, Harvard University Press, 1992, pp. 361–68.

Deckard, Sharae. "Deformed Narrators: Postcolonial Genre and Peripheral Modernity in Mabanckou and Pepetela." *Locating Postcolonial Narrative Genres*, edited by Walter Goebel and Saskia Schabio, Routledge, 2013, pp. 92–107.

Dunton, Chris. "Entropy and Energy: Lagos as City of Words." *Research in African Literatures*, vol. 39, no. 2, 2008, pp. 68–78.

Egbunike, Loiusa Uchum. "One Way Traffic: Renegotiating the 'Been-To' Narrative in the Nigerian Novel in the Era of Military Rule." *Tradition and Change in Contemporary West and East African Fiction*, edited by Ogaga Okuyade, Rodopi, 2014, pp. 217–32.

Egya, Sule. "Idiom of Text: The Unwritten Novel in Recent Nigerian Fiction." *English in Africa*, vol. 39, no. 1, 2012, pp. 109–24. *African Journals Online*, https://www.ajol.info/index.php/eia/article/view/79873.

Erritouni, Ali. "Postcolonial Despotism from a Postmodern Standpoint: Helon Habila's *Waiting for an Angel*." *Research in African Literature*, vol. 41, no. 4, 2010, pp. 144–61.

Esty, Jed. *Unseasonable Youth: Colonialism, Modernism, and the Fiction of Development*. Oxford University Press, 2012.

Eze, Chielozona. "Cosmopolitan Solidarity: Negotiating Transculturality in Contemporary Nigerian Novels." *English in Africa*, vol. 32, no. 1, 2005, pp. 99–112.

Faloyin, Dipo. *Africa Is Not a Country: Notes on a Bright Continent*. W.W. Norton, 2022.

Fludernik, Monika. "The Metaphorics and Metonymics of Carcerality: Reflections on Imprisonment as Source and Target Domain in Literary Texts." *English Studies*, vol. 86, no. 3, 2005, pp. 226–44.

Habila, Helon. *Waiting for an Angel*. W.W. Norton, 2003.

Hay, Simon. "*Nervous Conditions*, Lukács, and the Postcolonial Bildungsroman." *Genre: Forms of Discourse and Culture*, vol. 46, no. 3, 2013, pp. 317–44.

Heaton, Matthew M., and Toyin Falola. "Framing Nigerian History in the Twenty-First Century." *The Oxford Handbook of Nigerian History*, edited by Toyin Falola and Matthew M. Heaton, Oxford University Press, 2022, pp. 1–18.

Hoagland, Erika. "The Postcolonial Bildungsroman." *A History of the Bildungsroman*, edited by Sarah Graham. Cambridge University Press, 2019, pp. 217–38.

Jameson, Fredric. "Third-World Literature in the Era of Multinational Capitalism." *Social Text*, vol. 15, Autumn 1986, pp. 65–88. *JSTOR*, http://www.jstor.org/stable/466493.

Jussawalla, Feroza. "Postcolonial Novels and Theories." *A Companion to the British and Irish Novel*, edited by Brian W. Shafer, Blackwell, 2005, pp. 96–111.

Kelley, Robin D.G. "On Violence and Carcerality." *Signs: Journal of Women in Culture and Society*, vol. 42, no. 3, 2017, pp. 590–600.

Mabanckou, Alain. *Black Moses: A Novel*. Translated by Helen Stevenson, The New Press, 2019.

Okuyade, Ogaga. "Traversing Geography, Attaining Cognition: The Utility of Journey in the Postcolonial African Bildungsroman." *Matatu*, vol. 49, 2017, pp. 358–85.

Pfingst, Annie, and Wangui Kimari. "Carcerality and the Legacies of Settler Colonial Punishment in Nairobi." *Legacies of Empire*, special issue of *Punishment & Society*, vol. 23, no. 5, 2021, pp. 697–722. *Sage Journals*, https://journals.sagepub.com/doi/10.1177/14624745211041845.

Phillips, Delores B. "'What do I have to do with all this?': Eating, Excreting, and Belonging in Chris Abani's *Graceland*." *Postcolonial Studies*, vol. 15, no. 1, 2012, pp. 105–25.

Slaughter, Joseph R. *Human Rights, Inc.: The World Novel, Narrative Form, and International Law*. Fordham University Press, 2007.

Steemers, Vivian. "Liberation and Commodification of a Postcolonial Author: The Case of Alain Mabanckou." *Journal of the African Literature Association*, vol. 8, no. 2, 2014, pp. 195–218. *Taylor & Francis Online*, https://www.tandfonline.com/doi/abs/10.1080/21674736.2014.11690233.

Stern, Kristen. "Between France and Me: Ta-Nehisi Coates, Alain Mabanckou, and Transatlantic Mis-readings of Race." *Journal of the African Literature Association*, vol. 3, no. 2, 2017, pp. 201–17.

Stitt, Jocelyn. "Postcolonial Life-Writing." *The Bloomsbury Introduction to Postcolonial Writing: New Contexts, New Narratives, New Debates*, edited by Jenni Ramone, Bloomsbury, 2018, pp. 177–90.

Toivanen, Anna-Leena. "Uneasy 'Homecoming' in Alain Mabanckou's *Lumieres de Pointe Noire*." *Studies in Travel Writing*, vol. 21, no. 3, 2017, pp. 327–45.

Walker, Gavin. "The Late Foucault and the Allegories of Theory," *South Atlantic Quarterly*, vol. 121, no. 4, 2022, pp. 645–53. *Duke University Press*, https://read.dukeupress.edu/south-atlantic-quarterly/article/121/4/645/319603/IntroductionThe-Late-Foucault-and-the-Allegories.

Young, Crawford. *The Postcolonial State in Africa: Fifty Years of Independence, 1960–2010*. University of Wisconsin Press, 2012.

12

"FOR EVERY CHILD, EVERY RIGHT"

Reading Postcolonial Bildungsromane of the 1990s across the United Nations Convention on the Rights of the Child

Prathim-Maya Dora-Laskey

"It doesn't matter," she said. "Life is full of stupid things and sometimes we just have to do them."
—SHYAM SELVADURAI, *Funny Boy*

Only that once again they broke the Love Laws. That lay down who should be loved. And how. And how much.
—ARUNDHATI ROY, *The God of Small Things*

Building towards Denationalizations

What happens when a universalist, ethical, and legalistic framework of childhood is applied to South Asian Bildungsromane? Framed as an "international agreement on childhood" and declared "the world's most ratified human rights treaty" how does the United Nations Convention on the Rights of the Child (UNCRC),[1] which came into effect in September 1990, frame the legalistic and idealistic underpinnings of human rights narratives following in its wake? This chapter will study two celebrated postcolonial Bildungsromane from the 1990s, namely Shyam Selvadurai's Lambda-winning *Funny Boy*, published in 1994, and Arundhati Roy's Booker-winning *The God of Small Things*, published in 1997, in the consequential context of the UNCRC to investigate how personhood and circumstances reified by protagonists Arjie (*Funny Boy*) and Rahel and Estha (*The God of Small Things*) may be constituted in an international mode.

When Leela Gandhi alludes to "the conditions under which the Bildungsroman can be said to have arrived and been 'received' in post/colonial" spaces, it is a reminder that the postcolonial Bildungsroman is a genre under constant attention and reconstruction (57). The postcolonial articulation of the Bildungsroman represents, as Ericka A. Hoagland insists, simultaneously a reconfiguring of the genre as well as an independent literary tradition (237). In light of these political and literary incertitudes, I propose—instead of reading the literary as a parallel to human rights discourse—to read these literary narratives as a key reflection of the discourse on human rights. In doing so, the validity of both literary and rights narratives is enhanced in a direct, albeit hypothetical, way that follows the work of Joseph Slaughter. (As a reminder, in the decade in which these novels were published, Sri Lanka ratified its acceptance of the UNCRC in July 1991; India ratified the UNCRC in December 1992.) *Funny Boy* and *The God of Small Things* notably showcase the *Bildung* of a post-independence generation in Sri Lanka and India—Rahel, Estha, and Arjie are born in nation-states that are already independent of British rule and are part of a generation that must construct their development via the impromptu sites and contexts of postcolonial disharmony.

Simon Hay's identification of the fundamental contradiction between the prospects and practices of *Bildung* (development, formation, social stability), on the one hand, and the project of postcolonial self-determination and discordance on the other is embodied clearly in both novels (317). In the background to the childhoods studied in this chapter, several socio-political and cultural issues may be glimpsed in postcolonial Kerala and Sri Lanka. *The God of Small Things* provides insights on issues including women's rights, women's property rights, environmentalism, globalization, caste and racial oppression, and democratic rights; *Funny Boy* provides a reading of minority disenfranchisement, civil war, and the dissatisfactory state of ethnic relations and gay rights in multicultural Sri Lanka. The chaotic history of pre-communist Kerala at the beginning of the Marxist guerilla movement termed "Naxalite" (in the 1970s) and pre-civil war Sri Lanka (in the 1970s and early 1980s) are also strong historical markers in the novels. Thus, the children's victimization can be seen as structural, grounded in the growing political instability of the nation and its inability to resolve ethnic conflict.

As Slaughter observes, in many postcolonial Bildungsromane, "the genre's traditional conclusive event of social, civil, and self-integration is perpetually postponed, so that the sovereign, undivided human personality remains a vanishing (plot) point beyond the frame of the text" (235). In essence, this translates Franco Moretti's description of working-class Bildungsroman protagonists as "youth without the right to dream" (x). In the two novels studied here, this indicates that within the nation local strictures such as "Love Laws" and "stupid things...we just have to do" are regulatory social structures that are stringently fundamental yet significantly *arbitrary* and inexact. The fifty-six articles comprising the universalist UNCRC usefully shift the discussion away from the language of "rules" and towards the language of "rights." Thus, the UNCRC may be applied as useful and *neutral* articulations/calibrations that allow us to address the ways in which these novels of the 1990s communicate the postcolonial victimization of children in the process of *Bildung*—allowing us to triangulate between the protagonists, the national context, and universalist ideals.[2] For instance, in urging nondiscrimination on the basis of "the child's or his or her parent's or legal guardian's race, color, sex, language, religion, political or other opinion, national, ethnic or social origin, property, disability, birth or other status," the UNCRC immediately helps us identify, consistently and categorically, the ethnic discrimination that Arjie is subject to and the property discrimination the twins Rahel and Estha are subject to because of their mother's female sex (Article 2). Equally, the inaction of the family and the state is directly antithetical to "the best interests of the child," especially in the absence of "appropriate legislative, administrative, social and educational measures to protect the child from all forms of physical or mental violence, injury or abuse, neglect or negligent treatment, maltreatment or exploitation, including sexual abuse" (Articles 3, 19). Thus, instead of disregarding the postcolonial problems in the novels (ethnic conflict, secular inheritance rights) as a particularly unfortunate and personal set of circumstances, the UNCRC validates reader discomfort by engaging with these issues through specific language; through its "legal tautology," as Joseph Slaughter has it, the language of human rights demonstrates it is "of common sense" (77).

Bakhtin's description of the European Bildungsroman as an arbitrary category "requiring only the presence of the hero's development and emergence in the novel" (20) is challenged by what Barbara Harlow notes as the "historical and historicizing presuppositions" implied by the Western tradition (78). Harlow suggests these "resistance narratives" operate as "interventions into the historical record" (98, 116). This is one of the reasons it seems relevant and pertinent to use the UNCRC as an index, as it represents a global rather than colonial standard. In urging that the child assumes "a constructive role in society," or that societies are to undertake "preparation of the child for responsible life in a free society," the UNCRC very nearly replicates the definitive resolution of the traditional Bildungsroman where protagonists are expected to find their place in society (Articles 40, 29.1[d]). In the postcolonial context, some elements of the UNCRC are generous enough to accommodate a range of interpretations, for example "shall protect the child against all other forms of exploitation prejudicial to any aspects of the child's welfare" (Article 36); most are highly specific in naming interdictions and ideals such as child soldiers, children with disabilities, refugee children, adoptive children, and so on. The classic assumption of the Bildungsroman genre that childhood ought to be a period of preparation for adulthood is subverted by postcolonial crises and contexts such as the instability of the postcolonial state. Of the forty-one articles in Part I of the UNCRC dealing with principles related to children's well-being, nearly all apply to the postcolonial novels under consideration, with several being citable for violation. Even those not directly applicable, such as ones dealing with child soldiers or children with disabilities, nevertheless retain a sort of force as Arjie is implicated into working with a terrorist organization and postcolonial children are frequently beset by disability, as Clare Barker's excellent *Postcolonial Fiction and Disability: Exceptional Children, Metaphor and Materiality* demonstrates. Hoagland's summary of the postcolonial Bildungsroman in its diverse forms as ultimately being about "survival" (v) is borne out in *Funny Boy* and *The God of Small Things*. The "best interests" urged by the UNCRC are, naturally, not strictly universal, but are rather shaped by the surrounding postcolonial socio-political context and access to resources. We shall bear this in mind as we apply the UNCRC to these late-twentieth-century postcolonial novels.

Naturally, we will appreciate that the protagonists' subject positions are structurally in relation to national history, grounded in the growing political instability of the postcolonial nation and its inability to resolve ethnic conflict due to historically enshrined exclusionary practices. For instance, several elements of Rahel, Estha, and Arjie's developmental predicaments and societal challenges can be connected to postcolonial legislation, such as the Hindu Succession Act in India or the Sinhala Only Act in Sri Lanka.[3] Ultimately, this chapter will propose that the protagonists' personal *Bildung* and development of personhood moves them beyond their interpellation as "national representatives" to choose identities and communities freely based on their emotional affiliations for "others" (including denationalizing forces and characters associated with domestic secessions such as Jegan in *Funny Boy* and Velutha in *The God of Small Things*). The possibilities afforded in these novels for the protagonists to seek subjectivity outside the nation and the openness of the protagonists in *Funny Boy* and *The God of Small Things* to think of themselves in modalities such as "cosmopolitan" (c.f. Nussbaum) or "planetary" (c.f. Spivak "'Planetarity'") support this chapter's universalist, UNCRC-centred reading of *Bildung*. The three sections of this chapter indicate the growing devolution of the postcolonial state. While the first section details the denationalizations endemic to late-twentieth-century postcolonial nations, the second section analyzes the unhomeliness experienced—especially by minorities—within the nation-state. The third and final section sketches the protagonists' internationalist options between globalization and "planetarity."

The UNCRC ratifications[4] remind us that, while economic deregulation has been the chief cause of the waning of individual nation-states since the late twentieth century, international human rights developments are also, fortunately, a part of this vanguard. Saskia Sassen has argued the growth of international influence at the expense of the nation-state's power as a "denationalization."[5] The dismissal of the nation-state as a viable category may be hasty. In fact, Elleke Boehmer shows that, rather than eschewing the nation, victimized minorities such as those studied in this chapter "tend to explore and attempt to *adapt* the nation as a site through which their relational brand of politics may be organized," especially as "the nation encourages a sense of *belonging to*; it provides channels through which [they] can mobilize and take part in public debate" (*Women* 210). Sassen's vision of denationalization, however, is also pertinent to the two novels under consideration as it classifies the late-twentieth-century postcolonial state as a divisive rather than unitary condition. In postcolonial states, in particular, the affective value of a nation-state is increasingly destabilized in the absence of an imperial antagonist (such as Britain in the pre-independence era) or intra-regional conflict (as in the case of subcontinental Partition).[6] The global politics of the late twentieth century, which functions as the temporal and cultural backdrop to *Funny Boy* and *The God of Small Things*, is particularly disposed to Sassen's idea of "denationalizing" as it describes precisely the situation of outlying provinces (Kerala in *The God of Small Things*) and ethnic minorities (Tamils in *Funny Boy*) as what was previously "bundled up and experienced as a unitary condition—the national assemblage of territory, authority, and rights—now increasingly revealed to be less unitary and exclusive than is suggested in modern representations of the modern nation-state" (*Territory* 457–58). Given this decline of the nation-state due to pressure from within (secession) and without (globalization), the emergence, popularity, and possibility suggested by international human rights agreements such as the UNCRC are particularly beneficial.[7]

Arjie, Estha, and Rahel have frequently been read as victims of circumstance. This chapter reads them as victims of history, as their victimization is due to the postcolonial state's historical lack of accountability and incompetence in facilitating basic human rights. To this effect, an application of the values of the UNCRC, whose ratification occurred just a few years ahead of the first publication of these novels, corroborates that the children's victimhood that seems to be rooted in the domesticity of their individual families may be read also in a political and postcolonial frame. The child protagonists aggregate agency and *Bildung* through their "history from below," which although interstitial and seemingly insignificant provides a version of history that is typically subsumed by that of the nation-state. While the legalistic guidelines set out in the UNCRC are practical in their ability to articulate and calibrate forms of suffering, the children's subject position as victims *in relation to* national history remains germane and animates analyses of their development and subjectivity.

They are also specifically identified as victims in the narrative. In *Funny Boy*, Arjie is literally and legally a victim of his time; he is a victim of the anti-Tamil pogrom of 1983 and is headed for "the refugee camps that have been set up for victims of the riots" (Selvadurai 304). Fittingly, Arjie has been discussed as a "narrator-victim" (Jayawickrama 125) and as part of a victim diaspora and is seen as a "hapless victim" (Salgado, "Writing Sri Lanka" 13). In *The God of Small Things*, the victim status is less obvious but still strongly articulated in the text. The omniscient narrative voice believes the children need to be told, "You were only children. You had no control. You are the *victims*, not the perpetrators" (Roy 191).[8] More specifically, the narrative suggests that national history is itself responsible for the victimization: "This was an era, imprinting itself on those who lived in it. History in live performance" (309).[9] Even at the level of plot, the child protagonists are trapped by the history that took place long before their birth, such as the laws governing daughters' inheritance rights through the Hindu Succession Act in India (which leaves the twins' Syrian Christian mother impoverished and dependent) or the Sinhala Only Act in Sri Lanka (which stealthily enshrines linguistic and ethnic segregation and discrimination in the Sri Lankan constitution).[10] The theme of inheritance identified as central to the English Bildungsroman by Moretti and others, in characters as diverse as Tom Jones, Jane Eyre, or Elizabeth Bennet, is foiled by the specificity of postcolonial existence in *Funny Boy* and *The God of Small Things*. What does one inherit without citizenship? How does one inherit while female?

The historical nature of their predicament is especially pertinent since, as the "Love Laws" and "stupid things...we just have to do" mentioned in the epigraphs suggest, what we might consider private decisions (relationships and sexual choices) are instead issues of an uncertain social contract that identify and reify the child's identity, place in the community, and agency within social and national structures. The "touchable" subjects are only allowed to consort with other "touchables" in order that they may cultivate class and caste hegemony (in *The God of Small Things*); the ethnic segregation of Tamil and Sinhala categories must be policed so the populace may be divisively governed (in *Funny Boy*). The children's loyalty to Velutha, their Dalit friend (in *The God of Small Things*), or a romantic crush on Shehan, a Sinhala (in *Funny Boy*), are both relationships with "outsiders" to their community. These affections intersect, fatefully, with larger issues of postcolonial policy and governance such as the political appointment of a vice-principal to a prominent Colombo school (in *Funny Boy*) or local elections in a small Kerala village (in *The God of Small Things*).

Temporally sited in the generational aftermath of independence and previous anti-colonial independence movements, the protagonists have notional ideas of agency and "freedom." This may be seen, for instance, in the child protagonists' confidence that they can do what they want, since "It's a Free Country" (Roy 197). In *Funny Boy*, Arjie becomes a representative of his entire generation: "This young man is a prime illustration of what this country is coming to" (Selvadurai 139).[11] In *The God of Small Things*, the seven-year-old twins are exhorted to behave: "Don't forget that you are Ambassadors of India" (Roy 282). Although Arjie, Estha, and Rahel are subjected to expectations in that they are required to represent the country as model citizens ("this country," "Ambassadors of India"), and thereby interpellated as such, they are depicted as Other and subaltern. Nevertheless, they are discursively tied to the nation. Sujala Singh unequivocally asserts that the protagonists of *Funny Boy* and

The God of Small Things are engaged in "representing the nation" (13), and asks if the children "represent a world of the past, a world preserved or do they represent the dynamic instabilities of an uncertain future" (15).[12] Similarly, Andrew Lesk asks if Arjie can "in any way serve as a template upon which to draw the emerging nation-state?" (34). While these depictions of the postcolonial state as "uncertain" (Singh) and "emerging" (Lesk) decades after independence suggest the idea of a "de-nation," it nevertheless interpellates the children to an (unstable and immature) state. Although Slaughter does not reference the UNCRC in *Human Rights, Inc.*, he sees the subjectivity of the postcolonial subject as a child, characterizing the "movement of the subject from pure subjection to self-regulation" as a "plot trajectory of the dominant transition narrative of modernization, which both the Bildungsroman and human rights law take for granted" (9).

In a related manner—*Bildung*, modernization, and human rights law intersect when Arjie, Rahel, and Estha experience the "government" as a constant, omnipresent, and *amplified* manifestation. In *Funny Boy*, Arjie is continuously "immers[ed] in the present" through the immediacy of his response to national events (Salgado, "Writing Sri Lanka" 9). In *The God of Small Things*, the bureaucratic functions of the government are perceived by the twins to pervade all aspects of their lives: literally from birth to death. Estha believes that if they had been born on a state-run public transport bus, they would have received free bus tickets for the rest of their lives (Roy 3); he also believes that anyone who dies on a zebra (pedestrian) crossing will have their funerals underwritten by the government (4). Such notions of benevolent forms of bureaucratic governance and influence seem due to a conviction that the government is all-powerful. Estha and Rahel later extend the scope of government to regulations that govern living as well: ordered to behave in a socially sanctioned manner—to "jolly well behave"—the twins decide "the government" is the place where people are "sent" if they fail to "jolly well behave" satisfactorily (148, 150).

Despite this omnipresence of the nation-state, however, indications that these novels are set against a backdrop of denationalization reverberate within the narrative. The fading cohesiveness and solipsism of the state are obvious not only through internal national dissensions but also in the way the narratives position the child protagonists as articulating (childish) forms of appeal to world powers.[13] The UN, for instance, is invoked as a figurative refuge in *The God of Small Things* when life as unwelcome guests in their uncle's house becomes untenable: the children daydream that Ammu, their mother, might work for the United Nations in The Hague and hire a Dutch nanny to look after them.[14] After the alleged government-aided pogrom against Tamil populations in 1983 in *Funny Boy*, demonstrations against the Sri Lankan government in Canada and England signal both international judgment and cosmopolitan, transnational support for the victims (Selvadurai 302–03).[15] Although Arjie, Rahel, and Estha were born decades after independence, the entrenched ethnic[16] and class issues that predate independence severely interfere with the "atmosphere of happiness, love, and understanding" the UNCRC entreats for child citizens.[17] While *Funny Boy* and *The God of Small Things* parenthetically extend the span of South Asian childhood to locales and cultures that were—especially at first publishing—previously unrepresented in English literature, they simultaneously internationalize the Bildungsroman narrative in another way. Because of an increased international transaction of capital (globalization) and governance (e.g., the UN), the other aspect of the internationalization of the narrative comes from the adult location (immigration) of two of the three protagonists as settlers in Canada (Arjie) and the USA (Rahel). The nation-state is plainly unable to contain the narrative arcs of the protagonists, and this inability is at least in part because the postcolonial nation has stealthily enshrined linguistic and ethnic segregation and discrimination in the national constitution, thus making life inhospitable for our protagonists.

Since "There's No Place Like Home"

"Home," a word that commonly encompasses both domesticity as well as community and nationality, is a complicated and contested space in *Funny Boy* and *The God of Small Things*, where the characters experience various forms of insecurity through a lack of a stable and viable home space.[18] The UNCRC suggests that governments "help with housing" if the family is unable to afford one (Article 27), but beyond that, it takes for granted that most children will have a home, advocating only in the context of the loss of that home due to war, civil war, or some other similar privation (Articles 16, 18, 22, 32). By these standards, despite the ostensible middle-class position of the children, the child protagonists of this chapter suffer. Arjie's family home in *Funny Boy* is effectively razed by the ethnic riots of 1983; the twins in *The God of Small Things* have been shuttled between various homes because Ammu has been duped of both education and inheritance on account of being born female.[19] Simultaneously, the term "home" seamlessly works also to emphasize the postcolonial nation-state and its inability to equitably house ethnic and gender minorities despite the outpouring of the rhetoric of "home" and "family" during decolonization. In the absence of an affective community, home—in both its domestic as well as national sense—becomes rather an arena where conventional expectations and regulations are reiterated and reified incessantly. Notions of home are troubled as well by the lack (Rahel) or destruction (Arjie) of physical homes, which precipitates immigration. Thus, the protagonists' exiles to Canada (Arjie) and the USA (Rahel) are a telling indictment of the lack of refuge offered by the postcolonial home country and simultaneously an indication of the viability of a cosmopolitan world.[20]

Further, in *Funny Boy*, the constructed history of Sri Lanka as proposed by the dominant Sinhala power attempts to erase the Tamil community's existence by repudiating depictions of Tamil culture, in ways that violate Article 30.[21] In the section titled, "The Best School of All," the school's Sinhala Drama Society reenacts the Mahavamsa or "tale of Vijaya, the father of the Sinhala nation and his arrival on the shores of Lanka and his conquest of Kuveni, the Yaksha princess" (Selvadurai 275). In this, the national mythology of the Mahavamsa elides important elements of Sri Lanka's multicultural history, such as the arrival of the Tamils or Sri Lanka's location as a colony of the Tamil Chola empire.[22] This limited national myth, which conflicts with several of the UNCRC's appeals, specifically diversity (Article 17[b] and 17[d]), sets the stage for the effective erasure of the Tamil community via state-sponsored violence and is directly tied to Arjie's loss of home at the end of the novel. As a particularly final and literal form of unhomeliness, the destruction of the family home finds an echo in the previous erasure of the Tamil community. Arjie's last look at the home in which he has lived all his life is a study of loss on several levels:

> I pushed open the gate. Something was different from the last time I was there. The house looked even more bare, even more desolate than before. Then I realized what had happened and I stared at our house in shock. Everything that was not burned had been stolen. Whatever had remained intact, furniture, uncharred beams, doors, windows, even the hinges and drainpipes, had been taken. How naked the house appeared without its door and windows, how hollow and barren with only scraps of paper and other debris in its rooms. (310–11)

The veritable disappearance of the home both as a communal and family space, as well as a physical structure, in a short span of time marks Arjie's loss as both unexpected and accelerated. At the end of *Funny Boy*, on the cusp of immigrating to Canada as a refugee, Arjie walks away from his childhood home, recognizing the worthless nature of the home space, which has served as neither shelter nor sanctuary. At the point of figurative departure, Arjie doesn't "bother to close the gate" as "there was no reason to protect it against the outside world anymore" (312). It is revealing that he sees the home not as shelter but something *to be* sheltered; his shift away from the scene effectively breaks his physical connection to the nation and foreshadows his relocation in new communities in a new homeland.

Various instances of unhomeliness in *The God of Small Things* are intensified when the possibility of a home that shelters its inhabitants seems improbable—even at a literal level. Estha, for instance, is afraid after being sexually abused by the Orangedrink Lemondrink Man in the movie theatre that he will be tracked down and abused again and that his uncle's home will offer him no protection. Ironically, when the children leave their current home to find shelter in "the History House," it offers them even less protection. Their lack of belonging in "the History House" is an aesthetically tidy motif—since the children have no place in history—but it is troubling in every other way. Additionally, as dependents of Ammu, a female guardian, bereft of adequate education or inheritance, the lack of protection, and indeed of physical shelter itself, is a gravely political depiction of the married Syrian Christian woman's lack of inheritance. Therefore, although the children's subjectivity is forged in the absence of a stable home space, it is not a mere personal account but a political one and speaks to personal and communal disenfranchisement at several levels and locations.[23] Thus, I disagree with Susan Stanford Friedman's estimate that Roy's use of family space to address the politics of the state is intellectually effective as it "demonstrates how feminist geopolitics engages locationally—that is to say—spatially—with power relations as they operate both on the nation and within the nation" (117). Indeed, ideas of family spatiality are observable in the circumstances of Estha's "return," where he is treated as an object devoid of subjectivity or community and becomes yet another instance of "unhomeliness" that is in direct contravention of the UNCRC's urging. While Article 10 of the UNCRC proposes that children "whose parents reside in different States shall have the right to maintain on a regular basis, save in exceptional circumstances, personal relations and direct contacts with both parents" and Article 9.3 proposes that, if children are "separated from one or both parents," attempts should be made "to maintain personal relations and direct contact with both parents on a regular basis," none of these opportunities are offered to Estha.

Worse, the child protagonists are unable to take their lack of an "atmosphere of happiness, love, and understanding" seriously as their understanding of crisis is comparative—they are conscious that they forge their subjectivity against the backdrop of larger national tragedies. In *The God of Small Things*, for instance, Rahel's consciousness determines that "personal despair could never be desperate enough" because "Worse Things had happened. In the country she came from, poised forever between the terror of war and the horrors of peace, Worse Things kept happening" (Roy 19).[24] In *Funny Boy*, Arjie's sexual and political subjectivity is forged in the fires that overtake Colombo during the genocidal anti-Tamil pogrom of 1983; "all the

Tamil houses there are burnt and the trouble has begun to spread" (Selvadurai 287). Not only do these crises of socio-political collapse and denationalization disrupt the inherent optimism of the European Bildungsroman, but they also suggest that no matter how tragic and central personal *Bildung* may be, they are dwarfed by the enormity of post-independence national issues, paradoxically, in the contexts of increasing globalization and denationalization. As a way of defying what may be mistaken for a fungible fate in the light of the children's—self-reportedly—negligible trauma, an application of UNCRC standards allows us to verify that, although it is indeed possible that "Worse Things had happened," the events the children are involved in and the oppressions they are subject to are not inconsequential and ought not to be normalized.

Set against "the vast, violent, circling, driving, ridiculous, insane, unfeasible, public turmoil of a nation," "the relative smallness" of personal stories matter less than the dominant narrative of "'History' with a capital 'H'" (Roy 20).[25] In *Funny Boy*, government officials disseminate confidential electoral information to the rioting mobs in Colombo, making it easier for the mob to target Tamil Houses (Selvadurai 289). This betrayal of the democratic process leads to Arjie's defeated observation at the end that "the government had won" (291) (i.e., the government had won not an election, but rather a pyrrhic victory over its minority citizens by encouraging violence against them). In *The God of Small Things*, the upcoming election damages members of a grassroots radical movement (the Naxalite movement) and leads to the betrayal of the children's friend (and mother's lover) Velutha.

Troubling the personal experiences and notions of "home" further in *Funny Boy* and *The God of Small Things* are separatist radical movements within the nation that may be massed under a "terrorist" label (by the nation-state). These threats to the cohesiveness of the state and the myth of a national community (since there's no place like home) are quintessential postcolonial movements unravelling the postcolonial moment through dissension, secession, and civil war. As Hoagland references in the context of other postcolonial Bildungsromane, the foreclosure of possibility in times of civil war and civil unrest fractures the socialization necessary for a successful *Bildung* (235). In the novels, the "Liberation Tamil Tigers of Tamil Eelam (LTTE)" (in *Funny Boy*) and the Marxist Naxalite movement (in *The God of Small Things*) menace the idea of a stable nation-home while simultaneously endangering the domestic-home, and thus impart unhomeliness on two counts. In her essay, "Postcolonial Writing and Terror," Elleke Boehmer describes postcolonial terrorism as subject to two bearings: "the globalized and hybridizing inflection and a resistance inflection" (143). Interestingly, the two novels represent both forms of state-identified "terrorism"—the hybridizing (the Indian-Marxist movement), as well as the resistant (the secessionist LTTE). Moreover, these movements are central to the children's growth in subjectivity as they align themselves emotionally with members of these anti-national "communities." When Arjie becomes attached to Jegan (LTTE) and Rahel and Estha to Velutha (Marxist), they partake not only in a notional compromising of the nation, but these relationships—their self-selected community—imperil their domestic space in literal and metaphoric ways. They have become small, quiet participants in large-scale rebellions on a denationalizing level.

The threat of Marxist class violence as dangerous to home and nation is made immediate and perceptible in *The God of Small Things* when the family's car is stuck in the middle of a Naxalite protest march and Baby Kochamma is ridiculed by one of the marchers. Her deep humiliation during this encounter becomes narratively exaggerated by her irrational equation of a working-class marcher with the working-class figure with whom the family has most contact—Velutha.[26] Baby Kochamma's outrage at being bested by someone she considers beneath her results in the extreme violence that marks the baiting, assault, and betrayal of Velutha, a socialist advocate and the children's hero and friend. Similarly, within the connected stories that make up the outline of *Funny Boy*, Jegan is inserted into Arjie's life through the offices of his two absent parents—an invisible mother and a dead father—whose separate letters jointly charge Arjie's father to mentor him (Selvadurai 155–56). There are several indications that Jegan has been involved with the Tamil Tigers,[27] and as the narrative progresses, we even receive something approaching an admission of his involvement with the Tigers from Jegan (212). Further, he attempts to involve and implicate Arjie by simultaneously providing him with information and demanding his silence (214). In fact, in both novels, the child protagonists are charged with the necessity of keeping secret the suspected terrorist involvement of their mentors and friends. The children's involvement in such a global plot—the secrecy, suspicion, and demands for participation/silence—does not reimagine their subjective resistance as resistance to terrorism in the service of the integrity of the nation.

In a variety of ways, from marginalization to erasure, from the breakdown of the family to the outright destruction of the family home, the children's pre-chosen communities fail to provide them with the appropriate protections and precipitate their estrangement. Their ethnic communities are compromised when they befriend outsiders (Velutha, Shehan); their national "imagined" community is delimited through immigration. In this area of home, spatial injustices and absences precipitate the child protagonists' subjectivities as several denationalized positions that are either diasporic (Arjie) or immigrant (Rahel).[28] This is a good juncture to turn our attention to the specific and progressive internationalist turn of the narrative.

Not surprisingly, their inhospitable and unhomely childhoods impact their adult point of view from the denationalized vantage point of return from a safer, Western location through either memory (Arjie in *Funny Boy*) or an actual physical homecoming (Rahel and Estha in *The God of Small Things*). Rahel's return to Ayemenem from the US—the much-vaunted "Amayrica" of the novel—is nevertheless comparable to Arjie's reminiscences from the physical safety of his Canadian immigration. America ("Amayrica") is a refuge in *The God of Small Things*—most outstandingly from family and community spaces that constitute home. In a foreign country, Rahel does not have to navigate the ancient laws of *us* and *other* her Malayalee Syrian Christian family is prone to impose; it is a land whose ironically immense possibility is suggested in the "may." The internationalist stance this suggests, however, is more profound than mere immigration or other traffic guided by globalization. The next section will deconstruct how globalization and intentional planetarity bring the protagonists of both Bildungsromane to the internationalism of the UNCRC.

Resisting Globalization and Developing Planetarity

If we are to ascertain the children's agency in this chapter, a consideration of the disjunctions between their globalized existence and "planetary" consciousness is in order. In *The God of Small Things*, Baby Kochamma, the aunt positioned as the twins' primary antagonist, is aligned with the normativity of global consumer capitalism. Her obsession with satellite television shows, instead of opening her up through exposure to the world and to others as one might imagine, rather instills in her a sense of fear and mistrust, spurred on by "new television worries about the growing numbers of desperate and dispossessed people" (Roy 29). This leads to her keeping everything "locked": "locked together in a noisy television silence," Baby Kochamma keeps the objects she wins in television contests "locked away in her cupboard" (28) and keeps "her doors and windows locked" (29). The repetition of "locked" aligns Baby Kochamma with the normativity of consumer capitalism and globalized media—institutions that are arguably sustained by fear and possessive acquisition. World events such as "ethnic cleansing, famine, and genocide" are comically seen "as direct threats to her furniture" (29). Rather than opening people up to the world, consumer capitalism and globalized media keep people "locked" in fear, separation, and possessiveness, as well as mistrust of others, particularly those who do not conform to the norms of the dominant culture.

Slaughter references the global consciousness as "part of the freight of globalization" even as he urges the pursuit of humanism despite seeing globalization as part of a continuum bounded by "colonialism, (neo) imperialisms, international humanitarianism, and multinational consumer capitalism" (123). Due to the growing influence of denationalization, there is an increased awareness of needing to find ways of accommodating the world within individual subjectivity—to make space for what Spivak has called a "planetary consciousness." In this section, the enlarged global consciousness must serve the child protagonists' entire experience of not only their world—but *the* world. While "cosmopolitanism" would be a satisfactory descriptor of the ways in which the three child protagonists Rahel, Estha, and Arjie negotiate denationalization and a more "worldly" sensibility, Spivak's formulation of planetarity seems a more fitting way of describing not merely the affective nature of their relationship with the world, but simultaneously an acknowledgment that they have the agency to configure their places as affective keepers and inheritors of the world. In reaching for this internationalist stance, these postcolonial Bildungsromane expand the possibilities for the child protagonists to find their place in the world beyond the postcolonial nation and make the application of the UNCRC appropriate and prescient.

Arjun Appadurai in *Modernity at Large* argues that globalization allows for creative and empowering opportunities for postcolonial subjects to negotiate modernity on their own terms. Roy, in her political writings and fiction, expresses a more critical stance towards globalization, one that is aligned with the perspective of critics including Gayatri Spivak and recognizes the ways in which economic and political inequalities are sustained or exacerbated by globalization. Spivak has noted, "The general culture of Euro-US capitalism in globalization and economic restructuring has conspicuously destroyed the possibility of capital being redistributive and socially productive in a broad-based way" (*Other Asias* 30). Thus, for critics who acknowledge that globalized culture is inextricably linked to the inequities of globalized economic systems, a postcolonial standpoint offers a critical perspective from which to not only critique but to reimagine human relations in a globalized world. In *Globalization and Postcolonialism: Hegemony and Resistance in the Twenty-first Century*, Sankaran Krishna argues,

> Although globalization is a movement that is suffusing the entire world with a form of production based on free-market capitalism and an attendant ideology of individualist consumerism, postcolonialism articulates a politics of resistance to the inequalities, exploitation of humans and the environment, and the diminution of political and ethical choices that come in the wake of globalization. If neoliberal globalization is the attempt at naturalizing and depoliticizing the logic of the market, or the logic of the

economy, postcolonialism is the effort to politicize and denaturalize that logic and demonstrate the choices and agency inherent in our own lives. (2)

Thus, although the children occupy positions within rapidly denationalizing, inhospitable postcolonial situations trending towards globalization, they tend to resist the hegemonies proposed by late-twentieth-century globalization. Rather, their postcolonial stance tends towards Robert J.C. Young's advocacy of the continuing necessity of postcolonial inquiry. In his 2012 essay "Postcolonial Remains," Young suggests that academic discomfort notwithstanding, we must deal with issues such as "poverty, inequality, exploitation, and oppression" that constitute the "transformative edge of the postcolonial" (19–20). In *Funny Boy* and *The God of Small Things*, their postcolonial standpoints function to effect and affect resistance to globalization, including "through its continuous expansion of who gets to be counted within the provenance of 'human'" and "in its critique of the very idea of nation-states as territorial enclosures of essences" (Krishna 172).

Globalization, as represented by foreign employment, foreign trade, and international tourism, casually marks the chronological, cultural, and corporate zeitgeist within the novels. While it may bring additional revenue and attention, corporate globalization exerts a deleterious effect on the formation of childhood development in *Funny Boy* and *The God of Small Things*. In *Funny Boy*, Arjie's family benefits from their involvement in tourism; in *The God of Small Things*, Western-style tourism is identified as the harbinger of huge environmental and cultural loss. In an essay on ecological collectivity in Roy's novel, Aarthi Vadde shows how "the ideologies of development and progress that permeated hegemonic narratives of globalization" are a pertinent way of reading tourism in Kerala state (523). In addition, this is a form of globalization abetted by the nation as Sreekumar and Parayil show in their study of the resort industry in Kerala. In claiming that the industry benefitted from assorted "tax subsidies, tax exemptions, and credit facilities" (530) while workers, farmers, and other non-investing citizens did not, Sreekumar and Parayil highlight the inequities inherent in the capitalist model.

At the end of the novel, the agency of the children may be measured against the fetishisms of late capitalistic globalization (cable television, global tourism) when, with "the simple, unswerving wisdom of children" (Roy 208), they offer the possibility of hybrid and affective approaches. Rahel and Estha's relationship, in which there is "No Each, No Other," proposes an understanding of being human that is based not on separation, competition, and exclusion, as in the global market economy and the national body politic; rather, it is based on interconnection. The twins' approach here is an ethical stance that aligns with Gayatri Spivak's notion of "planetarity," which intimates "to be human is to be intended toward the Other" (*Death of a Discipline* 73). While Spivak acknowledges her vision of planetarity is incomplete, stating, "there are connections to be made that I cannot make yet" (92), it is her description of the ethical potential of the textual that suggests how we might, in literary study, engage the planet as a ground for inquiry: "In this era of global capital triumphant, to keep responsibility alive in the reading and teaching of the textual is at first sight impractical. It is, however, the right of the textual to be so responsible, responsive, answerable" (101–02).

The textual in *Funny Boy* and *The God of Small Things* makes it clear through the narrative arcs and dialogic utterance of child protagonists that globalization is not the internationalist ideology they are aligned with. The children's agency can be seen both in their central refusal to blindly back kinship-based structures and social systems, as well as their membership in planetary systems through imagining ways of being. In *The God of Small Things*, the children recant their forced testimony against Velutha, a development that runs counter to the loyalty demanded of them by members of the extended family, precipitating their exile. In *Funny Boy*, Arjie's refusal to perform, in the manner that members of his ethnic faction at school want him to, nullifies the slim chance that the Sinhala minister will be convinced about the need for ethnic parity. The children's refusal to reproduce hegemonic traditions—whether Indigenous or foreign, whether beneficial or inexpedient—and their commitment to identifying through affection and self-chosen community is key to the formation of their subjective development. In making strictly regulated loyalties problematic, *Funny Boy* and *The God of Small Things* argue for a larger, more generous affective—planetary—subjectivity, although the move towards such generosity results in crises for the protagonists. In ways that are crucial to their development, the children's internationalism and planetarity reflect that of the UNCRC. Article 17, for instance, emphasizes that the child "has access to information and material from a diversity of national and international sources" as a way of building up generations of world citizens. Article 29.1(d) addresses the aspect of Spivak's planetarity, which we have used in this chapter, by urging that the child be encouraged to develop "the spirit of understanding, peace, tolerance, equality of sexes, and friendship among all peoples, ethnic, national and religious groups and persons of indigenous origin."

The development/*Bildung* of children in *Funny Boy* and *The God of Small Things* illustrates how, for these children at the end of the twentieth century, "finding their place in the world" may be literally of the "world" in a global and universalist rather than in a local way. However, because they ultimately have not been able to adequately explore and develop this planetarity or worldliness in a way that is authentic to the novel or the UNCRC guidelines we have used to balance fictional and real worlds, the national and local regulations in their worlds frustrate the normative development schedules of *Bildung*. Arjie's development as a male child is problematized by his continuing designation as "funny"; the twins are repeatedly denigrated for sundry infractions including reading backwards, shivering their legs, and blowing spit bubbles. After the traumatic betrayal of Velutha, the foremost complaint is that they are rendered further unnatural. "It's as if she doesn't know how to be a girl," they say of Rahel, while Estha is treated as an aphasic subhuman (Roy 34).

Punished disproportionately for small childhood mischief and misdemeanours, the children in both novels ultimately constitute their subjectivity by developing *as* children. Despite their narrative and critical interpellation, they are not national representatives—rather, they are depicted and advance as characters representing themselves in the world with a range of rich and intersectional interrelationships. Their growing subjectivity does expose that characteristically postcolonial discrepancy between idealistic national postulations and regulatory functions, such as notions of individual sovereignty and juridical equality. This is a breach that in a denationalized/globalized world might be filled by global agencies and doctrines such as the UN or the UNCRC. When these child protagonists slough off their interpellation as national representatives and delink themselves from postcolonial national aspirations, erasures, and insurrections, they gain the possibility of meaningful human connection unbounded by national or kinship allegiance.

Notes

1. As of 2014, *all* 192 members of the United Nations are signatories to the UNCRC, and all but two members have ratified it. The two holdouts are the United States and Somalia; all other signatories agree to appear before the UNCRC Committee in response to any charges that may be brought against them. The two South Asian countries studied in this chapter—Sri Lanka and India—ratified in 1991 and 1992, respectively (OHCHR).
2. This is not to blur the lines between real and fictional children, but merely to apply neutral and real standards to their narrative predicament.
3. The 1956 Hindu Succession Act in India pertains to "unwilled succession, among Hindus, Buddhists, Jains, and Sikhs." The act attempted to secularize and provide equitable distribution of property to heirs without gender discrimination; previously only male heirs were eligible to inherit. However, daughters were allowed as equal shares as sons only in 2005. The Official Language Act (No. 33 of 1956), commonly referred to as the Sinhala Only Act in Sri Lanka, passed by the government of S.W.R.D. Bandaranaike, declared Sinhala as the only official language despite the opposition of the Tamil-speaking minorities (about 26 per cent) in the country, who characterized the act as discriminatory. The act lessened the opportunities for Tamils to seek government employment and representation.
4. In September 1990, the United Nations adopted the Declaration of the Rights of the Child into the UN Convention. Although some form of this declaration had been circulating since the beginning of the twentieth century as the Geneva Declaration of the Rights of the Child promulgated by the League of Nations in 1924, and the version proclaimed by the UN General Assembly in 1959, the UN Convention on the Rights of the Child transforms the Declaration of 1959 into a legally binding international agreement. The UNCRC has since been commonly used to define violations of children's rights as it bears universal approval and is

5. the most "widely and rapidly" ratified treaty in the history of the UN. Working at the intersection of international law and (children's) human rights, the UNCRC oversees how signatory nations safeguard child welfare.
5. Sassen has expanded on these ideas in works from *Globalization and Its Discontents* to "Globalization or Denationalization?" and *Territory, Authority, Rights: From Medieval to Global Assemblages*.
6. The declining role of the nation-state has been described by other terms such as "post-nation" in Stuart Hall's "Whose Heritage? Un-settling 'The Heritage,' Re-imagining the Post-nation," and earlier as a "transnation" in Arjun Appadurai's *Modernity at Large*. The choice of Sassen's use of "denationalization" is predicated on being focused on international agreements and conventions instead of issues of sovereignty, territory, or diaspora.
7. As Sassen emphasizes, "Human rights are not dependent on nationality, unlike political, social, and civil rights, which are predicated on the distinctions between national and alien…Human rights override such distinctions and hence can be seen as potentially contesting state sovereignty and devaluing citizenship" (*Globalization and Its Discontents* 95). Under human rights regimes, states must take account of persons qua persons, rather than qua citizens. Human rights, hence, begin to impinge on the principle of nation-based citizenship and the boundaries of the nation.
8. Although the twins wear "the tragic hood of victimhood," *The God of Small Things* identifies Velutha as the greater victim (191).
9. Following Frantz Fanon and Cathy Caruth, they work on illuminating the prospects for annotating the novel in terms of its trauma. Outka, especially (like Jill Didur in the context of *Ice-Candy Man*) cautions against reading literature as case history, but offers the novel as "an opportunity to convey, rather than simply reproduce, traumatic experiences, granting the reader a position unavailable not only to the character, but to the actual victims of traumatic events" (34).
10. Several of the following are useful in understanding the origins of the ethnic conflict in Sri Lanka: Neil DeVotta's "From Ethnic Outbidding to Ethnic Conflict: the Institutional Bases for Sri Lanka's Separatist War"; Newton Gunasinghe's "Ethnic Conflict in Sri Lanka: Perceptions and Solutions"; and Robert C. Oberst's "Federalism and Ethnic Conflict in Sri Lanka."
11. A sense of disappointment and low expectation is set also in the idea that Arjie's generation is one that will potentially contribute to the "future ills and burdens of Sri Lanka" (224).
12. Taking the idea of representation further, Singh suggests the children are "straightforward allegories of the nation," as "the child marks a rupture between adults and nation states" (15).

13. This is due both to the machinations of the state itself, as well as radical and separatist forces (e.g., the Naxalites in *The God of Small Things* and the Liberation Tamil Tigers of Eelam [LTTE] in *Funny Boy*).
14. This daydream is particularly pathos-laden as we are given to understand that Ammu is minimally educated and is therefore unlikely to secure a UN position.
15. The novel suggests the government abetted the violence of the mob by releasing electoral information that distinguished the Tamil households from Sinhala ones.
16. Mithran Tiruchelvam and C.S. Dattatreya, in their casebook *Culture and Politics of Identity in Sri Lanka*, show how the binary nature of ethnicity in Sri Lanka was initiated and encouraged by British colonialism. Selvadurai certainly belabours this angle. Selvadurai represents the hybridity of Sri Lankan existence at its most fundamental—being the child of a mixed Tamil-Sinahala marriage—but does not allow Arjie to occupy a similar hybrid space, instead depicting him as a child of Tamil parents alone.
17. From the preamble to the UNCRC: "Recognizing that the child, for the full and harmonious development of his or her personality, should grow up in a family environment, in an atmosphere of happiness, love and understanding."
18. The title of this section comes from Rushdie's famous alternative reading in his essay collection *Step Across This Line*. Rushdie unpacks Dorothy's celebrated catchphrase, "there's no place like home" from Frank L. Baum's *The Wizard of Oz* thus: "The real secret…is not that 'there's no place like home,' but rather that there is no longer any such place as home" (57).
19. Female inheritance laws were considered inapplicable to Kerala Syrian Christians until challenged by Mary Roy in 1986. Amali Philips has a lucid analysis in "Stridhanam: Rethinking Dowry, Inheritance and Women's Resistance among the Syrian Christians of Kerala" that is very useful. See also Susan and Markos Vellapally's "Repeal of the Travancore Christian Succession Act, 1916 and Its Aftermath," and Susan Visvanathan's "Marriage, Birth and Death: Property Rights and Domestic Relationships of the Orthodox/Jacobite Syrian Christians of Kerala."
20. Malashri Lal and Sukrita Paul Kumar's *Interpreting Homes in South Asian Literature* is a particularly useful formulation of several issues considered in this section. See also Sharanya Jayawickrama's "At Home in the Nation? Negotiating Identity in Shyam Selvadurai's *Funny Boy*."
21. "In those States in which ethnic, religious or linguistic minorities or persons of indigenous origin exist, a child belonging to such a minority or who is indigenous shall not be denied the right, in community with other members of his or her group, to enjoy his or her own culture, to profess and practise his or her own religion, or to use his or her own language" (UNCRC).

22. Minoli Salgado has written at length on the use of the Mahavamsa or "Great Chronicle" in contemporary Sri Lankan fiction ("Rebirth of a Nation").
23. I find it inspirational that Mary Roy, who challenged the injustice of the Syrian Christian inheritance law in 1986, is Arundhati Roy's mother. For a legal retelling, see Sebastian Champappilly's "Christian Law of Succession and Mary Roy's Case."
24. The narrator continues that, in the context of postcolonial India, "personal despair could never be desperate enough," and therefore, "Nothing mattered much. Nothing much mattered. And the less it mattered, the less it mattered. It was never important enough. Because Worse Things had happened…Worse Things kept happening" (20). The repetition in this passage suggests that contrary to the belief that only the master narratives of dominant national history matter, the "small things" that are erased by national and global histories do indeed matter.
25. Their smallness is a real consideration. In their mother's eyes, "her twins seemed like a pair of small, bewildered frogs engrossed in each other's company, galloping arm in arm down a highway full of hurtling traffic. Entirely oblivious of what trucks can do to frogs" (42). This image of the twins' vulnerability contrasts with the knowledge, awareness, and consciousness of the child protagonists themselves.
26. Although Aijaz Ahmad has characterized Roy's treatment of Marxism as "spiteful" (104), Pranav Jani helpfully points out that the novel's "criticism of Marxism stands as a marker of its progressive and leftist politics—the rejection of a big idea that masquerades as the redeemer of the small but actually helps to crush it" (58).
27. Contextual clues indicating Jegan is to be viewed as an ex-Tiger (his place of origin, his evasiveness, and so on) are discussed in wonderful detail by Maryse Jayasuriya in her *Terror and Reconciliation: Sri Lankan Anglophone Literature, 1983–2009* (see, in particular, pages 116–18).
28. Sujala Singh accurately warns that the child protagonists "make rather unconvincing adults" on their return (15).

Works Cited

Ahmad, Aijaz. "Reading Arundhati Roy Politically." *Frontline*, 8 Aug. 1997, https://frontline.thehindu.com/cover-story/reading-arundhati-roy-politically-by-aijaz-ahmad/article38458826.ece.

Appadurai, Arjun. *Modernity at Large: Cultural Dimensions of Globalization*. Vol. 1, University of Minnesota Press, 1996.

Bakhtin, M.M. *Speech Genres and Other Late Essays*. Translated by Vern W. McGee, University of Texas Press, 1986.

Barker, Clare. *Postcolonial Fiction and Disability: Exceptional Children, Metaphor and Materiality*. Palgrave Macmillan, 2012.

Boehmer, Elleke. "Postcolonial Writing and Terror." *Wasafiri*, vol. 22, no. 2, 2007, pp. 4–7.

Boehmer, Elleke. *Stories of Women: Gender and Narrative in the Postcolonial Nation*. Manchester University Press, 2005.

Champappilly, Sebastian. "Christian Law of Succession and Mary Roy's Case," (1994) 4 SCC (Jour) 9. *ebc-india.com*, https://www.ebc-india.com/lawyer/articles/94v4a2.htm.

Friedman, Susan Stanford. "Feminism, State Fictions and Violence: Gender, Geopolitics and Transnationalism." *Communal/Plural*, vol. 9, no. 1, 2001, pp. 111–29.

Gandhi, Leela. "'Learning Me Your Language': England in the Postcolonial Bildungsroman." *England through Colonial Eyes in Twentieth-Century Fiction*, edited by Ann Blake et al., Palgrave Macmillan, 2001, pp. 56–75. *Springer Nature Link*, https://link.springer.com/chapter/10.1057/9780230599277_4.

Government of India. The Hindu Succession Act, 1956. *India Code*, https://www.indiacode.nic.in/handle/123456789/1713?locale=en.

Government of Sri Lanka. Official Language Act (No. 33 of 1956). *Common LII Sri Lanka Consolidated Acts*, http://www.commonlii.org/lk/legis/num_act/ola3301956180/.

Hall, Stuart. "Whose Heritage? Un-settling 'The Heritage', Re-imagining the Post-nation." *Whose Heritage? Challenging Race and Identity in Stuart Hill's Post-nation Britain*, edited by Susan L.T. Ashley and Degna Stone, Routledge, 2023, pp. 13–25.

Harlow, Barbara. *Resistance Literature*. Taylor and Francis, 1987.

Hay, Simon. "*Nervous Conditions*, Lukács, and the Postcolonial Bildungsroman." *Genre: Forms of Discourse and Culture*, vol. 46, no. 3, 2013, pp. 317–44.

Hoagland, Ericka A. *Postcolonializing the Bildungsroman: A Study of the Evolution of the Genre*. Purdue University, PhD dissertation, ProQuest Dissertations Publishing, 2006.

Jani, Pranav. *Decentering Rushdie: Cosmopolitanism and the Indian Novel in English*. Ohio State University Press, 2010.

Jayasuriya, Maryse. *Terror and Reconciliation: Sri Lankan Anglophone Literature, 1983–2009*. Lexington Books, 2012.

Jayawickrama, Sharanya. "At Home in the Nation? Negotiating Identity in Shyam Selvadurai's *Funny Boy*." *The Journal of Commonwealth Literature*, vol. 40, no. 2, 2005, pp. 123–39.

Krishna, Sankaran. *Globalization and Postcolonialism: Hegemony and Resistance in the Twenty-First Century*. Rowman & Littlefield, 2009.

Lal, Malashri, and Sukrita Paul Kumar. *Interpreting Homes in South Asian Literature*. Pearson Education India, 2007.

Lesk, Andrew. "Ambivalence at the Site of Authority: Desire and Difference in *Funny Boy*." *Canadian Literature*, vol. 190, 2006, pp. 31–46.

Moretti, Franco. *The Way of the World: The Bildungsroman in European Culture*. Translated by Albert Sbragia. New Edition, Verso, 2000.

Nussbaum, Martha C. *The Cosmopolitan Tradition: A Noble but Flawed Ideal*. Harvard University Press, 2021.

Outka, Elizabeth. "Trauma and Temporal Hybridity in Arundhati Roy's *The God of Small Things*." *Contemporary Literature*, vol. 52, no. 1, Spring 2011, pp. 21–53.

Philips, Amali. "Stridhanam: Rethinking Dowry, Inheritance and Women's Resistance among the Syrian Christians of Kerala." *Anthropologica*, vol. 45, no. 2, 2003, pp. 245–63.

Roy, Arundhati. *The God of Small Things*. Random House, 1997.

Rushdie, Salman. *Step Across This Line: Collected Nonfiction 1992–2002*. Vintage Canada, 2010.

Salgado, Minoli. "Rebirth of a Nation or the Incomparable Toothbrush: The Origin Story and Narrative Regeneration in Sri Lanka." *South Asian Review*, vol. 33, no. 3, 2012, pp. 239–56.

Salgado, Minoli. "Writing Sri Lanka, Reading Resistance: Shyam Selvadurai's *Funny Boy* and A. Sivanandan's *When Memory Dies*." *The Journal of Commonwealth Literature*, vol. 39, no. 1, 2004, pp. 5–18.

Sassen, Saskia. *Globalization and Its Discontents: Essays on the New Mobility of People and Money*. The New Press, 1998.

Sassen, Saskia. "Globalization or Denationalization?" *Review of International Political Economy*, vol. 10, no. 1, 2003, pp. 1–22.

Sassen, Saskia. *Territory, Authority, Rights: From Medieval to Global Assemblages*. Princeton University Press, 2008.

Selvadurai, Shyam. *Funny Boy*. McClelland & Stewart, 1994.

Singh, Sujala. "Postcolonial Children Representing the Nation in Arundhati Roy, Bapsi Sidhwa and Shyam Selvadurai." *Wasafiri*, vol. 19, no. 41, 2004, pp. 13–18.

Slaughter, Joseph R. *Human Rights, Inc.: The World Novel, Narrative Form, and International Law*. Fordham University Press, 2007.

Spivak, Gayatri Chakravorty. *Death of a Discipline*. Columbia University Press, 2023.

Spivak, Gayatri Chakravorty. *Other Asias*. Wiley-Blackwell, 2008.

Spivak, Gayatri Chakravorty. "'Planetarity' (Box 4, WELT)." *Paragraph*, vol. 38, no. 2, 2015, pp. 290–92.

Sreekumar, T.T., and Govindan Parayil. "Contentions and Contradictions of Tourism as Development Option: The Case of Kerala, India." *Third World Quarterly*, vol. 23, no. 3, 2002, pp. 529–48.

Tiruchelvam, Mithran, and C.S. Dattathreya, editors. *Culture and Politics of Identity in Sri Lanka*. ICES, 1998.

United Nations (UN). Convention on the Rights of the Child (UNCRC). General Assembly Resolution, 1990. *United Nations Human Rights Office of the High Commissioner*, https://www.ohchr.org/en/instruments-mechanisms/instruments/convention-rights-child.

United Nations Office of the High Commissioner for Human Rights (OHCHR). "Status of Ratification Interactive Dashboard." https://indicators.ohchr.org/.

Vadde, Aarthi. "The Backwaters Sphere: Ecological Collectivity, Cosmopolitanism, and Arundhati Roy." *MFS Modern Fiction Studies*, vol. 55, no. 3, 2009, pp. 522–44.

Vellapally, Susan, and Markos Vellapally. "Repeal of the Travancore Christian Succession Act, 1916 and Its Aftermath." *India International Centre Quarterly*, vol. 22, nos. 2/3, 1995, pp. 181–90.

Visvanathan, Susan. "Marriage, Birth and Death: Property Rights and Domestic Relationships of the Orthodox/Jacobite Syrian Christians of Kerala." *Economic and Political Weekly*, vol. 24, no. 24, 1989, pp. 1341–46.

Young, Robert J.C. "Postcolonial Remains." *New Literary History*, vol. 43, no. 1, 2012, pp. 19–42.

13

ORGANI(CI)ZATION OF THE AFRICAN INTELLECTUAL

Bildung and Representativeness in the Fiction of Chimamanda Ngozi Adichie

David Babcock

In this chapter, I use the novels of Chimamanda Ngozi Adichie to explore some of the paths available to the African intellectual in the contemporary world. Adichie's novels participate in a far-reaching conversation around the fate of the nationalist intellectual, a conversation dating back to the first generation of anti-colonial writers. Historically, the project of the postcolonial Bildungsroman has coincided with one of the foundational theoretical problems of postcolonial studies itself: how a speaker might come to represent an emergent national culture, when the very claim to speak on a people's behalf renders the speaker exceptional, and thereby alienates them from the people they would seek to represent. While scholarship has acknowledged that the originary models of nationalist *Bildung* have been displaced by more critical attitudes towards education and development, there has been much less thorough exploration of what alternative forms of *Bildung* have been formulated in the postcolony, how they work, where specifically they diverge from previous *Bildung* narratives, and to what historical pressures they respond.

Over the span of Adichie's literary career, intellectuals in her country of origin, Nigeria, have been in crisis, a crisis that mirrors those of many postcolonies across Africa and beyond. Addressing the widespread disappearance of the public intellectual in Nigeria, Reuben Abati offers the following assessment in a 2016 op-ed piece:

> Even when corporations and politicians in power draw intellectuals close; they end up usurping the powers of the intellectual, compelling him to hold his intelligence within the scope of the definition of his assignment...[T]here are classical cases of intellectuals in power making a difference, but that age appears ended, the disdain of intellectualism has turned politicians and corporate gurus into wise men that they are not, and the intellectual into an organic element of power. ("Public Intellectuals")

Abati invokes the Gramscian sense of "organic" intellectual here to refer to those who have become subservient organs of powerful interest groups, rather than independent voices speaking truth to power. Abati's vision for a revitalized intellectual is one who can "offer intelligent solutions to practical problems," particularly in "critical areas" such as "budgets, economic planning, [and] a currency crisis" ("Public Intellectuals"). This remedy is one that is commonly suggested in the politics of the postcolony: looking to technical expertise to transcend destructive partisan politics.[1]

The new claimants to national representativeness, then, comprise a wide-reaching professional class that includes politicians, technocratic experts, and cultural producers. The multipartite structure of this professional elite creates thorny questions about what it means to hold representative authority, however. How do any of these groups, let alone all, guarantee their ability to transcend their narrow agendas and represent a genuine national interest? How do they overcome the pressures "to hold [their] intelligence within the scope of...[their] assignment"?[2] Can the professional class engage in practices of self-formation that eventually legitimate the value of their specialized work for the larger community?

To offer a narrative form for such legitimizing development via the Bildungsroman would salvage a vital form of community-building potential for the novelist's work. Like all legitimacy claims, those of the intelligentsia are fictional; they do not provide—or even necessarily attempt—a full and adequate description of reality.[3] Rather, they introduce an *artificial* sense of narrative direction to reality, an imaginary momentum that can generate real collective energies. It is, in large part, the artificiality of the Bildungsroman's generic connection to national narrative that inspires deeply conflicted responses. The most influential accounts of the postcolonial Bildungsroman tend to read it as either (1) privileging certain characters as the sole representative subjects of a national *Bildung*, or (2) deconstructing all claims to national representativeness as such in favour of a more independent, critical form of agency.[4] Adichie's *Bildung* narratives eschew both paths. On the one hand, she remains interested in how members of the variegated professional class might direct their critical capacity towards some form of collective existence—sometimes the nation, sometimes transnational communities. On the other, she resolutely avoids designating any character as speaking *for* the national community; each subject of *Bildung* speaks in a highly personalized, singular voice.

I will argue that Adichie reinvents the Bildungsroman as an instrument of collective discourse by rethinking the ways that aspiring intellectuals figure their relationship to the community, abandoning a concept of the intellectual as authoritative voice of the people in favour of one where the intellectual acts as a conduit for a dense network of interpersonal traces. Correspondingly, the Bildungsroman's "representative" quality depends upon how sensitively it can be made to register those traces. In short, Adichie's interest in *Bildung* lies in the individual's capacity to materialize the discursive impacts of others, rather than to proffer their own voice as a collective one.

The Bildungsroman and the Postcolonial Intellectual

The Bildungsroman has long been a prevalent fictive site upon which collective energies are generated through an encounter between the individual and colonial histories. In Susan Z. Andrade's words, the

Bildungsroman is "a genre that is defined by the interrelation of self-development and national development" (*Nation* 115). At the same time, Andrade observes that critics have yet to account for the many kinds of interrelation that are possible, from direct political leadership and public participation to the development of intimate family structures.

The tensions generated by this interrelation of self and nation are largely anticipated by the Lukácsian critique of the genre: on one hand, the Bildungsroman is identified with the emancipatory energies of modernity, while on the other, it represents an ideological mechanism that symbolically contains unacceptably radical energies by taking "problematic individuals" and turning them into socially productive subjects (Lukács 132). Joseph Slaughter's *Human Rights, Inc.*, provides a particularly apposite application of the Lukácsian critique, showing how the Bildungsroman works to naturalize globally dominant forms of legal and political modernity. Slaughter argues the genre has served as a blueprint for tempering the most radical, revolutionary energies emerging from decolonial and postcolonial movements, effectively "domesticating" them (91). The Marxian-Lukácsian tradition in which Slaughter writes tends to theorize a world system that renders emancipation and containment reversible, insofar as every emancipation entails subsumption into another form of tutelage, some ideological "universal" that, in fact, only naturalizes the interests of the privileged minority. This reading of the Bildungsroman serves to critique a certain outcome for the intellectual: the achievement of individual liberation at the expense of the national collective.

Some theorists, however, see a more generative range of possibilities for this interplay of self and decolonizing nation. As part of his theoretical reconstruction of postcolonial *Bildung*, Pheng Cheah identifies an "organic" metaphor that imaginatively authorizes the individual to represent the nation:

> The novel of early or decolonizing nationalism almost invariably figured the emergent nation-people as a living organism suffering from the chronic malaise of colonialism. The remedy to this disease was always

> a form of *Bildung*, a concerted effort at reaching out to the colonized masses, educating and raising their awareness so that they might rationally organize themselves into a people…This exemplary lesson about the imperativity of national *Bildung* was invariably personified in the novel's protagonist whose formation or *Bildung* parallels and symbolizes that of the emergent nation because he is its first patriot and ideal citizen. (239)

The organic metaphor does crucial work because it both (1) lends coherence to the potentially chaotic multiplicity of the "masses," and (2) positions the intellectual as an essential catalyst for this coherence. The analogy is held together by a double mimesis. On the one hand, the intellectual protagonist is successful insofar as they *represent* the nation's distinctive attributes—and, in the end, the best and most hopeful ones. The people, in short, must recognize themselves in the protagonist of *Bildung*. On the other hand, it is implied that the people are only successful insofar as they *imitate* the protagonist, who offers a model for the people to mimetically perform. Mimesis results in powerful bonds, but it achieves those bonds through an appeal to sameness; if the people are to act collectively, it suggests, they must share some essential qualities—or cultural DNA, as it were—that ensures their organic unity. The work of the novel, and the Bildungsroman in particular, is to enunciate that DNA into being. As Cheah puts it, "Culture's political vocation lies in its ability to articulate society into an organic community, to transform the masses into a *dynamic self-generating whole* that approximates or actualizes the ideal of freedom" (236, emphasis added). It is an idealized vision, but one that captures the crucial notion of the novelist's work conferring autonomy upon the community. Any specific prescriptions a writer may issue for the good of the community are of secondary importance when compared to this transfiguring function of enabling the community to invent its own self-constituting forms.[5]

As Cheah acknowledges, however, this version of organicist *Bildung* can easily efface internal differences within the nation. This is well demonstrated by Andrade's *The Nation Writ Small*, which traces alternative genealogies of feminist postcolonial African Bildungsromane that use domestic settings as allegorical screens upon which stories about the nation can be told. In doing so, she draws upon Marxist and feminist insights about how the personal can always be political, not just allegorically but literally. These stories of *Bildung* tend to emphasize the debts and trade-offs the protagonist (whether female or male) incurs as they aspire to national representativeness, as well as the stories of marginalization and exclusion that mirror, both figuratively and literally, the protagonist's self-building.[6] Andrade also illustrates how the family structure itself can absorb these inequities and thereby come to reflect more macro-political pathologies within the nation itself. To read the African Bildungsroman's relationship to the nation, then, we need to attend not only to stories of mimetic performance but also to the stories of difference and inequity that haunt the organicist national narrative.

As numerous critics have noted, Adichie's novels are deeply interested in human relationships as a site of politics.[7] I will suggest, however, that Adiche's novels merge this commitment to the irreducibility of the human scale with a more explicit exploration of public participation. To merge these two scales of agency, Adichie adapts the Bildungsroman genre to rethink the activity of writing itself, as something that allows the intellectual to mediate the network of human relationships that have placed them in their privileged positions of expertise. Intellectuals thereby preserve the imprints of many more people than just themselves. Within this framework, it is the scope, depth, and—most significantly—diversity of these networks that must be cultivated to foreground the community's own powers of self-generation. Adichie's writer-protagonists thereby give rise to an ironic refiguring of the ideology of organic nationhood that Cheah ascribes to the postcolonial Bildungsroman, one subtended less by communion with the undifferentiated masses and more by the intellectual's diversity of affiliative commitments. Adichie thereby discovers a more supple way for the *Bildung* narrative to mediate the individual's experience with that of the imagined community.[8]

The Viable Hybrid: *Purple Hibiscus*

Within the generational narrative of African letters, Adichie's generation is distinguished from the prior ones by having no experience of direct colonialism.⁹ Writers in this generation confront colonialism through a species of post-memory; they experience colonialism's traumas, its residual institutional structures, its rippling social and political effects, even its neocolonial reinventions—all at a remove from the nationalist anti-colonial struggles that characterized the era of independence.¹⁰ Ogaga Okuyade observes, "The obvious failure of Africa's post-military democracies has made a tremendous number of third-generation writers feel a demand to construct their own values from the only material available to them—the events of their personal lives"; as a result, "this generation of African writers has withdrawn from nationalism" (141). Likewise, Daria Tunca has noted Adichie's own avoidance of writing politics at the national, geopolitical level and insisting on a study of "human relationships" apart from their purely political coordinates (112). Christopher E.W. Ouma argues that the demands of post-memory have led Adichie's first two novels to re-envision the very temporality of childhood, suggesting they are more productively read not as Bildungsromane, but as narratives of the alternative futures imagined within the everyday experiences of childhood: "an archive of previously silenced experiences, of micro-resistance and micro-political regimes, which lead to a transformation and a critical apprehension of the dominant narratives of the time" (41).

My reading takes Adichie's commitment to these alternative temporalities and scales of experience seriously, while still registering a consistent, experimental fascination with *Bildung* and its relationship to a national community. *Purple Hibiscus* focuses on the headwinds facing the first-generation post-independence intellectual in order to establish a complex genealogy for the later generation. It describes an adolescent protagonist, called Kambili, first coming to a sense of freedom from her overbearing, religiously intolerant, and violent father. The novel does not follow Kambili into adulthood, but at the end she is the character positioned to carry on the project of the national intellectual, since other possible candidates are dead, imprisoned, or exiled. The novel delineates her process of growth, which lies in determining her relationships to various adult role models. While each adult has a different kind of influence on her, her survival depends upon the successful hybridization of these elements. This is corroborated by the novel's titular image, the purple hibiscus, which is explicitly presented as a metaphor for freedom: "Aunty Ifeoma's experimental purple hibiscus: rare, fragrant with the undertones of freedom, a different kind of freedom from the one the crowds waving green leaves chanted at Government Square after the coup. A freedom to be, to do" (Adichie, *Purple Hibiscus* 16). The thriving of plants is itself a kind of *Bildung*, which in its originary German romanticist form evoked the idea of an open-ended, organic human flourishing.[11] While Adichie is far from embracing German romanticism in every respect, the novel still insists upon the purple hibiscus as a metaphor for a form of flourishing less constrained by ready-to-hand political ideologies, which, in her early life, Kambili experiences as overbearing and oppressive. This image encapsulates the kind of freedom this novel envisions for the emergent intellectual—not the large-scale freedom of revolutionary political movements, which consists in taking over the institutions of government to impose a new ideology upon the masses from the top down, but a more intimate, open-ended capacity to explore new forms of life. This metaphor also suggests the delicateness of this form of *Bildung*: many experimental hybrids are possible, but few survive.

Moreover, Kambili's narration makes the link between the purple hibiscus and her self-expression metonymic as well as metaphorical. Her time spent with these flowers coincides with her finding a voice: "Aunty Ifeoma's little garden…began to lift the silence" (16). This metonymy, investing the garden with the qualities of the liberal Aunty Ifeoma herself, hints at a nascent form of agency that eventually will include public expression, not least indicated by the fact that the novel itself is voiced in Kambili's own first-person narration. But even in this initial image, we can see how the *Bildung* represented by the purple hibiscus involves not just the transcendence of one's origins, but the preservation of multiple traces of one's precursors. Kambili's precursors will consist of all those relationships that have shaped her world view—even those that, as in the case of her father, imposed dogmatic, authoritarian, or otherwise uncompromising paradigms upon her behaviour. Even as she ultimately outgrows these paradigms, the diverse relationships that have influenced her will have combined in a viable way. It is this viability that is the signature of the novel's refiguration of *Bildung*.

Kambili's father looms large in her passage from childhood to adulthood. Eugene Achike is a product of the colonial, missionary *Bildung* that legitimized the British Empire's so-called civilizing mission. He is wealthy from inheriting colonial economic privileges, and is zealously active in the Catholic Church. At the same time, he does have a strong public consciousness; he owns one of the only newspapers that is openly critical of the Nigerian government. He represents a nationalist intellectual whose redemptive vision for the country is intimately bound up with the church. While powerfully invested in national independence, he has just as deeply internalized the colonial ideology, where *Bildung* coincides with the privileges that come with adopting European civilization. He refuses to have any contact with his "idol-worshipping" father, Papa-Nnukwu (47), and reacts violently when any of his family members show any trace of their Igbo roots. It is for this reason that Heather Hewett reads *Purple Hibiscus* as critiquing nationalist movements for their inherent repressiveness at the family level: "The irony of the story, of course, resides in Eugene's oppression of his own family while he fights for political freedom; but through staging this seemingly paradoxical predicament, *Purple Hibiscus* suggests the pervasiveness of despotism and the way it can ensnare even those who resist it" (89). The novel's answer to this despotism, according to Hewett, is found in the daughter's "pivotal act of claiming one's own voice," one that "captures unconscious intentions and feelings," a process that is facilitated by the generic mechanics of the Bildungsroman (87).[12] This act of "claiming" is indeed crucial, but the novel also deals extensively with the relational rootwork that enables this voice to emerge.

Kambili's growth begins only when she meets a figure capable of competing with her father's aura: Aunty Ifeoma, the novel's counterpoint to Papa Eugene. Ifeoma is also a product of a European education, but in its more liberal guise. This can be succinctly illustrated through her attitude towards Papa-Nnukwu, who is her father as well as Eugene's. Like Eugene, she does not identify directly with her father's Igbo traditions, but unlike him she respects traditional values with ironic distance rather than violent abjection. She tells Kambili, "Papa-Nnukwu was not a heathen but a traditionalist, that sometimes what was different was just as good as what was familiar, that when Papa-Nnukwu did his itu-nzu, his declaration of innocence, in the morning, it was the same as our saying the rosary" (Adichie, *Purple Hibiscus* 166). This liberal form of intellectualism makes peace with traditionalisms without directly aligning itself with them. At the same time, it acknowledges that Catholicism is itself a traditionalism, albeit one with a foreign provenance and, in the colonial context, a dangerous ethic of control. In so doing, it envisions an ethic of tolerance among all of Nigeria's ethno-cultural groupings.

Ifeoma's household is an essential catalyst for Kambili's *Bildung*, as a space dedicated to polyvocal speech rather than doctrinal silence. Ifeoma encourages her children to engage in philosophical and political debates, not offering her own opinion but supervising in a "proud-coach-watching-the-team way" (132). As opposed to the atmosphere of terrified, traumatized silence that pervades Kambili's house, we learn that "Laughter always rang out in Aunty Ifeoma's house...Arguments rose quickly and fell just as quickly" (140). The family space comes to model that of the liberal public sphere, where the stakes of speech are paradoxically both lower and higher: lower in the sense that conflict does not threaten the fundamental basis of the family/community, but higher in the sense that individuals' opinions are allowed to have significance relative to the collective. In both instances, the space is still supervised by a hierarchical authority figure, but the novel reminds us that there are different models for wielding that authority: the coordinating "coach" whose object is to see the diverse parts of the collective work together effectively, rather than the violent despot whose object is to ensure the collective acts as an obediently uniform entity.

The liberating effect Ifeoma's multivocal liberalism has on Kambili is clear, and Ifeoma remains the favoured role model through the novel's end, though even this tolerant liberalism is revealed to have its weaknesses. As the political situation of Nigeria becomes more dire and the regime becomes more repressive, Ifeoma eventually loses her job as a professor and is forced to move to America. When this happens, her temper gets shorter, and she loses the "proud-coach" patience she once had for impractical arguments (272). Liberalism, no matter how desirable at the individual level, is still dependent on material security, and fails to rise to the level of speaking for the people. It is more suited to gaining a sense of individual agency rather than representative agency, but this leaves it vulnerable to exile at the hands of factionalist violence. At novel's end, we are left with the unresolved dilemma of benign-but-ineffectual liberalism pitted against malignant traditionalisms that seek to violently appropriate the right to speak as the nation by occupying the power centres of the state.

Yet, within the novel's Bildungsroman structure, Aunty Ifeoma's essential role is as a necessary catalyst for Kambili's coming-to-speech; she provides a model of the intellectual capable of providing a counterpoint to Papa Eugene's missionary nationalism. Without Ifeoma's influence, Kambili might have rebelled, but she would have remained firmly within Eugene's intellectual and emotional orbit. Another important character in Kambili's development is Father Amadi, the kindly Catholic priest who cultivates personal relationships with the members of his community. His worldliness takes Kambili by surprise—exposing his shirtless body, playing sports with local children, and teaching a youth how to siphon gasoline from one car to another, for instance. Most significantly, he questions the condemnation of Igbo customs so zealously practised by her father. He incorporates Igbo songs into his Catholic practice, and shows deference to Papa-Nnukwu. This definitively demonstrates to Kambili that one can be fully Catholic while still honouring one's Igbo community. This nimbler negotiation of personhood and community leadership inspires Kambili, and she eventually falls in love with Father Amadi. He eventually elects to become a missionary in Germany, but they maintain an emotionally intense correspondence. This intimacy at a distance is typical of Kambili's network of relationships at the novel's end. While these individuals have been forced out of her life, they remain core to her sense of having a meaningful voice in society. This is instanced when she carries Father Amadi's letters "because they remind me of my worthiness"; this notion that her thoughts and actions matter more than her obedience is precisely what was withheld in her childhood home (303). Likewise, she says a few lines later, "I no longer wonder if I have a right to love Father Amadi; I simply go ahead and love him" (303). The actions themselves determine her form of life, not their constant evaluation by an abstract standard. Her experience of love is intense enough to become a self-justifying fact, a source of truth rather than a temptation away from it. Without her interactions with Ifeoma, Amadi, and others, Kambili would not have been likely to trust her own experience. To discover that one's words and actions matter requires a space that does not constantly nullify them.

This discovery is the novel's redemptive vision of *Bildung*, of human flourishing. My goal in this analysis has been to show that, in Adichie's figuration, the success of this *Bildung* depends, above all, on forming relationships with individuals at decisive moments in one's development. The resulting subject is organically related to these individuals not as parts of a single being but as a plant is to soil: not identical but still vitally connected. Her despotic father, and the form of postcolonial agency he represents, is found to be untenable despite Kambili's willingness to enter his tutelage and adopt his harsh ideology of national uplift. The decisive catalyst needed for her to develop from a beleaguered disciple into an intellectual, according to the novel, is the space provided by Aunty Ifeoma's garden: social space where one individual's personality may serve to open up space for another's. Once it has discovered its *capacity* for autonomy within the space opened by her relationship with Ifeoma, Kambili's personality then begins to grow on its own trajectory, determined by many other factors, other relationships. Even though the ideologies of Papa-Nnukwu, Eugene, and Ifeoma are ultimately found inadequate to her reality, they are not rejected outright. Rather, they survive in her attempts to balance her own critical independence with the various Catholic, Igbo, and liberal traditions she has internalized. Her existence as a viable hybrid bears the traces of those influential relationships, less as assent to the abstract ideologies themselves and more as a way of honouring the singular, complex individuals who embodied them for her. It is in this way that the novel attempts to reconcile one of the core dilemmas of the postcolonial Bildungsroman: how to develop an independent, critical voice that can actively participate in the shaping of society without losing the vital link with the concrete community whose culture(s) you would critique.

Representation through Relationships: *Half of a Yellow Sun*

Half of a Yellow Sun pushes this idea of relational *Bildung* to a further extreme, exploring the crisis of the intellectual class brought on by the Biafran revolution. It also aims to represent a more ambitious network of personalities and experiences, portraying 1960s Nigeria through the lens of three focalizing characters: Olanna, a twenty-something daughter of a wealthy industrialist who wishes to become a professor; Richard, a young British expat writer who is eager to adopt Biafra as his home country; and Ugwu, a teenaged houseboy for Odenigbo, a professor with radical politics. While all these characters undergo shifts throughout the novel, it is only Ugwu whose story properly evinces a process of *Bildung*. John Marx and Eleni Coundouriotis both read Ugwu's storyline as an underdog success story of the unaccredited intellectual, in which more formally trained and elevated intellectuals must eventually cede their representational authority to Ugwu, the peasant-become-autodidact-writer.[13] In this reading, the first generation of idealistic postcolonial intellectuals fails to lead their young nation away from crisis; they are first reduced to merely commenting on the sidelines, and then lose their will to speak altogether. Thus, *Half of a Yellow Sun* is a novel at least as concerned with how one loses one's voice as with how one finds it.

If the post-independence intellectuals find themselves at a dead end, then it leads to a further question: What kind of intellectual takes their place? For both Marx and Coundouriotis, Ugwu's authority comes from the diversity of his experience: (1) his straddling of Igbo village culture and university education, and (2) his first-hand experience of being impressed and fighting in the Biafran army. But there is a further question here of precisely *how* those experiences translate into the authority to represent the Biafran people—is this an alternate process of *Bildung*, and if so, then how does it work? As Michael Donnelly has observed, "With a little goading from Odenigbo, and an elite education at Odenigbo's expense, Ugwu apparently casts off his upbringing and assumes the position of the antiperspirant-wearing, toothpaste-using, book-reading bourgeois Biafran" (259). That is, by the time Ugwu comes to compose his text, he has already "cultivat[ed] his class capital" (259) and become "a comparatively privileged interpreter and recorder of the failed Biafran nation" (258). Thus, he arrives precisely at the same dilemma that plagued his forebears: whatever connection he has to the village population, it is no longer one of direct communion.

Moreover, the book that Ugwu writes, *The World Was Silent When We Died*, does not draw upon his personal experiences, and indeed, is conspicuously "silent about his own participation" (Donnelly 260). As a Biafran soldier, Ugwu has committed atrocities that later consume him with shame, including his participation in the group rape of a female bartender after a successful attack, something he resists at first but then succumbs to the peer pressure from his platoon. Later, when he is no longer a soldier, he is tormented by nightmares of his actions and begins writing about the war to displace his guilt. But it is precisely due to these secret motives that Ugwu quickly realizes his writing fails to be truly *representational*: "he would...never be able to describe well enough the fear that dulled the eyes of the mothers in the refugee camp when the bomber planes charged out of the sky. He would never be able to depict the very bleakness of bombing hungry people. But he tried, and the more he wrote the less he dreamed" (Adichie, *Half of a Yellow Sun* 498). His writing is a therapeutic relief from the shame that haunts him personally, but he ultimately rejects it because it emphatically fails to portray a collective experience. Meanwhile, he carefully avoids personal experience because he fears that the important women in his life would lose all respect for him if they knew what he had done (499). His failed attempts to write about Biafra in his own voice are overdetermined by avoidance of his own unspeakable actions; they are a form of silence as much as speech.

In place of his own experience, he attempts to blend the experience of the other characters in his narrow network of friendships. From Olanna, he borrows a harrowing anecdote about a woman on a train carrying the head of her child in a calabash. From his master-turned-mentor Odenigbo he takes the geopolitical and historical analysis through which to situate the war. He adopts what was originally Richard's book title, with his permission, after Richard abandons his project. There is formal symmetry here, as each of the novel's focalizing characters end up contributing something crucial. Ugwu's manuscript becomes a kind of vessel for their perspectives, while bearing the negative imprint of Ugwu's unaddressed shame and trauma. When Richard shares his title with Ugwu, for instance, "The World Was Silent When We Died," Ugwu does not think first of silence of the world's geopolitical superpowers to which Richard intends to refer; rather, he thinks of the look of silent hatred on the face of the young woman as he raped her (496). Ugwu's wartime experience shapes the writing of history, but in a thoroughly displaced and unacknowledged way.

For all these reasons, Ugwu is very far from the heroic intellectual of national liberation whose writing subsumes and distills the people's voice. His book is a chaotic hodge-podge of borrowed perspectives. There is no synthesis, no Hegelian *Aufhebung*, as we might see in a conventional Bildungsroman. Ugwu's emergence as an intellectual does not come from any moral growth, let alone superiority; it happens because his demons are the only psychic motivation powerful enough to actually complete the writing. Olanna never intends to commit her anecdotes to writing; Odenigbo loses his confidence as an intellectual and succumbs to an alcoholic dissipation; and Richard comes to realize the Biafran war is "not his story to tell" and abandons the project. So the other educated people who might have written the history of the Biafran war end up exhausting their limited energies elsewhere. The new intellectual is the one who, for private reasons that are nevertheless deeply connected to historical currents, uses whatever contingent material is at hand to quell their compulsion. It is also the person who honours and monumentalizes the experiences of their associates who did not have the time, motivation, or energy to publicize their experiences due to their own private traumas. The resulting document is a disjointed cross-section of these experiences, rather than the discovery of a strong unifying voice. Indeed, contra *Purple Hibiscus*, *Half of a Yellow Sun* proposes the challenging idea that the intellectual's vocation may not be to find their *own* voice but to endlessly supplement the fragmented voices of those in one's life who could have spoken but have been silenced by historical circumstance.

Seeking Symbiosis: *Americanah*

In Adichie's third novel, *Americanah*, she widens the scope of the intellectual's network even further to the transnational. It is in the shift between nations—from Nigeria to America and back—that we see Adichie's distinctive model of *Bildung*, in which the nascent intellectual discovers her capacity to facilitate the voices of others who would otherwise remain voiceless, rather than merely cultivating her own voice. When we first meet Ifemelu, the protagonist, she is already a successful blogger and speaker with a Princeton fellowship. Her blog attracts "thousands of unique visitors each month," making it a platform that, while modest by mass media standards, is enough to earn "good speaking fees" (Adichie, *Americanah* 7). Yet, despite her success, she is painfully aware of her increasing alienation from Nigeria, her country of origin. In America she finds herself struggling to connect with other immigrants from Nigeria and other African nations due to class and dialect barriers (10, 11). Despite her success in professional and romantic matters, her story is one of only superficial rootedness. Looking up old acquaintances who have moved back to Nigeria, she feels, "They were living her life. Nigeria became where she was supposed to be, the only place she could sink her roots in without the constant urge to tug them out and shake off the soil" (7). Once again, as in *Purple Hibiscus*, Adichie extends the organic metaphor of plant roots, giving it a vividness and depth that it normally lacks, reminding us that roots bond with the soil they are immersed in. The metaphor invites us to imagine this as an unpleasant experience, something one might feel the urge to "shake off." Adichie adds nuance to the oft-clichéd binary of rooted/rootless. Ifemelu *is* able to find roots in America. She establishes loving, caring relationships that give her some degree of space to develop a meaningful voice within both American and international cultural politics. Yet her life in America also makes her restless; she explains that "layer after layer of discontent had settled in her, and formed a mass that now propelled her" (8), and that her current relationship was like "being content in a house but always sitting by the window and looking out" (9). The novel thereby prepares a contrast between a merely viable organism and a flourishing one.[14]

Corresponding to her restless existence in America, the blog she writes there results in parallel ambivalences, particularly surrounding the relationship between author and audience.[15] In her blog, entitled *Raceteenth or Various Observations About American Blacks (Those Formerly Known as Negroes) By A Non-American Black* (4), the posts tend to be highly personal, drawing on chance conversations she has on train platforms ("Not All Dreadlocked White American Guys Are Down"), flights ("Badly-Dressed White Middle Managers from Ohio Are Not Always What You Think"), and at the hairdresser's ("A Peculiar Case of a Non-American Black, or How the Pressures of Immigrant Life Can Make You Act Crazy") (5, 22). While this blog resonates with American audiences sufficiently to propel her into a career, Ifemelu discovers that the nature of her connection with the audience is a troubled one. Her articles elicit passionate responses, ranging from the affirmative to the aggressive to the wildly unrelated, as internet posts do, but while she continues to believe strongly in the content itself, she grows strangely disconnected from her writing persona as her blog gets more successful:

> Now that she was asked to speak at roundtables and panels, on public radio and community radio, always identified simply as The Blogger, she felt subsumed by her blog. She had become her blog. There were times, lying awake at night, when…the blog's many readers became, in her mind, a judgmental angry mob waiting for her, biding their time until they could attack her, unmask her. (379)

This feeling of "subsumption," along with a fear of "unmasking," expresses an underlying distance between her sense of self and the face she shows to audiences. Moreover, the audience, even the supportive members, come to be imagined as a collective adversary. This adversarial feeling becomes even more pronounced when she begins getting invited to speak at diversity conferences, where she quickly realizes, "They did not want the content of her ideas: they merely wanted the gesture of her presence. They had not read her blog but they had heard that she was a 'leading blogger' about race" (377). The more successful the blog becomes, the more transactional the relationship between author and audience is.

In this phase of Ifemelu's *Bildung*, she inhabits a pathic version of the professionalized intellectual, where success paradoxically ends up nullifying the content and thus the impetus for her writing. As a result, she begins to starkly tailor her content to what appeals to her various audiences. At her talks "she began to say what they wanted to hear, none of which she would ever write on her blog, because she knew that the people who read her blog were not the same people who attended her diversity workshops." During her talks, she said, "America has made great progress for which we should be very proud." In her blog she wrote, "*Racism should never have happened and so you don't get a cookie for reducing it*" (378). Even though we may read the blog statement as more authentic to Ifemelu's character than the talk statement, the previous sentence implies that both statements are motivated by what the audience expects of her. Here, too, the substantive content comes to mean less than the continued success of the blog, which impedes Ifemelu's own continued evolution and flourishing. The writing, as elsewhere, is motivated by an imagined relationship with readers, but the adversarial tenor of this relationship poisons her ability to devote her energies to the pursuit of truth that initially motivated her.

After returning to Nigeria, Ifemelu discovers a different intellectual voice as a Lagos-based blogger. When she returns to Lagos, she re-establishes her blog, under the title *The Small Redemptions of Lagos*. This blog inspires different kinds of conversations than *Raceteenth*, with its predominantly American audience. Where before she wrote about racial politics in America from the perspective of an immigrant, here she writes to a primarily Nigerian audience from the perspective of a returnee. An article criticizing the "Nigerpolitan Club, a group of young returnees who gather every week to moan about the many ways that Lagos is not like New York," (519) prompts one commenter to share their own experiences, writing "Thank God somebody is finally talking about this," while another commenter begins a tangent about the privileged political status of returnees that "sparked more responses than the original post had" (520). Even more significantly, another post, on women who live rich lifestyles by taking rich lovers, causes a friend, Ranyinudo, to phone her angrily: "Anyone who knows me will know it's me!" To which Ifemelu replies, "That's not true Ranyi. Your story is so common…So many women lose themselves in relationships like that" (520–21). These responses suggest a sphere in which her choice of words and topics *does* make a difference, because it creates the opportunity for readers to enunciate collective experiences that may otherwise have gone unspoken. In contrast to the more predictable range of comments to *Raceteenth*, Ifemelu seems to draw vitality from these responses, "reveling in the liveliness of it all, in the sense of herself at the surging forefront of something vibrant" (520). Where the responses to *Raceteenth* appear to reflect pre-set opinions and long-reified talking points, *The Small Redemptions of Lagos* generates new discourse, conversations that would not be possible without Ifemelu's intervention. Both writer and readers draw verbal life from one another, creating a more promising image of *Bildung*'s "dynamic self-generating whole" (Cheah 236).

Moreover, Ifemelu's writing life and her personal life are more fully integrated in this new situation. Her greatest expression of satisfaction comes near the end of the novel, when she re-establishes a relationship with her first love, Obinze. The novel reads:

> She wrote her blog posts wondering what he would make of them. She wrote of a fashion show she had attended, how the model had twirled around in an ankara skirt, a vibrant swish of blues and greens, looking like a haughty butterfly…She wrote about the waterlogged neighborhood crammed with zinc houses…and of the young women who lived there, fashionable and savvy in tight jeans, their lives speckled stubbornly with hope: they wanted to open hair salons, to go to university. They believed their turn would come. *We are just one step away from this life in a slum, all of us who live air-conditioned middle-class lives,* she wrote,

> and wondered if Obinze would agree…She was at peace: to be home, to be writing her blog, to have discovered Lagos again. She had, finally, spun herself fully into being. (585)

True, she does connect imaginatively with the people and sights of Lagos, but it is her imagined readership, Obinze, that gives her writing cohesiveness, that transmogrifies her writing from hollow representation to a fabrication of being. This passage is reminiscent of Kambili's correspondence with Father Amadi at the end of *Purple Hibiscus*; Obinze as imagined reader, from a distance, provides a screen upon which Ifemelu can project her own formulations of freedom. Though the observations and ideas expressed are her own, they bear the imprint of this and other relationships she forms in Lagos. This allows her to develop a sense of her collective readership as one who may occasionally be critical, but who is fundamentally on her side, so to speak, unlike the "judgmental angry mob" who kept her awake in America (379). In this way, she is able to achieve the most important symbiosis between intellectual and public: (1) the sense that her particular words matter, rather than being pre-judged (positively or negatively) from the outset, and (2) her own sense that the substantive responses of the readers matter, rather than seeing them as merely an abstract number of "unique visitors." The organic metaphor proposed by the Bildungsroman theorists here takes the form of energy exchange, resulting in the collective sense that both writer and readers are being enriched by the act of enunciation.

Conclusion

To conclude, Adichie's novels unfold an evolving vision of how the intellectual can bridge the gap between personal and collective experience without collapsing either sphere into the other. To this end, she not only *employs* the Bildungsroman but *refines* it, inviting us to reconsider the multifarious paths available to *Bildung* with ethical and social nuance. In *Purple Hibiscus*, the most classically structured Bildungsroman of the three, she introduces the metaphor of the viable hybrid as a form of growth that preserves the traces of personal relationships, rather than the superseded ideologies that shaped them. In her next two novels, Adichie incorporates the *Bildung* narrative into more formally ambitious, multi-vocal structures to re-envision how the subject of *Bildung* might situate itself among a multitude of perspectives and influences. In *Half of a Yellow Sun*, it is the nascent intellectual's written work itself that comes to bear the traces of past relationships; Ugwu's intellectual project does not succeed until he puts aside his own will-to-voice and begins to transmit the experiences of his friends and acquaintances, both living and dead. In the limited particularity of these channelled relationships, Ugwu's assemblage can gesture towards a larger cross-section of the social whole— one that includes professionals, village dwellers, and child soldiers— without claiming that any of them speak for all of Biafra. Finally, Ifemelu's blog in *Americanah* provides her with a sense of true collective agency only when it elicits *others* to write authentically, strangers connected to Ifemelu only virtually but who are moved by her words to produce their own.

Though the historical conditions and stakes are very different in these three novels, the common thread is that the vital intellectuals are the ones who, through the relationships that motivate their writing, come to bear the imprints of a network of individuals with whom they have lived through intimate experiences. Rather than incorporating these shared experiences and perspectives into a more totalizing, empowered form of selfhood, as more conventional Bildungsromane attempt to do, Adichie formulates *Bildung* narratives that allow their protagonists to commune with a community without subsuming it. In each of these novels there remains a process of self-formation, of cultivation, of passing through many dysfunctional states to a more functional one. Adichie posits a different outcome for this self-formation, however; her mature intellectuals do not stand above the collective history but are caught in its currents without the reassurance of redemption; their relationship to their constituency is to be understood less as moral exemplar than as a kind of communicative medium, comparable to a photographic contact sheet or an electric conduit. The more their writing is an act of subjective survival, the closer it vibrates to the traumas and histories that it seeks to both commemorate and escape.

Notes

1. In a 2021 speech in praise of activist Akin Osuntokun, Abati suggests the elite's co-optation has diverted its focus onto the fatal partisanship of "religion, geography and ethnicity" ("Consistency").
2. Alexander Thurston, in "The Politics of Technocracy in Fourth Republic Nigeria," usefully details the ways that technocrats' claims to be apolitical are paradoxically politicized by various parties, particularly those with the goal of neoliberal reform. See especially pages 222–27.
3. My purpose here is not to affirm or celebrate any intelligentsia's legitimacy claims, past or present. The African intelligentsia generates interesting and creative ways to reinvent national narratives in response to historical crises, but these solutions are far from seamless, univocal, or invulnerable to critique.
4. In what follows, I focus more on theorists and critics of the former category who connect the Bildungsroman to a collective national discourse, since I believe Adichie's fiction is more deeply in dialogue with this theoretical orientation. For typical instances of more critical-individualist readings of the postcolonial Bildungsroman, see Austen, Hay, Mickelsen, and Okuyade.
5. For a stark illustration of this dynamic, one could turn to Achebe's polemical pamphlet, *The Trouble with Nigeria*, whose stated goal is not to establish Achebe himself as a leader, but to offer prescriptions that will "create an atmosphere conducive to [the] emergence [of good leaders]" (2).
6. Andrade's most paradigmatic examples of this point are Tsitsi Dangarembga's *Nervous Conditions* and Nuruddin Farah's *Maps* (*Nation* 114–64).
7. See Andrade ("Adichie's Geneologies"), Hewett, Leetsch, Okuyade, and Tunca.
8. Benedict Anderson's classic *Imagined Communities* is particularly pertinent here in its reflections on *media* as a set of technologies through which communities can come into being on a mass scale. See especially chapter 3 (37–46). As we will see, Adichie's most fully developed instances of updated *Bildung* involve the innovative use of media as a catalyst for community.
9. See Mkandawire (80) and Adesanmi and Dunton (14).
10. See Hirsch.
11. This open-ended concept of *Bildung*, which I derive from Pheng Cheah's *Spectral Nationality* (see chapter 1, "The Rationality of Life," 17–60, for an elaboration of the concept's complexity in German romanticism), is a key point of distinction between my capacious understanding of the Bildungsroman, which encompasses unforeseen, experimental possibilities for education and self-formation, and a more restrictive, Lukácsian understanding, which emphasizes, as a constitutive feature, the teleological reconciliation with and legitimation of existing hierarchies of power. See Slaughter (94) and Ouma (104).

12. For another perspective on *Purple Hibiscus* as a discovery of voice, with an emphasis on women entering the public sphere, see Courtois.
13. See Coundouriotis (225–36) and Marx (70–76).
14. Stefanie Reuter correctly discerns a much lengthier process of *Bildung* in *Americanah*, which includes the early "development of a critical consciousness regarding the categories of race and gender" (3). My reading does not intend to dispute this argument; rather, in the context of my particular reflections on the intellectual, I have elected to focus more narrowly on the evolution of Ifemelu's writing persona.
15. For an extensive analysis of how Ifemelu's blogging evolves in the novel, see Duce.

Works Cited

Abati, Reuben. "Consistency in Public Intellectual Advocacy: Akin Osuntokun's Role in Nigeria's Ideas Industry." *This Day*, 16 Jan. 2022, https://www.thisdaylive.com/index.php/2022/01/16/consistency-in-public-intellectual-advocacy-akin-osuntokuns-role-in-nigerias-ideas-industry/.

Abati, Reuben. "Where Are the Public Intellectuals?" *The Guardian*, 23 Jan. 2016, https://guardian.ng/opinion/where-are-the-public-intellectuals/.

Achebe, Chinua. *The Trouble with Nigeria*. Heinemann, 1983.

Adesanmi, Pius, and Chris Dunton. "Nigeria's Third Generation Writing: Historiography and Preliminary Theoretical Considerations." *English in Africa*, vol. 32, no. 1, 2005, pp. 7–19.

Anderson, Benedict. *Imagined Communities: Reflections on the Origin and Spread of Nationalism*. Verso, 1998.

Andrade, Susan Z. "Adichie's Genealogies: National and Feminine Novels." *Research in African Literatures*, vol. 42, no. 2, 2011, pp. 91–101.

Andrade, Suzan Z. *The Nation Writ Small: African Fictions and Feminisms, 1958–1988*. Duke University Press, 2011.

Adichie, Chimamanda Ngozi. *Americanah*. Anchor, 2014.

Adichie, Chimamanda Ngozi. *Half of a Yellow Sun*. Anchor, 2007.

Adichie, Chimamanda Ngozi. *Purple Hibiscus*. Algonquin, 2003.

Austen, Ralph A. "Struggling with the African Bildungsroman." *Research in African Literatures*, vol. 46, no. 3, 2015, pp. 214–31.

Cheah, Pheng. *Spectral Nationality: Passages of Freedom from Kant to Postcolonial Literatures of Liberation*. Columbia University Press, 2003.

Coundouriotis, Eleni. *The People's Right to the Novel: War Fiction in the Postcolony*. Fordham University Press, 2014.

Courtois, Cédric. "Third-Generation Nigerian Female Writers and the Bildungsroman: Breaking Free from the Shackles of Patriarchy." *Growing Up a*

Woman: The Private/Public Divide in the Narratives of Female Development, edited by Soňa Šnircová and Milena Kostić, Cambridge Scholars Publishing, 2015, pp. 100–19.

Donnelly, Michael A. "The Bildungsroman and African Sovereignty in Chimamanda Ngozi Adichie's *Half of a Yellow Sun*." *Law & Literature*, vol. 30, no. 2, 2017, pp. 245–66.

Duce, Violeta. "Social Media and Female Empowerment in Chimamanda Ngozi Adichie's *Americanah*." *The European Legacy*, vol. 26, nos. 3–4, 2021, pp. 243–56.

Hay, Simon. "*Nervous Conditions*, Lukács, and the Postcolonial Bildungsroman." *Genre: Forms of Discourse and Culture*, vol. 46, no. 3, 2013, pp. 317–44.

Hewett, Heather. "Coming of Age: Chimamanda Ngozi Adichie and the Voice of the Third Generation." *English in Africa*, vol. 32, no. 1, 2005, pp. 73–97.

Hirsch, Marianne. *The Generation of Postmemory: Writing and Visual Culture after the Holocaust*. Columbia University Press, 2012.

Leetsch, Jennifer. "Love, Limb-Loosener: Encounters in Chimamanda Adichie's *Americanah*." *Journal of Popular Romance Studies*, vol. 6, 2017, pp. 1–16.

Lukács, Georg. *Theory of the Novel*. Translated by Anna Bostock. MIT Press, 1974.

Mickelsen, David J. "The Bildungsroman in Africa: The Case of *Mission terminée*." *The French Review*, vol. 59, no. 3, 1986, pp. 418–27.

Mkandawire, Thandika. "Three Generations of African Academics: A Note." *Transformation*, no. 28, 1995, pp. 75–83.

Marx, John. *Geopolitics and the Anglophone Novel, 1890–2011*. Cambridge University Press, 2012.

Okuyade, Ogaga. "Weaving Memories of Childhood: The New Nigerian Novel and the Genre of the *Bildungsroman*." *Ariel*, vol. 41, nos. 3–4, 2011, pp. 137–66.

Ouma, Christopher E.W. *Childhood in Contemporary Diasporic African Literature*. Palgrave Macmillan, 2020.

Reuter, Stefanie. "Becoming a Subject: Developing a Critical Consciousness and Coming to Voice in Chimamanda Ngozi Adichie's *Americanah*." 2015. *SSRN*, http://dx.doi.org/10.2139/ssrn.2808396.

Slaughter, Joseph R. *Human Rights, Inc.: The World Novel, Narrative Form, and International Law*. Fordham University Press, 2007.

Thurston, Alexander. "The Politics of Technocracy in Fourth Republic Nigeria." *African Studies Review*, vol. 61, no. 1, 2018, pp. 215–38.

Tunca, Daria. "Chimamanda Ngozi Adichie as Chinua Achebe's (Unruly) Literary Daughter: The Past, Present, and Future of 'Adichebean' Criticism." *Research in African Literatures*, vol. 49, no. 4, 2018, pp. 107–26.

14

(BE)COMING OF AGE IN POSTMILLENNIAL HONG KONG LITERATURE

Between Humans and Things in Hon Lai-chu's Works

Helena Wu

With its colonial history and atypical postcoloniality, Hong Kong is no stranger to the coming-of-age narrative. To start with, one should not forget that British Foreign Secretary Lord Palmerston, discontented with the acquisition of the territory as an outcome of the First Opium War in 1841, famously described Hong Kong as "a barren island with hardly a house upon it" (Tsang 14). This rock-bottom image was the starting point of the coming-of-age formula mainstreamed by officials over the centuries to follow. On the eve of the outbreak of the Second World War, in 1937, British historian Geoffrey Robley Sayer described the period between 1841 and 1862 as the "birth, adolescence and coming of age" of Hong Kong as a British colony. With time, the rags-to-riches discourse and the coming-of-age motif fused with the city's grand narrative, which has maintained an emphasis on (economic) growth regardless of Hong Kong's reversion of sovereignty from Britain to the People's Republic of China in 1997. Despite the upheavals during the negotiation period in the 1980s, and the transitional era after the signing of the Sino-British Joint Declaration in 1984, the idea of "stability and prosperity" was for the most part acknowledged by both London and Beijing as the past, present, and future blueprint of the city. The prevalent "discourse of the market," which was generally uninterrupted by the 1997 handover, was interpreted as thus: the "'market mentality' that characterizes many of Hong Kong's people is related to Hong Kong's peculiar situation as a colony, decades after most of the rest of the world's colonies had become independent" (Mathews et al. 15). The touristic gaze invited by the post-handover government is an exemplar of this market discourse:

> In the tumultuous years since then, this "barren rock" has been transformed from a sleepy collection of 20 or so villages into a dynamic metropolis of gleaming skyscrapers that form one of the world's most iconic skylines and reflect Hong Kong's status as "Asia's world city." ("Hong Kong Heritage")

In fact, what complicates the case of Hong Kong is that the trope of coming of age has been simultaneously employed, but in different ways, in texts ranging from analytical writings and fictional works to counternarratives. For instance, reflecting the political turmoil, exile, and diaspora during the Cold War era, Hong Kong refugee literature exhibited the characteristics of the Bildungsroman, despite the fact that many of the protagonists were perceived to have failed in their attainment of individuality (Wong).

During the 2014 Umbrella Movement and in its aftermath, scholars in the humanities and social sciences observed the emergence of a "new generation of the Hong Kong people" (Pang 170)—the "Umbrella Generation" (Hui and Lau). The collective perception of a generational shift was retrospectively a manifestation of a new mode of coming of age that valorized human rights, freedom, and democracy, as in the demands of the civil disobedience campaign. Differing from the aforementioned market discourse, bottom-up community-based subjectivity was contradistinguished from the adherence to the status quo as instilled by the grand narrative. In this regard, the coming-of-age narratives in post-2014 Hong Kong have become increasingly "rhizomatic," using Deleuze and Guattari's term, in that its discourse is not monodirectional (3–25). Characterized by its nonhierarchical and decentring nature, the rhizome, as opposed to roots that exist within the hierarchical order of a tree and that is associated with a linear mode of thinking, offers multiple points of entry to critically reflect on the inconsistencies and the internal contradictions enveloping Hong Kong as a "postcolonial anomaly."[1] In the post-handover age, just as decolonization has been challenged by unequally voiced narratives and identities, each competing for their own story of "Hong Kong," Hong Kong offers a pertinent site to explore the changing agency of (and within) coming of age with respect to its various functions in the mainstream and alternative representations of the city (S. Chan).

With an eye to the broader framework of the Bildungsroman, this chapter will offer a revisionist look at the genre and its fluid recontextualization in postmillennial Hong Kong literature. By examining selected works composed by Hon Lai-chu (1978–), a representative Hong Kong writer who emerged during the first decade of the twenty-first century, I will show how the writer problematizes the narratives of transition and transformation, the taken-for-granted growth formula, and the human-thing relationship in the city, with an aim to probe how and whether or not coming of age is attainable given the atypical and sometimes dubious postcolonial condition of Hong Kong. As the search for meaning, subjectivity, and self-expression continues, but is at times disrupted by external forces, this chapter asks: How do we position the postcolonial Bildungsroman in the context of Hong Kong when the goal of coming of age and the society's value system have become increasingly divergent? As a response to this question, I will argue that Hon Lai-chu's work deconstructs the mainstreamed logic of growth at both literal and allegorical levels through the representation of bodily degeneration (often into objects), contributing to the development of this distinctive feature characterizing post-handover, postmillennial Hong Kong literature.

The Application of the Bildungsroman in Hong Kong Literature

In a broad definition, the Bildungsroman genre follows the development of a child or an adolescent until he or she reaches a point in adulthood. Personal growth, formative changes, critical moments of transition, and the pursuit of goals are the featured themes frequently explored in this genre, which originated in Germany and gained popularity in the nineteenth century. In modern and contemporary Chinese-language literature, the idea of coming of age has been applied in various scenarios—from navigating the fictional world and reflecting social reality to negotiating with different existing institutions—resulting in different contextualized meanings, crossing over late Qing, the May Fourth period, and beyond. The reading of the Bildungsroman can as well be extended to the context of Hong Kong.

According to *Xiang Gang wen xue da xi* (*The Compendium of Hong Kong Literature*), Hong Kong is a "fluid literary and cultural space," and its literature is the diverse, multifaceted outcome of this networked relationship (L. Chan, Foreword 16–17).[2] Likewise, the distinctiveness and the locality possessed by Hong Kong literature has been proven by its status as a site of cultural memory and topophobia and by the multiple conscious and subjective positionings it embodies (L. Chan, "Sense of Place"; Chow, "Between Colonizers"). For instance, Wang Der-wei has called for rethinking the Bildungsroman by highlighting the unconventional articulation of the "passing of the modern and post-modern ages" in the works of Hong Kong writer Dung Kai-cheung, declaring the genre encompasses an old-new divide: "old Bildungsroman teach us nothing, it has by now been reduced to a kind of literary hard labour" (Wang 84). Prior to Wang's recontextualization of the Bildungsroman to address the city's "post-colonialist, post-society situation," Mary Wong laid the groundwork by examining Hong Kong Cold War literature but without submitting to the dominant perspective that it was built on the division of the left-right political camps. To this end, Wong demonstrated the possibility of rereading past narratives and renewing their interpretations by overcoming this blind spot in previous practices of literary criticism. Wong's concluding remark, furthermore, signalled that coming-of-age narratives should not be limited to a person's growth, nor narrowed down to the scope of a single generation: "In the case of Hong Kong in the 1950s, their stories of formation crisis were to be completed only with the coming of the second generation" (155).

In sum, the notion of the Bildungsroman has yielded a wide range of cultural meanings, political undertones, and social implications with respect to its different manifestations, applications, and their contexts. Considering the entangled forces accumulated from Hong Kong's coloniality and postcoloniality, the direction of coming of age has varied not only with time but also across space, be it narrative, communal, or psychological. On the one hand, progress in the form of financial gain penetrated the official discourse and was largely uninterrupted by the colonial-postcolonial transition, as mentioned earlier. On the other hand, writers with a postcolonial sensibility—such as Xi Xi in her notable creation of "Floating City" and "Fertile Town," and Dung Kai-cheung in his rendition of "Visible Cities"—have repeatedly questioned the "hegemonic representation of Hong Kong as a capitalist success" (Cheung, "The Hi/stories" 568). These allegorical portrayals of Hong Kong highlighted the intentional abstraction and trivialization of the actual urban space during the transitional era, which witnessed the signing of the Sino-British Joint Declaration in 1984 and the undertaking of the handover in 1997. Esther Cheung regarded the act of "weaving their stories of Hong Kong with rich resources from history, legend, gossip, myth, and above all, their own imagination" as a means to reconstruct everyday life and "re-politicize the social and cultural history" at times of crisis; thus, the postmillennial era has deepened the rethinking of colonial and postcolonial experiences, alongside the growth of local consciousness and the intensification of a locally oriented personal belonging in society (Cheung, "The Hi/stories" 568; Law).

In 1998, Hon Lai-chu, the Hong Kong-born-and-bred writer, published her debut essay at the age of fourteen in a local newspaper and her first book, *Shu shui guan sen lin* (*The Water Pipe Forest*). By 2010, Hon had received an honourable mention at the prestigious Dream of Red Chamber Award, among other titles, such as the Hong Kong Arts Development Council Artist of the Year, the Hong Kong Book Prize, and the Hong Kong Biennial Award for Chinese Literature

(Fiction). Outside of her home city, she has won accolades presented by the Unitas Literary Association (in 2006) and *China Times* (in 2008) in Taiwan and was named a resident by the University of Iowa at its International Writing Program in 2010, demonstrating the agility of her works and her readership in the Sinosphere and beyond. In her creative works, Hon is known for her portrayal of dysfunctional families, estranged individuals, and disoriented youths. She has unsettled the city's modus operandi with a surrealist brush, where language, signification, and boundaries are subject to dissolution. With an eye to how these narratives have resisted the discourse of the market, which has been installed since colonial times, and the ever-growing discourse of the state after the handover, can these narratives—underlined by their attention to things, animals, and the notion of change—be regarded as an alternative coming of age in postmillennial Hong Kong literature?

Becoming Things in Hon Lai-chu's World(s)

In Hon Lai-chu's corpus of work, a recurrent motif lies in the formulation of an absurd, but no less in-your-face, connection between humans and things, which I will interpret at the levels of the textual and the material in the following. Published in 2008, *Feng zheng jia zu* (*The Kite Family*) consists of six short stories that offer a glimpse of the fictive realm created by Hon. Her human protagonists often undergo transformations into things, material and immaterial, such as furniture in "Lin mu yi zi" ("Forrest Woods, Chair"), a kite in "Feng zheng jia zu" ("The Kite Family"), and air in "Bei shang lu guan" ("Heartbreak Hotel"). At other times, the protagonists' obsession with things is depicted in the collection of teeth in "Men ya" ("Front Teeth"), brains in "Huai nao dai" ("Spoiled Brains"), and even family members in "Gan mao zhi" ("Notes on an Epidemic"). These entangled themes have also found expression in Hon's novel-length works. One can find the recycling of human remains in *Hui hua* (*Grey Flower*); the fragmentation of the body into skin, muscle, ligaments, and soft bone in *Feng shen* (*Mending Bodies*); the transformation of a human into a balloon and the attainment of a weightless state in *Li xin dai* (*The Border of Centrifugation*); and face-dissecting and face-switching in

Kong lian (*Empty Face*). Meanwhile, Hon often explores different animate and inanimate agencies in her short stories. In the anthology *Shi qu dong xue* (*Losing Caves*), cats find their way into the stories "Shi qu dong xue" ("Losing Caves") and "Piao ma" ("Drifting Horse"),[3] rabbits in "Mao tu" ("Flurry Rabbit"), and rats in "Qing xi" ("Cleansing"). In *Ren pi ci xiu* (*Human Skin Embroidery*), tattoo art is contemplated through the magnification of human body parts such as skin and pores. On many occasions, Hon's works have been described as a conveyance of a Kafkaesque sensation (Dung 6–7). One apparent reason comes from her frequent depiction of a surrealistic, inexplicable transformation in an everyday setting. Whereas Franz Kafka's "Metamorphosis" portrays Gregor Samsa's gradual psychological change with respect to his body's man-to-insect transition, Hon's characters seem to exist outside of dominant logic—or simply the laws of physics such as gravity—as they face physical transformation and unexpected displacement in a matter-of-fact manner.

This rite of passage that transgresses the boundaries between human, thing, and animal reminds us of Wang's enthusiastic call for "a fresh look at the Bildungsroman" in view of historical consciousness at the "turning-point in history" (84). Considering the degrees and the extent of changes subjected to the human body and its habitat, Hon's persistent depiction of transformation as deformation and degeneration encompasses an unconventional "coming of age" that is tied to nonhuman counterparts. The opposition to the master narrative—where the city's status quo is emphasized and changes are mostly limited to growth in economic terms—also mirrors the "post-productivist" and "post-materialist" values that took root in postmillennial Hong Kong after a wave of social movements and preservation campaigns (Veg 73; Ma 710). In this regard, Hon's works could paradoxically be regarded as anti-Bildungsroman, for their resilience to domineering power relations and narrative closure, and postcolonial Bildungsroman, for subverting the master itinerary of growth.

To begin with, the absurdity of Hon's stories is accentuated by the lack of differentiation between humans and things. On the one hand, Hon channels and amplifies the feeling of being a misfit through her protagonists' estrangement to their own bodies and their surroundings.

On the other hand, there is always a surprising calmness in the occurrence of any unexpected phenomena, as if they were only natural, or even necessary. In "Forrest Woods, Chair," the namesake protagonist Forrest Woods is first presented in a conversation between his mother and a potential customer called M: "The mother...had just informed M that Forrest Woods had officially become a chair" (Hon, *The Kite Family* 105).[4] Following an account given by the narrator, the voice of Forrest Woods appears as he introduces himself: "I am a chair, and I can be any kind of chair you wish" (106). The difficulties in discerning the location of Forrest Woods's subjectivity in the body of a chair or a human being not only highlights the intentional confusion of the boundaries between forms, organic and inorganic, but also brings about an upfront, otherwise neglected closeness that puts readers in the shoes of an object (in this case, a chair). As the story develops, Forrest Woods behaves more and more like a chair and constantly reflects on his lived experience as a chair. For instance, "living as a chair" (121) is what Forrest Woods tells L, a customer looking for a chair to cure her back pain who would later provide a vantage point to the story upon Forrest Woods's complete transformation into a chair. If the Kafkaesque metamorphosis has inserted a mode of the fantastic by blurring the line between real and unreal (see Jackson), then the ironic ending of "Forrest Woods, Chair" strikes (back) at the realm of the real by destabilizing the norms in everyday life through ridiculing the neoliberalist logic that dominates consumer society:

> Mrs. Woods asked, "So, is he a fully qualified chair?"
> L replied firmly, "He's the most outstanding chair I have ever seen."
> (Hon, *The Kite Family* 124)

While it is uncertain whether Forrest Woods was still cognitively able to learn of the compliment he received, he seemed to have given more contributions to the local economy and international mobility as a chair than in his original form: he "has become a professional engaged in chair work" who "couldn't tear himself from his job," and "his dedication led to the opportunity for him to go abroad" (124). The prolongation of Forrest Woods's work life as a chair might easily recall Marx's theory of alienation, which criticizes the objectification of humans through labour. Nevertheless, a double irony is present in Hon's rendition of Forrest Woods in that he willingly learned to become a chair and embraced his chair form with joy.

In this regard, Leung Ping-kwan's contemplative questions urge a new way of understanding the positioning of things in the contemporary world:

> How do we face the new patterns that are engendered by different practices of thing production and consumption in consumer society? How do we look at the accumulation of things and the objectification of humans? How do we position ourselves in the entangled relationship between things and humans? Can we, after all, re-evaluate and rethink the impact of the material cast by poetic language, poetic images, and prints? (Leung, "Sui wu xin zhuan" 567, my translation)

While thing-chanting has been a literary device long employed in classical Chinese poetry, Leung observed its gradual decrease in number since the May Fourth period in Mainland China and the emphasis on the psyche during the 1950s and 1960s in Hong Kong and Taiwan. Against the backdrop of the twentieth century, Leung has pointed out how materiality is often overlooked in existing discourses and how objects are limited to a one-sided understanding as goods and commodities according to the logic of consumer society. From a dually physical and affective perspective, Leung has argued for what he calls the "heart-thing relation" (*xin wu guan xi*), which constellates the embodiments possessed by things, the actuality derived from the physical dimension, the attributes and values assigned by humans to things, and the connection between humans and things in the material realm (566). Meanwhile, what makes Leung's intervention crucial is not just the critical depth he offers beyond the planes of phenomenology, philosophy, and literary criticism, but also his situatedness in Hong Kong literature as a representative writer. To move from a contemplative angle (by Leung) to an interpretive aspect (of Leung's own works), Rey Chow's analysis of Leung's thing-chanting poems—such as "Feng huang mu" ("The Flame Tree") and "Lao zhi min di jian zhu" ("An Old Colonial Building")—offers a simultaneously close and distant reading of "Hong Kong" and the things that compose it at a meta-level (Chow, "Things"). Chow has argued that the material aspect of the urban space is actually what "transports" Hong Kong and highlights Hong Kong's condition as a "port" and a "passageway" corresponding to the city's colonial condition:

> The immanence and centrality of the material in his poems becomes both an expression of the commonplace-clichéd, ordinary, unremarkable things, things which are simply there—and a common place, the place where people meet, things converge, and mutualities and reciprocities are actively reinvented. (182)

To this end, the transformation of Forrest Woods into a chair could as well be read as a newly invented path for an alternative coming of age, where a "common" point between humans and things is likewise attained. Therefore, the more intensified and radicalized contacts between humans and things actually bespeaks the city's pseudo-postcolonial condition, which has unfolded with time in the postmillennial era.

Last but not least, the visuality embedded in Hon's texts brings in another aspect of materialization that involves the material existence of the texts. Considering the recurrent use of pictographs in conceiving the names of the characters, the two Chinese characters denoting Forrest Woods—*lin* (forest) and *mu* (wood)—bring together three identical radicals, *mu*, that can be recombined to form *lin*, which is the source of wood in nature. As characters' names are often recycled in Hon's works, this also leaves behind an intertextual linkage within Hon's fictive realm. For instance, as one moves across the four stories collected in *Human Skin Embroidery*, the names of the characters transit from Fire (*huo*) and Forest Fire (*lin huo*) to Wood (*mu*), all deriving from the radicals *mu* and *huo*, which generates the word *fen* (burning) that aligns with the connecting theme of pain and failed relationships in the collection (Hon, *Human Skin Embroidery*). Here the semiotic and visual power of the pictograph brings about a sensorial reading experience that enables one to perceive the text as signs as well as objects, hence turning "the reader into a spectator" (Stewart 9). In other words, the reader is a spectator who comes to witness the becoming of Hon's characters as both human subjects and material objects.

Be-Coming of Age with Changes

In the transposition between humans and things, the hermeneutic negotiation of identity is complicated by the self and the surrounding environment in both empirical and phenomenal terms. As such, lamenting the irretrievable human form as a loss could lead to an identity crisis, which is close to Hong Kong's response to the approaching handover in its cultural production and consumption during the 1980s and 1990s (Abbas; Cheung, *Fruit Chan's* 8–9, 30). However, in the worlds fabricated by Hon, the fluid positionings and the multiple roles available for humans, things, and animals, in fact, transgress the binary understanding of human and nonhuman without inserting any judgmental commentary. Through this fluidity and binary understanding, I contend, Hon's worlds have revealed that the postcolonial coming of age in the context of Hong Kong arrived with a renewed understanding of identity, one that is volatile and accepted as highly performative, as well as open to change.[5]

In "The Kite Family," the nameless protagonist narrates her family history from a first-person perspective through the stories of her maternal grandmother, mother, aunt, and sister. Regardless of the story's plot, Hon's special attention to things persists, as has been hinted by the title of the work, in this case the images of tethered flying objects like a kite and a helium balloon tied to a human body. For instance, the grandmother's obese body being *compared* to "a rainbow-colored balloon, floating up into the sky until it pops" is the exact wording of the narrating protagonist (Hon, *The Kite Family* 36–37), while the sister insists on becoming a kite—the image of the kite is externalized by her minute body size and light body weight—and the narrator of the story habitually flies her sister into the sky *as a kite*. A scene with similar superimposed images appears in another novel by Hon, *The Border of Centrifugation*, where a girl called Bird asks a balloon vendor to fly her to the sky as a balloon. The condition of uprootedness and the search for home are nothing new to Hong Kong literature. During the 1980s, Xi Xi famously portrayed Hong Kong as a "floating city" that was "neither sinking nor rising," among other figurative images that conveyed a suspended state (3). Interestingly, Xi Xi's approach to the story "Fu cheng zhi yi" ("Marvels of a Floating City") was inspired by the surrealist work of Belgian painter René Magritte, and the story highlights the role of the surreal in negotiating with ambivalent sentiments and identities in flux between a colonial status and an uncertain future. Nevertheless, Xi Xi's tales of Hong Kong—often magical and playful—were quite different from other refugee literature and nationalist narratives that would continue to emerge (Leung, "Xiang Gang de gu shi" 11–29). The transition from the works produced by the Southbound literati to the emergence of local writers has been signified by the articulation of a postcolonial identity in Hong Kong's literary history and the newer generation's willingness "to negotiate with cliché images, to rediscover the colonial process, and to rewrite local history" (Cheung, "Voices of Negotiation" 604). The rediscovery of past cultural memory in Hon's works and Hon's distinctive turn in embracing both the imaginary and the real have arguably effectuated another moment of coming of age in postmillennial Hong Kong literature.[6]

Going back to *The Border of Centrifugation*, Hon conjured a pathos called the "drifting disease," which originated from "humans' inability to change their perception of reality despite the passing of time"—as a result, humans cannot find a way out and become trapped "in an illusion that is more realistic than the moment occurring" (Hon, *Centrifugation* 171–72, my translation). As part of Hon's signature style, this troubled psyche is spelled out in both physiological and cognitive terms: the loss of balance and the sense of centrifugation—the driving force of drifting—is caused by the dissipation of memory, determinacy, orientation, and existential weight. To complicate this, the Chinese terminology for centrifugation, *li xi*, literally means "distance from the heart." While some characters (like Bird's father) simply drift away and disappear into thin air, others (like Bird's mother) try to ground themselves with the help of tools. This may explain why rope structures such as nets, strings, and knots constitute recurrent things other than balloons in this book. Most of all, what makes *The Border of Centrifugation*, as well as "The Kite Family," different from other narratives on drifting in Hong Kong literature is how Bird handles the situation—she cuts herself loose from her mother's attachments, which keep her from flying away, while willingly embracing drifting, whether or not it is a nearly inevitable disease for every human being as the story progresses. In this regard, what the narrator-protagonist ponders in "The Kite Family"— "I'll never know if my sister secretly wished I'd let go of the rope and let the wind blow her somewhere she'd never dreamed of, much less been"—might be answered in *The Border of Centrifugation* (Hon, *The Kite Family* 93). When Bird asks the balloon vendor to help her "return" to the sky, the man reminds her that any fall would render her "shattered into bits and pieces" before "getting there"; nonetheless, Bird demonstrates she is unafraid of the flight, but the skyward journey also channels a passage to an unquantifiable place that lies outside of symbolic order:

> [Bird:] "But it is my destination, there."
> [Man:] "Do you mean death?"
> [Bird:] "It is mid-air, there." (Hon, *Centrifugation* 229, my translation)

Between boldness and indifference, a mentality that readily accepts what is deemed absurd or impossible in the dominant discourse is actually values and psychological change, and the calm response towards uncertainty is somehow the revelation of change attained by Hon's protagonists.

Intriguingly, the unquestionable conversion between humans and things contrasts the doubt cast on once assertive human relations such as familial roles—not just in "The Kite Family," but also in "Heartbreak Hotel" and "Notes on an Epidemic" from the same collection. Identities are interchangeable and human relationships, biological or not, only become recognized at the time of role-playing. In "The Kite Family," the identities of the protagonist's family members—such as when she refers to her "aunt"—are in doubt in latter parts of the story:

> "Do you know who I am?" I asked. She shook her head slightly, and I continued, "How could you let a stranger into your home like this?"
> She finally looked at me. "You remind me of someone."
> ...I stepped inside because I saw the shadow of the grandmother I had never met. From then on, I called on my aunt every morning at about the same time...I knew that she had to be my aunt and no one else. (Hon, *The Kite Family* 67–68)

Whereas the feature of indeterminacy can easily be understood as a literary technique in postmodernist literature, Hon's works do not conform to postmodernism's discredit or denial of the real. Although "Hong Kong" is never directly named in the worlds fabricated by Hon in her texts, extratextual references are made to real-life happenings. These include but are not limited to the 2013 dock workers strike in *The Border of Centrifugation* and the community-driven preservation campaigns against the authorities' Land Resumption Ordinance in *Grey Flower* and *Losing Caves*—in addition to the looming presence of law enforcement figures such as bailiffs, judges, and the police in *The Border of Centrifugation*, *Mending Bodies*, and *Grey Flower*. Against this backdrop, and with awareness of the situated present of the writer, the absurdist elements in Hon's works should be scrutinized beyond their face value. Between the actual and the fictional, the oblivious states, dysfunctional relationships, and dismantling of identities actually constellate, if not simulate, a series of experiential encounters with changes in different forms during the process of reading. Hon's characters, especially children, welcome changes, which explains their high level of adaptability to external circumstances. In "The Kite Family," the protagonist contemplates the "role" of being a child as an adult:

> I suppose I should have adjusted more quickly to the rapid [pace] at which things were changing. When I was still a child, I played the role of a child along with others my age, even though we weren't entirely naïve.

> It was much later that I realized everyone [was] doing essentially the same thinking at each stage of life. (Hon, *The Kite Family* 41)

This indicator of change foreshadows the destabilization of familial relationships in later parts of the story.

Likewise, "Notes on an Epidemic" features identities like "Father," "Brother," and "Grandmother" (note the quotation marks) as roles to be assigned to different individuals who will then perform in a contractual "family." Following the unexplained disappearance of the other Mother and Father (note the capitalization), the protagonist-narrator becomes a member of a, or just another, make-believe "family" under the doctor's advice. Just as the fade-in/fade-out of different family members is simply handled by finding a "replacement" or a "fill-in," the story opens with nothing other than a reflection on change: "In reality, we'd changed much more than we knew" (Hon, *The Kite Family* 191, 227–28). Intriguingly, towards the end of the story, readers learn that sometimes it was not the role or the person who changed but how it was played out, which was subjected to circumstantial factors and shifts in dynamics. Before the protagonist sees "the man who played 'Younger Brother'" off,

> he begged me to write him a letter of recommendation which verified not only that he had performed the role of "Young Brother" here, but also that his performance had been exemplary and that he was well qualified to act as a "Young Brother" in another household. (229)

The idea of the marketplace is reprised in "Heartbreak Hotel," where humans can buy and consume one another while participating in a companionship engendered by each other's physical presence. For example, following a sudden collapse of a building, the loss of homes is not treated in a sentimental manner; the displaced individuals are simply ushered into different rooms in the hotel by the manager and the clerk.

While all these bizarre events and unorthodox behaviours chronicled in Hon's stories share a performative and participatory characteristic, their subversive nature also allows them to do away with the hierarchy usually normalized in a grand narrative. I contend that coming of age is rhizomatically simulated in the worlds constructed in Hon's corpus of work, where the fluctuating subjectivities, human or not, and the slippery boundary between human and thing are actually two sides of the same coin. Going back to "The Kite Family," during the autopsy of the obese grandmother, things that belonged to different family members—ranging from pearl necklaces, wedding rings, toys, unfinished sweaters, jewellery, keys, and scraps of paper to pebbles—are retrieved from her stomach. Through the ingestion of largely inorganic things and the dissection of a once-organic body, the undifferentiated interiority and exteriority permeates the positioning partaken by humans and things and further implicates a nondifferentiation between the human body, the form of a thing, and their situated environment. With regard to interchangeable subject-object relations, how Hon's characters cease to be human, to a certain extent, entails a matter of choice as well as a state of mind—of whether to accept such a change of role and form or not.

Meanwhile, coming of age can be manifested not only at a personal level but also on a generational scale. In addition to the stark difference between Bird and her parents in *The Border of Centrifugation*, the four-part *Grey Flower* also portrays a change of attitude towards land across generations. The first section opens with the shelling of a rubber plantation by Japanese forces in an unnamed territory, followed by the fleeing of Mi-on's parents with her and her sister to a foreign land by boat. The second section begins with Chan Kwai, Mi-on's daughter, delivering a baby by Caesarean section, but its general focus is on the sleepless urban life led by Chan's generation under mass surveillance. The third part features the first-person speaker "I" who is presumably Chan Kwai's child and distinguishes themselves from the passiveness of his/her parents' generation, who used to seek temporary refuge from authorities by hiding in basements. "I"—the fourth generation in the book—further debunks the myth of the "grey fog," contrasting with the grown-ups' refusal to admit its cause is from the circulation of human ashes in the air. As their friend Wah-wah concludes, "we are not able to hold similar values with the majority of people, which causes us to be excluded sometimes and feel frustrated at other times. This is all because our parameters exceed the normative area" (Hon, *Grey Flower* 176, my translation). Different from their refugee grandmother and indifferent mother, "I" has a habit, shared by Wah-wah, of smelling and tasting the flowers in their habitat, which were said to be cultivated by human ashes, creating a symbolic overturn in the uprootedness of the previous generation. In sum, the recurrent generational change captured in Hon's works encompasses a *be-coming of age*, which has unsettled any monolithic coming of age model in the post-handover, postmillennial era.

Conclusion

In this last section, I hope to make clear that my study did not intend to restrict Hon's works within the classification of coming-of-age narratives. Rather, my intention was to highlight the critical perspectives made available by the scholarship of the Bildungsroman genre to scrutinize the postcolonial sensibilities involved. Apart from his oft-cited discussion of youth as a "specific image of modernity" in the European Bildungsroman, it is noteworthy that Franco Moretti also delineated that the development of the Bildungsroman was "not a straight line but a tree, with plenty of bifurcations for genres to branch off from each other" (234). While the "postcolonial Bildungsroman" is generally understood as a response to colonialism, the decolonizing power residing in the Caribbean Bildungsroman—which "explore[s] precisely the complexities and contradictions of growing up in a region where (neo-)colonial relationships exacerbate an already oppressive patriarch"—bespeaks the possibility of the quest for alternate identities, as long as a critical distance can be kept from the colonialist or the dominant value system (Lima 858). While Maria Karafilis attributed the protagonist's reconciliation with the dominant and the native cultures as one of the salient features of the Bildungsroman "modified" by postcolonial writers, Homi Bhabha's theory of hybridity upon the formation of postcolonial culture and identity has been put into practice in the postcolonial Bildungsroman. In the case of the African postcolonial Bildungsroman, Hoagland observed the presence of an "anti-Bildungsroman tradition" such as "the depiction of a broken, or even impossible, maturation process, and an ethical critique of the society into which the protagonist seeks entrance" (220). In the context of Hong Kong, the juxtaposition of Wong's investigation of refugee literature as Bildungsroman and Wang's support of Dung Kai-cheung's works as a "new Bildungsroman" have demonstrated the transformation inherently experienced by the genre itself and literary criticism methods in respect of the changing sociopolitical landscape. In this light, the term "Bildungsroman" functions as an analytical tool in self-contained, if not entirely singular, cases, hence explaining the disruption and the discontinuity in the coming-of-age discourse when it is viewed in its entirety at a meta-level—in addition to the classification of "new" and "anti-Bildungsroman" (Wang; Xi). Coming back to Hon's works that emerged in the postmillennial era, the unstable identities actually allow humans to reconnect with things, and the out-of-place-ness experienced by her characters also facilitates a process to adapt to and engage with changes—this is what I call "be-coming of age" in a postcolonial landscape with things and places.

My conceptualization of "be-coming of age" is inspired by Stuart Hall's formulation of cultural identity as "a matter of 'becoming' as well as of 'being'":

> It belongs to the future as much as to the past. It is not something which already exists, transcending place, time, history and culture. Cultural identities come from somewhere, have histories. But, like everything which is historical, they undergo constant transformation. (225)

The idea of "becoming" resonates the intratextual and extratextual interactions between multiple narrative strands in Hon's works and the rhizomatic trajectories undertaken by her characters, as in their journeys to the sky, unknown caves, nameless cities, fictitious homes, and dysfunctional places, among others. In this chapter, I have shown that transformation—be it of the body, values, or ways of seeing—is an integral element in the cosmos penned by Hon. Albeit the absurd settings, many of Hon's protagonists come of age with alterity in their own different ways, for instance, by achieving alternate forms

("Forrest Woods, Chair"; "The Kite Family"; *Mending Bodies*), identities ("Notes on an Epidemic"), relationships ("Heartbreak Hotel"), states (*The Border of Centrifugation*), and places (*Grey Flower*). I have intentionally refrained from using the qualifier "new" here due to the nonconformist traits shared by these characters, who embrace and practise the process of change by diverting from the dominant discourse.

The focus of my discussion in this chapter was mainly on Hon's works produced before the arrival of a series of critical moments and social events—such as the 2014 Umbrella Movement, the 2019 Anti-Extradition Law Amendment Bill (Anti-ELAB) Movement, and the COVID-19 pandemic—to highlight the local subjectivity that resides in cultural memory and is incubated in creative voices. Hon's fictional work demonstrates the cultural potential of the human-nonhuman relation that has foregrounded the local population's responses to the city's increasingly questionable status quo in the large-scale social events that would take place in the years that followed. Meanwhile, in the turbulent times of 2020 and 2021, Hon chose to use prose to document the destabilizations and uncertainties that have become actual in her home city: in a diary format, *Hei ri* (*Darkness Under the Sun*) follows Hon's chain of thought over the course of the Anti-ELAB movement from April 1 to November 28, 2019, with flashbacks to the Umbrella Movement, which appears as a series of diary entries dated between September 28 and October 23, 2014; just as Hon's reflection of her everyday life in Hong Kong continues to interact with the private and the public, human and nonhuman in *Ban shi* (*Half Eclipse*).[7] The disproportionate image of a half and a potentially full eclipse, conveyed by both titles, not only disturbs the celestial and the human scales figuratively, but also brings light to a number of astronomical objects and bodies—some named (e.g., "the sun") and some unnamed (e.g., the cause of the shadow)—beyond mere symbolism. As Hon ends her prose writing titled "Zhong yin sheng huo" ("Liminal Life") collected in *Half Eclipse* with the line "When things fall apart, the city grows a thick and sturdy twig. This is an atypical plant" (435, my translation),[8] the nonhuman, by travelling from Hon's fictional to nonfictional work, persists as a form of literary expression to cope with the disastrous impacts of injustice and unfreedom, as well as trauma that has become nearly unspeakable.

Notes

1. The concept of "postcolonial anomaly" was raised by Chow ("Between Colonizers") as early as in the 1990s to describe Hong Kong's atypical postcoloniality upon the pending transferral of its sovereignty from Britain to the People's Republic of China. Decades apart, Chu (60) confirms this particulate state of the city in the post-handover context.
2. This chapter adopts Mandarin Pinyin romanization, while all the titles are pronounced in Cantonese as the works were written in Hong Kong.
3. When pronounced in Cantonese, the title of this story reads "puma."
4. In the original text, the said character is called "I," not "M," as in the translation published.
5. This, to a certain extent, recalls the use of magical realism, which can be regarded as "a genre that results from the complex interaction between aesthetic forms and their historicity" (Siskind 851). Although it was reported that renowned Hong Kong author Leung Ping-kwan (Yasi) once revealed in an introduction to his first collection of stories (with some work published as early as in 1975) that he had drawn on "magical realism to explore the absurdity of Hong Kong" (Minford 5), at the time of writing, I chose not to dwell too much on the discussion of magical realism in the scope of this chapter. One reason is to avoid a premature discussion that might result in over-appropriation in the context of Hong Kong literature. The other reason is that over the years Hon narrativizes the living experience in post-handover Hong Kong not only in fictional work but also in prose such as *Darkness Under the Sun* and *Half Eclipse* during the high time of social unrest, as will be delineated at the end of this chapter. Nonetheless, the discourse on magical realism in the context of postcolonial literature provides a useful reference to understanding the complexities between formal and aesthetic approaches in postcolonial writings and, to borrow from Siskind, the "historical, cultural and political determinations" (849).
6. Apart from the reference to Xi Xi, the featuring of a matriarchy lineage in "The Kite Family" also recalls Wong Bik-wan's *Lie nü tu* (*Portraits of Martyred Women*).
7. A similar attempt can be traced to the publication of Hon's first essay collection titled *Hui jia* (*Going Home*), where Hon reflects on her relocation to an outlying island (still within Hong Kong) and her memories of the city in the wake of the Umbrella Movement.

8. From the original title "Zhong yin sheng huo" 中陰生活, the term *zhong yin* is associated with the concept of *antarābhava* (in Sanskrit) or *bar do* (in Tibetan), which is understood as "a transitional state between death and rebirth...during which time the transitional being prepares for rebirth" (Buswell and Lopez 49). The closing line of this piece of writing by Hon is: 「城市在分崩離析的時候，長出了粗壯的枝椏，這是一株特異的植物」(*Half Eclipse* 435). The four-character Chinese idiom *fe beng li xi* 分崩離析 applied by Hon coincides with the Chinese translated title of Nigerian writer Chinua Achebe's acclaimed 1958 English-language novel *Things Fall Apart*, where the title of the novel was inspired by Irish poet William Butler Yeats's post-First World War work "The Second Coming." On a final note, in the context of African literature, Cajetan Iheka in *Naturalizing Africa* also sees the importance in re-examining humans' relationship to the nonhuman world and in doing away with human exceptionalism as an integral part of postcolonial resistance and in theorizing what he calls the "aesthetics of proximity" that "challenge a human-centered literary world by positing scenarios where various beings interact" (55).

Works Cited

Abbas, Ackbar. *Hong Kong: Culture and the Politics of Disappearance*. Hong Kong University Press, 1997.

Bhabha, Homi K. *The Location of Culture*. Routledge, 2004.

Buswell, Robert E., and Donald S. Lopez. *The Princeton Dictionary of Buddhism*. Princeton University Press, 2014.

Chan, Leonard. "Sense of Place and Urban Images: Reading Hong Kong in Hong Kong Poetry." *The Oxford Handbook of Modern Chinese Literatures*, edited by Carlos Rojas and Andrea Bachner, Oxford University Press, 2016, pp. 399–416.

Chan, Leonard, editor. Foreword. *Xiang Gang wen xue da xi 1919–1949* (*The Compendium of Hong Kong Literature 1919–1949*), Hong Kong Commercial Press, 2016, pp. 1–25.

Chan, Stephen C.K. "Delay No More: Struggles to Reimagine Hong Kong (for the Next 30 Years)." *Inter-Asia Cultural Studies*, vol. 16, no. 3, 2015, pp. 327–47.

Cheung, Esther M.K. *Fruit Chan's Made in Hong Kong*. Hong Kong University Press, 2009.

Cheung, Esther M.K. "The Hi/stories of Hong Kong." *Cultural Studies*, vol. 15, nos. 3–4, 2001, pp. 564–90.

Cheung, Esther M.K. "Voices of Negotiation in Late Twentieth-Century Hong Kong Literature." *The Columbia Companion to Modern East Asian Literature*, edited by Joshua S. Mostow et al., Columbia University Press, 2003, pp. 604–09.

Chow, Rey. "Between Colonizers: Hong Kong's Postcolonial Self-writing in the 1990s." *Diasporas*, vol. 2, no. 2, 1992, pp. 151–70.

Chow, Rey. "Things, Common/Places, Passages of the Port City." *Ethics after Idealism: Theory, Culture, Ethnicity, Reading*, Indiana University Press, 1998, pp. 168–90.

Chu, Yiu-wai. *Found in Transition: Hong Kong Studies in the Age of China*. SUNY Press, 2018.

Deleuze, Gilles, and Félix Guattari. *A Thousand Plateaus*. Translated by Brian Massumi, University of Minnesota Press, 2004.

Dung, Kai-cheung. Foreword. *Feng zheng jia zu* (*The Kite Family*), by Hon Lai-chu, Unitas Publishing, 2008, pp. 6–7.

Hall, Stuart. "Cultural Identity and Diaspora." *Identity, Community, Culture, Difference*, edited by Johnathan Rutherford, Lawrence and Wishart, 1990, pp. 222–37.

Hoagland, Ericka A. "The Postcolonial Bildungsroman." *A History of the Bildungsroman*, edited by Sarah Graham, Cambridge University Press, 2019, pp. 217–38.

Hon, Lai-chu. *Ban shi* (*Half Eclipse*). Acropolis, 2021.

Hon, Lai-chu. *Feng shen* (*Mending Bodies*). Unitas Publishing, 2010.

Hon, Lai-chu. *Feng zheng jia zu* (*The Kite Family*). Unitas Publishing, 2008.

Hon, Lai-chu. *Hei ri* (*Darkness Under the Sun*). Acropolis, 2020.

Hon, Lai-chu. *Hui hua* (*Grey Flower*). Unitas Publishing, 2009.

Hon, Lai-chu. *Hui jia* (*Going Home*). Hong Kong Literature House, 2020.

Hon, Lai-chu. *The Kite Family*. Translated by Andrea Lingenfelter, East Slope, 2015.

Hon, Lai-chu. *Kong lian* (*Empty Face*). Unitas Publishing, 2017.

Hon, Lai-chu. *Li xin dai* (*The Border of Centrifugation*). Ink Publishing, 2013.

Hon, Lai-chu. *Mending Bodies*. Translated by Jacqueline Leung, Two Lines Press, 2025.

Hon, Lai-chu. *Ren pi ci xiu* (*Human Skin Embroidery*). Aco, 2020.

Hon, Lai-chu. *Shi qu dong xue* (*Losing Caves*). Ink Publishing, 2015.

Hon, Lai-chu. *Shu shui guan sen lin* (*The Water Pipe Forest*). Po Po Workshop, 1998.

"Hong Kong Heritage—A Look Back." *Brand Hong Kong*, https://www.brandhk.gov.hk/html/en/Other/HongKongHeritage.html.

Hui, Po-Keung, and Kin-Chi Lau. "'Living in Truth' versus *Realpolitik*: Limitations and Potentials of the Umbrella Movement." *Inter-Asia Cultural Studies*, vol. 16, no. 3, 2015, pp. 348–66.

Iheka, Cajetan. *Naturalizing Africa: Ecological Violence, Agency, and Postcolonial Resistance in African Literature*. Cambridge University Press, 2017.

Jackson, Rosemary. *Fantasy: The Literature of Subversion*. Routledge, 1981.

Kafka, Franz. "Metamorphosis." Translated by Willa and Edwin Muir. *Franz Kafka: The Complete Stories*, edited by Nahum N. Glatyer, Schoken Books, 1971, pp. 89–139.

Karafilis, Maria. "Crossing the Borders of Genre: Revisions of the 'Bildungsroman' in Sandra Cisneros's 'The House on Mango Street' and Jamaica Kincaid's 'Annie John.'" *The Journal of the Midwest Modern Language Association*, vol. 31, no. 2, 1998, pp. 63–78.

Law, Wing-sang. "Xiang Gang ben tu yi shi de qian shi jin sheng" ("The Present and the Past of Hong Kong Local Consciousness"). *Reflexion*, vol. 26, 2014, pp. 113–51.

Leung, Ping-kwan. "Sui wu xin zhuan, yu xin pai hui: Tan yong wu shi" ("On Thing-chanting Poetry"). *Ye Si juan (Yasi Collection)*, edited by Fung Ng, Cosmo Books, 2014, pp. 553–67.

Leung, Ping-kwan. "Xiang Gang de gu shi: Wei shen me zhe me nan shuo?" ("The Story of Hong Kong: Why Is It So Hard to Tell?") *Hong Kong Literature as/and Cultural Studies*, edited by Esther M.K. Cheung and Yiu-wai Chu, Oxford University Press, 2001, pp. 11–29.

Lima, Maria Helena. "Imaginary Homelands in Jamaica Kincaid's Narratives of Development." *Callaloo*, vol. 25, no. 3, 2002, pp. 857–67.

Ma, Ngok. "Value Changes and Legitimacy Crisis in Post-industrial Hong Kong." *Asian Survey*, vol. 51, no. 4, 2011, pp. 683–712.

Mathews, Gordon, et al. *Hong Kong, China: Learning to Belong to a Nation*. Routledge, 2008.

Minford, John. "See Mun and the Dragon." Introduction. Translated by Wendy Chan et al. *Dragons: Shorter Fiction of Leung Ping Kwan*, edited by Laura Ng and John Minford, Chinese University of Hong Kong Press, 2020, pp. 1–5.

Moretti, Franco. *The Way of the World: The Bildungsroman in European Culture*. Translated by Albert Sbragia, Verso, 1987.

Pang, Lai-kwan. "Arendt in Hong Kong: Occupy, Participatory Art, and Place-Making." *Cultural Politics*, vol. 12, no. 2, 2016, pp. 155–72.

Sayer, Geoffrey Robley. *Hong Kong 1841–1862: Birth, Adolescence and Coming of Age*. Hong Kong University Press, 1980.

Siskind, Mariano. "Magical Realism." *The Cambridge History of Postcolonial Literature*. Vol. 2, edited by Ato Quayson, Cambridge University Press, 2012, pp. 833–68.

Stewart, Susan. *On Longing: Narratives of the Miniature, the Gigantic, the Souvenir, the Collection*. Duke University Press, 1993.

Tsang, Steve. *A Modern History of Hong Kong*. Bloomsbury, 2004.

Veg, Sebastian. "Legalistic and Utopian: Hong Kong's Umbrella Movement." *New Left Review*, vol. 92, 2015, pp. 55–73.

Wang, Der-wei. "Hong Kong Miracle of a Different Kind: Dung Kai-cheung's Writing/action and Xuexi niandai (The Apprenticeship)." *China Perspectives*, no. 2011/1, 2011, pp. 80–85.

Wong, Mary Shuk-han. "The Voyage to Hong Kong: Bildungsroman in Hong Kong Literature of the 1950s." *Diasporic Histories: Cultural Archives of Chinese Transnationalism*, edited by Andrea Riemenschnitter and Deborah L. Madsen, Hong Kong University Press, 2009, pp. 143–55.

Xi, Xi. "Marvels of a Floating City." Translated by Eva Hung. *Xi Xi: Marvels of a Floating City and Other Stories*, edited by Eva Hung, Research Centre for Translation, Chinese University of Hong Kong, 1997, pp. 2–27.

Xi, Xu. "Unattainable Maturity: Yu Hua's *Cries in the Drizzle* as an Anti-bildungsroman." *Reading China against the Grain: Imagining Communities*, edited by Carlos Rojas and Mei-Hwa Sung, Routledge, 2021, pp. 30–41.

V

IDENTITY POLITICS AND THE POSTCOLONIAL BILDUNGSROMAN

15

AMOS TUTUOLA AND THE NOVEL OF TRANSFORMATION

Gregory Byala

The Bildungsroman and the Right of Passage

The central problem of the postcolonial Bildungsroman is the genre's relation to its own form. This connection is vexed in two ways: firstly because of the fragility of the Bildungsroman itself, and secondly because of the ideological preconditions that make the Bildungsroman an unusual if not inherently self-defeating model for postcolonial narratives of maturation. Recent scholarship in the field has therefore needed to address two questions: What is the postcolonial Bildungsroman, and why would postcolonial writers, attempting to write outside of the structures of domination, adopt a genre whose history and ideological formations are distinctly European and colonial?

These two questions can be resolved into one. If the Bildungsroman charts, among other things, the development of the protagonist's social and political identity, how can the form accommodate subjects whose sovereignty and integrity have been compromised in advance by colonial institutions? This is the question that Maria Helena Lima asks in her work on the Caribbean Bildungsroman. For Lima, the tension between maturation and alienation requires what she describes as "genetic transculturation" ("Decolonizing Genre" 433), which enables the form to respond to the material, economic, and social conditions of its production. Simon Hay has similarly noted the tension between the form's generic elements and its social function. As Hay describes it, the interstice between the postcolonial condition and the Bildungsroman's ethos can never be closed. Instead, the fissure between form and place, between origin and application, creates the possibility for resistance. Other critics, including Erika Hoagland, José-Santiago Fernández-Vázquez, Pheng Cheah, and others, have likewise emphasized the genre's capacity to disrupt colonial practices and assumptions from within. Although they differ in important ways, these critical interventions jointly demonstrate that the postcolonial Bildungsroman responds to the legacy of colonialism with a series of subversive tactics that attempt to construct—if only through ghostly mirror images—the very societies that colonial and neocolonial administrations have vitiated.

In her seminal work on the African Bildungsroman, Hoagland develops what she refers to as the "three great symbolic tasks" that all postcolonial Bildungsromane undertake. They are as follows: "first, an active syncretic literary-cultural aesthetic that acknowledges the deep and diverse epistemological and ontological traditions of pre- and postcolonial societies; second, its dialogic engagement with pre-colonial, colonial, and postcolonial history; and third, its attempts—not always successful—to offer an alternative to the master narrative of compromise and accommodation in the self-formation process" (229). Originally published in 1954, Amos Tutuola's second novel, *My Life in the Bush of Ghosts*, provides an instructive case, in no small measure because its defamiliarizing practice anticipates the elements that constitute the postcolonial Bildungsroman as Hoagland envisions it. Escaping from slave traders at the age of seven, the unnamed narrator of the novel enters an otherworldly realm in which he matures. During his attempted *nostos*, the narrator moves from one town of ghosts to another. Within and between each, he is routinely captured, enslaved, and transformed.

Although *My Life in the Bush of Ghosts* resembles the postcolonial Bildungsroman, it is essential to recall that Tutuola's work remains alien to this tradition. The theme of maturation that he explores develops more properly from the rite of passage.[1] In an essay published in 1957, Gerald Moore notes this connection: "All his heroes or heroines follow out one variant or another of the cycle of the heroic monomyth, Departure—Initiation—Return" (qtd. in Lindfors 49). Speaking directly to *My Life in the Bush of Ghosts*, Moore argues the novel "may thus be seen as a kind of extended initiation or 'rite of passage'" (53). In his study of Nigerian literature, Ato Quayson draws a similar connection, noting that "in the case of the boy in the *Bush of Ghosts*, we can even say that he acquires heroic stature in a process of maturation akin to the structure of an initiation right" (51–52). What makes Tutuola's novel interesting is that its variations on the trajectories of personal and social development propose a separate lineage for the novel of development. From the outset, Tutuola's text inverts the procedures of maturation, so that, while present, they are robbed of their habitually socializing importance. Marriage, education, and military service appear, but their inversion has the effect of undermining the ideological legitimacy they possess outside of what Quayson (following Arthur Gennep's taxonomy of the rite of passage) terms the novel's "liminal phase" (56–57). As a result, maturation does not prepare the narrator for reabsorption into the social world but makes the prospect of reconciliation impossible. Rather than a novel of formation, *My Life in the Bush of Ghosts* is a novel of transformation.

Scholars of the Bildungsroman debate whether absorption into the collective is a fundamental requirement of the form. For example, Lima notes that the *telos* of self-constitution remains largely imaginary. Most novels, even the nineteenth-century texts from which it was later theorized, rarely coincide with the genre's theoretical standard. According to her, this ideal is "even less possible in the Caribbean context," to which we can append African contexts, "where a history of foreign domination, slavery, imperialism, and neocolonialism parallels a not always evident heritage of revolt, resistance and struggle to assert cultural and intellectual freedom" ("Imaginary Homelands" 859). Building on the work of Pheng Cheah, Hoagland similarly observes that the "depiction of a broken, or even impossible, maturation process, and an ethical critique of the society into which the protagonist seeks entrance, which typifies the anti-Bildungsroman tradition, may also be discerned in the postcolonial Bildungsroman" (219–20). As a result of this impossible process, Fernández-Vázquez has argued that "the protagonists of African Bildungsromane often find themselves incapable of choosing between two sets of values, an internal conflict which remains unsolved at the end of the narrative" (89). Tutuola's work gives evidence of this struggle. Following his ghostly sojourn, during which the narrator is brought to the brink of death by his encounter with mythologized figures of education and technological consumption, he can no longer rejoin the culture from which he has become detached. Rather than facilitate his reabsorption, the bush of ghosts destroys the connections that previously defined collective social identity. As Hoagland notes, the postcolonial Bildungsroman offers two potential outcomes, either "the protagonist triumphs over the crises sown by colonialism's influence, or the protagonist is left even more disenfranchised and disillusioned" (228). In *My Life in the Bush of Ghosts*, Tutuola erases this distinction. The narrator triumphs over—in the sense that he escapes—the liminal space of the novel, thereby fulfilling the rite of passage, only to discover that, having been corrupted by it, he can no longer remain comfortably in the outer world. Maturation has produced a liminal subject pulled in two directions. To borrow Fernández-Vázquez's formulation, "liminality emerges as a metaphorical representation of the double consciousness of the postcolonial subject" (88).

In his work on the African Bildungsroman, Ralph A. Austen argues that a "common feature" that unites it with its European counterpart is "an engagement with historical change" (215). In the tension between its interior and exterior space, Tutuola's novel stages precisely this engagement. The central character matures both within and against historical time. He occupies a landscape that is structured by history and totally free from its coordinates. To illustrate this point, two aspects of the novel can be marshalled: the first is the representation of slavery, and the second is the invocation of technology. Set against each other, these motifs illustrate the degree to which Tutuola's novel functions by inverting the relationship between the individual and history that forms the ordinary ground of the Bildungsroman. Slavery is both a historical echo, calling into the novel the ghosts of West Africa, and an ongoing condition—free from historical specificity—that defines the novel's metaphorical interest in the troubling reality of modernization.

In the third paragraph of chapter one, a significant temporal dislocation occurs:

> In those days of unknown year, because I was too young to keep the number of the year in my mind till this time, so there were many kinds of African wars and some of them are as follows: general wars, tribal wars, burglary wars and the slave war which were very common in every town and village and particularly in famous markets and on main roads of big towns at any time in the day or night. These slave-wars were causing dead luck to both old and young of those days, because if one is captured, he or she could be sold into slavery for foreigners who would carry him or her to unknown destinations to be killed for the buyer's god or to be working for him. (Tutuola, *Bush of Ghosts* 18)

Even if one accepts the narrator's justification for why he cannot locate the initial action in time, the fact that he can, by the end of the novel, precisely tally how long he has spent in the bush of ghosts (twenty-four years) makes this evasion illogical. The year, if he wished to provide it, would be the product of a simple sum. The erasure therefore preserves the novel's temporal ambiguity. Every attempt to claim a definitive history inevitably encounters inconsistencies, the most obvious of which is the appearance in the seemingly historical space of technological elements ranging from the wristwatch to the telegraph. In their confused adaptations, the presence of technological references challenges any attempt to locate the novel in time.[2]

One defence of the novel's anachronism is to observe that its technological references occur by way of analogy. For example, the radio that appears in chapter six, "A Cola Saved Me," exists exclusively as simile: "But as he was carrying the wood away, dancing and staggering on, he met over a million 'homeless-ghosts' of his kind who were listening to my cry as a radio" (Tutuola, *Bush of Ghosts* 50). The same applies to the Television-handed ghostess, the most complex representation of technology in the novel. The narrator describes her as follows: "But when she told me to look at her palm and opened it, nearly to touch my face, it was exactly as a television, I saw my own town, mother, brother, and all my playmates" (165). It is possible that the narrator, eventually familiar with these objects, utilizes their forms to explain his past experiences. However, the problem here is twofold. The first is that the Television-handed ghostess refers to herself by this name, and, in so doing, demonstrates that the existence of technology within the bush of ghosts cannot be strictly a matter of reflection (166). Secondly, these technologies have specific histories, both in terms of their development and their emergence in West Africa. Making sense of the narrator's knowledge of them therefore requires mapping the development of these artifacts against the length of the plot and the persistence of slavery at the novel's conclusion.[3]

One way to resolve this tension is to absolve the novel of temporal responsibility. In so doing, we liberate it into what Laura Murphy calls its "mythic" landscape (*Metaphor* 49). This reading has the obvious advantage of allowing the temporal displacements to sit easily against one another. The X-ray, radio, telegraph, and television cease to be historical markers that locate the action in time. Instead, they become individual mythemes whose emergence constitutes the novel's synthetic condition. Given the departure the novel stages from reality in every other dimension, why should it be asked to remain temporally consistent? Why should we insist that a novel populated by the Flash-eyed mother and the king of the Smelling Ghosts preserves the unities of time and place?

A second possibility is that the novel exists on two temporal planes. The movement into the bush of ghosts, which takes place directly after the narrator encounters what he calls "the 'FUTURE SIGN'" (Tutuola, *Bush of Ghosts* 21), is not only a spatial crossing—a lateral or metonymic movement into a contiguous space of maturation, a space that is always present, ordering the possible by determining its boundaries—but also a temporal shift, a movement from the past into the present-future. In support of this assertion, we might recall that the novel's technological references exist only in the bush of ghosts.

Abstracted from the ordinary social realm, although not sequestered from it entirely, the bush of ghosts reconfigures the material form of colonial exchange. It is the place of slavery to, and desired escape from, the endless process of production, consumption, and transformation that constitutes Tutuola's frightening mythological vision of his contemporary world. By comparison, the frame narrative, from which the narrator flees and to which he attempts to return, is the space of history and tradition. Its pre-industrial nature is deliberately marked the moment the narrator re-enters it. Standing once again beneath the "Future Sign," the narrator is captured by slave traders. As he is put to work, he distinguishes the world he returns to from both the one he has just departed and the one he will eventually inherit: "Because there was no other transport to carry loads more than by head *as now-a-days*, so I was forced to carry heavy loads which three men could not carry" (167, emphasis added). Although it initially appears that technology gives at least retrospective meaning to the experience of the ghostly realm, it is in fact the interstitial and imaginative realm of the ghosts that elucidates the violation that modernity imposes. Myth makes sense of modernity by exposing modernity's inherently monstrous heart. When they surface, the emblems of modernization therefore demonstrate that the fantasy of the novel's centre is Tutuola's grotesque rendering of the modern condition on the verge of its own transfiguration into what Achille Mbembe has called the "postcolony."

The radio that appears in chapter six illustrates this effect. What it symbolizes is the reduction of the human form to technological utility. Throughout the novel, the body is always a potential site for enslavement. However, in the bush of ghosts, the body's enslavement can be tethered to modern forms of technological production, even when those forms are abstracted to grotesque parodies of folkloric configurations. At every moment, the body can be robbed of its humanity and made to operate in service to a supervening authority that reduces it to purely equipmental value. Trapped in a log and terrorized by a snake—figures so elemental that they appear to defy any coordination with technological progress—the boy becomes an implement that can be exploited for entertainment. The same is true of the work he conducts in nontechnological manifestations. In the form of a horse or pitcher, the narrator's labour conveys prestige on the ghosts that extract it from him. This work likewise illustrates, as Matthew Omelsky has shown, that Tutuola's "creaturely modernism" collapses the distinction between the bodily and the technological as a way of depicting "West Africa as a global nexus of consumer culture, commodity flows, and social relation" (68). Even when he evades technological capture, his presence in the modernizing space requires that he become, as Ewa Macura-Nnamdi has powerfully argued, the essential element of the capitalist system: namely, the object and subject of an eternally consuming culture.[4]

Passage into the bush of ghosts involves a set of inversions that call into question the notion of development. One such inversion occurs in chapter four. When he asks for something to drink, the narrator receives "urine as it was their water" (Tutuola, *Bush of Ghosts* 34). In addition to inaugurating the theme of abjection that runs throughout the novel, this substitution prepares for the inversion of developmental stages. Shortly after this moment, the narrator falls in love with a ghost and wishes to marry her. Before the ceremony can be completed, the reverend who presides over it insists that the boy undergo a second baptism. The demand yields the following reversal: "Rev. Devil was going to baptize me with fire and hot water as they were baptizing for themselves there" (60). This excruciating counter-induction permits a further terrifying mirror image to arise: "Rev. Devil preached again for a few minutes, while 'Traitor' read the lesson. All the members of this church were 'evil-doers'. They sang the song of evils with evil's melodious tune, then 'Judas' closed the service" (61). This episode is prelude to the narrator's second marriage, which takes place in the chapter entitled "In the Nameless Town." While the first is a parody of religious union, the second marriage provides an idealized—and ultimately unsupportable—vision of ideal domesticity. Unlike the various containers in which he is continually detained, the home to which "the Superlady" brings the narrator possesses the markers of successful middle-class life. Their connubial space contains a bathroom outfitted with soap and sponges, a dressing room where the narrator's hair is combed, a dining room in which they consume tea, a parlour that contains an "easy chair with cushions," and two maids who oversee the required housework (121). It would appear, midway through, that the narrator has achieved one model of success that the European novel often places at its close. However, from this point onward, the novel progressively divests the narrator of his human qualities. He moves steadily towards a ghostly mirror image that allows him to pass in the world of spirits but forever corrupts his ability to rejoin the world of the frame narrative.

The "Valley of Loss and Gain" encapsulates the process of cultural and economic transfer that defines the bush of ghosts. In order to proceed across this geographical space, the narrator and Superlady must first disrobe. Once they have traversed the valley, they adopt (gain) the clothes that have been left behind (lost) by a pair of ghosts travelling in the opposite direction. In this particular iteration of what he calls "exchange," the narrator relinquishes the elements of his comfortable, middle-class life, his "trousers, shirt, tie, socks, shoes, hat, golden ring with…costly wrist watch," and receives "only…animals skins" in return (152–53). As this scene makes clear, the fantasy of bourgeois comfort that sustains at least one strand of the European Bildungsroman is not an end point of maturation but a stage in the counter-development of the narrator. Two chapters later, after the narrator and Superlady divorce, their marriage riven by the birth of their half-human/half-ghost child, the narrator's unmaking eventuates in the following realization: "I had already become a real ghost" (157).

Echoing some of the concerns that Lima and Hoagland develop about the inability of the postcolonial Bildungsroman to generate narratives of self-development, acculturation to the spectral world alienates the narrator from the world to which he finally returns. One marker of this is the series of wounds that haunt him when he departs the spectral space: "But as my body was full of sores, so it was debarring my boss getting loads from those who were giving him the job" (167). Entering the second half of the frame narrative, the narrator carries the illness of the ghost world with him. The man who purchases and attempts to resell the narrator addresses his lack of utility directly:

> If I take you to the market once more and if nobody buys you on that market day as well so if I am returning from the market to the town I will kill you on the way and throw away your body into the bush, because you are entirely useless for any purpose, even I have told several of my friends to take you free of charge but none of them accepts the offer, because I can no longer remain with you and your sore which is smelling badly to everybody, even the smell is also disturbing my friends and all my customers to come to my house again before I bought you. (168–69)

Eventually, the narrator's sores dissipate, but this resumption of health does not signify his reabsorption. The penultimate paragraph makes clear that transport from the terrifying landscape of loss and enslavement into the domestic space is only temporary, and though the narrator, now grown, does not intend to reside in the liminal space forever, it remains alluringly behind him as a place of further education:

> After that I hinted to them about the "SECRET-SOCIETY of GHOSTS" which is celebrated once in every century. I told them that as it is near to be celebrated I like to be present there so that I may bring some of its news to them and other people. But when both of them heard so again from me, they said that I will not go to the Bush of Ghosts again in their presence. Of course they said this of their own accord, because I dreamed a dream that I am present when this "Secret Society of Ghosts" is performing and I believe so, because my dream always comes to the truth in future, however it may be. So you will hear about this news in due course. (174)

Even after he escapes, the ghost world continues to structure the narrator's experience. One effect of this recalibration is an erosion of the hierarchical relationship between the narrator, his older brother, and his mother. Return from the world of ghosts does not entail an acceptance of the rules that exist beyond its limits. The dream supersedes maternal and fraternal authority, so that the final act of the novel, its final proclamation, is both a promise of new knowledge (the promise of future stories) and an act of disobedience. The re-emergence at the close of the novel of the "Future Sign" suggests that the bush of ghosts is not a place that can be fully distinguished from the world it attempts to keep at bay. The dream that hovers over the novel's conclusion is the inevitable assault of modernity, a force that is welcomed and feared, that satisfies desire and creates endless need. In the movement into and out of the liminal space, Tutuola's novel therefore charts two forms of maturation: the personal development of the self in conversation with society and the development of society in confrontation with global capital. In both cases, the experience of the bush—of modernity and technology—is ultimately corrupting. In this sense, *My Life in the Bush of Ghosts* is a novel of undevelopment or anti-development.[5]

Myth and Meaning in the Bush of Ghosts

If we wish to assign meaning to the specific elements of the novel, three possibilities arise. The first approach, common among many early critics, is to trace Tutuola's themes, images, and setting to sources in Nigerian folklore. In practice, this approach develops an image of Tutuola's work as almost entirely derivative.[6] A second method, common among early critics, particularly Western critics who were struck by what they perceived as his profound originality, is to treat the elements of his fiction symbolically. Hoisting them clear of specifically Nigerian antecedents, the constituent elements of the text become universal types: the hero, the hunter, the mother, the quest. This possibility invites a mythic reading in which the sources of Tutuola's images are less significant than their morphology. A mythic reading begins with the tension between "good" and "bad" that arises in the opening chapter and extends to the variety of oppositions that can be arranged vertically against it: clean/dirty, freedom/captivity, self/other, and so on.[7] A third possibility is that the elements of Tutuola's fiction are products of what Ato Quayson refers to as Tutuola's "opulent imagination" (49). Following this possibility, the final approach invites a psychoanalytic reading. Criticism of Tutuola that enlists the image of the "nightmare" to describe (if not explain) the novel's terrifying nature displays what a reading of this kind entails. Although they can be disentangled, the most complete reading of the novel requires holding these possibilities in solution.

The general pattern of Tutuola's fiction has led many critics to treat his work as a single work retold multiple times. The formula Bernth Lindfors provides in his instructive essay on Tutuola's relationship to Nigerian folklore illustrates this continuity:

> All six of Tutuola's longer works follow a similar narrative pattern. A hero (or heroine) with supernatural powers or access to supernatural assistance sets out on a journey in quest of something important and suffers incredible hardships before successfully accomplishing his mission. Invariably he ventures into unearthly realms, performs arduous tasks, fights with fearsome monsters, endures cruel tortures, and narrowly escapes death. Sometimes he is accompanied by a relative or by loyal companions; sometimes he wanders alone. But he always survives his ordeals, attains his objective, and usually emerges from his nightmarish experience a wiser, wealthier man. The story is told in an unorthodox way by curiously expressive idiom which is nearly as unpredictable as the bizarre adventures he undergoes in outlandish fantasy world. (277)

Tutuola's novels are undoubtedly formulaic. But every generalization runs the risk of obscuring the differences between texts. A brief outline of the novels that bookend *My Life in the Bush of Ghosts* demonstrates that entry into and exit out of the novel's interior space matters greatly. In *Simbi and the Satyr of the Dark Jungle*, the female protagonist enters the haunted space of the novel in search of "Poverty" and "Punishment." After she completes the preparatory rituals, she waits at the "junction of three paths" (12) from which she is kidnapped and sold into slavery. What ensues is the odyssey homeward, during which she fulfills her initial epistemological ambition. By comparison, the Palm-Wine Drinkard willfully traverses the land of the dead in hopes of recovering his beloved tapster. The difference between the two gestures is clear: Simbi desires education, while the Drinkard craves the solace of continued consumption. *My Life in the*

Bush of Ghosts provides a third variation on the general principle of the quest. The narrator has no desire to leave home. He is forced from it by the condition of war and enters the bush of ghosts unexpectedly, overstepping a boundary he does not know exists. He seeks neither knowledge nor pleasure.

In his essay on *The Palm Wine Drinkard*, Chinua Achebe argues that the tension between production and consumption provides the text's essential meaning. Reading the opening sentences of the book, Achebe condenses its "huge social and ethical proposition" to the following statement: "A man who will not work can only stay alive if he can somehow commandeer to his own use the labor of people either by becoming a common thief or a slave-owner" (102–03). It follows for Achebe that the novel's true quest is not for the return of the tapster but the perfect relationship between work and rest that summons its narrative and moral urgency. A similar economic impulse lies behind the young narrator's entrance into and experience of the bewildering landscape of the bush of ghosts. Before he enters the liminal space, the boy is vulnerable to capture because his mother, "a petty trader who was going to various markets every day to sell her articles" (Tutuola, *Bush of Ghosts* 17), is unable to offer protection. In the absence of maternal supervision—a key element of the plot that initiates that novel's long and complex rendering of motherhood—his father's others wives, both of whom despise the boy because he and his brother stand to become "rulers of [their] father's house and also all his properties after his death" (17), quietly escape when war approaches, treacherously sacrificing the narrator and his brother to the approaching army of slave traders. In the opening chapter, two forms of work are therefore brought into relation: the economy of petty trading and the system of forced labour.

As Ewa Macura-Nnamdi has noted, one of the most salient features of the bush of ghosts is the degree to which those who perform work are erased. Labour undoubtedly occurs, but those who are responsible for it are perpetually obscured. Beginning with this important observation, Macura-Nnamdi usefully moves the critical frame of reference away from slavery towards consumption. As she reads it, the novel stages the logic of speculative finance-capitalism. The chief figure for this reading is the mouth, which sanctifies consumption by rendering it part of a larger, more pronounced, and ultimately more pernicious process of production. Drawing her reading from the eighteenth-century logic of insurance, which rendered objects (including slaves) valuable at the moment of their annihilation, Macura-Nnamdi offers a powerful reading of the logic that "haunts the entire narrative: the capitalist logic of the production of value out of the destruction of what are supposed to but do not embody it" (43). It is important to note that this logic is largely, though not entirely, bracketed in the novel. It exists in the interstitial space of maturation and transformation. Although it develops out of the slave trade, it achieves its full dimension in the internal section of the novel, where the process of exploitation broadens to contain the capturing effects of both global markets and endless consumption. In this section of the book, the narrator is the subject and object of this consumptive need.

The Novel and Education

It is common in the critical literature surrounding Tutuola to remark upon his education. Here are two examples. The first comes from Geoffrey Parrinder's foreword: "Tutuola's writing is original and highly imaginative. His direct style, made more vivid by his use of English as it is spoken in West Africa, is not polished or sophisticated and gives his stories unusual energy. It is a beginning of a new type of Afro-English, rather than Yoruba; it is perhaps fortunate that his schooling ended too early to force his story-telling into a foreign style" (10). The second is from Gerald Moore's previously cited essay: "to write in his manner without comparable visionary power and imaginative intensity would not only be foolish but, for a more fully educated writer, affected as well. The most valuable part of Tutuola's example is his confidence. This confidence transforms even his apparent disadvantages into special virtues, for his fragmentary education seems to have left him in tune with the greatest imaginative life of his race, whilst his command of West African idiom enables him to create a style at once easy and energetic, naïve and daring" (qtd. in Lindfors 57).

How Tutuola learned (in a Christian school) and for how long (only six years) inform evaluations of his use of English, his competency in handling the novel, the depth of his originality, and the legitimacy of his representative status. Even if the novel itself were not an already ideologically pregnant form, the fact that the conditions of its production required the preparatory apparatus of colonial education reveals the extent to which African novel writing developed in tension with European power. Writers like Achebe, Camara Laye, Tayeb Salih, and others address the tension between the novel as a form situated largely in European ideology of family, nationhood, identity, and maturation, and the novel as a vehicle for staging resistance to forms of colonial inscription that efface Indigenous incarnations of these values. Part of this problem includes (as Ngũgĩ wa Thiong'o and others have argued) the mental colonization that takes place through the ideological implements of education and language.

Without reference to Tutuola, something like this question lies at the centre of "The Novelist as Teacher," in which Achebe argues that the African writer must animate traditional knowledge both to preserve and activate its contemporary value. Speaking at a conference in Italy, Tutuola provided a vision of his work that underscored this intention. As he presented it, his work exported Yoruba culture by making its hidden knowledge public: "I tried my best to bring out for the people to see the secrets of my tribe—I mean, the Yoruba people—and of Nigerian people, and African people as a whole. I'm trying my best to bring out our traditional things for the people to know a little about us, about our beliefs, our character, and so on" (Finely 148). Unlike the one Tutuola imagines, Achebe's intended audience is not Western. The ideal novel Achebe envisions would rescue African consciousness from the debilitating effects of colonialization. He imagines a novel that restores faith in traditional practices and elevates the landscape of Nigeria into a fit subject for self-confident art.

For Tutuola's early West African readers, no such claims for the educational value of his work could be made. Tutuola, they said, had not preserved traditional Yoruba mythology but perverted it. He appealed strictly to Western readers who could find in his naive, unlettered use of English and in his inaccurate translations of Fagunwa and the folkloric tradition emblems of African simplicity and atavism. If we turn the coordinates of this critique around, and if we apply to Tutuola the aspirations that Achebe sets for himself—to instruct rather than bewilder—it is possible to read Tutuola as a writer who engages with development in historical terms. What his novel can be read to present is a vision of African society in confrontation with modes of exploitation. Noting this broader historical engagement does not mean Tutuola is somehow divorced from the oral tradition of Nigerian folklore his work obviously engages and celebrates. My claim is that his work is not confined to that resource and instead manages through its imagery and structure to chart a critique of the institutions that constitute colonial African society, both as this society makes demands on the individual and as it sits in relation to processes of industrial development that arrange Nigeria's connection to the broader flow of global capital. Education is one of those institutions, and its appearance in the novel demonstrates how substantially *My Life in the Bush of Ghosts*, anticipating the deconstructive posture of the African Bildungsroman that Hoagland and others have delineated, subverts its socializing function. In Tutuola's work, education—a foundational principle of the Bildungsroman—does not produce a stable subject but a wandering, ghostly inversion.

Several moments in the novel address education directly. One occurs in chapter seven, where "a young ghost" teaches the narrator "some simple ghosts' language" (Tutuola, *Bush of Ghosts* 56). Another takes place at the end of the novel, when the narrator encounters his dead cousin: "After some weeks he handed me to one of the principles of his schools as a new scholar, then I started to learn how to read and write. In the evening my cousin would be teaching me how to be acting as a dead man and within six months I had qualified as a full dead man" (152). A third, less obvious illustration appears in chapter five. After he is transformed into a cow, the narrator is incapable of communicating his human identity.

> But one day, when they noticed that I was always standing or cast down in the same place and not eating the grasses or roaming about as other

cows were doing, then they started to flog me with heavy clubs and also illtreat me as they were treating wild or stubborn cows, so I was feeling much pain and still I was unable to eat the grasses or to be doing as other cows were doing. Their aim was that if they flog me I would eat the grasses and do as other cows, but after they had tried all their efforts and failed then they thought that I was sick. (44)

Several elements are at work in this moment, including the violence implicit in socialization and the pathologizing of individual identity. The whole episode is governed by a prevailing need for conformity: the boy should be as other cows. Unable to amend himself to the demands of the "cow-men," the boy is sold to a woman who plans on sacrificing him to cure her daughter's blindness. Together, these episodes demonstrate that Tutuola's novel is, in one sense, a novel of education, but one in which the self is not constructed but deformed.

In his influential essay on Tutuola, Achille Mbembe proposes the concept of the "wandering subject." Reading his metaphysics into and out of Tutuola's writing, he discovers a world in which delirium (the loss of reason, the loss of self) defines the conditions of the subject. Achebe's distinction between labour and leisure evaporates in Mbembe, replaced by what the latter calls "the work of life": "In Tutuola's universe, the self appears not as an entity, created once and for all, but as a *subject au travail*, in the making. Work itself is a permanent activity. Life is sketched out through successive shapes that constitute just as many lived experiences. It flows forth like the tide" (16). Because, according to Mbembe, the non-Western self is not self-identified; the work of life requires the ability to metamorphose, a process the boy achieves in the ghostly realm:

> The act par excellence of morphing consists in constantly exiting out of oneself, going beyond oneself in an agonizing, centripetal movement that is all the more terrifying as the possibility of returning to the center is never assured. In this context, where existence is tethered to very few things, identity can only live its life in a fleeting mode. Inhabiting a particular being can only be temporary. It is essential to know how to disguise this particular being, reproduce it, split it, retrieve it as

necessary. Not to be ahead of oneself literally means running the risk of death. (19)

As the traditional markers of development turn inward upon themselves, exposing the deeper structure of development as such, the repeated episodes of physical transformation call into question the notion of the stable subject that is necessary for traditional maturation. As he becomes a horse, a cow, a cadaver, and more, the narrator's physical metamorphoses problematize and enliven the notion of subjectivity that sits at the heart of the Bildungsroman. The paradox of the novel, however, is that the boy never fully changes. Even when he is a cow or pitcher, the narrator remains essentially himself, so that there is within the wandering subject, even at the point of accepting its ghostliness, something that Mbembe's critique does not fully touch: a self that persists through and against the material configurations that detain it.

Following a line similar to the one I am proposing here, Jennifer Wenzel has argued that the elements of Tutuola's fiction must be understood in relation to the economy of extraction. In her reading of *The Palm-Wine Drinkard*, Wenzel observes a "closed circuit of production and consumption" in the relationship between the hero and his lost tapster. Connecting this circuit to "the intricate and multivalent relationships among palm, petroleum, and publishing" that she finds in Tutuola and Ben Okri, Wenzel argues that "what tapsters see are not merely liminal, posthumous, or subterranean visions of the 'bewitching' or the fantastic, but also networks of production, consumption, and exploitation, as they survey the Nigerian economic landscape from the treetops" (450). In other words, the liminal space, which is often treated as an escape from reality, a place of nightmare, provides access to what holds that reality together. The nightmare is not the absence of reality but greater access to its (trans)formative elements.

In *My Life in the Bush of Ghosts*, Tutuola offers another vision of this kind. In the otherworldly landscape, he discovers the forces of modernity that are arranged against the self. As the narrator confronts this spectral space, he is transformed into a being that is corrupted by knowledge, desire, and consumption. The stable subject has become Mbembe's wandering form, tethered to itself but subject to deformations that leave the stamp of the modern upon it.

Notes

1. As Fernández-Vázquez has argued, the two forms are not radically distinct: "The structure of the prototypical Bildungsroman is linear and reproduces, from a naturalistic perspective, the three stages the anthropologist Joseph Campbell has identified in traditional rites of passage: separation, initiation, and return" (95).
2. The excellent work Laura Murphy has done on the echoes of slavery in West African literature is instructive. In an earlier article, published in 2007, Murphy proposes a precise time frame for the novel. Placing her emphasis squarely and justifiably on the word "foreigner" that appears in the third paragraph, Murphy concludes that the novel is "explicitly set in the midst of the slave trade" ("Into the Bush of Ghosts" 144). She further qualifies this assertion: "It may even be that Tutuola's narrator is referring precisely to the rampant slave raiding that threatened even the most remote villages in the early nineteenth century during the Yoruba civil wars, and which fed thousands of its victims into the trans-Atlantic slave trade" (145). In *Metaphor and the Slave Trade in West African Literature*, published in 2012, Murphy revises this view of the novel's temporality, arguing, "Tutuola does set his novel in a kind of mythic time" (49). It is this later version of the novel's temporality I will take up.
3. Tutuola's reference to the television is complicated by the fact that, prior to constructing the Television-handed ghostess, he had never seen one. Television broadcasting in Nigeria did not commence until 1959 (Nwulu et al.).
4. Macura-Nnamdi's reading of the boy's transformation into a pitcher provides striking support for this claim: "The boy is transformed into a sacrificial object whose greatest merit lies in his permanently open mouth" (31).
5. In this description of modernity as both alluring and repulsive, I am indebted to Simon Gikandi's "African Literature and Modernity." Briefly addressing *The Palm Wine-Drinkard*, Gikandi argues that "despite [its] invocation of a premodern world, Tutuola's fable is constantly haunted by the claims of the modern it seeks to foreclose" (3).
6. Owomoyela's *Amos Tutuola Revisited* exemplifies this attitude.
7. In his review of *My Life in the Bush of Ghosts*, V.S. Pritchett makes brief mention of this possibility: "Fear of the jungle, fear of the dead, fear of being eaten, despair in suffering and disgust, are the main emotions of the book, but occasionally there is a slightly comic note and a suggestion of symbolism or

allegory" (qtd. in Lindfors 22–23). Pritchett does not attempt to define the meaning of the novel's potential symbolism, presumably because that meaning, if it exists definitively and not merely as "suggestion," is off limits. The novel's "dreadful meaningfulness" can never be stated in terms other than ideally sociological ones, and Tutuola, for all his intuitive artistry, must remain an emblem of the first man, speaking from time immemorial in a language that frightens but never signifies.

Works Cited

Achebe, Chinua. *Hopes and Impediments: Selected Essays*. Doubleday, 1989.

Achebe, Chinua. "The Novelist as Teacher." *Hopes and Impediments: Selected Essays*, Doubleday, 1989, pp. 40–46.

Austen, Ralph A. "Struggling with the African Bildungsroman." *Research in African Literatures*, vol. 46, no. 3, 2015, pp. 214–31.

Cheah, Pheng. *Spectral Nationality: Passages of Freedom from Kant to Postcolonial Literatures of Liberation*. Columbia University Press, 2003.

Fernández-Vázquez, José-Santiago, "Recharting the Geography of Genre: Ben Okri's *The Famished Road* as a Postcolonial Bildungsroman." *Journal of Commonwealth Literature*, vol. 37, no. 2, 2002, pp. 85–106.

Finely, Mackenzie. "Constructing Identities: Amos Tutuola and the Ibadan Literary Elite in the Wake of Nigerian Independence." *Yoruba Studies Review*, vol. 2, no. 2, 2018, pp. 147–74.

Gikandi, Simon. "African Literature and Modernity." *Texts, Tasks, and Theories: Versions and Subversions in African Literatures*. Vol. 3, edited by T.R. Klein et al., Editions Rodopi, 2007, pp. 3–20.

Hay, Simon, "*Nervous Conditions*, Lukács, and the Postcolonial Bildungsroman." *Genre: Forms of Discourse and Culture*, vol. 46, no. 3, 2013, pp. 317–44.

Hoagland, Ericka A. "The Postcolonial Bildungsroman." *A History of the Bildungsroman*, edited by Sarah Graham, Cambridge University Press, 2019, pp. 217–38.

Lima, Maria Helena, "Decolonizing Genre: Jamaica Kincaid and the Bildungsroman." *Genre: Forms of Discourse and Culture*, vol. 26, no. 4, 1993, pp. 431–59.

Lima, Maria Helena, "Imaginary Homelands in Jamaica Kincaid's Narratives of Development." *Callaloo*, vol. 25, no. 3, 2002, pp. 857–67.

Lindfors, Bernth. *Critical Perspectives on Amos Tutuola*. Three Continents Press, 1975.

Macura-Nnamdi, Ewa. "Mouthwork." *Ariel: A Review of International English Literature*, vol. 49, no. 4, 2018, 23–51.

Mbembe, Achille. "Life, Sovereignty, and Terror in the Fiction of Amos Tutuola." *Research in African Literatures*, vol. 34, 2003, pp. 1–26.

Murphy, Laura. "Into the Bush of Ghosts: Specters of the Slave Trade in West African Fiction." *Research in African Literatures*, vol. 38, no. 4, 2007, pp. 141–42.

Murphy, Laura. *Metaphor and the Slave Trade in West African Literature*. Ohio University Press, 2012.

Nwulu, Nnamdi I., et al. "Television Broadcasting in Africa: Pioneering Milestones." 2010 Second Region 8 IEEE Conference on the History of Communications, 2010, pp. 1–6.

Omelsky, Matthew. "The Creaturely Modernism of Amos Tutuola." *Cultural Critique*, vol. 99, 2008, pp. 66–96.

Owomoyela, Oyekan. *Amos Tutuola Revisited*. Twayne Publishers, 1999.

Parrinder, Geoffrey. Foreword to *My Life in the Bush of Ghosts*. *The Palm-Wine Drinkard and My Life in the Bush of Ghosts*, by Amos Tutuola, Grove Press, 1984, pp. 9–15.

Quayson, Ato. *Strategic Transformations in Nigerian Writing*. Indiana University Press, 1997.

Tutuola, Amos. *The Palm-Wine Drinkard and My Life in the Bush of Ghosts*. Grove Press, 1984.

Tutuola, Amos. *Simbi and the Satyr of the Dark Jungle*. Faber and Faber, 2015 (1955).

Wenzel, Jennifer. "Petro-Magic-Realism: Toward a Political Ecology of Nigerian Literature." *Postcolonial Studies*, vol. 9, no. 4, 2007, pp. 449–64.

16

COMING OF AGE WITH AMBIGUOUS IDENTITIES AND A SENSE OF SHAME

Zoë Wicomb's *You Can't Get Lost In Cape Town* and David Dabydeen's *The Intended*

Elizabeth Jackson

The Bildungsroman, or coming-of-age novel, has often been described as a narrative of the young protagonist's "quest for identity" as he/she develops to maturity. For instance, in defining the Bildungsroman, Abrams's *Glossary of Literary Terms* refers to the protagonist's development of a "recognition of his or her identity and role in the world" (132). However, in opposition to the notion that an identity is a single, predetermined quality that a person must "recognize," cultural theory has emphasized the fluid, constructed, relational nature of all identities. From this perspective, although identity is largely determined by the relationship between self and Other, all identities (group and individual) are never monolithic or static, but always multifaceted, discontinuous, and constantly shifting and evolving. Postcolonial theorists like Homi Bhabha and Stuart Hall have provided further insight into the construction of hybrid identities, particularly in diasporic situations. In implicit recognition of the complex, and often difficult, process of identity construction, Chris Baldick has offered a more nuanced description of the maturation process in the Bildungsroman as "a *troubled* quest for identity" (24, emphasis added). Although Baldick does not elaborate on his use of the word "troubled" in this context, I would like to suggest that it is particularly applicable to those whose identities have been regarded by dominant groups as inferior and/or ambiguous. In this sense, the postcolonial Bildungsroman explores the process of identity construction for young people whose journey toward maturation is *troubled* by cultural othering and/or cultural ambiguity.

This chapter compares two postcolonial novels that reimagine the traditional Bildungsroman by focusing on the ways in which feelings of shame and self-loathing in the young protagonist are generated not only by racist colonial ideologies but also by their own sense of ambiguous cultural identity. In Zoë Wicomb's *You Can't Get Lost in Cape Town*, the identity development of Frieda Shenton is complicated by her status as a young woman categorized by the South African government as "Coloured" during the apartheid era. Although her parents encourage her to emulate the manners, speech, and appearance of white people (for example, by cultivating the "correct" accent and straightening her hair), she is not accepted as white in apartheid South Africa, and neither does she fit in among her black classmates at the University of the Western Cape. In an illuminating review of the novel in the *New York Times*, Bharati Mukherjee wrote, "Race laws are most cruelly operative when unseen and presumably unenforced, internalized—the test of the artist lies in exploring the varieties of self-imposed oppression" (7). Thus, Frieda's self-imposed oppression is shown to be rooted in a racist patriarchal culture that produces a sense of shame, exacerbated by her ambiguous designation as a "Coloured" woman.

Similarly, the unnamed first-person narrator in David Dabydeen's loosely autobiographical novel *The Intended* often experiences a deep sense of self-loathing and shame during his teen years in 1970s London, not only because of dominant racist ideologies but also because of a series of colonial displacements that generate an insecure sense of identity and belonging. Descended from Indian indentured labourers in Guyana, the narrator of *The Intended* migrates to Britain as an adolescent during the early 1970s and finds himself in what he describes as "the regrouping of the Asian diaspora in a South London schoolground" (Dabydeen 8). Having nothing in common with his Indian and Pakistani school friends except for brown skin, the narrator describes himself as "an Indian West-Indian Guyanese, the most mixed-up of the lot" (8). The novel explores the narrator's shifting, conflicting, and often painful feelings of shame and self-loathing as he navigates his own ambiguous identities and his striving to be accepted in upper-middle-class white British society. However, as in *You Can't Get Lost in Cape Town*, the protagonist's conventional upward trajectory in the manner of the traditional Bildungsroman is undercut by narrative strategies that highlight not only the damage wrought by toxic colonial ideologies but also the arbitrary and often ill-fitting nature of fixed categories of identity.

Racial and Cultural Identity

As Marcia Wright notes in her introduction to *You Can't Get Lost in Cape Town*, "Wicomb's protagonist, Frieda Shenton, and her immediate family resolutely defy any easy categorization" (vii). Officially classified as Coloured under the apartheid regime, the Shenton family pride themselves on being better educated than others in their rural community, on their growing command of the English language, and on the father's Scottish ancestor. The term "Coloured" as it was used in apartheid South Africa ostensibly described non-Indian people who were considered to be of mixed racial heritage—somewhere between the racial categories of Black and White. However, the reductive category of Coloured is in itself—like many ascribed identities—remarkably imprecise. As Wright points out, "the social arena in Little Namaqualand into which Frieda is born encompasses a confusing array of identities," along with their associated stereotypes (viii). Imposing an arbitrary hierarchy of identities on a diverse population, the National Party, which came to power in 1948, enacted the so-called Population Registration Act, categorizing all South Africans into four primary "racial categories": "White," "Coloured," "Indian," and "Bantu" (or Black). Each person had to carry an identity card declaring his or her race classification, which determined entitlement to educational facilities, to residential areas, to employment, and even to association, all of which were strictly segregated. In a further attempt to maintain what was thought to be racial "purity," the Immorality Act prohibited sex between people assigned to different racial categories. Wright explains,

> When the Population Registration Act rubrics were dictated, "Coloured" subcategories distinguished "Cape Coloured", "Cape Malay" (Muslims), "Griqua", and "other Coloured". These reflected potential fault lines to exploit in a policy of divide and rule. But the overarching categories "Coloured", "European" (or "White"), "Bantu" (African), and "Asian" (or "Indian") served as racial categories for juridical purposes. Members of the same families received different racial classifications. Assignments could be altered each year, unilaterally by officials or following appeal. (xix)

Although the scope for reassigning an individual person's racial category clearly demonstrates the obviously arbitrary and illogical nature of the apartheid system (to say nothing of its egregious injustice), the people classified as Coloured were arguably in the most ambiguous position of all. Along with the Indians, but without their clear ethnic designation, the Coloured people occupied a position between the Blacks at the bottom of the apartheid hierarchy and the whites at the top. As noted by Carol Sicherman, "Frieda belongs to a racial category whose ambivalence has often led to denial and self-betrayal" (202). Placing this situation in a longer historical context, she argues, "Wicomb's characters find their 'roots in shame' about coloured historical origins in miscegenation and slavery," which led in turn to a shameful Coloured "history of collaboration with Apartheid" (197). Although Wicomb in effect condemns this "complicity by coloured people, especially those with more education and power," she is "not without compassion for the characters who seek a modicum of power and 'respectability' at the expense of blacks and 'inferior' coloureds; the trap they have fallen into is one set by apartheid" (198).

The uneasy, ambivalent position of Coloured people in apartheid South Africa is explored in a number of ways in *You Can't Get Lost in Cape Town*, most obviously in the aspirations of the Shenton family to an educated, respectable, English-speaking status. As Rob Gaylard observes, "They have in fact internalized the racism that is endemic to South Africa and seek to escape (in so far as this is possible) the stigma and shame associated with colour and racially distinctive features" (189). For instance, they straighten their hair and anxiously scrutinize everyone's skin colour: "Truida, in spite of her light skin, came from a dark-complexioned family and there was certainly something nylonish about her hair" (Wicomb, *Can't Get Lost* 14). Growing up in a community and a society that inculcates such attitudes, Frieda's developing consciousness is loosely traced throughout the narrative, which has been described by some (e.g., Donnelly, Driver, Gaylard) as a series of linked stories instead of a novel. The various chapters or stories provide episodic views of her life as she prepares to journey to a prestigious school in Cape Town as one of its first Coloured students, as she later studies at the University of the Western Cape, as she prepares to migrate to Britain, and finally as she returns to South Africa as an outsider in her ostensible homeland. It is on her return visit to Cape Town as a young adult that Frieda's friend Moira muses on the uncomfortable self-image of South Africans designated as Coloured: "Just think, in our teens we wanted to be white, now we want to be full-blooded Africans. We've never wanted to be ourselves" (Wicomb, *Can't Get Lost* 156). However, being oneself—or, more precisely, constructing one's identity—is a challenging process for anyone, and not least for those whose identities have been deemed inferior and/or ambiguous.

Despite the efforts of the South African apartheid regime to reduce and codify all identities in racial terms, there has never been any such thing as a single, homogenous "Coloured" identity. As Andrew van der Vlies explains: "Sometimes but not always deployed as a synonym for mixed-race, the label in fact named (and names) a heterogeneous community encompassing a wide array of ethnic heritages and histories" (13), including the descendants of Black Africans and white Europeans, as well as various Aboriginal or Indigenous Peoples speaking different languages. Therefore, "South Africans of mixed race *and* autochthonous ancestry were thus included under this label, and questions of racial purity remain contentious in the coloured community to the extent to which it constitutes itself today" (14). Frieda's mother is specifically identified in the narrative as Griqua, a particular form of "mixed race" designation with a rich and complex history, as outlined by Dorothy Driver, who explains that the Griqua people were pastoralists until they lost all right to the land in the Native Lands Act of 1913. They had "abandoned their original nomadic life as well as their Khoi language when they started having contact, through marriage and barter, with the South African Dutch settlers from 1652. They started speaking the Dutch language and later, Afrikaans, which developed from Dutch" (47).

In this context, it is also important to note the historical hierarchy of languages in South Africa, in which English has traditionally been associated with the educated (white) elite. The white South Africans whose first language is Afrikaans tend to be descended from the Dutch settlers and tradesmen who began arriving in the Cape during the 1600s, often bringing slaves from varying ethnic backgrounds. Inevitably, as Christine Anthonissen points out, the language of the dominant community (Dutch) became the language of cross-cultural communication throughout the region, even after slavery was officially abolished in 1808. Interestingly, Anthonissen also argues that "the community that was later referred to as the Coloured community of the Cape most likely produced the first speakers of Afrikaans" (29). As the British gradually gained dominance in this region throughout the nineteenth century, many of the (white) Dutch-speaking farmers moved away to the interior and to the eastern parts of the country, beyond the bounds of the Cape Colony, leaving behind a large Afrikaans-speaking "Coloured" community. Thus, the Afrikaans language was already associated with a lower socio-economic status, even before the British gained official ascendancy after the Anglo-Boer War (1899–1902).

As we have seen, the ability of Frieda's family to speak English, instead of the Afrikaans of their Coloured neighbours, sets them apart in their community. Indeed, Rob Gaylard argues that Frieda's initial crisis of identity is created by her family who defines themselves (and her) as English-speaking and therefore as "respectable": "The fact that the Shentons are the only English-speakers in their community (her father is the schoolteacher) immediately defines her as other than or different from her peers; it creates a distance which she is expected to maintain" (179). After she is sent away to a prestigious English-speaking school in Cape Town as one of its first Coloured pupils, the subsequent narrative of Frieda's development to maturity is essentially a narrative of her gradual questioning and then distancing herself from the attitudes and anxieties of what Marcia Wright calls "the coloured petty bourgeoisie" (viii).

If Frieda, in *You Can't Get Lost in Cape Town*, experiences her own identity as ambiguous while she is growing up, so too does the unnamed narrator of David Dabydeen's semi-autobiographical coming-of-age novel, *The Intended*. This narrator, descended from South Asian indentured labourers in Guyana, is sent by his family during his adolescence to join his father in London. However, the father soon abandons his son, leaving him to be brought up in the social services system provided by the local government in a relatively poor area of South London. There on his own during the early 1970s, the young narrator faces not only poverty and racism but also the unwholesome influence of friends whose life choices revolve around profiting from drugs, pornography, and prostitution. Determined to construct a better life for himself, the narrator studies hard at school and eventually wins a scholarship to Oxford University. If this seems like an unlikely scenario, it is worth noting it is based on the real-life experience of the author, David Dabydeen, who had the exact same background and faced the exact same plight during his own teen years (also in the early 1970s) but still won a scholarship to Cambridge University. Although neither *You Can't Get Lost in Cape Town* nor *The Intended* can be taken as strictly autobiographical, it is interesting to note the parallels between the protagonists and the authors in both texts. Wicomb, like her protagonist Frieda Shenton, grew up in a Coloured community in South Africa and attended the University of the Western Cape before migrating to Britain in 1970. Both authors are not only creative writers but also academics, with Wicomb based at the University of Strathclyde and Dabydeen at the University of Warwick. One striking difference, it seems, is that while Wicomb's protagonist suffers from what Gaylard aptly describes as her family's "suffocating insistence on bourgeois respectability" (183), Dabydeen's protagonist suffers from a total absence of family during his teen years.

In *The Intended*, the narrator's first impressions at his new school in South London are worth quoting at some length because they dramatically illustrate not only his sense of displacement and unbelonging, but also his sense of ambiguous identity:

> It was the regrouping of the Asian diaspora in a South London schoolground. Shaz, of Pakistani parents, was born in Britain, had never travelled to the sub-continent, could barely speak a word of Urdu and had never seen the inside of a mosque. Nasim was more authentically Muslim, a believer by upbringing, fluent in his ancestral language and devoted to family. Patel was of Hindu stock, could speak Gudjerati; his mother, who once visited the school to bring her other son, wore a sari and a dot on her forehead. I was an Indian West-Indian Guyanese, the most mixed-up of the lot. (Dabydeen 8)

Thus, we see the narrator succinctly comparing himself with the other boys who look like him, noting their diversity but realizing he has no understanding of his own identity. Observing a Sikh man on the London underground, the narrator wonders whether he, too, would have been wearing a turban if the British had not taken his ancestors away to the Caribbean: "I had no knowledge whatsoever of India, no inkling of which part my ancestors came from, nor when they left, nor even their names" (17). However, regardless of the specific cultural backgrounds of people regarded as Other, there has often been a tendency to lump them all together into ill-fitting categories like "Coloured" in South Africa or "Paki" (among other inappropriate epithets) in Britain. In *The Intended*, the narrator's Afro-Caribbean friend Joseph vividly articulates the nature of the reductive white gaze: "All the time they seeing you as animal, riot, nigger, but you know you is nothing, atoms, only image and legend in their minds" (74).

Shame

In an essay significantly entitled "Shame and Identity: The Case of the Coloured in South Africa," Zoë Wicomb writes that "the shame is located in the very word 'coloured', a category established by the Nationalist government's Population Registration Act of 1950, where it was defined negatively as 'not a White person or a Black'" (123). In *You Can't Get Lost in Cape Town*, Frieda's upbringing imparts intense feelings of shame and self-loathing because of her ascription as Coloured in a racist society, combined with her female gender in a sexist society. In every society, there are social attitudes that associate the female body with shame. These include ideologies of female "modesty" that require women in some societies to cover their heads and bodies (regardless of the heat and discomfort),[1] strong social pressures in other societies for women's bodies to conform to particular sizes and shapes, and victim blaming when women's bodies and/or clothes allegedly "tempt" men to harass them or even attack them. Intense critical scrutiny of young women's bodies and clothing appears to be ubiquitous, so it should not be surprising that so many women (particularly *young* women) are ashamed of their own bodies. Neither should it be surprising that this shame is exacerbated for women whose "race" or ethnicity intensifies the hostility of the dominant gaze.

In the chapter entitled "Waiting for the Train," the teenage Frieda's painful self-consciousness, anxiety about the male gaze (and risk of harassment), and unhappiness with her own body will all be familiar to many women from their teen years (or for some, throughout their lives):

> I am not the kind of girl whom boys look at. I have known this for a long time, but I still lower my head in public and peep through my lashes. Their eyes leap over me, a mere obstacle in their line of vision. I should be pleased; boys can use their eyes shamelessly to undress a girl. (Wicomb, *Can't Get Lost* 21)

> The boys do not look at me and I know why. I am fat. My breasts are fat and, in spite of my uplift bra, flat as a verkoek. (22)

However, Frieda has to grapple not only with conventional female teenage anxieties about her physical attractiveness but also with anxieties about being noticeably different from those around her. When two other girls arrive on the train platform, they stand close to Frieda and her father, "perhaps seeking protection from the boys" who have been wolf whistling at them. Instead of thinking about the plight of those girls who are being teased by the boys, Frieda is preoccupied with her own sense of shame:

> I hope that Pa will not speak to me loudly in English. I will avoid calling him Father for they will surely snigger...But we all remain silent and I am inexplicably ashamed. What do people say about us? Until recently I believed that I was envied; that is, not counting my appearance. (25)

Frieda's fears are confirmed when one of the boys approaches her while her father is temporarily away to inquire about the delayed train: "[The boy's] eyes are narrowed with unmistakable contempt. He greets me in precise mocking English...The boy's voice is angry and I wonder what aspect of my dress offends him" (33). While worrying that her superior education offends the people around her, Frieda is at the same time conscious of her labouriously straightened hair and other aspects of her appearance that make her feel inadequate: "Now I look at my hands, at the irrepressible cuticles, the stubby splayed fingernails, that will never taper. This is all I have to show, betraying generations of servants" (27).

Sadly, the young Frieda seems to accept other people's derogatory views of her. At the University of the Western Cape, she gives up her seat at the library to a fellow student because of his "darting resentful looks" at her: "No doubt I am in the seat that he has come to think of as his own...The hatred in his lingering look is unmistakable" (42–43). Instead of feeling resentful for being regarded and treated as an inferior, Frieda vacates the seat and reports once again feeling ashamed of her body: "I blush for the warm imprint of my buttocks which has not yet risen from the thin upholstery" (43). Later, in the most tragic part of the novel, Frieda denies her Coloured identity in order to undergo an abortion at a white woman's home in Cape Town.

The passage illustrates not only the open contempt towards Coloured people that generates Frieda's sense of shame but also the ways in which her identity is complicated by the apparent disjuncture between her appearance, speech, and manners: "'You're not Coloured, are you?' It is an absurd question...Is she blind? How will she perform the operation with such defective sight? Then I realise: the educated voice, the accent has blinded her" (78). Here we see an obvious example of what Homi Bhabha describes as mimicry. If, as Bhabha argues, the discourse of mimicry is constructed around ambivalence—"almost the same but not quite" ("Of Mimicry" 544)—the inherent ambivalence of Frieda's identity as a Coloured woman with an elite education works to her advantage in these particular circumstances. She has learned to mimic the speech and mannerisms of white South Africans so well that in this situation her camouflage is effective, perhaps partly because of the nurse's (unconscious?) desire to believe Frieda is white. Another interesting point in Bhabha's argument is that "mimicry emerges as the representation of a difference that is itself a process of disavowal" (541). Certainly, in this situation Frieda disavows her own identity, denying she is Coloured, to which the quack nurse replies: "Good...One must check nowadays. These Coloured girls, you know, are very forward, terrible types...This is a respectable concern and I try to help decent women, educated, you know. No, you can trust me. No Coloured girl's ever been on this sofa" (Wicomb, *Can't Get Lost* 78–79). If it is attitudes like these that cause Frieda's desire to emigrate, she is nevertheless still anxious about her Coloured appearance on the eve of her emigration: "If my hair should drop out in fistfuls, tired of being tugged and stretched and taped, I would not be surprised...What will I do in the damp English weather?...What will I do when it matts and shrinks in the English fog?" (93). Although the narrative skips over Frieda's experiences in Britain, it does show her visit (perhaps a permanent return?) to South Africa several years later with "bushy" hair and self-respect, as we shall see.

David Dabydeen, too, writes eloquently about the shame of the young person from an ethnic group regarded as Other or inferior in a racist society. Indeed, the narrator's feelings of shame are an important element of his consciousness in *The Intended*, and several passages are worth quoting at some length because they poignantly and courageously express how he feels in 1970s Britain as a teenage boy of South Asian ancestry. When his friend Nasim ends up in the hospital due to injuries associated with a racist attack, the narrator regards him not with sorrow or empathy or righteous anger, but with shame and fear of weakness:

> I watched him, not knowing what to say, distressed, feeling a bitter contempt...His wounds were meant for all of us, he had suffered for all of us, but he had no right to. It was Nasim's impotence which was so maddening, the shamefulness of it. I knew immediately that Patel, Shaz and I could never be his friends again, because he had allowed himself to be humiliated. We would avoid him in school because he reminded us of our own weakness, our own fear. (Dabydeen 14–15)

The narrator adds that Nasim's brother, "who had managed to escape with a few bruises, hung around us disconsolately, the red stripes on his face like badges of shame" (15). Mentally distancing himself from Nasim's family in the hospital, the narrator reflects on the wider implications of his own identity and his associated feelings of shame and embarrassment:

> I knew then that I was not an Asian but that these people were yet my kin and my embarrassment. I wished I were invisible.
> It was the same feeling of shame that all of us, whether Indo-West Indians or real Indians, felt at the sight of our own people...Whenever an Asian sat next to us on the Tube, dressed in a turban or a sari, we would squirm with embarrassment, frozen in silence. (15)

However, the narrator's thoughts and feelings are always complex and conflicting. Alongside the shame he unfortunately feels at being associated with people of Asian background, he also at times feels a sense of kinship borne of a shared history of colonial and postcolonial displacement:

> In the London Underground we were forced into an inarticulacy that delved beneath the stone ground and barrier of language, whether Urdu, Hindi or Creole, and made for a new mode of communication: as the train trundled through a dark tunnel we flashed glances at one another, each a blinding recognition of our Asian-ness, each welding us in one communal identity. In the swift journey between Tooting Bec and Balham, we re-lived the passages from India to Britain, the long journeys of a previous century across unknown seas towards the shame of plantation labour; or the excitement with which we boarded *Air India* which died in a mixture of jet-lag, bewilderment and waiting in long queues in the immigration lounge at Heathrow. (16)

If the narrator's feelings about his "Indian" identity are fraught with shame and inner conflict, his feelings about his *West* Indian identity are even more so. These feelings are apparently rooted in colonial culture and unfortunately internalized by the colonized. Concurring with Gramsci's notion of ideology as "the broad sense of a world-view, knowledge, culture and ethics" imposed by the bourgeoisie (Bidet xxv), Althusser contends that once people have been interpellated into a particular ideology, they take on the world views of the dominant class, even seeing themselves through the gaze of those who dominate them. In *The Intended* the narrator recalls his own mother back in Guyana remarking that white people are "good, kind people, not nasty and stupid like we colonial trash. Is great curse will come on this country if the white people pack up and go" (Dabydeen 92) Perhaps the best illustration of the narrator's own internalization of these attitudes is his reaction to the sight of a group of noisy young Black West Indians on a London bus late at night:

> I wished they would behave, act respectfully, keep quiet...I'm different really. I come from their place, I'm dark-skinned like them, but I'm different, and I hope the whites can see that and separate me from that lot. I'm an Indian really, deep down I'm decent and quietly spoken and hard-working and I respect good manners, books, art, philosophy. I'm like the whites, we both have civilisation. If they send immigrants home,

> they should differentiate between us Indian people and those black West Indians. I was glad I was sitting next to Shaz, one of my own, with brown skin and straight hair. (127)

Several points are worth noting here, beyond the obvious stereotyping. Firstly, when the narrator experiences friendliness from one of the Black West Indians he has been condemning in his mind, he immediately feels further shame for having had such vile racist thoughts: "The small gesture of friendship made me feel deeply ashamed of myself. I didn't seem to know what to think anymore. Everything was so complicated, all this sudden hate and sudden companionship" (128). The second point is the irony of the narrator having such censorious thoughts of some lively young people he sees on this particular bus journey, when he and Shaz have just been to a seedy red light district in London, frequenting sex shops and "peep shows." Thirdly, the narrative calls attention to the inconsistency of the young narrator's identifications: Here he identifies himself as Indian, whereas at other times he is distancing himself from this identification.

Moreover, throughout this gritty but elegantly written novel the white people in the narrator's insalubrious part of London emerge as very different from his idealized colonial vision of them. In particular, their lives appear to revolve around drunkenness, football, pub brawls, commercial sex, and scrawling obscene graffiti wherever they go. Although the narrator does not make the point explicitly, the narrative clearly shows the mass of British whites in that area to be patently inferior to the people they look down upon. Ironically, however, he holds tenaciously to his colonial prejudices, writing: "I suddenly long to be white, to be calm, to write with grace and clarity, to make words which have status" (141), although obviously most white people do *not* write well, and obviously the narrator already does. Like Frieda in *You Can't Get Lost in Cape Town*, he is an aspiring writer and an avid student of English literature. As such, the narratives of both novels trace the growth of the young narrators into artists.

Narrative Strategies

In the Bildungsroman there is typically a double perspective: that of the child or young person experiencing the vicissitudes of life as he/she develops to maturity, and that of the older narrator recounting the experiences of his/her younger self. This is true, for instance, of Pip in Charles Dickens's *Great Expectations* and of Stephen Dedalus in James Joyce's *A Portrait of the Artist as a Young Man*. Mario Relich points out, however, that in *The Intended*,

> Dabydeen...provides a triple perspective, for his unnamed young man makes a sharp distinction between his experiences as a child in what was then British Guiana, and as a teenager living in the Balham district of London. The third perspective comes from his vantage point as a university student on a scholarship at Oxford. (46)

However, although the coming-of-age novels by Dickens, Joyce, and Charlotte Brontë (among many others) are narrated in chronological order, in Dabydeen's novel "the childhood recollections tend to disrupt the narrative of adolescent experiences in *The Intended*, often unexpectedly" (46). This has the effect of unsettling the conventional upward trajectory of a young protagonist in the traditional Bildungsroman. Here the nonlinear narrative questions the idea of smooth progress towards "success," suggesting on the contrary that childhood experiences remain an integral part of a person's identity and consciousness regardless of the status he/she eventually achieves (or fails to achieve). The fragmentary narrative also reflects the protagonist's everyday psychological experience of fragmentation, due to his sense of his own ambiguous identity.[2]

The chapters or linked stories in *You Can't Get Lost in Cape Town* are narrated in chronological order, but they are, as Rob Gaylard puts it, "subtle, indirect, often elliptical in their construction":

> In all but two stories Frieda is the focal character, but a double or multiple perspective is often created through a kind of counterpointing, as in "A Clearing in the Bush", where Frieda's experience is framed by Tamieta's reported monologue, or in the title story, where the extremity

> of Frieda's predicament is juxtaposed with the ordinary conversation of the two working-class "coloured" women seated near her on the bus. (178–79)

The effect of these multiple perspectives in both texts is to emphasize the discontinuous, constructed nature of identity, which is always shaped by experience and to some extent by choice. Taken together, the narratives suggest that "identity is complex rather than simple, provisional rather than final, constructed rather than given. It has to be continually negotiated" (186), particularly in complex, multifaceted postcolonial societies.

Given the manifold and continually evolving nature of identity, the endings of the two texts do not provide "resolutions" as such. Instead, Wicomb's text in particular traces the protagonist's developing consciousness as she begins to question some of the attitudes and dogmas she was brought up to accept, including patriarchal authority:

> God is not a good listener. Like Father, he expects obedience and withdraws peevishly if his demands are not met. Explanations of my point of view infuriate him so that he quivers with silent rage. For once I do not plead and capitulate; I find it quite easy to ignore these men. (Wicomb, *Can't Get Lost* 75)

Inevitably, Frieda develops a sense of distance from her family and their blind complicity with attitudes and arrangements that oppress them, as exemplified by her unthinkingly submissive mother who explains that "we all have to put up with things we don't understand" (4). We can infer that Frieda's privileged education in Cape Town has brought alienation from her family and her community, so that as a young woman she asks herself, "Why do I find it so hard to speak to those who claim me as their own?" (94). Similarly, the narrator of *The Intended*, upon receiving a letter from his mother back in Guyana (which coincides with his acceptance letter to Oxford), suddenly realizes that

> My sisters are strangers, I don't know them. I have forgotten what my mother looks like…I hold both letters in my hand and stare into the

mirror, wondering how I have changed, whether they would recognize me if I suddenly appeared in New Amsterdam, rattled the gate and called out in my English voice. (Dabydeen 152)

If, as Mark Stein argues, the postcolonial Bildungsroman should be best understood as a novel of transformation instead of a novel of development or formation, both Wicomb and Dabydeen present their individual protagonists as fundamentally *transformed* by their diasporic experiences. In both cases, the process of coming of age outside of their homelands has generated more complex cultural identities, so they are eventually able to step outside of the ways in which they have been interpellated in their homelands and see themselves as unique individuals not reduced to any one particular identity.

Beyond this, Stein suggests that the Black British (and by extension, postcolonial) novel of transformation "does not predominantly feature the privatist *formation* of an individual: instead the text constitutes a symbolic act of carving out space, of creating a public sphere" (30). Stein's emphasis on the "voicing" of an identity correlates with the views of Joseph Slaughter, who sees the postcolonial Bildungsroman as an "enabling fiction" that incorporates particular subjects into social and public spheres (4). Agreeing with Stein and Slaughter, I would nevertheless go further and argue that postcolonial Bildungsromane like *You Can't Get Lost in Cape Town* and *The Intended* not only "voice" an identity and incorporate it into the public sphere but also show the fundamental limitations of conventional categories of identity. These categories ("Coloured," "Asian," "Black") are not only reductive; they also reflect colonial ideologies that posit the white male as the norm and all other identities as alien. As Wicomb's and Dabydeen's texts suggest, the categories of identity for these "alien" subjects are not adept enough to take account of historical complexities, colonial and postcolonial displacements, and individual experiences and choices. The result, as the texts dramatize, can be confusion and shame for the young protagonist growing up in a racist society with an ambiguous sense of his/her own identity.

Notes

1. It is worth noting, however, that the use of the hijab has been—and continues to be—hotly debated throughout the world, not least in Iran, where mass protests have recently been enacted against mandatory veiling for women. On the other hand, some "hijab activists" have argued, for instance, that in the West, "women are forced to conform to sexualized media images and male-dominated expectations," so "it is 'the Western woman' who is the oppressed and unwitting victim of patriarchy and whose imprisonment can be read from her clothes (or lack of them)" (Tarlo 117). Indeed, the radical Islamist group Hizb ut-Tahrir encourages Muslim women to "assert their otherness from 'the West' by shunning Western fashions and adopting exclusively 'Muslim garments'" (Tarlo 104).
2. In *Black Skin, White Masks*, Frantz Fanon theorizes the psychopathologies generated by racism, with an exclusive focus on the experiences and perspectives of Black males. However, the experiences of the male and female protagonists of *The Intended* and *You Can't Get Lost in Cape Town*, respectively, are slightly different, not least because of the *ambiguity* of their racial and cultural identities.

Works Cited

Abrams, M.H. *A Glossary of Literary Terms*. 6th ed., Harcourt Brace Jovanovitch, 1993.

Althusser, Louis. *On the Reproduction of Capitalism: Ideology and Ideological State Apparatuses*. Translated by G.M. Goshgarian, Verso, 2014 (1971).

Anthonissen, Christine. "'With English the world is more open to you'—Language Shift as Marker of Social Transformation." *English Today*, vol. 29, no. 1, 2013, pp. 28–35.

Baldick, Chris, editor. *The Concise Oxford Dictionary of Literary Terms*. Oxford University Press, 1990.

Bhabha, Homi. *The Location of Culture*. Routlege, 1994.

Bhabha, Homi. "Of Mimicry and Man: The Ambivalence of Colonial Discourse." *Global Literary Theory*, edited by Richard Lane, Routledge, 2013, pp. 540–46.

Bidet, Jacques. "An Invitation to Reread Althusser." Introduction. *On the Reproduction of Capitalism: Ideology and Ideological State Apparatuses*, by Louis Althusser. Translated by G.M. Goshgarian, Verso, 2014, pp. xviv–xxviii.

Dabydeen, David. *The Intended*. Peepal Tree Press, 2010 (1991).

Donnelly, Kara Lee. "Metafictions of Development: *The Enigma of Arrival, You Can't Get Lost in Cape Town*, and the Place of the World in World Literature." *Journal of Commonwealth Literature*, vol. 49, no. 1, 2014, pp. 63–80.

Driver, Dorothy. "Transformation through Art: Writing, Representation, and Subjectivity in Recent South African Fiction." *World Literature Today*, vol. 70, no. 1, 1996, pp. 45–52.

Fanon, Frantz. *Black Skin, White Masks*. Translated by Charles Lam Markmann, MacGibbon and Kee, 1968 (1952).

Gaylard, Rob. "Exile and Homecoming: Identity in Zoë Wicomb's *You Can't Get Lost in Cape Town*." *ARIEL*, vol. 27, no. 1, 1996, pp. 177–89.

Hall, Stuart. "Cultural Identity and Diaspora." *Colonial Discourse and Post-Colonial Theory*, edited by Patrick Williams and Laura Chrisman, Columbia University Press, 1994, pp. 392–403.

Mukherjee, Bharati. "They Never Wanted to Be Themselves." *New York Times*, 24 May 1987, sec. 7, pp. 7–8.

Relich, Mario. "Literary Subversion in David Dabydeen's *The Intended*." *Journal of West Indian Literature*, vol. 6, no. 1, 1993, pp. 45–57.

Sicherman, Carol. Literary Afterword. *You Can't Get Lost in Cape Town*, by Zoë Wicomb, Feminist Press at the City University of New York, 2000 (1987), pp. 187–208.

Slaughter, Joseph R. *Human Rights, Inc.: The World Novel, Narrative Form, and International Law*. Fordham University Press, 2007.

Stein, Mark. *Black British Literature: Novels of Transformation*. Ohio State University Press, 2004.

Tarlo, Emma. *Visibly Muslim: Fashion, Politics, Faith*. Berg, 2010.

van der Vlies, Andrew, editor. *Race, Nation, Translation: South African Essays, 1990–2013*. Yale University Press, 2018.

van der Vlies, Andrew. "Zoë Wicomb's South African Essays: Intertextual Ethics, Translative Possibilities, and the Claims of Discursive Variety." van der Vlies, pp. 3–33.

Wicomb, Zoë. "Shame and Identity: The Case of the Coloured in South Africa." van der Vlies, pp. 114–27.

Wicomb, Zoë. *You Can't Get Lost in Cape Town*. Feminist Press at the City University of New York, 2000 (1987).

Wright, Marcia. Historical Introduction. *You Can't Get Lost in Cape Town*, by Zoë Wicomb, Feminist Press at the City University of New York, 2000 (1987), pp. vii–xxiv.

17

"NO SIGN OF IMPROVEMENT ANYWHERE"

Phantom Development in Seamus Deane's *Reading in the Dark*

Julieann Veronica Ulin

> Eternal youth. The secret of the insane.
> —SEAMUS DEANE, *Reading in the Dark*

I

On May 22, 1998, in a historic all-island vote, the peace accords of the Good Friday/Belfast Agreements were decisively approved by the people of the Republic of Ireland and Northern Ireland. The agreements concluded the period known as "the Troubles," three decades of sectarian conflict concentrated in the six counties of the North, rooted in the partition of Ireland effected in the Government of Ireland Act (1920) and maintained in the Anglo-Irish Treaty of 1921, and sparked by violent military, police, and civilian responses to the civil rights movements of a majority Catholic population facing job, housing, and electoral discrimination. While eruptions of violence in response to partition had occurred since the establishment of the border, the scale and duration of the 1968–1998 conflict, with over 3,500 killed and nearly fifty thousand injured, made the peace agreement in this deeply divided society remarkable. Political leaders on both sides of the negotiations hailed its ratification as the start of a "a new future based on mutual respect, concord and agreement" between nationalists and unionists ("Bertie Ahern Peace Referendum Press Conference").

In an interview with Seamus Deane just a few weeks after the vote, Mary Gray Davidson's interpretation of his novel *Reading in the Dark* as a Bildungsroman and "as a somewhat hopeful metaphor for Ireland" owes much more to the timing of the interview and an emergent peace than to the novel itself, which concludes in 1971, the year before what would be the bloodiest year of the conflict. Set in Derry, where the remains of the "blackened and gaunt" distillery where the IRA fought a "last-minute protest at the founding of the new state" in 1922 stand like "a burnt space in the heart of the neighborhood," Deane's novel belongs among other Irish fictions "in which ruin consistently returns to blight hopes of improvement or even renovation" (Deane, *Reading in the Dark* 33, 34; Deane, *Small World* 239). Yet Davidson's commitment to viewing the novel as "a boy's coming of age story" in which both he and Ireland emerge from "a troubled and violent past" leads her to forecast a successful attainment of a secure identity for the narrator beyond the novel's dead end: "the boy did not really discover his identity through his family, which leads me to think, well, he'll have to create his own identity." In his response to this imagined future for his narrator, Deane limits the applicability of the Bildungsroman in a way that anticipates contemporary critical interest in its troubled postcolonial manifestations:

> Well, the kind of identity that young man achieves is a little anorexic you know. The relationship between him and his parents, which is also a relationship between him and his past, and an attempt at interpreting it, does not in fact, what shall we say, sufficiently yield the kind of narrative that those novels that tell of a successful final celebration of identity generally do...So in that sense it's not at all a celebratory work about the achievement of identity. It's really rather a melancholy study of the attempt to forge an identity. (Davidson)

In classifying his novel as an "attempt to forge an identity," Deane both differentiates it from the achieved or attained *Bildung* and purposely echoes Stephen Dedalus's aim at the close of Joyce's Irish, colonial, and Catholic Bildungsroman, *A Portrait of the Artist as a Young Man*: "Welcome, O life! I go to encounter for the millionth time the reality of experience and to forge in the smithy of my soul the uncreated conscience of my race" (Joyce, *Portrait* 275–76). In discussions of *Reading in the Dark*, Deane acknowledges both *Portrait*'s position in the canon and his own efforts to "steer away from that shadow" (Rumens 28). While Deane invites comparisons to Joyce's novel and the mythic resonance of its protagonist's last name through repeated references to labyrinths and enclosures, his insistence on their capacity to entrap and his denial of a Joycean escape illuminates the impossibility of his own narrator's establishment of a coherent self within the context of the sectarian violence of Northern Ireland.

In *A Portrait of the Artist as a Young Man*, Ireland functions as the labyrinth that threatens Stephen's artistic development. The final section of its fourth chapter, with its careful attention to architecture, traces his journey from the darkened interior where he is asked to consider a priestly vocation to the open air of the strand where he chooses to chart his own artistic path. As a precursor to his departure, Stephen declares, "I will not serve that in which I no longer believe, whether it call itself my home, my fatherland, or my church: and I will try to express myself in some mode of life or art as freely as I can and as wholly as I can, using for my defense the only arms I allow myself to use—silence, exile and cunning" (Joyce, *Portrait* 268–69). In this credo, he imagines himself to be free from the labyrinthian demands of family, nation, and religion. In *Reading in the Dark*, Deane alludes to and alters this passage when the narrator thinks about the impact of his father's missing brother on their family: "I felt we lived in an empty space with a long cry from [Eddie] ramifying through it. At other times, it appeared to be as cunning and articulate as a labyrinth, closely designed, with someone sobbing at the heart of it" (Deane, *Reading in the Dark* 42). Here the labyrinth itself, rather than the one seeking to escape it, is "cunning and articulate." In Deane's representation of Derry, the city that would become the epicentre of the

Troubles, these enclosures and the pain they contain are realized repeatedly in physical form: the ring fort at Grinan where the narrator's uncle Eddie was executed, the abandoned air-raid shelters where rats are suffocated and burned out, the asylum at Gransha where the local man known as Crazy Joe is regularly committed and tortured. The narrator's fixation on discovering the sources of past pain sets him apart from narratives in which education, sexual development, confession, and vocational choice facilitate a move forward.

The clearest indication the narrator will remain within rather than escape the labyrinth of his family's past comes as he witnesses his mother's breakdown in a passage that alludes to Ariadne's string: "I picked [my mother's hairbrush] up and tugged at the strands of her hair caught in the wire bristles, winding them round my fingers, feeling them soften on my skin as though the tightness were easing off them into me. I felt it traveling inside, looking for a resting place, a nest to live in and flourish, finding it in the cat's cradle of my stomach and accumulating there" (148). Rather than charting an escape from the labyrinth, the strands here lead ever inward. This is one of the most embodied images in Deane's novel, one that makes clear that the narrator's brief temptation to flee from his home "into the safety of really foreign territory" cannot overcome his desire to "run into the maw of the sobbing" (147). These careful allusions to the labyrinth as a cunning structure that entices the narrator with the secret pain it contains allow Deane to craft a novel in which his narrator works relentlessly to uncover his family's history and inhabits that history so completely that his textual present and presence become ever more ghostly. By the end of *Reading in the Dark* the exilic path chosen by Dedalus that leads beyond the labyrinth (albeit temporarily between *Portrait* and *Ulysses*) seems an impossibility. If Dedalus's final diary entries see him embrace his strange name, reject his mother, and welcome life, Deane's own narrator will conclude the novel unnamed, haunting and haunted by his mother, and attaining only what Gregory Castle would call an "alienated and phantasmagoric" subjectivity (*Modernist Bildungsroman* 162).

As this book attests, many scholars of the Bildungsroman have noted both the inherent faults in its structure and the more pronounced cracks in its modern and postcolonial iterations, in which self-determinacy dependent on "wide cultural formation, professional mobility, [and] full social freedom," the mind's "special free mobility" to move from the local to the universal, and the twin self-making and nation-building projects that lead to integration within a community are particularly vexed (Moretti ix; Gadamer 14). Nearly every study and application of the Bildungsroman opens with a discussion of the problems with its form. Recent critical work on the modern Bildungsroman by Gregory Castle and Jed Esty has seen it as primarily "aspirational" rather than achieved and as contending with and exposing the "contingent, even fragile, logic of the old Bildungsroman" (Castle, "Destinies of *Bildung*" 483; Esty 16–17). The term itself has a built-in "mysterious ambiguity" (Gadamer 8). The "genre is insecure" and "a phantom" (Sammons 237, 243). Marc Redfield builds on this spectral trace in *Phantom Formations: Aesthetic Ideology and the Bildungsroman*, noting that, while literary criticism "is unable to guarantee the existence of a Bildungsroman," its familiarity as a category has "generated this ghost," and the structure, for all its flaws, "survives as a phantom" (43, 62, 63). In Redfield's, Castle's, and Esty's work, descriptions of the Bildungsroman acquire a haunted sensibility that is particularly evident in a novel such as *Reading in the Dark*, with its spectral protagonist obsessively returning to the past and living among fellow Derry residents "alive and inanimate, buried upright in the dead air that encased" (Deane, *Reading in the Dark* 193). Here what we might call the narrator's phantom development suggests not only absences around expected rites but a fixation around that which is lost or missing. The narrator joins the silenced, vanished, and ghostly company in the novel, integrated more with the conjured past than with any present.

For a postcolonial subject living in a contested state on a partitioned island, the problem of the Bildungsroman, with its focus on youth as embodying "a world that seeks its meaning in the *future* rather than in the past," is the proximity of that past (Moretti 5). In a preface written twenty years after he began *The Way of the World: The Bildungsroman in European Culture*, Moretti acknowledges that

Bakhtin's view of the Bildungsroman as a "mastering of historical time" requires "knowing how to keep history at a safe distance" (vii–viii). *Reading in the Dark* shows the impossibility of such a distancing effort for the narrator through the increasing pressure exerted on the apparently forward-moving narrative by the backstory. The reader, like the narrator, must work through a fragmented history received in confessions, hints, and overheard conversations. As Sarah L. Townsend asserts in her examination of the Bildungsroman narrative in Irish literature, such narratives "bear formal traces of the friction between the paradigm of development they attempt to chart and the forces that impede its progression" (338). Such formal traces, she argues, whether "distended or regressive narrative arcs, temporal discontinuity, unsociable retreat, inconclusive resolutions—register in narrative form both a keen awareness of the genre's incommensurability with Ireland's deeply uneven modernity and a keen objection to the violence of its application as a colonialist and capitalist developmental model" (345). In its form, specifically the "regressive narrative arc," "temporal discontinuity," and in its narrator's "unsociable retreat," *Reading in the Dark* registers this incompatibility of the Bildungsroman with Deane's Northern Irish subject.

Though the form of *Reading in the Dark* presents the illusion of *Bildung*, the increasing textual pressure exerted by the backstory resists ideologies of progressive development. The novel spans twenty-six years from 1945 to 1971, chronologically tracing the narrator's maturation from the age of five to thirty-one in forty-six dated episodes across the novel's three parts. With the first two parts spanning four to five years, and the final part seventeen years, the episodic form chosen for the novel, in which months, years, and in one case a decade are missing, reveals the disjunctive development of the narrator and implies that when he is not constructing his family's history from incomplete sentences, unanswered questions, hints, overheard stories, and conflicting confessions, he is dormant. For all the novel's apparent forward progression in time, its pull is inescapably backwards to the formation of Northern Ireland, to an October 1921 evening when Billy Mahon, "a drunken policeman with a gun, looking for a Catholic to kill," shoots the narrator's maternal grandfather's friend. As he is dying, the friend whispers the name of his killer and, a month later, the grandfather murders Mahon in retaliation. The narrator's unrelenting aim in the novel is the identification of the repercussions of these murders over the next half-century: that in 1922 the police infiltrate the IRA through an informer, that the informer is his mother's lover, that the police allow it to leak that his father's brother is the informer and he is (wrongfully) executed by his mother's father, that his mother protects her former lover when the truth is in danger of emerging, and that she marries his father years later and allows him to live and ultimately die with the belief that his brother was an informer.

In nearly every respect, the narrator's own individual development suffers from the contagion of this history. The ability to cultivate a self through education, marital, and vocational choices, and to inhabit a social role, is repeatedly undercut as the novel moves backward into the past even as its narrator ages. His mother's deep unease at what he learns, and the narrator's indecision about whether to tell his father the truth and spare him the shame of wrongly believing his brother to be a traitor, suspends his development as an individual and isolates him from his siblings and peers. As the family's backstory becomes more substantial, acquiring narrative shape and providing him a near-total causal explanation for the present, the narrator experiences only a phantom development, joining a community of revenants invited from the remnants of the constructed past. The present can only be experienced by him as a consequence of this past; the episodic form of the novel makes invisible any present not connected with that past. It becomes impossible to imagine him writing, as Stephen Dedalus does, "Welcome, O life!" (Joyce, *Portrait* 275). The older the narrator grows, the more he dwells imaginatively in the past and the more absent and arrested he appears in the present. Deane's novel does not make this condition endemic. We are not in the closing moments of Conor McPherson's play of just a year later, *The Weir*, in which a character remarks after an evening of storytelling, "We'll all be ghosts soon enough" (94). Rather, *Reading in the Dark* offers a narrative triptych in which the "proximity of the past" for the narrator, his mother, and the local figure Crazy Joe reveals its burden on those who can only view the present as the most insubstantial covering over the past (Deane 196).

Deane's backward-facing narrator, drawn to the conversational ellipses that punctuate the narrative accounts of the adults around him, suggests that the Joycean shadow over *Reading in the Dark* is not cast by *A Portrait of the Artist as a Young Man* but by the opening story of *Dubliners*, "The Sisters." The textual echoes between the two—repeated warnings by members of the narrators' families of the dangers of young children spending too much time with older figures, stalled confessions, gnomic ellipses, the tantalizing but ultimately false hope that a constructed backstory will allow for forward movement—link the narrator of *Reading in the Dark* with the *Dubliners* characters Deane identifies as "shades who have never lived, vicarious inhabitants of a universe ruled by others" (Deane, *Small World* 162). In "The Sisters," the narrator's opening meditation on paralysis has informed much of the foundational analysis of anti-development within Joyce's collection: "Every night as I gazed up at the window I said softly to myself the word *paralysis*. It had always sounded strangely in my ears, like the word *gnomon* in the Euclid and the word *simony* in the Catechism. But now it sounded to me like the name of some maleficent and sinful being. It filled me with fear, and yet I longed to be nearer to it and to look upon its deadly work" (Joyce, *Dubliners* 1). Deane echoes this attraction to illness, itself often used as an anti-development strategy, in the chapter that describes the death of the narrator's sister: "This was a new illness. I loved the names of the others—diphtheria, scarlet fever or scarlatina, rubella, polio, influenza…But this was a new sickness. Meningitis. It was a word you had to bite on to say it" (Deane, *Reading in the Dark* 13). In both texts, the narrators are drawn to older figures and to their potential confessions in a manner that is viewed suspiciously by surrounding adults as a kind of sickness in itself, a barrier to the narrators' own development. In "The Sisters," old Cotter hints obliquely at the dangers of the narrator spending so much time with the old priest:

—No, I wouldn't say he was exactly...but there was something queer... there was something uncanny about him. I'll tell you my opinion...

...

I have my own theory about it, he said. I think it was one of those...peculiar cases...but it's hard to say...

...

—I wouldn't like children of mine, he said, to have too much to say to a man like that.

...

—What I mean is, said old Cotter, it's bad for children. My idea is: let a young lad run about and play with young lads of his own age and not be...
—That's my principle, too, said my uncle. Let him learn to box his corner.

...

It's bad for children, said old Cotter, because their minds are so impressionable. When children see things like that, you know, it has an effect. (Joyce, *Dubliners* 1–3)

The reader, like the narrator, attempts to extract meaning from these unfinished sentences, stalled either by the narrator's censorious presence or the difficulty of finding language to expound upon the "queer," "uncanny," or "peculiar." Old Cotter's remarks identify the young narrator as different from his peers due to his association with the old priest. Haunted by old Cotter's unfinished sentences, the narrator dreams of the old priest's face desiring "to confess something...It began to confess to me in a murmuring voice" (3). The next morning, the narrator "couldn't remember the end of the dream." In the absence of this confession, the reader listens as a substitute backstory is constructed by the priest's sister and the narrator's aunt at the wake. It seems as if this "real story" is what the boy and aunt have been waiting for. When it comes—an accidentally dropped chalice had been the start of Father Flynn's trouble—it is framed by two "of courses," as if to underscore the certainty of the explanatory narrative structure. But this version of events feels unsatisfying when set against the possibilities inherent in the ellipses of old Cotter's version and inconclusive given how the story's closing ellipses erode the sense of finality that the backstory claims to provide.

Joyce's narrator, slipping silently into a chair after his sip of sherry to hear what his aunt and the priest's sister have to say, is not far from Deane's narrator, who likewise moves like a shade in the background, overhearing the adult conversations and continually ordered to return to the present. Initially sent to live with his dying grandfather, his questions about his family's past see him sent home for "getting too pale and too bound up with him" (Deane, *Reading in the Dark* 126). Even after this break, the narrator "still longed to get back to him, to keep at him until he told me" (127). The narrator's mother, responding to his similarly relentless questions, attempts to demarcate the past from the present and warns of the spectral consequences of failing to do so: "Child, she'd tell me. I think sometimes you're possessed. Can't you just let the past be the past? But it wasn't the past and she knew it" (42). When the narrator's father forcibly removes him from the presence of Crazy Joe in a late chapter, his father demands to know, "What were you sitting there with him for? Go and dance or talk with people your own age" (232). In both cases, Joyce's and Deane's narrators are pushed towards a normalized future-oriented world of youth, peers, and exercise as an antidote to their attraction to aged and infirm figures, isolation, and confessions of past deeds. While "The Sisters" is haunted by an elusive confession, Deane's narrator in *Reading in the Dark* pursues the past and extracts the necessary confessions, but his success in constructing his family's backstory offers no closure from it, only enclosure within it.

II

In *Reading in the Dark*, the Bildungsroman's everyday scenes of development, such as physical and sexual maturation, the creation of social bonds, education, confession, and marital and vocational closure, are repeatedly undermined by what Moretti calls the superindividual forces that appear in times of revolutionary crisis (54). Despite the repeated injunctions of the adults around him towards physical and social development (playing, fighting, dancing), the primary way in which the narrator's body is figured in the text is as a repository for past traumas carried into the present or as resisting a sexual future. The approach of knowledge, whether sexual or pertaining to his family's past, affects the narrator somatically. The narrator's first view of sex sickens him, and the text registers that memory's duration: "I saw two tinkers, a man and a woman, wrestling on the floor; I almost ran into their heaving foetor of split clothes and white skin. Vomit was rising up in my throat as I got out again into the field. *For ages afterwards*, I could envision them clearly, he butting back and forth on top of her, she writhing slowly, one leg in mid-air. I didn't know what I had seen, but I said nothing" (Deane, *Reading in the Dark* 78, emphasis added). In contrast to the classic Bildungsroman, in which the hero's mature body, "ripened via a series of amorous exploits ranging from the sensual to the sublime," reaches a "socially-sanctioned closing point" through marriage, the narrator of *Reading in the Dark* is initiated into a world of local history and folklore focused on sterility, abortive attempts at consummation, and absent conjugal rites (Miles 987; Esty 142). While these stories are circulated within the wider community, their impact on the narrator, and specifically the narrator's body, is distinct. While his brother Liam offers a pragmatic explanation for local folklore about a man who loses his genitalia after having sex with an otherworldly being right before his wedding ("the man was just scared of sex"), the narrator thinks, "I could understand someone being afraid of sex. It made me think of fire, glinting with greed and danger" (Deane, *Reading in the Dark* 178–79). The single kiss we see the narrator experience is immediately interrupted by the threat of violence as the girl's boyfriend appears and threatens to attack the narrator. When "the facts of life" are explained to him by his school's spiritual director, the narrator responds with a "slightly hysterical smile" and blocks out much of the explanation: "I couldn't do anything except stare at him and feel my head nodding every so often though I didn't know at what…The noise in my head was deafening" (155, 160). A late episode at a dancehall sees him similarly dissociated: "A girl from Cable Street approached and smiled in my direction. I bared my teeth at her, thinking I must look like [Crazy] Joe, a smiling non-smile semaphoring in the semi-darkness of the low-lit hall" (230). Even the final episode of the novel seems to indicate the narrator's marital status in an indeterminate way: "Everyone had moved out, gone away, got married" (243). Is he included here among everyone? In *Unseasonable Youth*, Esty writes, "Most of the novels of colonial adolescence examined here resist or forestall the traditional plot of libidinal closure in the Bildungsroman (heterosexual coupling and reproduction) and feature instead storylines driven by homoerotic investment, sexual indifference, homosexual panic, and same-sex desire" (22). The chief exceptions to the narrator's sense of fear and panic at the approach of sexual knowledge or expectations are in scenes in which he experiences sexual pleasure through reading a book about the 1798 rebellion or viewing a François Boucher painting from the 1700s. The narrator's resistance to the libidinal expectations of his adolescence in favour of vicarious visual and narrative pleasures found in the eighteenth century aligns with his backward-moving development throughout.

In classic Bildungsromane, as in the word itself, education broadens perspective and serves to dismantle "the continuity between the generations" and unlock a "hitherto unknown mobility" through the cultivation of the self and social bonds (Moretti 4). In Derry, the narrator finds his grandfather the subject of school lessons and learns that social bonds are organized around the burden of history in his deeply divided state. When the narrator throws a rock at a police car to summon them to interfere in a physical fight with his peers, his decision is interpreted not as an individual action but as part of a continuing cycle associating his family with the shame of informing. Rather than assaulting the narrator, Sergeant Burke instead decides to drive him home slowly to ensure that his community sees him in the company of the police, recognizing this will fuse his identity with that of his uncle in the community: "Once an informer, always an informer. That's what they'll say" (Deane, *Reading in the Dark* 101). Just as Sergeant Burke predicts, upon seeing the narrator, his classmates connect his perceived individual actions to those of his disgraced uncle Eddie and extend their implications out to the narrator's entire family: "Fuckin' stooly. Just like your uncle, like the whole lot o'ye" (100). The resulting ostracism the narrator experiences both from his peers and from his own family underscores the failure of any of his actions to be viewed as those of an individual. In times of such revolutionary crisis, the narrator's individual development becomes subject to what Moretti terms irresistible superindividual forces; the Bildungsroman structure is necessarily compromised in places where a classroom history lesson or a school fight can be figured as part of an ethno-religious struggle.

In a number of interviews about his novel, Deane notes the separation caused by formal education between the postwar generation of Northern Ireland and their parents; his narrator, however, cannot experience this individuation. During the "Retreat, March 1954" chapter, the narrator encounters *The Spiritual Exercises of St. Ignatius of Loyola* and he considers their use as a model for self-cultivation and development. In Nicholas Wiseman's preface to the 1847 edition, he emphasizes their transformative power for the reader, who will "come out from them restored to virtue, full of generous and noble thoughts, self-conquering and self-ruling, but not self-trusting, on the arduous path of Christian life" (xiii). Their dutiful reader will be "completely changed, and fitted for our future course" (xvii). Deane's narrator is drawn to this promise of self-rule and a determined future course as he witnesses the transformation of Loyola: "A man grew out of them, one whom I had never seen nor known, in all perfection, making choices in accord with that perfection. He was a star, sure and yet troubled, but always reducing his trouble gradually by accumulating certainty, by making decision after decision, knowing the more, the more trouble it took him to know" (Deane, *Reading in the Dark* 175). In the midst of this exercise, however, rather than finding in Loyola a model for imitation, the narrator recognizes the impossibility of such a solitary path. If Loyola seems to the narrator a star, he himself can only imagine himself as part of a constellation: "But when I imagined him so, then *I would see myself again* in a dither of light and dark, see my father again, see Eddie, re-recognize my mother, see them blur and fade, know that I too was blurred, was astray for not knowing how to choose" (175–76). Here the language of the epiphanic moment is reduced from its clear and singular depiction in Joyce's "Araby" ("I saw myself") or "The Dead" ("He saw himself") by the nature of its repetition ("then I would see myself again") (Joyce, *Dubliners* 28, 221).

The certainty and perfection the narrator sees in the *Spiritual Exercises* are threatened by his inability to isolate himself and retreat from his parents and his uncle Eddie. In what appears a deliberate echo of the spectral conclusion of the "The Dead" ("Other forms were near…His own identity was fading out into a grey impalpable world"), the narrator sees his identity "blur and fade" with theirs (*Dubliners* 224–25). Here there is no singular "I"-centred experience for the narrator, no ability to distinguish a self from among those who precede him. The *Spiritual Exercises*, with the clear path they chart for the inner cultivation of a life that follows and imitates a fixed model, leave the narrator all the more conscious of his failure to escape the constellation of influences upon his thoughts and actions that jeopardizes his ability to meet the challenge of "the method of 'election'; or choice of a state of life" (Wiseman xxii).

The narrator's failure of individuation appears in depictions of him in a postcolonial somatic state in which the connection between his present experience and the backstory that has marked his family as both internally suspect and as enemies of the state heightens the intensity of his physical sensations. As one self-explanation for his fixation on his family's past, the narrator thinks it must be rooted in "the accident of having been the one with the flecks of [his father's] dead and maltreated sister's blood on him" when his aunt coughs on him the last time he saw her alive (Deane, *Reading in the Dark* 45). When the father eventually confesses the shameful secret he believes, that his brother Eddie was a police informer killed by his own people, the narrator recognizes his reaction to the news is different from that of his brother Liam: "Liam's face was composed. He was feeling grown-up, I thought to myself. He can *take this into himself* better than I can, that's what he was thinking as I saw him look at me, and I knew I looked as thrown as he expected me to be" (140, emphasis added). The narrator's failure to remain "composed" and "grown-up" when confronted by revelations about the past distinguishes him from his brother, and the novel repeatedly shows how he carries past memories, whether his own or those relayed to him. At the end of chapter one, following the police interrogation of the family when the narrator is spotted by a known police informant while showing off a gun to his friends, the narrator describes how the memory haunts him: "*For long after*, I would come awake in the small hours of the morning, sweating, asking myself over and over, 'Where is the gun? Where is it? Where is the gun?' I would rub the sleep and fear that lay like a cobweb across my face. If a light flickered from the street beyond, the image of the police car would reappear and my hair would feel starched and my hands sweaty. The police smell took the oxygen out of the air and left me sitting there, with my chest heaving" (30, emphasis added). The police violation of their home and the interrogation and beating become an embodied memory, capable of being activated by a dream or a flickering light, registering in his breath, and felt in his hair, eyes, and hands. Crucially, the memory is linked to a man "known to be a police informer," the shameful role the narrator will come to learn is mistakenly attributed to his uncle Eddie, knitting this traumatic experience to his family's history (29).

It is in these representations of the narrator's body, and particularly how it almost exclusively registers trauma, fear, and grief, that his failure of individuation begins to emerge most clearly. When her dying father tells her that he ordered the execution of Eddie by mistake, and that the true informer was in fact her former lover, the narrator's mother reacts with a similarly physical manifestation of grief that will commence what the narrator calls "her long trouble" (125): "she began to shake and cry…She groaned, bent over as though her stomach ached" (123). The narrator's reaction to this sight is also rendered as physical and participatory: "my whole nervous system jumped and stood out before me like a constellation…my heart haunted by tremors" (124). Even the narrator's subsequent confession, a significant stage in the path towards self-knowledge, does not signal the requisite move "from the world without to the world within" since it concerns not his own actions but his knowledge of the actions of others (Miles 989). The narrator translates and then reads out all that he has learned to his parents in the Irish language that none of the three of them understand: his mother's father wrongly orders the execution of his father's brother, his mother warns the true informer and her former lover, his mother allows his father to live with the shame that his brother was an IRA informer. If confession is one path to self-knowledge and the "'conversion' to a new self," it can hardly succeed when the truth he speaks is only the knowledge of others rather than the self, the actions he relates those of others now dead or exiled (981). Deane's unnamed narrator might well join William Faulkner's Quentin Compson in experiencing a phantom selfhood in which even the body is not wholly one's own: "[Quentin's] very body was an empty hall echoing with sonorous defeated names; *he was not a being, an entity*, he was a commonwealth. He was a barracks filled with stubborn, back-looking ghosts" (Faulkner 7, emphasis added).

III

Alongside the narrator and his mother, the third figure in the novel's triptych depicting the consequences of the "proximity of the past" is Crazy Joe (Deane, *Reading in the Dark* 196). Through Deane's depiction of the communal silence surrounding Crazy Joe's past, his regular institutionalization within spaces in which he is further traumatized, and his sudden disappearance from the novel, he illuminates how the sectarian violence in the North can obscure other atrocities and offers a textual reminder that anti-development and exile can be the consequences of personal, and not only political, trauma. Crazy Joe occupies the space in the novel from August 1951 until December 1958. The period is one of deinstitutionalization in Northern Ireland, and Joe moves between confinement at Gransha, the local asylum, and Derry. Crazy Joe is introduced by way of events that happened in the past: "Something had happened when he was a young man and he had never been right since. He had no harm in him; the only harm in Joe had been done to him by someone else" (81). The novel never reveals what this "something" done by "someone" is. In a text that depicts a narrator working obsessively to discern a half-century of history from hints, allusions, and overheard snippets of conversation, the silence around what happened to Crazy Joe is total. When Crazy Joe's behaviour becomes troublesome or erratic, he is institutionalized at Gransha, which fails to have any rehabilitative effect: "when he came out again, he always seemed more disturbed, more upset" (195). Crazy Joe tells the narrator, "they'll beat the living daylights out of me in there, the male nurses" (197). The text signals the communal knowledge about the abuses within this space; the narrator is familiar with the rumours that "the only difference between the nurses and the inmates, they say, was the uniform" (197). Both the unrepresentatibility of the "something" that happened to Crazy Joe and the communal recognition of the failures and abuses of the institution where he is sent for correction suggest the invisibility and silence to which traumas outside the sectarian conflict are subject. When Crazy Joe visits the narrator's mother after he is released from Gransha, the narrator and his mother resist the full implications of his disclosures. The narrator describes Crazy Joe as "full of memories or fantasies from his stay in the asylum," which encodes the possibility that what he describes is not real (222). The novel shows the desire of even those who likewise suffer to put an end to such discomforting narratives: "His abiding memory of his time in the asylum was of beatings by male nurses, or being plunged in baths of freezing water if he irritated them in any way...Then he would weep, and my mother would rouse herself to tell him it was all right now, he was out of there, he wouldn't be going back; it was all over. But Joe would shake his head and say it wasn't" (223).

If the narrator's fixation on the past and his preoccupation with his grandfather are seen by his parents as threatening to his development, it is his relationship with Crazy Joe that is viewed as the greatest danger. In *Unseasonable Youth*, Esty writes that representations of stalled internal development are by no means limited to adolescents in colonial fiction: "As we interpret the inner life of youthful characters in modernist writing, it helps to remember that arrested development discourse in the period applied to a raft of social others, such as women, natives, and queer subjects" (22). In some cases, "queer and colonial versions of underdevelopment or 'backwardness' intersect," merging "Europe's internal and external others." As one such social Other, Crazy Joe uses the discourse of backwardness and underdevelopment to educate the narrator on the perils of remaining trapped in the past, even as he himself resists such institutional and coercive practices of rehabilitation and integration.

In *Anomolous States*, David Lloyd writes of the challenge issued by Irish literature to narratives of *Bildung* in which the "individual narrative of self-formation is subsumed in the larger narrative of the civilizing process, the passage from savagery to civility, which is the master narrative of modernity" (134). Crazy Joe's facility with this discourse is evident from his first appearance in the novel in the adult room of the local public library "on his own, standing at a lectern" (Deane, *Reading in the Dark* 81). He immediately places himself in the role of civilizing educator by telling the narrator that he can enter the adult section because it will benefit "a hot little savage like yourself [to] come under the cool shade of my educative influence" (82). José-Santiago Fernández-Vázquez sees postcolonial subversions of the Bildungsroman's emphasis on development as challenging the dominant imperialist discourses through mockery and irony. Crazy Joe's assumption of this role allows for a depiction of knowledge, education, and learning as processes that can arrest development and disrupt stable notions of time. He shows the narrator a painting of Marie-Louise O'Murphy by François Boucher and initiates one of the narrator's only experiences of pleasure or desire in the novel aside from his imagined talks with the heroine in a book he reads in the title chapter: "'Oh-ho,' Joe chortled, 'young Caliban sees beauty. The beauty of Boucher, young sir, will stir the sensibilities of even such an outcast as thou art,'" before taking the book away since "Too much too quickly will disturb the savage breast" (83). Crazy Joe's repeated references to the narrator as "idiot boy" (82), Caliban or young Caliban (83, 195, 199), "fool" (85), or "futile creature" (196) echo long-standing colonial discourse about educating and bringing the savage forward in time. But when Crazy Joe folds the eighteenth-century Marie-Louise O'Murphy into recent local history, confusing the narrator as to when she exists in time, he foregrounds the slippage between past and present that will come to define their mutual preoccupations.

Crazy Joe regularly points to the narrator's failure to develop, emphasizing the qualities of timelessness and immaturity that Fernández-Vázquez identifies as challenges to the traditional Bildungsroman. "Don't spend your life as a pupil," he tells him (197). Elsewhere he distinguishes between the narrator's physical and internal growth, linking the narrators's backward-facing glance with remaining underdeveloped as when, in a "manic rage," he demands of the narrator "Will you ever grow up? You're taller than you were and still so, *so* stupid. No sign of improvement anywhere…will you ever learn anything" (196)? The narrator will come to learn key elements of the family's backstory from Crazy Joe, but rather than leading to any "sign of improvement," this education suspends him. After revealing the identity of the true informer, Crazy Joe suggests that, while the burden of this knowledge might age the narrator ("you'll be a lot older"), the inability to forget has the opposite effect: "I'll be the same age as ever I was…Eternal youth. The secret of the insane…That's what punishment does; makes you remember everything" (200–01). There's an echo here of Deane's fellow Field Day writer Brian Friel's play *Translations*, where a character meditating on the virtues of forgetting says "To remember everything is a form of madness" (Friel 81). Crazy Joe's curse is not merely the unseasonable youth that Esty identifies but eternal youth with no possibility of moving forward. Neither he nor his stories can be integrated into the community.

Crazy Joe's final appearance in the novel comes in December 1958 as he sits with the narrator along the periphery of the local dancehall. Filled with discomfort at the prospect of dancing, the narrator thinks, "I must look like Joe" (Deane, *Reading in the Dark* 230). As Crazy Joe talks with him, encouraging him to "stay away from women" and "stick to your books," he also begins to touch the narrator's bare knee as he warns him of "filthy" women and the "sexual heat" of the drum beat (230, 231). Deane's novel invokes *Dubliners* here again, this time Joyce's "An Encounter" with its representation of the danger faced by a young narrator who meets an old man in a field while skipping school to seek more exciting adventures. Deane balances the narrator's frozen and disembodied reaction to Crazy Joe's touch with a clear representation of the extent of Crazy Joe's own trauma:

> He put his hand on my knee again. I ignored it. He rubbed my knee as though it were the crook of his walking stick. I looked at his hand moving on me. The noise in the hall was terrible. His teeth slid in and out as he stared me in the face…He rubbed my knee vigorously and at that I was lifted clean off the chair and planted on the ground. My father was

holding my shirt at the back of the neck and staring furiously at Joe. "Don't you ever lay a hand on him again, y'hear that?" Joe quailed and put one hand up across his face, saying nothing..."Stay away from Joe; he's sick in the head. What were you sitting with him for? Go and dance or talk with people your own age." (231–32)

When the narrator looks back at what will be his final vision of Joe in the novel, he is "as we left him, arm across his face and his wild eyes staring" (232). The next day, his mother warns him to stay away from Crazy Joe: "I spent too much time with him, she claimed, and he was not normal. I was never to let him touch me. He was odd. You mean he's queer? I asked. She shook her head almost in disbelief at the word. Then she shook her head again" (233). Crazy Joe vanishes from the novel from that point, ostracized through the threat of the physical violence and the fear of his touch. But in the final vision Deane gives of Joe, frozen in a position of attempting to wield off blows that have already been delivered in the past, he hints at trauma that remains unrepresented and which falls outside the scope of the sectarian conflicts.

IV

Whenever I teach *Reading in the Dark*, I end by asking the class if the narrator himself is a ghost. The initial reaction is an "of course not," followed by a rehearsal of all those actions that we see the narrator take: He cut down the rose bushes, didn't he? We've been reading about him for nearly 250 pages. But then there is a pause where they do the reading equivalent of the last moments of *The Sixth Sense*, or the *Fight Club*-style ending of Roddy Doyle's *Smile*, and cast their minds back over the narrative and ask, could all of that be possible if the narrator is a ghost? What do we really know about him anyway? He doesn't even have a name. A note of suspicion enters our discussions, not unlike the wariness that emerges in discussions of the dead or imaginary figures in *House of Splendid Isolation*, *Solar Bones*, or *Smile*. The narrator never solidifies into view. When he relates the folklore surrounding a local man who remains frozen at the place on the road where his plans to marry were interrupted, the narrator may well be describing himself: "You could look at Larry a thousand times, envisage him a thousand times, and still you had to look at him again the next time you passed to assure yourself that he was there" (Deane, *Reading in the Dark* 193). He is, like the description in the warning story told by the true informer McIllhenny, among those spirits "caught between this world and the next...never alive, never dead, just shadows in the air" (220–21). We return to the scene in which the narrator wanders the graveyard after his sister's death and reconsider the line "That was my first death" for how his use of the possessive allows the death to seem not only his sister's but his own (15). Deane's narrator is not a literal ghost. But in those closing discussions we usually find our way to thinking about how often in the novel moments that should signal development and rites of passage register only as absences. The dominance in the traditional Bildungsroman of the real, the rational, and the material over the spiritual elements is impossible to locate here; the narrator's obsession is with what is missing, imagined, phantom.

In one of the many cursed family narratives that weaves through the text, haunting manifests as "a force that blocked and stopped all movement" (171–72). In Deane's novel, the ostracized, silenced, and mad conditions of the narrator, his mother, and Crazy Joe are not general all over Northern Ireland, but for these three figures forgetting proves impossible. For the narrator, the Bildungsroman, with its promise of forward mobility and social integration, cannot survive alongside the overwhelming presence of his family's, and Northern Ireland's, backstory. In the penultimate chapter, even the move to university does not free the narrator from what he has learned: "I celebrated all the anniversaries: of all the deaths, all the betrayals—for both [parents]—in my head, year after year" (236). There is nothing in the novel to suggest that the narrator's siblings mark this forward move in time with the same return to the past; indeed, the character of Liam in the novel defeats any reductive attempt to extend the ghostly subjectivity of the narrator to the rest of his generation. It is for this reason that I find the concept of phantom development of such use in thinking about the narrator; it retains the sense that what can be apparent to one can be nonexistent to another. If, as the novel suggests, "Hauntings are, in their own way, very specific," how those histories affect those who receive their narrative is likewise specific (225): "Some of the things I remember, I don't really remember. I've just been told about them so now I feel I remember them, and want to the more because it is so important for others to forget them" (236–37). Gregory Castle writes that "one can conjure up ghosts or one can live with the living. Only the latter opens *Bildung* to the future" ("Destinies of *Bildung*" 499). It is this insistence on remembering on behalf of those who wish to forget that ultimately suspends, rather than enables, the narrator's development.

In *Truth and Method*, Gadamer points to the importance of forgetting as a path to development: "Only by forgetting does the mind have the possibility of total renewal, the capacity to see everything with fresh eyes, so that what is long familiar fuses with the new into a many leveled unity" (14). In Goethe, Eudo Mason argues, the "secret of happy and effectual living is not to have too good a memory" (32). The conclusion of *Wilhelm Meister* endorses "a constant denial of the past" and an "aversion to reflection" (982). Considering the impetus to immediately move forward from loss in *Wilhelm Meister*, Moretti notes that absence and death must not upset "the imminent and radiant conclusion" of the Bildungsroman: "Every void must be filled, every void can be filled without real losses. There is no room for doubt: we can easily reformulate [the injunction that follows Wilhelm Meister] 'Remember to live!' as 'Forget the dead!' Mourning does not become Wilhelm Meister" (48). *Reading in the Dark*, with its relentless focus on the narrator, his mother, and Crazy Joe, insists upon the recognition that becoming is suspended by mourning. After his grandfather's death, the narrator hopes that "the effect of what he had told me would magically pass away or reduce, even though I knew it could not but re-embed itself in my mother and go on living. We were pierced together by the same shaft" (Deane, *Reading in the Dark* 132–33). Though as a child, he can look critically on his mother and his aunt "turned inward toward one another…within the tiny globe of this kitchen," ultimately he will end in the same position with her, locked in silence: "I was to seal it all in too" (133, 242). The novel does not avoid the representation of the tremendous psychosocial consequences of this turn. In this decade in which the centenaries of the 1916 Easter Rising, the Anglo-Irish War, partition, and the Civil War, as well as the twenty-fifth anniversary of the new future ushered in by the 1998 Good Friday/Belfast Agreement bring to the fore questions of remembering and forgetting in Ireland, Deane's novel reminds us of the uneven allocations of the burdens of memory. Those in positions of relative power can shrug off such historical forces with indifference or when the past has grown tiresome. Late in Deane's novel, Sergeant Burke visits the narrator's mother, wanting to "clear up and put away for good" the troublesome aspects of history, to put "an end to it…a complete end, a real finish" (Deane, *Reading in the Dark* 213). This is the temporality and the narrative of the anti-ellipses: the full stop, the period. There is more than an echo of Haines's blithe aside to Stephen Dedalus that "It seems history is to blame" in Sergeant Burke's "Those were bad years…Northern Ireland had a cruel birth," offered as an explanation for the police terrorizing the narrator's family and orchestrating the execution of his uncle (215). Such platitudes and displacements are impossible for Deane's narrator, his mother, and Crazy Joe. In its narrator's commitment to carry forward the sufferings of the past, whether his own or another's, in its revelation of the power of the past to curtail the linear development of the subject, and, finally, in its creation of a textual absence for Crazy Joe's backstory that can never be heard and which may therefore be the most haunting of all, *Reading in the Dark* turns from a relentlessly individual-focused and forward-looking model to insist upon the recognition that, for some, even if "the only way [to] go on was by forgetting, forgetting," mourning is an incomplete and unending process punctuated by ellipses (240).

Works Cited

"Bertie Ahern Peace Referendum Press Conference." *APTV*. Story No. 79929, 5/23/1998, http://www.aparchive.com/metadata/youtube/45b51d7b5af86bf1dcb3c36eb698ab09.

Castle, Gregory. "Destinies of *Bildung*: Belatedness and the Modernist Novel." *A History of the Modernist Novel*, edited by Gregory Castle, Cambridge University Press, 2015, pp. 483–507.

Castle, Gregory. *Reading the Modernist Bildungsroman*. University Press of Florida, 2006.

Davidson, Mary Gray. "Ireland's Ghosts." Interview. *Common Ground: Radio's Weekly Program on World Affairs*. The Stanley Center for Peace and Security. Program 9823, 6/9/1998, https://stanleycenter.org/common-ground/irelands-ghosts/.

Deane, Seamus. *Reading in the Dark*. Vintage International, 1998.

Deane, Seamus. *Small World*. Cambridge University Press, 2021.

Esty, Jed. *Unseasonable Youth: Modernism, Colonialism, and the Fiction of Development*. Oxford University Press, 2012.

Faulkner, William. *Absalom, Absalom!* Vintage, 1990.

Fernández-Vázquez, José-Santiago. "Subverting the *Bildungsroman* in Postcolonial Fiction: Romesh Gunesekera's *Reef*." *Journal of Postcolonial Writing*, vol. 36, no. 1, 1997, pp. 30–38.

Friel, Brian. *Translations*. Samuel French, 1981.

Gadamer, Hans-Georg. *Truth and Method*. 2nd rev. ed., Continuum, 2004.

Joyce, James. *Dubliners*. Penguin, 1993 (1914).

Joyce, James. *A Portrait of the Artist as a Young Man*. Penguin, 1993 (1916).

Lloyd, David. *Anomolous States*. Duke University Press, 1993.

Mason, Eudo C. "Goethe's Sense of Evil." *Publications of the English Goethe Society*, vol. 34, 1963–64, pp. 1–53.

McPherson, Conor. *St. Nicholas and The Weir: Two Plays*. New Island Books, 1997.

Miles, David H. "The Picaro's Journey to the Confessional: The Changing Image of the Hero in the German Bildungsroman." *PMLA*, vol. 89, no. 5, 1974, pp. 980–92.

Moretti, Franco. *The Way of the World: The Bildungsroman in European Culture*. Translated by Albert Sbragia. New Edition, Verso, 2000.

Redfield, Marc. *Phantom Formations: Aesthetic Ideology and the Bildungsroman*. Cornell University Press, 1996.

Rumens, Carol. "Reading Deane." Interview. *Fortnight*, July–Aug. 1997, pp. 28–29.

Sammons, Jeffrey L. "The Mystery of the Missing Bildungsroman: or, What Happened to Wilhelm Meister's Legacy?" *Genre: Forms of Discourse and Culture*, vol. 14, no. 2, 1981, pp. 229–46.

Townsend, Sarah L. "The Drama of Peripheralized Bildung: An Irish Genre Study." *New Literary History*, vol. 48, 2017, pp. 337–62.

Wiseman, Nicholas. Preface. *The Spiritual Exercises of St. Ignatius of Loyola*, by Saint Ignatius of Loyola. Translated by Rev. Father Rothaan. Edited by Charles Seager, Charles Dolman, 1847.

18

REPLOTTING THE BILDUNGSROMAN THROUGH A QUEER POETICS

Ocean Vuong's *On Earth We're Briefly Gorgeous*

Rachel Ann Walsh

The Bildungsroman and the Posts of Imperialism and Neoliberalism
In February of 2020, before the pandemic radically intensified the pre-existing American inequalities that would make the COVID-19 virus devastatingly lethal in the US, novelist Tommy Orange interviewed his fellow debut novelist Ocean Vuong for San Francisco's City Arts and Lectures series. As often occurs at such events, and as their acclaimed, debut novels warrant, their conversation begins with expressions of mutual adoration; Vuong praises Orange's 2018 "genre-bending" novel, *There There*, and then locates his own stylistically dexterous 2019 novel *On Earth We're Briefly Gorgeous*, which, as reviewers have routinely commented, troubles the boundaries between the epistolary novel, autofiction, and lyric poetry, within the braided traditions of the Bildungsroman and Künstlerroman, or artist novel. Lingering over this characterization, Vuong cites James Baldwin's autobiographical novel, *Go Tell It on the Mountain*, as his model and elaborates that Baldwin prevents the reader from moving forward through the linear plot of the classic Bildungsroman in which, Joseph Slaughter remarks, the universalized, bourgeois individual develops

within the "Westphalian unities of nation-time and nation-space" to assume their civil responsibilities within society (92). *Go Tell It on the Mountain* both declines the Westphalian temporalities of the classic European iteration of the genre and foregoes what Viet Thanh Nguyen has identified as the American Bildungsroman's ratification of the "dominant national values" of upward social mobility, self-reliance, "patriarchal domination over women" ("Remasculinization" 135, 132), and, to return to Vuong's delineation of the American strain of the genre, "historical amnesia" ("Conversation with Tommy Orange"). In Vuong's estimation, Baldwin's novel refuses the erasures of history that the forward movement of plot can engender and confronts readers with a nonlinear "prehistory":

> What you got in that book was Baldwin going into church in Harlem and expounding on every person that made his main character possible…And he talked about the great migration of black bodies from the South to the North…And he never told the story, which is so powerful for me, because you read that book and you say, "*when are we gonna go forward in the plot?*" *And he never reveals it.* ("Conversation with Tommy Orange," emphasis added)

Vuong's reading of *Go Tell It* serves as an explanatory reminder of why James Baldwin appears among the artists he cites in the acknowledgements page appended to *On Earth We're Briefly Gorgeous*. The parallels between these two native and diasporic sons, the one of Harlem who, in *Go Tell It on the Mountain*, dramatizes the inheritance of the Black diaspora of slavery and the Great Migration, and the other of south Hartford, Connecticut, and the Vietnamese diaspora, are unstated yet enunciated when Vuong concludes by underlining that *On Earth* is, like Baldwin's *Go Tell It*, both a coming-of-age novel, as well as an artist statement novel. *On Earth We're Briefly Gorgeous* is a Künstlerroman that announces its artist statement through its repudiation of modernity's plot line of linear progress and its elucidation of the ways in which US imperialism and neoliberalism disqualify the queer, Vietnamese refugee from the category of the sovereign, citizen-subject.

I open this chapter with Vuong's lengthy citation of Baldwin's *Go Tell It on the Mountain* because it serves as a reminder that, Yogita Goyal notes, "race has always been entangled with form" (31), and literary forms and conventions linked to national ideals undergo transformations when repurposed by those positioned at national and global peripheries. By using the "coming-of-age" novel to depict the intergenerational traumas of the US's war against Vietnam, *On Earth* intervenes in what Quan Manh Ha and Mia Tompkins identify as the "American imperialistic education" that greatly redacts the experiences of Vietnamese subjects and erects false divides between younger generations of racialized, immigrant, and refugee children and those that precede them (201). In so doing, as Jennifer Cho has flagged, Vuong's novel breaks with the "'model minority' framework that promises the realization of the American Dream through individual determination, hard work, and civic compliance" (Cho 134). Indeed, in its form and plot, *On Earth* is a novel marked by uncertainty. Little Dog, who, like the author, is a young poet, writes an impossible letter to his mother, Rose, or Hong, whose limited English is determined by her socioeconomic precarity and whose Vietnamese is truncated by war. The question evoked by Little Dog's epistolary address to his mother mirrors the different forms of precarity his family and community experience throughout his life. In looping fragments and episodes that revisit and revise the novel's lyrical tableaus, Little Dog sifts through his inherited memories of the US's war against Vietnam as his adolescence unfolds against the backdrop of the US invasion of Iraq and the loss of his lover, Trevor, to opioid addiction. Trevor's overdose, in turn, indexes the broader devastation wrought by the escalation of neoliberalism and forms a link in the chain of what Rachel Lee terms the "disabling infrastructures" (193) that bind the chemical warfare used in Vietnam to the environmental toxins to which Rose and her fellow nail salon workers are exposed and the practices of the post-9/11 biopolitical security state that Little Dog incisively describes as "one nation, under drugs, under drones" (Vuong, *On Earth* 183). Recalling Viet Thanh Nguyen's trenchant observation that "the real American war was this entire American Century—a long and uneven expansion marked by a few periodic high-intensity conflicts, many low-intensity skirmishes, and the steady drone of a war machine's ever-ongoing preparations" (*Nothing Ever Dies* 7), *On Earth* depicts the waning American century as a palimpsest of wars and their terrible, domestic reverberations. Illustrative of these reverberations, Little Dog claims the Trump-era intensification of white nationalism as one of his wars and informs his mother, "I'm not with you 'cause I'm at war. Which is one way of saying it's already February and the president wants to deport my friends. It's hard to explain" (*On Earth* 173). In sum, the novel's recursive circuits between Little Dog's inherited and lived memories of war and socio-economic disasters of neoliberal abandonment capture the destabilized present and foreclosed future that Little Dog and his community inhabit.

 The novel's refusal to gesture towards any stable future promised by the classic Bildungsroman's and the Künstlerroman's shared plotting of the protagonist/artist's development bears a kinship with the "antagon[ism]" Lisa Lowe locates in many mid-twentieth-century Asian American novels canonized as coming-of-age texts, such as John Okada's *No-No Boy* and Carlos Bulosan's *America Is in the Heart*, both of which, Lowe emphasizes, foreclose any possibility of closure or "the reconciliation of Asian American particularity within a narrative of development" (*Immigrant Acts* 51). Unlike these forebearers, however, *On Earth*'s positioning of Little Dog's mother as his interlocutor complicates the ways in which these male-authored novels rehearse a cis-heteropatriarchal, nationalist narrative in which the "racialized subject...becomes a citizen when he identifies with the paternal state...by subordinating his racial difference" and disavowing the "feminized and racialized 'motherland'" (Lowe, *Immigrant Acts* 56). The tired trope of the "abject Asian mother"[1] found in novels of this era, as well as Chinese American Bildungsromane of the 1980s that "reenact exclusionary processes of violence" ("Remasculinization" 132) against Asian women,[2] is radically revised in Vuong's novel. Responding to a pre-emptive defence that his mother announces into the silence between them, "'I'm not a monster. I'm a mother,'" Little Dog reassures her she is not a monster and then confesses, "What I really wanted to say was that a monster is not such a terrible thing to be. From the Latin root, *monstrum*, a divine messenger of catastrophe, then adapted by the Old French to mean an animal of myriad origins...To be a monster is to be a hybrid signal, a lighthouse: both shelter and warning at once" (Vuong, *On Earth* 13). A diasporic human animal of "myriad origins"—born of a Vietnamese sex worker, Lan, and a white American GI, and bastardized by war—Rose's body is shaped by the monstrous traumas of the war and the quotidian traumas of poverty and patriarchal violence.

The novel's plotting of Rose's and Little Dog's respective and intertwined experiences of being positioned as monstrous subjects within the dominant white, heteronormative culture of the US is, in Cho's compelling reading, illustrative of how the novel "refute[s] notions of teleological progress that undergird discourses of refugee, Asian American, and queer assimilation in the U.S." (138). In their respective readings, Cho and, elsewhere, Ha and Tompkins, have elucidated that *On Earth* responds to the discursive construction of Cold War-era Vietnam and the Vietnamese refugee as a recipient of what Mimi Thi Nguyen theorized as the US's "gift of freedom." In its imperial benevolence, the US, Nguyen argues, "first diagnoses some peoples as anomalous and anachronistic and then intervenes to mediate and guide 'their natural developments' toward the world historical project of modernity" (M. Nguyen 43). The Vietnamese refugee, she notes, is hailed as being forever indebted to their imperial saviour and always falling short of demonstrating that they have made good on the gift. To this line of argument, Cho draws on the work of Lee Edelman and Jack Halberstam to add that Little Dog's queerness renders him "incompatible with the reproductive futurism of the nation...the queer figure has already 'failed' the future" (138) and thus is imagined as failing to redeem the US's gift of freedom.

Following Cho and Ha and Tompkins, I maintain that, as a queer Vietnamese refugee, Little Dog does not so much fail the future as he is denied one. *On Earth* metabolizes the insights of queer of colour theorists such as David Eng, Roderick Ferguson, and José Esteban Muñoz by signalling how, along the co-articulated lines of race, ethnicity, nationality, and sexuality, racialized queer folk are imagined as out of time with modernity and disallowed a future.[3] As Esteban Muñoz wrote in his measured response to Edelman's imperative that queer subjects must "abjur[e] fidelity to a [reproductive] futurism" (4), racialized and racialized queer subjects do not have a guaranteed future to reject. They "are not the sovereign princes of futurity" (Muñoz 95). *On Earth* avows this reality through its unspooling of how Little Dog's experience of coming out to his mother becomes an "exchang[e] of truths" (Vuong 133) in which his mother shares that, due to the deprivation their family experienced as a consequence of the war, she was forced to abort his older brother in a hospital that "'still smelled of smoke and gasoline'" (135). Their exchange is followed by Little Dog's recounting of an attack on a young queer boy in Vietnam and the Pulse Nightclub shooting where young men of colour "rummaging the dark, each other, for happiness" (137) were targeted. It is only, Little Dog reflects, through carelessness that one can imagine "survival [as] easy" (137).

The novel's attention to the often-foreclosed futures of racialized and queer subjects is, I hold, central to its critique of the cost at which the fraudulent gift of freedom is tendered. As Little Dog tells his mother, "the calf is most free when the cage opens and it's led to the truck for slaughter. All freedom is relative—you know too well—and sometimes it's no freedom at all, but simply the cage widening far away from you" (Vuong, *On Earth* 216). Little Dog's analogy of the calf being led to slaughter serves as a reminder that freedom is one of modernity's privileged criteria for, Lowe argues, the racialized subject to be incorporated into the category of the human. Within modern liberalism, "freedom" serves as a civilizational yardstick by which some "subjects, practices, and geographies are placed at a distance from 'the human'" (*Intimacies* 3), and literary genres such as the autobiography and the novel, Lowe emphasizes, can serve as vehicles for either maintaining this distance or tendering the promise of its closure. Vuong's interruption of the Bildungsroman's *and* Küntlesrroman's shared plots of development and liberation rejects this promise. Instead of positioning the figure of the artist as a neoliberal entrepreneur of the self or, in its earlier iteration, the self-autonomous human subject, Little Dog is installed, like other protagonists of diasporic coming-of-age novels, as "an archiver of memory and of the zeitgeist of [his] place and time" (Quintana-Vallejo 5). He surveys the still-unfolding aftermaths or "posts" of US imperialism and reveals the ruse of sovereignty attached to the figure of the human. In one of the novel's lyrics that simultaneously operates as a joke that withholds its punchline, Little Dog tells his mother, "They say nothing lasts forever and I'm writing to you in the voice of an endangered species" (Vuong, *On Earth* 176). In the reading that follows, I examine the queer poetics through which Vuong repurposes the Bildungsroman and Küntlesrroman and how its underexamined use of animals operates as a leitmotif for lyrically archiving moments of exposure, trauma, and care shared between multiracial and queer subjects whose precarity is determined by their historically uncertain relationship to the category of the human. In keeping with readings advanced by Lee and Neumann, who have respectively explored how *On Earth* valorizes "non-essentialized and open forms of proximity" (Neumann 288) through its "multilingual poetics" and depicts "emotional and erotic support labor" (Lee 194) as a form of resistance to the chemical weaponry of US empire and neoliberalism, I argue that Vuong's use of animals and animality, the latter of which has historically been ascribed to racialized, colonial, and queer subjects, reaffirms the porosity and dependency of human-animals and thus reimagines the artist at the centre of the Künstlerroman.

"In the voice of an endangered species": Beyond the Sovereign Author, towards an Archive of Diasporic Creatures

For all that Vuong's novel is a Künstlerroman, Little Dog's education and identity as a poet are not cast as a realization of "the gift of freedom," and the novel actively thwarts any reading of his education and success in the literary marketplace from being absorbed into the adjacent, post-1965 model minority myth of Asian American upward social mobility. In part I, the novel gestures towards this narrative as a road deliberately not taken when Little Dog informs his mother of an earlier and since destroyed letter in which he recounted his development as a writer, "How I, the first in our family to go to college, squandered it on a degree in English. How I fled my shitty high school to spend my days in New York lost in library stacks, reading obscure texts by dead people, most of whom never dreamed a face like mine floating over their sentences—and least of all that those sentences would save me" (Vuong, *On Earth* 15). Little

Dog's rueful characterization of his undergraduate English studies as wasteful alludes to the imperative—enshrined in US work and student visa allocations—that Asian immigrants and refugees must justify their presence within the body politic of the nation by contributing to its wealth through their professionalization in business and STEM fields.[4] This expectation, Christopher T. Fan notes, is more pronounced in texts by Chinese American authors such as Ling Ma's *Severance*, but it is also appears in *On Earth*'s depiction of the "trope of the college classroom as a symbol of race and class" (83).

In the novel's use of this trope, however, *On Earth* does not elaborate on the redemption Little Dog experiences through literature (i.e., how "those sentences would save me"), nor does it position the classroom—college or otherwise—as a gateway to citizenship in which, to review Lowe's formulation, racial difference is transcended through a repudiation of the abject Asian mother and feminized motherland (Lowe, *Immigrant Acts* 56). Rather, the novel illuminates the linkages between English language acquisition, that vaunted criterion for national belonging and upward social mobility, and heteropatriarchal masculinity, both of which cast Little Dog and Rose in an uncertain relationship to the conjoined categories of citizen and human. Beginning with one of the novel's many accumulative transitions, Little Dog recounts an episode in which his ability to speak English is violently questioned by his white male classmates who had "already mastered the dialect of damaged American fathers" (Vuong, *On Earth* 24). His mother later responds by urging him to be a "real boy" and defend himself by using the "bellyful of English" (25) that she herself does not have. Her pleas are accompanied by their adoption of a ritual in which Little Dog drinks "'American milk'": "I'd drink it down, gulping...both of us hoping the whiteness vanishing into me would make more of a yellow boy...The milk would erase all the dark inside me with a flood of brightness" (26). Consuming the mother's milk of the nation-state in which heteronormative masculinity is co-articulated with whiteness, they speculate, will enable Little Dog to override the "racialized vision of the feminized Asian American male" (Eng, *Racial Castration* 3).

The memory of Little Dog's failure to verbally assert himself as a "'real boy'" who has mastered both American English and his racialized queerness brushes up against another in which he, Rose, and Lan attempt to buy oxtail to make *bún bò huê*. Little Dog describes Rose's faltering attempt to order in Vietnamese and then, abandoning language, pantomiming the physical attributes of an ox to communicate her order: "You moved, carefully twisting and gyrating so he could recognize each piece of this performance: horns, tail, ox" (Vuong, *On Earth* 30). Met with derisive laughter that quiets into confused pity, Rose and Little Dog are bound together by shame— her wet face mirroring Little Dog's humiliating recognition of the insufficient store of his "'bellyful of English.'" In Birgit Neumann's reading of *On Earth*, this scene indexes the novel's theorization of how "linguistic insufficiency threatens the integrity of the body and our embodied sense of self" (285). Notably, Rose's linguistic dispossession, established after the recalled imperial French of her childhood is met with confusion and after a Spanish-speaking worker is unable to communicate with her, threatens her bodily integrity by aligning her with the animal she mimics. As Mel Y. Chen remarks, despite long-running and continuing debates, language remains the defining attribute used to distinguish "the animal" (inevitably posited as an abstraction) and the human. "Who and what are considered to possess 'language,' and the qualities afforded to it within that location, are factors that influence how identification, kinship, codes of morality, and rights are articulated, and how affection and rights themselves are distributed" (Chen 91). Little Dog, Lan, and, more pronouncedly, Rose are situated outside the racializing codes of kinship and morality that organize national belonging. They do not exhibit a fluency in English (the required language of the American citizen-consumer) nor, as the Spanish-speaking worker's solicitation demonstrates, are they legible within a racial schema that reductively situates Spanish (without any consideration of its many dialects) as the dominant language of the racialized precariat.

Their illegibility within this racial and linguistic matrix is later historicized when the novel more overtly addresses the selective inclusion and erasure of Asian immigrants within US law. Little Dog cites an 1884 Texas court case in which a judge blocked the prosecution of a white railroad worker who had murdered a Chinese labourer due to a legal precedent that defined a "human being" only within the racializing categories of white, Mexican, and Black. Little Dog concludes, "The nameless yellow body was not considered human because it did not fit in a slot on a piece of paper" (Vuong, *On Earth* 63). Marked as yellow subjects who do not fit within these categories and whose words are "suddenly wrong everywhere, even in our mouths" (31), Little Dog and his family flee the store with only Wonder bread, mayonnaise, and moon rings to nourish them, and he vows to never be "wordless" and begins his "career as our family's official interpreter. From then on, I would fill in our blanks, our silences…I code switched. I took off our language and wore my English, like a mask, so that others would see my face, and therefore yours" (32). Neumann underlines that the advent of Little Dog's "career" as the family's advocate and translator is symptomatic of how translation "radically re-forms the individual, reconfiguring him along the terms, concepts and connotations of another" (290)—in this example, those determined by the global propagation of American English as the lingua franca of global capitalism. Through its temporal marker, "from then on" the novel appears to memorialize this episode as inaugurating a linear narrative of Little Dog's subject formation as an autonomous citizen. Yet the novel does not continue to plot Little Dog's career path. As he helps his grandmother knead the strained muscle tissue of his mother's back and affirms that the moon rings she and his grandmother wear do, indeed, reveal their happiness, Little Dog anchors himself in the shared vocabulary of his family. "Because gunshots, lies, and oxtail—or whatever you want to call your god—should say *Yes* over and over, in cycles, in spirals, with no other reason but to hear itself exist. Because love, at its best, repeats itself" (34). Little Dog's translation of "another portion of America" (33) and his reaffirmation of his mother's happiness is, by the novel's characterization, a recursive valorization of his matrilineal inheritance. Rather than the mother being installed as an abstraction or metonym for the mother country, that, as in earlier Asian American iterations of the Bildungsroman, must be abandoned in order to engage in the dual projects of "self-authoring as self-fathering" (Chu 42) and translation-as-masquerade (Neumann 290), *On Earth* elegizes the education Little Dog receives from Lan and Rose.

Little Dog's education, moreover, does not merely facilitate his paradigmatic entrance into the liberal public sphere, nor does it follow the affirmative Bildungsroman tradition of "plotting human personality development…as the normative story of modern socialization, liberation, and emancipation" (Slaughter 145). The binaristic promise of liberation within the liberal public sphere and the accompanying guarantee of safety within the private sphere are revealed for the lies they are. The divisions between public and private do not exist when, for queer diasporic subjects, the latter is always under threat of invasion. The novel addresses this when Little Dog admits that his letter is not a private communiqué for only his mother: "It could be, in writing you here, I am writing to everyone—for how can there be a private space if there is no safe space, if a boy's name can both shield him and turn into an animal at once?" (Vuong, *On Earth* 33–34). Within the soundscape of their apartment, where his grandmother, Lan, hears July fourth firecrackers as exploding mortars, Little Dog slowly unfolds the origin of his name, given to him by his grandmother, that acts as both a significatory talisman against evil spirits and an inscription of animality. Little Dog's name is later contrasted with the undisclosed name given to him at birth, translated in English as "Patriotic Leader of the Nation" (20), and bestowed upon him by a shaman in Vietnam who correctly intuits his father's desire to shore up his own masculinity through the identity of his newly born son. The withheld name immediately becomes a prophecy ironized by the family's displacement.

The novel's redaction of the name of the father is characteristic of what David L. Eng has termed a methodology of queer diaspora. Queer diaspora operates as a theoretical framework that resists post and neocolonial forms of social belonging by "declining the normative impulse to recuperate lost origins, to recapture the mother or motherland, and to valorize dominant notions of social belonging and racial exclusion…It simultaneously complicates the homogenizing narratives of...economic development as a guiding beacon of (neo)liberal rights and freedom" (*Feeling of Kinship* 13–14). *On Earth* rejects the heteropatriarchal fantasy of self-determination *through* national recuperation and questions the Bildungsroman's promise of being incorporated (to borrow from Slaughter once more) into the human through literature and self-authorship. Little Dog may be saved by the sentences he reads when his face floats above texts within the canons of European and American literature that exclude him, but the novel incisively critiques the liberal humanist criterion of "transcendence" still espoused by the Anglo-American literary marketplace. "They will tell you," he warns his mother, "that to be political is to be merely angry, and therefore, artless, depthless...They will tell you that great writing 'breaks free' from the political...uniting people toward universal truths" (Vuong, *On Earth* 186). While "great writing" may break free, Little Dog emphasizes that the hegemonically white gatekeepers of the literary marketplace position minoritized authors of colour as native informants who must paradoxically write and represent the traumas of the communities for whom they are presumed to speak while still shoring up national mythologies.

Cathy Park Hong rightly points out that Vuong's often-rehearsed biography as a Vietnamese refugee and the acclaim that his 2016 poetry collection, *Night Sky with Exit Wounds*, received, have been deployed by reviewers and interviewers in "a single American myth of individual triumph" (Park Hong 51). For Park Hong, this myth is part of an "ethnic literary project [that] has always been a humanist project in which nonwhite writers must prove they are human beings who feel pain...My books are graded on a pain scale. If it's a 2, maybe it's not worth telling my story. If it's a 10, maybe my book will be a bestseller" (49). Park Hong's critique of the Anglo-American literary marketplace and the pressures it exerts on authors of colour echoes Little Dog's observation, "They will write their names on your leash and call you necessary, call you urgent" (185). In a widely shared Instagram post, Vuong has addressed the misreadings produced by white critics who, with barely disguised resentment, have read texts by authors of colour as "tragic" and "morbid," and in so doing, entirely flatten the range of their stylistic techniques and affects ("At the risk"). He draws attention in particular to critics who evaluate and devalue works by "colonial subjects" as "'uneven'" or "'incohesive,'" to which he trenchantly responds, "To write 'cohesion' as a colonial subject is to write a lie" ("At the risk").

On Earth's critique of the comforting and cohesive lies expected from colonial subjects is expressed, in part, through the novel's refusal to cast Little Dog in the role of the emergent auteur whose ability to write "universal truths" of humanity would establish him as both a sovereign citizen and self-fashioning neoliberal subject. Rather, the novel repeatedly casts Little Dog as an archivist of a multiracial and multigenerational precariat—that which he likens to "a shipwreck—the pieces floating, finally legible" (Vuong, *On Earth* 190). In a section of part III that announces his letter as one among many false starts and iterations, "Dear Ma—Let me begin again" (173), Little Dog's memories and observations about authorship are configured as a series of ironic axioms that severely undermine the intertwined constructs of the Bildungsroman protagonist and neoliberal self "responsibly self-authored, and one that owes no sense of its formation to a past trace in time" (Chen 77). Responding to his mother's question, "what does it mean to be a writer?" Little Dog starkly announces,

> Seven of my friends are dead. Four from overdoses. Five, if you count Xavier who flipped his Nissan doing ninety on a bad batch of fentanyl.
> I don't celebrate my birthday anymore. (Vuong, *On Earth* 174)

Authorship is not valorized by its promises of present and future selfhood; Little Dog understands it as paying witness to the foreclosure of any future. The novel's repeated references to what has been euphemistically mistermed the "opioid epidemic"—as if its viral devastation were a naturally occurring phenomena that did not capitalize on the co-morbidities of poverty, unemployment, privatized health care, and corporations unfettered by regulations—are interwoven with fragmented memories of Trevor's slow death-by-addiction, allusions to the US's post-9/11 military operations, and the violence of militarized heteronormative masculinities. An encounter between Little Dog and an older white man, dependent on an oxygen tank, wearing a hat reading "'*Nam Vet 4 Life*" (179) later echoes in a memory of Little Dog translating for his mother the red, spray-painted threat *FAG4LIFE* inscribed on their front door as "Merry Christmas" (180–81). Both slogans tragically, and in the latter example, ironically, assert a fatal allegiance to a discursive articulation of whiteness and imperial masculinity that, as the veteran's oxygen tank suggests, is terminal and terminating. Shorn together, these fragments of violent ruin and strangulating allegiance map the relationship between the "escalating violence of neoliberal economics" (Masco 7) and fatal costs of white heteronormative masculinity and US imperialism. The novel's diasporic archive insistently links the expansion of slow death in the post-welfare US to the long history of its distribution of fast death in its imperial wars. These parallels are drawn when Little Dog riffs off the word "corpus" and explains,

> I never wanted to build a "body of work," but to preserve these, our bodies, breathing and unaccounted for, inside the work…The truest ruins are not written down. The girl Grandma knew back in Go Cong, the one whose sandals were cut from the tires of a burned-out army jeep, who was erased by an air strike three weeks before the war ended—she's a ruin no one can point to. A ruin without location, like a language.
>
> After a month on the Oxy, Trevor's ankle healed, but he was a full-blown addict. (Vuong, *On Earth* 175)

In the white space between these two cruelly truncated biographies of the nameless girl from Go Cong and Little Dog's first love, the novel allows the echoes that exist between these two "ruins" to travel across a space that denies any collapsing or "transcending" of the differences of gender, nationality, and race that determine their lives and their deaths. Little Dog's endeavour to document the unaccounted ruins excluded from the dominant narratives of his inherited and experienced wars thus seeks spatially and temporally to imagine an archive that cannot cohere within a patriarchal and colonial order of things but instead is organized by a queer poetics.

"To have the ruined lives of animals tell a human story": Animality and Memory

On Earth's queer poetics is evident in the novel's depiction of animality and its recurrent use of nonhuman animals as a leitmotif of diaspora, vulnerability, and the policed borders of the human. From the novel's opening passage, in which Little Dog discloses that he is writing to engage in time travel—"to get back to the time"—the novel's recursive routes are marked with animal bodies. In the novel's opening passages, Little Dog tunnels back in time to the moment when his mother stared in horror at a taxidermied buck mounted over a soda machine at a rest stop. "I think now of that buck, how you stared into its black glass eyes and saw your reflection, your whole body, warped in that lifeless mirror. How it was not the grotesque mounting of a decapitated animal that shook you—but that the taxidermy embodied a death that won't finish, a death that keeps dying" (Vuong, *On Earth* 1). The distorted reflection of his mother in the dead mirror of the buck's eyes, and her horror at the displayed animal being forever trapped in the spectacle of its execution, predicts the novel's many returns to the intergenerational trauma of the US's aggression against Vietnam. Rose's horror at "a death that keeps dying" is later mirrored in Little Dog's inquiry, "When does a war end? When can I say your name and have it mean only your name and not what you left behind?" (Vuong, *On Earth* 12).

Little Dog's irresolvable question, first emerging from the image of his mother gazing at her reflection in the eyes of the slaughtered and preserved buck, hovers over his later imagining of Lan and Rose's survival at a checkpoint in Vietnam. In keeping with queer archival practices that imagine in "an affective register irreducible to traditional historical inquiry [that seeks to confront] what has been forgotten, abandoned, discredited, and otherwise effaced" (Freeman xxii–xxiii), the novel does not directly address the fact that they encounter this checkpoint during the year of the Tet Offensive. The novel pointedly only historicizes their experience through the Chinese zodiac sign of his mother's birth year when Little Dog revises an earlier refrain, "It is a beautiful country," by clarifying, "It is a beautiful country because you are still in it. Because your name is Rose, and you are my mother and the year is 1968—the Year of the Monkey" (Vuong, *On Earth* 44). The novel's periodization of Lan and Rose's confrontation with the soldiers through the zodiac figure of the monkey serves as a lyrical end point to the novel's serpentine movements between Lan's story and the story of Vietnamese patriarchs consuming the brain of a still-alive macaque monkey, drugged with vodka and morphine, to ensure their virility and the continuation of their family lines. Both stories are about creatures all too often installed as abstractions; "the animal," as Jacques Derrida, Donna Haraway, and others have long decried (even as the former failed to move beyond his own lamentation) appears as a universal category, and often animalized, Vietnamese women, in the colonial tropeologies produced in American media, are conflated with land to be invaded and conquered. At different turns, the novel alludes to these tropes through its itemization of the generic elements of Lan and Rose's story, "A woman, a girl, a gun. This is an old story, one anyone can tell. A trope in a movie you can walk away from if it weren't already here, already written down" (35). Lan, who becomes a sex worker after she is disowned from her family for leaving a marriage she was coerced into entering, is, indeed, a trope in many late 1970s and 1980s Hollywood films about the US's war against Vietnam. Typified by Stanley Kubrick's *Full Metal Jacket*, such films and popular media depict the "Vietnamese woman [as] the ultimate Gook, different from the American soldier through race, culture, language, and gender. She is the complete and threatening object of both rapacious desire and murderous fear, the embodiment of the whole mysterious, enticing, forbidding, and dangerous country of Vietnam" (Nguyen, *Nothing Ever Dies* 64).

In the novel's framing of Lan and Rose's encounter with the US soldiers armed with M-16s, they are introduced as stock figures in a deliberately cinematic tableau. The novel's lyricism borrows from the visual strategies of film by including a description that zooms in on the "beautiful country" populated by US soldiers guarding a "gate made of concertina and weaponized permission" (Vuong, *On Earth* 35), with fields burning beneath circling Huey helicopters. The novel's repeated use of the second person, such as when Little Dog characterizes their story as "a human story. Anyone can tell it. Can you tell?" (38), interpellates the reader as one who has consumed, either in whole or as visual quotations, the films and media in which Vietnamese women are framed as the brutalized objects of desire and fear. His question, "Can you tell?" is an inquiry into narration and observation—do "you" have the capacity to see what has been historically redacted?—and it enfolds the reader into a "you" principally inhabited by his mother. In so doing, the novel reminds the reader of the distance and proximity between themselves and Rose, as well as Little Dog's own distance and proximity to Rose and Lan's story.[5]

The tensions at play between the "you" and their relationship to this "human story" are amplified by the narrative of the brutalized macaque. As the novel reminds us, "It is a beautiful country... depending on who you are" (Vuong, *On Earth* 36). Within this beautiful, patriarchal nation, under siege by US imperialism, Lan, her infant daughter, Rose, and the macaque are disposable creatures. The story of the men consuming the brain of the macaque to ward off the threat of impotence and thereby ensure the viability of the nation is tightly interlaced with Lan and Rose surviving the checkpoint. After noting that macaques are the "most hunted primates in Southeast Asia," the novel shifts to the future tense and predicts the slow death this creature will experience before returning to the present tense in which Lan holds her child and repeats the slogan of American exceptionalism in hopes it will function as a password to secure their safe passage, "Yoo Et Aye numbuh won. No bang bang" (42). Lan's pleas are followed by Little Dog's explanatory note that macaques exhibit traits once and still thought to be the sole cognitive province of humans: "They are able to recall past images and apply them to current problem solving. In other words, macaques employ memory in order to survive" (43). Little Dog's retelling of what the novel later reveals are stories he first receives from his mother situates Rose, Lan, and the macaque as creatures that trouble biopolitical borders. In his reimagining, their survival is contingent on Rose's proximity to whiteness when an American soldier reads Rose for "the whiteness showing from her yellow body" (42) and her possible kinship to him and his fellow servicemen. "He could be her father, he thinks...He considers them, rifle gripped tight, his eyes on the girl with American blood before the American gun" (42). This speculative moment of empathy, inspired by a proximity to whiteness, emphasizes how their survival is dependent on the US's racial calculus and alludes to the post-1965 reading of Asian Americans as best positioned to be "disappear[ed]" into whiteness and the US's "amnesiac fog" (Park Hong 35). Reading this scene for its allegorical dimensions, Cho observes that it forecasts how the "the future of Vietnam and its refugees are dependent on the patriarchal lineage and tutelage of the United States to survive" (142). I argue, though, that, through the proximities Little Dog maps between the macaque and those whom US imperialism positions as outside of the human, the novel provides a decidedly different lesson.

Returning to the Vietnamese men who consume the macaque and absorb its memories into their bodies, Little Dog asks, "Who will be lost in the story we tell ourselves? Who will be lost in ourselves?" (Vuong, *On Earth* 43). The novel's question is then answered in Little Dog's revision of his grandmother's words as, "*Hands up. Don't shoot. Yoo Et Aye numbuh won. Hands up. No bang bang*" (43). Lan's statement, italicized to alert us to Little Dog's curative citation of it, is prefaced by words of protest that directly recall the Ferguson uprising of 2014. The recombination of Lan's desperate and phonetically represented utterance of US empire with a statement of protest against the state-sanctioned murder of unarmed Black people, whose Blackness has long been criminalized, both locates the US's war against Vietnam within an ongoing history of its extra-legal violence against Black people and racialized peoples of the Global South and refuses to allow the terrible contingency of Lan's and Rose's survival to recede from the horizon. Their ability to pass through the checkpoint on the basis of the soldier's recognition of Rose's "American blood" does not afford them freedom. Within the biopolitical calculus of US imperialism, the novel emphasizes, they have only been temporarily incorporated into the category of the human, long enough to pass through its "widening cage" (93). The momentary understanding of their lives as worthy of being preserved is a brief illumination likened to the light that "flickers" over the macaque's "hollowed mind," which is then linked to the light that "flickers" in the muzzle of a rifle that remains aimed at them (44).

"Tell a Human Story": Dependency and the Multitude

Just as Lan and Rose's safe passage through the checkpoint is situated as an episode within an archive that traverses borders of species, generations, nation-states, and the US's organizing racial schemas, Little Dog's letter travels a wayward, recursive path that refuses a progressive plot. From one angle, the novel's refusal is in keeping with what Slaughter has identified as one of the defining characteristics of the postcolonial Bildungsroman: "the genre's traditional conclusive event of social, civil, and self-integration is perpetually postponed, so that the sovereign, undivided human personality remains a vanishing (plot) point beyond the frame of the text" (215). From another, though, *On Earth* does more than defer the "vanish[ed] (plot) point" of the "sovereign, undivided human personality." It avows the multitude, figured in the novel's bestiary and Little Dog's relationships to Rose, Lan, and Trevor. In the novel's final sequence, Little Dog inhabits pasts and landscapes that collapse into one another. Following the voice of a hurt cow through the tobacco field where he and Trevor experienced their most sexually intimate moments, he finds his mother and begs her to share, once more, the story of the Vietnamese elders' consumption of the macaque. A request that reveals his inheritance of her stories, Little Dog acknowledges his debt to Rose's storytelling even as he admits the divide between them. "Ma, I don't know if you've made it this far in this letter...You always tell me it's too late for you to read, with your poor liver, your exhausted bones...That reading is a privilege you made possible for me with what you lost" (Vuong, *On Earth* 240). Positing a counterfactual that is also a projection into a future, Little Dog imagines Rose as a young girl with "a room full of books with parents who will read you bedtime stories in a country not touched by war. Maybe then, in that life and in this future, you'll find this book and you'll know what happened to us" (240). Little Dog's nano-Bildungsroman in which Rose is installed as the protagonist gives way to his flight from the present they inhabit together and the past that happened to them. As Little Dog attempts to outrun the dismantling of his world that he knows will come—the loss of Trevor, Lan, his friends from "speed and heroine nowhere their scarless veins," the sale of the tobacco farm where he met Trevor—he loses his human form and is absorbed into the novel's organizing bestiary. Buffalos become moose, moose transform into dogs, and the pack of dogs gives way to a "whole troop" of macaques with "the crowns of their heads cut open, their brains hollowed out" (241). Inhabiting a collective figured in the bodies of animals, shedding the fiction of the self-contained and sovereign human, the novel affirms its queer poetics of dependency and exposure.

Notes

1. In Patricia P. Chu's *Assimilating Asians*, she observes that in numerous texts authored by Asian American men, "the Asian immigrant mother [is depicted] as a proponent of problematically construed Asian values or as a person whose claims to American-born son's care and loyalty somehow threaten his capacity to establish his autonomy, masculinity, and American subjectivity" (54).
2. Viet Thanh Nguyen situates these Chinese American Bildungsromane within the context of the post-Vietnam attempts to recuperate and restore cisheteropatriarchal authority and reads them as a "project of Asian American remasculinization both within and against the dominant American remasculinization, for it partakes in American patriarchy's attempts to continue the masculinization of political and economic public life" while opposing its historical Orientalism ("Remasculinization" 133).
3. See David Eng's *Racial Castration: Managing Masculinity in Asian America*, Roderick Ferguson's *Aberrations in Black: Toward a Queer of Color Critique*, and José Esteban Muñoz's *Cruising Utopia: The Then and There of Queer Futurity*.
4. As Christopher T. Fan argues, post-1965 Asian American literature has been heavily shaped by the ascendancy of China as a global economic power and the US's adoption of immigration policies that sought to recruit highly skilled Asian immigrants in the STEM fields. He tracks this influence in texts such as Ling Ma's *Severance* and terms it "science fictionality," and defines it as "a fantasy that associates a certain mode of production (industrialization) with certain kinds of people (STEM professionals)—[it] conjure[s] new forms when its imagined locus of industrialization shifts from the US to China and its imagined ideal subjects begin to resonate with the prestige of global capital over against the racial form of nationally specific identities" (Fan 92). Notably,

Vuong himself first majored in business and rationalized his decision at the time as one of following the well-trodden path of Asian American authors who, like Chang-Rae Lee, first fulfilled their familial obligation for economic success and then became authors in their forties and fifties ("Conversation with Tommy Orange").

5. My reading of Vuong's use of the second-person "you" is indebted to Ben Lerner's *The Hatred of Poetry* where he offers a reading of Claudia Rankine's use of the second-person "you" in her *Citizen: An American Lyric*.

Works Cited

Baldwin, James. *Go Tell It on the Mountain*. Alfred A. Knopf, 2016 (1953).

Chen, Mel Y. *Animacies: Biopolitics, Racial Mattering, and Queer Affect*. Duke University Press, 2012.

Cho, Jennifer. "'We were born from beauty': Dis/inheriting Genealogies of Refugee and Queer Shame in Ocean Vuong's *On Earth We're Briefly Gorgeous*." *MELUS*, vol. 47, no. 1, Spring 2022, pp. 130–53.

Chu, Patricia P. *Assimilating Asians: Gendered Strategies of Authorship in Asian America*. Duke University Press, 2000.

Derrida, Jacques. *The Animal That Therefore I Am*. Translated by David Wills, Fordham University Press, 2008.

Edelman, Lee. *No Future: Queer Theory and the Death Drive*. Duke University Press, 2004.

Eng, David L. *The Feeling of Kinship: Queer Liberalism and the Racialization of Intimacy*. Duke University Press, 2010.

Eng, David L. *Racial Castration: Managing Masculinity in Asian America*. Duke University Press, 2001.

Fan, Christopher T. "Science Fictionality and Post-65 Asian American Literature." *American Literary History*, vol. 33, no. 1, 2021, pp. 75–102.

Ferguson, Roderick. *Aberrations in Black: Toward a Queer of Color Critique*. Duke University Press, 2003.

Freeman, Elizabeth. *Time Binds: Queer Temporalities, Queer Histories*. Duke University Press, 2010.

Goyal, Yogita. *Runaway Genres: The Global Afterlives of Slavery*. New York University Press, 2019.

Ha, Quan Manh, and Mia Tompkins. "'The truth is memory has not forgotten us': Memory, Identity, and Storytelling in Ocean Vuong's *On Earth We're Briefly Gorgeous*." *Rocky Mountain Review of Literature*, vol. 75, no. 2, Fall 2021, pp. 199–220.

Lee, Rachel. "Affective Chemistries of Care: Slow Activism and the Limits of the Molecular in Ocean Vuong's *On Earth We Are Briefly Gorgeous*." *Journal of Transnational American Studies*, vol. 13, no 1, 2022, pp. 193–223.

Lerner, Ben. *The Hatred of Poetry*. Farrar, Strauss and Giroux, 2016.

Lowe, Lisa. *Immigrant Acts: On Asian American Cultural Politics*. Duke University Press, 1996.

Lowe, Lisa. *The Intimacies of Four Continents*. Duke University Press, 2015.

Masco, Joseph. *Theatre of Operations: National Security Affect from the Cold War to the War on Terror*. Duke University Press, 2014.

Muñoz, José Esteban. *Cruising Utopia: The Then and There of Queer Futurity*. New York University Press, 2009.

Neumann, Birgit. "'Our mother tongue, then, is no mother at all—but an orphan': The Mother Tongue and Translation in Ocean Vuong's *On Earth We're Briefly Gorgeous*." *Anglia*, vol. 138, no. 2, 2020, pp. 277–98.

Nguyen, Mimi Thi. *The Gift of Freedom: War, Debt, and Other Refugee Passages*. Duke University Press, 2012.

Nguyen, Viet Thanh. *Nothing Ever Dies: Vietnam and the Memory of War*. Harvard University Press, 2016.

Nguyen, Viet Thanh. "The Remasculinization of Chinese America: Race, Violence, and the Novel." *American Literary History*, vol. 12, no. 1, 2000, pp. 130–57.

Park Hong, Cathy. *Minor Feelings: An Asian American Reckoning*. One World, 2020.

Quintana-Vallejo, Ricardo. *Children of Globalization: Diasporic Coming-of-Age Novels in Germany, England, and the United States*. Routledge, 2020.

Slaughter, Joseph R. *Human Rights, Inc.: The World Novel, Narrative Form, and International Law*. Fordham University Press, 2007.

Tolentino, Jia. "Ocean Vuong's Life Sentences." *The New Yorker*, 3 June 2019, https://www.newyorker.com/magazine/2019/06/10/ocean-vuongs-life-sentences.

Vuong, Ocean. "At the risk of sounding too obtuse, I wonder what it is about white critics." *Instagram Stories*, 11 Sept. 2021, https://www.instagram.com/accounts/login/?next=/ocean_vuong/.

Vuong, Ocean. "Ocean Vuong in Conversation with Tommy Orange." *City Arts & Lecture*, 3 Feb. 2020, https://www.cityarts.net/event/ocean-vuong/#transcript.

Vuong, Ocean. *On Earth We're Briefly Gorgeous*. Penguin, 2019.

19

CHILDLESSNESS AND THE FEMALE NIGERIAN BILDUNGSROMAN

Julia Wurr

Better to be ugly, to be crippled, to be a thief even, than to be barren. We had both been raised to believe that our greatest day would be: the birth of our first child, our wedding and graduation days in that order. A woman may be forgiven for having a child out of wedlock if she had no hope of getting married, and she would be dissuaded from getting married if she didn't have a degree. Marriage could immediately wipe out a sluttish past, but angel or not, a woman had to have a child.

—SEFI ATTA, *Everything Good Will Come*

As the epigraph above vividly illustrates, Sefi Atta's *Everything Good Will Come*, published in 2005, negotiates female self-formation between the conflicting priorities of individual *Bildung* and formal education, on the one hand, and of both societal and internalized gendered expectations such as marriage and—above all—motherhood, on the other hand.[1] In fact, Atta's debut novel presents Enitan, the novel's protagonist, and her best friend Sheri's actively tackling such gendered expectations as crucial to the two characters' processes of self-formation. In these processes, the issue of childlessness and the stigma attached to it play a prominent role. While Sheri has to come to terms with being infertile—a result of her desperate attempt to perform an abortion on herself after being raped in her early adolescence—Enitan withstands massive pressure when it takes her several years to carry a child to full term in her early thirties:

> Niyi's [Enitan's husband's] relations began to press, "Is everything all right?" They looked at my stomach before looking at my face. Some scolded me outright. "What are you waiting for?" My mother invited me to her vigils; my father offered to send me overseas to see other doctors. I asked why they harassed women this way. We were greater than our wombs, greater than the sum of our body parts. (Atta 188)

Her initial Aristotelian self-affirmation notwithstanding, Enitan feels "shrunk to the size of [her] womb" (189) when, after a miscarriage, an emergency operation, and two more years of trying to become pregnant, she agrees to undergo fertility treatment. Eventually, Enitan gives birth to a daughter, and she is filled with love and joy. At the same time, however, the protagonist confounds expectations when, on the day of her child's naming ceremony, she leaves her husband to become an advocate for women prisoners. In the supposed climax of the novel's numerous baptismal scenes, the protagonist thus transforms the meaning of such rites. Having opted against the tradition of naming her daughter after her own recently deceased mother, Enitan also decides to escape the exclusively vertical narrative of being a daughter, wife, and mother herself. Instead, she prioritizes lateral growth and horizontal kinship in the form of sisterhood—a decision that extends the climax of the novel's baptismal scenes to the protagonist's own metaphorical rebirth and baptism at the end of the novel.

Like *Everything Good Will Come*, Flora Nwapa's *Efuru*, first published in 1966, and Buchi Emecheta's *The Joys of Motherhood*, published in 1979, also focus on the role of childlessness in processes of female self-formation.[2] All of these novels can be read as Bildungsromane, and, although their protagonists grow up under very different circumstances, all of these texts critically explore the great procreative pressure their female protagonists have to endure from their adolescence onwards. However, rather than perpetuating gendered expectations by exclusively concentrating on how motherhood influences female self-formation, the novels emphasize how the pressure to have children informs their protagonists' development from childhood to adulthood. So, while none of the novels opposes motherhood per se—in fact, all three protagonists want and have children—the novels undermine the dichotomy between motherhood and childlessness by exploring what role the strained spectrum in between plays in the self-formation of young girls, childless women, childless mothers—but also childfree women. Considering what an important role motherhood, particularly in the stereotyped form of the Mother Africa trope, has played in literary representations of African women (Stratton 39–55; Oloruntoba-Oju and Oloruntoba-Oju 5–6), the novels' foregrounding of the nexus between coming of age and childlessness offers great subversive and analytical potential. Read together,[3] these three novels and their common focus on the nexus between coming of age and childlessness consequently promote interesting reflections on the connection between reproduction and the generic conventions of the Bildungsroman: through their disturbance of the procreation plot,[4] these novels help to examine to what extent repronormativity—although not always uncritically accepted—has informed the ideological and generic suppositions in the continuous history of rewriting the Bildungsroman.

The Bildungsroman and Social Reproduction

Given that in its eighteenth- and nineteenth-century form the Bildungsroman predominantly featured young men as protagonists (Amoko 199), it does not seem surprising that the nexus between coming of age and childlessness has received scant attention in discussions of the generic conventions of the genre. In fact, at first sight, analyzing childlessness in the Bildungsroman might seem counterintuitive. After all, are Bildungsromane not all about children? However, approaching the Bildungsroman from the angle of childlessness is not only revealing for the study of the three Bildungsromane at hand, but it also yields interesting insights in the ongoing rewritings of the Bildungsroman's—highly volatile—generic conventions (Redfield 10; Austen 220–21; Hirsch 302). Broadly defined as a "novel that follows the development of the hero or heroine from childhood or adolescence into adulthood, through a troubled quest for identity" (Baldick 35), the Bildungsroman typically negotiates tensions between individuation and socialization—that is, issues that are intricately linked with questions of reproduction in both its social and biological forms.

Given that the Bildungsroman flourished at a time when society was "increasingly structured through sexuality" (Miller 240), it does not seem surprising that reproduction, both in its ideological sense but also in the sense of life making (Ferguson), continues to resurface as an—albeit not unquestioned—foil in the Bildungsroman's generic conventions. As, moreover, the idea of self-development that the Bildungsroman epitomizes rose simultaneously with heterosexual gendering (Miller 240), this foil bears traces of heteronormativity. While these traces might be less discernible in Bildungsromane with a chronological plot, they manifest themselves especially in Bildungsromane with teleological plots.[5] Determined by the end point, these teleological Bildungsromane often culminate in marriage (Hirsch 305–06). Interestingly, however, many Bildungsromane do not just end in marriage (Fernández-Vázquez 97), but are also—either implicitly or more explicitly—framed by procreation. If procreation serves as the implicit prerequisite of any Bildungsroman, this fact is ironically highlighted in the mid-eighteenth-century example of Laurence Sterne's *Tristram Shandy*, or rendered hauntingly explicit in the opening chapter of Nuruddin Farah's 1986 novel, *Maps*. While in the former, the novel's autodiegetic narrator reaches the point of his birth in volume III only, in the latter, the protagonist consciously experiences the agonizing process of his own birth (Hoagland 217). Besides being a prerequisite, procreation also often marks the end of traditional Bildungsromane: either it ensues as an implicit consequence of the marriage plot, or it results more explicitly in the creation of children. In fact, Aaron Matz argues that with regard to most Victorian Bildungsromane,

> the telos of these novels is only partly marriage; marriage is a station or position that makes possible a different telos, which is reproduction. Indeed, if we think of the bourgeois ideology of nineteenth-century fiction not simply as the normative union of the heterosexual couple, but also as the perpetuation of bourgeois order (and therefore life) through the birth of children, then we can see more clearly the main action of those concluding chapters of the typical Victorian novel. (12)

If this *telos* is already present in the late eighteenth century's prototypical example of Goethe's *Wilhelm Meisters Lehrjahre*, whose protagonist finally settles down as a husband and father (Austen 220), it is particularly visible in a number of Bildungsromane stemming from the nineteenth century, that is, from the time in which both the Bildungsroman and heteronormativity gained massive momentum. While Louisa May Alcott's *Little Women* also ends with a house full of children, Matz illustrates the role of childbirth in other nineteenth-century Victorian Bildungsromane such as *Jane Eyre*, *David Copperfield*, and *Middlemarch*: in *Jane Eyre*, Rochester regains his vision to discover that his first-born son has inherited his eyes; Dickens peoples the penultimate chapter of *David Copperfield* with three children; and *Middlemarch* ends with the indication that Dorothea has had the first of two children (12).

Although the Bildungsroman's historical connections to nation building and its role in socially reproducing capitalist and imperialist structures, as well as liberal subjects, has been duly marked (Lea 18–19; Hoagland; Hay 319–23), the negotiation of reproduction in the form of childbirth has remained curiously implicit. This could be due to the ambiguous status of children in the Bildungsroman. Although at first sight, Bildungsromane appear to be all about children, upon closer inspection, the child protagonist, while seemingly omnipresent, is often minimized through the ironic distance of the mature narrator (Hirsch 298). As a result, children as individuals or historical beings often appear less immediately present than the construct of the child as a carrier of social meaning—or more specifically, as an "emblem of reproduction" (Sheldon 35). If actual children thus often remain visibly absent, their implied presence in the procreation frame gains more relative importance.

The Postcolonial Bildungsroman and Childlessness

Especially when tying in with those inflections of the (anti-) Bildungsroman that criticize the dominant order into which the protagonist fails or refuses to enter (Hoagland 219; Hay 330), the genre has proven to be a particularly popular choice for postcolonial writers. Given the historical connections between Western self-realization and colonialism (Hoagland 225), the Bildungsroman might nonetheless seem a paradoxical choice in postcolonial fiction (Fernández-Vázquez 86). In much of this uneasy relationship between the Bildungsroman and the postcolonial, the figure of the child plays a prominent role. Firstly, "by describing the child's initiation in terms of a successful exploration of the external world, the Western novel of education opens the path for the colonial enterprise, with its narrative of adventure and conquest of distant lands" (91). Secondly, and on a more abstract level, "the whole idea of an evolution from childhood to adulthood—that is, from a primitive to a fully developed state of being—constitutes one of the images that has made the colonial enterprise possible" (Fernández-Vázquez 86; see also Hay 322). In fact, as Jo-Ann Wallace notes,

> an idea of "the child" is a *necessary precondition* of imperialism—that is, that the West had to invent for itself "the child" before it could think a specifically colonialist imperialism...it was an idea of "the child"—of the not yet fully evolved or consequential subject—which made thinkable a colonial apparatus dedicated to, in [Thomas] Macaulay's words, "the improvement of colonized peoples." (qtd. in Fernández-Vázquez 86)

In addition to the colonial instrumentalization of the construct of the child, problematic equations of postcolonial individuals and even entire postcolonial nations with children continue to serve as a template for reductionist readings of many postcolonial Bildungsromane. In their equation of discourses of independence and postcolonial nation building with narratives of attaining adolescence and adulthood, such readings overstrain parallels between young protagonists and the "experience of the new nations" (86), and thus reduce postcolonial Bildungsromane to allegories of postcolonial nations reaching maturity.

The focus on childlessness complicates such reductionist readings by highlighting the ambiguous position of children in the Bildungsroman, especially in its postcolonial inflections. However, while the reading of postcolonial Bildungsromane as national allegories has been thoroughly discussed (Fernández-Vázquez 86), the nexus of coming of age and childlessness has only been mentioned in passing: Austen briefly discusses British-born Kenyan writer Marjorie Oludhe Macgoye's 1986 Bildungsroman *Coming to Birth*, a novel in which the protagonist's struggles to bear a child take precedence over her formal education. If Austen aptly describes the protagonist's development as a "postcolonial opposition to the 'bookish' Bildungsroman" (224), the wider implications of childlessness in the Bildungsroman still remain to be explored.

Rewriting Childlessness in the Bildungsroman

> Between childhood and adulthood there was no space to grow laterally, and whatever our natural instincts, our parents were determined to clip off any disobedience. (Atta 49)

As mentioned in the introductory remarks of this chapter, in her coming of age, Enitan, the protagonist of Sefi Atta's *Everything Good Will Come*, increasingly distances herself from teleological expectations of longitudinal progress and vertical growth. Instead, she begins to look for lateral growth in the form of political participation and sisterhood. By concentrating on the role of alternative forms of kinship and female activism, she begins to rewrite the vertical narrative of being a daughter, wife, and—finally—mother. While at first sight, such a renegotiation of reproduction and kinship could be read as reminiscent of recent—and often Western—feminist frameworks (see, for instance, Clarke and Haraway),[6] the two other novels discussed in this chapter, that is, *Efuru* and *The Joys of Motherhood*, provide earlier and more direct intertextual reference points to such renegotiations. In fact, by interweaving historical time with Indigenous procreative models and myths, these novels constitute very early subversions of procreative teleologies. Underpinning their exploration of colonial and Indigenous forms of patriarchy with Indigenous models of childlessness and gender-fluidity, as well as social parenthood, *Efuru* and *The Joys of Motherhood* do not only defy the myth of progress through Westernization but, what is more, they also demonstrate how colonization stifled Indigenous forms of female agency and power (Robolin 84; Katrak 159–63; Andrade 101; Amadiume, *Male Daughters* 119–33), and how—by imposing binary understandings of sexual difference—colonialism eroded the flexibility of pre-colonial Igbo gender systems (Amadiume, *Male Daughters* 15, 89–98, 119; "Bodies, Choices" 53). As Ifi Amadiume explains, pre-colonial Igbo gender systems were much more flexible and featured forms of nonbiological, social motherhood, as well as institutions such as woman-to-woman marriage and the gender role of "male daughters," who—without having to become married—could remain in their natal homes, where they could conceive children by lovers (Amadiume, "Bodies, Choices" 59). Both novels allude to such Indigenous alternatives to biological and patrilinear reproduction, especially social motherhood and the practice of the "male daughter." At the same time, by referring to the myth of Uhamiri, a female water deity who grants her followers beauty and wealth but no children, both texts also include an Indigenous model of childlessness.

Efuru

> Efuru slept soundly that night. She dreamt of the woman of the lake, her beauty, her long hair and her riches. She had lived for ages at the bottom of the lake. She was as old as the lake itself. She was happy, she was wealthy. She was beautiful. She gave women beauty and wealth but she had no child. She had never experienced the joy of motherhood. Why then did women worship her? (Nwapa 221)

As indicated in its famous ending, *Efuru*, "the first published novel written by an African woman" (Nnaemeka 140), dispels the myth of the joy of motherhood and the Mother Africa trope by means of the myth of Uhamiri, an ancient matriarchal water goddess (Stratton 88–90; Oloruntoba-Oju and Oloruntoba-Oju 5–6). Ending in a rhetorical question, the answer to which the text has just provided, the novel shows how its protagonist, a follower of the goddess, sleeps soundly and has vivid visions of childfree Uhamiri. This stands in stark contrast to the beginning of the novel when Efuru, the novel's eponymous protagonist, desperately longs to become a mother and undergoes a long ordeal in order to become pregnant. During her first marriage, the protagonist heeds a healer's complicated advice (Nwapa 24–26) and finally does give birth to a daughter. However, Efuru's husband leaves her for another woman, and Efuru's daughter dies. Efuru returns to her father's home, but although the protagonist eventually remarries, she soon realizes she might not be able to bear any more children herself. Not wanting to hinder her second husband from reproducing, Efuru begins to look for another wife for him. At the same time, however, the protagonist changes her own priorities. As she increasingly dreams of Uhamiri, Efuru not only begins to follow the deity's instructions (one of which forbids women to have sexual intercourse with their husbands on Uhamiri's special day) but also begins to re-evaluate her own childlessness (Oloruntoba-Oju and Oloruntoba-Oju 9). While *Efuru* initially depicts its protagonist's fervent wish to become a wife and mother, the novel thus gradually substitutes the myth of the joy of motherhood with the Indigenous myth of Uhamiri.

Highlighting the complex process of how Efuru overcomes the immense procreative pressure in her community, the novel frequently juxtaposes Efuru's thoughts and emotions with the reactions and prevailing opinions in her social environment. In Efuru's social environment, motherhood is considered the ultimate goal, whereas childlessness is regarded as a curse, a failure (Nwapa 165) and leads to social stigma, rejection, and malicious gossip (174–75). Both to illustrate the considerable effort it takes Efuru to withstand this procreative pressure, and to provide representational space to what she refrains from uttering, the text makes Efuru's thoughts and emotions accessible to the reader through internal focalization. Devastated for being "considered barren" (165), the protagonist finds little solace in the fact that, as she has had a child herself, she is not a childless woman but a childless mother (Whitehouse and Hollos 128). Instead, she hopes for another of "those sweet dreams about her [Uhamiri]" (Nwapa 165)—a wish Efuru is granted after she realizes Uhamiri "cannot give [her] children, because she has not got children herself" (165). Having realized this, Efuru is not only able to accept her own inability to reproduce, but is rewarded for this acceptance with her most beautiful vision of Uhamiri so far (165). In the end, the novel presents its protagonist as not only childfree but also as warm-hearted, helpful, and as a successful trader—thus providing a model of female self-formation that does not only dissolve the dichotomy of motherhood and childlessness, but which also transcends reductively defining women in terms of their reproductive role (Oloruntoba-Oju and Oloruntoba-Oju 6).

In this renegotiation of childlessness, *Efuru* tightly interweaves narrative, myth, and a dynamic portrayal of historical time (Lu 128–31). It thereby subverts both the *telos* of motherhood and the myth of an exclusively Indigenous form of patriarchy. By invoking the matriarchal myth of Uhamiri while also drawing on historical events to portray a strong community of women in active subversion of colonial rule (Stratton 88; Andrade 100), the novel de-romanticizes the ideology of motherhood found in Nwapa's male fellow writers (Stratton 39–55, 89–90). At the same time, it "places Achebe's characterization of Igbo society as strictly patriarchal and excessively masculinist under revision" (Stratton 90), and instead serves as a reminder of the pernicious effects of colonialism on women (Stratton 88). Although, prior to colonization, there was no complete sexual equality—as is most visible in practices such as female genital mutilation and polygamy—"the traditional, patriarchal control over a woman's body...was balanced, at least, by a woman's participation in the political sphere" (Katrak 162–63). Under colonial domination, however, the more flexible Igbo gender system was disrupted (Robolin 84) and "traditional sexist structures within Igbo society were reinforced by Western sexual mores dictated by Victorial [sic] morality and Christian missionary zeal, for instance, the Victorian belief that a woman's place was in the home and not in the space of business or politics" (Katrak 160–61). As a result, "administrative, evangelical, legal, and economic institutions and social structures—in addition to educational ones—in colonial life converged to systematically remove African women from the domain of social and cultural power to which they were privy prior to the advent of colonialism" (Robolin 84).[7]

Although the novel strongly emphasizes Indigenous forms of female agency and solidarity (for instance, Nwapa 106–11, 216–17; Andrade 99–100), the text's negotiation of childlessness does not establish new dichotomies. While the myth of Uhamiri provides the main impetus for both Efuru's re-evaluation of childlessness and her development in general, the novel still includes the information that motherless Efuru was raised by Dr. Uzaru's mother, a Western-educated woman (Nwapa 96; Lu 137). Interestingly, however, this information is mentioned only in passing and does not suggest that Efuru's reconceptualization of childlessness is mainly due to some Westernized influence. In fact, the text only states that Efuru "learnt cooking, baking and sewing from the doctor's mother" (Nwapa 96), skills missionaries often taught girls to prepare them for Christian marriage and motherhood (Katrak 162). Thus reflecting that education as introduced by the British increased gender inequality (162), this information complements the myth of Uhamiri in two ways. While it, firstly, implies that a "very respectable" and headstrong woman (Nwapa 96) served as a role model for Efuru, it also briefly alludes to social parenthood as another option in the spectrum between childlessness and motherhood (Lu 137). Throughout the whole novel, it is consequently strong matriarchal figures who—in lieu of the Bildungsroman's typical mentors—foster Efuru's formation—a formation that is not framed as logocentric education but in terms of the protagonist's turn to female networks.

In general, *Efuru* rewrites generic conventions by delinking the Bildungsroman's functions and temporalities from procreative teleologies. Beginning where traditionally most Bildungsromane end, that is, with marriage (which, in Efuru's case, is unconventional as she enters into it without her father's consent) (7), the novel subverts the procreative plot by showing how Efuru's main coming of age does not culminate in marriage but in turning to female solidarity when she becomes a worshipper of Uhamiri. Thus, rewriting both logocentric notions of *Bildung* and the temporal setting of the Bildungsroman, *Efuru* renegotiates the trope of childlessness not only on the level of plot but—by not depicting the protagonist as a child herself— the novel also iterates the trope of childlessness in its temporal frame. Thereby actualizing the absent presence of children in many Bildungsromane, the text questions schematic developmental stages and their concluding demarcation by gendered conventions such as marriage or reproduction in the genre. So although some critics suggest the novel's plot does not use the myth of Uhamiri or Igbo gender flexibility to their full potential (Amadiume, "Bodies, Choices" 60; see also Jell-Bahlsen 253; Krishnan 9), *Efuru*'s formal properties profoundly subvert some implicit repronormative functions and temporalities that underlie the Bildungsroman's generic genealogy.

The Joys of Motherhood

> "God, when will you create a woman who will be fulfilled in herself, a full human being, not anybody's appendage?" [Nnu Ego] prayed desperately. "After all, I was born alone, and I shall die alone…Yes, I have many children, but what do I feed them on? On my life, I have to work myself to the bone to look after them; I have to give them my all. And if I am lucky enough to die in peace, I even have to give them my soul. They will worship my dead spirit to provide for them…When will I be free?"… "Never, not even in death. I am a prisoner of my own flesh and blood."
> (Emecheta 209–10)

Featuring the end of *Efuru* as its own title and displaying numerous other similarities with Nwapa's text, Buchi Emecheta's novel, *The Joys of Motherhood*, can be read as "pick[ing] up where [*Efuru*] left off" and as "us[ing its] characters to continue to explore more possible ways to view and experience motherhood and marriage in an increasingly industrialized and capitalized Nigeria" (Lu 135). In fact, *Efuru* and *The Joys of Motherhood* share numerous similarities. Both texts allude to the gender-fluid practice of "male daughters." Explicitly representing how Ona, Nnu Ego's mother, stays in her father's house, refuses to marry, but has a relationship with Nnu Ego's father, the later text renders explicit to what *Efuru* only alludes to when its eponymous protagonist returns to her father's house after her separations. Moreover, in both novels, the protagonists come from Igbo villages, and their mothers die during childbirth. Not only do both protagonists marry twice, but both Efuru and Nnu Ego also withstand great pressure because of their difficulties in conceiving children (Stratton 111). However, as Stratton remarks, "Emecheta underscores the irony of Nwapa's question [at the end of the novel] by departing from Nwapa's narrative. Nnu Ego spends most of her adult life in Lagos and she eventually experiences 'the joy(s) of motherhood' many times over. As a result, her life becomes a cumulation of miseries" (111), and—despite her having seven surviving children, Nnu Ego dies alone at the side of a road. Reiterating *Efuru*'s turn towards Uhamiri's childless cult, *The Joys of Motherhood* closes with the remark that, although people start "appeal[ing] to her to make women fertile" (Emecheta 254), Nnu Ego does not answer any prayers for children.

While at first sight it might seem that the protagonist in *The Joys of Motherhood*—with her continuing adherence to the ideal of motherhood—does not manage to grow into an independent individual (Robolin 82), the novel reframes the temporal generic conventions of the Bildungsroman so skillfully that it offers a simultaneous representation of Nnu Ego's desperate wish for hers to be a teleological narrative resulting in motherhood and of the great pain this causes her. Thus demonstrating how much its protagonist wishes for her story to *be* a teleological Bildungsroman, the novel not only illustrates how much this form needs to be rewritten if it is not to crush its own protagonist under procreative pressure, but the text already begins this process of rewriting. Besides the novel's interweaving of historical time and myth, it is mainly the text's temporal reframing that rewrites the generic conventions of the Bildungsroman.

Undermining not only the *telos* of motherhood implied in its own title but also the implicit procreation plot of many Bildungsromane, *The Joys of Motherhood* features a frame of death and childlessness instead of a frame of procreation and motherhood. Reversing any forward and procreative motion, the novel opens with a backwards movement of its protagonist. After she discovers that her child has just died, "Nnu Ego back[s] out of the room" (Emecheta 1) and tries to commit suicide. Through an almost cinematic depiction, in which the time of narration approximately equals narrated time, Nnu Ego's shock and desperation at having lost her baby are vividly illustrated; they find verbal expression when, hindered from jumping from Carter Bridge, she exclaims, "'But I am not a woman any more! I am not a mother any more'" (65). Intercalating the background story of Nnu Ego's own conception into a drastic rendering of child death and the protagonist's attempted suicide, *The Joys of Motherhood* therefore criticizes an exclusively procreative framing of female identity from the beginning. Throughout the novel, the text upholds this criticism by means of its chapter headings. At first sight, most of these chapter headings ("The Mother," "The Mother's Mother," "The Mother's Early Life," "First Shocks of Motherhood," "A Failed Woman," and "The Canonised Mother") might be seen as "revolving around [Nnu Ego's] success and failure as a mother" (Katrak 166). However, the content of the chapters continually questions both the idealization and the absolute privileging of motherhood, especially by presenting death as a counterpoint to childbirth:

> The first chapter of the novel is called "The Mother." It tells of Nnu Ego's attempted suicide following the death of her first baby. The second chapter, "The Mother's Mother," concludes by relating the death of Nnu Ego's mother, Ona, in childbirth, while the circumstances of Nnu Ego's own death are recounted in the final chapter, ironically entitled "The Canonised Mother." (Stratton 113)

Even though on the surface level it might seem that in *The Joys of Motherhood* "womanhood is defined exclusively as motherhood" (Katrak 166), the novel subverts the *telos* of motherhood by rewriting the procreative expectations of the Bildungsroman. In fact, the novel not only presents Nnu Ego's increasing disillusionment with "the joys of motherhood" as her most important development, but it also reframes the predominant procreative plot of the Bildungsroman by interrupting the cycle of reproduction by means of a frame of death.

Despite Nnu Ego's initial refusal to dismiss her prioritization of motherhood, the novel does not cast Nnu Ego's motherhood as the end point of her self-formation. Instead, the latter results from Nnu Ego's disillusionment with idealized motherhood and from the agency she gains when she refuses to grant other childless women children after her own death. If Nnu Ego thus gains a certain level of agency after she dies, this agency does not result from procreation, that is, from the fact that her children perpetuate her memory or that she herself helps women to procreate, but, in contrast, it stems from her refusal to be continually reduced to producing children (Robolin 88). On the level of form, Nnu Ego's growing disillusionment, desperation, and concomitant changing stance on procreation are conveyed by the increasing use of free indirect discourse towards the end of the novel (for instance, Emecheta 208, 219). Faced with numerous injustices when she is pregnant with twins again, Nnu Ego begins to prefer death over motherhood, and her desperation gains a much more immediate and urgent note: "Oh, God, please kill her with these babies she was carrying, rather than let the children she had hoped for so much pour sand into her eyes" (208).

In Nnu Ego's process of self-formation, the use of myth plays an important, albeit more ambiguous, role than in *Efuru*. In *The Joys of Motherhood*, the myth of Uhamiri is invoked through Nnu Ego's *chi*, her guiding spirit. This *chi* is an enslaved woman who refused to be buried alive with her mistress, Nnu Ego's father's wife. When Agbadi, Nnu Ego's father, impregnates Ona, Nnu Ego's mother, his wife falls ill and dies. When the enslaved woman struggles to survive, she is hit on the head with a cutlass and buried with her mistress. As Nnu Ego is born with a mark on her head similar to the one the cutlass left on the enslaved woman's head, the latter is said to be her *chi*. At first, Nnu Ego thinks her *chi* is punishing her by not granting her any children as revenge for being murdered (Emecheta 3) and implores her to stop haunting her: "'O my chi, why do you have to bring me so low? Why must I be so punished? I am sorry for what my father did and I am sure he is sorry too. But try to forgive us'" (30). Increasingly, however, her *chi* becomes a more positive presence for Nnu Ego, and the protagonist learns that "her *chi* would not give her a child because she had been dedicated to a river goddess before Agbadi took her away in slavery" (30). As Florence Stratton argues, "the slave woman is, then, in this revised version of her story, an avatar of both Efuru and Uhamiri" (112). However, while Uhamiri grants her worshippers wealth and beauty but no children, this is reversed in *The Joys of Motherhood*:

> Just as Efuru dreams of Uhamiri, so Nnu Ego dreams of her *chi*. But what the slave woman offers her is not beauty or wealth but the one gift that Uhamiri withholds from her worshippers: children. Emecheta intensifies the irony by making the offer subject to certain economic conditions. Thus, while as yet financially secure, the apparently barren Nnu Ego dreams of her *chi* taunting her by holding out a beautiful baby boy and then vanishing. Shortly afterwards, Nnu Ego gives birth to a son who dies in infancy. Some time later when she and her husband are experiencing privation, Nnu Ego has a similar dream. On this occasion the baby is extremely dirty, and her *chi*, mocking Nnu Ego with laughter, tells her she can have as many babies of this kind as she wants. Soon Nnu Ego, who has repeatedly implored her *chi* to allow her to conceive, is encumbered with a bevy of children that she cannot afford to feed, clothe, or educate. Like *Efuru*, then, *The Joys of Motherhood* defines its heroine's experience through her psychic identification with a deity. But while the myth of Uhamiri specifies a paradigm of female transcendence, the slave woman's story tells of entrapment and defeat. (112)

Despite these differences, however, in the end, "in her refusal to answer prayers for children, Nnu Ego becomes after death, as the enslaved woman, her *chi*, had before her, like Uhamiri" (119). Not only does the story of the *chi* thus evoke the myth of Uhamiri, but, as its presence changes from a bad omen to a positive presence and even a role model throughout the novel, it also creates a similar structure as the use of myth in *Efuru*, that is, a chiastic re-evaluation of childlessness and motherhood that opens up the spectrum in between by offering the option of being childfree and of female solidarity. While Nnu Ego's economic conditions prevent her from realizing the full potential of female solidarity, and she understands "that she would have been better off had she had time to cultivate those women who had offered her hands of friendship" (Emecheta 247, see also Derrickson), female friendship plays a prominent role from the beginning in the negotiation of coming of age and childlessness in the next novel, *Everything Good Will Come*.

Everything Good Will Come

> "You have not grown up," she [Mother of Prisons] said. "You're still a child…Shame on you. Shame. Bringing another child into the world." (Atta 273)

In many ways, *Everything Good Will Come* continues the re-evaluation of childlessness and the role it plays in the developments of the female protagonists in *Efuru* and *The Joys of Motherhood*. In addition to including allusions to myths of infertility, the novel reiterates elements such as the doubling of characters and a cooking strike (Emecheta 148–52). Moreover, and similarly to *Efuru*, *Everything Good Will Come* also relegates Westernized influences on the protagonist's education to the background (Feldner 177), instead foregrounding *Bildung* in the sense of social learning (Austen 218). Most importantly, however, in *Everything Good Will Come*, Enitan's decision to leave her husband on the day of her daughter's naming ceremony to become an activist for female prisoners does not simply appear as an intertextual reference to *The Joys of Motherhood*, but as a continuation of this motif. While *The Joys of Motherhood* employs the gendered trope of the prisoner to explore the relationship between slavery, colonialism, and motherhood (Emecheta 153, 209–10; Robolin 78–79), *Everything Good Will Come* reifies and rewrites this trope. After a reading in support of imprisoned journalists, Enitan is imprisoned for one night herself. During her hours in an overcrowded prison cell, she almost has another miscarriage when she is confronted with the dire reality of female prisoners who are detained without trial (Atta 264–81). Sensing Enitan's unfamiliarity with the fate of the underprivileged, one of the detainees accuses the protagonist of still being a child herself. According to the detainee, Enitan's decision to have a child underlines rather than changes the protagonist's inexperience. Fittingly called "Mother of Prisons," this detainee thus powerfully questions the status of motherhood as the *telos* of female growth. Brief though her imprisonment is, it leaves a lasting impression on Enitan. Instead of continuing to follow the linear narrative of development as a wife and mother, Enitan becomes an advocate for women prisoners. As her husband objects to this, Enitan leaves her marriage, which, for her, has become a prison itself. While Enitan's father challenges his daughter's comparison of women to prisoners by raising the question of choice and agency, Enitan uses the metaphor of "women in home prisons" (326) to describe "a condition of the mind" (326–27).

In its continuance of Nwapa's and especially Emecheta's re-evaluation of childlessness in processes of female self-formation, *Everything Good Will Come* relies on—but at the same time critically questions—the generic conventions of the Bildungsroman. Although the novel has a linear and conventional structure consisting of four chronological parts, it continually challenges the seemingly inextricable link between the conventionalized steps in a girl's life—education, but also menarche, the loss of virginity, marriage, and motherhood—and coming of age. In order to do so, it focuses on events that counterpoint the alleged importance of said steps, and it has its autodiegetic narrator comment on and question exclusively linear narratives of vertical and longitudinal female growth towards motherhood, while presenting female solidarity as a chance for lateral growth instead. From the beginning, the novel focuses on the tension between gendered expectations and the narrator's own inclinations:

> From the beginning, I believed whatever I was told, downright lies even, about how best to behave, although I had my own inclinations. At an age when other Nigerian girls were masters at ten-ten, the game in which we stamped our feet in rhythm and tried to outwit partners with sudden knee jerks, my favorite moments were spent sitting on a jetty pretending to fish. My worst was to hear my mother's shout from the kitchen window: "Enitan, come and help in here." (Atta 7)

While through scenes such as the above the novel illustrates Enitan's attempts at distancing herself from gendered expectations, it simultaneously demonstrates how difficult her socialization makes it for her *not* to measure her own progress in terms of bodily growth and fertility: "I worried about breaking school rules, failing exams. I even worried about being skinny, and for a while I worried that I might be a hermaphrodite, like an earthworm, because my periods hadn't started. Then they did and my mother killed a fowl to secure my fertility" (52).

In order to criticize the repronormative measurement of female development in terms of fertility, and to reframe the experiences that Enitan's younger self underwent, the novel substitutes the typical ironic distance of the mature narrator (Hirsch 298) with supportive and solidary comments of the older narrator, such as the following:

> People say I was hot-headed in my twenties. I don't ever remember being hot-headed. I only ever remember calling out to my voice. In my country, women are praised the more they surrender their right to protest. In the end they may die with nothing but selflessness to pass on to their daughters; a startling legacy, like tears down a parched throat. (Atta 179)

While the autodiegetic narrator thus opens the last of the novel's four parts by openly criticizing how little voice women have, at the same time she presents a complicated picture of conflicting desires throughout this part. In fact, the novel juxtaposes different scenes connected to gendered expectations in order to forego a linear narrative of progress. The following excerpt, in which Enitan refuses to serve her husband and his friends drinks and he stops speaking to her, shows how much the protagonist oscillates between her wish for emancipation and a family:

> In my 29 years no man ever told me to show respect. No man ever needed to. I had seen how women respected men and ended up shouldering burdens like one of those people who carried firewood on their heads, with their necks as high as church spires and foreheads crushed...As far back as my grandmother's generation we'd been getting degrees and holding careers. My mother's generation were the pioneer professionals.

> We, their daughters, were expected to continue. We had no choice in the present recession…It was an overload of duties, I thought, sometimes self-imposed. And the expectation of subordination bothered me most… But no one I knew had left a man because he sulked, and I wanted a family, and I'd seen how Niyi grieved for his…I got pregnant and shortly after had a miscarriage. (186–87)

When, after two years, Enitan has still not carried a child to full term, she becomes increasingly desperate to become pregnant, and she even relinquishes her voice in order to become a mother:

> In no time at all Niyi and I began to quarrel about the fertility regime… I stared at other people's children imagining their soft, sticky hands in mine, worked myself into false morning sickness and cursed out loud when my periods started…Soon I convinced myself that it was a punishment; something I'd done, said, I remembered the story of Obatala who once caused women on earth to be barren. I made apologies to her. I remembered also, how I'd opened my mouth once too often and thought that if I said another bad word, had another bad thought, I would remain childless, so I swallowed my voice for penitence. (189)

While in their negotiations of childlessness, the earlier two Igbo novels invoke the matriarchal myth of Uhamiri in support of their protagonists, in *Everything Good Will Come*, Enitan's encounter with the Yoruba god Obatala has a much more ambivalent effect. In her earlier and formative relationship with Mike, an artist, Enitan admires Mike's artistic take on Obatala, who portrays "the creator of the human form" (112) as "a naked woman with muscular shoulders, in black and white beading" (111). However, when Enitan finds Mike with another woman, the protagonist smashes Mike's Obatala (Atta 154–55; Owonibi and Gaji 116–18). Years later, when Enitan desperately tries to become pregnant, she questions her past choices—of destroying Obatala, but also of speaking up. Until she finds out she is pregnant again, she thus remains silent.

Although Enitan was born in the year of Nigerian independence, and even though the novel tightly interweaves her development with the historical background of the time, *Everything Good Will Come* is neither just a national allegory nor does it employ Bildungsroman conventions without reflecting on them critically. In fact, the novel, through juxtaposition and narratorial comments, shows the great influence that conventions—including myths—have on the protagonist—and how long it takes her to be able to reach the critical distance she displays towards them in her ulterior narration. In its negotiation of childlessness and focus on lateral growth, the novel consequently not only foregoes vertical narratives but questions metanarratives altogether:

> When people speak of turning points in their lives it makes me wonder. I can't think of one moment that made me an advocate for women prisoners in my country. Before this, I had opportunities to take action, only to end up behaving in ways I was accustomed, courting the same old frustrations because I was sure of what I would feel: wronged, helpless, stuck in a day when I was fourteen years old. Here it is: changes came after I made them, each one small. (Atta 332)

If *The Joys of Motherhood* casts Nnu Ego's disillusionment and the agency she gains after her death as the ending of its story, *Everything Good Will Come* further undermines the nexus of coming of age and becoming a wife and mother. The future-bound focus of the novel's title, assumed at the very end of the novel, seems to confirm this: although Enitan has become a mother, the use of the title in the last scene suggests there is a further goal to reach.

The Postcolonial Bildungsroman: From Childless to Childfree?

What *Everything Good Will Come* shares with *Efuru* and *The Joys of Motherhood* is not just the common focus on the role of childlessness in processes of female self-formation but also the structural subversion of the dichotomy between childlessness and motherhood. Most strikingly, all three novels collapse the initial dichotomous evaluations of motherhood as the desirable goal and of childlessness as a calamity into a structure that dissolves the teleological end point of motherhood into a spectrum that—without rejecting motherhood per se—covers not only the opposite ends of de-idealizing motherhood and introducing childfree options, but which, by focusing on criticizing procreative pressure, mainly negotiates the ground in between. In order to do so, the novels disturb the procreation plot and structurally displace motherhood. While the novels all feature absent mothers (two of whom died in childbirth) (Owonibi and Gaji 112), so that motherhood is not portrayed as the starting point, the texts do not use motherhood as their climax or end point either. Thus replacing the teleological frame of motherhood with a focus on childlessness, the novels manage to portray how their female protagonists are pressured into, if not reduced to, producing children, especially sons, while at the same time countering this reduction of women to their reproductive abilities by featuring a diverse cast of women. In this, the combined use of doubling and a critical stance towards procreative myths plays a prominent role. In all three novels, structures of doubling serve as "a major narrative strategy" to present "intersecting stories of other women as they experience the combined burdens of womanhood, blackness, and poverty" (Wilson-Tagoe 189), and "to challenge some of the orthodoxies of male literary representation" (Stratton 117). Although the structure of paired women is already present in *Efuru* and *The Joys of Motherhood*, *Everything Good Will Come* modifies the use of doubling found in the earlier novels. While *Efuru* and *The Joys of Motherhood* feature both actual and mythical doubles, in *Everything Good Will Come*, mythical doubles give way to actual doubles. Rather than serving as a means of antitheses (117), in Atta's novel, doubling serves as a means of "composite characterization," which helps to "reshape the classic *Bildungsroman* to reflect the various ramifications of the feminine condition" (Wilson-Tagoe 189).

With their focus on the role of gendered expectations of procreation in their protagonists' processes of self-formation, the three Bildungsromane discussed in this chapter might, in a more reductionist reading, be simplistically interpreted as the difficult coming-of-age stories of women in a patriarchal society (Okuyade 152–53). While none of these texts are opposed to motherhood as such, all of them portray their protagonists' development mainly in terms of their increasing disillusionment with the idealization and privileging of motherhood, and with the procreative pressure this entails. In doing so, the novels rewrite the procreation plot found in many Bildungsromane, and they thereby also demonstrate that procreative pressure is not just an issue in the societies they portray but is also present in the genre itself. Thus, the three novels reveal that many teleological Bildungsromane do not only rely on the assumption that children are not fully formed people—an assumption often underlined by the generic ironic distance of the mature narrator—but that they also often feature the end point of reproduction. The novels discussed here can consequently not just be read as a criticism of patriarchal practices—of both Indigenous and colonial origin—in the respective societies. In fact, through their focus on childlessness and the processes of social learning it engenders, these novels transcend a mainly logocentric understanding of *Bildung* and unmask double standards in natalist/anti-natalist discourses. They show that while natalist pressure is framed as a problem of the Global South (as becomes visible in discourse on the correlation of demographic development, birth control, and progress), it is also deeply inscribed in the repronormative narrative conventions of a genre that originated in the Global North.

In order to diversify these vertical and longitudinal genre conventions, the three novels rewrite narratives of being a daughter, wife, and mother into stories of lateral growth and solidarity. While rewriting has always been part of the long history of the Bildungsroman, and subversions of hetero- and repronormative poetics can also be found in other, especially queer, Bildungsromane (Miller), *Efuru* and *The Joys of Motherhood* constitute very early examples of such rewriting. By using Indigenous myths, these novels not only gradually debunk the idealization of motherhood but they also dismantle the myth that patriarchy is an exclusively Indigenous phenomenon of allegedly underdeveloped societies and that it might be overcome by modernization along Western lines. In fact, by also alluding to more flexible Igbo gender roles, as well as by rewriting the temporality of the Bildungsroman through the depiction of their protagonists' development after childhood, *Efuru* and *The Joys of Motherhood* question beliefs of adults as fully formed people, and they render visible the present absence of children in many Bildungsromane. Thus actualizing the trope of childlessness on the level of form, the novels differentiate childlessness on the level of content by opening a spectrum that also spans childfree options. Reading these—and further—postcolonial Bildungsromane with regard to tropes of childlessness consequently does not only approach the Bildungsroman from a perspective that has so far remained mostly implicit. It also shows how postcolonial studies can help to further develop approaches that explore the interdependence of narrative and reproduction, which, so far, often come from the field of queer theory (see, for instance, Edelman, Roof, McBean).

Notes

1. A heartfelt thank you to my colleagues at the University of Oldenburg for discussing the outline of this chapter with me, and to Anika Mikulski for her excellent research assistance.
2. The novels discussed in this chapter achieve their critique of procreative pressure mainly by focusing on their female protagonists' coming of age. Nigerian writer Ayòbámi Adébáyò's 2017 debut novel *Stay with Me* would constitute a further interesting case study, as it expands the focus on coming of age and childlessness by exploring how the pressure to procreate affects women *and* men—with the former, however, being the ones who suffer the most.
3. Due to the early subversive potential of Nwapa's and Emecheta's novels, this chapter does not read the three novels as a series of teleological growth organized into generations. Although female Nigerian writers are often grouped into first to third generations, the focus will instead be on the intricate networks of similarities between the texts.
4. I borrow the expression "procreation plot" from Matz (10).
5. Hirsch differentiates between the two: "The distinction between the 'developmental,' 'exemplary' plot, on the one hand, and the 'mimetic,' 'chronological' one, on the other, goes back to E.M. Forster's differentiation between 'life by values' and 'life by time'" (306).
6. For a critique of the universalization of Western feminist theories, see Mohanty.
7. For differences in female independence within various Igbo societies, see Stratton (112).

Works Cited

Adébáyò, Ayòbámi. *Stay With Me*. Canongate, 2018.
Alcott, Louisa May. *Little Women*. Oxford University Press, 2008 (1868–1869).

Amadiume, Ifi. "Bodies, Choices, Globalizing Neocolonial Enchantments: African Matriarchs and Mammy Water." *Meridians*, vol. 2, no. 2, 2002, pp. 41–66.

Amadiume, Ifi. *Male Daughters, Female Husbands: Gender and Sex in an African Society*. Zed Books, 2015 (1987).

Amoko, Apollo. "Autobiography and Bildungsroman in African Literature." *The Cambridge Companion to the African Novel*, edited by Abiola Irele, Cambridge University Press, 2009, pp. 195–208.

Andrade, Susan Z. "Rewriting History, Motherhood, and Rebellion: Naming an African Women's Literary Tradition." *Research in African Literatures*, vol. 21, no. 1, 1990, pp. 91–110.

Atta, Sefi. *Everything Good Will Come*. Interlink, 2016 (2005).

Austen, Ralph A. "Struggling with the African Bildungsroman." *Research in African Literatures*, vol. 46, no. 3, 2015, pp. 214–31.

Baldick, Chris. "*Bildungsroman*." *Oxford Dictionary of Literary Terms*, Oxford University Press, 2008, p. 35.

Clarke, Adele, and Donna Haraway, editors. *Making Kin Not Population: Reconceiving Generations*. Prickly Paradigm, 2018.

Derrickson, Teresa. "Class, Culture, and the Colonial Context: The Status of Women in Buchi Emecheta's *The Joys of Motherhood*." *International Fiction Review*, vol. 29, no. 1, 2002, pp. 40–49.

Edelman, Lee. *No Future: Queer Theory and the Death Drive*. Duke University Press, 2004.

Emecheta, Buchi. *The Joys of Motherhood*. Heinemann, 2008 (1979).

Farah, Nuruddin. *Maps*. Penguin, 2000 (1986).

Feldner, Maximilian. "Returning to Nigeria: Teju Cole's *Every Day Is for the Thief* (2006) and Sefi Atta's *Everything Good Will Come* (2005)." *Narrating the New African Diaspora*, edited by Maximilian Feldner, Palgrave Macmillan, 2019, pp. 165–84.

Ferguson, Susan. "Social Reproduction: What's the Big Idea?" *PlutoPress*, https://www.plutobooks.com/blog/social-reproduction-theory-ferguson/.

Fernández-Vázquez, José-Santiago. "Recharting the Geography of Genre: Ben Okri's *The Famished Road* as a Postcolonial *Bildungsroman*." *The Journal of Commonwealth Literature*, vol. 37, no. 2, 2002, pp. 85–106.

Graham, Sarah, editor. *A History of the Bildungsroman*. Cambridge University Press, 2019.

Hay, Simon. "*Nervous Conditions*, Lukács, and the Postcolonial Bildungsroman." *Genre: Forms of Discourse and Culture*, vol. 46, no. 3, 2013, pp. 317–44.

Hirsch, Marianne. "The Novel of Formation as Genre: Between Great Expectations and Lost Illusions in Studies in the Novel." *Genre Norman NY*, vol. 12, no. 3, 1979, pp. 293–311.

Hoagland, Ericka A. "The Postcolonial Bildungsroman." Graham, pp. 217–38.

Jell-Bahlsen, Sabine. "Flora Nwapa and Oguta's Lake Goddess: Artistic Liberty and Ethnography." *Dialectical Anthropology*, vol. 31, 2007, pp. 253–62.

Katrak, Ketu H. "3. Womanhood/Motherhood: Variations on a Theme in Selected Novels of Buchi Emecheta." *The Journal of Commonwealth Literature*, vol. 22, no. 1, 1987, pp. 159–70.

Krishnan, Madhu. "Mami Wata and the Occluded Feminine in Anglophone Nigerian Literature." *Research in African Literatures*, vol. 43, no. 1, 2012, pp. 1–18.

Lea, Daniel. "Bildungsroman." *The Routledge Dictionary of Literary Terms*, edited by Peter Childs and Roger Fowler, Routledge, 2006, pp. 18–20.

Lu, Nick T.C. "Between Tradition and Modernity: Practical Resistance and Reform of Culture in Flora Nwapa's *Efuru*." *Research in African Literatures*, vol. 50, no. 2, 2019, pp. 123–41.

Matz, Aaron. "Hardy and the Vanity of Procreation." *Victorian Studies*, vol. 57, no. 1, 2014, pp. 7–32.

McBean, Sam. "Digital Intimacies and Queer Narratives." *The Edinburgh Companion to Contemporary Narrative Theories*, edited by Zara Dinnen and Robyn Warhol, Edinburgh University Press, 2018, pp. 132–44.

Miller, Meredith. "Lesbian, Gay and Trans Bildungsromane." Graham, pp. 239–66.

Mohanty, Chandra Talpade. "Under Western Eyes: Feminist Scholarship and Colonial Discourses." *Boundary*, vol. 2, nos. 12.3/13.1, 1984, pp. 333–58.

Nnaemeka, Obioma. "From Orality to Writing: African Women Writers and the (Re)Inscription of Womanhood." *Research in African Literatures*, vol. 25, no. 4, 1994, pp. 137–57.

Nwapa, Flora. *Efuru*. Waveland Press, 2013 (1966).

Okuyade, Ogaga. "Narrating Growth in the Nigerian Female Bildungsroman." *The AnaChronisT*, vol. 16, 2011, pp. 152–70.

Oloruntoba-Oju, Omotayo, and Taiwo Oloruntoba-Oju. "Models in the Construction of Female Identity in Nigerian Postcolonial Literature." *Tydskrif Vir Letterkunde*, vol. 50, no. 2, 2013, pp. 5–18.

Owonibi, Sola, and Olufunmilayo Gaji. "Identity and the Absent Mother in Atta's *Everything Good Will Come*." *Tydskrif Vir Letterkunde*, vol. 54, no. 2, 2017, pp. 112–21.

Redfield, Marc. *Phantom Formations: Aesthetic Ideology and the Bildungsroman*. Cornell University Press, 1996.

Robolin, Stéphane. "Gendered Hauntings: *The Joys of Motherhood*, Interpretive Acts, and Postcolonial Theory." *Research in African Literatures*, vol. 35, no. 3, 2004, pp. 76–92.

Roof, Judith. *Come as You Are: Sexuality and Narrative*. Columbia University Press, 1996.

Sheldon, Rebekah. *The Child to Come: Life after the Human Catastrophe*. Minnesota University Press, 2016.

Sterne, Laurence. *The Life and Opinions of Tristram Shandy, Gentleman.* Knopf, 1991 (1759–1767).
Stratton, Florence. *Contemporary African Literature and the Politics of Gender.* Taylor & Francis, 1994.
Whitehouse, Bruce, and Marida Hollos. "Definitions and the Experience of Fertility Problems: Infertile and Sub-Fertile Women, Childless Mothers, and Honorary Mothers in Two Southern Nigerian Communities." *Medical Anthropology Quarterly*, vol. 28, no. 1, 2014, pp. 122–39.
Wilson-Tagoe, Nana. "The African Novel and the Feminine Condition." *The Cambridge Companion to the African Novel*, edited by Abiola Irele, Cambridge University Press, 2009, pp. 177–94.

AFTERWORD

Sarah Brouillette

This book makes a great case for the Bildungsroman as a form that has been of productive and even signal interest to postcolonial writers. Previous scholarship on the Bildungsroman has established it as a genre often present in the shape of a departure from it—and this is the source of its longevity, as it is made newly relevant whenever a writer struggles with it (see Castle; Esty). Conceptually rich and complicated in ways that help writers define themselves and their own projects, it is as a genre, as Jed Esty argues, an "empty set" that is present in literary history mainly through its "negation, deviation, variation, and mutation" (18). Yet this volume's charting of the Bildungsroman's postcolonial afterlives reminds us it is also very full—its available meanings and applications overdetermined by the genre's relation to colonial history. Deviation from its scripts is part of an anti-colonial imagination that is explored across the chapters here, because the Bildungsroman's particular ways of seeing and scripting a life make it complicitly colonial. A primary instance is, as José-Santiago Fernández-Vázquez studies, the coming-of-age narrative in which the colonial subject is associated with childhood, trapped in an early stage of nondevelopment that the colonizer ushers them out of. The postcolonial Bildungsroman dwells in the racism and violence that are the subtext of the tale of colonial maturation.

For me, a representative text here will always be Tsitsi Dangarembga's *Nervous Conditions*, in which Tambu's development is presented ironically from a future vantage, with an awareness of what she has had to enact and endure to achieve her "liberation" from her rural village. Mainly, the novel impugns the *Bildung* as a script imposed by the Rhodesian colonial education system, which would select only a few Black children for cultivation and development towards European models of success—towards England itself, eventually, if one progresses far enough to move on to Oxbridge, with the help even of a Rhodes Scholarship, itself a prestigious engine of *Bildung*. Of course, the very presence of the white colonial elite in Rhodesia doling out its ostensible largesse to a few select candidates, funded largely by profits derived from Africans working in mines, nullifies any claims to benevolence they might want to make.

Like Dangarembga's novel, the contributions to this book tell us that the suppositions of the *Bildung* narrative have always been in question, as postcolonial engagement with the form was always wary and dismantling. What is there to say, then, about the situation in which we find the Bildungsroman today? This postcolonial wariness is intensified and heightened, I want to argue, such that the Bildungsroman has become a residual form—an almost purely historical imaginary, whose contemporary relevance is precisely as something definitively behind us. There are determinate historical transformations at work here. The conditions that made the Bildungsroman a primary literary and social form no longer exist, and reading this book made me reflect on how obscene it would be to lament this fact.

Let's dwell further on the association between underdevelopment and childhood. In this story, the individual and the nation are joined in their relative infancy, to be overcome through their maturation via colonial administration of what amounts to enlightened modernity: individualism, secularity, science and reason, and—crucially—integration into the capitalist economic order through urbanization, growth in waged workforce participation, infrastructure development, and the administrative nation-state extracting and controlling taxation and public spending. The infantile stage of agrarianism would thereby be displaced by industrialization and market expansion overseen by colonial and then postcolonial technocrats, which would increase general wealth and therefore raise "living standards," before finally a growing tertiary service sector would signal the relative leisure and ease of the fully developed wealthy nation. A capitalist *Bildung* set to take place in every postcolony.

Yet this was all a massive deception. The reality instead has been one of uneven urbanization and of accumulation of wealth for a few, but without significant growth in formal employment, and without sustained or prolonged development in the form of state distribution of taxes for social services and infrastructures. Looking at the case of Tanzania, Phillip Neel has recently shown that "premature deindustrialization" best describes the situation there today, signalling not just a trajectory of nondevelopment in one nation but rather a "major change in the structural character of growth in developing economies" writ large (97). The idealist end point of "'maturity' defined by the final ascent of 'postindustrial' employment in services" (99) has not only failed to materialize: "countries are jumping from a largely rural economy marked by high levels of subsistence to an increasingly urban and seemingly postindustrial economic base at lower and lower income levels, with shorter and shorter periods of industrialization in between" (102). This limits any positive wage gains and any of development's beneficial outcomes, while "still accompanied by many of its negative externalities, such as environmental pollution and mass eviction conducted in the name of urban development" (103). People living in cities looking for work are not finding formal industrial employment. Instead, they are turning to informal work, and to fitful handicraft production and semi-services, which means accepting pay that isn't regulated by legal minimums while enduring forms of work discipline—responsibilities to family, the sheer need to survive—that really cannot be escaped nor fought against through labour agitation.

This is the global deformation and disintegration of work that defines our present. Phil Jones points to "sections of the global populace rendered outside of the economy proper," though still dependent on it, in generalized conditions of "sluggish growth, proletarianization and declining labor demand." Often educated but "cut adrift from the formal labour market," they will take on almost any work as "grim sanctuary" that does little to alleviate poverty (3–4). They live by moving in and out of relation to a capitalist system that is "no longer creating enough new jobs for the growing numbers brought into the sphere of capital," with its "ever slowing rate of job creation and the ever more rapidly expanding pool of workers dependent on a wage" (18). To describe what results from these conditions, Alcinda Honwana develops the idea of "waithood," and argues that across Africa more and more young people "are living in a period of suspension between childhood and adulthood," as they cannot find work, cannot afford to live alone, cannot get married and start families. "This state of limbo is becoming pervasive and is gradually replacing conventional adulthood," she argues, as their crises of "joblessness and restricted futures" become increasingly common ("'Waithood'" 28).

While capitalism continues to define the terms of social relations—one has to pay to eat, one has to find work to earn money—secure opportunities to enter into the labour circuit are continuously diminishing. The kinds of work that are today's global dominant, such as contingent service work, informal work, low-wage work, and microwork, cannot really be squared with any developmentalist script, let alone with the *Bildung* as the classic structure of capitalist narrative life, of life in narrative. Those trapped in only fitful and partial relation to any formal economy, in waithood, in conditions of absent futurity, are in a situation that "will never be narrativizable" ("The Irreconcilable" 112), Joshua Clover writes. The Bildungsroman is no longer for us! We are instead now in the age of—if anything—the picaresque. Honwana refers to *desenrascar a vida*, *débrouillage*, and improvisation: hustling, or "making it up as you go along," the effort to "assess challenges and possibilities and plot scenarios conducive to the achievement of specific goals." The average working life is defined now by tactical "daily struggles that respond to immediate needs rather than longer-term strategies designed to achieve broader ends" ("Youth" 2436).

Clover argues that, as these conditions intensify, the novel itself will cease to exist as "an orienting form." "Do not all such forms pass from hegemony and then from relevance, heralding not a new form to orient us in the old world but rather that world's exhaustion?" he asks ("The Irreconcilable" 101). I would only add to his account that observers of postcolonial print see this happening already (see Harris;

Harris and Hållén). The print container for text is itself becoming a residual form, displaced instead by the smartphone: the device that one has on one's person already as one moves throughout the day, the means of finding and securing work, negotiating temporary arrangements, remaining flexible and contactable. The material and the textual are connected here. The Bildungsroman has been a key novel genre—if not the urgenre of the novel, as the very *story of stories*, with its generative narrativity of beginning, middle, and conclusive end. The print form of the novel was appropriate for a particular kind of consumer with some disposable income and leisure time, while the protagonism of a certain kind of character was suited to the print book that took some time to read and that engaged one in the cohesive story of a life from its sprouting to its fruition. Today everything is different. We find instead the not-quite-subject—the character in waithood and hustle—with a life given shape in more ephemeral forms: flash fictions, social media image captions, quick accessible poems that amuse and prop you up, self-published digital works released in short installments and read for free on platforms. To read has become a digital device-based picaresque experience that accompanies people hustling from opportunity to opportunity, taking what comes. If this kind of post-print reading is not quite the new global dominant, I have little doubt it will be.

There is another kind of protagonism worth mentioning here too: the protest movements that emerge as "those surplus to the needs of capital and empire grow, and grow restless" ("Fanon" 43), as Clover puts it. Their energy stems from the economic and social pressures they suffer, as well as from their "pervasive political marginalisation," Honwana argues, as the feeling of being "trapped" in a "prolonged state of youth" combines with a sense that "national political structures create serious obstacles to real change and new politics" ("Youth" 2430). There appears to be no new politics, no futurity, instead a threatening planetary nonfuturity: this is the context for what Clover describes as "surplus rebellions," the resurgence of urban riots by "the planetary *classes dangereuses*." They are "increasingly united not by their role as producers but by their relation to state violence, organized along raced and racializing lines" ("Fanon" 43–44), Clover writes; while for

Honwana, one further key is their disposition against the political classes who cannot be the agents of anything new. The Bildungsroman belongs to those outmoded political classes—it is a genre of order in a time of order's unravelling. This is another reason for its denouement, its diminishing global relevance, its failure to convince.

Consider in this context—our age of disorder—Tsitsi Dangarembga's most recent novel, *This Mournable Body*, the last in her Tambu trilogy. It finds our protagonist in Harare trying to find work and housing with everyone else converging in the city. She must countenance every kind of cruelty and depredation to try to make a living, including, as part of her work for a tourism company, allowing members of her own family to be turned into a curiosity for eco-tourists attracted to spectacles of village life in Africa. Tambu worked hard to leave her village behind and endured a lot of psychic turmoil in the process. Now she returns to the homestead to reproduce it in the form of a saleable pastiche. The villagers agree because they need money and other goods, such as clothing and medicine: the limitations of the rural village's capacity to sustain life produce the simulation villager as worker.

This is more than an anti-Bildungsroman. Dangarembga is digging the genre's grave. She shows how its scripts helped to turn Tambu into someone who, to fulfill "aspiration," will bear—even become herself— an "unutterable occurrence" (*Mournable Body* 204). Not stopping there, though, she also makes you look squarely at the misfit between the Bildungsroman's conditions of existence and contemporary realities. The people arriving in huge numbers from rural areas at Harare's Fourth Street Bus Terminus find women and boys "selling airtime, vegetables, mazhanje, and matohwe fruit" (188), and what work will they find for themselves, in turn? Unemployment is nearly universal. Tambu has managed to find a job—her boss hates that their office building overlooks the filth and poverty of the bustling bus terminal— but it is at an unbearable cost, and she's left miserable. And what about everyone else? The Bildungsroman is decaying, but it never was a portent of generalized development for all human beings. It was part of the rise of a very few people to positions of wealth, security, and power, and the consignment of everyone else to, at best (if they are lucky!) pantomime.

Works Cited

Castle, Gregory. *Reading the Modernist Bildungsroman*. University Press of Florida, 2006.

Clover, Joshua. "Fanon: Absorption and Coloniality." *College Literature*, vol. 45, no. 1, Winter 2018, pp. 39–45.

Clover, Joshua. "The Irreconcilable: Marx after Literature." *After Marx: Literature, Theory, and Value in the Twenty-First Century*, edited by Colleen Lye and Christopher Nealon, Cambridge University Press, 2022, pp. 101–15.

Dangarembga, Tsitsi. *Nervous Conditions*. The Women's Press, 1988.

Dangarembga, Tsitsi. *This Mournable Body*. Greywolf Press, 2018.

Esty, Jed. *Unseasonable Youth: Modernism, Colonialism, and the Fiction of Development*. Oxford University Press, 2012.

Harris, Ashleigh. "Hot Reads, Pirate Copies, and the Unsustainability of the Book in Africa's Literary Future." *Postcolonial Text*, vol. 14, no. 2, 2019, https://www.postcolonial.org/index.php/pct/article/view/2383.

Harris, Ashleigh, and Nicklas Hållén. "African Street Literature: A Method for an Emergent Form beyond World Literature." *Research in African Literatures*, vol. 51, no. 2, Summer 2020, pp. 1–26.

Honwana, Alcinda. "Youth, Waithood, and Protest Movements in Africa." ECAS 2013 5th European Conference on African Studies: African Dynamics in a Multipolar World, pp. 2427–47.

Honwana, Alcinda. "'Waithood': Youth Transitions and Social Change." *Development and Equity*, edited by Dick Foeken et al., Brill, 2014, pp. 28–40.

Jones, Phil. *Work without the Worker: Labour in the Age of Platform Capitalism*. Verso, 2021.

Neel, Phillip. "Broken Circle: Premature Deindustrialization, Chinese Capital Exports, and the Stumbling Development of New Territorial Industrial Complexes." *International Labor and Working-Class History*, vol. 102, 2023, pp. 94–123.

CONTRIBUTORS

David Babcock is an associate professor of English at James Madison University, and is an affiliated faculty member of the university's African, African American, and Diaspora Studies Center. His research focuses on how the anglophone novel imagines the work of intellectuals and other professionals in postcolonial and globalizing contexts. He is currently completing a book manuscript on the ideology of professionalism in contemporary world anglophone literature, and beginning a second project focusing on how contemporary African professionals use literary genres to understand their relationship to their constituencies. He has co-edited, with Peter Leman, a special issue of the *Journal of Commonwealth and Postcolonial Studies* entitled "Law and Literature from the Global South." His work has also appeared in *PMLA*, *Cultural Critique*, the *Journal of the African Literature Association*, *Modern Fiction Studies*, *Diaspora*, *Novel*, and *Contemporary Literature*.

Sarah Brouillette is a professor in the Department of English at Carleton University in Ottawa. She is the author of three books: *Postcolonial Writers in the Global Literary Marketplace* (2007), *Literature and the Creative Economy* (2014), and *UNESCO and the Fate of the Literary* (2019).

Gregory Byala completed his doctoral work at Yale University. His writing has appeared in *Samuel Beckett Today/Aujourd'hui*, *The Dictionary of African Biography*, *Bryn Mawr Review of Comparative*

Literature, Comparative Literature Studies, Theater Journal, and more. He is currently an associate professor at Temple University, in Philadelphia.

Deena Dinat received his PhD in English literature from the University of British Columbia in 2022. His research investigates the relationship between processes of subjection, capital accumulation, and the construction of nationhood in contemporary world literature. He has also published work on the writing of Imraan Coovadia, as well as collaborative research on "eco-xenophobia" and its impact on conservation. Upcoming work theorizes film adaptation as a means of tracing the transit of empire, and brings together Herman Melville's Billy Budd, Sailor, Claire Denis's Beau Travail, and Mati Diop's Atlantics. He lives and teaches on the unceded, traditional and ancestral land of the Musqueam, Squamish, and Tsleil-Waututh Peoples in Vancouver, British Columbia.

Prathim-Maya Dora-Laskey teaches English literature and women's, gender, and sexuality studies at Alma College after attending graduate school on three continents. An alumna of Stella Maris College, Chennai, their awards include scholarships from the Mellon Foundation, the Pennathur Foundation, and a Violet Morgan Vaughan award at the University of Oxford. A poetry editor at JaggeryLit magazine and a current moderator at SAWNET (South Asian Women's Net @sawnet.org), they have published work in Contemporary South Asia, Interventions: International Journal of Postcolonial Studies, South Asian Review, and Hypatia: A Journal of Feminist Philosophy. Their poetry has previously appeared in Yemassee, Mirror Magazine, Cerebrations, Eclectica Magazine, The Scriblerus Arts Magazine, and several anthologies. A monograph, Trans(formations) and Tenderness: Rhetorics and Resources to Support Transgender Youth in the US, is out soon (2025).

José-Santiago Fernández-Vázquez is a full professor in the Department of Modern Philology at the University of Alcalá (Madrid, Spain), where he teaches linguistics, literary studies, and history. He has published several studies on postcolonial literature and contemporary British fiction, literary censorship, persuasive language, multimodal critical discourse studies, and ecolinguistics.

Ericka A. Hoagland is a professor in the Department of English and Creative Writing at Stephen F. Austin State University, where she regularly teaches courses in world literature and science fiction. She has contributed essays to *A History of the Bildungsroman* (2019), *To Boldly Go: Essays on Gender and Sexuality in the Star Trek Universe* (2016), and co-edited the 2010 collection, *Science Fiction, Imperialism, and the Third World: Essays on Postcolonial Literature and Film*.

Elizabeth Jackson is a recently retired Senior Lecturer in Literatures in English at the University of the West Indies in Trinidad. She has a BA from Smith College (USA) and a PhD from the University of London (UK). Her publications include numerous articles in peer-reviewed journals and three single-authored books: *Global Childhoods and Cosmopolitan Identities in Literature* (2022), *Muslim Indian Women Writing in English* (2017), and *Feminism and Contemporary Indian Women's Writing* (2010).

Feroza Jussawalla is Professor Emerita at the University of New Mexico. She has taught in the United States for forty years, including also at the University of Utah and the University of Texas at El Paso. She is the author of *Family Quarrels: Towards a Criticism of Indian Writing in English* (1985), one of the earliest works on what would become postcolonial literature. Since then, she has edited or co-edited *Interviews with Writers of the Postcolonial World* (1992), *Conversations with V.S. Naipaul* (1997), *Emerging South Asian Women Writers: Essays and Interviews* (2016), *Memory, Voice, and Identity: Muslim Women's Writing from across the Middle East* (2021), and *Muslim Women's Writing from across South and Southeast Asia* (2023). Her collection of poems, *Chiffon Saris* (2003), was published by Kolkotta's Writers Workshop and Toronto South Asian Review. She has published numerous articles, poems, and conference presentations.

Andrew David King is a doctoral student in English at UC Berkeley, where they serve as the director of the Disabled Students Advocacy Project. They hold an MFA from the Iowa Writers' Workshop and an MA in philosophy from Central European University, and were formerly Provost's Visiting Writer and Visiting Assistant Professor in the University of Iowa's Department of English, as well as Research Assistant at the Walt Whitman Archive. Previous critical work has appeared in *boundary 2*, *Journal of Arts & Communities*, *The Routledge Companion to Working-Class Literature* (2024), *A Field Guide to the Poetry of Theodore Roethke* (2020), *Care and Disability: Relational Representations* (2025), and more.

Aruna Krishnamurthy is a professor of English at Fitchburg State University. Her research areas include travel writing in India, the vernacular novel in India, and eighteenth- and nineteenth-century class and gender issues in Britain. She is the editor of *The Working-Class Intellectual in Eighteenth- and Nineteenth-Century Britain* (2009).

Simone Maria Puleo is an assistant professor of Italian and Italian American studies at Central Connecticut State University. He earned a PhD in comparative literary and cultural studies from the University of Connecticut in 2020. His interests include Italian and Italian American studies, world literature, cosmopolitanism, and international relations. His research focuses on global literary production dating from the eighteenth century to contemporary times.

Peter Ribic teaches English at EF Academy in Pasadena, California. His writing on global fiction and the political economy of development has appeared in the *Journal of Commonwealth Literature*, the *Journal of Postcolonial Writing*, the *Journal of Popular Culture*, and *Literary Geographies*.

Arnab Dutta Roy is an assistant professor of English at Florida Gulf Coast University. He received his PhD in comparative literary and cultural studies from the University of Connecticut. His research is located at the intersection of postcolonialism, human rights theory, and modern South Asian literature, and has appeared or is forthcoming in journals including the *Journal of Global Postcolonial Studies*, *South Asian Review*, *American Book Review*, *Literary Universals Project*, *Comparatist*, *Humanities*, and *APA Studies on Asian and Asian American Philosophers and Philosophies*. He has co-edited two volumes on the postcolonial Bildungsroman: *The Postcolonial Bildungsroman: Narratives of Youth, Representational Politics, and Aesthetic Reinventions*, and *The Postcolonial Bildungsroman and the Character of Place* (forthcoming). He teaches both graduate and undergraduate courses on world literature and postcolonial theory.

Craig Smith is a tenured English instructor at Northwestern Polytechnic, in Grande Prairie, Alberta. He has written several articles on the fiction of J.M. Coetzee, and has also published work on cetacean personhood in Zakes Mda's *The Whale Caller* and on the conjunction of conservative aesthetics and political radicalism in the early fiction of Ngũgĩ wa Thiong'o. More recently, he has been focusing on the need for a reinvigorated sense of the grey zone in Holocaust pedagogy, and this work will be included in an edited collection on new approaches to teaching Holocaust literature.

Antonette Talaue-Arogo is an associate professor in the Literature Department at De La Salle University Manila, where she obtained her PhD in literature in 2016. She was a participant in the School of Criticism and Theory at Cornell University in 2009. Her scholarly works appear in internationally published edited collections. Her research is focused on critical theory, especially cosmopolitanism, postcolonialism, and decolonization/decoloniality, and gender studies.

Paul Ugor is a professor in the Department of English Language and Literature at the University of Waterloo, Ontario. His research and teaching interests are in the areas of African literature and cultures, anglophone postcolonial world literature, and global Black studies. He is the author of *Nollywood: Popular Culture and Narratives of Youth*

Struggles in Nigeria (2016), and co-editor of several collections including *Youth and Popular Culture in Africa: Media, Music, and Politics* (2021); *African Youth Cultures in a Globalized World: Challenges, Agency and Resistance* (2015); a special issue of *Postcolonial Text* (2013); a special issue of *Review of Education, Pedagogy, and Cultural Studies* (2009); and a special issue of *Critical African Studies* (Spring 2023). Recently, he completed work with Bonny Ibhawoh on an edited volume, *Narrating Transitional Justice: Memory in the Age of Truth and Reconciliation*, due to be published by McGill-Queens University Press in fall 2025.

Julieann Veronica Ulin is an associate professor of English at Florida Atlantic University. She received her PhD in English from the Keough-Naughton Institute for Irish Studies at the University of Notre Dame, where she was the Edward Sorin Postdoctoral Fellow in the Humanities. She holds a MA in English from Fordham University and a BA in English from Washington and Lee University. The chapter in this book began life as part of her undergraduate honours thesis on *Reading in the Dark*, a novel recommended to her by Marc Conner. At Notre Dame, she had the opportunity to take courses taught by Seamus Deane. A version of this chapter was delivered there at the 2022 Seamus Deane at Notre Dame: The Legacy memorial conference. She is grateful for the development made possible by extraordinary teachers.

Rachel Ann Walsh is an associate teaching professor in the English Department and International Studies Program at Bowling Green State University in Ohio. Her research focuses on multi-ethnic literature of the US and transnational and global literature that operate as archives of the intergenerational traumas of settler-colonialism, slavery, apartheid, and US imperialism. Her work, ranging from studies of South African literature of the apartheid to depictions of neoliberalism and anti-Asian violence in contemporary transnational literature, has been published in *Contemporary Literature*, *Twentieth-Century Literature*, *Radical Philosophy Review*, and the interdisciplinary journal, *Society and Space: Environment and*

Planning. She has a forthcoming chapter in the collection *Human Rights in the Age of Drones: Critical Perspectives on Post-9/11 Literature, Film and Art* with Palgrave Macmillan.

Maria Su Wang is an associate professor of English at Biola University (La Mirada, California), where she teaches courses in world literature, British literature, and the history and theory of the novel. She has published articles on the Victorian novel in *Narrative* and *Victorian Review*, and is currently completing a book manuscript on the narrative techniques of Victorian realism in relation to concepts from the founding figures of classical sociology, such as Émile Durkheim, Georg Simmel, and Max Weber.

Bethany Williamson is an associate professor of English at Biola University (La Mirada, California), where she teaches courses in British and world literature, literary theory, and academic writing. She is the author of *Orienting Virtue: Civic Identity and Orientalism in Britain's Global Eighteenth Century* (2022). She has also published articles on the global eighteenth century, environmental humanities, and literary pedagogy in refereed journals such as *Eighteenth-Century Fiction*, *Journal for Early Modern Cultural Studies*, *South Atlantic Review*, and *ABO: Interactive Journal for Women in the Arts, 1640–1830*.

Helena Wu is Canada Research Chair and Assistant Professor of Hong Kong Studies at the University of British Columbia, Vancouver. She has written on the topics of Hong Kong cinema, literature, and media for peer-reviewed journals such as *Interventions: International Journal of Postcolonial Studies* (2018), *Global Media and China* (2020), *Journal of Chinese Cinemas* (2020), *Asian Cinema* (2022), and *Screen* (2024). Her work on the concept of *jianghu* (rivers and lakes) has been published in *Chinese Martial Arts and Media Culture* (2018), and *HKU Journal of Chinese Studies* (2023). She is the author of *The Hangover after the Handover: Places, Things and Cultural Icons in Hong Kong* (2020), where she explores the manifestation of local icons and relations.

Julia Wurr is Junior Professor of Postcolonial Studies at the Institute for English and American Studies at the Carl von Ossietzky University of Oldenburg, Germany. Published as *Literary Neo-Orientalism and the Arab Uprisings: Tensions in English, French and German Language Fiction* (2022), her doctoral research focused on Neo-Orientalist forms of othering, as well as on the postcolonial Middle East and North Africa region. Her current research project on "reproductive imperialism" explores the nexus between narrative, social, and biological reproduction in (post)colonial texts and contexts. Her research interests include postcolonial medical and health humanities, biocapitalism, reproductive studies, South Asian and Arab anglophone literature, as well as Orientalism and Neo-Orientalism, and she is involved in research projects on critical AI studies and migration studies. She serves as the vice-president of GAPS, the Association for Anglophone Postcolonial Studies, and she is associate editor of the *Journal of Postcolonial Writing*.

INDEX

Abacha, General Sani, 256, 259
Abani, Chris, xxx
Abati, Reuben, 300, 320n1
Abrams, M.H., 102n1
Achebe, Chinua, xxiii, 55–57,
  320n5, 343n8, 361, 363, 446
Adalla, Carolyne, xxx
Adébáyò, Ayòbámi, 460n2
Adhikari, Mohamed, 211
Adichie, Chimamanda Ngozi, xxx,
  xl, 3, 299–301, 304–07, 311–
  14, 318–19. *See also*
  Americanah; *Half of a*
  Yellow Sun; *Purple Hibiscus*
adolescence, xxvii, xxxvi, 29, 35,
  133, 402, 438–39, 440, 442
The Adventures of Huckleberry
  Finn (Twain), xxiii
aesthetics, 108, 110–11
Affective Communities (Gandhi),
  124
Africa
  Eurocentric caricatures of, 267
  exclusion from global
    modernity, 256
  modernization, 265
  postcolonial democracies, 305
  postcolonial states, 265
  violence of "the colonial political
    economy," 255
African American women, 97
African Bildungsroman
  anti-Bildungsroman tradition
    in, 339–40
  autobiography in, xxxv
  and carceral politics, 255–58,
    263–66
  contradictions within, 252–53
  disillusionment and
    Afropessimism, 254
  feminist genealogies of, 303
  historical time in, 352
  introduction of different
    character types, xl
  "male destiny" in, 266, 268n2
  popularity of, xxxvii, 254
  protagonist's inability to self-
    actualize, 266, 340, 352
  theoretical debates on, 350
  ur text of, xxxv
  Western readership for, 260–62,
    267–68

481

youth coming-of-age twinned with postcolonial nationhood, 252–53, 304

See also African postcolonial democracies; African war Bildungsroman; AIDS Bildungsroman

African literature, xxix, 39, 55–56, 252, 304–05, 363. *See also* African Bildungsroman

African postcolonial Bildungsroman, 99

African war Bildungsroman, xxix–xxx, 255

African writers
  born in postcolonial era, 304–05
  dilemmas/challenges of, 363–64
  and traditional/indigenous culture, 363
  Western readers and publishers, 260–62
  See also Achebe, Chinua; Adichie, Chimamanda Ngozi; Iweala, Uzodinma; Kourouma, Ahmadou; Mabanckou, Alain; Soyinka, Wole

Africanfuturism, 29–30, 37–38, 40, 48

Afrikaans (language), 376

agency
  of child protagonists, 277–78, 287–88, 290
  conditions and constraints of, 133, 153, 301
  of female protagonists, 116, 309, 319, 447, 451, 457
  individual versus collective, 309
  lack of, 62, 444, 454

of the postcolonial subject, xiv, 137, 305

Aguilar, Filomeno V., Jr., 114

Aguinaldo, Emilio, 109

Agyeya (S.H. Vatsyayan), 162

AIDS Bildungsroman, xxx, 255

Akata Witch (Okorafor), 48

Akkad, Moustapha, 86

Alcott, Louisa May, 441

al-Hakim, Tawfiq, xxviii

Ali, Monica, xxvi

Al-Kassim, Dina, 208

Allah Is Not Obliged (Kourouma), xxx

Al-Mousa, Nedal M., xxviii, xxix

al-Mukhtar, Umar, 86, 92

al-Tayib Salih, xxviii

Althusser, Louis, 383

America Is in the Heart (Bulosan), 418

American Bildungsroman, 73, 416

American Born Chinese (Yang), xxxvi

American Century, 417–18

American exceptionalism, 431

Americanah (Adichie), 314–18, 319, 321n14

An Imperfect Blessing (David), xxxix, 209, 210–15

Anand, Mulk Raj, xxii, 55

Anantanarayanan, M., xxxi

Ananthamurthy, U.R., xiii

Anatomy of Criticism (Frye), 132

Anderson, Benedict, 57, 71, 320n8. *See also Imagined Communities*

Andrade, Susan Z., 301–02, 303–04

Anglo-American literary marketplace, 426

Anglo-Boer War, 376
animals
    in Hong Kong literature, 333
    love for, 118–19
    non-Western people seen as, 193–94, 197
    precarious status of, xlii
    in queer poetics, 421, 423, 429–34
Anomalous States (Lloyd), 407–08
Another Life (Walcott)
    "Adamic task," 138, 143, 148, 150
    as anti-Bildungsroman, 149–56
    division and repetition, 137–49
    friendships/love, 146–47, 150–51
    narrator of, 132, 145, 146
    nonhuman universe, 143, 153–55
    as postcolonial Bildungsroman, xxxviii, 131–37, 151–52
    self-actualization, 146, 152–53
    suicides, 138, 148, 150
    summary of, 134–35
    sunlight as metaphor, 140–41, 151
Anthonissen, Christine, 376
anti-apartheid movement (South Africa), 213–14
anti-Bildungsroman, 62, 149–56, 159, 329
anti-colonialism, xxiv–xxvi, 74, 110, 231, 305
anti-development, xx, xxii, 61–62, 228, 359, 398, 406, 467–68
Anti-Extradition Law Amendment Bill (Anti-ELAB) Movement, 341
Antigua, xxxiii–xxxiv, 15
Anzaldúa, Gloria, 85
apartheid (South Africa), xxxix, 207–10, 213, 219, 372–76, 387. *See also* South Africa; Truth and Reconciliation Commission (TRC)
Appadurai, Arjun, 288
Appiah, Kwame Anthony, 122–23
Aquino, Benigno, Jr., 120
Aquino, Corazon, 120
Arabian Nights, 59
Arabic Bildungsroman, xxviii–xxix
Arabic literature, 60
Arendt, Hannah, 60, 141
Arjie (protagonist, *Funny Boy*), 272, 274–79, 283–86, 290
Armah, Ayi Kwei, 254
Arnold, Matthew, 10, 108
"arrested development discourse," 255
artist as entrepreneur, 420
artist novel, 415. *See also* Künstlerroman
Arya Samaj movement, 170, 172–73, 176, 177
Ashk, Upendranath, xxxviii, 160, 162, 165–67. *See also* Chetan (protagonist, *Falling Walls*); *Falling Walls*
Asian Americans
    authors/literature, 418, 434–35n4
    feminization/remasculinization of, 422, 434n2
    immigrant mothers, 418, 434n1
    as model minority, 421
Assimilating Asians (Chu), 434n1

INDEX   483

Atta, Sefi, xlii, 437
Aufhebung (Hegelian concept), 21, 313
Austen, Jane, xiii, xvii, 15
Austen, Ralph A., 260, 352, 443
Australia, 14, 20
authors of colour/nonwhite writers, 426
autobiographical narrative, xxxv, 84, 135, 215, 420
autonomous subject of modernity, 108, 251, 256, 420, 424. *See also* liberal subject; neoliberal subject; unitary subject
autophylography, 138
Ayyub, Dun al-Nun, xxviii
Azim, Firdous, 16
Azure (protagonist, *Thirteen Cents*), 216–22

Baartman, Saartje, 49n1, 221
Babcock, David, xl
Bakhtin, Mikhail, 78, 134, 135, 159, 224n6, 274, 396
Bakshi, Sandeep, xxvii
Baldick, Chris, 371–72
Baldwin, James, 415–17
Barad, Karen, 48
Barker, Clare, 275
Barney, Richard A., 21
Barre, Siad, 84, 88, 99
Bassi, Shaul, 77
Bataille, Georges, 220
Baudrillard, Jean, 220
Baugh, Edward, 131, 136
Beah, Ishmael, xxx
Beasts of No Nation (Iweala), xxx, 3

Bechdel, Alison, xxxvi
Beddow, Michael, 33
Bedi, Rajinder, 180n1
Bennet, Elizabeth (protagonist, *Pride and Prejudice*), 241, 277, 466
Berlatsky, Noah, 30
Berlin Conference, 11
Berlusconi, Silvio, 95
Bhabha, Homi
    on hybridity, 75, 85, 339, 371
    on mimicry, 110, 381
    on the nation, xxxix, 72, 207
    on universal progress, 21–22
Biafran revolution, 311
Bildung
    alternative forms of, 299–307, 310–11, 314, 317–19, 321n14
    as capitalist, 467–68
    and colonialism, xxxiii, 307
    contested nature of, 111, 239, 272, 466
    cosmopolitan subject of, 116–25, 275
    of female protagonists, 268n2
    as inconclusive/unfinished, 107, 111, 116, 122, 164, 177
    as journey to decolonized identity, 60, 74, 302–03
    meaning of, xvi, xx, 8–9, 21, 108, 153, 155, 320n11, 407–08
    of the nation, 209, 228–31, 233, 245, 299, 305
    as national reconciliation, 210–15
    in a posthuman era, 32, 38, 43, 46–47
    in science fiction, 34, 38

stunted by war, xxx
as trauma, 40–41, 43, 45–46
See also Adichie, Chimamanda Ngozi; Azure; Chetan; children/childhood; development; education; Kambili; Rodrigues; subject formation; Waleed; Wang Meng

Bildungsroman
bourgeois ideology of, 18, 23, 33–34
defining features of, 58, 102n1, 133, 160–64, 251, 301–02, 326, 425
definitions of, xvi–xvii, 102n1, 326, 371
as didactic, 94
of/in formation, 107–12
as "future-facing," 40, 395–96
German origins of, xiii, xvi–xvii, 4, 58, 60, 83, 159, 326
heteronormativity in, 441
history and evolution of, xvi–xix, xxxiv–xxxvi, 4–5, 58–61, 465–70
introduction to, xiii–xv
as narrative of development, 133
popularity in postcolonies, xiv, 60–61, 252, 254, 465
scope of genre, 32–34, 160, 183–84
social reproduction in, 439–42
See also American Bildungsroman; British Bildungsroman; classical Bildungsroman; colonial Bildungsromann; coming-of-age narratives; Continental Bildungsroman; Cosmopolitan Bildungsroman; dissensual Bildungsroman; female Bildungsroman; nationhood/national development; Philippines Bildungsroman; postcolonial Bildungsroman; Western Bildungsroman

Bildungsroman: scholarship on
by critical theorists, xiv–xv, 131–34
instability/fragility of genre, 183–84, 394–95, 465
the "postcolonial turn" in, xiv–xv, 83–84, 160
See also Cheah, Pheng; Esty, Jed; Fernández-Vázquez, José-Santiago; Hoagland, Erika; Jussawalla, Feroza; Lima, Maria Helena; Moretti, Franco; Slaughter, Joseph

Bildungsweg, 35

Binti trilogy (Okorafor)
Africanfuturism in, 37–38, 40, 48
Meduse, 31, 37, 38, 41, 42, 47, 49n1
plot of, 30, 38, 41, 43–46
posthumanism in, 38–39, 46–47, 49
protagonist's development, 38, 40, 42–49
as reconstitution of Bildungsroman, 30–32, 36–38, 46–47
role of trauma in, 39–43, 46
See also science fiction (SF) Bildungsroman

Black British fiction, xiv, 387
Black diaspora, 416
Black Moses (Mabanckou), xl, 255, 261–66
Black Skin, White Masks (Fanon), 388
Blackness/Black people, 152, 432. *See also* African American women; African diaspora; African writers
Blixen, Karen, 68–69
blogs, 315–18, 319
Boehmer, Elleke, 276, 285
The Border of Centrifugation (*Li xin dai* by Hon Lai-chu), 326, 328, 333–35, 338, 341
borders
   of bodies and species, 46, 429, 431, 433
   "border culture," xxxvii, 85
   of genres, 33
   of geographies, 74–76
Bouchane, Mohamed, 94
Boucher, François, 402, 408
bourgeois social order, 11, 161, 163, 224n5, 378, 383, 441
bourgeois subject, 13, 312, 377, 415–16
Bové, Paul, 4
Braun, Michael, 83
Brennan, Timothy, 69
Brison, Susan, 42
British (colonial) education, 55, 56, 65–66
British Bildungsroman, 12
British Empire, 227, 230, 307
British India, 24n3
British novel—nineteenth century, 14–15, 159, 163

Brontë, Charlotte, 17, 58, 385
Brouillette, Sarah, xxiv, xlii–xliii
Buckley, Jerome, 35–36, 162
The Buddha of Suburbia (Kureishi), 62
Buddha/Buddhism, xiii, 201–02
Bulosan, Carlos, 418
Burger, Bettina, 47
Burnett, Joshua Yu, 40
Burroughs, Edgar Rice, 243
Butler, Judith, 76, 217
Byala, Gregory, xli, xlii

Cabral, Amilcar, 231
Caliban, 408
Cambridge University, 377
Campbell, Joseph, 21, 55, 58, 367n1
Canada, xv, 234, 280, 281, 282
Cape Town, xli, 210, 213, 219, 375, 377, 380, 386
capitalism
   authoritarian, 233
   bourgeois, 224n5
   and consumerism, 287, 288, 356
   crony capitalism, 114
   global, xx, 120, 424, 466–68
   mercantile, 11
   postcolonial, 219
   racial capitalism, xxxix, 214, 222
   speculative finance-capitalism, 361
carceral colonialism, 267
carceral politics, 263–64
carceral states Bildungsroman, xl, 255–56, 267
Card, Orson Scott, 35

Caribbean Bildungsromane, 132,
  339, 349. *See also* Walcott,
  Derek
Caribbean history, 133, 137
Caribbean literature, xxix
Carter, Angela, xxvii
Casetti, Francesco, xxv–xxvi
Castle, Gregory, 32, 34, 161, 163,
  164, 177, 395, 412
Castries (St. Lucia), 132–35, 138,
  142–43, 149, 153
categorization problematized, xxi,
  32–34
Catholic Church, 99, 185, 199, 307–09
censorship, 86
Cereus Blooms at Night (Mootoo),
  xxix
Césaire, Aimé, 21–22
Chandrasekera, Vajra, 49n1
Chatterjee, Partha, 74
Cheah, Pheng
  and death-dealing state, 216
  "organic" metaphor of anti-
    colonialism, xxv, 231, 240,
    302–03
  theories of *Bildung*, 112, 320n11
  theories of postcolonial
    Bildungsroman, 228, 350
  See also Spectral Nationality
chengzhang xiaoshuo, xxix
Chetan (protagonist, *Falling
  Walls*), 160, 168–70, 172–76,
  178–80
Cheung, Esther, 327
chi, 451–52
childlessness, 438, 443–47, 453–54, 456–60
children/childhood

agency of children, 277–78,
  287–92
"best interests of the child,"
  273–74, 275
child as protagonist in
  Bildungsroman, 441–42
child soldiers, xxx, 274, 419
effect of corporate globalization
  on, 289
idea of the child as enabling
  imperialism, xxi, xxii, 5–6,
  7–8, 442–43
in South Asian Bildungsroman,
  271–72
testifying at South Africa's
  TRC, 209
and underdevelopment, 466–67
victimization of children, 273–74, 276–77
See also childlessness; United
  Nations Convention on the
  Rights of the Child
  (UNCRC)
China, People's Republic of, 323,
  331, 356, 434n4
China's Great Leap Forward, 232,
  233
Chinese American authors, 422
Chinese American Bildungsromane,
  418, 422, 434n2
Chinese literature, xxix, 5, 326,
  331. *See also* thing-chanting
  (Chinese poetry)
Cho, Jennifer, 417, 419
Chow, Rey, 154, 331–32, 342n1
Christian proselytism, 98–99, 185,
  191
Chu, Patricia P., 434n1
civilizing project, 5, 9, 23

INDEX   487

Clark, Arthur C., 211
classical Bildungsroman
  childhood equated with the colonized, 5–6, 7
  and civilizing projects, 9, 23
  as colonialist, 4, 13–14, 15
  education and colonial tutelage in, 6–8, 10–11, 23
  features of, xviii
  geographical mobility in, 11–12, 23
  hero of, 5, 11–13, 18, 21, 23
  historicism in, 20–22
  individualism in, 12–13
  mentors in, 6–7, 8, 10
  and mercantile capitalism, 11
  non-Western origins of, 4–5
  notions of culture in, 9–10
  progress and humanism, 8–9
  rationalism and secularism in, 19
  repression/annihilation of otherness, 16–18, 23
  and stable futures, 418
  suppression of fantasy and supernatural, 18–20
Clover, Joshua, 468
Cobham-Sander, Rhonda, 151
Cockley, David, 261
Coconut (Matlawa), 3
Coetzee, J.M., 259
Cold War, 324, 419
Collins, Larry, 75–76
colonial Bildungsroman, xvii–xviii, xix
colonial education, 55–59, 110, 169–170, 363, 466. *See also* education
colonial modernity, xviii–xxi, xxiv, 466. *See also* modernity
The Colonial Rise of the Novel (Azim), 16
colonial trauma, xxiv, 39, 137. *See also* trauma
colonial violence/atrocities, 92–93
colonialism
  American colonialism in Philippines, 109–10
  as backdrop in postcolonial Bildungsroman, 67–69, 107, 159–61, 302–03, 339
  effects on gender relations (Nigeria), 446–47, 453
  Italian colonialism in East Africa, 86–94, 101
  legacies of, 116, 161, 235–36, 304–05, 350
  as worldview in classic Bildungsroman, 5–23, 108–09
  See also anti-colonialism; colonial education; colonial trauma; colonial violence/atrocities; colonization of the mind (Ngũgĩ); colonized subject; imperialism; Orientalism
colonialist Bildungsroman, xix–xxi, xix–xxii, xxii–xxiii
colonization of the mind (Ngũgĩ), 363
colonized subject, 13, 164–65, 170, 241
"Coloured" identity—apartheid South Africa, 372, 373–75, 377, 380–81
Comberiati, Danielle, 103n6

comic books, xxxv
Coming to Birth (Macgoye), xxiii, 443
coming-of-age narratives
   of the African diaspora, 85, 94–95
   in African postcolonies, 253
   as Bildungsromane, xiii
   by Caribbean writers, xxix
   in Chinese-language literature, 326
   and colonialist ideologies of childhood, xx
   and intergenerational trauma, 417
   plots of, xxvii–xxviii
   as popular postcolonial genre, xxviii, 3–4, 55
   and queer identity, xxvii
   travel and individuation in, 263
   young protagonist's quest for identity in, 371
   See also Hong Kong literature
"Commonwealth Literary Prize," 260
The Compendium of Hong Kong Literature (*Xiang Gang wen xue da xi*), 320n2, 326
Confessions of an AIDS Victim (Adalla), xxx
Congo-Brazzaville, 261, 262, 264, 265
Congolese revolution, 265
Conrad, Joseph, xviii, xx
Contarini Fleming (Disraeli), 12
Continental Bildungsroman, 159
"contrapuntal readings," 15
Cosmopolitan Bildungsroman, 107–25

cosmopolitanism
   of Bildungsroman as genre, xv
   critical theories of, 122–24
   as inclusionary, 107
   "new cosmopolitanisms," 125
   in Philippines Bildungsroman, 112, 116, 122
   versus planetarity, 287–88
   as "strategic bargain with universalism," 123
Costa, Raffaele, 86
Coundouritotis, Eleni, 311
COVID-19 pandemic, 341, 415
Cracking India (Sidhwa), 57, 74–75
Crane, Ralph, xxx–xxxi
"creolization," xxv
Crowley, Dustin, 40
Cruz, Isagani R., 120
Cuba, 109
cultural hybridity. *See* hybridity/hybrid subjectivity
Culture and Imperialism (Said), 4, 12, 14

Dabiri, Emma, 47
Dabydeen, David, 372, 387
Dalit identity, xiv, 61, 278
Damrosch, David, 111–12
Dangarembga, Tsitsi, xiv, xxxii–xxxiii, xxxiii, 85, 228, 465–66. *See also Nervous Conditions*; *This Mournable Body*
Daniel Deronda (Eliot), xxxiv
Dante, Alighieri, 141
Darkness Under the Sun (*Hei ri* by Hon Lai-chu), 341
Dash, J. Michael, 155

David, Nadia, xxxix, 209. *See also An Imperfect Blessing* (David)
David Copperfield (Dickens), 55, 441
Davidson, Mary Gray, 392
Davis, Angela, 267
Dawood, Alia (protagonist, *An Imperfect Blessing*), 210–12
De, Shobhaa, xxvi
de Vries, Fred, 216
Deane, Seamus, xli–xlii, 22, 392
death, anti-economy of, 220–22. *See also* slow death
Debre Libanos monastery massacre, 92
Dedalus, Stephen (protagonist, *Portrait of the Artist*), 74, 385, 393, 394, 397, 413
Defoe, Daniel, 5
Del Boca, Angelo, 90, 103n6
Deleuze, Gilles, 76, 325
denationalization (of postcolonies), 275–76, 279–80, 284–85, 287–88
"dependency school" of economic development, 231
Derrida, Jacques, 64–65, 78, 430
Derry (Ireland), 392, 393, 395, 402
Desai, Anita, xiii
development
  arrested, stalled; maldevelopment, xxxiv, 255, 407–08, 470
  of the child, xv, 290–91, 294n17, 326
  of colonies; as rationale for colonization, xx, 5–6, 10, 23, 465–67
  critiques of, 299
  of female protagonists, xlii, 453–55, 458–59
  inversions of, by Tutuola, 356, 364, 366
  linear/historicist nature of, xlii, 20–22, 142, 413, 454
  of protagonist in classic Bildungsroman, xiii–xiv, xx–xxi, xlii, 94, 102n1, 112, 133, 183, 349, 425, 440
  of protagonist in postcolonial Bildungsroman, xxix–xxx, xxxiv, 228, 272
  tropes of, in colonialist Bildungsroman, xx
  twinned development of protagonist and nation, 6–7, 184, 189, 224n6, 252–53, 301–02, 359
  See also anti-development; *Bildung*; developmental time; developmentalism, ideology of; education; maturation; phantom development; underdevelopment
developmental time, 229, 234–42. *See also If We Dream Too Long* (Goh)
developmentalism, ideology of, 228–34, 240, 246, 289, 425–26, 466–68
diaspora Bildungsroman, xxxvii, 83, 85–86, 99, 101. *See also La mia casa è dove sono* (Scego)
diaspora populations
  Africans, xiv, xv, 94–95, 98–101, 314, 416

Asians in UK, 372–73, 378
  popularity of Bildungsroman with, 60
  queer identities, 425
  second-generation, 85
  Vietnamese in America, 416
  See also hybridity/hybrid subjectivity
Dickens, Charles, xiii, xvii, 4, 59, 385, 441
Dinat, Deena, xxxix
Discourse on the Origin of Inequality (Rousseau), 140
discrimination, 58, 273, 277, 280, 292n3, 391. *See also* racism
disillusionment, literature of, xl, 229, 253–54, 258
Disraeli, Benjamin, 12
dissensual Bildungsroman, 61–62
Divakaruni, Chitra Bannerjee, 77
Dongala, Emmanuel, xxx
Donnelly, Michael, 311
Dora-Laskey, Prathim-Maya, xl
Dostoyevsky, Fyodor, 243
Driver, Dorothy, 376
Dubliners (Joyce), 398–400, 403–04, 409
Duiker, K. Sello, xxxix, 209. *See also Thirteen Cents* (Duiker)
Dung Kai-cheung, 326, 327, 340
Dutch East India Company, 200
Dutch merchants, 198–201
Duterte, Rodrigo Roa, 115, 119

eco-critical theory, xv
Edelman, Lee, 419
education
  "American imperialist education," 417
  college classroom as trope, 422
  contested as route to self-realization, 402–04, 408
  critiqued by postcolonial writers, 299, 364–65, 421, 425
  as cultivation of the self, 162, 169, 178–80, 397, 402
  educational value of the novel, 362–65
  in Indian Bildungsroman, xxxi
  as meaning of *Bildung*, xvi
  and rationalism/positivism, 18–19
  for social control/socialization, 10
  into social violence, 218, 220–22
  as theme in classic/colonialist Bildungsroman, xxi, 23, 133–34, 442
  Western/European modes of, 307, 311
  See also colonial education
Efuru (Nwapa), 438, 443–49, 451, 458
El Filibusterismo (Rizal), 112
Eliot, George, xvii, xxxiv, 58
Elites and Illustrados in Philippine Culture (Hau), 113–14
elites of postcolonial nations, 113–14, 123, 300–01
Emecheta, Buchi, xlii, 438, 449
Empire (Hardt and Negri), xxxiv
employment/work in global economy, 467–68, 470
Empty Face (*Kong lian* by Hon Lai-chu), 329
Ender's Game (Card), 35–36

Endō, Shūsaku, xxxix. *See also Silence* (Endō)
Eng, David, 419, 425, 434n3
England, 6, 15, 17, 73, 191, 280, 466
English as colonial language, 55, 58–59, 62–63
English Bildungsroman, 277
English language/speakers of, 363, 376–77, 422–23
English literary studies, 24n3
Enlightenment, xviii, xx, 7, 19–20, 109–10, 256
environment: theme in postcolonial Bildungsroman, xxxiii–xxxiv
Enyi Zinariya people, 44–45
epics, 5
epistemic violence, 6, 17, 23, 24, 40
Eritrea, 86
Erritouni, Ali, 261
Erwin, Lee, 13
Erziehungsroman, 132
Esty, Jed
    comparison of colonialist/postcolonialist Bildungsroman, xxii
    on development/anti-development, 37, 62
    on globalization, 184
    maturation foreclosed, 239
    as scholar of Bildungsroman, 83, 134, 254, 395, 465
    as scholar of colonialist Bildungsroman, xvii–xviii, xix–xx, 402, 407
Eteraz, Ali, 62
Ethiopia, 86
European Bildungsroman, 274, 284, 339, 357

Everything Good Will Come (Atta), 437–38, 443, 453–57, 458
exoticization of Third World Bildungsroman, 260
exploitation of people and planet, xxxiii, 364
extraction/extractivism, xxxiv, 366
Eyre, Jane (protagonist, *Jane Eyre*), 277

fairy tales, 19
Falling Walls (Ashk), xxxviii, 160–67, 176–80. *See also* Chetan (protagonist, *Falling Walls*); Shadiram, Pandit (*Falling Walls*)
Fan, Christopher T., 422, 434n4
Fanon, Frantz, 13, 90, 231, 388
Farah, Christina Ali, 94
Farah, Nuruddin, 85, 94, 440
fast death, 428
Faulkner, William, 406
Feder, Helena, xxxiii–xxxiv
female Bildungsroman, xvii, xxvii, xxix, 58, 268n2
female Nigerian Bildungsroman
    childlessness in, 438, 443–48, 453–54, 456–60
    doubling in, 458
    female self-formation in, 437–39, 446, 451, 457
    gender fluidity in, 444, 448, 459
    gendered social expectations, 437, 439, 445, 454–56, 458–59, 460n2
    lateral growth of protagonist, 438, 443, 454, 459

motherhood in, 450-51, 454,
 457-58
patriarchy (Indigenous and
 colonial) in, 444, 458-59
sisterhood/female solidarity,
 438, 443, 447, 452-54, 459
social motherhood, 444, 447
subversion of procreative
 teleologies in, 444, 447-450,
 459
See also Adichie, Chimamanda
 Ngozi
feminist theories, 460n6
Ferguson (USA) uprising, 432
Ferguson, Roderick, 419
Fernández-Vázquez, José-Santiago
 comparison of colonialist/
  postcolonialist
  Bildungsroman, xxii
 as scholar of Bildungsroman,
  xxxvi, 83, 367n1, 465
 as scholar of colonialist
  Bildungsroman, xx-xxi
 as scholar of postcolonial
  Bildungsroman, xviii-xix,
  xix, 77, 350, 352, 408
Fernando, Lloyd, 245
Filipino-foreigners ("Fil-foreign"),
 114, 115, 120-21, 124
Fish, Stanley, 64, 77
Flanagan, Victoria, 38
Fludernik, Monika, 258
folktales, 58
Fondo, Blossom, 156n1
The Forever War (Haldeman), 35
"Forrest Woods, Chair" (Hon Lai-
 chu), 330-31, 332, 341
Forster, E.M., 58
Foucault, Michel, 7, 133, 154, 219

Frames of War (Butler), 76
freedom
 in cosmopolitan thought, 125
 of individuals in classic
  Bildungsroman, 7, 8, 163,
  239
 from neo/colonial oppression;
  national liberation, xii, xxx,
  179-80, 230, 232, 278
 from societal/family strictures,
  305-07, 318
 US's "gift of freedom," xlii,
  419-21
 See also carceral colonialism;
  carceral politics; carceral
  states Bildungsroman
Freedom at Midnight (Collins and
 Lapierre), 75-76
Friedman, Susan Stanford, 283
Friel, Brian, 409
*From Third World to First: the
 Singapore Story, 1965-2000*
 (Lee), 229, 230-32, 234
Frow, John, xxxv, 183
Frye, Northrop, 131-32, 135
Fumagalli, Maria Cristina, 141
fumie, trampling on, 185-87, 192,
 198, 201, 203
Fun Home (Bechdel), xxxvi
Funny Boy (Selvadurai), 271-72,
 275-78, 280-86, 289-91
future
 Bildungsroman as "future-
  facing," 40, 395-96
 as disallowed/foreclosed, 419-
  20, 427
futurity, xxxvii, xliii, 112, 228, 420,
 468, 469

Gadamer, Hans-Georg, 111, 153, 155, 412
Gaeffke, Peter, 162, 180n2
Gandhi, Leela, 8–9, 108, 124, 125n1, 272
Gandhi, Mahatma, 56, 72–73, 165
Garcia Márquez, Gabriel, xxii
Gayland, Rob, 375, 376, 377–78, 385–86
gender inequality, 379, 447
Gennep, Arthur, 351
genre, theories of. *See* Bildungsroman: scholarship on
Germany
　humanism, 8–9
　idealists, xvi
　literary tradition, 83
　nationalism, 58
　origin of Bildungsroman, xiii, xvi–xvii, 4, 58, 60, 83, 159, 326
　romanticism, 4, 159, 306, 320n11
　values, 60
Gessel, Van C., 187
Ghermandi, Gabriella, 94
Ghosh, Amitav, xiii
ghosts in classical Bildungsroman, 19, 20
Gibson, William, 233
Gikandi, Simon, xxxviii, 55, 367n5
The Girl in the Tangerine Scarf (Kahf), 62
Glissant, Édouard, 152, 154–56
global capitalism. *See* capitalism
Global North, 459
global political economy, xxiv. *See also* capitalism

Global South, xiii, xxxiii, 113, 432, 459
globalization
　anxieties in globalized world, xli
　contrasted with "planetarity," 275, 287–92
　and destabilization of nation-state, 184, 276, 284
　impact on postcolonial coming-of-age, xxviii
　and increased inequality, xxiv
　of trade and finance, 123, 280
　violence of, xxxiv
Globalization and Postcolonialism: Hegemony and Resistance in the Twenty-First Century (Sankaran), 288
Glossary of Literary Terms (Abrams), 371
Go Tell It on the Mountain (Baldwin), 415–17
The God of Small Things (Roy), 71, 271–72, 275–87, 289–91
Goethe, Johann Wolfgang von, xvi, xxii, 4, 7–9, 60, 134. *See also Wilhelm Meisters Apprenticeship*
Goh, Poh Seng, 228, 229, 234–35, 238–39, 242, 245. *See also If We Dream Too Long*
Goh Keng Swee, 231–32
Going Home (*Hui jia* by Hon Lai-chu), 342n7
Good Friday/Belfast Agreement, 391, 413
Gordon, Ian, xxxvi
gothic tales, 19
Graham, Sarah, xvi, 33, 83, 160

Graham, Shane, 210
Gramsci, Antonio, 300, 383
graphic novels, xxxv–xxxvi
Grass, Gunter, 69
Gravel Heart (Gurnah), 3
Graziani, Rodolfo, 90–91
Great Expectations (Dickens), xxi, 4, 11, 12, 14, 17, 20, 59, 385
Gregorias (character, *Another Life*), 135, 138, 140–41, 146, 148, 153
Grey Flower (*Hui hua* by Hon Lai-chu), 328, 336, 338–39, 341, 342n7
Griqua people, 376
Guattari, Félix, 76, 325
Gunesekera, Romesh, 3
Gupta, Charu, 173
Gurnah, Adulrazak, xiv, 3
Guyana, 377, 383, 386
Gwee Li Sui, 245

Ha, Quan Manh, 417, 419
Habila, Helon, xl, 255
Halberstam, Jack, 419
Haldeman, Joe, 35
Half Eclipse (*Ban shi* by Hon Lai-chu), 341
Half of a Yellow Sun (Adichie), xxx, 311–14, 319
Hall, Peter, 35–36, 48
Hall, Stuart, 340, 371
Haraway, Donna, 430
Hardie, Melissa, xxxv, 183
Hardt, Michael, xxxiv
Harlow, Barbara, 274
Harrex, Syd, 78
Harris, Michael, xxxi
Hau, Caroline S., 112–13

haunting/haunted subjects, 411–12
Hay, Simon, 184, 272, 350
Hayi ibn Yaqdhan (Tufail), 5
Hegel, Georg Wilhelm Friedrich, 21–23, 134, 153, 155, 221. See also *Aufhebung* (Hegelian concept)
Heinlein, Robert, 35
Helff, Sissy, xxvi
Herder, Johann, 9
hero's journey as trope, 58, 122, 125n5
heteronormativity, 440, 441
Highway, Tomson, xiv
Himba people, 30, 40, 43–45
Hindi as national language, 165
Hindi cinema, xxxi
Hindi novel, 159, 160, 161–64
Hindu Mahasabha movement, 170, 173
Hindu Succession Act, 275, 277
"historical amnesia," 416
historicism, 20–23
History of Japan (Kaempfer), 200
Hizb ut-Tahrir, 388n1
Hoagland, Erika
  commentary on Farah's *Maps*, 94
  genealogy of the genre, xxxvi–xxxvii, 134
  as postcolonial theorist, xxiv, 132, 164
  as scholar of African Bildungsroman, xxxv, 99, 255, 350–52
  as scholar of Bildungsroman, xxvii, 83, 272, 275

INDEX   495

as scholar of postcolonial
Bildungsroman, 284–85,
350, 352, 357
theories of colonialist/
postcolonialist
Bildungsroman, xix, xxix–
xxx, 67, 184, 339–40
Holden, Philip, 230, 243, 246n1
home as contested concept, 275,
280–87
Hon Lai-chu—literary works of
absurdism/magic realism in, xli,
329, 336–38
as anti-Bildungsroman, 329
coming-of-age as generational,
338–39
early work and awards, 327–28
humans, things and animals,
328–33, 335, 338, 340
key themes, 328
notions of identity in, 333–39,
340–41
pictographic features of, 332–33
prose/nonfiction writing, 341
transformation as deformation
and degeneration, 329
trauma and unfreedom in, 342
See also The Border of
Centrifugation (Li xin dai);
Darkness Under the Sun
(Hei ri by Hon Lai-chu);
Empty Face (Kong lian);
"Forrest Woods, Chair";
Going Home (Hui jia); Grey
Flower (Hui hua); Half
Eclipse (Ban shi); Human
Skin Embroidery (Ren pi ci
xiu); The Kite Family (Feng
zheng jia zu); Losing Caves
(Shi qu dong xue); Mending
Bodies (Feng shen); The
Water Pipe Forest (Shu shui
guan sen lin)
Hong, Cathy Park, 426
Hong Kong
under British and Chinese rule,
323–25, 333, 342n1
coming-of-age in, xl–xli
discourses of market and
growth, 324
as "fluid cultural space," 326
as a "postcolonial anomaly,"
325, 342n1
"post-materialist" values in,
329
as pseudo-colonial, 332
representations of, 323, 325,
327, 342n5
urban space in, 332
See also Anti-Extradition Law
Amendment Bill (Anti-
ELAB) Movement;
"Umbrella Generation";
Umbrella Movement
Hong Kong literature
"be-coming of age," 339, 340–
41
of Cold War era, 326
and magical realism, 342n5
of postmillennial era, 325–28,
334
"rags to riches," 323
and refugee literature, 324, 340
as rhizomatic, 325, 338
of the "Umbrella Generation,"
324–25
Honwana, Alcinda, 468
Hua, Yu, xxix

human rights
    as interpretive lens, 271–72
    in postcolonial Bildungsroman,
        xxxii–xxxiii, 261
    and the postcolonial state, 276–
        77
    recognition and violations of,
        207, 254–55, 276
    and South Africa, xxxix
    See also United Nations
        Convention on the Rights of
        the Child (UNCRC)
Human Rights Inc. (Slaughter), 77,
    279, 302
Human Skin Embroidery (Ren pi ci
    xiu by Hon Lai-chu), 329,
    332
humanism; liberal humanism, xviii,
    xx, 8–9, 108–09, 122–23,
    287, 426
Hussein, Kadija, 84, 100–101
hybridity/hybrid subjectivity
    complexity of, 187
    in the diaspora Bildungsroman,
        85–86, 89, 93, 371
    of diaspora communities, 99
    in Filipino literature, 124–25
    in life of Igiaba Scego, 89
    of Parsis in India, 75
    in the postcolonial
        Bildungsroman, xxxvii, 84
    in postcolonial culture, 339
    of protagonist in Purple
        Hibiscus, 310

identity
    categories of, 387
    construction of, 371–72
    marginalized, xxxviii

    politics of, xxvi–xxvii, xli, 29
    racial and cultural, 373–78
Idris, Suhayl, xxviii
If We Dream Too Long (Goh),
    xxxix, 234, 235, 240, 242–43
Ifemelu (protagonist, Americanah),
    314–17, 319
Ifeoma, Aunty (character, Purple
    Hibiscus), 306–10
Igbo people and culture, 307–10,
    444, 446, 448–49, 459,
    460n7
Iheka, Cajetan, 343n8
Ihimaera, Witi, xiv
Ilmonen, Kaisa, xxv, xxix
Imagined Communities (Anderson),
    320n8
The Immolation (Goh), 234
imperial benevolence/saviour, 419
imperial imagination, 185–92, 192
imperialism
    and the colonialist
        Bildungsroman, xix–xxiii,
        xxxii, 13–16, 164
    as context/setting, 187, 287,
        351, 415–16
    epistemic violence of, 6, 17, 24
    and European competition, 185,
        190–91
    as master code of postcolonial
        Bildungsroman, 164
    and precondition of concept of
        child, xxi–xxii, 5–8, 442–43
    of United States (US), 416, 420,
        428, 431–32
    See also capitalism; colonialism
In the Castle of My Skin
    (Lamming), 3, 6, 132, 228

India
   class divisions, 165
   "coming of age" as nation, 180
   cult of violence in, 173
   Hindu Succession Act, 275, 277, 292n3
   identity, 383–84
   literary traditions, 161
   partition of, 70, 75–76, 168
   transition to independence, 159, 161
   youth, 160
   See also Naxalite (Marxist) movement
Indian Bildungsroman, xxxi, xxxvii, 60, 78, 280
   See also The God of Small Things (Roy)
indigeneity; Indigenous peoples
   cultural identity, xxx, 56, 67–68
   forms of female agency, 447
   forms of patriarchy, 444, 446
   gender fluidity, 444
   knowledge valued, 68–69
   models of childlessness, 444
   myths, 459
   selfhood, xxiii
   valued, 65–69
   writers' use of Bildungsroman, xviii
individualism, 12–13, 159. *See also* autonomous subject of modernity
Individualroman, 13
inequality—global economic, 289
inheritance, 277–78, 283
Inoue (Japanese magistrate), 191, 199, 201

intellectuals
   acting in the national interest, 299–301
   African intelligentsia, 320n3
   bridging of personal and collective experience, 318–19
   new vocation of, 313–14
   "organic"/public, 299–301
   peasant-become-intellectual, 311–13
   postcolonial, 301–04, 311
   professionalization of, 316
   transnational scope of, 314–18
The Intended (Dabydeen), 372, 377–78, 381–87
interiority, aesthetics of, 162
Ireland
   civil war, 413
   Irish as colonized subjects, 164
   language and literature, 392, 396, 405, 407–08
   nationalism, 74
   partition of, 391, 413
   twentieth-century history of, 391–92
   uneven modernity of, 396
Italian postcolonial studies, 89
Italy
   Blackness in, 101, 104n10
   citizenship legislation, 91, 103n7
   colonialism; colonial history suppressed, 84, 85, 86–91, 94, 102n4, 103n6
   diaspora in, 98–99, 101, 103n8
   racism in, 95–96, 104n9
   treatment of migrants, 85, 91

498   INDEX

Iweala, Uzodinma, xxx, 3. *See also
  Beasts of No Nation*

Jackson, Elizabeth, xli
Jal, Emmanuel, xxx
James, C.L.R., 150
James, Henry, 58
Jameson, Frederic, 65, 72, 215, 233,
  245, 268n1
Jane Eyre (Brontë), xxi, 17, 19, 20,
  441
Japan, 185–86, 189–90, 195, 199–
  201
Japanese Christians, 185, 187, 193–
  200
Japanese literature, 192
Jean Christophe (Rolland), 167
Jegan (character, *Funny Boy*), 275,
  285
Jinnah, Muhammad Ali, 56, 75
Joannou, Maroula, xxvii
Johnny Mad Dog (Dongala), xxx
Jones, Phil, 467
Jones, Tom (protagonist, *The
  History of Tom Jones, a
  Foundling*), 277
Joyce, James
  anti-development theme of, 398
  Künstlerroman of, 164
  personal/national return to
    origins, 73–74
  and protagonist's self-
    realization, 393
  reclaiming language, 59, 63, 69
  reimagined Bildungsroman,
    xvii, xviii, 159
  youth in novels of, xx
  See also Dubliners; *A Portrait of
    the Artist as a Young Man*

The Joys of Motherhood
  (Emecheta), 438, 443, 448–
  53, 458
Jussawalla, Feroza, xix, xxii–xxiii,
  xxxvii, 252

Kaempfer, Engelbert, 200–201
Kafka, Franz, 69, 329
Kahf, Mohja, 62
Kala, Violet, xxx
Kambili (protagonist, *Purple
  Hibiscus*), 305–10, 318
Kant, Immanuel, 7–8, 108, 109
Kanthapura (Rao), 62–63
Karafilis, Maria, 339
Keller, Gottfried, xvi
Kenya, xiv
Kerala (India), 272–73, 276, 278,
  289, 294n19
Khoi language, 376
Khouma, Pap, 94
Kim (Kipling), xxiii
"Kim, Huck, and Naipaul"
  (Jussawalla), 58
Kincaid, Jamaica, xxxiii–xxxiv
King, Andrew David, xxxviii
King, Martin Luther, Jr., 72
Kipling, Rudyard, xiii, xvii, xx,
  xxiii, 109, 110. *See also Kim*
The Kite Family (*Feng zheng jia zu*
  by Hon Lai-chu), 328
Kittler, Friedrich, xxxv
"knowing subalterns," xiv
Koh Tai Ann, 235, 237
Kok Seng Tan, 245
Koolhaus, Remi, 233
Kourouma, Ahmadou, xxx
Krishnamurthy, Aruna, xxxviii
Kuala Lumpur, 234

Kubrick, Stanley, 211, 430
Kultur (culture), 111
Künstlerroman
    classic form of, 418
    in colonialist Bildungsroman, xx
    modernist form of, 162, 164
    in postcolonial writing, 97, 133, 135–36, 145, 165, 255, 420–21
    as subgenre, 102n2, 132–33
Kureishi, Hanif, xxvi, 62
Kuruvilla, Gabriella, 94
Kwang Meng (protagonist, *If We Dream Too Long*)
    acquiescence of, 240–42
    and colonial architecture, 235–36, 238
    dull life of, 235, 238–41, 245–46
    and "generational lateness," 227–28, 242
    literary education of, 243–44
    memories of Chinatown, 236–38
    Shakespearean quote, 241–43
    stealing of office time, 244–45

La mia casa è dove sono (Scego), 83–90, 97–102
A la recherce du temps perdu (Proust), 168
labyrinth as metaphor, 393–94
Lacanian theory, 16, 18
Lagos, 316–18, 449
Lahore, 176
Lamming, George, 3, 6, 132, 228
Lampedusa, 99
Lane, M. Travis, 138
Lapierre, Dominique, 75–76
Laye, Camara, xxxv, 363
Lee, Rachel, 417
Lee Kwan Yew, 227, 229–34
L'Enfant Noir (Laye), xxxv
Lesk, Andrew, 279
Lessing, Doris, xxvii
Leung Ping-kwan, 331–32, 342n5
Levy, Michael, 34
Lewis, R.W.B., 73
Li, Hua, xxix
liberal humanism. *See* humanism
liberal subject, 441. *See also* autonomous subject of modernity; neoliberal subject
liberalism, 308–09, 420, 425. *See also* freedom; humanism
Liberation Tamil Tigers of the Tamil Eeelam (LTTE), 285–86
Libya, 86
Lim, Catherine, 245
Lima, Maria Helena, xxxii, 32, 77, 83, 349, 357
Lindfors, Bernth, 360
Lindow, Sandra, 31, 48
Lingala (language), 262
Lion in the Desert (Akkad), 86
Liptak, Andrew, 46
L'Italia in Africa (Italian Ministry of Foreign Affairs), 90–91
Little Dog (protagonist, *On Earth We're Briefly Gorgeous*)
    as archivist of precarity, death, and ruins, 427–28
    death of lover Trevor, 417, 427, 434
    education and identity of, 421–28
    language skills of, 422–25

letters written by, 417, 421, 427, 433
name of, 425
queerness/coming out of, 419, 420
racial whitening of, 422–23
relationship with mother, 417, 418–21, 424–25, 429–30
Little Women (Alcott), 441
Lloyd, David, 407–8
The Location of Culture (Bhabha), 75
Loh Kah Seng, 233
Lomba (protagonist, *Waiting for an Angel*), 255, 256–61
Lombardi-Diop, Cristina, 103n6
London, UK, xli
A Long Way Gone: Memoirs of a Boy Soldier (Beah), xxx
Losing Caves (*Shi qu dong xue* by Hon Lai-chu), 329, 336
Lowe, Lisa, 418, 420, 422
Loyola, St. Ignatius of, 403
Lukács, Georg, 134, 302
Lyde, L.W., 6

Ma, Ling, 422, 434n4
Mabanckou, Alain, xl, 255, 261–62
Macao, 191
macaque, eating of, 430–34
Macaulay, Thomas, 6, 56, 442
Macgoye, Marjorie Oludhe, xxiii, 443
Macherey, Pierre, 16
Macura-Nnamdi, Ewa, 356, 361–62, 367n4
magical realism, xxvi, xli, 69, 342n5
Magritte, René, 334

Magwitch (protagonist, *Great Expectations*), 14, 17, 18, 20
Maher, Ashley, 36–37, 48
Mais, Roger, 132
Malay nationalism, 230
Malaysia, 227, 230, 234, 243
Malcolm X, 91
"male daughter," 444, 448
Mamdani, Mahmood, 208
The Man Died (Soyinka), 257
Mandela, Nelson, 72
Mansfield Park (Austen), 15
Maoism, 230
Maps (Farah), 85, 94, 440
Marcos, Ferdinand, 114
Markandaya, Kamala, xxx
Marshall, Paula, 156n1
Marx, John, 311
Marx, Karl, 22
Marxism, xv, 261, 285, 302, 304
masculinity
    of British colonials, 173, 243
    as cisheteropatriarchal authority, 422, 434n2
    in colonial/postcolonial India, 163, 169–74
    imperial, 428
    and insecurity, 175
    violence of, 427
Masks of Conquest: Literary Study and British Rule in India (Viswanathan), 55
Matlawa, Kopano, 3
maturation
    in African Bildungsroman, 39–41, 253, 255, 264
    in carceral Bildungsroman, xl
    of Chetan (*Falling Walls*), 160–61, 164, 175, 178–79

in colonial contexts, 465–66
in diaspora Bildungsroman, xxxvii, 85, 101
in graphic novels, xxxvi
impossibility for neo/colonized subjects, 107, 264, 340
in modernist Bildungsroman, 163
in postcolonial Bildungsroman, 124, 240, 349, 371–72
in traditional Bildungsroman, 84, 109, 112, 163, 183, 239, 363, 366
in Tutuola's writing, xli, 350–52, 354, 359
Matz, Aaron, 440, 441
Maus (Spiegelman), xxxvi
Mbembe, Achille, 216, 221, 355, 365
McClatchy, D.J., 131
McCulloch, Fiona, xxvii
McKinley, William, 110
McPherson, Conor, 397
"media ecologies," xxxv
Meeting the Universe Halfway (Barad), 48
Memmi, Albert, 90
Memoirs of a Spacewoman (Mitchison), 36, 37, 47
Memory of Departure (Gurnah), 3
Mending Bodies (*Feng shen* by Hon Lai-chu), 328, 336, 341
mentors, 6–7, 8, 10
The Merchant of Venice (Shakespeare), 241
"Metamorphosis" (Kafka), 329
Middle Passage, 155
Middlemarch (Eliot), 441

Midnight's Children (Rushdie), xxx–xxxi, 56, 57, 64–65, 69–71
migrant deaths at sea, 99–100
Miller, Meredith, xxviii
mimicry (Bhabha), 381
missionaries, 189–92, 447
The Mistress of Spices (Divakaruni), 77
Mitchison, Naomi, 36–37, 47
"model minorities," 417, 421
modernist Bildungsroman, 161, 163–64
modernity
  African, 255–56, 259, 267
  associated with youth, 252–53, 339
  capitalist, 161
  as challenge to tradition, xiv, xlii
  civility as master narrative of, 408
  colonial, xviii–xxi, xxiv, 466
  contradictions and "monstrosities" of, xxii, 266, 355, 359, 366, 367n5
  European, 203n1
  global, xxxix, 256, 267, 419
  in Indian Bildungsroman, 163, 169, 172, 175, 178, 180
  naturalized in classic Bildungsroman, 302
  postcolonial, xxvii, 151, 259, 288
  rights and freedoms of, xxiii, 302, 420
  in Singapore, 233, 237
  Western, 3–5, 19, 108
  See also liberalism

Modernity at Large (Appadurai), 288
Mogadishu, 84
monsters/monstrous subjects, 418–19
Moore, Gerald, 351, 362
Mootoo, Shani, xxix
Moretti, Franco
    on capitalist modernity, 161, 178, 224n5, 239
    as scholar of Bildungsroman, xxxiv, 60, 101, 111, 339, 395–96
    on superindividual forces, 400, 403
    on theme of inheritance, 277
    on youth and modernity, 18, 163, 273
Moses (protagonist, *Black Moses*), 261–66, 267
Mother Africa trope, 439, 444
Mukherjee, Bharati, 372
Mukherjee, Upamanyu Pablo, xxxiii
Muñoz, José Estaban, 419
Murphy, Laura, 354, 367n2
"The Muse of History" (Walcott), 136
Mussolini, Benito, 90–91
My Days (Narayan), 59
My Life in the Bush of Ghosts (Tutuola)
    capitalism/consumerism in, 362
    education as deformation, 364–65
    interpretations of, 359–62
    inversions/subversions in, 356–57
    maturation of protagonist, xli, 350–52, 354, 359
    as myth, 354–55
    as novel of anti-development, 359, 362
    as a novel of transformation, xli, 351
    plot of, 350, 352, 356–58, 361
    slavery/enslavement in, 352–55, 361, 362, 367n2
    technology in, 352–56
    temporal ambiguity, 353–54
My Son the Fanatic (Kureishi), 62
myth, 20, 24n4, 354–55

Naipaul, V.S., 132
Narayan, R.K., xxiii, xxx, 3, 55, 57, 59, 67, 243, 244
Nat King Cole, 88
nation as "imagined community" (Anderson), 57, 71
The Nation Writ Small (Andrade), 303
"national allegories," 3, 65, 71, 137, 242, 252–53, 268n1, 293n12, 443, 457
national subjects, creation of, 207–09
Nationalist Thought and the Colonial World (Chatterjee), 74
nationhood/national development
    allegories of, 65, 242, 268n1
    as key trope of Bildungsroman, 251, 441
    literature as a tool of, 112–14
    as necropolitical, 216
    and neoliberal elites, 113–14

in postapartheid South Africa,
  207–11, 212–13
in the postcolonial
  Bildungsroman, 56–58, 61
in postcolonial thought, 71–72
twinning of protagonist's and
  nation's development, 184,
  228, 302, 395
violence of, 215–16
nation-state
  as capitalist/administrative,
    466
  critique of, 289
  decline and destabilization of,
    184, 276, 293n6
  masculinity and whiteness of,
    422
  as modern/rights-based, xxix,
    xxxii
  as organic, 251
  and sense of home/belonging,
    61, 281
  violence/exclusions of, 217, 218,
    222
  See also denationalization;
    postcolonial states
Native Believer (Eteraz), 62
native informants, 426
Naturalizing Africa (Iheka), 343n8
Naxalite (Marxist) movement, 273,
  285
Nayar, Pramod, xiv–xv, 61, 62
necropolitical power, xxxix, 209,
  216
Neel, Philip, 467
Negri, Antonio, xxxiv
Nehru, Jawaharlal, 56
neocolonialism
  in Africa, 46

and Christian proselytism, 99
as context of postcolonial
  Bildungsroman, xv, 39, 113,
  124, 231, 305, 350–51
in India, 69
neoliberal subject, 427
neoliberalism/neoliberal
  globalization, xxxiv, 267,
  288–89, 415–18, 421, 428
Nepaulsingh, Colbert, 131, 136
Neruda, Pablo, 97
Nervous Conditions
  (Dangarembga), xxxiii, 85,
  228, 465–66
Netland, John, 187
Neumann, Birgit, 423, 424
New Criticism, 108
New Story movement (India), 162
New Zealand, xiv
Ng, Linda, 40
Ngũgĩ wa Thiong'o, xiv, xxiii, 3,
  55–56, 66–68, 254, 363
Nguyen, Mimi Thi, 419
Nguyen, Viet Thanh, 416, 417,
  434n2
Nietzsche, Friedrich, 22
Nigeria
  and Biafran revolution, 311
  capitalist economy of, 366, 448
  carceral politics of, 256, 258
  decimation of publishing and
    education sectors, 259
  feminist writers, xlii
  folklore, 359, 360
  literature of, 351
  loss of public intellectuals, 300
  as multi-ethno-cultural, 308
  neoliberal economy of, 267

political despotism of, xl, 255,
  256–58, 261, 267, 308
  See also Abacha, General Sani
Nigerian Bildungsroman. *See*
  female Nigerian
  Bildungsroman
Night Sky with Exit Wounds
  (Vuong), 426
Nixon, Rob, xxxiii
Njamba Nene and the Cruel Chief
  (Ngũgĩ), 68
Njamba Nene and the Flying Bus
  (Ngũgĩ), 68
Nobel Prize for Literature, 3
Noli Me Tangere (Rizal), 111, 112
nomadism, 76
No-No Boy (Okada), 418
non-realist genres, xxvii
Northern Ireland, 391, 396
Nussbaum, Martha, 123, 125, 275
Nwapa, Flora, xlii, 438

Obama, Barack, 96
Obatala (Yoruba deity), 456
Okada, John, 418
Okorafor, Nnedi, 29–31, 36–41,
  46–49
Okri, Ben, 366
Okuyade, Ogaga, 253–54, 263, 305
Olney, James, 138
Omar (grandfather of Igiaba
  Scego), 91–93
Omelsky, Matthew, 356
O'Murphy, Marie-Louise, 408
On Earth We're Briefly Gorgeous
  (Vuong)
  animal-human relations, 421,
    423, 429–33
  artist reimagined in, 421
  bestiary in, 433–34
  checkpoint scene, 429, 431–33
  as coming-of-age narrative, 416
  critique of liberal humanism,
    426–27
  foreclosure of future, 418–21,
    427
  and intergenerational trauma,
    417
  as Künstlerroman, 416, 417,
    421
  language, humanness, and
    national belonging, 422–25
  macaque, eating of, 430, 431–
    34
  plot of, 417–18
  queer poetics of, xlii
  racialization, 431–32
  and US film tropes, 430–31
  See also Little Dog (protagonist)
opioid epidemic, 417, 427, 428
opium wars, 323
oral storytelling, xxxi, 57, 364
Orange, Tommy, 415
The Order of Things (Foucault),
  133, 154
"organic" metaphor, 302–03
Orientalism
  and colonial power, 110
  critiques of, 107, 108, 120
  discourses of, 12, 22
  distancing of historical, 434n2
  and East-West binary, 187,
    188–89
  in European views of Japan, 190
  theorized by Said, 109, 111
  See also Kipling, Rudyard; Said,
    Edward; "White Man's
    Burden" (Kipling)

Orientalism (Said), 111
Ormsbee, Michael, 32–34, 37
Ostry, Elaine, 29, 46–47
otherness, 16–18, 19, 31, 39
Ouma, Christopher E.W., 305
Out of Africa (Blixen), 68
Overseas Contract Workers (OCW), 115, 120
Overseas Filipino Intellectuals, 114, 120–21
Overseas Filipino Workers (OFW), 114–15, 120
Oxford University, 377

Palmerston, Lord, 323
The Palm-Wine Drinkard (Tutuola), 360–61
Paradise (Gurnah), 3
Parameswaran, Uma, 78n2
Paranjape, Makarand, xxxi
Parayil, Govindan, 289
Parrinder, Geoffrey, 362
Parsis (of India), 75–76
patriarchy/patriarchal domination, 388n1, 416, 434n2, 444, 446, 459
Patron Saints of Nothing (Ribay), xxxvii–xxxviii, 107, 112, 115, 116–25
People's Action Party (PAP), 227, 229–30, 233, 236, 238, 241
Peterson, Carla, 5
phantom development, 391, 395, 397, 411–12. See also *Reading in the Dark* (Deane)
Phantom Formations: Aesthetic Ideology and the Bildungsroman (Redfield), 395

Philippine Bildungsroman, 107, 112, 115, 125n1, 125n4
Philippine-American War, 109
Philippines
    colonial history, 107, 109–10
    elites of, 113–14, 123
    epics and heroes, 120
    as exporter of labour, 115
    as imagined nation, 115–16, 125n2, 125n4
    legislated curriculum ("Rizal Bill"), 112–13
    "migration revolution," 114–15
    post-independence history, 114, 120
    represented as poor, 124
    war on drugs, 115, 117, 119, 120–22
Philosophy of Right (Hegel), 153
picaresque, 5, 168, 264, 468, 469
pilgrimage, xiii, 44
Pip (protagonist, *Great Expectations*), xxii, 12, 14, 15, 17, 18, 385
planetarity, 275, 290–91
"planetary consciousness," 287
plantations, 15, 243, 338, 383
Pointe-Noir (Congo), 263, 264, 265, 266
Ponzanesi, Sandra, 86–87, 103n6
Population Registration Act (South Africa), 373, 374, 379
A Portrait of the Artist as a Young Man (Joyce), 66–67, 73–74, 136, 385, 393
Portuguese merchants, 191
postcolonial Bildungsroman

anti-colonial and nationalist feeling in, xxiv–xxvi, xxv, 61, 65–69, 74, 251–52
and anti-colonialism, xxiv–xxvi
childlessness in, 442–43
compared with colonialist Bildungsroman, xxii–xxiii
compared with traditional Bildungsroman, 84
contradictions/dilemmas of, 251–53, 272–73, 299, 311, 325, 349–52
cross-cultural models of, xxviii–xxxii
indefinite postponement of self-realization, 273, 357, 433
internationalization of, 280
key features of, 63, 67
narrative forms of, xxxiv–xxxvi, 385–87
as a novel of transformation, 387
protagonist's coming-of-age twinned with national self-determination, 228, 252
protagonist's embrace of indigeneity, 65–70, 71
as realist genre, 58, 62–63, 65
reconfiguring of, 272
as resistance narrative, 67
revised coming-of-age plots in, xxvii–xxviii
theories of, xviii–xix, 301
unsettled futurity in, 228
and "writing back" to colonizers, 4
See also African Bildungsroman; AIDS Bildungsroman; anti-Bildungsroman; Arabic Bildungsroman; carceral states Bildungsroman; Caribbean Bildungsromane; Chinese American Bildungsromane; diaspora Bildungsroman; female Nigerian Bildungsroman; Hong Kong literature; Indian Bildungsroman; Philippine Bildungsroman; postcolonial science fiction Bildungsroman; posthuman science fiction Bildungsroman; queer Bildungsroman; reverse Bildungsroman; science fiction (SF) Bildungsroman; South Asian Bildungsroman

The Postcolonial Bildungsroman (ed. Roy and Ugor)
aim and scope of book, xv–xvi
authors' contributions and themes, xxxvi–xliii
postcolonial Bildungsroman, theorists of. *See* Cheah, Pheng; Esty, Jed; Fernández-Vázquez, José-Santiago; Hoagland, Erika; Jussawalla, Feroza; Lima, Maria Helena; Moretti, Franco; Slaughter, Joseph

Postcolonial Environments (Mukherjee), xxxiii

Postcolonial Fiction and Disability: Exceptional Children, Metaphor and Materiality (Barker), 275

INDEX 507

postcolonial literature, 55–58, 61, 65, 71–72, 77–78, 252
postcolonial resistance, 343n8
postcolonial science fiction Bildungsroman, 32
postcolonial sovereignty, 216, 221, 222
postcolonial states
  corruption, cronyism, and cruelty, 267
  denationalization of, 275, 276, 279–80, 284, 285, 287, 288
  as divisive versus unitary, 276
  failure to enshrine rights, 280
  See also states/state power
postcolonial subjects. See under subject formation
postcolonial theory, 91, 108–09, 204n5, 334. See also Bhabha, Homi; Gandhi, Leela; Hall, Stuart; Said, Edward; Spivak, Gayatri
Postcolonial Theory: A Critical Introduction (Gandhi), 125n1
Postcolonizing the Bildungsroman: A Study of the Evolution of the Genre (Hoagland), 67
posthuman science fiction Bildungsroman, 38
posthumanism/posthuman era, 29, 30, 39, 46, 48
postmillenial era, 327, 329, 332, 339, 340
postmodernism, xxvii, 63–64, 70, 79n3, 336
Potts, Matthew, 187–88
Practical Criticism, 108

precarity/precariat, 217–18, 417, 427
"The Prelude" (Wordsworth), 141
Premchand, Munshi, 161, 162
primitive accumulation, xxxiv
print book, demise of, 469
Pritchett, V.S., 367–68n7
protagonists
  arrests and "arrested development" of, 255
  coming of age with alterity, 340–41
  reconciliation with indigenous/ national culture, 67–69, 339
  as returning hero, trope of, 116
  and twinned development with nation, 6–7, 184, 189, 224n6, 252, 301–02, 359
  writers as, 304
  See also agency; children/ childhood; maturation of protagonist; self-actualization/self-cultivation; subject formation
protest movements, 469–70
Proust, Marcel, 167–68, 180n1
Puckett, Kent, 133, 134
Puleo, Simone Maria, xxxvii
Punjabi poets/poetry slams, 176
Purple Hibiscus (Adichie), 3, 94, 305–11, 314, 318

Quayson, Ato, 152, 351, 359
queer Bildungsroman, xxvii–xxviii
queer diaspora, 425–26
queer of colour theorists, 419
queer poetics, xlii, 428, 429, 434
queer subjects, 416, 419–420

queer theory, xv, 460

race studies, 72
racial capitalism, xxxix, 214, 222
Racial Castration: Managing Masculinity in Asian America (Eng), 434n3
racialized queer subjects, 419, 423
racism
    blogging about, 315–16
    experienced by postcolonial subjects, xli, 423–24
    in Guyana, 383–84
    internalized, 383–84
    in Italian society, 85, 95–96
    of Portuguese missionaries, 188, 192–98
    in postcolonial Bildungsroman, 465
    and racial construction of gender, 264
    racial stereotypes, xli
    racialization in law, 424
    in South Africa, 375, 379–81
    See also apartheid—South Africa
Rahel and Estha (twin protagonists, *The God of Small Things*), 272, 275–79, 285–86
Ramazani, Jahan, 136
Rao, Raja, xxx, 55, 62–63
"Reading Barbara Kingsolver's *Poisonwood Bible*" (Jussawalla), 58
Reading in the Dark (Deane)
    as "attempt to forge identity," 391–92
    compared to Joyce's *Portrait of the Artist*, 393
    education, 402–04, 408
    forgetting in, 412–13
    interpreted as coming-of-age story, 392
    narrator's embodiment of trauma, 400–02, 404–06
    narrator's failure to develop, 397, 408–09
    narrator's fixation on the past, xli–xlii, 394, 396–400
    phantom selfhood, 395, 406, 410–11
    plot and historical span of, 396–97
    superindividual forces in, 400, 403
    trauma of Crazy Joe, 394, 397–98, 400, 401, 406–13
    as troubled postcolonial Bildungsroman, 392–95
realism
    in classic Bildungsroman, xxvii, 58, 64, 78, 159, 161
    in postcolonial Bildungsroman, 58, 62–63, 71, 162, 164. *See also* magical realism
Redfield, Marc, 10, 107–8, 110, 395
Reguero, Jay (protagonist, *Patron Saints of Nothing*), 116–25
Relich, Mario, 385
remittances, 115
Renan, Ernest, 71
reparations (for apartheid), 208
repronormativity, 439
residential schools, xiv
Reuter, Stefanie, 321n14
reverse Bildungsroman, 77

Rhodesia, xxxiii. *See also* Zimbabwe
Ribay, Randy, xxxvii, 107, 112, 116, 124
Ribic, Peter, xxxix
Richardson, Dorothy, xxvii
rite-of-passage, xxii, xvi, 21. *See also* "coming-of-age" narratives
Rizal, José, 111, 113, 115, 118
Robin Hood, 265–66
Robinson Crusoe (Defoe), 5
Rockwell, Daisy, 165–66, 168, 176
Rolland, Romain, 167
Roman Catholics. *See* Catholic Church
Romeo, Caterina, 103n6
Roosevelt, Theodore, 109, 110
Rousseau, Jean-Jacques, 140
Roy, Arundhati, 71, 272, 283, 287–89, 295n23, 295n26. *See also The God of Small Things*
Rushdie, Salman
    and alternative modernities, xxii
    empire writes back, xxv
    indigeneity ("Indianness") reclaimed, xxiii, xxx, 69–70
    literary ancestry of, 59–60
    as postmodernist, 59, 63–64
    as realist, 63–64
    scholarship on, 56
    stabbing of, 64
    use of Bildungsroman genre, xiii
    use of oral tradition by, xxxi
    See also Midnight's Children

Said, Edward, 4, 12, 14, 20, 22, 109, 111

Saint Lucia, 135, 138, 142–43
Salih, Tayeb, 363
Sammons, Jeffrey, xvi
Sankara, Thomas, 257
Sankaran Krishna, 288–89
Sansalvadore, Giovanna, 103n6
Sanyal, Kalyan, 219
Sartre, Jean-Paul, 243
Sassen, Saskia, 276
The Satanic Verses (Rushdie), 56, 57, 64
Sayer, Geoffrey Robley, 323
Scego, Ali Omar, 84, 87–88
Scego, Igiaba
    as author, 83, 101–2
    diaspora experience of, 84–85, 89, 91, 96–98
    family history, 84–85, 87–88, 92–93, 100–01
    on Italian colonialism, 86, 89–90, 94, 101
    racism experienced by, 95–98
    See also La mia casa è dove sono
Schoene-Harwood, Berthold, xxvii–xxviii
science fiction (SF) Bildungsroman, 29, 30, 33–36, 40
"scientific socialism," 265
Scott. Sir Walter, 243
"The Second Coming" (Yeats), 343n8
Second World War, 323
self-actualization/self-cultivation, 61–62, 93, 137, 146, 164, 184–85
self-immolation, 17
Selvadurai, Shyam, 272, 294n16. *See also Funny Boy*
Seng, Goh Poh, xxxix

Severance (Ma), 422, 434n4
sexual abuse/violence, 87, 216, 218–20, 282, 312–13
Shadiram, Pandit (character, *Falling Walls*), 169–71, 173
Shakespeare, works of, 243
Sharmarke, Abdirashid Ali, 88
Shenton, Frieda (protagonist, *You Can't Get Lost in Cape Town*), 372–73, 375–77, 379–81, 385–86
Sicherman, Carol, 374
Sidhwa, Bapsi, xxx, 57, 74–75
Silence (Endō)
    European-Japanese trade relations, 189, 190–91
    Jonassen's perspective, 198–202
    Kichijiro's perspective, 185, 192–98
    postcolonial analysis of, 187–89
    racism of Rodrigues, 188, 192–98
    Rodrigues' Eurocentric worldview, 189–92
    Rodrigues' spiritual dilemma, xxxix, 187–89
    as transimperial text, 184–85, 186, 202
    triangulation of perspectives, 185–87, 192, 202–03
    See also fumie, trampling on
silk trade, 191
The Silver Pilgrimage (Anantanarayanan), xxxi
Simbi and the Satyr of the Dark Jungle (Tutuola), 360
Simmons, Harry (character, *Another Life*), 133, 135, 138, 146, 148–50

Singapore
    as authoritarian developmental state, xxxix, 245
    colonial architecture of, 235–36, 237–38
    depoliticized independence, 229, 238–39, 246
    as "a heart without a body," 230, 231
    and immobilization of the masses, 233
    as model capitalist economy, 228–33
    as mundane, 233–34, 239
    national literature of, 229, 245–46
    postcolonial identity of, 229–34
    refashioning of national subjects, 232–33
    separation from Malaysia, 227, 230
    utilitarian architecture of, 232–33, 235–38
    See also People's Action Party (PAP); Singapore Story as state narrative
Singapore Story as state narrative, 229, 230–34, 235, 245
The Singapore Story: Memoirs of Lee Kwan Yew (Lee), 229, 230, 232–33
Singh, Sujala, 278–79
Sinhala language, 275, 277, 292n3
Sino-British Joint Declaration, 323, 327
Sitze, Adam, 208
Slaughter, Joseph
    on African Bildungsroman, 267–68

comparison of colonialist/
    postcolonialist
    Bildungsroman, xxii–xxiii
defining features of postcolonial
    Bildungsroman, 273, 387,
    433
on human rights and
    Bildungsroman, xxxii–
    xxxiii, 77, 254, 272, 274, 279
on humanism and globalization,
    287
scholarship on Bildungsroman,
    xiv, xviii, xvi, 83, 94, 302,
    415–16
slavery/enslavement
    as backdrop in Austen's novels,
    15
    in USA, 416
    in West African literature,
    367n2, 451–52
slow death, 428
slow violence, xxxiv
A Small Place (Kincaid), xxxiii–
    xxxiv
Smith, Craig, xl
Smith, Vanessa, xxxv, 183
Smith, Zadie, 59, 71
Somali immigrants and refugees,
    84, 85, 87, 99–100
Somalia, 84–85, 87–89, 97, 99–100
Song for Night (Abani), xxx
South Africa
    "Coloured" identity in, 211–12,
    214–15, 224n4, 373–75, 377
    language hierarchy in, 376
    and politics of death, 216–17,
    220–22

and post-apartheid subject
    formation, xxxix, 207–09,
    212–16, 219, 222–23
those "born too late," 210
violence of post-apartheid
    society, 216–19, 221–23
See also Truth and
    Reconciliation Commission
    (TRC)
South Asia, xiii, xv, xxvi, xxix,
    280, 377, 382
South Asian Bildungsroman, xi,
    xxx–xxxi, xl, 271. *See also
    Funny Boy* (Selvadurai); *The
    God of Small Things* (Roy);
    Midnight's Children
    (Rushdie)
South London, 377, 378
Southeast Asia, xv
Soyinka, Wole, 56, 155, 257
Spanish language, 423
Spanish-American War, 109
Spectral Nationality (Cheah), 111,
    116
Spiegelman, Art, xxxvi
spiritual Bildungsroman, xxxix
*The Spiritual Exercises of St.
    Ignatius of Loyola*, 403–04
Spivak, Gayatri, 6, 17, 74, 151, 275,
    287–91
Sreekumar, T.T., 289
Sri Lanka
    anti-Tamil pogroms/ethnic
    riots, 277, 281, 283–84
    ethnic segregation, 278
    international condemnation of,
    280
    ratification of UNCRC, 292n1

representation in fiction, xxxi, 272–73, 280
Sinhala dominance in, 281–82
Sinhala Only Act, 275, 277, 292n3
social inequalities, 273
See also Funny Boy (Selvadurai); Liberation Tamil tigers of the Tamil Eeelam (LTTE)
St. Lucia, 132
St. Omer, Dunstan ("Gregorias"), 133
Star Trek, 31
Starship Troopers (Heinlein), 35
states/state power
  carceral politics of, 263–65
  in classical Bildungsroman, 222
  despotism of, 259
  experienced by children, 279
  in modernity, 216
  as necropolitical, 209
  in post-apartheid South Africa, 210
  protection from, 217
  as regenerative in classical Bildungsroman, 209
  See also postcolonial states
Stay with Me (Adébáyò), 460n2
Steemers, Vivian, 262
Stein, Mark, xiv, 387
Steinecke, Hartmut, 13
Sterne, Lawrence, 440
Stevenson, Robert Louis, 243
Stiegler, Bernard, 140
Stitt, Jocelyn, 252
Straits Times, 243, 245
Stratton, Florence, 449, 452

subject formation
  in colonialist Bildungsromane, xvii–xviii
  of Little Dog (*On Earth We're Briefly Gorgeous*), 424
  in post-apartheid South Africa, 215–16, 219–23
  of postcolonial subjects, xli, 228, 352, 395–96
  in science fiction Bildungsromane, 36
  See also national subjects
Sufi traditions, xiii
Suncatcher (Gunesekera), 3
supernatural events, 19
Swami and Friends (Narayan), 3, 57, 59, 65–68, 74
Syrian Christians, 277, 283, 286

Taft, William Howard, 110
Taiwan, 328, 331
Talaue-Arogo, Antonette, xxxvii–xxxviii
Tambu (protagonist, *Nervous Conditions*), 465–66, 470
Tamil people, 276, 277, 278, 281, 283, 292n3. *See also Funny Boy* (Selvadurai); Sri Lanka
Tanzania, xiv, 467
"terrorism" and "terrorist" groups, 284, 285
Tet Offensive, 429
"the Troubles," 393–94
There There (Orange), 415
thing-chanting (Chinese poetry), 331
Things Fall Apart (Achebe), 343n8

"Third-World Literature in the Era
  of Multinational Capitalism"
  (Jameson), 72
Thirteen Cents (Duiker), 209
This Mournable Body
  (Dangarembga), 470
Thumboo, Edwin, 245
Tobin, Robert, 18
Tolentino, Rolando B., 115
Tompkins, Mia, 417, 419
Tong, Su, xxix
tourism, xxiv, 289, 290, 470
Tower Society, 8, 9, 10
Townsend, Sarah L., 396
*Tragedy and Postcolonial
  Literature* (Quayson), 152
transimperial world, 202
Translations (Friel), 409
transnationalism, xxix
trauma
  of abusive parenting, 169–71
  of apartheid, 208, 210, 213
  of the *Bildung* process, 40
  in colonialist Bildungsromane, 39
  of colonization (Caribbean), xxiv, 137
  of Crazy Joe, 406–13
  experienced by children, 284
  in postcolonial Bildungsromane, 39, 43, 46, 84
  theory of, 30, 43
  of Vietnam war, 429
  of war, poverty, and patriarchal violence, 419
travel narratives, 12
TRC Literature, 209–10, 223n3
Triangular Road (Marshall), 156n1
Trinidad, xxix

Tristram Shandy (Sterne), 440
Trocki, Carl A., 233
Truman, Harry, 230
Truth and Method (Gadamer), 412
Truth and Reconciliation
  Commission (TRC), xxxix,
  207, 211–15, 218, 222–23,
  223n1-2, 224n7
The Truths and Lies of Nationalism
  (Chatterjee), 74
Tufail, Ibn, 5
Tunca, Daria, 305
Tutuola, Amos, 350–51, 359–67.
  See also *My Life in the Bush
  of Ghosts*; *The Palm-Wine
  Drinkard*
Twain, Mark, xiii, xxiii. See also
  *The Adventures of
  Huckleberry Finn* (Twain)
Tynyanov, Yury, 32

Ugwu (protagonist, *Half of a
  Yellow Sun*), 311–14, 319
Uhamiri (female deity), 444, 445, 447, 449, 451, 452
Ulin, Julieann Veronica, xli–xlii
Ulysses (Joyce), 136
"Umbrella Generation," 324
Umbrella Movement, 324, 341, 342n7
UN Resolution 289 (Somalia under
  UN trusteeship), 88
underdevelopment, 407, 466
unitary subject, 16, 47. See also
  autonomous subject of
  modernity
United Nations Convention on the
  Rights of the Child
  (UNCRC), xl, 271–77, 280–

81, 283, 291–92, 292–93n4,
    294n17, 294n21
United Nations (UN), 280
United States of America (USA)
    and colonization of Philippines,
        109–10
    heteronormative culture of, 419
    immigrants and immigration
        policy, 280–81, 314, 434n4
    imperialism and imperial wars,
        416, 420, 428, 432
    and legal erasure of Asian
        immigrants, 424
    racial schemas of, 433
    as setting for Bildungsroman,
        xlii
    war against Vietnam, 417, 430,
        432
    war with Spain, 109
    and white nationalism, 418
universal subject, 415–16
University of Strathclyde, 377
University of the Western Cape,
    372, 375, 377, 380
University of Warwick, 377
Unseasonable Youth (Esty), 402,
    407

Vadde, Aarthi, 289
van der Vlies, Andrew, 375
Veltroni, Walter, 99
Velutha (character, *The God of
    Small Things*), 275, 278,
    284–86, 290, 291
Victorian Bildungsroman, 440–41
Victorian morals and beliefs, 446
Vietnam, 417, 419, 420, 430
Vietnam War, 109, 429, 430, 432

Vietnamese diaspora and refugees,
    416, 417, 419
Vietnamese women, 430–32
Viljoen, Shaun, 216
Villon, François, 142
violence
    of colonialist-capitalist
        development, 396
    experienced by queer folk, 420
    experienced by Crazy Joe, 406–
        07
    as gendered and colonial, 221
    in national subject-formation,
        215–16
    in northern Ireland, 405
    in post-apartheid South Africa,
        216–18
    in postcolonial Bildungsroman,
        465
    in the postcolony, 219
    ritualized, 221
    of universities as institutions,
        49n1
    See also precarity; sexual
        abuse/violence
Viswanathan, Gauri, 24n3, 55
Vita Nuova (Dante), 141
voice, loss of, 311
Vuong, Ocean, xlii, 415–16, 420–
    21, 426–27, 434–35n4. *See
    also Night Sky with Exit
    Wounds*; *On Earth We're
    Briefly Gorgeous*

Wachal, Chritopher B., 187
Wager-Lawlor, Jennifer, 37
"waithood," 468
Waiting for an Angel (Habila), xl,
    255, 256–61

Walcott, Derek, xxxviii, 131–34, 137, 139, 149, 152–53
Waleed (protagonist, *An Imperfect Blessing*), 213–15
Wallace, Jo-Ann, 5, 442
Walsh, Rachel Ann, xlii
Wang, Martha Su, xxxviii–xxxix
Wang Der-wei, 326, 329, 340
War Child: A Child Soldier's Story (Jal), xxx
war crimes, 92
war narratives, 99. *See also* African war Bildungsroman
Waste Not Your Tears (Kala), xxx
The Water Pipe Forest (*Shu shui guan sen lin* by Hon Lai-chu), 327
Waters, Sarah, xxvii
Watson, Jini Kim, 237, 242
The Way of the World: The Bildungsroman in European Culture (Moretti), 395–96
Weep Not, Child (Ngugi), 3, 66, 67, 69
The Weir (McPherson), 397
Wenzel, Jennifer, 366
Western Bildungsroman, xxxi, 252, 261
What the Twilight Says (Walcott), 153
white beauty norms, 97–98
White Egrets (Walcott), 149
white gaze, 378
white literary critics, 426–27
"The White Man's Burden" (Kipling), 109, 110
White Mythologies (Young), 22
white nationalism, 418
white privilege, 188
White Teeth (Smith), 59, 71
whiteness
    in the colonial imagination, 384
    and imperial masculinity, 428
    in South Africa, 211–12
    in USA, 422, 431–32
Who Fears Death (Okorafor), 48
Wicks, Amanda, 41
Wicomb, Zoë, 372, 379, 387
Wieland, Christoph Martin, xvi
Wilhelm Meister's Apprenticeship (Goethe)
    as example of classic Bildungsroman, xxxii, 4–5, 8–12, 14, 134, 159
    heteronormativity in, 441
    moving forward from loss in, 412
    national and class analysis in, 60
    and rationalist subjectivity, 19
    as ur text, xvi–xvii
Wilhelm Meisters Lehrjahre. *See Wilhelm Meister's Apprenticeship* (Goethe)
Williams, Raymond, 9–10
Williamson, Bethany, xxxviii–xxxix
Winterson, Jeannette, xxvii
Wiseman, Nicholas, 403
Wong, Mary, 326, 340
Woolf, Virginia, xviii, xx, 159, 162, 167, 177
Wordsworth, William, 141
world literature, 111–12
Wright, Marcia, 373
writing as activism, 256–57, 259
Writing Wrongs (Nayar), 61
Wu, Helena, xl, xli

Wurr, Julia, xlii
Wynter, Sylvia, 152

Xi Xi, 327, 334

Yang, Gene Luen, xxxvi
Yap, Arthur, 245
Yeats, William Butler, 343n8
Yeo, Robert, 245
Yoruba people and culture, 362, 363, 367n2, 456
You Can't Get Lost in Cape Town (Wicomb), 372–77, 379–81, 385–87
Young, Robert J.C., 22, 289

young adult (YA) fiction, 29, 46, 47
youth
    education of, xxxi
    "frozen youth," xxii
    and global capitalism, xx
    as master trope of classic Bildungsroman, 252
    in postcolonial society, xxviii
    and twentieth-century India, 161

Zahrah the Windseeker (Okorafor), 48
Zaire, 264
Zimbabwe, xiv

www.ingramcontent.com/pod-product-compliance
Ingram Content Group UK Ltd.
Pitfield, Milton Keynes, MK11 3LW, UK
UKHW042332230126
467268UK00003B/180